Earl Aubec and other stories

By the same author

The Tale of the Eternal Champion
New Omnibus Editions, revised and with new introductions by the author.

1 Von Bek
2 The Eternal Champion
3 Hawkmoon
4 Corum
5 Sailing to Utopia
6 A Nomad of the Time Streams
7 The Dancers at the End of Time
8 Elric of Melnibone
9 The New Nature of the Catastrophe
10 The Prince with the Silver Hand
11 Legends from the End of Time
12 Stormbringer
13 Earl Aubec
14 Count Brass*

Also: A Warrior of Mars

Science Fiction

The Sundered Worlds
The Shores of Death
The Winds of Limbo
The Wrecks of Time

Omnibuses

A Cornelius Quartet
A Cornelius Calendar

Three Love Stories
(Behold the Man, Breakfast in the Ruins, Constant Fire) *

Comic Capers
(The Jerry Cornell Stories, w. Jack Trevor Story) *

Colonel Pyat

Byzantium Endures
The Laughter of Carthage
Jerusalem Commands
The Vengeance of Rome †

Other novels

Gloriana; or, The Unfulfill'd Queen
The Brothel in Rosenstrasse
Mother London

Short stories and graphic novels

Casablanca
Sojan (juvenile)
My Experiences in the Third World War
Lunching with the Antichrist*
The Swords of Heaven, The Flowers of Hell (with Howard Chaykin)
The Crystal and the Amulet (with James Cawthorn)
etc.

Non-fiction

The Retreat from Liberty
Letters from Hollywood (illus. M. Foreman)
Wizardry and Wild Romance
Death is No Obstacle (with Colin Greenland)

Editor

New Worlds

The Traps of Time
The Best of *New Worlds*
Best SF Stories from *New Worlds*
New Worlds: An Anthology
Before Armageddon
England Invaded
The Inner Landscape

Records

With *The Deep Fix*:

The New Worlds Fair
Dodgem Dude
The Brothel in Rosenstrasse etc.

With *Hawkwind*:

Warriors at the Edge of Time
Choose Your Masques
Zones
Sonic Attack etc.
Also work with *Blue Oyster Cult*, Robert Calvert etc.

For further information about Michael Moorcock and his work please send SAE to Nomads of the Time Streams, 18 Laurel Bank, Truss Hill Road, South Ascot, Berks, UK. or PO Box 451048, Atlanta, Georgia, 30345–1048, USA.

* In preparation (Orion Books) † In preparation (Cape)

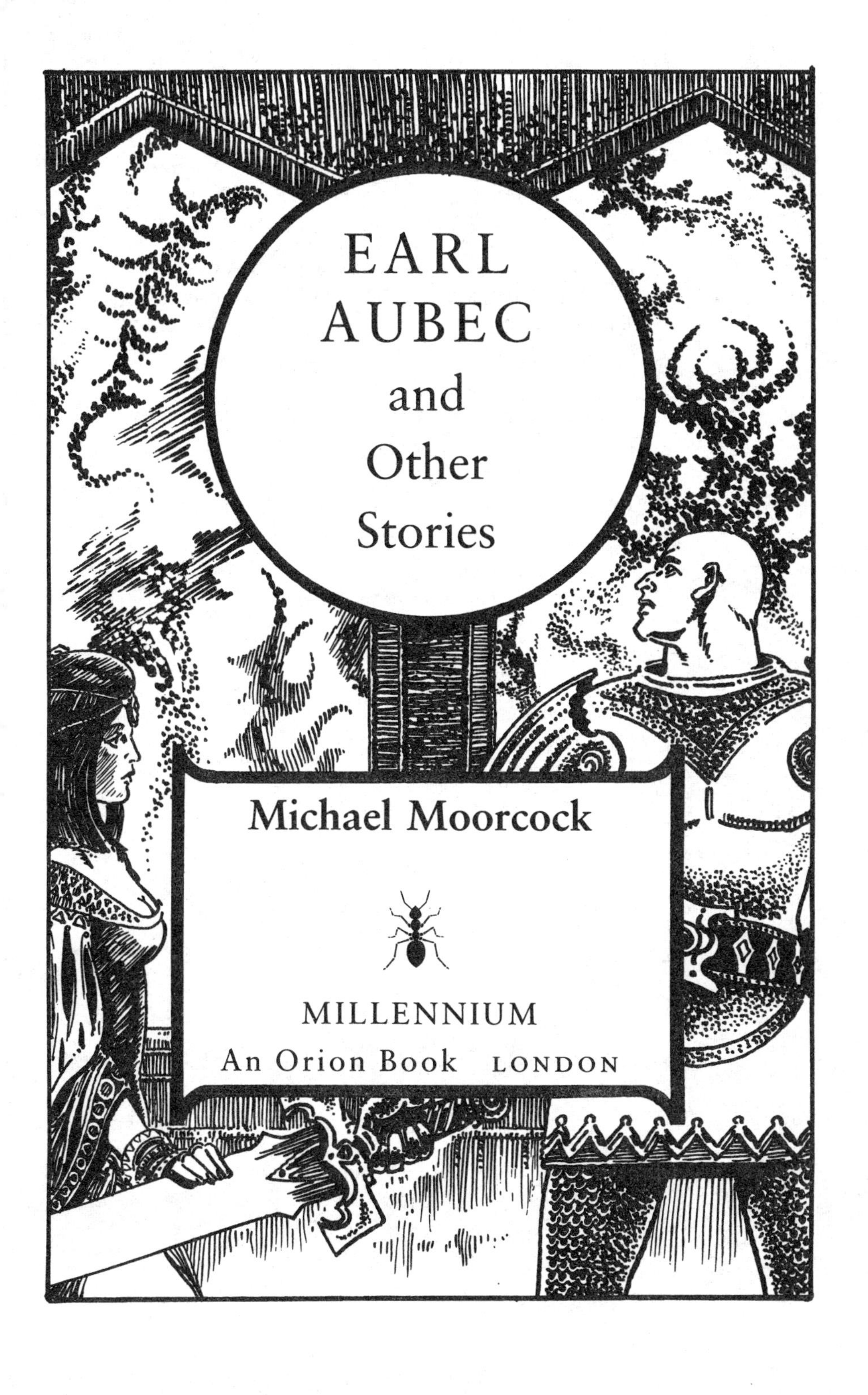
EARL
AUBEC
and
Other
Stories
Michael Moorcock
MILLENNIUM
An Orion Book LONDON

This edition first published in Great Britain in 1993 by
Millennium
An imprint of Orion Books Ltd
Orion House, 5 Upper St Martin's Lane
London WC2H 9EA

A CIP catalogue record for this book is available from the
British Library

ISBN: (Csd) 1 85798 047 6
(Ppr) 1 85798 048 4

Millennium

Book Twenty-Nine

Printed and bound in Great Britain by
Clays Ltd. St Ives plc

Dear Reader,

These stories were written over the course of my whole working life which began in 1955 when I was fifteen. By 1957 I was a professional editor, producing TARZAN ADVENTURES, one of the last juvenile magazines to carry as much text as strip. It became for a while a junior version of the US pulps I enjoyed – a mixture of PLANET STORIES (my favourite) and JUNGLE STORIES (whose best writing was in its shout-lines: 'Ki-Gor – Jungle Lord – tracks zombie spoor to the Congo's dungeon of despair in *Voodoo Slaves for the Devil's Daughter*').

Before I edited TARZAN I had done several fanzines and had sold a variety of features and stories. My first fantasy hero to receive national distribution was *Sojan the Swordsman*, who owed more than a little to John Carter of Mars and who travelled the skies of his far-off planet in an airship. Around the same time I was beginning to write what would become the Eternal Champion sequence, but was sidetracked from any serious ambition by the easy money to be made from comic strips. I became a juvenile Fleet Street hack. Between leaving Amalgamated Press and winding up in a Covent Garden pub at six in the morning, usually with an unclear sense of where I'd been for the past few hours, I would spend a small fortune.

I like to think I got through an entire journalistic career, from golden years to gutter while still a teenager. After I'd seen the future and it was called El Vino, I took my guitar and left. Within a couple of months I somehow wound up on top of a melting glacier in the Arctic Circle.

While sitting on the peak of Mount Portafjället and waiting for the mist to lift I had the nearest thing to a revelation. When I returned to England I decided to concentrate on my adult fiction. *The Mountain* is pretty much a straight account of the expedition to Arctic Lappland which caused me to revise any ideas I had previously had about writing conventional social fiction. I made the climb with my friend David Harvey who has published some deep thinking on economics and geography since we got off that glacier and has also written *The Condition of Post Modernity*, about the best and most sensible book on the subject.

In 1959 I had sold my first adult sf story to NEW WORLDS, the collaboration with Barry Bayley called *Peace on Earth*. Most of those early stories were sold to E.J. Carnell, editor of NEW WORLDS, SCIENCE FANTASY and SF ADVENTURES, who published them in the magazine he felt most appropriate. *Going Home* appeared in SF ADVENTURES. *The Greater Conqueror* was actually written for an existing cover painting which the remarkable Gerard Quinn had done for SCIENCE FANTASY. There were probably few full-time writers of periodical fiction in those days who did not at some stage write to accomodate available pictures. Whole novels, including two of mine, were written to existing cover artwork and titles, much as one writes lyrics for existing tunes . . .

I also worked for SEXTON BLAKE LIBRARY. One of my first jobs was writing the readers' letters. It was then I met Jack Trevor Story who was doing filmscripts for Anna Neagle and Adam Faith and writing Sexton Blake novels in his spare time, producing some of his funniest comic thrillers. He would change Sexton Blake's name, make him a solicitor instead of a private detective, and publish the same book with Secker and Warburg to excellent reviews in the Sunday heavies. It's no wonder that I never did quite understand what standards were being applied, except gormless snobbery, by the likes of Cyril Connolly who set a literary tone in his day and once called his friend Ian Fleming 'a master craftsman' for writing books which were never up to the professional standard demanded by SEXTON BLAKE!

From the start I have written both popular and literary fiction. Unlike many, I have received generous notices and suffered very little for my choice of subject and technique but I was often advised to change my name if I ever wanted to be taken seriously . . .

For me there was an inherent irony worthy of Molière in that advice. I write all kinds of fiction because I enjoy reading all kinds of fiction. I have played and enjoyed many kinds of music. Should you only read Jane Austen because people won't take you seriously if you read anything else? Or only listen to Mozart? Or only look at one school of painting? I have a good many ideas for stories and have been blessed with sturdy, energetic peasant genes. I like to use a form which suits the story best. Some stories are less demanding than others and some less ambitious. Some are meant to amuse and nothing else. Some are the work of an unskilled tyro. None, however, was written simply for the money but most were commissioned. I am still inclined to write short stories only when asked.

In 1962 a collaboration with Jim Cawthorn, a Sexton Blake story *Caribbean Crisis*, was published under what was known as a house name, 'Desmond Reid', but none of the other scores of Desmond Reid titles were anything but edited by me. By the early sixties I was writing both features and fiction for Carnell's magazines and a whole variety of weeklies and monthlies, including BIBLE STORY WEEKLY and PEOPLE'S FRIEND. I specialized in fantastic adventure stories, westerns, historicals, science and architecture. I have no idea of the volume I turned out in those years and even now can't distinguish a story of mine from someone else's. Everything, including my fiction, was done at white heat, frequently to a very close deadline, and I did not know any other way of working, so the large proportion of these stories were written in matter of hours and very, very rarely more than a day, which will doubtless explain some sour notes, at least in the earlier stories.

Because of my habit of working to commission, I rarely had much contact with the U.S. magazines. *Earl Aubec* was one of the few stories I sent, via Carnell who had become my agent, to Cele Goldsmith, the innovative editor of AMAZING STORIES and FANTASTIC ADVENTURES, two of the longest running pulps. She was the first U.S. editor to recognize the talents of Ballard, Disch, Zelazny, Samuel R. Delany and others. She commissioned Fritz Leiber's new Gray Mouser stories, published Philip K. Dick and gave the so-called sf new wave an enormous boost. With Judith Merrill, another ground-breaking editor not sufficently noted in the histories, Goldsmith did much to raise the standards and aspirations of US sf writers.

Cele Goldsmith bought Earl Aubec and retitled it 'Master of Chaos'. I was encouraged to send her a short Elric story, *The Last Enchantment*, which I wrote before *Stormbringer*. Goldsmith left the magazines and the story was lost. It was not until after Carnell's death that his successor, Leslie Flood, found it and let me have it. I had completely forgotten I had written it. It is published here as *Jesting With Chaos*.

The Deep Fix was written for Carnell, who chose the name James Colvin from the railway guide (I had preferred 'Mendoza') because I had two other contributions in the same issue of SCIENCE FANTASY. It was my first attempt to use the machinery of the sf story to explore perceptions of reality, something of an obsession with English writers to this day, as well as Americans like Philip K. Dick and Thomas M. Disch, who knowingly used sophisticated symbolism in their work and who tended to be published in the more accepting British magazines. Carnell was reluctant to run *The Deep Fix* but was persuaded by Ballard to do so. Meanwhile I was busy persuading Carnell to run Ballard's *The Terminal Beach*. It was how we got our 'off-beat' stories published at that time.

By 1964 I was editing NEW WORLDS which had been taken over by a firm previously best known for its semi-pornographic crime thrillers, the most popular of which were by the notorious Steve Frances, who had actually been responsible for backing the earliest issues of NEW WORLDS in the forties, but was exiled to Spain after his 'Hank Janson' novels aroused the moral outrage of our paternal watch-dogs. NEW WORLDS was to be the firm's respectable front. I wrote very few new stories during that period. When Compact Books, publishers of the magazine, suddenly asked me to put an sf list together for them (it would include Merrill, Disch and others) one of the easiest to produce was a 'James Colvin' collection, *The Deep Fix*. *The Real Life Mr Newman* was rapidly written for that collection and manuscripts sent on to a copy-editor whose normal job was correcting Hank's spelling and grammar. No proofs were seen. By the time the book appeared, thoroughly rewritten by the copy-editor, I had lost the original manuscript. This version is what I have been able to piece together and clean up a bit.

Goodbye, Miranda . . . was one of the short stories I ran in NEW WORLDS, as well as *The Time Dweller* and *Escape from Evening*. *Islands* appeared in a pin-up magazine called GOLDEN NUGGET which for a while I edited for the same publisher. I needed the fee. Nobody who ever worked for NEW WORLDS made money at it. *The Mountain* first appeared in French, courtesy Maxim Jakubowski, and stories like *Wolf*, *Consuming Passion*, *The Lovebeast*, *Environment Problem* first appeared in various Compact publications, some sleazier than others. Some of the stories I wrote in that period, including the short version of *Behold the Man*, have not been reprinted here. By 1967 I was writing mostly Jerry Cornelius stories for various publications, including much of the underground press, and these appear in *The New Nature of the Catastrophe*.

The Golden Barge was my first completed novel to survive. I am rather glad that my earlier *The Hungry Dreamers* was eaten by rats in Ladbroke Grove. It deserved its fate. It was a piece of maudlin self-promotion about low life in Soho. *The Golden Barge* would probably never have seen the light of day had not David Britton and Michael Butterworth discovered it in a laundry box at my house in Yorkshire in the late 1970s. It is published here pretty much as it was written in 1957 or thereabouts.

Some Reminiscences of the Third World War was first published by Britton and Butterworth's famous Savoy firm in Manchester but I wrote *Crossing into Cambodia* first, for Maxim Jakubowski, who published it this time in English. It is a very specific homage to Isaac Babel, one of the great 20th century short story writers, killed by the KGB on Stalin's orders. His daughter Nathalie now lives in Washington and we met when the Old Vic put on a new production of Babel's play *Marya*. Babel inspired the other stories in the sequence, but less directly.

I wrote *Mars* for Robert Holdstock and Chris Evans, who edited a fine, short-lived series, *Other Edens*. I wanted to see if you could still write a story about the E.R. Burroughs/Ray Bradbury Mars which exploratory rockets had shown did not exist. Since then there have been many convincing demonstrations that it is possible.

The Frozen Cardinal was written for PLAYBOY on request but never sent in after I saw their 'rewrite sheets' and discovered that it was not only the pictures which were sanitized with a bit of air-brushing. British magazines paid worse but cut less. Years later, slightly revised, *The Frozen Cardinal* also appeared in *Other Edens*.

Waiting for the End of Time was written for the short-lived sf magazine VISION OF TOMORROW edited by Philip Harbottle from Newcastle. *Hanging the Fool* was commissioned for *Tarot Tales* by Rachel Pollack and Caitlin Mathews. *The Opium General* appeared in a story collection of that title. *The Stone Thing* was written for my friend, the late Eric Bentcliffe, who published a wonderful fanzine TRIODE, while *The Last Call* was done in the same vein at the request of FANTASY TALES. *My Life* was produced for B. S. Johnson and Giles Gordon for their anthology *You Always Remember The First Time*. It is a lie, written on the assumption that, since all the other contributors were probably going to lie, I might as well as make mine a big one. *A Museum of the Future* was commissioned by David Johnson for a *Daily*

Telegraph science supplement and is a piece of simple polemic with more than a nod to H. G. Wells. *To Rescue Tanelorn . . .* is one of my few fantasy stories to show some slight influence of Morris or Dunsany. It was also written for Carnell who, as I recall, lost the last page of the manuscript but published the story anyway. It was reprinted with the ending missing and is published here with the page restored. To the best of my knowledge nobody, including myself, ever noticed.

Although, of necessity, I must have something of the attitude of a mother cat to her litters, I still have considerable affection for the majority of these stories. Some of the least comely are probably the ones I remember most fondly and those that have done well for themselves I am proud of. Some are a little embarrassing, a bit loud, a bit coarse, but they were all written with pleasure in the hope they would give pleasure and I offer them without further apology since, anyway, they are not really mine any more. The act of publishing a story makes it at once the property of the reader. In the end it is the reader who decides what a story is worth. Therefore, with great respect, I dedicate this collection of stories to you, the reader, with my thanks.

Yours,
Michael Moorcock

Contents

1. The Beginning
Earl Aubec, 3
Jesting with Chaos, 16
The Greater Conqueror, 26

2. The Middle
Going Home, 65
Hanging the Fool, 79
Consuming Passion, 96
Wolf, 104
Environment Problem, 110
The Opium General, 119
A Dead Singer, 127
The Lovebeast, 145
The Ruins, 155
The Golden Barge, 163
The Deep Fix, 283
The Real Life Mr Newman, 332
Goodbye, Miranda, 364
Islands, 367
Some Reminiscences of the Third World War, 383
(*'Casablanca'*
'Going To Canada'
'Leaving Pasadena'
'Crossing Into Cambodia')
Mars, 447
The Frozen Cardinal, 461
Peace on Earth, 471

3. The End
The Mountain, 483
The Time Dweller, 493
Escape from Evening, 509
Waiting for the end of time . . . 534

. . . And Somewhere Else
The Stone Thing, 547
The Last Call, 551
My Life, 555
The Museum of the Future, 559

. . . And Another Beginning . . .
To Rescue Tanelorn . . . 567

1: *The Beginning*

Earl Aubec

From the glassless window of the stone tower it was possible to see the wide river winding off between loose, brown banks, through the heaped terrain of solid green copses which blended very gradually into the mass of the forest proper. And out of the forest, the cliff rose, grey and light-green, up and up, the rock darkening, lichen-covered, to merge with the lower, and even more massive, stones of the castle. It was the castle which dominated the countryside in three directions, drawing the eye from river, rock, or forest. Its walls were high and of thick granite, with towers; a dense field of towers, grouped so as to shadow one another.

Aubec of Malador marvelled and wondered how human builders could ever have constructed it, save by sorcery. Brooding and mysterious, the castle seemed to have a defiant air, for it stood on the very edge of the world.

At this moment the lowering sky cast a strange, deep-yellow light against the western sides of the towers, intensifying the blackness untouched by it. Huge billows of blue sky rent the general racing greyness above, and mounds of red cloud crept through to blend and produce more and subtler colourings. Yet, though the sky was impressive, it could not take the gaze away from the ponderous series of man-made crags that were Castle Kaneloon.

Earl Aubec of Malador did not turn from the window until it was completely dark outside; forest, cliff, and castle but shadowy tones against the overall blackness. He passed a heavy, knotted hand over his almost bald scalp and thoughtfully went towards the heap of straw which was his intended bed.

The straw was piled in a niche created by a buttress and the outer wall and the room was well-lighted by Malador's lantern. But the air was cold as he lay down on the straw with his hand close to the two-handed broadsword of prodigious size. This was his only weapon. It looked as if it had been forged for a giant – Malador was virtually that himself – with its wide crosspiece and heavy, stone-encrusted hilt and five-foot blade, smooth and broad. Beside it was Malador's old, heavy armour, the casque balanced on top with its somewhat tattered black plumes waving slightly in a current of air from the window.

Malador slept.

His dreams, as usual, were turbulent; of mighty armies surging across the blazing landscapes, curling banners bearing the blazons of a hundred nations, forests of shining lance-tips, seas of tossing helmets, the brave, wild blasts of the war-horns, the clatter of hooves, and the songs and cries and shouts of soldiers. These were dreams of earlier times, of his youth when, for Queen Eloarde of Klant, he had conquered all the Southern nations – almost to the edge of the world. Only Kaneloon, on the very edge, had he not conquered, and this because no army would follow him there.

For one of so martial an appearance, these dreams were surprisingly unwelcome, and Malador woke several times that night, shaking his head in an attempt to rid himself of them.

He would rather have dreamed of Eloarde, though she was the cause of his restlessness, but he saw nothing of her in his sleep; nothing of her soft, black hair that billowed around her pale face, nothing of her green eyes and red lips and her proud, disdainful posture. Eloarde had assigned him to this quest and he had not gone willingly, though he had no choice, for as well as his mistress she was also his Queen. The Champion was traditionally her lover – and it was unthinkable to Earl Aubec that any other condition should exist. It was his place, as Champion of Klant, to obey and go forth from her palace to seek Castle Kaneloon alone and conquer it and declare it part of her Empire, so that it could be said Queen Eloarde's domain stretched from the Dragon Sea to World's Edge.

Nothing lay beyond World's Edge – nothing save the swirling stuff of unformed Chaos which stretched away from the Cliffs of Kaneloon for eternity, roiling and broiling, multicoloured, full of monstrous half-shapes – for Earth alone was Lawful and constituted of ordered matter, drifting in the sea of Chaos-stuff as it had done for aeons.

In the morning, Earl Aubec of Malador extinguished the lantern which he had allowed to remain alight, drew on greaves and hauberk, placed his black plumed helm upon his head, put his broadsword over his shoulder and sallied out of the stone tower which was all that remained whole of some ancient edifice.

His leathern-shod feet stumbled over stones that seemed partially dissolved, as if Chaos had once lapped here instead of against the towering Cliffs of Kaneloon. That, of course, was quite impossible, since Earth's boundaries were known to be constant.

Castle Kaneloon had seemed closer the night before and that, he now realized, was because it was so huge. He followed the river, his feet sinking in the loamy soil, the great branches of the trees shading him from the increasingly hot sun as he made his way towards the cliffs. Kaneloon was now out of sight, high above him. Every so often he used his sword as an axe to clear his way through the places where the foliage was particularly thick.

He rested several times, drinking the cold water of the river and mopping his face and head. He was unhurried, he had no wish to visit Kaneloon, he resented the interruption to his life with Eloarde which he thought he had earned. Also he, too, had a superstitious dread of the mysterious castle, which was said to be inhabited only by one human occupant – the Dark Lady, a sorceress without mercy who commanded a legion of demons and other Chaos-creatures.

He arrived at the cliffs by midday and regarded the path leading upward with a mixture of wariness and relief. He had expected to have to scale the cliffs. He was not one, however, to take a difficult route where an easy one presented itself, so he looped a cord around his sword and slung it over his back, since it was too long and cumbersome to carry at his side. Then, still in bad humour, he began to climb the twisting path.

The lichen-covered rocks were evidently ancient, contrary to the speculations of certain philosophers who asked why Kaneloon had only been heard of a few generations since. Malador believed in the general answer to this question – that explorers had never ventured this far until fairly recently. He glanced back down the path and saw the tops of the trees below him, their foliage moving slightly in the breeze. The tower in which he'd spent the night was just visible in the distance and, beyond that, he knew, there was no civilization, no outpost of Man for many days' journey North, East, or West – and Chaos lay to the South. He had never been so close to the edge of the world before and wondered how the sight of unformed matter would affect his brain.

At length he clambered to the top of the cliff and stood, arms akimbo, staring up at Castle Kaneloon which soared a mile away, its highest towers hidden in the clouds, its immense walls rooted on the rock and stretching away, limited on both side of the cliff, Malador watched the churning, leaping Chaos-substance – predominantly grey, blue, brown, and yellow at this moment, though its colours changed constantly – spew like the sea-spray a few feet from the castle.

He became filled with a feeling of such indescribable profundity that he could only remain in this position for a long while, completely overwhelmed by a sense of his own insignificance. It came to him, eventually, that if anyone did dwell in the Castle Kaneloon, then they must have a robust mind or else must be insane, and then he sighed and strode on towards his goal, noting that the ground was perfectly flat, without blemish, green, obsidian, and reflecting imperfectly the dancing Chaos-stuff from which he averted his eyes as much as he could.

Kaneloon had many entrances, all dark and unwelcoming, and had they all not been of regular size and shape they might have been so many cave-mouths.

Malador paused before choosing which to take, and then walked with outward purposefulness towards one. He went into blackness which appeared to stretch away forever. It was cold; it was empty and he was alone.

He was soon lost. His footsteps made no echo, which was unexpected; then the blackness began to give way to a series of angular outlines, like the walls of a twisting corridor – walls which did not reach the unsensed roof, but ended several yards above his head. It was a labyrinth, a maze. He paused and looked back and saw with horror that the maze wound off in many directions, though he was sure he had followed a straight path from the outside.

For an instant, his mind became diffused and madness threatened to engulf him, but he battened it down, unslung his sword, shivering. Which way? He pressed on, unable to tell, now, whether he went forward or backward.

The madness lurking in the depths of his brain filtered out and became fear and, immediately following the sensation of fear, came the shapes. Swift-moving shapes, darting from several different directions, gibbering, fiendish, utterly horrible.

One of these creatures leapt at him and he struck at it with his blade. It fled, but seemed unwounded. Another came and another and he forgot his panic as he smote around him, driving them back until all had fled. He paused and leaned, panting, on his sword. Then, as he stared around him, the fear began to flood back into him and more creatures appeared – creatures with wide, blazing eyes and clutching talons, creatures with malevolent faces, mocking him, creatures with half-familiar faces, some recognizable as those of old friends and relatives, yet twisted into horrific parodies. He screamed and ran at them, whirling his huge sword, slashing, hacking at them, rushing past one group to turn a bend in the labyrinth and encounter another.

Malicious laughter coursed through the twisting corridors, following him and preceding him as he ran. He stumbled and fell against a wall. At first the wall seemed of solid stone, then, slowly it became soft and he sank through it, his body lying half in one corridor, half in another. He hauled himself through, still on hands and knees, looked up and saw Eloarde, but an Eloarde whose face grew old as he watched.

'I am mad,' he thought. *'Is this reality or fantasy – or both?'*

He reached out a hand, *'Eloarde!'*

She vanished but was replaced by a crowding horde of demons. He raised himself to his feet and flailed around him with his blade, but they skipped outside his range and he roared at them as he advanced. Momentarily, while he thus exerted himself, the fear left him again and, with the disappearance of the fear, so the visions vanished until he realized that the fear preceded the manifestations and he tried to control it.

He almost succeeded, forcing himself to relax, but it welled up again and the creatures bubbled out of the walls, their shrill voices full of malicious mirth.

This time he did not attack them with his sword, but stood his ground as calmly as he could and concentrated upon his own mental condition. As he did so, the creatures began to fade away and then the walls of the labyrinth dissolved and it seemed to him that he stood in a peaceful valley, calm and idyllic. Yet, hovering close to his consciousness, he seemed to see the walls of the labyrinth faintly outlined, and disgusting shapes moving here and there along the many passages.

He realized that the vision of the valley was as much an illusion as the labyrinth and, with this conclusion, both valley and labyrinth faded and he stood in the enormous hall of a castle which could only be Kaneloon.

The hall was unoccupied though well-furnished, and he could not see the source of the light, which was bright and even. He strode towards a table, on which were heaped scrolls, and his feet made a satisfying echo. Several great metal-studded doors led off from the hall, but for the moment he did not investigate them, intent on studying the scrolls and seeing if they could help him unravel Kaneloon's mystery.

He propped his sword against the table and took up the first scroll.

It was a beautiful thing of red vellum, but the black letters upon it meant nothing to him and he was astounded for, though dialects varied from place to place, there was only one language in all the lands of the Earth. Another scroll bore different symbols still, and a third he unrolled carried a series of highly stylized pictures which were repeated here and there so that he guessed they formed some kind of alphabet. Disgusted, he flung the scroll down, picked up his sword, drew an immense breath, and shouted:

'Who dwells here? Let them know that Aubec, Earl of Malador, Champion of Klant and Conqueror of the South claims this castle in the name of Queen Eloarde, Empress of all the Southlands!'

In shouting these familiar words, he felt somewhat more comfortable, but he received no reply. He lifted his casque a trifle and scratched his neck. Then he picked up his sword, balanced it over his shoulder, and made for the largest door.

Before he reached it, it sprang open and a huge, manlike thing with hands like grappling irons grinned at him.

He took a pace backward and then another until, seeing that the thing did not advance, stood his ground observing it.

It was a foot or so taller than he, with oval, multi-faceted eyes that, by their nature, seemed blank. Its face was angular and had a grey, metallic sheen. Most of its body was composed of burnished metal, jointed in the manner of armour. Upon its head was a tight-fitting hood, studded with brass. It had about it an air of tremendous and insensate power, though it did not move.

'A golem!' Malador exclaimed for it seemed to him that he remembered such man-made creatures from legends. 'What sorcery created *you*!'

The golem did not reply but its hands – which were in reality composed of four spikes of metal apiece – began slowly to flex themselves; and still the golem grinned.

This thing, Malador knew, did not have the same amorphous quality of his earlier visions. This was solid, this was real and strong, and even Malador's manly strength, however much he exerted it, could not defeat such a creature. Yet neither could he turn away.

With a scream of metal joints, the golem entered the hall and stretched its burnished hands towards the earl.

Malador could attack or flee, and fleeing would be senseless. He attacked.

His great sword clasped in both hands, he swung it sideways at the golem's torso, which seemed to be its weakest point. The golem lowered an arm and the sword shuddered against metal with a mighty clang that set the whole of Malador's body quaking. He stumbled backward. Remorselessly, the golem followed him.

Malador looked back and searched the hall in the hope of finding a weapon more powerful than his sword, but saw only shields of an ornamental kind upon the wall to his right. He turned and ran to the wall, wrenching one of the shields from its place and slipping it on to his arm. It was an oblong thing, very light, and comprising several layers of cross-grained wood. It was inadequate, but it made him feel a trifle better as he whirled again to face the golem.

The golem advanced, and Malador thought he noticed something familiar about it, just as the demons of the labyrinth had seemed familiar, but the impression was only vague. Kaneloon's weird sorcery was affecting his mind, he decided.

The creature raised the spikes on its right arm and aimed a swift blow at Malador's head. He avoided it, putting up his sword as protection. The spikes clashed against the sword and then the left arm pistoned forward, driving at Malador's stomach. The shield stopped his blow, though the spikes pierced it deeply. He yanked the buckler off the spikes; slashing at the golem's leg-joints as he did so.

Still staring into the middle-distance, with apparently no real interest in Malador, the golem advanced like a blind man as the earl turned and leapt on to the table, scattering the scrolls. Now he brought his huge sword down upon the golem's skull, and the brass studs sparked and the hood and head beneath it was dented. The golem staggered and then grasped the table, heaving it off the floor so that Malador was forced to leap to the ground. This time he made for the door and tugged at its latchring, but the door would not open.

His sword was chipped and blunted. He put his back to the door as the golem reached him and brought its metal hand down on the top edge of the shield. The shield shattered and a dreadful pain shot up Malador's arm. He lunged at the golem, but he was unused to handling the big sword in this manner and the stroke was clumsy.

Malador knew that he was doomed. Force and fighting skill were not enough against the golem's insensate strength. At the golem's next blow he swung aside, but was caught by one of its spike-fingers which ripped through his armour and drew blood, though at that moment he felt no pain.

He scrambled up, shaking away the grip and fragments of wood which remained of the shield, grasping his sword firmly.

'The soulless demon has no weak spot,' he thought, *'and since it has no true intelligence, it cannot be appealed to. What would a golem fear?'*

The answer was simple. The golem would only fear something as strong or stronger than itself.

He must use cunning.

He ran for the upturned table with the golem after him, leaped over the table and wheeled as the golem stumbled but did not, as he'd hoped, fall. However, the golem was slowed by its encounter, and Aubec took advantage of this to rush for the door through which the golem had entered. It opened. He was in a twisting corridor, darkly shadowed, not unlike the labyrinth he had first found in Kaneloon. The door closed, but he could find nothing to bar it with. He ran up the corridor as the golem tore the door open and came lumbering swiftly after him.

The corridor writhed about in all directions, and, though he could not always see the golem, he could hear it and had the sickening fear that he would turn a corner at some stage and run straight into it. He did not – but he came to a door and, upon opening it and passing through it, found himself again in the hall of Castle Kaneloon.

He almost welcomed this familiar sight as he heard the golem, its metal parts screeching, continue to come after him. He needed another shield, but the part of the hall in which he now found himself had no wall-shields – only a large, round mirror of bright, clear-polished metal. It would be too heavy to be much use, but he seized it, tugging it from its hook. It fell with a clang and he hauled it up, dragging it with him as he stumbled away from the golem which had emerged into the room once more.

Using the chains by which the mirror had hung, he gripped it before him and, as the golem's speed increased and the monster rushed upon him, he raised this makeshift shield.

The golem shrieked.

Malador was astounded. The monster stopped dead and cowered away from the mirror. Malador pushed it towards the golem and the thing turned its back and fled, with a metallic howl, through the door it had entered by.

Relieved and puzzled, Malador sat down on the floor and studied the mirror. There was certainly nothing magical about it, though its quality was good. He grinned and said aloud:

'The creature *is* afraid of something. It is afraid of itself!'

He threw back his head and laughed loudly in his relief. Then he frowned. 'Now to find the sorcerers who created him and take vengeance on them!' He pushed himself to his feet, twisted the chains of the mirror more securely about his arm and went to another door, concerned lest the golem complete its circuit of the maze and return through the door. This door would not budge, so he lifted his sword and hacked at the latch for a few moments until it gave. He strode into a well-lit passage with what appeared to be another room at its far end – the door open.

A musky scent came to his nostrils as he progressed along the passage – the scent that reminded him of Eloarde and the comforts of Klant.

When he reached the circular chamber, he saw that it was a bedroom – a woman's bedroom full of the perfume he had smelled in the passage. He controlled the direction his mind took, thought of loyalty and Klant, and went to another door which led off from the room. He lugged it open and discovered a stone staircase winding upward. This he mounted, passing windows that seemed glazed with emerald or ruby, beyond which shadow-shapes flickered so that he knew he was on the side of the castle overlooking Chaos.

The staircase seemed to lead up into a tower, and when he finally reached the small door at its top he was feeling out of breath and paused before entering. Then he pushed the door open and went in.

A huge window was set in one wall, a window of clear glass through which he could see the ominous stuff of Chaos leaping. A woman stood by this window as if awaiting him.

'You are indeed a champion, Earl Aubec,' said she with a smile that might have been ironic.

'How do you know my name?'

'No sorcery gave it me, Earl of Malador – you shouted it loudly enough when you first saw the hall in its true shape.'

'Was not *that*, then, sorcery,' he said ungraciously, 'the labyrinth, the demons – even the valley? Was not the golem made by sorcery? Is not this whole cursed castle of a sorcerous nature?'

She shrugged. 'Call it so if you'd rather not have the truth. Sorcery, in your mind at least, is a crude thing which only hints at the true powers existing in the universe.'

He did not reply, being somewhat impatient of such statements. He had learned, by observing the philosophers of Klant, that mysterious words often disguised commonplace things and ideas. Instead, he looked at her sulkily and over-frankly.

She was fair, with green-blue eyes and a light complexion. Her long robe was of a similar colour to her eyes. She was, in a secret sort of way, very beautiful and, like all the denizens of Kaneloon he'd encountered, a trifle familiar.

'You recognize Kaneloon?' she asked.

He dismissed her question. 'Enough of this – take me to the masters of this place!'

'There is none but me, Myshella the Dark Lady – and I am the mistress.'

He was disappointed. 'Was it just to meet you that I came through such perils?'

'It was – and greater perils even than you think, Earl Aubec. Those were but the monsters of your own imagination!'

'Taunt me not, lady.'

She laughed. 'I speak in good faith. The castle creates its defences out of your own mind. It is a rare man who can face and defeat his own imagination. Such a one has not found me here for two hundred years. All since have perished by fear – until now.'

She smiled at him. It was a warm smile.

'And what is the prize for so great a feat?' he said gruffly.

She laughed again and gestured towards the window which looked out upon the edge of the world and Chaos beyond. 'Out there nothing exists as yet. If you venture into it, you will be confronted again by creatures of your hidden fancy, for there is nothing else to behold.'

She gazed at him admiringly and he coughed in his embarrassment. 'Once in a while,' she said, 'there comes a man to Kaneloon who can withstand such an ordeal. Then may the frontiers of the world be extended, for when a man stands against Chaos it must recede and new lands spring into being!'

'So that is the fate you have in mind for me, sorceress!'

She glanced at him almost demurely. Her beauty seemed to increase as he looked at her. He clutched at the hilt of his sword, gripping it tight as she moved gracefully towards him and touched him, as if by accident. 'There is a reward for your courage.' She looked into his eyes and said no more of the reward, for it was clear what she offered. 'And after – do my bidding and go against Chaos.'

'Lady, know you not that ritual demands of Klant's Champion that he be the queen's faithful consort? I would not betray my word and trust!' He gave a hollow laugh. 'I came here to remove a menace to my queen's kingdom – not to be your lover and lackey!'

'There is no menace here.'

'That seems true . . .'

She stepped back as if appraising him anew. For her this was unprecedented – never before had her offer been refused. She rather liked this solid man who also combined courage and imagination in his character. It was incredible, she thought, how in a few centuries such traditions could grow up – traditions which could bind a man to a woman he probably did not even love. She looked at him as he stood there, his body rigid, his manner nervous.

'Forget Klant,' she said, 'think of the power you might have – the power of true creation!'

'Lady, I claim this castle for Klant. That is what I came to do and that is what I do now. If I leave here alive, I shall be judged the conqueror and you must comply.'

She hardly heard him. She was thinking of various plans to convince him that her cause was superior to his. Perhaps she could still seduce him? Or use some drug to bewitch him? No, he was too strong for either; she must think of some other stratagem.

She felt her breasts heaving involuntarily as she looked at him. She would have preferred to have seduced him. It had always been as much her reward as that of the heroes who had earlier won over the dangers of Kaneloon. And then, she thought, she knew what to say.

'Think, Earl Aubec,' she whispered. 'Think – new lands for your queen's Empire!'

He frowned.

'Why not extend the Empire's boundaries farther?' she continued. 'Why not *make* new territories?'

She watched him anxiously as he took off his helm and scratched his heavy, bald head. 'You have made a point at last,' he said dubiously.

'Think of the honours you would receive in Klant if you succeeded in winning not merely Kaneloon – but that which lies *beyond*!'

Now he rubbed his chin. 'Aye,' he said, 'Aye . . .' His great brows frowned deeply.

'New plains, new mountains, new seas – new populations, even – whole cities full of people fresh-sprung and yet with the memory of generations of ancestors behind them! All this can be done by *you*, Earl of Malador – for Queen Eloarde and Klant!'

He smiled faintly, his imagination fired at last. 'Aye! If I can defeat such dangers here – then I can do the same out there! It will be the greatest adventure in history! My name will become a legend – Malador, Master of Chaos!'

She gave him a tender look, though she had half-cheated him.

He swung his sword up on to his shoulder. 'I'll try this, lady.'

She and he stood together at the window, watching the Chaos-stuff whispering and rolling for eternity before them. To her it had never been wholly familiar, for it changed all the time. Now its tossing colours were predominantly red and black. Tendrils of mauve and orange spiralled out of this and writhed away.

Weird shapes flitted about in it, their outlines never clear, never quite recognizable.

He said to her: 'The Lords of Chaos rule this territory. What will they have to say?'

'They can say nothing, do little. Even they have to obey the Law of the Cosmic Balance which ordains that if man can stand against Chaos, then it shall be his to order and make Lawful. Thus the Earth grows, slowly.'

'How do I enter it?'

She took the opportunity to grasp his heavily muscled arm and point through the window. 'See – there – a causeway leads down from this tower to the cliff.' She glanced at him sharply. 'Do you see it?'

'Ah – yes – I had not, but now I do. Yes, a causeway.'

Standing behind him, she smiled a little to herself. 'I will remove the barrier,' she said.

He straightened his helm on his head. 'For Klant and Eloarde and only those do I embark upon this adventure.'

She moved towards the wall and raised the window. He did not look at her as he strode down the causeway into the multicoloured mist.

As she watched him disappear she smiled to herself. How easy it was to beguile the strongest man by pretending to go his way! He might add lands to his Empire, but he might find their populations unwilling to accept Eloarde as their Empress. In fact, if Aubec did his work well, then he would be creating more of a threat to Klant than ever Kaneloon had been.

Yet she admired him, she was attracted to him, perhaps, because he was not so accessible, a little more than she had been to that earlier hero who had claimed Aubec's own land from Chaos barely two hundred years before. Oh, he had been a man! But he, like most before him, had needed no other persuasion than the promise of her body.

Earl Aubec's weakness had lain in his strength, she thought. By now he had vanished into the heaving mists.

She felt a trifle sad that this time the execution of the task given her by the Lords of Law had not brought her the usual pleasure.

Yet perhaps, she thought, she felt a more subtle pleasure in his steadfastness and the means she had used to convince him.

For centuries had the Lords of Law entrusted her with Kaneloon and its secrets. But the progress was slow, for there were few heroes who could survive Kaneloon's dangers – few who could defeat self-created perils.

Yet, she decided with a slight smile on her lips, the task had its various rewards. She moved into another chamber to prepare for the transition of the castle to the new edge of the world.

Thus were the seeds sown of the Age of the Young Kingdoms, the Age of Men, which was to produce the downfall of Melnibone.

Jesting with Chaos

Through the blue and hazy night ran a shuddering man. He clutched terror to him, his bloated eyes full of blood. First behind him and then seemingly ahead of him came the hungry chuckles, the high whispered words.

'Here toothsome. Here sweetmeat.'

He swerved in another direction, moaning. Like a huge husk he was, like a hollow ornament of thin bone, with his great, rolling head swaying on his shoulders resembling a captive balloon, the wet cavern of his wide mouth fully open and gasping, the yellow spikes of teeth clashing in his head.

Awkwardly he ran, sometimes scuttling like a wounded spider, sometimes lurching, mooing to himself through the tall and ancient forest, his feet sinking into the carpet of wet, pungent bracken and rotting roots. He held in his hand, that long, white, metal-coloured claw, a glowing black talisman, held it out and cried:

'Oh Teshwan – aid me, Teshwan. Aid me . . .'

In the sluggish brew that was the contents of his rolling skull a few words swam to the surface and seemed to lie there, moving with the tide of his mind. And the voice which spoke them was sardonic: *'How can Teshwan aid thee little mortal?'*

But this relic of disoriented flesh could not form a coherent thought; could not answer save to scream its fear. So Teshwan took his presence away and it was left to the horseman to find the horror-crazed man.

Elric of Melniboné heard the voice and recognized the name. He sensed other, more ominous, denizens lurking about him in the forest.

Moodily he curled his hands about the reins of his mount and jerked its head, guiding it in the direction of the screams. He only casually considered aiding the man and he rode his horse towards him more from curiosity than anything. Elric was untroubled by the terrors that the forest held, regarding them as another, more normal man might regard the omnipresent song of birds and the rustle of small rodents in the undergrowth.

*

Great tremblings shuddered through Slorg's ruined body and he still heard the sharp whisperings. Were they carried on the air or were they slithering about in his jellied brain?

He gasped as he turned and saw the white-faced horseman riding like a grim, handsome god into the moonglazed glade.

The horseman's long, sharply delineated skull was leper-white, as if stripped of flesh, and his slightly slanting eyes gleamed crimson. He wore a jerkin of black velvet caught at the throat by a thin silver chain. His britches, too, were of black cloth, and his leather boots were high and shining. Over his shoulders was a high-collared cape of scarlet and a heavy longsword slapped at his side as he pulled his steed to a standstill. His long, flowing hair was as white as his face. The horseman was an albino.

The shock of confronting this new and more tangible figure jerked Slorg back into half-sanity and broken words sidled from his lips.

'Who are you? Aid me! I beg you, aid me!'

Elric laughed lightly. 'Now why should I, my friend? Tell me that.'

'I have been – been profaned – I am Slorg. I was once a man – but those . . .' He rocked his body and flung his rolling head backwards, the curved lids falling down to cover his bulging eyes. 'I have been profaned . . .'

Elric leaned forward on the pommel of his saddle and said lazily: 'This is none of my business, Master Slorg.'

The great head darted forward, the eyes snapped open and Slorg's long lips writhed over his teeth like a camel's. 'Address not me by a mundane title! I am Siletah Slorg – Siletah of Oberlorn – rightfully – rightfully.'

The title was unknown to Elric.

'My apologies, O Siletah,' he mocked, 'for now I observe a man of rank.'

'A man no longer,' whispered Slorg and he began to sob. 'Help me.'

'Are you, then, in danger?'

'Aye, danger – my kinsmen have set the Hungry Whisperers upon me; do you not hear them?'

And Elric cocked his head to listen. Yes, he heard sibilant voices now, *'Where are you, morsel?'*

'Oh, help me, help me,' begged Slorg and lurched towards Elric. The albino drew himself up and pulled his horse back.

'No closer,' he warned. 'I am Elric of Melniboné.'

Slorg's tattered face squeezed itself into a frown. 'Ah, the name and the face,' he mumbled to himself, 'the face and the name. Elric of Melniboné. *Outcast!*'

'Indeed,' smiled Elric, 'but no more than you, it seems. Now I must bid you farewell and suggest, by way of friendly advice, that you compose yourself soon. It is better to die with dignity, Siletah Slorg.'

'I have powers, outcast of Melniboné – I have powers, still! Help me and I will tell you secrets – such secrets!'

Elric waved a disdainful hand. A moonbeam caught for an instant the flash of the rare actorios ring which reposed on his finger. 'If you know me, you should also know that I'm no merchant to bargain. I ask nothing and give nothing. Farewell!'

'I warn you, Elric – I have one power left. I can send you screaming from this place – into another. It is the power which Teshwan gives all his servants – it is the one he never takes back!'

'Why not send your hungry friends into this other place?'

'They are not human. But if you leave me, I shall lay my last enchantment upon you.'

Elric sighed. 'Your last, perhaps, but not the last or the first to be laid upon me. Now I must go and search for a quieter place than this where I can sleep undisturbed.'

He turned his horse and his back on the shaking remnant of a man and rode away.

He heard Slorg calling again as he entered another part of the forest, untainted by the Siletah or those he had termed the Hungry Whisperers.

'Teshwan – return! Return to do me one last service – a deed of vengeance – a part of our bargain, Teshwan!'

A short time later Elric heard a thin, wailing scream come flowing out of the night behind him and then the whole forest seemed alive with horrible laughter. Satiated, triumphant, chuckling.

His mood altered by his encounter, Elric rode through the night, not caring to sleep, and came out of the forest in the morning, glad of the sight of the green plateau stretching ahead of him.

'Well,' he mused, 'Teshwan disdained to aid Slorg and it seems there is no enchantment on me. I am half regretful. Now Slorg resides in the bellies of those he feared and his soul's at home in Hell.'

Then the plateau changed quite suddenly to grey rock.

Swiftly Elric wheeled his horse. The plateau and the forest was behind him. He spurred his mount quickly forward and the plateau and forest faded away to leave a vast and lonely expanse of flat, grey stone. Above him the sun had disappeared and the sky was bright and white and cold.

'Now,' said Elric grimly into silence, 'it seems I was wrong in my assumption.'

The plateau – its atmosphere – reminded him of another environment in which he had once found himself. Then he remembered clearly a time years before when he and two companions had sought an ancient volume called the Dead God's Book. Their questing had led them to a cavern guarded at its entrance by the symbol of the Lords of Chaos. In that cavern they had discovered an underground sea which had had unnatural qualities. There was the same sense of a sardonically amused *presence* here as there had been in the Caverns of Chaos.

Teshwan was a Lord of Chaos.

Hastily Elric pulled his runesword Stormbringer from its thick scabbard.

The sword was dead.

Normally the blade, forged by unhuman smiths for Elric's royal ancestors, was alive with sentience – throbbing with the life force it had stolen from a hundred men and women whom Elric had slain. Once before it had been like this – in the Caverns of Chaos long ago.

Elric tightened his lips, then shrugged as he replaced the sword in its scabbard.

'In a world completely dominated by the Forces of Chaos,' he said, 'I cannot rely on the powers which normally aid me in my sorcery. Thank Arioch I have a good supply of drugs about me, or I would indeed be doomed.'

In earlier times Elric had relied on his soul-stealing runesword to give him the energy which, as an albino, he lacked intrinsically, but recently he had rediscovered a cleaner way of counteracting his deficiency, by taking herbs he had discovered in the Forest of Troos where many unlikely things grew, both flora and fauna.

'By my father's plague-infested bones,' he swore. 'I must find a way off this granite plain and discover who, if anyone, rules in this world. I have heard of the powers invested in Teshwan's worshippers – and I seem to remember a hint of why the Lords of Chaos confer such peculiar talents upon them.'

He shuddered.

He began to sing a ululating hate-song of old Melniboné. Elric's ancestors had been clever haters. And on he rode beneath the sunless sky.

He could not tell how much time had passed before he saw the figure standing out strongly against the featureless horizon.

Now on the flat waste of stone there were two points at which the monotony was broken.

Elric – white, black and scarlet on a grey gelding.

The morose man, black hair lying like a coat of lacquer on his rounded skull, dressed in green, a silver sword dangling in his right hand.

Elric approached the man who raised his eyes to regard the albino.

'This is a lonely place,' said the stranger, sucking at his fleshy cheeks, and he stared at the ground again.

'True,' replied Elric halting his horse. 'Is this your world or were you sent here, also?'

'Oh, it's my world,' said the man, without looking up. 'Where are you bound?'

'For nowhere, seeking something. Where do you journey?'

'I – oh, I go to Kaneloon for the Rites, of course.'

'All things, it is said, are possible in the World of Chaos.' Elric murmured, 'and yet this place seems unusually barren.'

The man looked up suddenly, and jerking his lips into a smile, laughed sharply.

'The Rites will alter that, stranger. Did you not know that this is the Time of The Change, when the Lords of Chaos rest before re-forming the world into a fresh variety of patterns?'

'I did not know that,' said Elric. 'I have come here only recently.'

'You wish to stay?'

'No.'

'The Lords of Chaos are fickle. If you wished to stay they might not let you. Now that you are resolved to leave, they might keep you here. Farewell. You will find me therein! He lifted his sword and pointed. A great palace of greenstone appeared at once. The man vanished.

'This, at least, will save me from boredom,' Elric said philosophically, and rode towards the palace.

The many-pinnacled building towered above him, its highest points hazy and seeming to possess many forms, shifting as if blown by a wind. At the great arch of the entrance a huge giant, semi-transparent, with a red, scintillating skin, blocked his way. Over the archway, as if hanging in the air above the giant's proud head, was the Symbol of Chaos, a circle which produced many arrows pointing in all directions.

'Who visits the Palace of Kaneloon at the Time of the Change?' enquired the giant in a voice like limbo's music.

'Your masters, I gather, know me – for they aided their servant Slorg in sending me hither. But tell them it is Elric of Melniboné, nonetheless – Elric, destroyer of dreaming Imrryr. Kinslayer and outcast. They will know me.'

The giant appeared to shrink, to solidify and then to drift in a red mist, pouring like sentient smoke away from the portal and into the palace. And where he had been a portcullis manifested itself to guard the palace in the giant's absence.

Elric waited patiently until at length the portcullis vanished and the giant re-formed himself.

'My masters order me to inform you that you may enter but that, having once come to the Palace of Kaneloon, you may never leave save under certain conditions.'

'Those conditions?'

'Of these they will tell you if you enter. Are you reckless – or will you stand pondering?'

'I'll avail myself of their generosity,' smiled Elric and spurred his nervous horse forward.

As he entered the courtyard, it appeared that the area within the palace was greater than that outside it. Not troubling to seek any mundane explanation for this phenomenon in a world dominated by the Lords of Chaos, Elric instead dismounted from his horse and walked for nearly a quarter of a mile until he reached the entrance of the main building. He climbed the steps swiftly and found himself in a vast hall which had walls of shifting flame.

In the glow from the fiery walls, there sat at a table at the far end of the hall nine men – or at least, men or not, they had assumed the form of men. Different in facial characteristics, they all had the same sardonic air. In the centre of these nine was the one who had first addressed Elric. He leaned forward and spoke words carefully from his red lips.

'Greetings to you, mortal,' he said. 'You are the first for some time to sit with the Lords of Chaos at the Time of the Change. Behold – there are others who have had the privilege.'

A rent appeared in the wall of flame to disclose some thirty frozen human figures, some men and some women. They were petrified in positions of many kinds, but all had madness and terror in their eyes – and they were still alive. Elric knew.

He lifted his head.

'I would not be so impertinent, my lords, as to set myself beside you all insofar as powers are concerned, but you know that I am Elric of Melniboné and that my race is old; my deficient blood is the royal blood of the Kings of the Dreaming City. I have little pity or sentiment of any kind within me, for sentiment, whether love or hate, has served me badly in the past. I do not know what you require of me, and I thank you for your hospitality nonetheless, but I believe that I can conduct myself better in most ways than can any other mortal.'

'Let us hope so, Elric of Melniboné, for we would not wish you to fail, know that. Besides, you are not fully mortal as humans understand the word. Now, know you that I be Teshwan, and these need not be named and may be addressed singly or collectively by the name of Lords of Chaos.'

Elric bowed politely. 'Lord Teshwan – my Lords of Chaos.'

They returned his bow by slightly inclining their heads and broadening a trifle their sardonic, crooked smiles.

'Come,' said Teshwan briskly, 'sit here beside me and I will inform you of what we expect. You are more favoured than others have been, Elric, and, in truth, I welcomed the opportunity given me by my vengeful servant Slorg before he died.'

Elric climbed upon the dais and seated himself in the chair which appeared beside Teshwan. About him the walls of flame soared and tumbled, mumbled and roared. Sometimes shadow engulfed them, sometimes they were bathed in light. For a while they all sat in silence, pondering.

At last Teshwan spoke.

'Now,' he said decisively. 'Here's the situation in which we have decided to place you. You may leave only if you can create something which it has never occurred to us to create.'

'But you, surely, are the Masters of Creation?' said Elric in puzzlement. 'How may I do this?'

'Your first statement is not strictly true and in qualifying it I can give you a hint of the answer to your question. We of Chaos cannot make anything new – we may only experiment with combinations of that already created. Do you understand?'

'I do,' said Elric.

'Only the Greatest Power, of which we know little more than do humans, can create fresh conceptions. The Greatest Power holds both Law and Chaos in perpetual balance, making us war only so that the scale will not be tilted too far to one side. We wish not for power – only for variety. Thus every time we weary of our domain we let our old creations fade and conceive new ones. If you can bring a fresh element to our domain, we shall free you. We create jokes and paradoxes. Conceive a better joke and a better paradox for our entertainment and you may leave here.'

'Surely you expect the impossible from me?'

'You alone may assess the truth of your question. Now, we begin.'

And Elric sat and watched, pondering his problem, as the great Lords of Chaos began their mighty experiments.

The walls of fire slowly flickered and faded and again he saw the vast and barren plain of flat stone. Then the air darkened and a sighing wind began to moan over the plain. In the sky clouds blossomed in myriad shapes, alien, dark, unfamiliar, blacks and smoky orange, at the same time familiar . . .

The rock heaved like lava, became liquid, rearing upwards and as it reared it became giants, mountains, ancient beasts, monsters, gryphons, basilisks, chimerae, unicorns. Forests bloomed, their growths huge and exotic, elephants flew and great birds crushed boiling mountains beneath their feet. Fingers of brilliant colour climbed the sky, criss-crossing and blending. A flight of wildly singing lions fell from the firmament towards the forest and soared upwards again, their music lonely.

As the forest melted to become an ocean, a vast army of wizened homunculae came tramping from its depths dragging boats behind them. For a short while they marched over the seething waters and then, with precision, began, in ordered style, to climb into the flaring sky. When they had all left the ocean behind them, they righted their boats, set their sails, laughed and screamed and shouted, waved their arms, climbed into the boats and with fantastic speed streamed towards the horizon.

All creation tumbled and poured, malleable in the Domain of Chaos. All was gusto, craze and roaring terror, love, hate and music mingled.

The sky shook with multi-coloured mirth, blossoming white shot through with veins of blue and purple and black, searing red, splattered with spreading flowers of yellow, smeared, smeared, smeared with ghoulish green. Across this seething backdrop sped bizarre shapes.

The Lords of Chaos shouted and sang their weird creation and Elric, shouting also, thought the frozen statues he had seen were weeping and laughing.

A grotesque combination of man and tree sent roots streaming towards the earth to tug mountains from the caverns it exposed and set them, peak first, like inverted pyramids, into the ground. Upon the flat surfaces dancers appeared in bright rags which fluttered and flared around them. They were warped, unhuman, pale as dead beauty, grinning fixedly and then Elric saw the strings attached to their limbs and the silently laughing puppet-master bearlike and gigantic, controlling them. From another direction sped a small, blind figure bearing a scythe that was a hundred times bigger than the bearer. With a sweep, he cut the strings and, with that action, the whole faded to be replaced by a gushing brilliance of green and orange flame which formed itself into streamers of zig-zagging disorder.

All this went on around them. The Lords of Chaos smiled to themselves now, as they created, but Elric frowned, watched with wonder and no little pleasure, but puzzled how he might emulate such feats.

For long hours the pageant of Chaos continued as the Lords took the elements of Elric's world and shook them about, turned them inside out, stood them on end, made startling, strange, beautiful, unholy combinations until they were satisfied with the constant movement of the scene about them, the perpetual shifting and changing.

They had set a pattern that was no pattern, which would last until they became bored with their domain again and brought about another Time of the Change.

Then their heads turned and all regarded Elric expectantly.

Teshwan said a trifle wearily, 'There – you have seen what we can do.'

'You are artists, indeed,' said Elric, 'and I am so amazed by what I have witnessed that I need a little time to think. Will you grant it me?'

'A little time – a little time only – we want to see what you prepare for us while the excitement is still upon us.'

And Elric placed his white albino's head upon his fist and thought deeply.

Many ideas occurred to him, only to be discarded, but at length he straightened his back and said: 'Give me the power to create and I will create.'

So Teshwan said smilingly, 'You have the power – use it well. A joke and a paradox is all we require.'

'The reward for failure?'

'To be forever conscious.'

At this, Elric shivered and put his mind to concentrating, searching his memory until a manlike figure formed before him. Then he placed features on its head and clothes on its body until there stood before Elric and the Lords of Chaos a perfect replica – of Elric.

Puzzledly, Teshwan said: 'This is splendid impertinence, I grant you – but this is nothing new – you already sit there beside us.'

'Indeed,' replied Elric, 'but look in the man's mind.'

They frowned and did as he asked. Then, smiling, they nodded: 'The paradox is good,' said Teshwan, 'and we see your point. We have, for an eternity, created the effect. You, in your pride and innocence, have created the cause. In that man's mind was all that could ever exist.'

'You have noted the paradox?' asked Elric, anxious that the correct interpretation had been divulged.

'Of course. For though the mind contains the variety beloved of we of Chaos, it contains the order that those barren Lords of Law would foist on the world. Truly, young mortal, you have created everything with a stroke. And thank you, also, for the joke.'

'The joke?'

'Why truly – the best joke is but a simple statement of truth. Farewell. Remember, friend mortal, that the Lords of Chaos are grateful to you.'

And with that, the whole domain faded away and Elric stood on the grassy plain. In the distance he observed the city of Bakshaan which had been his original destination, and nearby was his horse to take him there.

He mounted, flapped the reins, and, as the grey gelding broke into a trot, he said to himself: 'A joke indeed, but it is a pity that men do not laugh at it more often.'

Reluctantly, he headed for the city.

The Greater Conqueror

CHAPTER ONE

He felt he was much more than one man. Not one god, even, but many . . . There seemed to be a hundred other entities writhing within him. Writhing to release themselves. Every limb, every projection of bone seemed to be part of another being.

He lay on the fur-strewn bed, sweating, dominated by movement in his mind and body which he was incapable of controlling. Alexander the Great groaned in torment.

The buxom Corinthian woman spat into the rushes on the floor of the tavern.

'That for the God-King!'

But the silence around her put a stop to her enlarging the theme. The Thracian known as Simon of Byzantium lifted his bronze cup, the sleeve of his silk-trimmed jerkin falling back down his bronze arm, and sucked sweet Persian wine into his throat. He sensed the discomfort the other roisterers felt towards the woman and, because he could be cautious, dropped his arm from her thick waist and pushed her from him.

He looked down his long nose. His scarred face moved and he smiled as he addressed an old Persian soldier.

'You say you were in the army Darius led against Alexander?'

'That's right – a charioteer. His cavalry ran rings round us.'

'What did you think of him?'

'Alexander? I don't know. I was quite close to him at one stage and saw a spearman get a blow at him – struck him in the thigh. He yelled – not in pain but when he saw his own blood flowing. He couldn't believe it. For a short time he was an open target as he stared down at his thigh, dabbing at the blood with his finger and inspecting it. Then he shouted something – I didn't recognize the language – and was in command of himself again. They said the wound healed unnaturally quickly.'

'He claims to be the son of Zeus,' the Corinthian woman said from the shadows, 'but many Persians say he's evil Ahriman's spawn.'

Simon pursed his lips and fingered his wine cup. 'Perhaps he's just a mortal,' he suggested, 'a mortal of unusual vitality?'

'Perhaps,' the Persian soldier said. 'I only know he's conquered the world.'

'I heard he halted his Indian campaign at the River Indus – why should he do that?' Simon said.

'His Macedonians say they forced him to stop, but I cannot believe that. Even Alexander must tire – that's my theory. I think he needed to rest and recuperate. Throughout his campaigns he's hardly slept; must move on continually as if driven to conquer. Who knows what spurred him to conquest – or what made him put a temporary halt to his victories?'

'The Indians have an ancient and mighty religion of which we know little,' said a middle-aged and scrawny trader from Carthage. 'Could their Gods be stronger than ours? Stronger than Alexander?' He pulled at his grey-streaked beard. His many rings glinted in the ill-lit place.

'Such talk is heresy these days,' cautioned the Persian, but it could be seen that he was contemplating this idea.

'People talk of nothing but the Macedonian,' said the swarthy trader. 'From the Bosphorus to the Nile they curse or praise him. But what is he other than a man who has been lucky? Events have shaped him, not he them. He owes much to his foresighted father King Philip, and that warped mother Queen Olympias, both of whom, in their separate ways, prepared the world for his conquests. What reason for instance did he have for his meanderings in Persia some years ago? Why, instead of pressing on, did he embark on a wild goose chase after Darius? He had no reason save that events were not ready for him.'

'I like to think this of great men, also.' Simon smiled. 'But I would join his army for my own convenience.'

'So that's why you're in Babylon. I wondered about you, my friend. Where are you from?' The Carthaginian poured himself more wine from a skin.

'I was born in Thrace, but I'm Byzantine by adoption. I've spent seven years there as Captain of Infantry. But now I've the urge to see the East and since Alexander goes East, decided to attach myself to his army. I hear he's in Babylon now.'

'That's true. But you might find him hard to meet – obviously he is not personally concerned with the hiring of mercenaries.' The

Persian's tone was friendly.

'I've heard this man – or God – spoken of so often that I've a mind to meet him if that's possible.'

'Good luck to you, friend. He'll either kill you or promote you. He's a man of extremes.'

'Are not all great conquerors?'

'You're marvellous learned for a mercenary.' The Carthaginian grinned.

Simon picked up his scabbarded short-sword from the bench.

'And you're marvellous curious, friend. Know you not that all Arts are encouraged in Byzantium, just as they were in ancient Greece – including the Arts of Reading and Philosophy.'

The Persian laughed. 'That's the story Byzantium tells. I for one do not believe that any city could be so enlightened. All you Westerners yearn for a Greece that never was – your whole philosophy is based on a need for perfection; a perfection you can never attain because it never existed. Believe me, the gutters of Byzantium still stink!'

'Not so strongly as Persian jealousy,' Simon said, and left before he was called upon to take the argument to its conclusion.

But behind him in the tavern the Persian had not been angered. Instead he was laughing, wiping his mouth with his arm stump.

Simon heard the laughter as he crossed the dim Square of the Bazaar, almost deserted of merchants and customers. The sun was still setting. It was nearly curfew. A few merchants baling their goods looked up as he strode, a tall, gaunt, fighting man, in smooth old leather, towards the Street of the Bronzeworkers where he had a friend.

Around him, golden Babylon squatted like an ancient monster, containing all knowledge, all secrets, her stepped houses, palaces, and temples soaking the last of the sun into their burnished hides. He walked up the steeply rising street and came at length to a small white house without windows. He knocked.

For a while he waited patiently as darkness came. Eventually bolts were withdrawn on the other side of the door and it was opened. An eye gleamed. The door opened wider.

Wizened Hano smiled welcomingly. 'Come in, Simon. So you reached our splendid Babylon!'

Simon stepped into the house. It was very dark, over-hot, with the unpleasantly bitter smell of metal. The old Phoenician clutched at his arm and led him down the dark passage.

'Will you be staying in Babylon, my boy?' Hano said, and then, before Simon could answer this question: 'How's the sword?'

'I intend to see Alexander,' Simon said, disliking the old man's touch though he liked Hano greatly. 'And the sword is excellent, has kept its edge in a dozen fights – I intend to hire it to Alexander.'

Hano's grip tightened as they entered a dark, smoky room, a red brazier gleaming in its centre. Around the smoke-stained walls were weapons – swords, shields, lances – and several couches and small tables were scattered on the floor. The smoke caught in Simon's lungs and he coughed it out. Hano pointed to a couch. 'Sit down, Simon.' He shuffled towards his own couch on the other side of the brazier, stretched himself at full length and scratched his hooked nose.

'Alexander has many swords.'

'I know – but if you granted me a favour it might facilitate my meeting him.'

'I owe you friendship and more,' Hano said, 'for you saved me from an unpleasant death that time in Thebes nine years ago. But though I sense what you want of me I am reluctant to agree to it.'

'Why?'

'An old man's caution, maybe, but the stories I've been hearing of late have been disquieting. Alexander claims himself son of Zeus, Jupiter Ammon. Others say that the Persian evil one Ahriman possesses him. All or none of this may be true – but every oracle from here to Pela is prophesying turmoil and trouble for the world and the king who rules it. Perhaps you would be wiser to join some ordinary caravan travelling east?' Hano pulled back his woollen robe, revealing a pale and unlovely leg. He poised his wrinkled hand and then almost hurled it at a spot on his leg and began to scratch at the place with his talons of nails.

'I'm sick of this prattle of gods and demons. Can no one be content simply to believe in men and what men could be if they ceased blaming their misfortunes on unseen gods rather than on their own ineffectiveness? Life's not easy, it is a hard task to live it well and with grace – but, by Hades, let's not complicate it with deities and water-nymphs!'

Simon spat into the brazier which flared and spluttered.

Hano scratched at his thigh, drawing back more of his robe to do so, revealing a greater expanse of unhealthy flesh.

'I have seen supernatural manifestations of evil, my boy.'

'You have seen what a muddled brain wished you to see.'

'What matter? Now, let's end this conversation before you yell more heresies and have us both arrested.'

'Heresy and treason combined if Alexander's chest-puffing claim be true.' Simon looked away from the old man's thin legs and stared into the brazier.

Hano changed the subject.

'In Utopia,' he said to Simon, 'you'd yet be seeking further perfection. You call yourself a realist, Simon – perfection is not a reality.'

'Realities can be created,' said Simon.

'True,' Hano agreed. 'But by the same logic, realities can be made unreal – unrealities made real. What if there *were* super-natural beings? How would you fit them into your theory?'

'The situation will never arise.'

'Let us hope so.'

The Phoenician turned his old twisted face towards Simon. The brazier light stained it a reddish brown, showing the wrinkles of mingled cynicism, fatalism, and good nature. Hano said at length: 'Very well.'

He got up and moved about the crowded room taking a pot from one shelf, a skin of wine from another.

Soon the smell of herbs came from the pot on the brazier as Hano brewed wine for his guest.

'You'll help.' Simon said.

'Alexander owes me a favour. But he has strange ways of repaying debts and I'd not normally be foolish enough remind him of this one.'

'What did you do for him?'

'Set the handle of a star-metal blade with black opals.'

'That was a favour!' Simon laughed.

Hano scowled, but genially. 'Know you not what that meant? It meant he could not directly handle iron or anything likely to conduct its force to his body. Black opal is one of the few gems which will serve to negate the flow.'

'So?'

'So Alexander has a weakness. Iron will harm him.'

'If I had such a secret I would kill the man who held it.' Simon said reflectively.

'Not if you were Alexander and the man was dear to Olympias.'

'*You* know Queen Olympias!'

'Olympias wishes me kept alive so I can feed her with secrets.'

'Dark secrets, I'll warrant, if the stories of her are half-true.'

'They do not touch the real truth about her.'

'Does she really sport with snakes at these rites?'

'Aye – and black goats are present too.'

Simon swore.

Hano handed him a cup of hot wine. As he drank he said: 'I'm impatient to meet the God-King – how will you help?'

'I'll give you a letter and a token to take to Alexander. But be wary, my boy. Be wary.'

CHAPTER TWO

Though he rarely admitted it, the idea of a supernatural world of gods and spirits disturbed Simon. Had it been practicable he might have become a militant atheist but instead he kept his opinions secret for the most part and did his utmost not to question them or even think of them.

When he reached the great golden palace of Alexander he paused and stared up at it with admiration. It was illuminated by hundreds of torches many of which, on long poles, surrounded the palace. Others flared on its many ramparts.

Two guards came forward. They were Babylonians in high helmets with oiled hair and beards. Their javelins threatened him.

In poor Babylonian Simon said:

'I come to see King Alexander – I have a token and a letter for him.'

They treated him with some respect, though they divested him of his sword and led him to the main gate where, after conversation he was admitted.

He was made to wait several times, being studied and questioned by a variety of viziers and minions of the king, but at last he was ushered into a large chamber.

Big windows let in the flickering torchlight. A great bed of brass, silver, and gold, heaped with silks and furs, was in the centre of the room.

Alexander was sitting up in bed. He had been sweating, Simon could see. His nose told him the same story.

The odour, in fact was bad. Far worse than ordinary perspiration. Simon couldn't place the smell.

With a degree of nervousness Simon approached the huge bed.

Suddenly, King Alexander grinned and stuck out a handsome hand.

'You have a letter for me, I hear – and a token?'

'I have, sire.' Simon gave the letter and the little talisman to Alexander, studying the king's strange face. In a way it was boyish; in another ancient and sensuous. He had a long nose and thick lips, heavily lidded eyes, and brown, curly hair. Simon was taken aback by the king's lack of ceremony, by his friendly grin. Was this the God-King? The spawn of evil?

Alexander read the letter quickly, nodding to himself.

'Did Hano tell you of my debt to him?'

'No, sire,' Simon said tactfully.

'He has many secrets, Hano – but he's an old man and, in his generosity, keeps few to himself, I've heard.'

'He seems curiously tight-lipped, sire,' Simon replied, anxious for his friend's life, 'and even I who saved his life one time in Thebes can never get a full reply to any question I ask him.'

Alexander looked up sharply, staring Simon in the face with peculiarly wide eyes.

'So you wish to join my army. Hano recommends you as a fighting man – suggests you join my staff. I choose my officers with care, Simon of Byzantium.'

'I wish only a trial, sire.'

'You shall have it.'

Alexander studied the letter again.

'You're from Byzantium, I note. My father Philip was repulsed by that city some years ago – but that does not mean I can have no love for the city – perhaps the contrary. It's well known I disliked him and can admire a city which withstood his attack.' Alexander smiled again. 'Though she did not hold out for long against Philip's son, did she?'

'No, sire.'

Alexander had an almost tangible vitality, but he was evidently unwell. This ailment was not solely confined to his body, either, Simon felt.

Alexander mused, caressing the little amulet.

'I have need of a herald – a man who can travel between wherever I am campaigning and the capital of Macedonia.'

'I thought Persia was your base these days, sire.'

'You've been listening to Greek and Macedonian criticism, no doubt. They say I've forsaken my own lands for the fleshpots and honours of the East. That's a lie. It is too far to travel back always to Pela. Persia offers a better base for my operations. There are still a few acres of the world left for me to conquer, Simon – and they all lie eastwards.'

Alexander sank back into his silks, eyeing the Thracian.

'You'll serve my mother and myself as a messenger.'

Simon put his hand to his lips and said courteously: 'I had rather hoped to go with the army, sire.'

Alexander frowned slightly. 'And so you will, of course. No doubt there'll be fighting for you – and new knowledge. I'm pleased that you're literate. Most of my captains are chosen for several qualities – courage, loyalty – and learning. You appear to have courage and learning – but I must find out about your loyalty, you understand.'

Simon nodded. 'That is logical, sire.'

'Good, then –' Alexander broke off as the doors of the chamber opened behind Simon. The Thracian turned to stare at the door.

A vizier, in long cloth-of-gold robes, hurried into the room.

He prostrated himself before the king's bed.

'Son of Zeus,' he mumbled, 'a message.'

'Is it secret?'

'No, sire – they say it is already common knowledge.'

'Then speak – what is it?' Alexander propped himself into a sitting position again.

'A massacre, sire – in Lonarten – a troop of your Macedonian horse went berserk, killed many hundreds of women and children. There are rumours of cannibalism and unhealthy rites . . .' The vizier stopped as a smile crossed Alexander's sensuous lips. 'The people are asking for your interference – for compensation.'

Alexander smiled again. Simon was sickened by the sight. The king could be seen to grip hold of the bed-clothes as if attempting to control himself. He groaned once, slightly.

With effort he said: 'We must call a halt to – we must stop . . .' Then he flung back his handsome head and bellowed with laughter. It was a laughter totally evil, a horrible, malicious joy which seethed around the room, echoing and roaring in Simon's horrified ears.

'Seize the complainers,' Alexander shouted, 'we'll sell them as eunuchs to the harems of Turkey. Teach them that the ways of a god are not the ways of a mere king – teach them not to question the word or actions of the Son of Zeus!'

Hurriedly, the vizier backed out of the room.

Simon, forgetful for his own safety, leaned forward and shouted into Alexander's twisted face:

'You are mad – for your own sake do not let this massacre continue. Your unruly troops will cause a revolution – you will lose your empire.'

Alexander's eyes opened even wider. A hand leapt from the silks and furs and seized Simon's ear. The mouth curled and even teeth moved as Alexander snarled:

'For you I will *invent* a death!'

Simon grasped the wrist attempting to wrest himself from Alexander's grip. He was sickened, trembling and shaken by the strength in one so evidently ill. He felt the presence of something more than common insanity. What had changed the pleasant, practical soldier into this manifestation of evil? How could such different qualities exist in one body? Terror clouded his mind.

With a wrench he was free of the king's grasp and backed panting away from him.

'They said you were Ahriman's spawn – and I did not believe them,' he gasped.

Alexander grimaced, flung back the bed-clothes and leapt to the ground, advancing towards Simon, with hands outstretched.

'I am Zeus's son – born of god and mortal to rule the world. Abase yourself, heretic, for I have the power to send you to Hades!'

'All men have that power,' Simon said, turned and ran for the great doors, tugged them open and, before he could be stopped fled down the shouting corridors, blind to everything but the need to escape from the screaming madman behind him.

He remembered little of the flight, of the two fights, in the first of which he somehow gained a weapon, of his breathless running through the streets of Babylon with hordes of soldiers seeking him out.

He ran.

He had run himself virtually to death when several warriors pinned him in a blind alley and he turned, snarling like an animal to defend himself. Crouching, sword raised, he waited for them as they cautiously advanced.

They had not expected such ferocity. He had cut the first soldier down in a trice and sliced the flesh from another's arm.

In front of him, as if superimposed on the real scene before him, was the great, sensuous head of Alexander still roaring with crazy laughter.

Simon had seen madmen many times. But Alexander had more than madness. He slashed with his sword and missed his target, fell forward, rolled on his back, brought his sword across his face to deflect a blade which had hurtled down through the confused night. He edged back, flung himself sideways, slashing, scrambled up and brought the edge of his sword up to chop a man's jugular.

Then he was running again, every limb aching, but a terrible fear, a fear of more than death or torture, driving, driving him onward to escape.

When the silent, dark-robed men appeared out of the night and surrounded him he cut at one but his sword seemed to meet metal, his hand went numb and the blade fell to the stones of the streets.

Alexander's face rose before him, laughing, laughing. The roaring, evil merriment filled his head, then his whole body until it seemed that he, Simon, was Alexander, that he was enjoying the bloody joke, the evil, malignant glee pouring wildly from his shaking body.

Then peace of a kind, and hazy, mysterious dreams where he saw strange shapes moving through the smoke from a million red and glowing braziers.

Simon felt a hard, smooth surface beneath his back.

He opened his eyes warily.

A lean, white, thin-lipped face looked kindly down at him.

'I am Abaris,' he said.

'Simon of Byzantium,' said the Thracian.

'You have witnessed darkness?' It was only half a question.

'Yes,' Simon replied, bemused.

'We are men of light. The Magi welcome you. You are safe here.'

'Magi? They are priests in Persia – but you're not Persian.'

'That is so.'

'Abaris? There is an Abaris of legend – a wizard, was he not – a priest of Apollo who rode on an arrow?'

The Magi made no reply to this, simply smiled.

'You have incurred the wrath of Alexander. How long would you say you had to live?'

'A strange question. I'd say as long as my wits were sharp enough to evade the searchings of his soldiers.'

'You would be wrong.'

Simon pushed himself upright on the wide bench and looked around him. Two other priests sat regarding him from across the bare room. Daylight filtered in from a hole in the ceiling.

'Do I really owe you my life?'

'We think you do – but you are in no debt. We wish we could give such concrete aid to all enemies of Alexander.'

'I am not his enemy – he is mine.'

'You have witnessed what he is – can you still say that?'

Simon nodded. 'I am his enemy,' he agreed and then amended this with: 'Or at least the enemy of what he represents.'

'You are exact – we also are the enemies of what Alexander represents.'

Simon put his head on one side and smiled slightly. 'Ah – let us be careful. He is insane, that is all. He represents material evil, not supernatural.'

Briefly, Abaris looked impatiently away, frowning. Then his features resumed their earlier look.

'It is a bold thing to be an unbeliever in these times.'

'Bold or not – it is what I am.' Simon swung his legs off the bench. He felt incredibly weak.

Abaris said: 'We Magi worship Ormuzd. Simply – Alexander represents Ahriman.'

'These are the twin facets of your single deity are they not?' Simon said. He nodded. 'I know a little about your cult – it's cleaner than most. You worship Fire, Sun, and Light – with a minimum of ritual.'

'True. A man who is confident in his soul needs little ritual.'

Simon was satisfied by this.

'We would be grateful if you would ally yourself with us, the Magi,' Abaris said quietly. 'In return we will protect you from Alexander's minions as best we can.'

'I told you – and I do not wish to seem ungrateful – my wits will keep me safe from the Macedonian's warriors.'

'We refer to his supernatural minions.'

Simon shook his head. 'I respect your beliefs – but I cannot accept them personally.'

Abaris leaned forward and said urgently, softly:

'Simon, you must aid us. Alexander and his mother are both possessed. For years we have been aware of this. For years we have attempted to fight the forces possessing them – and we are losing. You have seen how Ahriman controls Alexander. You must aid us!'

Simon said: 'You have cloaked the simple fact of Alexander's madness in a shroud of supernatural speculation.'

Abaris shook his head, saying nothing. Simon continued:

'I have seen many men go mad with riches and power – Alexander is another. When he dies his good works will survive but the evil will be eliminated by time.'

'You are naïve, young man. Why, Achilles believed that . . .' Abaris bit his lip and lapsed into silence.

'Achilles? He died a thousand years ago. How do you know what he believed?'

Abaris turned away. 'Of course, I could not know,' he said. His eyes were hooded.

'You give me cause to think you really are the Abaris of legend,' Simon smiled. He was joking. But even to his ears the joke rang true.
Abaris said: 'Can a man live for more than a thousand years?'
'No,' Simon said, 'no.' He said it almost savagely, for it was what he wished to believe.

Out there, in a palace of Babylon, there was *evil*, he thought. But it was not, could not be – *must* not be supernatural.
Abaris now said:
'Alexander has reigned almost thirteen years – a mystic number. Our oracles prophesied that the turning point would come after thirteen years of rule. Now, as we fear, Alexander and the forces which act through him will bring an unchecked reign of evil to the world – or else, and the chance is small, he will be stopped.'
'You wish me to aid you in this. I must dissent. To help you I would have to believe you – that I cannot do.'
Abaris seemed to accept this. When he next spoke it was in a detached, trancelike voice.
'Ahriman – the multiplicity of Ahrimans whom we designate by the one name – selected Olympias many years ago. He needed a vessel through which to work and, at that time, no mortal had been born who would serve Ahriman's purpose. So he took possession of poor Olympias. Philip, that great and wronged man, went regularly to the Isle of Samothrace on pilgrimage and, one year, Olympias made it her business to be there also. A love potion was all she needed. Philip was enamoured of her. They had a son – Alexander . . .'
Simon said wearily: 'This is mere gossip such as old women make in the markets.'
'Ormuzd protect you if you ever learn the truth,' was all Abaris said.
Simon rose shakily. 'If there is anything I can do to repay you – some material act, perhaps – I am very willing.'

Abaris thought for a moment. Then he took a scroll from his robe. He unrolled it and glanced over the weird script. It was not Persian, Simon knew, but what it was he could not tell.
Abaris handed the scroll to Simon. 'We'll furnish you with a horse and a disguise. Will you go to Pela for us? Will you deliver a message to our brothers?'
'Willingly,' Simon said, though he was aware that to journey to the capital of Macedonia would be courting danger.
'They live in secret,' Abaris told Simon, 'but we will tell you how to

find them. Also we will furnish you with weapons, a horse and a disguise of some sort.'

'I'd be grateful for that,' Simon smiled.

'We'll give you a day for resting and allowing the herbs we'll give you to drink to do their work – then you can start off. You should have little trouble here, for our magic will protect you and we know a secret way out of the city.'

Simon lay back on the bench. 'Healing herbs will be very welcome,' he said, 'and something to help me take a dreamless sleep . . .'

CHAPTER THREE

Outside, the courtiers glanced at one another, not daring to enter the room where a man groaned.

A short, clever-looking man in ornate war-gear turned to a calm-faced, sensitive man.

'Why was he so anxious to apprehend the Thracian, I wonder, Anaxarchus?'

The sensitive man shook his head. 'I have no idea. I hear he was from my home city, Abdera, before he went to Byzantium. For all my people say that the folk of Abdera are stupid, some very clever men were born there.'

'And you, of course, are one,' the soldier smiled ironically.

'I must be – I am a philosopher attached to Alexander's train,' Anaxarchus said.

The warrior took several nervous paces up the corridor, wheeled around, cursing. 'By the Salamander's breath, are we never to finish our conquests? What is wrong with Alexander, Anaxarchus? How long has he been like this? Rumours came to Egypt, but I discounted them.'

'He is ill, Ptolemy, that is all,' Anaxarchus said, but he did not believe his own words.

'That is *all*! Even if I had not heard the Oracle of Libya speak of terrible strifings in this world and the others I would be troubled. Things are happening. Anaxarchus – doom-clouds are covering the world.'

'Gloomy, Ptolemy – he is only sick. He has a fever.'

Another awful groan came from behind the doors, a terrified and terrible groan of awful agony. Neither did it seem to represent physical pain but some deeper agony of spirit.

'An unusual fever,' Ptolemy said savagely. He strode towards the doors, but Anaxarchus blocked his passage.

'No, Ptolemy – you would not emerge with your sanity intact, I warn you.'

Ptolemy looked at the scholar for a moment, then turned and almost ran down the corridor.

Inside the locked room, the man – or god – groaned terribly. It was as if the bones of his face were breaking apart to form individual beings. What was he? Even he could not be sure. For years he had been certain of his own power, confident that his greatness was his own. But now, it was obvious to him, poor, tormented Alexander, that he was nothing – nothing but a vessel, an agent through which many forces worked – and even those forces were united under a common name. He knew then also, that they had entered many others in the past that, if his strength broke, they would enter many more until their work was done.

Part of him begged for death.

Part of him attempted to fight that which was in him.

Part of him planned – crime.

Simon, cloaked and armed, clamped his knees against his steed's back and galloped over the sparsely-covered plains of Babylon, the folds of his cloak flying behind him like the wings of a stooping hawk.

The horse snorted, its sturdy legs flashing, its eyes big and its heart pounding.

For two hours, Simon had ridden in safety.

But now the cold night air above him was alive with dreadful sounds.

He drew his sword from its scabbard and rode on, telling himself that the noises were the flapping wings of vultures.

Then a shape came swooping in front of him. He caught a glimpse of a pale, human face. But it was not entirely human. Snakes twined on its head, blood dripped from its eyes. The horse came to a sudden halt, reared whinnying.

Simon closed his eyes against the sight.

'The herbs the Magi gave me have induced visions,' he told himself aloud in shaking tones.

But he could not believe it. He had seen them.

The Eumenides – the Furies of legend!

For the face had been that of a woman.

Now the sounds came closer, ominous. Simon urged the frightened horse onwards. Sharp female faces with serpents in place of hair, blood streaming from malevolent eyes, hands like talons, swooped and cackled about him. It was nightmare.

Then, quite suddenly, there came a dull booming sound from the distance, like the far-away sound of surf. Nearer and nearer it came until the night opened to brightness, a strange golden light which seemed to break through the blackness, splintering it into fragments. The winged creatures were caught in the glare, wheeled about uncertainly, shrieking and keening.

They were gone.

The light faded.

Simon rode on. And still he insisted to himself that what he had witnessed was hallucination. Something done to his weary brain by the potion the Magi had given him.

The rest of the night was full of nauseous sound, glimpses of things which flew or wriggled. But, convinced that he dreamed, horrified yet keeping close hold on sanity, Simon pushed the steed onwards towards Pela.

Horse and man rested for only a few hours at a time. The journey took days until, at length, eyes sunken in his head from tiredness, face grey and gaunt and mind numb he arrived at the Macedonian capital and sought out the Magi in the clay-built slums of the city.

Massiva, head of the secret order in Pela, was a tall, handsome Numidian. He greeted Simon warmly.

'We were informed of your coming and did our best, when you came close enough, to ward off the dangers which Alexander's minions sent against you.'

Simon did not reply to this. Silently, he handed over the scroll.

Massiva opened it, read it, frowning.

'This we did not know,' he said. 'Olympias has sent aid to Alexander in Babylon.'

The priest offered no explanation, so Simon did not ask for one.

Massiva shook his head wearily. 'I do not understand how one human can endure so much,' he said, 'but then she has other aid than human . . .'

'What are these stories about her?' Simon asked, thinking that he might at last find some truth where before he had heard nothing but rumour and hints.

'The simple facts concerning her activities are common knowledge here,' Massiva told him. 'She is an ardent initiate of a number of mystery cults, all worshipping the dark forces. The usual unpleasant rites, secret initiations, orgiastic celebrations. Three of the main ones, supposedly having no communication with one another, are the cults of Orpheus, Dionysius and Demeter. It's hinted that Alexander was conceived at one of these rites. In a way that is the truth – for Olympias was selected by the Dark One when she was a girl participating in the rites of a similar cult.'

Simon shook his head impatiently at this. 'I asked you for facts – not speculation.'

Massiva looked surprised. 'I indulged in no speculation, my friend. Why, the whole city lives in fear of Olympias and her friends and servants. Evil is so thick here that ordinary folk can hardly breathe for its stink.'

Simon said shortly: 'Well, I hope the information is useful to you. I've paid my debt, at least. Now, can you recommend a tavern where I can stay?'

'I can recommend none well, in this cursed city. You might try the *Tower of Cimbri*. It's comfortable, so I've heard. But be wary, take iron to bed with you.'

'I'd do that in any event,' Simon grinned, 'with Alexander after my blood and me staying in his home city.'

'You're courageous, Thracian – do not be foolish.'

'Don't worry, friend.' Simon left the house, remounted his horse and rode it towards the tavern quarter, eventually locating the *Tower of Cimbri*.

He was about to enter when he heard the sound of running from an alley which ran along the side of the building. Then a girl screamed. Drawing his sword he ran into the alley and, because he had become so hardened to sights of horror, hardly noticed the misshapen creatures menacing a frightened girl, save that they were armed and evidently powerful. The girl's eyes were round with fear and she was half-fainting. One of the twisted men put out a blunt paw to seize her, but wailed out its pain as Simon's sword caught it in the shoulder blades.

The others turned, reaching for their weapons. Simon cut two down before they could draw their swords. The fourth swung at Simon but was too clumsy. He died in a moment, his neck cloven.

Instead of thanking him, the girl stared down at the corpses in terror.

'You fool,' she muttered.

'Fool?' Simon was taken aback.

'You have killed four of Queen Olympias's retainers – did you not recognize the livery – or their kind?'

'I'm a stranger in Pela.'

'Then leave now – or be doomed.'

'No, I must see that you are safe. Quickly – I have a horse waiting in the street.' He supported her with one arm though she protested and helped her into the saddle.

He got up behind her.

'Where do you live?'

'Near the west wall – but hurry, by Hera, or they'll find the corpses and give chase.'

Following her directions, Simon guided the horse through the evening half-light.

They came to a pleasant, large house, surrounded by a garden which in turn was enclosed in high walls. They rode through the gate and she dismounted, closing them behind her. An old man appeared in the doorway to the courtyard.

'Camilla? What's happening?'

'Later, father. Have the servants stable the horse and make sure all the gates are locked – Olympias's retainers attempted to kidnap me again. This man saved me from them – but four are dead.'

'Dead? Gods!' The old man pursed his lips. He was dressed in a loose toga and had a stern, patrician face. He was evidently a nobleman, though his black-haired daughter was most unlike him.

Quickly, Simon was ushered into the house. Servants were summoned bringing bread, cheese, and fruit. He ate gratefully. As he ate he told as much of his personal story as he wished to divulge. The patrician, Merates, listened without commenting.

When Simon had finished, Merates made no direct remark but instead said, half to himself:

'If King Philip had not continued his line, there would be peace and achievement in this war-wrecked world. I curse the name of Alexander – and the she-snake who bore him. If Alexander had been left to his father's teaching, he might well have carried on the great plan of Philip. But his warped mother put different ideas into his head – turned him against his father. Now there is evil on every wind, it blows east and west, south and north – and the hounds of darkness rend, slaver, and howl in Alexander's bloody wake.'

Camilla shuddered. She had changed her street robe into a loose, diaphanous gown of blue silk. Her long, black, unbound hair fell down her back, gleaming like dark wine.

She said: 'Now, though Alexander's off on his conquests, Olympias terrorizes Pela more than ever before. All comely youths and girls are sought out to take part in her ghastly rituals. For ten or more months she has tried to encourage me to join until, at last, her patience failed and she attempted to kidnap me. She will know that someone killed the servitors – but she need not know it was you, Simon.'

Simon nodded mutely. He found it difficult to speak as he breathed in the girl's dark beauty, intoxicated by it as he had never before been.

They were troubled times. Times of high deeds and feats of learning; times of obscene evil and wild daring. Alexander mirrored his times. With one breath he would order a massacre, with another honour a conquered city for its courage in withstanding him. His great horse Bucephalus bore his bright armoured master across the known world. Fire destroyed ancient seats of civilization, wise men were slain and innocents drowned in the flood tide of his conquests. Yet he caused new cities to be raised and libraries to be built. Men of learning followed in his train – this pupil of Aristotle – and he was an enigma to all. Greece, Persia, Babylonia, Assyria, Egypt, all fell to him. Four mighty races, four ancient civilizations bore Alexander's yoke. People had speculated on whether he was a force for darkness or enlightenment – whether he would rend the world to fragments or unite it in lasting peace. An enigma.

But now the year was 323 BC and Alexander was aged 32. He had ruled over twelve years – soon he would have reigned thirteen . . .

In the dark caverns of creation, existing within a multiplicity of dimensions, vital evil thrived, chuckling and plotting – crime.

For thirteen years had the forces of Light and Darkness warred in poor Alexander's soul and body, unbeknownst to the proud, grandiose and arrogant world-conqueror. But now the stars proclaimed that a certain time had come.

And Alexander suffered . . .

Riders galloped towards the corners of the world. Bright banners whipped in the wind as armies sped across the lands around the Mediterranean. Ships groaned with the weight of armoured soldiers. Blood flowed like wine and wine like water. Corpses roasted in guttering castles and the earth shook to the coming of Alexander's cavalry.

And now messengers rode to the camps of his captains, recalling them. They were needed. The final conquest was to be made. But it would not be Alexander's triumph. The triumph would belong to a greater conqueror. Some called him Ahriman.

Hastily now Alexander's captains mounted their chariots and

headed towards Babylon. Many had to cross oceans, continents.

Every oracle prophesied doom – some said for Alexander, some said for the world. Never, they said, had evil clouded the world as much as now.

Ahriman had prepared the world through Alexander.

Soon the Powers of Light would be destroyed for ever and, though it might take many more centuries of completion, Ahriman could begin his plans of conquest and, finally, destruction.

There were more vehicles for his plans.

CHAPTER FOUR

Simon lazed back on a bench and ran his hand over Camilla's warm shoulders.

'Do not the heroes of legend always claim such reward from the maidens they rescue?' he asked mockingly.

She smiled at him affectionately.

'The Camilla of legend, if you remember, had nought to do with men. I've a mind to emulate her.'

'A sad waste.'

'For you, perhaps, but not for me . . .'

Simon pretended to sigh. 'Very well,' he said, 'I can see I shall have to wait until you eventually succumb to my undoubted attraction.'

Again she smiled. 'You have been here a week and I have not fallen yet.'

'It was good of your father to give me the position of Captain of his Bodyguard, particularly since he is risking arrest if Olympias should ever discover that I slew her servants.'

'Merates is a good and wise man,' Camilla said seriously, 'one of the few left in Pela, these days. He was close to Philip and admired him greatly. But Philip's son would have nothing to do with his father's councillors so now Merates lives in quiet retirement.'

Simon had already learnt that Camilla was the foster daughter of Merates, that she had been born to a loved and trusted Paeonian slave who had died when she was a child.

He had grown to respect the old nobleman and planned, though it was dangerous for him, to stay in Pela and probably settle there. He had already fallen in love with Camilla.

And so he courted her and although she gave him no reason to cease this courtship, on the other hand she did not encourage him overmuch. She knew him for a soldier-of-fortune and a wanderer.

Perhaps she wanted to be certain of him.

But they were dark times and Simon, rationalist though he was, could not be unaware of them. He sensed the gathering storm and was restless.

One day as he was instructing a group of slaves in the art of using the shield, Merates came hurrying into the courtyard.

'Simon – a word with you.'

The Thracian propped his sword against the wall and went with Merates into the house.

There were tears in Merates's eyes when he spoke.

'Camilla is gone. She had to go on an errand in the market – a regular monthly visit to settle our score with the merchants with whom we trade. She has been gone four hours – she is normally gone one . . .'

Simon's body grew taut. 'Olympias? Do you think . . .?'

Merates nodded.

Simon turned, went swiftly to his quarters where he buckled on his leather belt bearing the scabbarded sword the Magi had given him.

He flung a blanket over his horse's back, rode it from the stable, ducking his head beneath the door beam, through the gates of the house and down the streets of Pela to the city centre.

He inquired in the market for her. She had not been seen there for well over two hours. Thinking swiftly, he headed for the slums of the city, dismounted outside a certain door and knocked.

Massiva, the black Numidian priest answered the door himself. He was dressed like a slave – evidently disguised.

'Come in, Simon. It is good to see you.'

'I wish aid, Massiva. And in return I may be able to help you.'

Massiva ushered him inside.

'What is it?'

'I am certain that Queen Olympias has kidnapped Camilla, Lord Merates's daughter.'

Massiva's expression did not change. 'It is likely – Camilla is reputed beautiful and a virgin. Olympias seeks such qualities. Either she will corrupt Camilla and force her to take an active part in the rites – or else she will make her take a passive part.'

'Passive? What do you mean?'

'The blood of virgins is needed in several spells.'

Simon shuddered.

'Can you help me? Tell me where I may find her!'

'The Rites of Cottyttia begin tonight. That is where to look.'

'Where do they take place?'

'Come, I will draw you a map. You will most likely perish in this, Simon. But you will be convinced that we have spoken truth in the past.'

Simon looked at the Negro sharply. Massiva's face was expressionless.

They called her Cotys and she was worshipped as a goddess in Thrace, Macedonia, Athens, and Corinth. For centuries her name had been connected with licentious revelry – but never had she prospered so well than where Queen Olympias danced with snakes in her honour. Though only part of a greater Evil One, she flourished and grew on the tormented souls of her acolytes and their victims.

The house stood on its own on a hill.

Simon recognized it from Massiva's description. It was night, silver with rime and moonlight, but there were movements in the shadows and shapes of evil portent. His breath steaming white against the darkness, Simon pressed on up the hill towards the house.

A slave greeted him as he reached the door.

'Welcome – be you *Baptae* or heretic?'

Baptae, Simon had learned from Massiva, was the name that the worshippers of Cotys called themselves.

'I come to take part in tonight's Cottyttia, that's true,' Simon said and slew the slave.

Inside the house, lighted by a single oil-lamp, Simon located the door which opened on reeking blackness. He bent and entered it and soon was creeping downwards, down into the bowels of the hill. The walls of the tunnel were slippery with clammy moss and the air was thick and difficult to breathe. The sharp sound of his sword coming from its scabbard was comforting to Simon.

His sandalled feet slipped on the moss-covered stones of the passage and, as he drew nearer to his goal, his heart thudded in his ribcage and his throat was tight for he now had something of the emotion he had felt when confronted by Alexander's insanity.

Now he heard a low chanting, half ecstatic moaning, half triumphant incantation. The sound grew louder, insinuating itself into his ears until he was caught for a moment in the terrible evil ecstasy which the Cottyttian celebrants were feeling. He controlled himself against an urge to flee, the even stronger urge to join them, and continued to advance, the rare steel sword gleaming in his fist. The iron was a comfort, at least, though he still refused to believe that there was any supernatural agency at work.

Almost tangibly the evil swirled about him as he pressed on and here his rational, doubting nature was to his advantage. Without it, he might easily have succumbed.

The chanting swelled into a great roar of evil joy and through it he heard a name being repeated over and over:

'*Cotys. Cotys. Cotys. Cotys.*'

He was half hypnotized by the sound, stumbled towards a curtain and wrenched it back.

He retreated a pace at what he saw.

The air was thick with incense. Golden light flared from tall black candles on an altar. From the altar rose a pillar and tied to the pillar was Camilla. She had fainted.

But it was not this that sickened him so much as the sight of the things which swarmed about the altar. They were neither men nor women but neuter. Perhaps they had once been men. They were young and good-looking, their hair long and their faces thin, the bones prominent and the eyes flickering with malignant glee. Naked, to one side of the altar, Simon saw an old woman. Her face was that of a woman of sixty, but her body seemed younger. Around it twined great serpents, caressing her. She crooned to them and led the chanting. Young women danced with the neuters, posturing and prancing.

'*Cotys. Cotys. Cotys.*'

The candles spurted seething light and sent shadows leaping around the walls of the caverns. Then a peculiar golden orange brightness appeared at the top of the column to which Camilla was tied and seemed to twine and coil down the pillar.

Other shapes joined the dancing humans. Twisted shapes with great horns on their heads and the faces of beasts, the hooves of goats.

Simon moved forward, his sword held before him in instinctive protection against the evil in the cavern.

'Cease!' A name came to his lips and he shouted it out: 'In the name of Ormuzd – cease!'

A huge swelling of unhuman laughter came from the boiling brightness on the pillar and Simon saw figures form in it. Figures that were man-shaped and seemed to be at the same time part of the structure of a huge face, lined and pouched with a toothless, gaping mouth and closed eyes.

Then the eyes opened and seemed to fix themselves on Simon. The smaller figures writhed about it and it laughed again. Bile was in his throat, his head throbbed, but he gripped the sword and pushed his way through the sweating bodies of the worshippers. They grinned at him maliciously but did not attempt to stop him.

He was lost in the pull of those malicious eyes.

'Ormuzd is too weak to protect thee, mortal,' the mouth said. 'Ahriman rules here – and will soon rule the world through his vessel, Alexander.'

Still Simon pushed his way towards the pillar, towards Camilla and the leering face above her.

'Ormuzd will not aid thee, mortal. We are many and stronger. Behold me! What do you see?'

Simon made no reply. He gripped the steel blade tighter and advanced closer.

'Do you see us all? Do you see the one these revellers call Cotys? Do you see the Evil One?'

Simon staggered forwards, the last few paces between him and the entity coiling about the pillar. Olympias now pushed her face forward, the snakes hissing, their forked tongues flickering.

'Go to her, Thracian – my son knows thee – go to her and we'll have a double sacrifice this night.'

With his free hand, Simon pushed against the scaly bodies of the snakes and sent the woman staggering back.

With trancelike deliberation he cut the bonds that held Camilla to the pillar. But many hands, orange-gold hands, shot out from the column and gripped him in a shuddering, yet ecstatic embrace. He howled and smote at the hands and, at the touch of steel they flickered back again into their scintillating parent body.

Then he felt the clammy hands of the acolytes upon his body. Sensing that he had some advantage, Simon dragged a bunch of herbs from his shirt – herbs which Massiva had given him – and plunged them into the candle flames. A pungent aroma began to come from the flaring herbs and the naked worshippers dropped back. The apparition itself seemed to fade slightly, its light less bright.

Simon sprang at the shape, his sword flashing like silver and passing through the hazy face which snarled and laughed alternately. The sword clanged on the stone of the column. Desperately, he drew back his arm to strike another blow, his whole body weakened. He felt like an old, worn man.

'Ormuzd!' he shouted as he struck again.

Again the face snarled at him; again the golden hands shot out to embrace him so that his body thrilled with terrible weakening joy.

Then Simon felt that he was all his ancestors and a knowledge came to him, the knowledge of darkness and chaos which his forebears had possessed.

And this knowledge, though terrifying, contained within it a further knowledge – the awareness that the Forces of Darkness had been vanquished in the past and could be vanquished again.

This gave him strength. Ahriman-Cotys realized that from somewhere Simon had gained renewed energy and its shape drew in on itself, began to slide down the pillar towards Camilla.

But Simon reached her, tugged her away from the column and onto the ground. Then he drew back his arm and flung the flaming herbs into the face of the apparition.

A horrid growling sound filled the air, and, for a moment, the face faded entirely.

Simon grasped Camilla and fell back through the crowd, slashing at their naked bodies with his bright sword. Blood flowed and faces reappeared, bellowing with laughter.

Many little faces joined in the merriment, piping their mirth and detaching themselves from the greater entity to fall upon the blood of the slain.

Simon observed, with a degree of relief, that the beings could not pass through the smoke from the herbs and, by this time, the whole room was full of the pungent odour.

'Nothing can destroy us, mortal!' Ahriman-Cotys bellowed. 'Slay more – give me more! You may escape now – but I will sport with you both soon. The huntsmen of my servitor, Olympias, will hound you across the earth. You cannot escape. And when you are ours – you will both become the most willing of my slaves . . .'

Simon reached the doorway of the cavern, turned, bearing the insensible Camilla, and ran up the slippery tunnel.

Now he knew. Now he could no longer rationalize. He had seen too much.

Now he knew that reason had passed from the world and that the ancient gods had returned to rule once more.

CHAPTER FIVE

The body was strong enough. Ahriman had tested it to his satisfaction. He had given the vessel superhuman strength and vitality which it had used for what it thought were its own purposes.

Alexander, though he possessed little of his own personality now, was ready. Soon entire populations would be the slaves of Ahriman, their bodies bent to him. Darkness such as the world had never known would come. Ormuzd and the Forces of Light would be vanquished for ever.

Ahriman had many facets – many names. Shaitan was another.

Now Alexander's captains gathered. They were loyal to him, would do his bidding – would become Ahriman's agents in bringing Hell to the surface of the Earth.

323 BC. A time of omens of evil. A turning point in history.

Alexander rose from his bed. He walked like an automaton and called for his slaves. They washed him, dressed him, and clad him in his golden armour.

'Hail, Jupiter-Ammon!' they intoned as he strode from the room and walked steadily to the chamber where his generals and advisors awaited him.

Ptolemy stood up as Alexander entered. His master seemed no different, yet there was a strange, detached air about him.

'Greetings, Jupiter-Ammon,' he said bowing low. Normally he refused to designate Alexander by the name of the God – but this time he was wary, remembering perhaps how Alexander had killed his close friend Clitus in Bactria.

Anaxarchus also bowed. The remaining ten did the same.

Alexander seated himself in the middle of the long table. The leather joints of the golden armour groaned as he bent. There was food and maps on the table. He stuffed a bit of bread into his mouth and unrolled a map, chewing. The twelve men waited nervously for him to speak.

Studying the map, Alexander held out his goblet. Ptolemy filled it with wine from a long-necked bottle of brass. Alexander drank it in a single gulp. Ptolemy replenished the cup.

Simon and Camilla had fled from Pela. The night was like a clammy cloak about them and lightning split the sky, rain hurling itself like tiny spears against their faces.

Camilla rode slightly behind Simon, following him in a terror-filled flight towards the East.

There was no other direction they might go and Simon needed to find Abaris the Magi and get his help, though Alexander still dwelled in Babylon.

Behind them now they heard the Huntsmen of Olympias – great dogs baying, horns sounding, and wild shouts urging the hounds on.

And these huntsmen were not mortal – but loaned to Olympias by Ahriman that they both might sport with the fleeing humans.

They caught glimpses of their pursuers – things of legend. Offspring of Cerberus, the three-headed dog which guarded the gates of Hades – dogs with the tails of serpents and with snakes twining round their necks; great, flat, hideous-eyed heads, and huge teeth.

The huntsmen rode on the progeny of Pegasus, winged horses which skimmed over the ground, white and beautiful, fast as the North Wind.

And on the backs of the horses – the huntsmen. The grinning shades of dead villains, spewed from Hades to do Ahriman's work. Beside them loped the leopard-women, the Maenades, worshippers of Bacchus.

Behind all these came a screaming multitude of ghouls, demons and were-beasts, released from the depths of Hell.

For two weeks they had been thus pursued and Simon and Camilla were well aware that they could have been caught many times. Ahriman – as he had threatened – was sporting with them.

But still they pushed their horses onwards until they had reached the Bosphorus, hired a boat, and were on the open sea.

Then came the new phantoms to haunt them. Sea-shapes, rearing reptilian monsters, things with blazing eyes which swam just beneath the surface and occasionally put clawed hands on the sides of the boat.

Simon realized at last that all this was calculated to torment them and drive them mad, to give in to Ahriman's evil will.

Camilla, Simon could see, was already beginning to weaken. But he kept tight hold of sanity – and his purpose. Whether the Fates wished it or not, he knew what he must do, had taken upon himself a mission. He refused to attend to anything but that – and his strength aided Camilla.

Soon, Simon knew, the Evil One would realize that he could not break his spirit – then they would be doomed for Ahriman had the power to snuff them out. He prayed to Ormuzd, in whom he now believed with a fervour stemming from his deep need of something to which he could cling, and prayed that he might have a little more time – time to get to Babylon and do what he had taken upon himself to do.

Over the barren plains of Asia Minor they rode and all the nights of their journey the wild huntsmen screamed in their wake until Simon at least could turn sometimes and laugh at them, taunting them with words which were half-mad ravings.

He had little time, he knew.

One night, while great clouds loomed across the sky, they lost their way.

Simon had planned to follow the Euphrates on the banks of which was built Babylon, but in the confusion of the shrieking night he lost his way and it was not until the following morning that they sighted a river.

With relief, they rode towards it. The days were theirs – no phantoms came to torment them in the sunlight. Soon, Simon knew with a feeling of elation, they would be in Babylon with Abaris and the Magi to aid them against the hordes of Ahriman.

All day they rode, keeping to the cracked bed of the river, dried in the heat of the searing sun. When dusk came, Simon calculated, they should reach the outskirts of Babylon. Which was well, for their horses were by now gaunt skeletons, plodding and tripping in the river bed, and Camilla was swaying, pale and fainting, in the saddle.

The sun began to go down lividly on the horizon as they urged the weary horses forward and already in their ears they heard the faint howling of the Maenades, the insane howlings of Cerberus's spawn. The nightmare of the nights was soon to begin again.

'Pray to Ormuzd that we reach the city in time,' Simon said wearily.

'Another such night and I fear my sanity will give way,' Camilla replied.

The howling, insensate cries of the Bacchae grew louder, in their ears and, turning in the saddle, Simon saw behind him the dim shapes of their pursuers – shapes which grew stronger with the deepening darkness.

They turned the bend in the river and the shape of a city loomed ahead.

But then, as they drew closer, Simon's heart fell.

This desolate, jagged ruin, this vast and deserted place was not Babylon! This city was dead – a place where a man, also, might die.

Now the armies of Alexander gathered. And they gathered, unbeknownst to them, not for material conquest but for a greater conquest – to destroy the power of Light and ensure the powers of Darkness of lasting rule.

Great armies gathered, all metal and leather and disciplined flesh.

323 BC and a sick man, drawing vitality from a supernatural

source – a man possessed – ruled the known world, ordered its fighting men, controlled its inhabitants.

Alexander of Macedonia. Alexander the Great. Son of Zeus, Jupiter-Ammon. He had united the world under a single monarch – himself. And, united, it would fall . . .

In Babylon, oldest city of the ancient world, Alexander gave his orders to his captains. One hundred and forty-four miles square was Babylon, flanking each side of the great River Euphrates, embanked with walls of brick, closed by gates of bronze. Dominating the city was the Temple of Baal, rising upwards and consisting of eight storeys gradually diminishing in width, ascended by a flight of steps winding around the whole building on the outside. Standing on its topmost tower, Alexander surveyed the mighty city which he had chosen as the base for his military operations. From here he could see the fabulous hanging gardens built by Nebuchadnezzar, laid out upon terraces which were raised one above the other on arches. The streets of the city were straight, intersecting one another at right angles.

Babylon, which had brooded for centuries, producing scientists, scholars, artists, great kings, and great priests, splendid warriors, and powerful conquerors. Babylon, whose rulers, the Chaldaeans, worshipped the heavenly bodies and let them guide their law-making.

Babylon, city of secrets and enlightenment. Babylon, soon to be abased by the most terrible blight of evil the world had known. The forces of light were scattered, broken by Alexander's conquerings, and Alexander himself had become the focus for the forces of evil. Soon the world would sink into darkness.

Desperately the adherents of Light strove to find a way to stop him, but they were weakened, outlawed. Little pockets of them, chief of these being the Magi of Persia, strove to stand against him – but it was almost futile. Slowly, surely, implacably, evil Ahriman and his minions were gaining ascendancy.

And Simon of Byzantium had failed to reach Babylon and contact the Magi.

Simon and Camilla had never seen such a vast city. The crumbling walls encompassed a fantastic area . . . Where they were still intact three chariots might have passed each other on them and they were over 100 feet high. Broken towers rose everywhere, hundreds of them, twice as high as the walls.

But the wind moaned in the towers and great owls with wide, terrible eyes hooted and glided about them, seeming the city's only occupants.

Camilla reached over and found Simon's hand. He gripped it to give her a comfort he did not himself feel.

Behind them they still heard the hunters. Wearied, they could go no further and their tired brains told them that here, among ruins, they would find no hiding place.

The slow clopping of their horses' hooves echoed in the empty city as they followed a broad, overgrown avenue through jagged shadows thrown by the broken buildings. Now Simon could see that the city had been destroyed by fire. But it was cold, chillingly cold in the light of the huge moon which hung overhead like an omen of despair.

The cries of the huntsmen joined the hoots of the owls, a horrid cacophony of fearful, foreboding sound.

But now they could no longer run before their hunters. Fatalistically they must wait – to be caught.

Then suddenly, ahead of them. Simon saw a dark shape framed against the moonlight. He drew his sword and halted his horse. He was too tired to attack, waited for the figure to approach.

When it came closer it flung back the cowl of its cloak and Simon gasped in relief and astonishment.

'Abaris! I was going to seek you in Babylon. What are you doing here?'

'Waiting for you, Simon.' The priest smiled gently and sympathetically. He, also, looked dreadfully worn. His long un-Persian face was pale and there were lines about his mouth.

'Waiting for me? How could you have known that I should lose my way and come here?'

'It was ordained by the Fates that you should do so. Do not question that.'

'Where are we?'

'In the ruins of forgotten Nineveh. This was a great city once, larger than Babylon and almost as powerful. The Medes and Babylonians razed it 300 years ago.'

'Nineveh,' Camilla breathed, 'there are legends about it.'

'Forget those you have heard and remember this – you are safe here, but not for long. The remnants of Ormuzd's supporters fled here and form a strong company – but not so strong that we can last for ever against Ahriman's dreadful minions.'

'Now I realize what happened,' Simon said. 'We followed the Tigris river instead of the Euphrates.'

'That is so.'

Behind them the wild baying came closer. Abaris signed to them to follow him.

Abaris led them into a dark sidestreet and then into a maze of alleys choked with fallen masonry, weed-grown and dank. By a small two-storied house which was still virtually intact, he stopped, withdrew a bolt and motioned them inside. They took their horses with them.

The house was much larger inside than it seemed and Simon guessed that it consisted of several houses now. There were about two hundred people in the large room behind the one they had entered. They sat, squatted, and stood in positions of acute weariness. Many were priests. Simon recognized several cults.

Here were Chaldaeans, the ruling caste of Babylon, proud and arrogant-seeming still, Egyptian priests of Osiris, a Hebrew rabbi. Others Simon did not recognize and Abaris whispered answers to his questions. There were Brahmin from India, Pythagoreans from Samos and Crotona in Etrusca, Parsees from the deserts of Kerman and Hindustan, Druids from the far North, from the bleak islands on the world's edge, blind priests of the Cimmerians who, history told, were the ancestors of the Thracians and Macedonians.

Alexander had destroyed their temples, scattered them. Only in the far North and the far East were the priests of Light still organized and they had sent deputations to Nineveh to aid their brothers.

And Alexander's wrath had been mainly turned on the Zoroastrians, the Persian and Chaldaean Magi, strongest of the sects who worshipped the powers of Law and Light.

Here they all were, weary men, tired by a battle which required no material weapons yet sapped their vitality as they strove to hold Ahriman at bay.

Abaris introduced Simon and Camilla to the gathering, and he appeared to know the best part of their story, how they had been present at the Cottyttia, how they had fled from Pela, hounded by the infernal hordes, crossed the Bosphorus and came, at length, to fallen Nineveh.

Outside, Nineveh's streets were filled with a hideous throng, weird beasts of all kinds, dead souls, and malevolent denizens of Hell. Three-headed, snake-tailed dogs, winged horses, chimerae, basilisks, sphinx, centaurs and griffins, fire-spewing salamanders. All roamed the broken streets hunting for Ahriman's prey. But there was an area where they could not pass – an area which gave out emanations which meant death for them, so they avoided this area.

For the meantime, Simon and Camilla were safe. But it was stalemate, for while they were in Nineveh, secure against the forces of evil, Alexander strode the golden towers of Babylon and readied the world for the final conquest.

CHAPTER SIX

Abaris told Simon: 'Alexander slew your friend Hano, the Phoenician a week ago.'

Simon cursed: 'May the Harpies pluck his eyes from his skull!'

Camilla said: 'Do not evoke the Harpies, also. We have enough to contend with.'

Abaris half smiled, waved his hand towards a small table in a corner of the room. 'You had better eat now. You must be very tired.'

Gratefully the pair began to eat, drinking the spiced wine of the Magi – a wine which was unnaturally invigorating. Abaris said, while they ate:

'Ahriman dwells constantly, now, in Alexander's body. He intends to make a final campaign, north and east, to subdue the barbarian tribes of Gaul and the Dark Island, crush the Indian kings, and rule the entire world. And, it seems, he will be able to do all this through his vessel, Alexander – for the whole world already responds to Alexander's whims; he commands the fighting men and a host of subject kings and princes. It will be an easy matter . . .'

'But he must be stopped,' Simon said. 'Have you no means of stopping him?'

'For months we have tried to fight the forces of evil, without success. We have almost given up and wait for the coming of Darkness.'

'I believe I know what can be done,' Simon said, 'and it will be a cleaner method than that used by any of you. With your aid I must get to Babylon – and with your aid I will do what I must.'

'Very well, my friend,' Abaris said, 'tell me what you need.'

Kettle-drums beat and brazen trumpets sounded. The dust swelled into the heated air before the feet of Alexander's armies. Coarse soldiers' voices bellowed orders and the captains rode in military pomp at the head of their armies. Plumes of dyed horse-hair bobbed bright beneath the sun, horses stamped, bedecked in trappings of blue and red and yellow, bronze armour glinted like gold and shields clashed against javelins, lances rose like wheat above the heads of the marching men, their tips bright and shining.

Hard-faced warriors moved in ordered ranks – men from Macedonia, Thrace, Greece, Bactria, Babylon, Persia, Assyria, Arabia, Egypt, and the Hebrew nations.

Millions of fighting men. Millions of souls trained for slaying and destruction.

And ordering them, one man – Alexander the Great. Alexander in his hawk-like helm of gold, standing on the steps of the Temple of Baal in Babylon and readying his hosts for the final conquest. Alexander in the trappings of a Persian monarch, absolute ruler of the civilized world. In his right hand a gleaming sword, in his left the sceptre of the law giver. In his body, possessing it, flowing through it, dominating it – black evil. Ahriman, Master of Darkness, soon to commit the absolute crime – the destruction of Law, the birth of the Dark Millennium.

Around Babylon, mighty armies were camped and it was easy for Simon to enter the city, for many mercenaries had flocked to fight beneath Alexander's banner.

Wrapped around the Thracian was what seemed to be a simple stained black soldier's cloak, but inside, lining it, was richer stuff marked with curious symbols, the Cloak of the Magi, it served to ward off evil and kept Simon, for the time being, safe from Ahriman's attentions.

That day he stood in the square surrounding the Temple of Baal and heard Ahriman speak through Alexander. It was dangerous for him to do this, he knew, but he had to see the man again.

Alexander addressed the populace.

'People of Babylon, my warriors, the morrow sees the start of our final conquests. Soon no spot of soil, no drop of ocean shall be independent of our Empire, I, Jupiter-Ammon, have come to Earth to cleanse it of heretics, to destroy unbelievers and bring the new age to the world. Those who murmur against me shall die. Those who oppose me shall suffer torments and will wish to die. Those who would halt my plans – they shall never die but will be sent living to Hades. Now the armies are marshalled. Already we control most of the world, save for a few patches to the North and a few to the East. Within months these, also, will be ours. Worship us, my people, for Zeus has returned from Olympus, born of a woman named Olympias, father of the son, son and father are One. We are Jupiter-Ammon and our will is divine!'

The people screamed their exultation at these words and bowed low before the man-god who stood so proud above them.

Only Simon remained standing, clad in his bagged and dusty cloak, his face thin, and his eyes bright. He stared up at Alexander who saw him almost immediately, opened his mouth to order the unbeliever destroyed, and then closed it again.

For long moments the two men stared into one another's eyes – the one representing total evil, the other representing the forces of Light. In that great, hushed city nothing seemed to stir and the air carried only faint sounds of military preparation from behind the city walls.

There was a peculiar communication between them. Simon felt as if he were looking into the Abyss of Hell and yet sensed something else lurking in the eyes – something cleaner that had long since been subdued and almost erased.

Then he was in motion, running for the steps that wound upwards around the Temple of Baal.

He bounded up the steps, twenty, fifty, a hundred and he had still not reached Alexander who stood like a statue awaiting him.

The God-Emperor turned as Simon finally reached the upper level. As if Simon were not there he strode back through the shaded pillars and into the building. That was where Simon confronted him.

Sunlight lanced through the pillars and criss-crossed the place in a network of shadow and light. Alexander now sat on a huge golden throne, his chin resting in one hand, his back bent as if in meditation. Steps led up to the dais on which the throne was placed. Simon stopped at the first step and looked up at the conqueror of the world.

Alexander leaned back in his throne and clasped his hands in front of him. He smiled slowly, at first a smile of irony which twisted into a grin of malice and hatred.

'There is a sacred bull in Memphis,' Alexander said slowly, 'which is called Apis. It is an oracle. Seven years ago I went to Memphis to hear the sacred bull and to ascertain whether it had, indeed, oracular powers. When it saw me it spoke a rhyme. I have remembered that rhyme for seven years.'

Simon drew the Cloak of the Magi closer about him. 'What did it say?' he asked in a strained half-whisper.

Alexander shook his head. 'I did not understand it until recently. It went:

The City that thy father lost shall fall to thee,
The City that gives birth to fools shall bear a sword.
The City that thy father lost shall be its home.
The City that thou mak'st thy home shall feel its edge.'

Simon brooded over this for a moment and then he nodded, understanding.

'Byzantium, Abdera, Byzantium – Babylon,' he said.

'How sharp is the sword?' Alexander asked and changed shape.

A dazzling orange-golden haze burst upwards and a black and scarlet figure stood framed in the centre. It vaguely resembled Alexander but was twice as high, twice as broad, and bore a weirdly wrought staff in its hand.

'So!' Simon cried. 'At last you show your true shape. You bear the Wand of Ahriman, I see!'

'Aye, mortal – and that only Ahriman may bear.'

From beneath the Cloak of the Magi, Simon produced a short javelin and a small shield of about ten inches in diameter. He held the shield in front of his face and through it could see unnerving and alien shapes where the figure of Ahriman stood. He was seeing the true shape of Ahriman, not the warped and metamorphosed body of Alexander.

He drew back his arm and hurled the javelin at a certain spot in the intricate supernatural pattern.

There came an unearthly groaning and muttering from the figure. It threw up its arms and the wand flickered and sent a bolt of black lightning at Simon who put up his shield again and repelled it, though he was hurled back against a far column. He leaped to his feet, drawing his sword and saw that, as Abaris had told him, Alexander had resumed his usual shape.

The God-King staggered and frowned. He turned and saw Simon standing there, sword in hand.

'What's this?' he said.

'Prepare to fight me, Alexander!' Simon cried.

'But why?'

'You must never know why.'

And Simon leaped forward.

Alexander drew his own lovely blade, a slim thing of strong tempering, of glowing-star-metal with a handle of black onyx.

The iron clashed with a musical note, so fine were both blades and the two men feinted, parried, and stabbed, fighting in the Greek manner, using the points of their swords rather than the edges.

Alexander came in swiftly, grasped Simon's wrist and pushed his sword back, bringing his own sword in, but Simon sidestepped just in time, and the blade grazed his thigh. Alexander cursed a very human curse and grinned briefly at Simon in the old, earlier manner.

'You are swift, my friend.'

Simon disliked this. It was harder to fight such a lighthearted and likeable warrior than the thing which Alexander had earlier been. It was almost unjust – yet the action had to be made.

In and out of the network of light and shadow the two men danced, skipping away, coming in close, swords flashing, and the music of their meeting echoing about the Temple of Baal.

Then Alexander's soldiers came running into the place but Alexander cried:

'Stand back – I do not know why this man attacked me, but I have never fought such a swordsman before and would not miss the privilege. If he wins – free him.'

Bewildered, the guards retreated.

For hours the fight continued, each man evenly matched. Dusk came, sunset flooding the Temple with blood-red rays. Like two archetypal gods they fought on, thrusting, parrying, employing every tactic at their command.

Then Alexander, whose earlier sickness had wearied him, stumbled and Simon saw his opportunity, paused, deliberating the act, then rushed upon his opponent and struck him a terrible thrust in the lung.

'Go – be Charon's guest!' he cried.

Alexander went hurtling back to land with a crash, sprawled on the steps of the dais. Again the watching warriors rushed forward, but Alexander waved them back.

'Do not tell the people how I met my end,' he gasped. 'I have united the world – let it stay united in the confidence that a – a – god created that unity. Perhaps that will serve to ensure peace . . .'

Dismissed, the guards returned, wondering, down the steps of the Temple and Simon and the dying Alexander were left alone in the half-light while a wind blew up and sent a cold chill through the silent columns.

'I remember you now,' Alexander said, blood beginning to trickle from his mouth. 'You are the Thracian. What happened – I remember interviewing you and then the rest is hazed in blackness and chaos – what happened then?'

Simon shook his head.

'Call it madness,' he said. 'A madness, which came upon you.'

In the shadows behind the throne he saw a black mist begin to form. Hurriedly he shouted: 'Abaris – quickly!'

The priest appeared then. He had slipped up the steps and had been standing behind a column. Others followed him. He motioned them in. They began a weird and beautiful chanting, advancing towards the hazy form behind the throne, making peculiar passes in the air.

After them, Camilla appeared and stood framed in a gap between two columns, the wind ruffling her hair.

Alexander grasped Simon's arm. 'I remember a prophesy – one made by the Oracle of Memphis. How did it go?'

Simon quoted it.

'Yes,' Alexander gasped. 'So you are the sword which the City of Fools, Abdera, bore . . .'

'What shall we remember of you, Alexander?' Simon asked quietly as there came a commotion behind the throne which was now surrounded by chanting Magi. He looked up. The priests seemed to be straining to hold back some horrible force which whimpered and moaned at them, yet was still very strong.

'Remember? Will not the world always remember me? My dream was to unite the world and bring peace. But a nightmare interrupted that dream, I think . . .'

'Your father's dream and yours,' Simon said.

'My father – I hated him – yet he was a good and wise king, and moulded me for a purpose. Aristotle was my teacher, you know. But I had other indoctrination. My mother Olympias, taught me peculiar things which I cannot remember now.'

'Let us hope no one shall ever know them again,' Simon breathed.

'What has happened?' Alexander asked again. Then his eyes closed. 'What did I do?'

'You did nothing that was not for the good of the world,' Simon told him. Alexander was dead. 'But,' the Thracian added quietly as the Emperor's grip loosened and the limp hand fell to the marble of the step, 'that which possessed you wrought harm. You could not help it. You were born to perish . . .'

He rose and called: 'Abaris. Abaris – he is dead.'

The chanting ceased. The black shape still hovered there, veins of orange-gold, black, and scarlet throbbing in it like blood-vessels. Simon and the priests fell back.

The shape shot towards Alexander's corpse, sank down over it. The corpse jerked but then was still again. For an instant a face – the face Simon had seen at the Rites of Cotys in Pela – appeared.

'There will be others, never fear!' Ahriman said and vanished.

Abaris went over to Alexander's corpse and made a pass over the wound. When Simon looked there was no sign of a wound.

'We'll say he died of a fever,' Abaris said softly. 'It was well known that he was ill. They will believe us – we will let the Chaldaeans speak in Babylon for they long ruled the people before Alexander's coming.'

Simon said: 'I knew that clean steel could end this matter for us.'

Abaris looked at him a trifle cynically.

'Without our magic to drive Ahriman out of Alexander's body for the time you needed, you would never have succeeded.'

'That's true, I suppose.'

Abaris continued:

'That was the solution. Ahriman works through many people – but he needs a single human vessel if he is to carry out his Great Plan. Several have been born in the past – others will be born again. Fanatical conquerors who will set out to rule the world. Men with superhuman vitality, the power of dominating great masses of people and driving them to do that one man's will. Yes, Ahriman – under whatever name he takes – will try again. That is certain.'

'Meanwhile,' Simon said as Camilla came up to him, 'we have succeeded in halting Ahriman this time.'

'Who knows?' Abaris said. 'History will show if we were in time or not.'

Simon said gravely: 'I am not sure what Alexander, himself, was. He could have been a force for good or evil. He was something of both. But the evil gained ascendency towards the end. Was I right to kill him? Could not his course have been turned so that the good in him could have continued his plan to unite the world in peace?'

'That may have been possible,' the priest said thoughtfully, 'but we men set limits to our endeavours – it is easier that way. Perhaps, in time, we will not stop short but will learn to choose the harder paths and so achieve more positive results. As it is we strive merely to keep a balance. One day Alexander's dream may be realized and the world united. Let us hope that the unity will be inspired by Ormuzd. Then it may be possible to build.'

Simon sighed and made his body relax.

'Meanwhile, as you say, we'll strive for balance alone. Pray to Ormuzd, priest, and pray that men will one day cease to need their gods.'

'That day may come and, if I am right, the gods themselves will welcome it.'

Abaris bowed and left Simon and Camilla staring at one another. For a long time they remained so before embracing.

2: The Middle

Going Home

They were like eagles of silver flashing towards the smoky blue sun.

They were like the hopes of men, those slim ships, as they headed through the afternoon towards outer space. They were beautiful and it was still a little difficult for many of the watchers to believe in them. They were gone in the time it takes a man to dream a dream – swiftly, yet they seemed to take a long, long while before they were lost from sight. Then the watchers dispersed, not quite sure if it had happened. And if it had – then what did it mean? What would the five ships find?

Men and women went slowly back to the cities. There were only two cities on the planet. They were enough. That night, they celebrated.

They celebrated and they forgot what they were celebrating, if they had ever known. The drinking houses were open until morning, and when they had finished drinking, the men returned, dazed, to their wives, or went to talk with friends. But they didn't sleep.

They didn't sleep because they were trying to remember something. People asked one another half-formed questions, but no one had an answer to give in return.

And the five ships, like eagles of silver, were now silently ploughing through space, towards a planet which the men on board called 'Home' – but they were self-conscious about using the word. For home was three centuries ago and hundreds of light years away, and they were not at all sure whether they had a right, any more, to use the word.

The speed of the five ships increased.

They became dark silhouettes in the blaze of space, they merged into grey shadows and the men in the bellies of the ships would have screamed loudly had they not already gagged themselves and strapped themselves in the couches of dark green velvet, hung with tassels of gold and scarlet. They were rich those ships, for the men who rode them were the darlings of Veildo, their world. The ambassadors to 'Home.'

And the captain, alone, was clear about why they were going.

*

Captain Hardrek unbuckled the belt which held his sword and gun. He let it fall on to a chair of yellow-cushioned gold. On one wall of the large cabin were the duplicate instruments which told him the condition of the five ships which were now moving, without difficulty, through hyper-space. Hardrek walked across the soft-carpeted cabin and studied the instruments with satisfaction. He had been afraid that not all the ships would make the transition, and he was glad that he had been wrong in his fears.

He lowered his strong body into a deep chair. On the polished wooden table beside him was a brass box of herbal cigarettes. He took one and lit it. He closed his eyes, relaxing, and hardly heard the doorbell ring. It rang again and he said: 'Enter.'

Malarak came in, his scarlet lieutenant's uniform as neat as always. He rested one dark-skinned hand on the butt of his energy-gun, saluting Hardrek with the other.

Hardrek smiled and waved an arm at the chair on the other side of the table. 'Sit down, Malarak, and have a cigarette. We did pretty well, I think.'

Malarak nodded and made an attempt to return his captain's smile. But his squat, hard face wasn't built for smiling. Malarak took life seriously and was embarrassed when other people didn't seem to take it so. He was given to brooding. He reached over and lifted the box towards him, extracting one of the herb-filled paper tubes. He was a man who spoke when he was spoken to, so he said nothing. He was also sensitive, and hoped that he was wrong when he thought the captain was laughing at him silently.

Captain Hardrek yawned before he said: 'Well, Malarak? We're having a good trip and there won't be any technical worries until we break out. What's on your mind? Or did you come to congratulate me?'

'I just wanted to talk to you, sir. I don't really know why I came. I just wanted to talk . . .'

Hardrek began chewing little pieces of skin off his lower lip. The herbs in the cigarettes did that – dried the skin and made it flake, but the chewing was more of a habit than the smoking. He always did it when he felt uncomfortable.

He said calmly: 'Are the men happy?'

'Well – I suppose they are, sir, yes.'

'What's the matter with them?' Hardrek had not expected any trouble quite so soon, but he sensed it now. 'I haven't noticed anything, Malarak. They can't be dissatisfied with the conditions – they can't have had second thoughts and want to return. You know the number of enthusiastic volunteers we had. This is a big mission – an historic mission . . .' Hardrek stopped himself, smiling ironically. I'm beginning to sound like the politicians, he thought. 'They're aware of this, I know,' he continued, 'and they all wanted to come. We're going home.'

'*Why*, sir?' Malarak blurted. 'That's what's troubling them – and me – now they've started to think about it – now there's two months of waiting ahead. We're going home; but that's not enough.' He frowned, continuing at a slower pace:

'None of us have reasons, really. We don't know why we left – and we don't know why we're going back. All we know is that our ancestors came and settled on Veildo. Soon after this they destroyed most of the records pertaining to their reasons for leaving Earth, as well, of course, as those other records. We know, now – though they tried to clean that bit of history of the records as well – *how* they managed to settle on Veildo.'

'They wiped out the original inhabitants, yes,' Hardrek said quietly. 'We don't like to admit it, even now, do we? Even after three centuries we feel guilty about the sins of our ancestors. Well, they must have done, too.' He thought over what Malarak had said. Then he murmured:

'We don't know why we left – and we don't know why we're going back. Well, I know. Lieutenant Malarak. The first part of the question answers the second, doesn't it? We're going back in order to find out why we left in the first place. We want to set the record straight, to know our own history, however dark. Why did they leave Earth? That's one thing our conquering ancestors did manage to keep a secret.'

'Is that a good enough reason for going back, sir?'

'It's the only one,' Hardrek smiled. 'Make sure the men know that we have a mission. We're going to find out why we ran away from home . . .'

The ships pressed onwards towards 'Home' while the news got around among the men that they had a purpose for going there, after all.

But the reason wasn't enough for them. They began to speculate.

There were many obvious reasons for their ancestors to have left Earth – overcrowding of the home planet, political differences, persecution, war, just plain restlessness. And almost every man had a different theory. The crews began to argue among themselves, mainly out of boredom. Who was right?

Then some became so certain that they used force to back up their arguments. Captain Hardrek had difficulty in straightening things out, but he managed it.

When they were done with fighting, the men, wondering still, settled down at last. Settled down to wait and see. This was now their smiling catch-phrase – Wait-and-See. Two months had nearly passed and they were nearing 'Home.'

'Home' was the planet called Earth, the third from its sun. The ships materialized painlessly, just on the edge of the system. The ships were a credit to their designers and the men who had lovingly built them. They were far better than the ships which had left Earth three hundred years before to land, eventually, on Veildo. They were lovely things, slim and fine. Even the gun-mountings were beautiful as the ships, like eagles of silver, cruised in towards Sol, bound for Terra.

There are many names to call a planet, but this one was called 'Home.'

Hardrek, in full dress uniform of scarlet and ice-blue, sword and energy-gun buckled firmly, was nervous as he stood beside his operator who was attempting radio contact with Earth. The operator was sending signals on all the wavelengths he could muster. Hardrek smiled as he thought of the havoc they must be playing with communications down there. Then he thought that they might not have radio of any kind – not now. They might have found something better, something different, in three centuries.

But at last the operator got through to someone. The voice was puzzled and Hardrek had difficulty in understanding the words. The language had changed quite a lot. The voice he heard was not speaking the lilting speech of Veildo. The words were clipped and harsh to Hardrek's sensitive ears. He didn't like the sound of them.

'*Who are you? What is your call-signal? Are you in difficulty? Use your vision if you can. I can't see you.*'

But the ships were not equipped for vision, and Hardrek ordered his operator to inform the Earthman of this before he told him who they were. The operator spoke slowly into his microphone, pained by the harsh rasping tones in his ears:

'We are not equipped for vision,' he said.

There was a longer silence than there should have been at the other end. Eventually there came back: 'Message received. Repeat: Who are you?'

The operator said: 'We are a friendly fleet from Veildo, a planet in a Rim System. Of the same race as the men of Earth. May we land?'

The puzzled voice eventually came through: 'Message received. You may land. Stand by to receive instructions.'

Hardrek spoke swiftly through the intercom, readying his ships for planetfall.

The ships, like eagles of silver, fell gracefully towards the planet called 'Home.'

They landed almost delicately on the ice-fields of the North, standing upright in the sunshine, gleaming and silver and waiting... Waiting to see.

The welcoming party was not large.

It was contained in one big wingless aircraft, bulbous, sleek and most unpleasing to the eyes of the Veildomen who sometimes put the considerations of design before those of function. It was not Good Taste. There was nothing beautiful about this ship which, fast as it was, seemed to wallow through the air. It came to rest about fifty metres from the five spacecraft.

Because of the extreme cold, Hardrek and his men were forced to wear their space-suits since they had no heavy clothing with them. The Earthmen who came to meet them were wrapped in shapeless garments resembling animal fur. Hardrek, whilst cursing their caution, thought it wise of them to choose a place like this to meet strangers. He approached them, his lieutenants behind him.

The fur-swathed leader of the Earthmen said, raspingly: 'Welcome, sir. Welcome to Earth. Would you be good enough to accompany us back to the capital?'

Hardrek nodded clumsily: 'We should be glad to.' He switched over his speaker and said, so that only his own people could hear him: 'We are returning with these men. I do not expect trouble of any kind – but be prepared for treachery. We have been out of touch with Earth for three centuries and they are obviously somewhat wary of us, otherwise they would not have met us here, in the wilderness. It would be as well for us to imitate their caution.'

He allowed the Earthmen to lead him inside the aircraft, even as he spoke. Hardrek looked around the interior of the vessel and concealed his distaste well.

It was functional enough – but it lacked even the beauty which functional things could have. It was ugly – as bad inside as it was out. The Earthmen took off their heavy furs and the Veildomen noted, depressed, that they were dressed in overalls, undistinguished, of a drab, brownish colour. After Hardrek and his men had rid themselves of their space-suits and stood in bright contrast to the Earthmen, one of the welcoming party put out a hand to Hardrek. The captain took it and introduced himself. The Earthman had a soft hand and a soft smiling face. He said: 'Orvin is my name, Captain Hardrek.'

Hardrek noticed that the Earthmen were apparently unarmed. He was glad, now, that the wearing of the space-suits had necessitated the leaving behind of his own party's swords and guns. There were introductions all round and the people of Earth were friendly and bland.

The aircraft was now moving South. In their heavy cloaks of blue and their scarlet uniforms, trimmed with gold, the Veildomen sat uncomfortably on the tubular steel seats and tried not to notice that the ship was devoid of decoration, colour or character.

It was also, they saw, unarmed.

'Earth has changed, I suppose, since your ancestors left, Captain,' smiled Orvin, sitting down next to Hardrek.

Hardrek hated himself for it, but he was beginning to feel superior to these drably dressed men. He said: 'Three hundred years, sir, brings many changes.'

'Oh.' said Orvin, 'not so many as all that, Captain. You'll probably find Earth, on the surface at least, much the same as your forefathers knew it. I suppose you have studied our planet in the records they left?'

'There weren't many records,' Hardrek said. 'Most of them were – destroyed – unfortunately. We don't know a great deal about Earth. It will be interesting to see the planet since most of its aspects will be new to us.'

Orvin nodded: 'Our libraries are extensive,' he said. 'You are naturally free to make use of them. Many pioneers left Earth for the stars after the hyperspacial craft were built. You will forgive us if we do not recognize the names of the families which colonized –'

'Veildo,' Hardrek told him, 'it was the old name for the planet – not an Earth name.'

'So your planet is populated by another intelligent race?'

'They died out,' Hardrek said nervously. 'There were very few left when our ancestors came to Vieldo. They died out . . .'

Orvin said nothing. He glanced towards the nose of the ship which was transparent. 'We are nearing the capital,' he told Hardrek. 'The President will be pleased to see you. We have few visitors – not many of the children of Earth return to the home planet. You are the first in over a hundred-and-fifty years.' His voice was a monotone, rehearsed, unfeeling. He pointed: 'There – I think you can see the city, now.'

The city was built in a perfectly square area measuring about forty kilometres. All the buildings were of the same height and of the same pattern. At regular intervals were small green parks, oval splashes of colour in the grey mass of concrete and steel. Hardrek shuddered.

The place was in direct contrast to the slender towers of his home city with its tree-lined avenues and wide spaces, its statues and its delicate colourings. He was sure that the Earth of his ancestors had not been like this. What had happened here? He began to despise these soft men of Earth with their total lack of taste. They seemed to have no art at all, not even a rudimentary sense for the visual arts.

He tried a question:

'I suppose your literature and painting has undergone considerable changes in three centuries,' he smiled, 'I hope I can take some examples back to Veildo.'

Orvin said vaguely: 'Ah, yes – well, we don't have much time for that sort of thing these days, you know. There are no neurotics left on Earth. We are all very happy.'

Hardrek was angry then. Angry for no apparent reason. A boiling, frustrated anger which ran about inside him and which he couldn't let out. He wanted to tell Orvin something, but he didn't know how to put his emotion into coherent words. He controlled his anger and sat back until it was replaced by a dull feeling of disappointment and frustration.

The ship circled in and landed on the roof of one of the grey buildings. Overhead the sky was beautiful as the sun set, colouring the clouds with a score of subtle shades. It was as beautiful as Veildo's sky – but so very different. Delighted as he left the aircraft, Hardrek stood for a moment and looked at that sky, almost jubilant in his appreciation.

Orvin, walking ahead, stopped and turned round. He frowned, perplexed. 'The President is expecting us, Captain,' he hinted firmly.

Hardrek cursed to himself and followed the soft man to the entrance of a lift. They all got in and the lift began to hum downwards.

They haven't had any visitors for one hundred and fifty years, the captain thought, and they give us a welcome like this! What's wrong with Earth? This isn't what it used to be like. This planet is decadent – it has no life. But why? *Why?*

They met the President, a pink-faced man with short grey hair.

They met the President, that was all.

There was no ceremony, no chance for Hardrek to make use of his mentally prepared speech. They were invited to refresh themselves in the rooms which were set aside for them. Later, they would attend the dinner which was to be given for them. They went despondently to the rooms and sat around wondering, privately, what was wrong.

Every man in the party felt the sense of anti-climax.

Hardrek, as he sat talking to Malarak, felt it most of all.

'If this is Earth,' Hardrek said, 'they can keep it. I'll be glad to get back to Veildo.'

'No wonder our ancestors left, sir,' said Malarak softly, sadly.

'Earth wasn't like this three centuries ago,' Hardrek reminded his lieutenant. 'It was a thriving planet – it was active in all the fields of human endeavour. It sent its sons to the other planets of its System, to the stars – it had a tremendous wealth of artistic talent. The dramacord was beginning to replace the novel as the new literary form. Vermer's "psychic painting" techniques were beginning to be used to brilliant effect. We know this – our own records at least show that. Three centuries ago there seemed to be a new renaissance on Earth. Now look at it.' He mimicked Orvin's words: '"There are no neurotics left on Earth. We are all very happy."' Hardrek swore and laughed. 'Why – if we wanted to, we could take Earth with just the five ships we have. We could take it back and make the soft little people sit up. We'd give them some neurotics, then.'

Malarak was uncomfortable: 'I don't think we're welcome here, sir. I think we should find out about our ancestors and then get out.'

Hardrek snorted. 'Over twenty years of perfecting the ships and training the crews. More time than that spent in speculating what wonderful new achievements the men of Earth would have made when we got here. Two months of travelling through the blazing insanity of hyperspace – and now we do what we came to do and leave. Is that what you want, Malarak?'

'What else is there to do, sir?'

Hardrek shook his head impatiently, but he didn't answer Malarak. He couldn't. He had expected many things of Earth. He had been prepared for a hostile reception, possibly, to be threatened with superior armament – but there seemed to be no weapons of any kind discernible. Peace, he reflected cynically, hung like a pall over the planet. He had thought that they might find the planet experiencing a new Dark Age. He had even readied himself to find a desolate planet, ruined by war – or even a deserted planet. But he had not expected the polite, unenthusiastic welcome that Orvin and the President had given him – the sight of a planet which seemed to have no artistic flowering now, when once it had produced books, music and painting which still inspired Veildo artists who had never seen Earth. What had happened to Earth? When he visited the library, he hoped he would find out. There would be an indication, there, at least.

Hardrek and his party, at the appointed time, traipsed into the President's featureless dining hall and sat down to eat. The food was good, but unimaginatively prepared. They ate it, but they didn't like it. The President seemed only vaguely interested when he said to Hardrek:

'Tell me about your planet, Captain. I gather it is an Earth-type.'

Aware that the President was conscientiously making conversation, Hardrek answered him quite briefly: 'Yes, sir, it is. We have a comparatively small population with two large cities and a number of small townships. You might call Veildo a "rural planet." There is plenty of land available for those who desire to make use of it. We are a freedom-loving people.'

'The men of Earth always were that,' smiled the President, and he seemed to display a genuine feeling for a moment. He looked almost sad. Hardrek didn't know why – couldn't find any special meaning in the President's statement.

'We have our records of wars, of course,' Hardrek said, 'but they were small wars and soon over. There is too much space on Veildo for people to quarrel for long. As for our Art . . .' he noticed that the President was looking uncomfortable and that the other Earthmen at the table seemed embarrassed, also. He stopped speaking and it was several seconds before the President said:

'Ah – yes . . .'

And then there was silence again for a little while. The President and Hardrek were both trying to think of something to say, something to chase away the silence.

At last, Hardrek said: 'Mister Orvin informed us that we could make use of your library, if we desired.'

'Of course,' the President said gratefully, glad of the change of subject. 'It is at your disposal. For how long did you expect to stay?'

Almost grimly, Hardrek said: 'As long as it takes to discover why our ancestors left Earth.'

'You are naturally welcome to stay as long as you wish,' the President was trying to make up for his apparent rudeness.

The meal continued – partly in silence, partly in strained conversation. Everybody was very uncomfortable indeed. It was a relief to leave the dining table and return to the rooms to talk savagely among themselves for a short while, to indicate their disgust, and to think before eventually going to sleep.

Hardrek wondered, sardonically, how the people ever managed to find their way about the characterless city. The ground car drew up outside a building, much the same as the rest.

Orvin was his guide. The other Veildomen were with him. Orvin said: 'The Archives. Shall we go in?'

The place was very clean inside. Neat and orderly. There weren't many people there – and those there were seemed to be employed in the Archives. Orvin consulted a huge plan of the building which had been placed on one wall of the main hall. 'We'll need the ninth basement for records regarding people who took ship from Earth at the time we want,' Orvin told Hardrek. They entered a lift and went down.

The custodian of the records was a sour-faced man who, in his own way, seemed pleased to see Hardrek and his party. He shook hands with all of them. 'What was the exact date of the expedition?' he asked Hardrek. The captain told him. The custodian pressed certain buttons on a huge container – it occupied the entire room. 'Name of the leader?'

'Callahan. Henry Callahan.' Hardrek supplied the rest of the information necessary. Within a few moments, the custodian was holding a printed card in his hand. 'This way,' he said and left the room. They walked down a long corridor and entered another room containing a microfilm projector and banks of filing cabinets.

'Now, let's see,' said the custodian to himself, consulting the card and glancing along the rows of cabinets. He found the one he wanted and pulled out a drawer. He took out a packet.

He read what was written on the packet and his sour face became serious. He replaced the packet in the cabinet.

He looked at Orvin. The custodian said nervously: 'Excuse me, gentlemen – I'm having some difficulty. There seems to be an error – something wrong with the system.'

Hardrek knew he was lying. He growled: 'What is it? What's in that box?'

The custodian waved his hand. 'Nothing, captain. The wrong coordinates. We can straighten this out in a short time. I'll get my assistant on the job.'

Hardrek could do nothing, for the moment. He was suspicious, but that was all. He agreed to accompany Orvin back to a waiting room.

They waited for over an hour and Hardrek and his men became

impatient. What had been written on the packet that had so upset the custodian?

Orvin left them, apologizing, saying that he would be back soon.

Malarak said, 'Something's cropped up, sir. Maybe the secret our ancestors brought from Earth was darker than we suspected. Perhaps the Earth people blame them for their current mediocrity?'

Hardrek cursed. 'I'd like to know what's happening! We've a right, I think.' His men agreed, their faces taut. 'By God,' Hardrek said savagely, 'if we don't find out – I'm going to tear this city apart until we do. *I'll burn it to the ground!*'

They were hurt and bewildered, those men. They had returned to their mother and they felt that their mother had rejected them. When this happens to children, their reactions are unpredictable. Sometimes they show their frustration in violence. Hardrek was beginning to hate Earth.

Sometime later, Orvin came back and, avoiding looking directly into Hardrek's face, said: 'The President would like to see you.'

The Captain seized Orvin by the slack material of his overalls and growled: '*We* want to see these records, little Earthmen! We want to see them, d'you hear?'

'Please,' Orvin struggled helplessly. 'Please, Captain. Let me go. The President will explain.'

With an oath. Hardrek flung Orvin aside. 'He'd better, by God!'

They marched out of the Archive Building in silence, anger surging through them. They entered the ground car and it took them to the Presidential Palace – a drab 'palace,' indeed.

The President's round face wasn't smiling. He said quickly, as Hardrek strode towards him: 'I'm afraid we must ask you and your ships to leave Earth immediately, Captain.'

'What?' Hardrek nearly shouted. '*Why?*'

'You should not have come here. Your ancestors should have warned you. I must order you to leave.'

'Tell me why,' Hardrek ordered harshly.

'Leave, Captain, please. It will be for our mutual good, I assure you. We cannot blame you, but . . .'

'If we leave Earth without knowing why, my friend – then we'll leave your city burning behind us. We'll devastate the planet!'

The President turned away. 'I ask you again – please leave Earth as soon as possible.'

Hardrek's face was bloodless. He wheeled about, signing to his men to follow him. An aircraft awaited them. It took them back to the Northern Icecap. The five ships, the sun turning them into tall fires of dancing golden light, waited . . .

Hardrek sat in his cabin, thinking. He was mad with anger, bewilderment and grief. He wanted to return to the capital – to loot and destroy – to show the Earthlings that he had meant what he said. And yet he was intelligent enough to know that control over these emotions was the thing for which he should fight. But he *had* to discover the reason why Henry Callahan's expedition had left the Earth. It was becoming even more of an obsession with him. The President had said that he should leave for their mutual good. Well, if feeling were to be mutual, he could attempt to make the people of Earth feel as he felt, as his crews felt. He got up and went to the central control cabin. He picked up a microphone: 'Prepare for take-off,' he said harshly.

The slim ships cruised slowly in towards the capital, guns pointing their cold snouts at the Presidential building. Hardrek spoke over the radio:

'This is Captain Hardrek, Commander of the Veildonian Fleet. We have guns trained on the Presidential Palace – guns capable of flinging megabombs and wiping out your city in moments. We wish to depart in peace, but will not do so until the records relating to the Callahan Expedition are given into our hands.'

Eventually, the President himself answered Hardrek.

'Captain, if we hand these records over to you – do we have your word that you will leave Earth and never return?'

Hardrek said cynically: 'With all due respect, Mr President, we have no desire to return to your sterile planet. There are many others which will reward visiting better, I think.' He knew that his words were childish – but he could not resist one bitter stab at the Earth culture which had so disappointed him.

'Then you may have the documents and film,' the President said slowly.

Hardrek was elated. He had won.

The silver ships climbed, bellowing, through the night sky, back towards Veildo.

The President of Earth and the Custodian of the Archives stood together on the roof of the Presidential Palace, watching the ships leave. The Custodian stared around at the drab, grey city – and hated it.

He had spent many years among the records. He had studied the history of Earth. He felt he knew what Earth lacked. He sighed with regret as the ships disappeared into the soft blackness above.

'We could never have protected ourselves against their – weapons – you know,' said the President. 'Those poor, sick people. To think that they are of the same race.'

'To think . . .' agreed the Custodian.

On board the flagship, Captain Hardrek sat in his cabin studying the documents on hs lap. He picked one of them up and read it through again. It began:

FACTS RELATING TO THE EXILE OF
HENRY CALLAHAN AND PARTY

Callahan was given three of the latest J-type Hyperspacial Craft on condition that neither he, nor his descendants, would make any attempt to return to Earth. 76 adult men, 54 adult women, 104 adolescent boys (judged incurable) and 89 adolescent girls (jic) were put aboard the HS Craft. All members of the party had been fully examined and under observation for periods ranging from 3–8 years. Psychologists were unanimous that their condition was hopeless and their existence on this planet detrimental to Earth's general wellbeing.

Callahan, who in earlier years had been a high-ranking officer in the since disbanded United Terran Space Fleet, was put in charge of the party. He, more than any other member of the party, had displayed paranoiac tendencies to an alarming degree.

President Lidén was quoted in contemporary newspapers as saying: 'At last our planet is free of the elements which might have destroyed our culture. The threat of war, the threat of dictatorship, the threat of cultural death is over. A new era for Earth has begun. An era of peace – an era of freedom.'

Callahan's party was the last such to be exiled from Earth. Since then, all potential neurotics have been treated and cured before reaching adolescence. The proof of Lidén's statement lies in the last two-hundred-and-fifty years of peace and prosperity which has existed, and which can only continue to exist, on our planet.

When he had finished reading, Hardrek began to laugh. 'You can't have one without the other, so it seems. Well, little Earth people, you threw your waste into space and we are the result. You complacent, ruined degenerates. We may be neurotics – but our neuroses lead us somewhere, and give us the strength, even, to overcome the neuroses when we've used them to our advantage.'

He was still grinning when he gave the orders for the ships to enter hyperspace.

As he completed the orders, Hardrek said cheerfully over the intercom: 'Good luck, men. We're going home.'

This time, he was not a bit self-conscious about using the word.

Hanging the Fool

I THE HERMIT

His wife, he said, had negro blood. 'It makes her volatile, like Pushkin.'

Watching him later, as he played the table, I saw him show panic twice. He recovered himself rapidly on both occasions. He would tap his wedding ring sharply with his right index finger. His hands were long, not particularly thin, and as tawny as the rest of him – a lion, lazy and cruel, quick as a dagger. 'Lord, lord,' he would say as his wife made her appearance every evening just before dinner, 'she is magnificent!' And he would dart towards her, eager to show her off. Her name was Marianne Max and she loved him in her careless way, though I thought it more a mother's affection, for she was at least ten years his senior.

He would escort her into the dining room and afterwards would never gamble. Together they would stroll for a while along the promenade. Frequently I saw them silhouetted with the palms and cedars, talking and sometimes embracing before returning to the hotel and the suite permanently booked to them. The Hotel Cumberland was older than most and cared more for pleasing its regular customers than attracting the new money which had come to St Crim; it was a little run down but maintained its elegance, its superiority over more modern buildings, especially those revivalist deco monstrosities which had risen across the bay on the French side, upon the remains of the old Ashkanasdi mansion, where the so-called Orient Express brought rich Americans in large numbers.

I had been spending the summer with my ex-wife, who had a villa just above the town, in the pine woods. Every evening I would go down to dine at the hotel and perhaps indulge in a little baccarat.

De Passoni was the chief reason for the regularity of my visits. The man was so supremely unselfconscious, so unguarded, few would have believed him a convicted murderer, escaped from the notorious Chatuz Fortress outside Buenos Aires some years earlier. There was no sign that he feared recognition or recapture. He appeared to live entirely for the day. And there was, of course, no deportation treaty between Argentina and St Crim.

I had not by the middle of the season found any means of approaching him, however. Every time I tried I had been rebuffed. His wife was equally impossible to engage in anything but light conversation.

She was the Countess Max, one of the oldest titles in Wäldenstein. Her first husband, Freddie Max, had been killed during the Siege, leading a cavalry charge against the Prussians across the ruins of the St Maria and St Maria Cathedral. She had remarried after a year, regaining her estates by her alliance with Prince Osbert, the new prime minister. He had died of influenza in 1912, whereupon she had appeared openly with de Passoni, who was already her lover, until the scandal had forced them to St Crim where they now lived in unofficial exile.

De Passoni had his own money, from his father's locomotive works, and it was this he gambled. He took nothing from her. Neither did she expect him to take anything. Residents of the Hotel Cumberland said they were a bloodless pair. I thought otherwise.

2 THE NINE OF PENTACLES

When I came home from North Africa, the following spring, my ex-wife told me that the couple had disappeared from the Hotel Cumberland, although their suite was still booked and paid for. There was a rumour that they were in the hills outside Florence and that the Italian police were resisting an attempt to extradite him. His father had investments in Milan and considerable influence with the authorities. My ex-wife became vague when I asked her for more details, a sure sign that she possessed a secret which she hoped would add to her power.

While she was in her private sitting room taking a telephone call my ex-wife's companion approached me that evening. The woman, Pia, knew through a friend of hers that Countess Max had been seen in Florence and then in Genoa. There was talk of her having bought and equipped a steam yacht. De Passoni had not been with her.

I asked Pia, who disliked me, why they should have left St Crim. She did not know. She shrugged. 'Perhaps they were bored.'

Returning, my ex-wife had laughed at this and then grown mysterious; my sign for leaving them.

I borrowed her horse and rode down to the cliffs above Daker's

Cove. The Englishman's great Gothic house was a shell now, washed by the sea he had attempted to divert. Its granite walls were almost entirely intact and the towers showed well above the water line even at high tide, when waves washed foam in and out of the tall windows, but the great weather vane in the shape of a praying mantis had broken off at last and lay half-buried in the sand of the cove. Daker himself had returned to England and built himself a castle somewhere in the Yorkshire Dales. He lived there the year round, I heard, a disappointed recluse. The remains of his great garden were as beautiful as ever. I rode the chestnut down overgrown paths. Rhododendrons, peonies, lilac and great foxgloves filled the beds, and the whole of the ground was pale blue with masses of forget-me-nots, the remaining memories of England.

What had he learned, I wondered, from all his experience? Perhaps nothing. This was often the fate of those who attempted to impose their own reality upon a resisting and even antagonistic world. It was both a failure of imagination and of spirit. One died frustrated. I had known so many politicians who had ended their days in bitterness. The interpreter, the analyst, the celebrant, however, rarely knew the same pain, especially in old age. Neither, I thought, was that the destiny of those whose politics sought to adjust genuine social ills, who responded to the realities of others' suffering.

The paths joined at an abandoned fountain, a copy of the Kassophasos Aphrodite. Even though she was half-obscured by a wild clematis which clambered over her torso and shoulders like a cloak, she retained her air of serene wisdom. I reined in my horse and dismounted.

Struck by her similarity to the Countess Max, I wondered if I, in my turn, were not imposing my own fancy on the reality.

3 THE ACE OF WANDS

I had returned to Paris for a few days. My investments there were under attack from some manipulations on the Bourse which it soon emerged were fraudulent. By careful covering I was able not only to counter the threat and recover my capital, but make a handsome and honest profit from those whose actions might well have caused me considerable financial embarrassment.

Hearing I was at my house my friend Frere came to see me. He had a message from my father to say that he had been taken ill and was in Lucerne to recover. My own business was over. I went immediately to

Switzerland to find my father in reasonable health and breathing almost normally. He was working on his book again, a catalogue of the important buildings destroyed in France and Belgium during the Great War. It was to be his acknowledgement, he said, to an irrecoverable moment in our history, when peace had seemed a natural condition of civilized mankind.

My father asked me to visit my brother at our estates. I had not been to Bek since the last family gathering immediately following the Armistice. Uncle Ricky was long since gone to Italy, obsessed as usual, with a woman, but my brother Ulrich, whom we called Billy, was running the place very well. He was most like my father, more prepared than I to accept such rural responsibilities.

When I left Lucerne the summer had come. Mountains were brilliant with wild flowers and the lake shone with the tranquillity of steel. The train wound down to the French border first and then travelled across to Germany. I changed in Nuremberg, which always reminded me of a gigantic toy, like the one made by the Elastolin firm, with its red castle and walls, its neat cobbles and markets, the epitome of a Bavarian's dream of his perfect past. I had a light lunch at the excellent station restaurant and was disturbed only once, by a gang of men, evidently ex-soldiers, who marched in military style through the lanes shouting of revenge against the French. I found this singularly disturbing and was glad to get on the train which took me to Bek's timeless woods and towers, her deep, lush fields, so like the countryside of Oxfordshire which I had explored while at Balliol before the War.

Billy met me himself, in a dogcart, having received my telegram that morning. 'You've been in Africa, I gather?' He looked me over. 'You'll be black as an Abyssinian, at this rate!' He was curious about my mining interests in Morocco and Algeria, my relations with the French.

Since I had taken French citizenship, I explained, I had had no trouble. But I was disturbed by the Rif and Bedouin rebels who seemed to me to be growing in strength and numbers. I suspected German interests of supplying them with weapons. Billy said he knew little of international politics. All he hoped was that the Russians would continue fighting amongst themselves until Bolsheviks, Whites, Anarchists, Greens, and whoever else there were, had all wiped one another out.

I had less unsophisticated views, I said. But I laughed. Ivy-covered Bek came in sight at last. I sighed.

'Are you ever homesick?' Billy asked as he guided the dogcart up the drive.

'For which home?' I was amused.

4 THE HIGH PRIESTESS

From Marseilles I took the train down the coast. The sun had given the olive trees and vines an astonishing sharpness and the white limestone glared so fiercely that it became for a while unbearable. The sea lacked the Atlantic's profundity but was a flat, uncompromising blue, merging with a sky growing hotter and deeper in colour with every passing hour until by three o'clock I drew the blinds and sat back in my compartment to read.

I determined not to go to Cassis where Lorna Maddox, the American, had told me she would wait until she returned to Boston in September.

I had met her at dinner when I visited Lord St Odhran at the opening of the grouse season, the previous summer. She had told an extraordinary story about her own sister receiving in the post a piece of human skin, about the size of a sheet of quarto writing paper, on which had been tattooed an elaborate and, she said, quite beautiful picture. 'It was the Wheel of Fortune, including all the various fabulous beasts. In brilliant colours. Do you know the Tarot?'

I did not, but afterwards, in London, I purchased a pack from a shop near the British Museum. I was curious.

Lorna's sister had no idea of the sender, nor of the significance of such a grotesque gift.

I discovered that the card indicated Luck and Success.

For at least a week, whenever I had time on my hands, I would lay out sets of cards according to the instructions in the book I had bought at the same time. I attempted to tell my own fortune and that of my family. I recall that even my Uncle Ricky had 'Safety' as his final card. But I made no notes of my readings and forgot them, though I still kept the pack in my luggage when I travelled.

'She was told by the police that the tattoo was quite recent,' Lorna had said. 'And that if the owner were still alive she would have a trace of the design still, on her flesh. The ink, apparently, goes down to the bone. The theory was that she had regretted having the thing made and had it removed by surgery only a month or so after it had been done.'

'You're sure it was a woman's skin?' I had been surprised.

'The police were pretty certain.'

'What did your sister do with the thing?' St Odhran had asked.

'The police held it for a while. Then they returned it to her. There was no evidence of foul play, you see. My brother wanted it. It fascinated him. I believe she gave it to him.'

I knew her brother. His name was Jack Hoffner and he often visited St Crim. I had no great liking for him. He was a bad loser at the tables and was reputed to be a cruel womanizer. Possibly the piece of skin had belonged to some deserted paramour. Had she sent it to Hoffner's sister as an act of revenge?

5 THE NINE OF WANDS

It was raining by the time I reached St Crim. Huge drops of water fell from the oaks and beeches on to tall irises and there was a sound like the clicking of mandibles. Mist gathered on the warm grass as my car drove from the station up the winding road to the white house with its gleaming red roof and English chimneys. The scent of gardenias in the rain was almost overwhelming. I found that I was suddenly depressed and looking back through the rain saw the sea bright with sunlight, for the cloud was already passing.

Pia waited for me on the steps, her hair caught in some multicoloured gypsy scarf. 'She's not here. But she'll be back.' Pia signed for a servant to take my bags from the car. 'She told me you were coming.'

'She said nothing of leaving.'

'It happened suddenly. A relative, I gather.'

'Her aunt?'

'Possibly.' Pia's tone had become almost savage and it was clear she had no intention of telling me anything else.

It had always been my habit not to enquire into my ex-wife's life but I guessed she had gone somewhere with a lover and that this was disturbing Pia unduly. As a rule she kept better control of herself.

My room was ready for me. As soon as I had bathed and dressed I took the car back to the Cumberland. Almost the first person I saw as I stepped through the revolving door into the foyer was the Countess Max who acknowledged my greeting with a warmer than usual smile. Her husband came hurrying from the elevator and shook hands with me. His palm was moist and cool. He seemed frightened, though he quickly masked his expression and his face grew relaxed as he asked after mutual friends.

'I heard you had gone to Genoa to buy a boat!' I said.

'Oh, these rumours!' Countess Max began to move away on de Passoni's arm. And she laughed. It was a wonderful sound.

I followed them into the dining room. They sat together near the open French doors, looking out to the harbour where a slender steam yacht was moored, together with several other large vessels chiefly the property of visitors. I was on the far side of the room and a party of Italians came in, obscuring my view, but it seemed to me that the couple talked anxiously while preserving a good appearance. They left early, after a main course they had scarcely started. About half-an-hour later, as I stood smoking on the balcony, I saw a motor launch leaving a trail of white on the glassy water of the harbour. It had begun to rain again.

6 THE LOVERS

By the following Sunday I suspected some radical alteration in the familiar routine of life at St Crim. My ex-wife had not yet returned and it was impossible for me to ignore the gossip that she had gone to Tangier with Jack Hoffner. Further rumours, of them disappearing into the interior wearing Arab dress, I discounted. If every European said to be disguised as a Touareg was actually in the Maghreb then I doubted if there were a single tribe not wholly Caucasian and at least ninety per cent female!

However, I began to feel some concern when, after a month, nothing had been heard from them while the *Shaharazaad*, the steam yacht owned by Countess Max, was reported to have docked in El Jadida, a small, predominantly Jewish port south of Casablanca. They had radio equipment aboard.

I took to laying out my Tarot pack with the Hermit as Significator. I constantly drew the Ten of Swords, the Ace of Wands and Justice, always for the future but the order frequently changed so that although sadness, pain and affliction lay forever in my future they were not always the finale to my life. The other card drawn regularly for the future was the Lovers.

We turn to such methods when the world becomes overly mysterious to us and our normal methods of interpretation fail.

I told myself that my obsession with the Tarot was wholesome enough. At least it lacked the spurious authenticity of psychoanalysis. That particular modern fad seemed no more than a pseudo-scientific form of Theosophy, itself pseudo-religious: an answer to the impact of the twentieth century which enabled us to maintain the attitudes and convictions of nineteenth-century Vienna. Everyone I knew was presently playing at it. I refused to join in. Certain insights had been made by the psychoanalystic fraternity, but these had been elevated to the level of divine revelation and an entire mystical literature derived from them. I was as astonished by society's acceptance of these soothsayers as I was by the Dark Age rituals in St Crim's rather martial sub-Byzantine cathedral. At least these had the excuse of habit. Doctor Freud was a habit I did not wish to acquire.

I remained at St Crim until early September when I received a letter from my ex-wife. She was recovering from typhus in a hospital run by the White Sisters in Tangier. She was alone and had no friends there. She asked me to cable funds to the British Embassy or have my agent help her. There was no mention of Jack Hoffner or de Passoni and the Countess Max.

I chose one card at random from my pack. It was the Wheel of Fortune. I went down to the hotel and telephoned my friend Vronsky. That afternoon his Van Berkel seaplane landed in the harbour and after a light supper we took off for North Africa, via Valencia and Gibraltar.

The machine was a monoplane of the latest type and was built to race. There was barely room for a small valise and myself. Vronsky's slightly bloated, boyish face grinned at me from the rear cockpit, his goggles giving him the appearance of a depraved marmoset. Since the Bolshevik counter-revolution Vronsky had determined to live life to the absolute, convinced that he had little time before someone assassinated him. He was a distant cousin of the Tsar.

The plane banked once over St Crim, her wooded hills and pale villas, the delicate stone and iron of her harbour and promenade, the mock-Baroque of her hotels. It would only be a matter of seven years before, fearing the political situation in Italy, she gave up her independence to France.

The plane's motion, though fluid, filled me with a slight feeling of nausea, but this was quickly forgotten as my attention was drawn to the beauty of the landscape below. I longed to own a machine again. It had been three years since I had crashed and been captured by the Hungarians, happily only a matter of weeks before the end of the War. My wife, a German national, had been able to divorce me on the grounds that I was a traitor, though I had possessed French citizenship since 1910.

Gradually the familiar euphoria returned and I determined, next time I was in the Hague, to order a new machine.

After refuelling stops we were in sight of Tangier within a few hours. As always, the shores of Africa filled me with excitement. I knew how difficult, once one set foot on that continent, it was to leave.

7 THE PAGE OF WANDS

The Convent of the White Sisters was close to the British Consulate, across from the main gate to the Grand Socco, an unremarkable piece of architecture by Arab standards, though I was told the mosque on the far side was impressive. Apart from the usual mixture of mules and donkeys, bicycles, rickshaws, the occasional motor car and members of almost every Berber and Arab tribe, there was an unusually large presence of soldiers, chiefly of the Spanish Foreign Legion. Vronsky spoke to a tall man he recognized from before the War. The exchange was in Russian, which I understood badly. There had been some sort of uprising in a village on the outskirts of the city, to do with a group of Rif who had come in to trade. The uprising was not, as it had first seemed, political.

'A blood feud,' Vronsky informed me as we crossed the square from the shade of the great palms, 'but they're not complaining. It brought them in from the desert and now they have a day's unexpected leave. They are going in there' – he pointed through the gate – 'for the Ouled Näil. For the women.' And he shuddered.

We knocked on a rather nondescript iron door and were greeted by a small black nun who addressed me in trilling, birdlike French which I found attractive. Since they did not accept divorce, I simply told her I was visiting my wife and she became excited.

'You got the letter? How did you arrive so soon?'

'Our aeroplane is in the harbour.' I lifted my flying helmet.

She made some reference to the miraculous and clapped her little hands. She asked us to wait but Vronsky said he had some business in the new town and arranged to meet me at the Café Stern in three hours. If I was delayed I would send a message.

The little negress returned with a tall olive-skinned old woman who introduced herself as the Mother Superior. I asked after my wife.

'She is well. Physically, she's almost fully recovered. You are Monsieur von Bek? She described you to me. You'll forgive me. She was anxious that it should only be you.'

The nun led me down whitewashed corridors smelling of vinegar and disinfectant until we entered a sunny courtyard which contained a blue mosaic fountain, two Arab workmen repairing one of the columns and, in a deck chair reading a book, my ex-wife. She wore a plain lawn dress and a simple straw cloche. She was terribly pale and her eyes still seemed to contain traces of fever.

'Bertie.' She put down her book, her expression one of enormous relief. 'I hadn't expected you to come. At least, I'd hoped –' She shrugged, and bending I kissed her cheek.

'Vronsky brought me in his plane. I got your letter this morning. You should have cabled.'

Her look of gratitude was almost embarrassing.

'What happened to Hoffner?' I asked. I sat on the parapet of the fountain.

'Jack's . . .' She paused. 'Jack left me in Foum al-Hassan, when I became ill. He took the map and went on.'

'Map?' She assumed I knew more than I did.

'It was supposed to lead to a Roman treasure – or rather a Carthaginian treasure captured by the Romans. Everything seemed to be going well after we picked up the trail in Volubilis. Then Michael de Passoni and Countess Max came on the scene. God knows how they found us. The whole business went sour.'

'Where did Hoffner come by a map?'

'His sister gave it to him. That awful tattoo.'

'A treasure map? The Wheel of Fortune?'

'Apparently.' The memory appeared to have exhausted her. She stretched out her arms. 'I'm so glad you're here. I prayed for you to come. I've been an absolute ass, darling.'

'You were always romantic. Have you ever thought of writing novels? You'd make a fortune.'

On impulse I moved into her embrace.

8 THE QUEEN OF PENTACLES

I remained at St Crim for several months while my wife grew stronger, though her mental condition fluctuated considerably. Her nightmares were terrifying even to me and she refused to tell me what they involved.

We were both curious for news of Jack Hoffner and when his sister arrived at the Cumberland for a few days I went down to see her. My visits to the town had been rare. In the evenings my wife and I played cards. Sometimes we read each other's Tarot. We became quite expert.

Lorna Maddox believed that her brother was dead. 'He hadn't the courage for any prolonged adventure – and North Africa sounds dangerous. I've never been there. Someone killed him, probably, for that map. Do you really think it was sent by a deserted mistress?'

'Perhaps by the one who actually inscribed the tattoo.'

'Or the person who commissioned it? I mean, other than the recipient, as it were?'

'Do you know more about this now?' I asked. We sat indoors looking through closed windows at the balcony and the bay beyond.

'I'm not sure,' she said. 'I think Michael de Passoni had it done.'

'To his victim?'

'Yes. To a victim.'

'He's murdered more than once?'

'I would guess so. I heard all this from Margery Graeme who had quite a long affair with him. She's terrified of him. He threatened to kill her.'

'Why would he have told her such secrets?' A waiter came to take our orders and there was a long pause before she could speak again.

She had magnificent blue eyes in a large, gentle face. She wore her hair down in a girlish, rather old-fashioned style identified with pre-War Bohemia. When she bent towards me I could feel her warmth and remembered how attractive I had found her when we had met in Scotland.

'Margery discovered some papers. Some designs. And a set of Tarot cards with the Wheel of Fortune removed. The addresses of several tattooists in Marseilles were there. And the piece of skin, you know, came from there. At least the postmark on the envelope was Cassis.'

'Everyone goes to Cassis.' I was aware of the inanity of my remark which had to do, I was sure, with my wish to reject her information, not because it seemed untrue but because it seemed likely. I was beginning to fear a moral dilemma where previously I had known only curiosity.

9 THE WHEEL OF FORTUNE

Business at last forced me to return to Paris. Dining at Lipp's in St Germain on the first evening of my arrival I was disturbed to see the Countess Max. De Passoni was not with her. Instead she was in the company of a dark man who was either Levantine or Maghrebi. He was strikingly handsome and wore his evening clothes with the easy familiarity which identified him, as we used to say, as some sort of gentleman.

Countess Max recognized me at once and could do nothing but acknowledge me. When I crossed to greet her she reluctantly introduced me to her companion. 'Do you know Moulay Abul Hammoud?'

'Enchanted, monsieur,' he said in the soft, vibrant voice I associated always with the desert. 'We have already met briefly, I believe.'

Now that we stood face to face I remembered him from a Legation reception in Algiers before the War. He had been educated at Eton but was the religious leader of the majority of clans in the Southern- and pre-Sahara. Without his control the clans would have been disunited and warring not only amongst themselves but making desultory raids on the authorities. Moulay Abul Hammoud not only kept order in large parts of the Maghreb but also maintained enormous political power, for upon his orders the desert Berbers as well as large numbers of urban Arabs, could forget all differences and unite to attack the French or Spanish.

It was commonly agreed that Moulay Abul was only awaiting the appropriate moment, while the benefits of colonial occupation outweighed the ills, before declaring the renewed independence of the Saharan kingdoms. His influence was also recognized by the British who acknowledged his growing power in North India and in their own Middle Eastern interests.

'I'm honoured to meet you again, sir.' I was impressed by him and shared a respect many had expressed before me. 'Are you in Paris officially?'

'Oh, merely a vacation.' He smiled at the Countess Max. She looked darker, even more exotic than when I had last seen her.

'Moulay Abul was of great service to me,' she murmured, 'in Morocco.'

'My wife has only recently returned. I believe you met her there. With Jack Hoffner?'

The countess resumed her familiar detached mask, but in spite of seeming ill-mannered I continued. 'Have you heard anything of Hoffner? He was meant to have disappeared in Morocco or Algeria.'

Moulay Abul interrupted quickly and with considerable grace. 'Mr Hoffner was unfortunately captured by hostile Tuaregs in Mauretania. He was eventually killed. Also captured, I believe, was the poor countess's husband. The authorities know, but it has not been thought wise to inform the Press until we have satisfactory identification.'

'You have some?'

'Very little. A certain map that we know was in Hoffner's possession.'

It seemed to me that the Countess Max tried to warn him to silence. Unconsciously the Moulay had told me more than he realized. I bowed and returned to my table.

It seemed clear that Hoffner and de Passoni had failed in their adventure and had died in pursuit of the treasure. Possibly Moulay Abul and Countess Max had betrayed them and the treasure was in their hands. More likely the answer was subtler and less melodramatic.

I was certain, however, that Moulay Abul and the Countess Max were lovers.

10 THE TEN OF SWORDS

The tragedy eventually reached the Press. By coincidence I was in Casablanca when the news appeared and while the local journals, subject to a certain discretion, not to say censorhip, were rather matter-of-fact in their reporting, the French and English papers were delighted with the story and made everything they could of it, especially since de Passoni was already a convicted murderer and Hoffner had a warrant for fraud against him issued in Berlin at the time of his disappearance.

The Countess Max emerged more or less with her honour intact. The Press preferred to characterize her as an innocent heroine, while my wife was not mentioned at all. Moulay Abul remained a shadowy but more or less benign figure, for the story had been given a Kiplingesque touch by the time the writers had licked it into a shape acceptable to a wide public.

The opinion was that de Passoni and Hoffner had duped the Countess Max, getting her to buy the steam yacht they needed to transport the treasure back to Europe as soon as it was in their possession. The map, drawn on the skin of a long-dead Roman legionary, had become the conventional object of boys' adventure fiction and we learned how the two adventurers had dressed as Bedouin and ridden into the Sahara in search of a lost city built by Carthaginians who had fled conquering Rome. More in fact was made of the mythical city than the map, which suited Hoffner's family, who had feared the sensational use journalists would have made of the bizarre actuality.

I was invited to dinner by General Fromental and his wife and should have refused had not I heard that Moulay Abul was also going to be present.

By chance it was a relatively intimate affair at one of those pompous provincial mansions the French liked to build for themselves in imitation of an aristocracy already considered impossibly vulgar by the rest of Europe. My fellow guests were largely of advanced years and interested neither in myself nor the Moulay, who seemed glad of my company, perhaps because we shared secrets in common.

When we stood together smoking on the terrace, looking out at palms and poplars, still a dark green against the deep blue of the sky, and listening to the night birds calling, to the insects and the occasional barking of a wild dog, I asked after the Countess Max.

'I gather she's in excellent health,' he said. He smiled at me, as if permitting me a glimpse of his inner thoughts. 'We were not lovers, you know. I am unable to contemplate adultery.'

The significance of his remark completely escaped me. 'I have always been fascinated by her,' I told him. 'We were frequently in St Crim at the same time. She and de Passoni lived there for a while.'

'So I understand. The yacht is moored there now, is it not?'

'I hadn't heard.'

'Yes. Recently. She had expressed some notion of returning to Wäldenstein but the situation there is not happy. And she is a cold-natured woman needing the sun. You've a relative there, I believe.'

'An ex-wife. You know her?'

'Oh, yes. Slightly. My other great vice is that I have difficulty in lying.' He laughed and I was disarmed. 'I make up for this disability by the possession of a subtle mind which appreciates all the degrees and shades of truth. Hoffner deserted her in Foum al-Hassan. I was lucky enough to play some small part in getting her back to Tangier. One should not involve women in these affairs, don't you think?'

'I rather understood they involved themselves.'

'Indeed. A passion for excitement has overwhelmed Western females since the dying down of war. It seems to have infected them more than the men.'

'Oh, our women have always had more courage, by and large. And more imagination. Indeed, one scarcely exists without the other.'

'They do define each other, I'd agree.'

He seemed to like me as much as I liked him. Our companionship was comfortable as we stood together in the warm air of the garden.

'I'm afraid my wife mentioned nothing of your help,' I told him.

'She knew nothing of it. That man Hoffner? What do you think of him?'

'A blackguard.'

'Yes.' He was relieved and spoke almost as if to someone else. 'A coward. A jackal. He had a family?'

'Two sisters living. I know one of them slightly.'

'Ah, then you've heard of the map?'

'The one you mentioned in Paris? Yes, I know of it. I don't think his sister recognized it for a map.'

'Metaphysically, perhaps, only?' His humour had taken a different colour. 'Oh, yes, there is a map involved in many versions of that design. I thought that was common knowledge.'

'You're familiar with the Tarot?'

'With arcana in general.' He shrugged almost in apology. 'I suppose it's in the nature of my calling to be interested in such things. Hoffner's death was no more unpleasant than any he would have visited on – on me, for instance.' He turned away to look up at the moon. 'I believe they flayed him.'

'So he's definitely dead. You saw the corpse?'

'Not the corpse exactly.' Moulay Abul blew smoke out at the sky. It moved like an escaped ifrit in the air and fled into invisible realms. 'Just the pelt.'

11 JUSTICE

My return to St Crim was in the saddest possible circumstances, in response to a telegram telling me that my wife was dead. When I arrived at the house Pia handed me a sealed envelope addressed to me in my wife's writing.

'You know she killed herself?' The voice was neutral, the eyes desolate.

I had feared this but had not dared to consider it. 'Do you know why?'

'It was to do with Hoffner. Something that happened to her in Africa. You know how she was.'

We went down to the kitchens where Pia made coffee. The servants were all gone, apart from the cook, who was visiting her sister in Monaco. The woman and her husband who had kept the house for her had found her body.

'She cut her wrists in the swimming pool. She used Hoffner's razor.'

'You don't know why? I mean – there wasn't anything she discovered? About Hoffner, for instance?'

'No. Why, did you hear something?'

I shook my head but she had guessed I was lying. Handing me the coffee cup she said slowly: 'Do you think she knew what was going on? With Hoffner and de Passoni?'

'She told you.'

'The Countess Max stayed with us for several days. She went down to the hotel. She plans to remain there until the funeral. Hoffner's sister is there, too. A bit of a reunion.'

'You think my wife was guilty? That she had a hand in whatever happened in Morocco?'

'She knew Hoffner was involved in every sort of beastly crime and that half the Berlin underworld was after him – not to mention the New York police and the French Secret Service. He betrayed men as well as women. She told me he was threatening her but I think she loved him. Some bad chemistry, perhaps. He excited her, at least. The Countess Max, on the other hand, was thoroughly terrified of him. He had a hold over her husband, you know.'

'So he forced them into his adventure?'

'Apparently. They needed a boat.'

I found that I could not bear to open the envelope my wife had left for me and walked instead down to the Hotel Cumberland where I found Lorna Maddox and Countess Max taking tea together in the cool of the salon. They both wore half-mourning in honour of my wife and greeted me with sincerity when I presented myself, asking me to join them.

'It must have been frightful for you,' said Lorna Maddox, 'the news. We were appalled.'

'Her nerves were terribly bad.' The Countess Max remained distant, though less evasive, less cool. 'I thought she was brave. To go inland with the men like that. I refused, you know.'

'But you believed the map?'

'I had no reason to doubt. Jack was completely convinced. The woman – the woman on whom it had been inscribed was – well, you know, of very good family over there. She was no more than a girl. The secret was passed from mother to daughter, apparently. God knows where Jack heard the story originally, but he made it his business to find her.'

'And seduce her,' said Lorna in a small, chilling voice.

'He was proud of that. I gather it was something of a challenge.' The Countess Max raised china to her lips.

'Surely he didn't – he couldn't . . . ?' I was glad to accept the chair Lorna Maddox offered me.

'Take the skin?' she said. 'Oh, no. That was sent to my sister by the girl's uncle, I gather. There was for a while some suspicion of a blood feud between her family and mine.'

'Moulay Abul put a stop to that.' The Countess was approving. 'Without his interference things might have become considerably worse.' She frowned. 'Though poor Michael's not entirely convinced of that.'

I was shocked. 'Your husband's still alive? I understood that he had died in North Africa.'

'Moulay Abul saved him also. Through his influence he was given up to the French police and is now at sea, escorted back to Buenos Aires by two Sûreté sergeants. He was relieved at first . . .'

She stared directly back into my eyes. 'He saw it.'

Although it was not yet five I ordered a cognac from their waiter. I marvelled at the self-control of such women. It was still impossible to guess their real feelings – one towards her brother, the other towards her husband.

There was little more to say.

'The matter's been resolved in the best possible way.' Lorna Maddox sighed and picked up a delicate cup. She glanced at me almost in amusement. 'You are very upset. I'm sorry. We were fond of your wife. But she would encourage men to such extremes, don't you think?'

I returned to the house and opened the packet, expecting some explanation of my wife's part in the affair. But she had written nothing.

The envelope contained a folded section of almost transparent skin on which had been tattooed a Wheel of Fortune. It had been wrapped around the Tarot card representing Justice. There was also a visiting card bearing the printed name of Moulay Abul Hamoud and on the reverse, in clear script, a few words – 'With my compliments. I believe this is morally, madame, your property.'

The note was, of course, unsigned.

Consuming Passion

I travel swiftly and cautiously over the soft, dry wood-shavings. All around me loom the canvas-covered piles of timber. It is on nights as dark as this that I enjoy my work; the fruits of my labours are that much more apparent.

I feel my mouth go dry, as dry as the wood I tread on; my breath comes quickly, in and out of my lungs; my heart pounds heavily against my ribs. Here is a place, a dark, quiet place with light dowelling stacked high. Fine kindling.

From my special little pocket, I extract my shiny petrol lighter. Press of a thumb, scrape of a wheel, a random spark shoots from flint to wick – and lights the invisible fumes. How perfect it is, this little pointed, flickering flame.

In my jacket pockets is paper, screwed up tight. I stuff it into gaps between the heaped dowels. Now I apply the flame.

Beautifully, the fire begins to lick explorative tongues delicately upwards, darting along the wood, further and further. The delicious smell of woodsmoke fills my lungs.

I stand back and I want to laugh at the flaming glory I have created. It will soon engulf the stacks of timber, but now I must run away. Far away. To be found here would mean that my days of creation would be over. It is warm, near the fire, and the night air chills me as I run.

Another Big Blaze
ARSON STRONGLY SUSPECTED
Is maniac at large?

Jordan Mennell reads the headline with a slightly thumping heart. A faint smile plays around his well-shaped mouth. His eyes, too bright for grey eyes, scan the columns avidly.

Once more a masterpiece accomplished.

This makes ten. Ten great works of heart. Ten triumphs; ten little note-books with ten collections of clippings pasted neatly in them. And they have a name for him now.

Pyro Jack!

His pseudonym.

Tomorrow I try for eleven. No more petty ignitions of garden bonfires; no more the occasional surreptitiously dropped match in a waste-paper bin. Big ones from now on. Vast timber yards, rubber dumps, petrol reservoirs. Like God I create the flame which destroys. Yes, I am a creator and a destroyer. The power is in my hands. The glory of leaping, yelling, roaring, soaring flames – the red, yellow and blue, the gold and the silver. The tall columns of smoke and the red glow on the skyline. And frantic, terrified little men hopping about, impotent and frightened.

Tomorrow, the eleventh and greatest ever creation. Tomorrow – Dennissen's the furniture store. No watchman; quite safe. Eight storeys of combustibles. A fitting monument to my power. Today, dull wood and fabric; lifeless. Tomorrow – a glorious, sentient mountain.

He pulls on the black trousers, the dark shirt, the soft-soled shoes; feels for the lighter, checks for paper. Paper safe and crinkly against his thigh; lighter hard and smooth.

He goes out of the brown and grubby back door from which the paint is peeling. He turns the rusty key in the stiff lock; picks a silent path through the rubble of the yard, past the dilapidated shed with the door which hangs on one hinge. Over the leaning fence and into the narrow, cindered alley.

Softly, he crunches along, keeping to the maze of alleyways which run between the identical banks of houses. Bright lights of the High Street before him. A sudden dash across it into the gloom of another narrow alley. But this one is of firm concrete, a wall on one side, a tall corrugated-iron fence on the other. The fence is pointed at the top, like triangular fingers clutching for the sky.

Panting now, after the exertion of the swift run across the deserted main street. A white-painted sign, white foam on the undulating sea of the corrugated fence. He removes his jacket.

With a quick movement, he sends the jacket sailing upwards so that it falls and hangs on the barbs of the fence. An agile jump and his hands are on the top of the fence, padded by his jacket. With little obvious effort, he hauls himself carefully over the fence and, hanging for a moment by one hand, grasps his jacket with the other and drops. The jacket comes with him, but it rips loudly as it comes. He put it on again and looks around him.

He can guess what the dark silhouettes are; old chests of drawers, ancient divans, bed-springs.

Now he takes out his sharp, steel knife and begins to force the lock on the door. He hacks at the wood which surrounds the lock and knows that this damage may be discovered. Good, he thinks, they will know that I am responsible.

I am in a dark passage full of the odours of wood-polish and veneer and cloth. I walk along the passage and find the stairway which leads down into the basement. I have been here before. I bought a chair in the second-hand department. That department is in the basement.

I know what I must do. I must ignite the furniture in the basement, then I must go quickly up to the eighth floor and light the fabrics they keep there. Then I must open some windows so that a breeze will fan the flames.

I take out my small pocket-torch and flash it around the basement. A carpet on the floor, wardrobes, tallboys, book-cases. Many of them frail-looking. All the better. A cupboard painted dull cream and very flimsy. The ideal spot, I take the paper from my pocket and put it along the bottom shelf of the cupboard. Some curtains partition off another piece of the department. I walk over to them and rip them down; they tear with a tiny tinkle of curtain rings.

Stuffing the curtains into other shelves of the cupboard, I take out my lighter. A great feeling of elation and power begins to surge through my body. I breathe heavily, my hand shakes a little, my heart is beating a frenzied tattoo against my rib-cage.

This is the ultimate of sensations, almost all I desire. I press my thumb on the lighter.

Nothing happens, a brief spark but that is all. I press it again, there is a tiny snap. I know that sound, the sound when the flint is finished. I moan in anguish and pass my hands through my hair in violent frustration. I glare with rage at the cupboard. And the cupboard bursts into flames.

Not with a delicate flicker of light, but with a sudden snap and a roar and it is burning; burning so brightly.

I stare at a cabinet and will it to burn. But nothing happens. Then I realize that the flames are licking nearer to me. I turn and run from the basement, up the stairs, three at a time, opening windows at every landing. Up another flight of stairs, and another, and another, until I am breathing very heavily and irregularly and I am at the top of the building.

But I realize I have no matches, no lighter, nothing with which to create another blaze. I feel frustrated among the rolls of cloth, the cotton and the nylon which will burn so well. I feel like a writer without a pen, an artist without his brushes. The canvas is before me, but I have nothing with which to paint it, to turn it into glowing beauty.

Anger once more consumes me. Is God so frustrated when He works *His* miracles? I wish with all my heart that the cotton and the nylon will burn. And it does. It begins to burn all around me, quite suddenly. I stand for a long moment and revel in the passionate wonder of the dancing flames. I breathe in the smell of the burning fabric.

Then I realize that if I stay and watch, I will no longer be alive. No longer will I be able to create more grandeur and magnificence. I turn and dash down the stairs. As I reach the last flight, I see a glow, a glorious glow, in the basement.

I fling open the door through which I entered and rush out into the yard. The fence stops me. Why hadn't I thought about the fence before? Leering, jeering fence! My teeth clench tightly, twisting my mouth. I sob in anger. And the fence begins to melt. A hole appears in it; drops of white-hot metal fall from the edges of the hole. I dash through, howling as a piece of molten iron drops on to my shoulder and sets my jacket ablaze. I tear off the garment and fling it behind me as I run down the alley the way I came. No one is in the High Street. I run across the road into the safety of the alley-ways behind the rows of houses. I moan softly to myself; the pain in my shoulder is agonizing.

Jordan Mennell sits in the shabby armchair reading his paper. He is dressed only in a pair of pyjama trousers and his right shoulder is crudely smothered in a large piece of medical plaster which is wrinkled and dirty.

The same faint smile is on his face, the same bright light in his eyes. He is reading his latest reviews.

One of the most disastrous fires in South London!
WHO IS PYRO JACK?

says one critic. Praise indeed! The critic mentions that the police suspect arson once more. And Pyro Jack, as the public knows Jordan Mennell, is credited. The eleventh big fire in the area within two weeks. Jordan Mennell has been able to see the flames from his bedroom window. He decides that this was the biggest. His unnamed critic agrees. And now Jordan Mennell has the power to create more great fires wherever he pleases. If his anger is sufficiently roused, he supposes, he can start a blaze anywhere he wishes. He is content.

The pain in his shoulder is great, but it will go away soon. His eyes follow the front-page columns, reading the speculations and assertions. He comes to a paragraph and the smile clears from his mouth as it opens slightly. The police have a clue. A charred jacket which was left on the scene of the fire.

For a moment, Jordan Mennell knows concern. But then he is his old self, his old powerful self. With his new talents, he can defy the police even though they may catch him. He knows what he is capable of, now. Concentration will help him channel his talent, he will not need to feel anger, there will be other emotions. Concentration and power. He has both.

I am dressing, ready to go to work, when there comes a terse knocking on the door of my house. I am puzzled but I finish dressing before I walk down the narrow stairs which creak, and reach out my hand to the handle of the door. As I turn it, I have an inkling of who my caller is. I open the door slowly and confront the man who stands on my step, his left foot close to a bottle of milk and a carton of eggs; his right foot on the cracked concrete of my path. His trousers are black, like his shoes; his raincoat is khaki and grubby. He wears a dark jacket, a striped shirt and a blue tie. He has a double chin and a small moustache and his eyes are deep blue under thick eyebrows. On top of his head is a brown felt trilby. He is, I feel certain, a plain-clothes policeman.

'Yes?' I enquire, shortly.

'Mr Jordan Mennell?' He knows who I am but I answer him all the same.

'Yes,' I tell him. I know the next words before he speaks them.

'I am a police officer. I wonder if I might come in and ask you a few questions?' His voice is gruff and he attempts a politeness which is not in his nature, there is a rock core beneath this very thin veneer.

What else can I say but 'Very well.'

He enters and I lead him into my small sitting-room. I indicate a chair and the movement sends spasms of pain through my throbbing shoulder. I manage to smile.

'What can I do for you, officer? Looking for burglars?'

'No, sir,' this he says slowly. 'It's about the big fire at Dennissen's.'

'I read about it this morning,' I say, keeping perfect control of myself. 'A terrible catastrophe.'

'Yes, sir. The whole place was gutted. Your jacket was found nearby.' This is an attempt to shock me. A bluff. But I am ready for this policeman with his shallow cunning.

'My jacket!' I manage to seem astounded. 'But that is impossible!'

'Your name was on a tag fixed inside the jacket, sir. Most of the right side of the jacket was burned, but much of it was left when we found it. Perhaps you would like to come along to the station and identify the jacket, sir?'

I feel anger coursing inside me, but I control my emotion and smile again. 'Very well, officer, but I am sure you are mistaken.' What can they do to me, anyway? I am invincible.

We reach the red-brick police-station and walk together along a cold marble passage, up a short flight of stairs and into a warm room. There is a gas-fire burning against one wall. A desk is before it and a coat-rack beside the entrance to the room. The desk has wire trays and papers on it – and a parcel. There is a small window which looks out on to the street. A grey street, with an occasional dull-coloured car flashing by, or a darkly-dressed man. These people should feel honoured that I bring such magnificent colour into their lives. But instead they resent me. It is wrong, but I must accept it.

The policeman walks over to the desk after shutting the door behind us. He unwraps the parcel and discloses the remains of the coat I wore last night.

I feel annoyed because I have been so careless. I had assumed that the jacket would have burned to ashes.

I feel another upsurge of power within me, just as a uniformed policeman enters. He begins to tidy up the desk.

'That is my coat,' I say, after having glanced at it.

'And,' I add grandly, 'I was responsible for all eleven fires you have been worrying about. I shall also be the cause of many more.'

'Pyro Jack, my God!' says the younger uniformed policeman. I bow slightly to him as he makes for the door with an armful of papers, bent on telling the news to his companions no doubt. After all, I am a personality whose work has been very much in the public eye recently. They may ask me for my autograph. I shall refuse.

However, I am still angry, but manage to retain a mask of calm.

The policeman is visibly shocked by my statement, but he recovers his composure enough to say 'In which case, Mr Mennell, perhaps you'd like to make a statement.'

'I have made all the statement I wish to make,' I reply. 'Now I must leave.'

'Oh, no you don't!' He moves forward to stop me as I make for the door.

I wheel around and glare at him, if only he would burn too, it would be easier for me.

He shrieks horribly as the flames lick at his flesh. But he has stopped by the time I reach the entrance of the police station.

'*Stop him!* That's Pyro Jack!' The young policeman yells shrilly, excitedly. Another policeman, entering the front of the building, moves forward to stop me. I burn his uniform. He begins to beat frantically at the flames.

I walk calmly out of the place and stroll along the street. A few minutes later, a police-car pulls up beside the pavement. I melt it.

The men inside scream in terror.

I laugh out loud, glorying in my magnificent power. The instinct of self-preservation is a wonderful thing.

People rushing. People shouting. People pushing. People grasping, People burning brightly like giant skipping fireflies, a glorious dance of death.

I walk on down the long brick-lined avenues, I stride along burning and melting anyone or anything which comes in my way. I can conquer the world, and turn it into leaping flames, like a second sun. It shall burn in the heavens as it did millions of years ago.

I thrill jubilantly and my steps are light and buoyant. An hour passes, then manlike, mis-shapen things shuffle clumsily towards me. They have a single broad eye and carry guns in thick-fingered hands.

'Stop, Mennell! Stop, or we shoot!'

Asbestos! Of course, I see it now, I cannot burn asbestos. And those guns can kill me. I shudder and wish that the guns would catch fire, too. They melt.

But the men in the asbestos suits draw nearer. They reach out their coarse, ungainly hands to grasp me.

I draw back, the indignity of it all appals me. I run away from them towards a tall building; a tall white building. The public library.

A woman shrieks as I rush inside but I ignore her and run on. The clumping of my pursuers' boots echoes down the corridor towards me. I dash into a high-roofed room lined with bookshelves.

The men come nearer and nearer, I stare wildly around me, looking for a route of escape – but I have entered through the only door. Framed in it now are the three asbestos-clad monsters.

It is unfair. They should herald me as master of the world, not treat me as if I were an abnormal beast. I am a supernormal man!

They spread out their arms and move in a cautious semi-circle towards me. I feel enraged at myself and admit that my own blind folly has led me to this trap.

'Back! Get back!' I roar, my voice reverberating round the lofty room. 'Back, or I will destroy you!' Still they come nearer, light glinting on their cyclops' eyes, their faceplates.

I scream at them, but the fools still advance. I deserve to burn myself, for my negligence. A flicker of flame appears on my trousers, runs sensuously up my leg, caresses my thigh. Frantically, I attempt to beat it out, but it is too late. I can start fires but cannot extinguish them – I have never wanted to.

I glare at the books. Voltaire, Dickens, Dostoevsky, Shakespeare, Conrad, Hemingway surround me, glaring back, mocking me. Their work will last, they seem to say. Mine is finished.

My anger sets tongues of orange flame writhing around the books. Everywhere on the shelves the books begin to burn. I feel the heat of my flaming clothes, the pain of the fire. Softly, at first, I begin to laugh. I have achieved some small measure of triumph.

Wolf

Whose little town are you, friend? Who owns you here? Wide and strong, you have an atmosphere of detached impermanence as you sit in the shallow valley with your bastion of disdainful pines surrounding you; with your slashed, gashed earth roads and your gleaming graveyards, cool under the sun. Here I stand in your peaceful centre, among the low houses, looking for your owner. Night is looming in my mind's back-waters.

I stop a long-jawed man with down-turned, sensuous lips. He rocks on his feet and stares at me in silence, his grey eyes brooding.

'Who owns this town?' I ask him.

'The people,' he says. 'The residents.'

I laugh at the joke, but he refuses to join me, does not even smile. 'Seriously – tell me. Who owns this town?'

He shrugs and walks off. I laugh louder: 'Who owns this town, friend? Who owns it?' Does he hate me?

Without a mood, what is a man, anyway? A man has to have some kind of mood, even when he dreams. Scornfully, I laugh at the one who refused to smile and I watch his back as he walks stiffly and self-consciously over a bridge of wood and metal which spans soft water, full of blossom and leaves, flowing in the sunlight.

In my hand is a cool silver flask loaded with sweet fire. I know it is there. I lift it to my mouth and consume the fire, letting it consume me, also. Blandly, we destroy each other, the fire and I.

My stomach is full of flame and my legs are tingling, as soft as soda water, down to where my feet ache. *Don't leave me, sweetheart, with your hair of desire and your mockeries hollow in the moaning dawn. Don't leave me with the salt rain rushing down my cold face.* I laugh again and repeat the man's words: 'The people – the residents!' Ho ho ho! But there is no one to hear my laughter now unless there are inhabitants in the white town's curtained dwellings. *Where are you, sweetheart – where's your taunting body, now, and the taste of your fingernails in my flesh*?

Harsh smoke drowns my sight and the town melts as I fall slowly down towards the cobbles of the street and a pain begins to inch its way through my stinging face.

Where's the peace that you seek in spurious godliness of another man – a woman? Why is it never there?

I regain my sight and look upwards to where the blue sky fills the world until it is obscured by troubled sounds which flow from a lovely face dominated by eyes asking questions which make me frustrated and angry, since I cannot possibly answer them. Not one of them. I smile, in spite of my anger and say, cynically: 'It makes a change, doesn't it?' The girl shakes her head and the worried noises still pour from her mouth. Lips as red as blood – splashed on slender bones, a narrow, delicate skull. 'Who – ? Why are you –? What happened to you?'

'That's a very personal question, my dear,' I say patronizingly. 'But I have decided not to resent it.'

'Thank you,' says she. 'Are you willing to rise and be helped somehow?'

Of course I am, but I would not let her know just yet. 'I am seeking a friend who came this way,' I say. 'Perhaps you know her? She is fat with my life – full of my soul. She should be easy to recognize.'

'No – I haven't . . .'

'Ah – well, if you happen to notice her, I would appreciate it if you would let me know. I shall be in the area for a short while. I have become fond of this town.' A thought strikes me; 'Perhaps you own it?'

'No.'

'Please excuse the question if you are embarrassed by it. I, personally, would be quite proud to own a town like this. Is it for sale, do you think?'

'Come, you'd better get up. You might be arrested. Up you get.'

There is a disturbing reluctance on the part of the residents to tell me the owner of the town. Of course, I could not afford to buy it – I asked cunningly, in the hope of discovering who the owner was. Maybe she is too clever for me. The idea is not appealing.

'You're like a dead bird,' she smiles, 'with your wings broken.'

I refuse her hand and get up quickly. 'Lead the way.'

She frowns and then says: 'Home I think.' So off we go with her walking ahead. I point upwards: 'Look – there's a cloud the shape of a cloud!' She smiles and I feel encouraged to such a degree that I want to thank her.

We reach her house with its green door opening directly on to the street. There are windows with red and yellow curtains and the white paint covering the stone is beginning to flake. She produces a key, inserts it into the large black iron lock and pushes the door wide open, gesturing gracefully for me to enter before her. I incline my head and walk into the darkened hallway of the house. It smells of lavender and is full of old polished oak and brass plates, horse-brasses, candlesticks with no candles in them. On my right is a staircase which twists up into gloom, the stairs covered by dark red carpet.

There are ferns in vases, placed on high shelves. Several vases of ferns are on the window-sill by the door.

'I have a razor if you wish to shave,' she informs me. Luckily for her, I am self-critical enough to realize that I need a shave I thank her and she mounts the stairs, wide skirt swinging, leading me to the upstairs floor and a small bathroom smelling of perfume and disinfectant.

She switches on the light. Outside, the blue of the sky is deepening and the sun has already set. She shows me the safety-razor, soap, towel. She turns a tap and water gushes out into her cupped hand. 'Still hot,' she says, turning and closing the door behind her. I am tired and make a bad job of shaving. I wash my hands as an afterthought and then go to the door to make sure it isn't locked. I open the door and peer out into the lighted passage. I shout: 'Hey!' and her head eventually comes into sight around another door at the far end of the passage. 'I've shaved.'

'Go downstairs into the front room,' she says. 'I'll join you there in a few minutes.' I grin at her and my eyes tell her that I know she is naked beneath her clothes. They all are. Without their clothes and their hair, where would they be? *Where is she? She came this way – I scented her trail right here, to this town. She could even be hiding inside this woman – fooling me. She was always clever in her own way. I'll break her other hand, listen to the bones snap, and they won't catch me. She sucked my life out of me and they blamed me for breaking her fingers. I was just trying to get at the ring I gave her. It was hidden by the blaze of the others.*

She turned me into a sharp-toothed wolf.

I thunder down the stairs, deliberately stamping on them, making them moan and creak. I locate the front room and enter it. Deep leather chairs, more brass, more oak, more ferns in smoky glass of purple and scarlet. A fireplace without a fire. A soft carpet, multicoloured. A small piano with black-and-white keys and a picture in a frame on top of it.

There is a white-clothed table with cutlery and plates for two. Two chairs squat beside the table.

I stand with my back to the fireplace as I hear her pointed-heeled shoes tripping down the stairs. 'Good evening,' I say politely when she comes in, dressed in a tight frock of dark blue velvet, with rubies around her throat and at her ears. There are dazzling rings on her fingers and I shudder, but manage to control myself.

'Please sit down.' She repeats the graceful gesture of the hand, indicating a leather chair with a yellow cushion. 'Do you feel better now?' I am suspicious and will not answer her. It might be a trick question, one never knows. 'I'll get dinner,' she tells me, 'I won't be long.' Again I've defeated her. She can't win at this rate.

I consume the foreign meal greedily and only realize afterwards that it might have been poisoned. Philosophically I reflect that it is too late now as I wait for coffee. I will test the coffee and see if it smells of bitter almonds. If it does, I will know it contains poison. I try to remember if any of the food I have already eaten tasted of bitter almonds. I don't think so. I feel comparatively safe.

She brings in the coffee smoking in a big brown earthenware pot. She sits down and pours me a cup. It smells good and, relievedly, I discover it does not have the flavour of bitter almonds. Come to think of it, I am not altogether sure what bitter almonds smell like.

'You may stay the night here, if you wish. There is a spare room.'

'Thank you,' I say, letting my eyes narrow in a subtle question, but she looks away from me and reaches a slim hand for the coffee pot. 'Thank you,' I repeat. She doesn't answer me. What's her game? She takes a breath, is about to say something, looks quickly at me, changes her mind, says nothing. I laugh softly, leaning back in my chair with my hand clasped around my coffee cup.

'There are wolves and there are sheep,' I say, as I have often said. 'Which do you think you are?'

'Neither,' says she.

'Then you are sheep,' say I. 'The wolves know what they are – what their function is. I am wolf.'

'Really,' she says and it is obvious that she is bored by my philosophy, not understanding it. 'You had better go to bed now – you are tired.'

'If you insist,' I say lightly. 'Very well.'

She shows me up to the room overlooking the unlit street and bids me good night. Closing the door, I listen carefully for the sound of a key turning, but the sound doesn't come. The room contains a high, old-fashioned bed, a standard lamp with a parchment shade with flowers pressed between two thicknesses, an empty bookcase and a wooden chair, beautifully carved. I feel the chair with my fingertips and shiver with delight at the sensation I receive. I pull back the quilt covering the bed and inspect the sheets which are clean and smell fresh. There are two white pillows, both very soft. I extract myself from my suit, taking off my shoes and socks and leaving my underpants on. I switch off the light and, trembling a little, get into the sheets, I am soon asleep, but it is still very early. I am convinced that I shall wake up at dawn.

I open my eyes in the morning and pale sunshine forces its way between gaps in the curtains. I lie in bed trying to go back to sleep, but cannot. I push away the covers, which have slipped partly off the bed, and get up. I go to the window and look down into the street.

Incredibly, a huge hare is loping along the pavement, its nose twitching. A lorry roars past, its gears grating, but the hare continues its imperturbable course. I am tensed, excited. I open my door and run along the passage to the woman's room, entering with a rush. She is asleep, one arm sprawled outwards, the hand dangling over the edge of her bed, her shoulders pale and alive. I take hold of one shoulder in a strong grip designed to hurt her into wakefulness. She cries out, sits up quivering.

'Quick,' I say – 'Come and see. There is a hare in the street!'

'Go away and let me sleep,' she tells me, 'let me sleep.'

'No! You must come and look at the big hare in the street. How did it get there?'

She rises and follows me back to my room. I leap towards the window and see with relief that the hare is still there. 'Look!' I point towards it and she joins me at the window. She, too, is amazed. 'Poor thing,' she gasps. 'We must save it.'

'Save it?' I am astounded. 'Save it? No, I will kill it and we can eat it.'

She shudders. 'How could you be so cruel?' The hare disappears around a corner of the street. I am furious and all the nerves of my body are taut. 'It has gone!'

'It will probably be all right,' she says in a self-conciliatory tone and this makes me more angry. I begin to sob with frustration. She puts a hand on my arm. 'What is the matter?' I shrug off the hand, then think better of it, I begin to cry against her breast. She pats me on the back and I feel better. 'Let me come to bed with you,' I plead.

'No,' she says quietly. 'You must rest.'

'Let me sleep with *you*,' I insist, but she breaks from my grasp and backs towards the door. 'No! Rest.'

I follow her, my eyes hot in my skull, my body full. 'You owe me something,' I tell her viciously. 'You all do.'

'Go away,' she says threateningly, desperate and afraid of me. I continue to move towards her, beyond the door, along the passage. She starts to run for her room but I run also, and catch her. I catch her before she reaches the room. She screams. I clutch at her fingers. I bend them back slowly, putting my other hand over her mouth to stop her horrible noises. The bones snap in the slim, pale flesh. Not all at once.

'You made me wolf.' I snarl. 'And sheep must die.' My teeth seek her pounding jugular, my nose scents the perfume of her throat. I slide my sharp teeth through skin and sinew. Blood oozes into my mouth. As I kill her, I sob.

Why did she suck the soul of me from the wounds she made? Why am I wolf because of her? Or did it always lurk there, needing only the pain she made to release the ferocity?

But she is dead.

I had forgotten. I had sought her in this pleasant town.

Ah, now the other is dead, too.

Let murder drown me until I am nothing but a snarling speck, harmless and protected by my infinitesimal size.

Oh, God, my bloody darling . . .

Environment Problem

'I've come about your advert,' said the demon.

'Advert?' Greg Morle coughed on the choking fumes already dispersing in the narrow, shabby room that had been his home for the past three months.

'You *did* put that advertisement in today's *Clarion*?' The demon's purple-tinged brows met in a frown. He was beginning to look worried in the manner of someone constantly browbeaten by some higher authority; a green, taloned finger scratched nervously behind his right horn. His long, spiked tail twitched.

From somewhere he produced a slightly charred copy of a newspaper, turned to the small-ad. section and began to read in a rapid monotone:

'"Young man, intelligent and resourceful, seeks any job offering large reward. Failing this, has one slightly soiled soul for sale."

That is *you*, isn't it? I do hope so, because . . .'

'Oh, yes, that's me all right,' Morle said hurriedly. 'No, well, you see – uh – I put the ad. in because I need a job – but I'm not prepared to work for peanuts. I never have been. I'm ambitious, you see. I'll take risks – if there's lots of loot at the other end. But I put the soul bit in only to attract someone's attention . . .'

The demon's face cleared a little.

'It served its purpose admirably, Mr Morle. Admirably. A lot of people still use pentagrams and other mumbo-jumbo – but we move with the times, we move with the times. No need for all that these days.' The demon moved towards an old, worn armchair. 'Mind if I sit down?'

'Go ahead,' Morle said, 'but I don't really think . . .'

A faint wisp of smoke came up from the leather as the demon sat down. He produced a briefcase – Greg hadn't noticed it before – and whisked some papers from it. The papers had a legal look to them. Greg felt a sensation in his stomach. He wondered if things weren't moving just a shade too fast.

'Er . . .' he said and cleared his throat. The demon looked up.

'You haven't had any other offers, Mr Morle?'

'Oh, no, but . . .'

The demon was plainly an expert at the hard sell. 'Now,' he said decisively, 'what policy do you want to take out? There are several extremely generous ones. For instance, a very popular policy is "Everlasting life, B, C or D". Then again, "Power J" is an interesting and lucrative policy. Of course,' the demon winked, 'there's always the "Attractive to Women Policy F", if you . . .'

'Look,' said Greg, 'if I sell you my soul – and I haven't said I'm going to yet – there are a couple of things I'd like to know. One is, when you get the soul what do you do with it? Two is, if I'm going to sell it can I experience just a little of what's in store for me when my time's up? That's fair, isn't it?'

The demon looked doubtful. 'Well, I suppose so, Mr Morle,' he said reluctantly, 'I suppose so. To answer the first question – um – *hellfire*. Nothing complicated, just bad old-fashioned hellfire. As to the second question – well, I'll have to have a word with my principals. No one's ever requested a trial – er – sample before. Still, I'll see what can be arranged. Hang on a moment . . .'

There was a *pop*, a foul smell of sulphur, and the demon wasn't there any more. Morle noticed he'd left his briefcase behind. Curious, he began to move towards it – but then the demon was back again, sitting in the armchair.

'Sorry I took so long,' he apologized, 'but sometimes I get back before I've left and it makes everything so confusing.' His voice once more took on a business-like tone.

'It seems to be in order. Just say the word and we'll have it all laid on for you.'

'I'll keep it in mind,' Greg said. 'Now, if I *do* sell my soul to you, I'll want twenty million British pounds for it. In sterling, dollars and German marks. Everlasting Life sounds attractive, but I can't see where you make anything out of it. What's the catch?'

'We stand only a slim chance of losing on Everlasting Life "A", Mr Morle, or the "Wandering Jew" policy as we – ha, ha – call it at the office. The other three policies have what you might call "escape clauses" on our behalf. For instance, "B" is Everlasting Life without immunity against disease – client could die of cancer or something – "C" omits the accident and murder clause, and "D" leaves out the suicide clause. Is there anything else, before we get down to business?'

Greg Morle prided himself on his cunning and his resourcefulness. That was why he had so rarely bothered to find a regular job. After all, someone of his ingenuity and talent shouldn't need to work in some mundane clerical post. He thought very carefully before answering.

'Yes,' he said at length, 'yes, there is. If you let me have twenty million in cash – where will it come from? I don't want to be picked up with twenty million quid in stolen money on me.'

The demon smirked. 'That's easy – and quite clever, if I may say so. There are, for instance, some twenty million working adults in Great Britain alone. Would there be much of a hue and cry if they all discovered, over a short period, that they had mislaid or overspent one pound? All we do is take a pound or its equivalent from each of six-and-two-thirds of a million people in three countries – or a little more if they can spare it. Simple really, isn't it? But foolproof!'

'Hm,' said Morle. 'It *sounds* all right . . .'

'It *is* all right. Take my word . . .'

'How do you pull it off, though?'

The demon put one taloned finger against the side of his hooked nose and winked. 'Trade secret,' he smiled.

'Yes, well . . .' Morle frowned heavily. He had to work out all the angles. He had to be sure. A clever fellow like himself *should* be able to make a deal with the devil that would work out to his advantage. He just had to think coolly, not get into a panic. He had to be *very* certain.

'There's another clause in the contract we'll prepare which states that if you are accused – yes, even *accused* – of having stolen the money, whether you are convicted or not, then the contract on our side is invalid, but you keep the money.' The demon's sell was getting even harder.

'Sounds all right,' Greg admitted reluctantly. Perhaps if he hung on long enough, he might get other concessions. He glanced cunningly at the demon, but the creatures seemed to have a firm look now about the set of its twisted mouth. 'Yes, well, now how about a taste of this hellfire?'

'Stand by!' said the demon and snapped his fingers.

It was horrible.

Flames licked everywhere, burning, searing. Greg Morle writhed in unceasing, indescribable agony. It seemed that his blood boiled in his veins, that his head was submerged in molten lead, that his body was sprayed with blazing petrol. It should have killed him, but it didn't. There seemed no end to it: no hope of release from the dreadful pain. And above the crackle of the eternal fires came the wails of countless other damned souls, an echoing cacophony, insensate, hopeless, forever tormented . . .

Yet . . . after what must have been eons . . . Greg began to notice a slight easing off. The agony was slowly leaving him: gradually he began almost to take a relish in the flames. There was just a trace of pain, perhaps, but even that was pleasantly stimulating. He began to relax. This was fine. He was getting used to the hellfire.

He chuckled contentedly. A bloke could get used to anything after a while. This wasn't at all bad. Well, well, well . . . He reckoned he was going to cheat the devil anyway, more or less . . . He was immune to the flames now.

Suddenly he was back in the room again. The demon was standing there looking at him anxiously.

Greg clutched at himself, shivering uncontrollably with cold. Seeing this the demon mumbled something and pointed at him. Greg felt better at once. He stretched and then lit a cigarette. He had a great sense of mental and physical well-being. He should have, really, he thought. After all, essentially, he was going to cheat the devil, and not many people could claim that! He smiled.

'What's so funny?' the demon asked.

'Oh, nothing really,' Morle said as casually as he could.

The demon's tail began to twitch with agitation. Then his face cleared a little, but not much. 'What happened to you – you don't look as if the hellfire did you much harm?'

'I'm not so sure about that,' Morle said, but he couldn't disguise his smirk of glee.

'After a time down there you begin to get used to it, is that it?' The demon's shoulders sagged. He sat down again.

'Well, yes . . .'

The demon rubbed his right horn mournfully.

'You'll make it sore if you keep doing that,' Greg told him. The demon stopped.

'I suppose you still want to sell your soul to us?'

'Yes, I do. I've decided – or almost. I just want to know if there was some mistake – should I have enjoyed it?'

'Of course you shouldn't!' the demon snapped. 'It's the – the – blessed adaptability of your race. You seem able to adapt to *any* environment after a while. Some adapt quicker than others – you're one of those.'

'I've always been able to fit in wherever I go,' Greg said contemplatively.

'Oh, shut up,' said the demon miserably. He just sat in the chair moodily burning holes in the leather with his index finger.

'It's a bit like going to the dentist, isn't it?' mused Greg. 'You're scared before you go, have a dose of pain while you're there – then after ten minutes of leaving you've forgotten all about the pain and everything's fine.'

'For you it is! I never wanted to come to this planet in the first place. There's more worries here than in the whole galaxy. I'm putting in for a transfer as soon as I can. I thought – hoped – you'd be different. I always hope that. But no, we're not often lucky. Next time-cycle round I'm off to Andromeda 3, even though business isn't so brisk there . . .'

Greg wasn't listening. He was too busy congratulating himself on getting the better of a bargain with the devil. 'Shall we get back to the subject in hand,' he said in a brisk, superior tone. 'You suggested this, you know.'

'*I* suggested it! I like that! Who put the advertisement in the paper? Who asks question after question and drives me out of my mind with problems? Who looks the biggest gifthorse they've ever seen in the mouth? I suggested . . .' He broke off, speechless. 'I should have kept up with my precognition lessons, then this might never have happened. I only wish I could make you suffer longer when you get there!'

'Well, you can't,' said Greg, aloof. 'If you're not careful I'll find a way to get in touch with your boss and tell him the way you handle prospective clients. Talk about rudeness!'

'All right,' the demon said hastily, 'all right, I'm sorry, Mr Morle. But you must admit that you and your race are rather trying at times. It's never been much of a job working here. Never really been worthwhile. It was slightly better in the old days – at least people had a healthy fear of us and we got the satisfaction of scaring the daylights out of 'em. Things aren't what they used to be, even here.' He sighed and fished in his briefcase.

'Here we are, "Money Contract" – have a look at it. I've filled in the relevant details. All you've got to do is sign it in your blood.'

'Hey!'

'What,' said the demon, 'is the matter now?'

'Blood! Do I have to cut myself?'

'Of course. It's one of the traditions that you sign in blood.'

'I thought you were all modernized – that you didn't go for that mumbo-jumbo stuff . . .?'

'We need the blood for our records,' the demon said. 'We have to keep records and we're more used to dealing in blood-samples than fingerprints.'

'Well . . .'

'Isn't it worth a scratch for twenty million pounds?'

'I suppose so.' Greg began to read the contract carefully. It was printed on something like paper-thin asbestos. Although couched in old-fashioned legal language, essentially it said what they had already discussed. He would receive twenty million pounds – with no catch – in return for his soul when he died.

'All right,' he grunted. 'It seems to be in order. I sign here, do I?'

'On the dotted line,' the demon agreed. He had taken a cigarette from Greg's pack and was smoking luxuriously. He blew out orange smoke and then followed it up with some green.

'You're smoking my last fag,' Greg said.

'In a few hours you can buy a cigarette factory if you want. Please sign the contract. I haven't got all this century . . .'

'That's still my last fag,' Greg persisted. 'And you're smoking it.'

'Sign! Sign!' the demon cried in exasperation. 'There's a razor blade just there on the draining board.'

Gingerly Greg picked up the razor blade. He looked at it and then at his wrist. 'What if I cut the jugular or whatever it is?'

'Cut your thumb, you fool. Your thumb!'

Greg paused, poising the blade. 'If you go on like that,' he said, 'I won't sign the thing – and I should think you need the commission . . .'

The demon looked dejected. 'How do you know I work on commission?'

'Don't you?'

'Well, yes, I do. I suppose it's obvious.' He ground the butt of the cigarette out in the ashtray.

'I worked as a salesman like you,' Greg said. 'Selling encyclopædias, as it happened. I got fired because I was rude to a client. What would happen to you?'

The demon shuddered. 'Stop it,' he said. 'It's already happened – I've been assigned here. I don't want an extension.'

'Then mind your manners,' grinned Greg. It was good to be able to threaten a demon.

'Why in the name of Satan do *I* always get the tough ones?' The demon hunched deeper into his chair. 'Cut your thumb and get on with it – please.'

Greg cut his thumb and signed the contract. The signature was a bit faint, what with the scratchy pen he was using and the thin cut he had made. 'There! Now get me the twenty million.'

'A pleasure,' said the demon sardonically and disappeared. He was gone ten minutes.

'What a job!' he gasped when he reappeared. 'Here you are.' He handed over a dozen bank- and cheque-books to Greg.

'What are these for?'

'Ingrate. We've done everything for you. Got the money and banked it. Don't worry, we've stuck to our end of the contract. You'll find everything's in order. You won't have any problems. Some of our technical boys rigged up perfect androids and used them to imitate you in six different places at once. Up-to-the-minute, modern *doppelgängers* – absolutely efficient and foolproof. Here are the details of the banks – papers signed and so on. We did it all the day before yesterday.'

Up to this moment, Greg hadn't fully been able to accept that it was all real. But seeing the bank-books in his hand did the trick. A slow smile began to spread across his face. Then he fainted.

When he woke up the demon was gone and Greg began his new life of wild debauchery that very afternoon.

It was only the awful beginning.

Greg Morle spent a hectic, colourful, frenzied, dissipated and short life.

Five people at least tried to murder him for the things he had done to them or theirs. The sixth person to make the attempt got life imprisonment. He had succeeded . . .

In life, Morle's riches had saved him from the law. In death, they helped avenge him against his murderer.

The last thing Greg Morle remembered was a blazing pain in the side of his head. Then he was standing before a long metal desk watching a large, fat demon writing something in a book.

The demon looked up and smiled.

'Aha, Mr Morle – you've been a credit to us. A credit!' He indicated a door. 'Go straight through, please. The master would like to congratulate you himself before you go on . . .'

Morle smirked and entered the door. He had led his wicked life and was now going to escape if not with impunity then at least with the minimum of discomfort. Not at all bad . . .

Satan was about twice Morle's height and was dressed in a lounge suit. He had a weary, beautiful face and his stance was just a little bored as he straightened from stoking the large fire in the ornate grate at the far end of the study.

'Ah, Mr Morle. An entity after my own – um – heart. I hope you aren't going to enjoy your stay with us. There's something we have to get you to sign – just the visitor's book. I trust you're not going to make a scene, hm?'

'No,' Greg said, smiling inwardly. 'No, sir. I don't think so.'

'Good man!' The statement seemed just a little ambiguous. 'Here's the book.' Satan brought it over and Greg signed it. 'So many of them do try to get out of it, you know. After all, the set-up's none of my creation. If I was to let anyone off then *my* head would roll. I have to answer to the higher-ups too, you know.'

Greg handed the book back to Satan.

Satan tugged at his goatee. 'Excellent. Well, Mr Morle, my congratulations again. A thoroughly wicked career. If only there were more like you . . .'

'Aren't there?' Greg said in some surprise, and then he was in the hellfire again.

Greg Morle screamed and screamed.

Then he went on screaming.

Every inch of him was in agony and it seemed to last forever. Perhaps it did, in ordinary terms of agony, but a small part of Greg's mind occasionally reminded him that it would stop eventually and then he would be all right. Now it didn't seem a great consolation. He writhed as the flames ate at his whole being. The stink of sulphur was in his nostrils, his mouth was clogged with a dreadful taste of burning flesh. On and on it went.

Fire was everywhere. He cried and begged and threatened but the pain went on.

Then, very gradually, Greg became aware that there was another figure near him, also writhing and screaming. It was a girl – a good-looking, well-shaped girl as far as he could tell.

The pain began to wear off as he got used to the fires. It was still bad, but he managed to take his mind off it now by taunting the damned soul who had joined him. But even this sadistic pleasure palled after a while; the girl must have arrived later than himself and was still suffering the worst, could hardly hear his taunts.

Soon a sense of well-being possessed him and he settled back to wait until his companion should have adapted too. He was looking forward to that. They could have some fun together – an eternity of fun once she had got used to the flames.

When the girl had adapted enough to take an interest in her surroundings she glared at Greg.

'Nice twin soul you turned out to be,' she said.

'Oh, come on, I never asked them to put you in with me,' Greg replied. 'But now we're here, there's no point in quarrelling. See how you've got used to the heat. It must be a fantastically high temperature – but we've adapted to it.'

The girl nodded. 'So that's what's happened.' She licked her lips and looked him over. 'Hm . . .'

Greg drifted through the flames towards her. They touched hands and he was glad that all earthly sensations seemed to continue to exist in hell.

Not at all bad, he thought again. A life of Riley up above, and now . . .

The girl winced. The flames were still troubling her a trifle.

'Don't worry,' Greg said. 'The flames have become our natural habitat, you see. We're very adaptable creatures . . .'

He bent forward to kiss her.

But he never got to touch her lips because then they switched off the hellfire.

It was all of a sudden agonizingly cold.

Greg began to scream again.

The Opium General

They had lived in a kind of besieged darkness for several weeks. At first she had welcomed the sense of solitude after the phone was cut off. They ignored the front door unless friends knew the secret knock. It was almost security, behind the blinds. From his ugly anxiety Charlie had calmed for a while but had soon grown morose and accusatory. There were too many creditors. The basement flat turned into a prison he was afraid to leave. When she had arrived three years ago it had seemed a treasure house; now she saw it merely as a record of his unrealized dreams: his half-read books, his comics, his toys, his synthesizers no longer stimulated him yet he refused to get rid of a single broken model Spitfire. They were tokens of his former substance, of a glorious past. When she suggested they go for a walk he said: 'Too many people know me in Notting Hill.' He meant the customers he had burned, taking money for drugs he never delivered, and the important dealers he had never paid. He tried to form a unity of his many frustrations: a general pattern, a calculated plot against him. A friend was murdered in a quarrel over sulphate at a house in Talbot Road. He decided the knife had been meant for him. 'I've made too many enemies.' This was his self-pitying phase.

She steered him as best she could away from paranoia. She was frightened by overt instability, but had learned to feel relaxed so long as the signs were unadmitted, buried. In response to her nervousness he pulled himself together in the only way he knew: the appropriate image. He said it was time for a stiff upper-lip, for holding the thin red line. She was perfectly satisfied, her sympathy for him was restored and she had been able to keep going. He became like Leslie Howard in an old war film. She tried to find somebody who could help him. This awful uncertainty stopped him doing his best. If he got clear, got a bit of money, they could start afresh. He wanted to write a novel: in Inverness, he thought, where he had worked in an hotel. Once away she could calm him down, get him to be his old self. But there remained the suspicion he might still choose madness as his escape. His friends said he habitually got himself into mental hospitals where he need feel no personal responsibility. He said, though, that it was chemical.

'Nobody's after you, Charlie, really.' She had spent hours trying to win round all the big dealers. She went to see some of them on her own. They assured her with dismissive disgust that they had written off his debts and forgotten about him but would never do buisness with him again. The landlord was trying to serve them with a summons for almost a year's unpaid rent and had been unnecessarily rude the last time she had appealed to him. She blamed herself. She had longed for a return of the euphoria of their first weeks together. There had been plenty of money then, or at least credit. She had deliberately shut out the voice of her own common sense. In her drugged passivity she let him convince her something concrete would come of his elaborate fantasies; she lent her own considerable manipulative powers to his, telling his bank-manager of all the record-companies who were after his work, of the planned tour, of the ex-agent who owed him a fortune. This lifted him briefly and he became the tall handsome red-headed insouciant she had first met. 'Partners in bullshit,' he said cheerfully. 'You should be on the stage, Ellie. You can be a star in my next road-show.' It had been his apparent good humoured carelessness in the face of trouble which made him seem so attractive to her three years ago when she left home to live here. She had not realized nobody in the music business would work with him any more, not even on sessions, because he got so loony. It was nerves, she knew, but he could be so rude to her, to everybody, and make a terrible impression. At the very last guest spot he had done, in Dingwalls, the roadies deliberately sabotaged his sound because he had been so overbearing. As Jimmy had told her gravely later: 'Ye canna afford to get up the roadies' noses, Ellie. They can make or break a set.' Jimmy had been Charlie's partner in their first psychedelic group, but had split the third time Charlie put himself in the bin. It was a bad sign, Jimmy told her, when Charlie started wearing his 'army suit', as he had done to the Dingwalls gig.

Over the past two weeks Charlie had worn his uniform all the time. It seemed to make him feel better. 'Look out for snipers, Algy,' he warned her when she went shopping. He kept the shutters of the front room windows closed, lay in bed all day and stayed up at night rolling himself cigarettes and fiddling with his little Casio synthesizer. He needed R&R, he said. When, through tiredness, she had snapped at him not to be so silly, playing at soldiers, he turned away from her sorrowfully: a military martyr, a decent Englishman forced into the dirty business of war. 'This isn't fun for any of us.' His father had been a regular sergeant in the Royal Artillery and had always wanted

Charlie to go to Sandhurst. His parents were in Africa now, running a Bulawayo grocery shop. He frequently addressed her as sergeant-major. Creditors became 'the enemy'; he needed more troops, reinforcements, fresh supplies. 'What about a cup of coffee, s'a'rnt-major?' and she would have to get up to make him one. His old friends found the role familiar. They didn't help by playing up to it. 'How's the general?' they would ask. He got out his military prints, his badges, his model soldiers, his aircraft charts. They were on every wall and surface now. He read Biggles books and old copies of *The Eagle*.

His last phone call had been to Gordon in Camden. 'Morning to you, field marshal. Spot of bother at this end. Pinned down under fire. Troops needing supplies. What can you get to us?' Gordon, his main coke-supplier, told him to fuck himself. 'The chap's gone over to the enemy.' Charlie was almost crying. 'Turned yellow. Made of the wrong bally stuff.' She pushed her long pale hair away from her little oval face and begged him to talk normally. 'Nobody's going to take you seriously if you put on a funny voice.'

'Can't think what you mean, old thing.' He straightened his black beret on his cropped head. He had always been vain but now he spent fifty percent of his waking time in front of the mirror. 'Don't tell me you're crackin', too.' He rode his motorbike to Brixton and came back with cash, claiming he had been cheated on the price. 'We're going to have transport and logistics problems for a bit, s'a'rnt-major. But we'll get by somehow, eh? Darkest before the dawn and so on.' She had just begun to warm to his courage when he gloomily added: 'But I suppose you'll go AWOL next. One simply can't get the quality of front-line chap.' All his other girl-friends had finally been unable to take him. She swore she was not the same. She made him a cup of tea and told him to go to bed and rest: her own universal remedy. It always seemed to work for her. Dimly she recognized his desperate reaching for certainties and order yet his 'general' was slowly wearing her down. She asked her mother to come to stay with her for a couple of days. 'You should be on your own, love,' said her mother. She was discomfited by Charlie's role. 'Get yourself a little place. A job.'

Ellie spread her short fingers on the table and stared at them. She was numb all over. He had made her senses flare like a firework; now she felt spent. She looked dreadful, said her mother. She was too thin, she was wearing too much make-up and perfume. Charlie liked it she said. 'He's not doing you any good love. The state of you!' All this in a murmur, while Charlie napped in the next room.

'I can't let him down now.' Ellie polished her nails. 'Everybody owes him money.' But she knew she was both too frightened to leave and felt obscurely that she had given him more than his due, that he owed her for something. There was nobody else to support her; she was worn out. It was up to him. She would get him on his feet again, then he would in turn help her.

'You'd be better off at home,' said her mother doubtfully. 'Dad's a lot calmer than he used to be.' Her father hated Charlie. The peculiar thing was they were very much alike in a lot of ways. Her father looked back with nostalgia to wartime and his Tank Regiment.

She and her mother went up to Tesco's together. The Portobello Road was crowded as usual, full of black women with prams and shopping bags, Pakistani women in saris, clutching at the hands of two or three kids, old hippies in big miserable coats, Irish drunks, gypsies, a smattering of middle-class women from the other side of Ladbroke Grove. Her mother hated the street; she wanted them to move somewhere more respectable. They pushed the cart round the supermarket. Her mother paid for the groceries. 'At least you've got your basics for a bit,' she said. She was a tiny, harassed woman with a face permanently masked, an ear permanently deaf to anything but the most conventional statements. 'Bring Charlie to Worthing for a couple of weeks. It'll do you both good.' But Charlie knew, as well as anyone, that he and Ellie's dad would be at loggerheads within a day. 'Got to stay at H.Q.' he said. 'Position could improve any moment.' He was trying to write new lyrics for Jimmy's band, but they kept coming out the same as those they'd done together ten years before, about war and nuclear bombs and cosmic soldiers. Her mother returned to Worthing with a set, melancholy face; her shoulders rounded from thirty years of dogged timidity. Ellie noticed her own shoulders were becoming hunched, too. She made an effort to straighten them and then heard in her mind Charlie (or was it her dad?) saying 'back straight, stomach in' and she let herself slump again. This self-defeating defiance was the only kind she dared allow herself. Her long hair (which Charlie insisted she keep) dragged her head to the ground.

That night he burned all his lyrics. 'Top Secret documents,' he called them. When she begged him to stop, saying somebody would buy them surely, he rounded on her. 'If you're so into money, why don't you go out and earn some?' She was afraid to leave him to his own devices. He might do anything while she was away. He'd have a new girl-friend in five minutes. He couldn't stand being alone. She had thought him sensitive and vulnerable when he courted her. They met in a pub near The Music Machine. He seemed so interested in her, at once charmingly bold, shy and attentive. He made her laugh. She had mothered him a bit, she supposed. She would have done anything for him. Could that have been a mistake?

'You've got to find out what you want,' said her sluttish friend Joan, who lived with an ex-biker. 'Be independent.' Joan worked at the health-food shop and was into feminism. 'Don't let any fucking feller mess you around. Be your own woman.' But Joan was bisexual and had her eye on Ellie. Her objectivity couldn't be trusted. Joan was having trouble with her old man yet she didn't seem about to split.

'I don't know who I am.' Ellie stared at the Victorian screen Charlie had bought her. It had pictures of Lancers and Guardsmen varnished brownish yellow. 'I was reading. We all define ourselves through other people, don't we?'

'Not as much as you do, dearie,' said Joan. 'What about a holiday? I'm thinking of staying at this cottage in Wales next month. We could both do with a break away from blokes.'

Ellie said she'd think about it. She now spent most of her time in the kitchen looking out at the tiny overgrown yard. She made up lists in her mind: lists of things they could sell, lists of outfits she could buy, lists of places she would like to visit, lists of people who might be able to help Charlie. She had a list of their debts in a drawer somewhere. She considered a list of musicians and A&R men they knew. But these days all Charlie had that people wanted was dope contacts. And nobody would let him have as much as a joint on credit any more. It was disgusting. People kept in touch because you could help them score. The minute you weren't useful, they dropped you. Charlie wouldn't let her say this, though. He said it was her fault. She turned friends against him. 'Why don't you fuck off, too? You've had everything I've got.' But when she began to pack (knowing she could not leave) he told her he needed her. She was all he had left. He was sorry for being a bastard.

'I think I'm bad luck for you.' Really she meant something else which she was too afraid to let into her consciousness. He was weak and selfish. She had stood by him through everything. But possibly he was right to blame her. She had let herself be entranced by his wit, his smiling mouth, his lean, nervous body so graceful in repose, so awkward when he tried to impress. She should have brought him down to earth sooner. She had known it was going wrong, but had believed something must turn up to save them. 'Can't we go away?' she asked him early one afternon. The room was in semi-darkness. Sun fell on the polished pine of the table between them; a single beam from the crack in the shutters. 'What about that mate of yours in Tangier?' She picked unconsciously at the brocade chair left by his ex-wife. She felt she had retreated behind a wall which was her body, painted, shaved, perfumed: a lie of sexuality and compliance. She had lost all desire.

'And have the enemy seize the flat while we're there? You've got to remember, sergeant-major, that possession is nine-tenths of the law.' He lay in his red Windsor rocker. He wore nothing but army gear, with a big belt round his waist, a sure sign of his insecurity. He drew his reproduction Luger from its holster and checked its action with profound authority. She stared at the reddish hair on his thick wrists, at the flaking spots on his fingers which resembled the early stages of a disease. His large, flat cheekbones seemed inflamed; there were huge bags under his eyes. He was almost forty. He was fighting off mortality as ferociously as he fought off what he called 'the mundane world'. She continued in an abstracted way to feel sorry for him. She still thought, occasionally, of Leslie Howard in the trenches. 'Then couldn't we spend a few days on Vince's houseboat?'

'Vince has retreated to Shropshire. A non-pukkah wallah,' he said sardonically. He and Vince had often played Indian army officers. 'His old lady's given him murder. Shouldn't have taken her aboard. Women always let you down in a crunch.' He glanced away.

She was grateful for the flush of anger which pushed her to her feet and carried her into the kitchen. 'You ungrateful bastard. You should have kept your bloody dick in your trousers then, shouldn't you!' She became afraid, but it was not the old immediate terror of a blow, it was a sort of dull expectation of pain. She was seized with contempt for her own dreadful judgement. She sighed, waiting for him to respond in anger. She turned. He looked miserably at his Luger and reholstered it. He stood up, plucking at his khaki creases, patting at his webbing. He straightened his beret in front of the mirror, clearing his throat. He was pale. 'What about organizing some tiffin, sergeant-major?'

'I'll go out and get the bread.' She took the Scottish pound note from the tin on the mantelpiece.

'Don't be long. The enemy could attack at any time.' For a second he looked genuinely frightened. He was spitting a little when he spoke. His hair needed washing. He was normally so fussy about his appearance but he hadn't bathed properly in days. She had not dared say anything.

She went up the basement steps. Powys Square was noisy with children playing Cowboys and Indians. They exasperated her. She was twenty-five and felt hundreds of years older than them, than Charlie, than her mum and dad. Perhaps I'm growing up, she thought as she turned into Portobello Road and stopped outside the baker's. She stared at the loaves, pretending to choose. She looked at the golden bread and inhaled the sweet warmth; she looked at her reflection in the glass. She wore her tailored skirt, silk blouse, stockings, lacy bra and panties. He usually liked her to be feminine, but sometimes preferred her as a tomboy. 'It's the poofter in me.' She wasn't sure what she should be wearing now. A uniform like his? But it would be a lie. She looked at herself again. It was all a lie. Then she turned away from the baker's and walked on, past stalls of fruit, past stalls of avocados and Savoys, tomatoes and oranges, to the pawn shop where two weeks ago she had given up her last treasures. She paid individual attention to each electronic watch and every antique ring in the window and saw nothing she wanted. She crossed the road. Finch's pub was still open. Black men lounged in the street drinking from bottles, engaged in conventional badinage; she hoped nobody would recognize her. She went down Elgin Crescent, past the newsagent where she owed money, into the cherry-and apple-blossom of the residential Spring streets. The blossom rose around her high heels like a sudden tide. Its colour, pink and white, almost blinded her. She breathed heavily. The scent came as if through a filter, no longer consoling. Feeling faint she sat on a low wall outside somebody's big house, her shopping bag and purse in her left hand, her right hand stroking mechanically at the rough concrete, desperate for sensation. Ordinary feeling was all she wanted. She could not imagine where it had gone. An ordinary life. She saw her own romanticism as a rotting tooth capped with gold. Her jaw ached. She looked upwards, through the blossom at the blue sky in which sharply-defined white clouds moved very slowly towards the sun, like cut-outs on a stage. She became afraid, wanting to turn back: she must get the bread before the scene ended and the day became grey again. But she needed this peace so badly. She grew self-conscious as a swarthy youth in a cheap black velvet suit went by whistling to himself. With only a little effort she could have made him attractive, but she no longer had the energy. Panic made her heart beat. Charlie could go over the top any minute. He might stack all the furniture near the doors and windows, as he had done once, or decide to rewire his equipment (he was useless at practical jobs) and be throwing a fit, breaking things, blaming her because a fuse had blown. Or he might be out in the street trying to get a reaction from a neighbour, baiting them, insulting them, trying to charm them. Or he might be at the

Princess Alexandra, looking for somebody who would trust him with the money for a gram of coke or half-a-g of smack and stay put until closing time when he promised to return: restoring his ego, as he sometimes did, with a con-trick. If so he could be in real trouble. Everyone said he'd been lucky so far. She forgot the bread and hurried back.

The children were still yelling and squealing as she turned into the square in time to see him walking away round the opposite corner of the building. He was dressed in his combat beret, his flying jacket, his army-boots, his sun-glasses. He had his toy Luger and his sheath-knife on his belt. She forced herself to control her impulse to run after him. Trembling, she went down the steps of the basement, put her key in his front door, turned it, stepped inside. The whole of the front room was in confusion, as if he had been searching for something. The wicker chair had been turned over. The bamboo table was askew. As she straightened it (for she was automatically neat) she saw a note. He had used a model jeep as a weight. She screwed the note up. She went into the kitchen and put the kettle on. Waiting for the kettle to boil she flattened the paper on the draining board:

> *1400 hrs. Duty calls. Instructions from HQ to proceed at once to battle-zone. Will contact at duration of hostilities. Trust nobody. Hold the fort.*
> *– BOLTON, C-in-C, Sector Six.*

Her legs shook as she crossed back to the tea-pot. Within three or four days he would probably be in a police-station or a mental hospital. He would opt to become a voluntary patient. He had surrendered.

Her whole body shook now, with relief, with a sense of her own failure. He had won, after all. He could always win. She returned to the front door and slowly secured the bolts at top and bottom. She pushed back the shutters. Carefully she made herself a cup of tea and sat at the table with her chin in her hand staring through the bars of the basement window. The tea grew cold, but she continued to sip at it. She was out of the contest. She awaited her fate.

A Dead Singer

In memory, among others,
of Smiling Mike and John the Bog

CHAPTER ONE

'It's not the speed, Jimi,' said Shakey Mo, 'it's the H you got to look out for.'

Jimi was amused. 'Well, it never did me much good.'

'It didn't do you no harm in the long run.' Shakey Mo laughed. He could hardly hold on to the steering wheel.

The big Mercedes camper took another badly lit bend. It was raining hard against the windscreen. He switched on the lamps. With his left hand he fumbled a cartridge from the case on the floor beside him and slotted it into the stereo. The heavy, driving drumming and moody synthesizers of Hawkwind's latest album, made Mo feel much better. 'That's the stuff for energy,' said Mo.

Jimi leaned back. Relaxed, he nodded. The music filled the camper.

Shakey Mo kept getting speed hallucinations on the road ahead. Armies marched across his path; Nazis set up road blocks; scampering children chased balls; big fires suddenly started and ghouls appeared and disappeared. He had a bad time controlling himself enough to keep on driving through it all. The images were familiar and he wasn't freaked out by them. He was content to be driving for Jimi. Since his comeback (or resurrection as Mo privately called it) Jimi hadn't touched a guitar or sung a note, preferring to listen to the other people's music. He was taking a long while to recover from what had happened to him in Ladbroke Grove. Only recently his colour had started to return and he was still wearing the white silk shirt and jeans in which he'd been dressed when Shakey Mo first saw him, standing casually on the cowling of the Imperial Airways flying boat as it taxied towards the landing stage on Derwentwater. What a summer that had been, thought Mo. Beautiful.

The tape began to go round for the second time. Mo touched the stud to switch tracks, then thought better of it. He turned the stereo off altogether.

'Nice one.' Jimi was looking thoughtful again. He was almost asleep as he lay stretched out over the bench seat, his hooded eyes fixed on the black road.

'It's got to build up again soon,' said Mo. 'It can't last, can it? I mean, everything's so dead. Where's the energy going to come from, Jimi?'

'It's where it keeps going to that bothers me, man. You know?'

'I guess you're right.' Mo didn't understand.

But Jimi had to be right.

Jimi had known what he was doing, even when he died. Eric Burden had gone on TV to say so. 'Jimi knew it was time to go,' he'd said. It was like that with the records and performances. Somc of them hadn't seemed to be as tight as others; some of them were even a bit rambling. Hard to turn on to. But Jimi had known what he was doing. You had to have faith in him.

Mo felt the weight of his responsibilities. He was a good roadie, but there were better roadies than him. More together people who could be trusted with a big secret. Jimi hadn't spelt it out but it was obvious he felt that the world wasn't yet ready for his return. But why hadn't Jimi chosen one of the really ace roadies? Everything had to be prepared for the big gig. Maybe at Shea Stadium or the Albert Hall or the Paris Olympia? Anyway, some classic venue. Or at a festival? A special festival celebrating the resurrection. Woodstock or Glastonbury. Probably something new altogether, some new holy place. India, maybe? Jimi would say when the time came. After Jimi had contacted him and told him where to be picked up, Mo had soon stopped asking questions. With all his old gentleness, Jimi had turned the questions aside. He had been kind, but it was clear he hadn't wanted to answer.

Mo respected that.

The only really painful request Jimi had made was that Mo stop playing his old records, including *Hey, Joe!* the first single. Previously there hadn't been a day when Mo hadn't put something of Jimi's on. In his room in Lancaster Road, in the truck when he was roading for Light and later The Deep Fix, even when he'd gone to the House during his short-lived conversion to Scientology he'd been able to plug his earbead into his cassette recorder for an hour or so. While Jimi's physical presence made up for a lot and stopped the worst of the withdrawal symptoms, it was still difficult. No amount of mandrax, speed or booze could counter his need for the music and, consequently, the shakes were getting just a little bit worse each day.

Mo sometimes felt that he was paying some kind of price for Jimi's trust in him. That was good karma so he didn't mind. He was used to the shakes anyway. You could get used to anything. He looked at his sinewy, tattooed arms stretched before him, the hands gripping the steering wheel. The world snake was wriggling again. Black, red, and green, it coiled slowly down his skin, round his wrist and began to inch towards his elbow. He fixed his eyes back on the road.

CHAPTER TWO

Jimi had fallen into a deep sleep. He lay along the seat behind Mo, his head resting on the empty guitar case. He was breathing heavily, almost as if something were pressing down on his chest.

The sky ahead was wide and pink. In the distance was a line of blue hills. Mo was tired. He could feel the old paranoia creeping in. He took a fresh joint from the ledge and lit it, but he knew that dope wouldn't do a lot of good. He needed a couple of hours sleep himself.

Without waking Jimi, Mo pulled the truck into the side of the road, near a wide, shallow river full of flat, white limestone rocks. He opened his door and climbed slowly to the grass. He wasn't sure where they were; maybe somewhere in Yorkshire. There were hills all around. It was a mild autumn morning but Mo felt cold. He clambered down to the bank and knelt there, cupping his hands in the clear water, sucking up the river. He stretched out and put his tattered straw hat over his face. It was a very heavy scene at the moment. Maybe that was why it was taking Jimi so long to get it together.

Mo felt much better when he woke up. It must have been noon. The sun was hot on his skin. He took a deep breath of the rich air and cautiously removed his hat from his face. The black Mercedes camper with its chrome trimming was still on the grass near the road. Mo's mouth felt dry. He had another drink of water and rose, shaking the silver drops from his brown fingers. He trudged slowly to the truck, pulled back the door and looked over the edge of the driver's seat. Jimi wasn't there, but sounds came behind the partition. Mo climbed across the two seats and slid open the connecting door. Jimi sat on one of the beds. He had erected the table and was drawing in a big red notebook. His smile was remote as Mo entered.

'Sleep good?' he asked.

Mo nodded. 'I needed it.'

'Sure,' said Jimi. 'Maybe I ought to do a little driving.'

'It's okay. Unless you want to make better time.'

'No.'

'I'll get some breakfast,' said Mo. 'Are you hungry?'

Jimi shook his head. All through the summer, since he had left the flying boat and got into the truck beside Mo, Jimi appeared to have eaten nothing. Mo cooked himself some sausages and beans on the little Calor stove, opening the back door so that the smell wouldn't fill the camper. 'I might go for a swim,' he said as he brought his plate to the table and sat as far away from Jimi as possible, so as not to disturb him.

'Okay,' said Jimi, absorbed in his drawing.

'What you doing? Looks like a comic strip. I'm really into comics.'

Jimi shrugged. 'Just doodling, man. You know.'

Mo finished his food. 'I'll get some comics next time we stop on the motorway. Some of the new ones are really far out, you know.'

'Yeah?' Jimi's smile was sardonic.

'Really far out. Cosmic wars, time warps. All the usual stuff but different, you know. Better. Bigger. More spectacular. Sensational, man. Oh, you want to see them. I'll get some.'

'Too much,' said Jimi distantly but it was obvious he hadn't been listening. He closed the note-book and sat back against the vinyl cushions, folding his arms across his white silk chest. As if it occurred to him that he might have hurt Mo's feelings, he added: 'Yeah, I used to be into comics a lot. You seen the Jap kind? Big fat books. Oh, man – they are *really* far out. Kids burning. Rape. All that stuff.' He laughed shaking his head. 'Oh, man!'

'Yeah?' Mo laughed hesitantly.

'Right!' Jimi went to the door, placing a hand either side of the frame and looking into the day. 'Where are we, Mo? It's a little like Pennsylvania. The Delaware Valley. Ever been there?'

'Never been to the States.'

'Is that right?'

'Somewhere in Yorkshire, I think. Probably north of Leeds. That could be the Lake District over there.'

'Is that where I came through?'

'Derwentwater.'

'Well, well.' Jimi chuckled.

Jimi was livelier today. Maybe it was taking him time to store up all the energy he'd need when he finally decided to reveal himself to the world. Their driving had been completely at random. Jimi had let Mo decide where to go. They had been all over Wales, the Peaks, The West Country, most parts of the Home Counties, everywhere except London. Jimi had been reluctant to go to London. It was obvious why. Bad memories. Mo had been into town a few times, leaving the Mercedes and Jimi in a suburban layby and walking and hitching into London to get his mandies and his speed. When he could he scored some coke. He liked to get behind a snort or two once in a while. In Finch's on the corner of Portobello Road he'd wanted to tell his old mates about Jimi, but Jimi had said to keep quiet about it, so when people had asked him what he was doing, where he was living these days, he'd had to give vague answers. There was no problem about money. Jimi didn't have any but Mo had got a lot selling the white Dodge convertible. The Deep Fix had given it to him after they'd stopped going on the road. And there was a big bag of dope in the truck, too. Enough to last two people for months, though Jimi didn't seem to have any taste for that, either.

Jimi came back into the gloom of the truck. 'What d'you say we get on the road again?'

Mo took his plate, knife and fork down to the river, washed them and stashed them back in the locker. He got into the driver's seat and turned the key. The Wankel engine started at once. The Mercedes pulled smoothly away, still heading north, bumping off the grass and back on to the asphalt. They were on a narrow road suitable only for one way traffic, but there was nobody behind them and nobody ahead of them until they left this road and turned on to the A65, making for Kendal.

'You don't mind the Lake District?' Mo asked.

'Suits me,' said Jimi. 'I'm the mad Gull Warrior, man.' He smiled. 'Maybe we should make for the ocean?'

'It's not far from here.' Mo pointed west. 'Morecambe Bay?'

CHAPTER THREE

The cliff tops were covered in turf as smooth as a fairway. Below them the sea sighed. Jimi and Mo were in good spirits, looning around like kids.

In the distance, round the curve of the bay, were the towers and fun-fairs and penny arcades of Morecambe, but here it was deserted and still, apart from the occasional cry of a gull.

Mo laughed, then cried out nervously as Jimi danced so near to the cliff edge it seemed he'd fall over.

'Take it easy, Jimi.'

'Shit, man. They can't kill me.'

He had a broad, euphoric smile on his face and he looked really healthy. 'They can't kill Jimi, man!'

Mo remembered him on stage. In total command. Moving through the strobes, his big guitar stuck out in front of him, pointing at each individual member of the audience, making each kid feel that he was in personal touch with Jimi.

'Right!' Mo began to giggle.

Jimi hovered on the edge, still flapping his outstretched arms. 'I'm the boy they boogie to. Oh, man! There ain't nothing they can do to me!'

'Right!'

Jimi came zooming round and flung himself down on the turf next to Mo. He was panting. He was grinning. It's coming back, Mo. All fresh and new.'

Mo nodded, still giggling.

'I just know it's there, man.'

Mo looked up. The gulls were everywhere. They were screaming. They took on the aspect of an audience. He hated them. They were so thick in the sky now.

'Don't let them fucking feathers stick in your throat,' said Mo, suddenly sullen. He got up and returned to the truck.

'Mo. What's the matter with you, man?'

Jimi was concerned as ever, but that only brought Mo down more. It was Jimi's kindness which had killed him the first time. He'd been polite to everyone. He couldn't help it. Really hung-up people had got off on him. And they'd drained Jimi dry.

'They'll get you again, man,' said Mo. 'I know they will. Every time. There isn't a thing you can do about it. No matter how much energy you build up, you know, they'll still suck it out of you and moan for more. They want your blood, man. They want your sperm and your bones and your flesh, man. They'll take you, man. They'll eat you up again.'

'No. I'll – no, not this time.'

'Sure.' Mo sneered.

'Man, are you trying to bring me down.'

Mo began to twitch. 'No. But . . .'

'Don't worry, man, okay?' Jimi's voice was soft and assured.

'I can't put it into words, Jimi. It's this, sort of, premonition, you know.'

'What good did words ever do for anybody?' Jimi laughed his old, deep laugh. 'You *are* crazy, Mo. Come on, let's get back in the truck. Where do you want to head for?'

But Mo couldn't reply. He sat at the steering wheel and stared through the windscreen at the sea and the gulls.

Jimi was conciliatory. 'Look, Mo, I'll be cool about it, right? I'll take it easy, or maybe you think I don't need you?'

Mo didn't know why he was so down all of a sudden.

'Mo, you stay with me, wherever I go,' said Jimi.

CHAPTER FOUR

Outside Carlisle they saw a hitchhiker, a young guy who looked really wasted. He was leaning on a signpost. He had enough energy to raise his hand. Mo thought they should stop for him. Jimi said: 'If you want to,' and went into the back of the truck, closing the door as Mo pulled in for the hitchhiker.

Mo said: 'Where you going?'

The hitchhiker said: 'What about Fort William, man?'

Mo said: 'Get in.'

The hitchhiker said his name was Chris. 'You with a band, man?' He glanced round the cabin at the old stickers and the stereo, at Mo's tattoos, his faded face-paint, his Cawthorn T-shirt, his beaded jacket, his worn jeans with washed-out patches on them, the leather cowboy boots which Mo had bought at the Emperor of Wyoming in Notting Hill Gate last year.

'Used to road for The Deep Fix,' said Mo.

The hitchhiker's eyes were sunken and the sockets were red. His thick black hair was long and hung down to his pale face. He wore a torn Wrangler denim shirt, a dirty white Levi jacket and both legs of his jeans had holes in the knees. He had moccasins on his feet. He was nervous and eager.

'Yeah?'

'Right,' said Mo.

'What's in the back?' Chris turned to look at the door. 'Gear?'

'You could say that.'

'I've been hitching for three days, night and day,' said Chris. He had an oil- and weather-stained khaki pack on his lap.

'D'you mind if I get some kip some time?'

'No,' said Mo. There was a service station ahead. He decided to pull in and fill the Merc up. By the time he got to the pumps Chris was asleep.

As he waited to get back into the traffic, Mo crammed his mouth full of pills. Some of them fell from his hand on to the floor. He didn't bother to pick them up. He was feeling bleak.

Chris woke when they were going through Glasgow.

'Is this Glasgow?'

Mo nodded. He couldn't keep the paranoia down. He glared at the cars ahead as they moved slowly through the streets. Every window of every shop had a big steel mesh grill on it. The pubs were like bunkers. He was really pissed off without knowing why.

'Where you going yourself?' Chris asked.

'Fort William?'

'Lucky for me. Know where I can score any grass in Fort William?'

Mo reached forward and pushed a tobacco tin along the edge towards the hitchhiker. 'You can have that.'

Chris took the tin and opened it. 'Far out! You mean it? And the skins?'

'Sure,' said Mo. He hated Chris, he hated everybody. He knew the mood would pass.

'Oh, wow! Thanks, man.' Chris put the tin in his pack.

'I'll roll one when we're out of the city, okay?'

'Okay.'

'Who are you working for now?' said Chris. 'A band?'

'No.'

'You on holiday?'

The kid was too speedy. Probably it was just his lack of sleep. 'Sort of,' he said.

'Me, too. Well, it started like that. I'm at university. Exeter. Or was. I decided to drop out I'm not going back to that shit heap. One term was enough for me. I thought of heading for the Hebrides. Someone I know's living in a commune out there, on one of the islands. They got their own sheep, goats, a cow. Nobody getting off on them. You know. Really free. It seems okay to me.'

Mo nodded.

Chris pushed back his black, greasy hair. 'I mean compare something like that with a place like this. How do people stand it, man. Fucking hell.'

Mo didn't answer. He moved forward, changing gear as the lights changed.

'Amazing,' said Chris. He saw the case of cartridges at his feet. 'Can I play some music?'

'Go ahead,' said Mo.'

Chris picked out an old album, *Who's Next*. He tried to slide it into the slot the wrong way round. Mo took it from his hand and put it in the right way. He felt better when the music started. He noticed, out of the corner of his eye, that Chris tried to talk for a while before he realized he couldn't be heard.

Mo let the tape play over and over again as they drove away from Glasgow. Chris rolled joints and Mo smoked a little, beginning to get on top of his paranoia. By about four in the afternoon, he was feeling better and he switched off the stereo. They were driving beside Loch Lomond. The bracken was turning brown and shone like brass where the sun touched it. Chris had fallen asleep again, but he woke up as the music stopped. 'Far out.' He dug the scenery. 'Fucking far out.' He wound his window down. 'This is the first time I've been to Scotland.'

'Yeah?' said Mo.

'How long before we reach Fort William, man?'

'A few hours. Why are you heading for Fort William?'

'I met this chick. She comes from there. Her old man's a chemist or something.'

Mo said softly, on impulse: 'Guess who I've got in the back.'

'A chick?'

'No.'

'Who?'

'Jimi Hendrix.'

Chris's jaw dropped. He looked at Mo and snorted, willing to join in the joke. 'No? Really? Hendrix, eh? What is it, a refrigerated truck?' He was excited by the fantasy. 'You think if we thaw him out he'll play something for us?' He shook his head, grinning.

'He is sitting in the back there. Alive. I'm roading for him.'

'Really?'

'Yeah.'

'Fantastic.' Chris was half convinced. Mo laughed. Chris looked at the door. After that, he was silent for a while.

Something like a half an hour later, he said: 'Hendrix was the best, you know. He was the king, man. Not just the music, but the style, too. Everything. I couldn't believe it when I heard he died. I still can't believe it, you know.'

'Sure,' said Mo. 'Well, he's back.'

'Yeah?' Again Chris laughed uncertainly. 'In there? Can I see him?'

'He's not ready, yet.'

'Sure,' said Chris.

It was dark when they reached Fort William. Chris staggered down from the truck. 'Thanks, man. That's really nice, you know. Where are you staying?'

'I'm moving on,' said Mo. 'See you.'

'Yeah. See you.' Chris still had that baffled look on his face.

Mo smiled to himself as he started the camper, heading for Oban. Once they were moving the door opened and Jimi clambered over the seats to sit beside him.

'You told that kid about me?'

'He didn't believe me,' said Mo.

Jimi shrugged.

It began to rain again.

CHAPTER FIVE

They lay together in the damp heather looking out over the hills. There was nobody for miles; no roads, towns or houses. The air was still and empty save for a hawk drifting so high above them it was almost out of sight.

'This'll do, eh?' said Mo. 'It's fantastic.'

Jimi smiled gently. 'It's nice,' he said.

Mo took a Mars Bar from his pocket and offered it to Jimi who shook his head. Mo began to eat the Mars Bar.

'What d'you think I am, man?' said Jimi.

'How d'you mean?'

'Devil or angel? You know.'

'You're Jimi,' said Mo. 'That's good enough for me, man.'

'Or just a ghost,' said Jimi. 'Maybe I'm just a ghost.'

Mo began to shake. 'No,' he said.

'Or a killer?' Jimi got up and struck a pose. 'The Sonic Assassin. Or the messiah, maybe.' He laughed. 'You wanna hear my words of wisdom?'

'That's not what it's about,' said Mo, frowning. 'Words. You just have to be there, Jimi. On the stage. With your guitar. You're above all that stuff – all the hype. Whatever you do – it's right, you know.'

'If you say so, Mo.' Jimi was on some kind of downer. He lowered himself to the heather and sat there cross-legged, smoothing his white jeans, picking mud off his black patent-leather boots. 'What is all this *Easy Rider* crap anyway? What are we doing here?'

'You didn't like *Easy Rider*?' Mo was astonished.

'The best thing since *Lassie Come Home*.' Jimi shrugged. 'All it ever proved was that Hollywood could still turn 'em out, you know. They got a couple of fake freaks and made themselves a lot of money. A rip off, man. And the kids fell for it. What does that make me?'

'You never ripped anybody off, Jimi.'

'Yeah? How d'you know?'

'Well, you never did.'

'All that low energy shit creeping in everywhere. Things are bad.' Jimi had changed the subject, making a jump Mo couldn't follow. 'People all over the Grove playing nothing but fake fifties crap, Simon and Garfunkel. Jesus Christ! Was it ever worth doing?'

'Things go in waves. You can't be up the whole time.'

'Sure,' Jimi sneered. 'This one's for all the soldiers fighting in Chicago. And Milwaukee. And New York . . . And Vietnam. Down with War and Pollution. What was all that about?'

'Well . . .' Mo swallowed the remains of the Mars Bar. 'Well – it's important, man. I mean, all those kids getting killed.'

'While we made fortunes. And came out with a lot of sentimental shit. That's where we were wrong. You're either in the social conscience business or show business. You're just foolish if you think you can combine them like that.'

'No, man. I mean, you can say things which people will hear.'

'You say what your audience wants. A Frank Sinatra audience gets their shit rapped back to them by Frank Sinatra. Jimi Hendrix gives a Jimi Hendrix audience what they want to hear. Is that what I want to get back into?'

But Mo had lost him. Mo was watching the tattoos crawl up his arms. He said vaguely: 'You need different music for different moods. There's nothing wrong with the New Riders, say, if you're trying to get off some paranoia trip. And you get up on Hendrix. That's what it's like. Like uppers and downers, you know.'

'Okay,' said Jimi. 'You're right. But it's the other stuff that's stupid. Why do they always want you to keep saying things? If you're just a musician that's all you should have to be. When you're playing a gig, anyway, or making a record. Anything else should come out of that. If you wanna do benefits, free concerts, okay. But your opinions should be private. They want to turn us into politicians.'

'I tol' you,' said Mo, staring intensely at his arms. 'Nobody asks that. You do what you want to do.'

'Nobody asks it, but you always feel you got to give it to 'em.' Jimi rolled over and lay on his back, scratching his head. 'Then you blame them for it.'

'Not everyone thinks they owe anything to anyone,' said Mo mildly as his skin undulated over his flesh.

'Maybe that's it,' said Jimi. 'Maybe that's what kills you. Jesus Christ. Psychologically, man, you know, that means you must be in one hell of a mess. Jesus Christ. That's suicide, man. Creepy.'

'They killed you,' said Mo.

'No, man. It was suicide.'

Mo watched the world snake crawl. Could this Hendrix be an imposter?

CHAPTER SIX

'So what you going to do, then?' said Mo. They were on the road to Skye and running low on fuel.

'I was a cunt to come back,' said Jimi. 'I thought I had some kind of duty.'

Mo shrugged. 'Maybe you have, you know.'

'And maybe I haven't.'

'Sure.' Mo saw a filling station ahead. The gauge read Empty and a red light was flashing on the panel. It always happened like that. He'd hardly ever been stranded. He glanced in the mirror and saw his own mad eyes staring back at him. Momentarily he wondered if he should turn the mirror a little to see if Jimi's reflection was there too. He pushed the thought away. More paranoia. He had to stay on top of it.

While the attendant was filling the truck, Mo went to the toilet. Among the more common bits of graffiti on the wall was the slogan 'Hawkwind is Ace'. Maybe Jimi was right. Maybe his day was over and he should have stayed dead. Mo felt miserable. Hendrix had been his only hero. He did up his flies and the effort drained off the last of his energy. He staggered against the door and began to slide down towards the messy floor. His mouth was dry; his heart was thumping very fast. He tried to remember how many pills he'd swallowed recently. Maybe he was about to O.D.

He put his hands up to the door-handle and hauled himself to his feet. He bent over the lavatory bowl and shoved his finger down his throat. Everything was moving. The bowl was alive. A greedy mouth trying to swallow him. The walls heaved and moved in on him. He heard a whistling noise. Nothing came up. He stopped trying to vomit, turned, steadied himself as best as he could, brushed aside the little white stick men who tried to grab at him, dragged the door open and plunged through. Outside, the attendant was putting the cap back on the tank. He wiped his big hands on a piece of rag and put the rag back into his overalls, saying something. Mo found some money in his back pocket and gave it to him. He heard a voice:

'You okay, laddie?'

The man had offered him a genuine look of concern.

Mo mumbled something and clambered into the cab.

The man ran up as Mo started the engine, waving money and green stamps.

'What?' said Mo. He managed to wind the window down. The man's face changed to a malevolent devil's mask. Mo knew enough not to worry about it. 'What?'

He thought he heard the attendant say: 'Your friend's already paid.'

'That's right, man,' said Jimi from beside him.

'Keep it,' said Mo. He had to get on the road quickly. Once he was driving he would be more in control of himself. He fumbled a cartridge at random from the case. He jammed it into the slot. The tape started halfway through a Stones album. Jagger singing *Let it Bleed* had a calming effect on Mo. The snakes stopped winding up and down his arms and the road ahead became steady and clearer. He'd never liked the Stones much. A load of wankers, really, though you had to admit Jagger had a style of his own which no one could copy. But basically wankers like the rest of the current evil-trippers, like Morrison and Alice Cooper. It occurred to him he was wasting his time thinking about nothing but bands, but what else was there to think about? Anyway how else could you see your life? The mystical thing didn't mean much to him. Scientology was a load of crap. At any rate, he couldn't see anything in it. The guys running all that stuff seemed to be more hung-up than the people they were supposed to be helping. That was true of a lot of things. Most people who told you they wanted to help you were getting off on you in some way. He'd met pretty much every kind of freak by now. Sufis, Hare Krishnas, Jesus Freaks, Meditators, Processors, Divine Lighters. They could all talk better than him, but they all seemed to need more from him than they could give. You get into people when you were tripping. Acid had done a lot for him that way. He could suss out the hype-merchants so easily these days. And by that test Jimi couldn't be a fake. Jimi was straight. Fucked up now, possibly, but okay.

The road was long and white and then it became a big boulder. Mo couldn't tell if the boulder was real or not. He drove at it, then changed his mind, braking sharply. A red car behind him swerved and hooted as it went past him through the boulder which disappeared. Mo shook all over. He took out the Stones tape and changed it for the Grateful Dead's *American Beauty*, turned down low.

'You okay, man?' said Hendrix.

'Sure. Just a bit shakey.' Mo started the Merc up.

'You want to stop and get some sleep.'
'I'll see how I feel later.'
It was sunset when Jimi said: 'We seem to be heading south.'
'Yeah,' said Mo. 'I need to get back to London.'
'You got to score?'
'Yeah.'
'Maybe I'll come in with you this time.'
'Yeah?'
'Maybe I won't.'

CHAPTER SEVEN

By the time Mo had hitched to the nearest tube station and reached Ladbroke Grove he was totally wasted. The images were all inside his head now: pictures of Jimi from the first time he'd seen him on TV playing *Hey, Foe* (Mo had still been at school then), pictures of Jimi playing at Woodstock, at festivals and gigs all over the country. Jimi in big, feathered hats, bizarre multi-coloured shirts, several rings on each finger, playing that white Strat, flinging the guitar over his head, plucking the strings with his teeth, shoving it under his straddled legs, making it wail and moan and throb, doing more with a guitar than anyone had done before. Only Jimi could make a guitar come alive in that way, turning the machine into an organic creature, simultaneously a prick, a woman, a white horse, a sliding snake. Mo glanced at his arms, but they were still. The sun was beginning to set as he turned into Lancaster Road, driven more by a mixture of habit and momentum than any energy or sense of purpose. He had another image in his head now, of Jimi as a soul thief, taking the energy away from the audience. Instead of a martyr, Jimi became the vampire. Mo knew that the paranoia was really setting in and the sooner he got hold of some uppers the better. He couldn't blame Jimi for how he felt. He hadn't slept for two days. That was all it was. Jimi had given everything to the people in the audience, including his life. How many people in the audience had died for Jimi?

He crawled up the steps of the house in Lancaster Road and rang the third bell down. There was no answer. He was shaking badly. He held on to the concrete steps and tried to calm himself, but it got worse and he thought he was going to pass out.

The door behind him opened.

'Mo?'

It was Dave's chick, Jenny, wearing a purple brocade dress. Her hair was caked with wet henna.

'Mo? You all right?'

Mo swallowed and said: 'Hullo, Jenny. Where's Dave?'

'He went down the Mountain Grill to get something to eat. About half an hour ago. Are you all right, Mo?'

'Tired. Dave got any uppers?'

'He had a lot of mandies in.' Mo accepted the news.

'Can you let me have a couple of quids' worth?'

'You'd better ask him yourself, Mo. I don't know who he's promised them to.'

Mo nodded and got up carefully.

'You want to come in and wait, Mo?' said Jenny.

Mo shook his head. 'I'll go down the Mountain. See you later, Jenny.'

'See you later, Mo. Take care, now.'

Mo shuffled slowly up Lancaster Road and turned the corner into Portobello Road. He thought he saw the black and chrome Merc cross the top of the street. The buildings were all crowding in on him. He saw them grinning at him, leering. He heard them talking about him. There were fuzz everywhere. A woman threw something at him. He kept going until he reached the Mountain Grill and had stumbled through the door. The café was crowded with freaks but there was nobody there he knew. They all had evil, secretive expressions and they were whispering.

'You fuckers,' he mumbled, but they pretended they weren't listening. He saw Dave.

'Dave? Dave, man!'

Dave looked up, grinning privately. 'Hi, Mo. When did you get back to town?' He was dressed in new, clean denims with fresh patches on them. One of the patches said 'Star Rider'.

'Just got in.' Mo leaned across the tables, careless of the intervening people, and whispered in Dave's ear. 'I hear you got some mandies.'

Dave's face became serious. 'Sure. Now?'

Mo nodded.

Dave rose slowly and paid his bill to the dark, fat lady at the till. 'Thanks, Maria.'

Dave took Mo by the shoulder and led him out of the café. Mo wondered if Dave was about to finger him. He remembered that Dave had been suspected more than once.

Dave said softly as they went along. 'How many d'you need, Mo?'

'How much are they?'

Dave said: 'You can have them for ten p each.'

'I'll have five quids' worth. A hundred, yeah?'

'Fifty.'

They got back to Lancaster Road and Dave let himself in with two keys, a Yale and a mortise. They went up a dark, dangerous stairway. Dave's room was gloomy, thick with incense, with painted blinds covering the window. Jenny sat on a mattress in the corner listening to Ace on the stereo. She was knitting.

'Hi, Mo,' she said. 'So you found him.'

Mo sat down on the mattress in the opposite corner. 'How's it going, Jenny?' he said. He didn't like Dave, but he liked Jenny. He made a big effort to be polite. Dave was standing by a chest of drawers, dragging a box from under a pile of tasselled curtains. Mo looked past him and saw Jimi standing there. He was dressed in a hand-painted silk shirt with roses all over it. There was a jade talisman on a silver chain round his throat. He had the white Strat in his hands. His eyes were closed as he played it. Almost immediately Mo guessed he was looking at a poster.

Dave counted fifty mandies into an aspirin bottle. Mo reached into his jeans and found some money. He gave Dave a five pound note and Dave gave him the bottle. Mo opened the bottle and took out a lot of the pills, swallowing them fast. They didn't act right away, but he felt better for taking them. He got up.

'See you later, Dave.'

'See you later, man,' said Dave. 'Maybe in Finch's tonight.'

'Yeah.'

CHAPTER EIGHT

Mo couldn't remember how the fight started. He'd been sitting quietly in a corner of the pub drinking his pint of bitter when that big fat fart who was always in there causing trouble decided to pick on him. He remembered getting up and punching the fat fart. There had been a lot of confusion then and he had somehow knocked the fat fart over the bar. Then a few people he knew pulled him away and took him back to a basement in Oxford Gardens where he listened to some music.

It was *Band of Gipsies* that woke him up. Listening to *Machine Gun* he realized suddenly that he didn't like it. He went to the pile of records and found other Hendrix albums. He played *Are You Experienced*, the first album, and *Electric Ladyland*, and he liked them much better. Then he played *Band of Gipsies* again.

He looked round the dark room. Everyone seemed to be totally spaced out.

'He died at the right time,' he said. 'It was over for him, you know. He shouldn't have come back.'

He felt in his pocket for his bottle of mandies. There didn't seem to be that many left. Maybe someone had ripped them off in the pub. He took a few more and reached for the bottle of wine on the table, washing them down. He put *Are You Experienced* on the deck again and lay back. 'That was really great,' he said. He fell asleep. He shook a little bit. His breathing got deeper and deeper. When he started to vomit in his sleep nobody noticed. By that time everyone was right out of it. He choked quietly and then stopped.

CHAPTER NINE

About an hour later a black man came into the room. He was tall and elegant. He radiated energy. He wore a white silk shirt and white jeans. There were shiny patent leather boots on his feet. A chick started to get up as he came into the room. She looked bemused.

'Hi,' said the newcomer. 'I'm looking for Shakey Mo. We ought to be going.'

He peered at the sleeping bodies and then looked closer at one which lay a little apart from the others. There was vomit all over his face and over his shirt. His skin was a ghastly, dirty green. The black man stepped across the others and knelt beside Mo, feeling his heart, taking his pulse.

The chick stared stupidly at him. 'Is he all right?'

'He's O-D'd,' the newcomer said quietly. 'He's gone. D'you want to get a doctor or something, honey?'

'Oh, Jesus,' she said.

The black man got up and walked to the door.

'Hey,' she said. 'You look just like Jimi Hendrix, you know that?'

'Sure.'

'You can't be – you're not, are you? I mean, Jimi's dead.'

Jimi shook his head and smiled his old smile. 'Shit, lady. They can't kill Jimi.' He laughed as he left.

The chick glanced down at the small, ruined body covered in its own vomit. She swayed a little, rubbing at her thighs. She frowned. Then she went as quickly as she could from the room, hampered by her long cotton dress, and into the street. It was nearly dawn and it was cold. The tall figure in the white shirt and jeans didn't seem to notice the cold. It strode up to the big Mercedes camper parked near the end of the street.

The chick began to run after the black truck as it started up and rolled a little way before it had to stop on the red light at the Ladbroke Grove intersection.

'Wait,' she shouted. 'Jimi!'

But the camper was moving before she could reach it.

She saw it heading north towards Kilburn.

She wiped the clammy sweat from her face. She must be freaking. She hoped when she got back to the basement that there wouldn't really be a dead guy there.

She didn't need it.

The Lovebeast

They must let me in – *I can love them. They must let me in!*

He is drifting, invisible, in the upper atmosphere and there is a longing in him. He has been there, and on the surface, for many centuries now – knowing what he needs but not quite strong enough to do anything to achieve it. He requires only an opportunity but it has never come. Not once in all those years has the world, as a whole, given him his opportunity. He doesn't know whence he came nor how he arrived on this planet. He cannot leave – he is in love.

He is a lonely beast, and his loneliness is heightened by his intelligence, which is very great.

Let me love you – let me.

For his love is selfless and he will not force it upon the world. His agony is terrible and it is true that in a hundred years or so he will die.

There is not much more time.

Curtis walked slowly down the middle of the village street, his blood tingling.

He entered Adam Turner's cluttered general store and listened to the jangling music until Turner came into the front of the shop. The old man switched off the radio and said:

'You've heard the latest report too, eh, Charlie?'

Curtis nodded. 'Is it really the end of the human race, Adam? The papers said it would be – some of *us* said it would be. But I don't think I ever believed it.'

'Do you believe it now, Charlie?'

'Yes.'

The tone of the newspapers had been too subdued – the voice of the news announcer had been grim and filled with fear. Charles Curtis believed it now. Curtis, the frustrated artist who painted signs for a living, had been able to conceive the end of humanity as something possible, much as he dreaded the idea. But radioactive fall-out would not be the cause, he had told himself – that was a bogey exploited by sensation-seeking newspapers and people who wanted to stop the manufacture of nuclear bombs.

Two years before, the East had set off three huge nuclear explosions in outer space and the West had responded with four even bigger ones. And so the ridiculous game of Who's-got-the-most-Power? continued until the upper atmosphere had become choked with radiation. The representatives of nations were worried but they wavered. One Premier had been pressured by his military chiefs to detonate just one more bomb – so others followed suit. And now the radiation was everywhere. People were dying all over the world – dying horribly. Populations were in a state of despair and agony.

The Sunday after the news had been released, Curtis had gone to church as usual, striving to recapture some of the faith that had been flagging in him gradually for the last five years. But he had not been successful. As far as Curtis was concerned, God had abandoned the Earth to its self-chosen fate.

'But is it *fair*, Adam?' he said. 'Is it fair? A few men in positions of power instruct their technicians and scientists to construct multi-megaton bombs so that they can demonstrate just how much personal power they held in their hands. They claim that they represent the peoples of their respective nations. Some of these people may even believe this in their hearts – they may be honest men. Yet they are only succeeding in killing us all – or most of us. Is there any chance, I wonder, of a few of us surviving?'

'There's nowhere to escape – nowhere in the world.' Adam Turner spoke dully. He was thinking of his long-dead wife and of his married daughter living in London. He was glad that his wife was dead.

'No chance, you think?' Curtis's eyes were wet.

'Who knows? A few may live – some may adapt. What's it called . . .?'

'Mutate,' supplied Curtis. 'But they won't really be human, will they? I mean, not like us. I wonder if it matters . . .'

The door of the shop opened as Mrs Vaughan came in. The bell didn't ring until after the door had closed again. The girl, recently married to a young farm worker, was buxom and pale. The shopping bag which had always been with her when she left her house was not on her arm.

'Have we got it?' Her voice was thick, almost hysterical. 'Have we got it, Mr Turner – Mr Curtis. *Have we?*'

'Christ!' Curtis turned away and leant both hands on the shop counter. Yes, they all had it. He could feel it in his bones – in his blood, in his flesh and his brain. In his soul, perhaps? It was there. Radiation sickness – the disease one never believed was real.

'Can't we get injections or something? He didn't say on the radio. Can't they stop it?'

'*No!*' Curtis wheeled around and confronted the frightened girl. 'No, No, Mrs Vaughan, there's nothing they can do. We're all going to die!'

'Shut up, Charlie!' Turner shouted. 'Shut up, you idiot!'

Curtis couldn't stop. He knew he shouldn't be reacting this way – but he simply couldn't stop: 'There's nothing any more, Adam – nothing to look forward to. No hope, no chance. No injections or safety precautions – no shelters. Nothing, Adam – absolutely nothing in the Universe that can save us. Do you realize that? In the whole of infinity there is nothing that can stop this. We are all going to suffer death – and we are not even going to die decently. We're going to rot away – our bones are going to crumble and the flesh fall away from them. The planet is stricken with the plague of man's foolishness and cowardice.

'Adam – we can't even die bravely – fighting . . .'

Curtis was dazed. Mrs Vaughan, terrified, shocked by his words, fled sobbing from the shop. Curtis shrugged and started to follow her out.

Turner said: 'You bloody fool. And you talk of cowardice.'

But Curtis wasn't afraid. Curtis was hurt and bewildered. More so than ever, now, he felt the wisdom of the Sanskrit *sultras*. Everything seemed illusory – a bad dream. Was it worth clinging to reality, still? Could he find comfort in believing that what was happening now didn't matter – that it was the ordained and irrevocable *karma* of the world to die in this way?

He began to walk towards the pub.

There was that line of Eliot's which everyone quoted when the poet's name was mentioned – the line from *The Hollow Men: This is the way the world ends – this is the way the world ends – not with a bang, but a whimper . . .* Curtis almost laughed. How precisely the poet had described the present situation. And now he remembered that line of Donne's, too – a line also pertinent to his present predicament: *Any man's death diminishes me – for I am involved in humanity . . .*

'Any man's death diminishes me.' Curtis had the same feeling. He knew, deep within him, what Donne meant. Curtis, too, sensed his own involvement. He felt as if he were part of some great being – a being which had possessed infinite potential but was now slowly dying, cell by cell. All over the world, the cells were crumbling and the great being which, in recent years, had come more and more to represent God to Curtis, was dying. And there was no other world, no after-life for a planet and its population, its mountains and its buildings and its forests. They were all the same thing and the whole set-up was destined to die and could never exist again in that form – the form which Curtis loved so much.

As the men of the world died in hopeless terror and slow agony, Curtis felt himself diminishing, being destroyed piece by piece – spiritually and physically. For in his own body, as in the body of the world, the sickness was intruding further – eating into him, rotting him, killing him body and soul.

The King's Head was open – it had not closed for long in the past two days – and Curtis entered its cool, dark confines, surprised to see that only a couple of the old men were sitting at the bar with their dogs lying beside them.

''Morning, Peter – 'morning Edward,' he said. The old men nodded and smiled. 'Where is everybody, Edward?'

'Dunno, Mister Curtis. Some's gone to church. Some's at home – not many's workin' today.' Edward Cray threw some money on the bar, the coins clattering loudly. He shouted: 'Pint of best, Henry!' He turned enquiringly to Curtis.

'That's what you'll have, eh, Mister Curtis?'

'Thanks, Edward – but you can't afford it on your pension, I'll get it.'

Cray smiled a thin, tired, old man's smile. 'Don't think I'll have to worry, Mister Curtis. I always promised myself I'd buy you one back some day – and I can do it now, can't I? I'm not so sure there'll be anyone to pay out next week's pension – nor whether there'll be anyone to collect it, either . . .'

Curtis thanked Cray as Henry, the landlord, put the brimming glass mug on the bar. He threw the money in the till, not even bothering to ring it up. He grinned at Curtis. But couldn't disguise the fear behind his eyes. 'Don't know why I bother to take money, Mr Curtis. But it's habit, you know – and for me to give the beer away would be an empty sort of generosity, wouldn't it?'

'I suppose so,' Curtis agreed.

The beer, he expected, was radioactive, too. Why, then, was he pouring it down his throat? Didn't taste any different . . .

He hoped Edward hadn't been hurt by Henry's talk of empty generosity. Curtis accepted the drink in the spirit the old man had offered it. He thanked Cray and offered to buy a fresh round. The two men nodded approval.

Peter Baker bent down with difficulty and scratched his black spaniel behind the ears. 'I hope she goes first,' he muttered. 'She'd pine without me.'

Edward chuckled: 'I'm an evil old man,' he said. 'My Janet always told me that. I'm near me time, anyway – but I get a funny sort of satisfaction, you might say, from knowing that all them others is going too. I won't be lonely, will I, Mr Curtis?'

'No, Edward,' Curtis said.

He drank his beer as quickly as he could.

'I'm off home now,' he told them. 'See you this evening, perhaps.'

'Aye,' Cray chuckled. 'Maybe, Mr Curtis – maybe . . .'

Trembling, Curtis left the pub and walked the hundred yards to his cottage, passing the houses where people sat – wondering and waiting. He unlatched the door of the cottage and went straight up the uncarpeted stairs.

Here, the single room of the upper storey had been converted by Curtis into a studio. His paintings were heaped everywhere, together with lettered signs and rough drawings. He kicked at the pile of finished signs, sending them scattering.

Did this impending horror help, he asked himself, when it came to painting? Could he create something worthwhile at last – as he died? A canvas was ready, prepared, on the easel. His brushes were on the table, with his palette and his colours. He inhaled the smell of linseed oil – the smell he loved. Could he paint a picture which would symbolize everything he felt – everything the world was feeling? He knew he could try and that his effort would come close to doing what he wanted to express. In the dark corner of the studio, hardly visible in the shadow, a camp bed had been erected. This was where he slept sometimes, when he had been working late. He couldn't bring himself to pick up the brushes, to mix his colours.

Instead, he walked towards the bed and lowered himself wearily on to it. He knew that his energy was failing – that all his vitality was being consumed by his body to resist the sickness in his bloodstream – to fight, though hopelessly. Well, at least I am fighting, he thought, Unconsciously, perhaps – but fighting, nonetheless.

He lay back with his hands folded on his chest.

Any man's death diminishes me . . .

If only there were something. Miracles were needed. Big miracles. There was no hope – nowhere in the Universe was there a spark of hope. If only there were . . .

He was beginning to go to sleep. Vague memories were combining with his wandering imagination so that he heard fragments of conversation that had never been, saw faces that were half-familiar, became aware of situations which he had never known before. Was this, perhaps, his last sleep . . .?

But something else was pervading his confused half-dream. A peculiar something – a feeling of – desperate warmth . . . Was this death? No . . .

Let me in. Let me love you – let me love . . .

Curtis did not dare break his tenuous, delicate link with . . . Himself? His subconscious? No, it was more than the usual dream-before-sleeping fantasy. This was something outside – something new.

Where are you? he asked silently. *What do you want?*

Then it burst through, filling all of him. His mind, his brain, his body was full of warmth – no longer desperate. Now it was joyous, grateful . . .

In all the days I have lived, I have begged you to be loved. For my sake, let me love you.

Where are you? Curtis was sitting up on the shaking bed. He had an impression, not only of love but of great intelligence. And the words . . . They were not actually from the source. Certainly the feeling was expressed in the words, but – *they were his own words!* The words he had used once in an old poem.

'Who are you?' he said aloud now.

Lovebeast loves world . . .

'What? Where are you from?'

Know not. My love is here, if you desire it . . .

It was becoming almost too much for Curtis's tired brain. Was he suffering from hallucinations induced by the sickness in him? Could he really believe this?

Please don't fear – please don't question. I can love you – love you all . . .

'But – how? What should we do to gain your love? When did you come? Did you hear of our plight?'

A million years I have been in love with you, but you have never given me the opportunity I needed to show you my love. Where is the rest of you? I can love it all – all of you . . .

Curtis felt frantic, but he was also filled with joy – fresh hope.

'We must all open ourselves to your love – is that it? Every one of us must allow himself to be loved.'

Yes! Yes! Communicate this to the rest of you. Let me love you – there is so little time left . . . For centuries, hundreds of centuries, I have wanted to love you and now, in the last few moments of my old age, I may yet be able to . . .

*

Curtis rushed for his station wagon, knowing that it would take at least three hours to reach the capital. But there was the means he needed to broadcast his message of hope to a world that had begun to accept the prospect of death with a hopeless, apathetic fatalism.

He was at last admitted to an office. A tired man sitting behind a desk said: 'You're not the only one who wants to use our transmitters, Mr Curtis. We've had dozens of applications, you know.'

Curtis said levelly: 'I appreciate that you must have. But I think my message may be instrumental in saving the world. You must admit that anything is worth trying.'

Please let me love you . . . The Lovebeast was still with him, its messages weirdly pathetic for one of its powers and intelligence. The world must accept its love, Curtis thought, as he reasoned with the man behind the desk. He was sure that if it did, then the world would be saved.

The official sighed: 'Very well, Mr Curtis. We'll announce your broadcast on all networks. The rest is up to you. I don't expect you to be successful, any more than all the other cranks we've allowed to broadcast. But you seem a trifle more reasonable and it's worth the chance. What is it you want to say exactly?'

Curtis was cautious, aware of the reception he would receive if he mentioned the Lovebeast beforehand.

'Just listen,' he said. 'Listen when I make my broadcast.'

I am ready to love you – as ready as I have been in a million years. Please – please – do not disappoint me now . . .

He waited impatiently for the people to make their announcement. Then he was escorted to a studio and had to wait patiently once more while networks were cleared. Then he was ready – ready to broadcast his message of hope to the world.

He stuttered his first words, conscious that his voice was going out to all people, translated into many different tongues.

'There . . . there is hope.' He had to force himself to speak clearly and calmly. 'Somewhere about the Earth there is a . . . being . . . an unhuman entity which has come from a different galaxy – perhaps a different dimension – and it can help us.

'It can help us.' Curtis spoke confidently now. 'Believe that. It is our only chance and we must take it. This entity can only help us if we allow it to. *If we let it into ourselves.* All we need to do is relax and let this being see that we are ready to receive its love – and its help.

'*We have nothing to lose.*

'I know you may think I sound like a madman – that many of you will disbelieve what I have told you. But I ask you all – every man, woman and child on the Globe – to test the truth of my words . . .' He glanced at the big studio clock. 'At twenty-four-hundred hours, GMT, be ready – open your hearts and minds to receive this entity's love. Remember, it is our chance for survival – our chance to correct the ghastly mistake we have made – our chance to live and make a better world. *Let him love you.*'

There was nothing more for Curtis to say. He hoped he had been coherent enough – that all the nations of Earth had given him a chance to be heard. There were three hours still to go.

'We'll keep playing the recording,' a technician said. The man was almost smiling. 'I hope to God you've got something – and I think you have.'

Curtis nodded to him: 'I hope everybody thinks so,' he said softly.

He had lost a great deal of faith in the human race during recent weeks and he was not sure, even now, because of their stupid pride, that they would accept this final chance. He hoped that they would – but how could he be certain? He could only wait – with the Beast for company.

Are you ready? Are you ready? love . . .

Not yet, he said, as he drove wildly home. *Not yet . . .*

When? There was longing and pain in the word.

Soon. There was a trace of uncertainty in his answer. *Soon*.

He is drifting closer to Earth, together with the poisoning radiation of which he is unaware – the radiation which has, ironically, given him the opportunity he had sought for so long. His vast, amorphous being encircles the world – waiting impatiently, expectantly – even humbly.

Soon. Soon I will love you all . . .

He will receive nothing from those he wishes to love. He desires nothing save the vessels for the huge love within him and around him. He can give. This is his purpose. To give. To give. To bestow love.

The Lovebeast drifts closer and closer.

Soon – soon.

Curtis scrambled from the station wagon and burst into Turner's still-open shop. Adam Turner, his friend, was waiting for him calmly.

'Well,' he said, 'we all heard your broadcast. I don't know what this is, Charlie, but I hope you're right. How do you know about this – this Beast of Love – whatever it is? How did you contact it?'

'I don't know,' Curtis replied. 'But I don't think that I've been the first individual to make contact with its "aura", anyway. Perhaps I've been the first to communicate with it, recognize it for what it is – an alien entity from a different part of the Universe. Maybe people under great emotional and intellectual stress are good "mediums" for contacting the Beast . . .'

There were only five minutes to go.

They went back into the living room behind the shop. They sat down.

Now but three minutes to go.

Adam was frowning.

Now – now. May I love you now?

Soon, Curtis told the Lovebeast. Soon.

Adam smiled: 'You know, Charlie, I *do* sense something . . .'

. . . One minute.

Yes, you are ready – I think – almost . . .

This is their last chance, Curtis thought desperately. Their last chance. They must take it!

Yes!

And then the love came.

All over the world, those who still lived felt its warmth flowing into them. Men who had never been happy before became overjoyed. Men remembered times when, for no reason at all, they had been caught up in a happiness resembling this – when they had been filled with love for the world, for no reason, for no reason. And now they knew from where this spirit had emanated. Love – pure, selfless love, flowed through the world, bringing hope to the hopeless. Comfort – new life.

Upon all the lands of the Earth, in all the people of every nation, in cities and villages, the forests and in the mountains and upon the plains, wherever men were living, the joy came – bursting upwards from within them. It filled them.

Of course, some had paid no attention to Curtis's broadcast – others had not heard it. But the majority of cells in that great Earth Body had seized their chance, opening up the breach the Lovebeast had so long yearned for. And the small minority were caught up in its love before they realized it.

It was a quality of love that made the people feel humble before it even as they rejoiced – for it was a love of such tenderness, such humility, such sympathy . . .

Pure love – selfless love.

The Lovebeast gave at last. Gave of his great store which had been building up within him for a million years. Gave and gave and gave until those who received him – and there were still left many millions – felt they could absorb no more of this wondrous joy. But they could.

And they did, as the Lovebeast lavished its love, generously and with tenderness.

And now the cry came from the minds of those millions united by the love of the Beast, sensing, at last, that they were all of the same flesh, all part of the same body. They were now unified in love – the same thing – involved – blended with one another. The cry came from the Earth:

YOU WHO LOVE US – SAVE US NOW FROM DESTRUCTION.

The Lovebeast fed its love to the object of its love. At first it was oblivious of the cry, not sensing it.

The world was sure of salvation. It looked forward to a new, brilliant phase in its history – a return to Grace . . .

OH, LOVEBEAST – SAVE US NOW . . .

The Lovebeast heard the words at last – and finally it understood them. But it was bewildered.

Save you? Save you – my love?

The Lovebeast was puzzled. What could this mean? A peculiar development. What was wrong?

He tried to grasp at the full significance of the words, but something stopped him. He couldn't quite reach them. The concept was – alien.

Save you? I cannot interfere. I love you. I love you, too much . . . I cannot save you – I can love you – This is my purpose – to love you. Love you – you – love – love – love.

The Ruins

Maldoon picked his way over the ruins, his sombre face speckled with gleaming drops of sweat as if he had covered it with jewels.

The ruins went away from him in all directions beneath the blue and glowing sky, spikes of masonry, jumbled concrete, pools of ash, so that the whole bleak landscape took on the aspect of sea-carved rocks at low tide. The sun shone and the ruins lay peacefully beneath; pale shadows having nothing ominous or mysterious about them. Maldoon felt safe in the ruins.

He took off his jacket and sat on a slab of concrete from which protruded rusted wires, curling back on themselves like a sculpture depicting space and time. In fact the ruins were that – a mighty sculpture, a monument created by the random and ambivalent machinations of mankind – a monument to time and space and to the sacrifices men had made to understand it. Maldoon realized his thoughts were rambling. He lit a cigarette and drank some water from his flask.

He had been travelling over the ruins for a long time, searching for signs of life but finding nothing. He was regretting the notion that had sent him into the ruins. There were no signs of the previous explorers who had not returned; no mark scratched on stone, no note, no shred of cloth, no skeleton. The ruins were barren.

Maldoon stood up, putting his flask away and dropping his cigarette into a crevice. He stared ahead of him at the jagged horizon, turned his body round. The strange thing was that his view to the horizon was never interrupted. No crumpled building or collapsing wall ever blocked his vision. The horizon was on all sides, giving him the peculiar sensation of standing in the centre of a huge disc which drifted in an infinity of blue sky.

He frowned. The sun was directly overhead and he had no idea which direction he had come from. Now that he considered it, he couldn't remember the sun changing its position or, for that matter, night ever falling. Hadn't the light always been so? Yet he thought he had been travelling for several days.

Slowly he began to make his way across the ruins again, stumbling sometimes, half-falling, jumping from slab of masonry to pile of broken bricks, leaning against the shattered wall of a house with one hand as he inched his way around the ash-pools which he mistrusted, though there was no cause for his wariness as he remembered.

At length, something close to panic began to fill him and he wished very strongly that he had not come to the ruins, wished that he was back amongst people again, amidst orderly streets of neat houses and solid, well-filled shops. He looked about him hopefully and, as if his wish had been answered by some magical spirit, he saw on the horizon a line of tall, complete-looking buildings which might possibly be part of a town.

His speed increased; his progress was no longer such hard going.

And, he noted, laughing at himself for his earlier fancies, the sun was beginning to set. With luck he could make the town before night.

He began to leap from point to point, but he had misjudged his distance from the town and night came while he was still about a mile away. But he was heartened further by the sight of the lights shining out of the buildings. Perhaps this was even the town he had left? One town was much like another, seen from the distance. With the lights to guide him he was soon at the town's outskirts. Here the streets were deserted, though illuminated by splendid lamps, and he guessed that the inhabitants had gone to bed. Getting closer to the city-centre, he heard traffic noises and saw cars moving through the streets, people on the boulevards, cafés open for business.

He ignored the notion that there was something incomplete about the city. He was tired and was seeing things in a peculiar perspective. Also the hot sun of the day might well have given him sunstroke.

The city was new to him, though familiar enough in its general layout. It was, like most cities he knew, planned around a central square with the main streets radiating from the square like spokes from a wheel, with an outer circle of suburbs.

Maldoon entered a café and ordered a meal. The proprietor was an old man with a gnomish face and a deferential manner. He put the plate of food before Maldoon, averting his eyes. Maldoon began to eat.

Presently a girl came into the café, glanced around at the few available seats and chose one opposite Maldoon. 'Is this seat taken?' she asked him.

He waved his fork and shook his head, his mouth too full for speech.

She smiled and sat down daintily. She picked up the menu and studied it, giving her order to the proprietor who received it with a little bow and hurried back to the kitchen.

'It's a beautiful night for the time of the year,' Maldoon said, 'isn't it?'

'Ah, yes . . ' She appeared to be confused.

'I'm sorry,' he said. 'I hope you don't think I'm . . '

'No, no.'

'I have just come in from the ruins,' he told her. 'I was doing a bit of exploring. They stretch for miles and miles. Sometimes I think they must cover the planet. Does anyone know?'

She laughed. 'You look tired – hadn't you better get some sleep?'

'I'm a stranger here. Can you recommend an hotel?'

'Not really. Being a resident, as it were, I don't know much about the hotels. There's one up the road, though, that looks all right.'

'I'll try that, then.'

Her meal was brought for her. She thanked the proprietor with a quick smile. He saw that she had ordered the same meal.

He let her eat without interruption. Now that he was seated, his body felt numb with tiredness. He looked forward to a good night's sleep.

The girl got up. She looked at him with curiosity. 'I'd better show you where that hotel is.' She smiled sympathetically.

'Oh, thanks.' He got up and left the café with her. As they walked along the street he thought of something. Shouldn't he have paid for his meal? He couldn't remember. But the owner of the café wouldn't have let him walk out like that, anyway, so it must be all right.

He walked along beside the girl, his shoulders feeling as if they were carrying a tremendous weight, his muscles aching and his legs weak.

How had he managed to cross such a huge area of the ruins? Surely he hadn't walked all that way? What way? How much way? Where way?

'Are you sure you can make it?' said the girl distinctly, her lips close to his ear. She spoke as if repeating herself.

'Yes.'

'Well come on, it's not much further.'

He followed her, but now he was crawling. He heard a voice that was not his own crying: 'Can somebody give me a hand?'

He lay on the uneven surface of the ruins and the sun was directly over his head. He turned and saw the horizon in the far distance, he turned his eyes in the other direction and there, too, were ruins stretching to the horizon. He felt like a giant spread-eagled and crucified on the ruins. As he pushed himself into a sitting position, his body seemed to diminish until he was normal size again.

Normal size? What was normal size? What yardstick had he with which to measure the ruins? They were of all sizes, all shapes. Yet not one of them, however high, blocked his view of the horizon.

He had lost his jacket and his cigarettes. He stood up unsteadily and stared around him.

Was he some kind of outcast? He couldn't remember. There had to be some reason for his being here. Someone had put him here? People from the city had taken the trouble to transport him here.

Or had they? And if they had, *why* had they?

The problem did not concern him for very long. He began to move over the ruins once again, pausing sometimes to inspect a building that seemed to have been sliced down the centre, leaving its floors intact and exposed like those of a doll's house. Yet he could find no clue to answer any of the questions which drifted and dispersed in his mind.

By now, he had forgotten about the city, even; had forgotten that he had had a jacket, that he had smoked cigarettes, felt no need for either.

Later, he sat down on a pile of broken tiles and looked around him. To his left a tower leaned. Though it seemed that something had crushed it from two angles, it still stood upright. His logic told him that it should have fallen, yet the tower was frozen there. He stopped looking at it, but too late to stop the rising sensation of fear which the sight created.

He got up and walked carefully away from the tower, not looking back, and then broke into a stumbling run.

But he saw that all the buildings seemed about to fall, all the towers and houses and columns were pitched at an angle, which said that they *must* fall.

Why hadn't he noticed it before? What was wrong?

With the fear, his knowledge of his identity began to re-emerge.

He remembered his name and a little of the past as far back as his visit to the city. Then he remembered his days-long journey over the ruins, beneath a sun that did not set, a sky that did not change, seeing on all sides the horizon which *should* have been obscured by the great piles of ruined architecture and yet was *not*.

He stopped, shaking with hatred of the ruins, striving to bring back a memory of *before* the ruins, but he could not.

What was this? Dream? Drug-vision? Madness? Surely there was something more than the ruins? Had the city been just an illusion?

He closed his eyes, his body tottering. In the darkness which came with the closing of his eyes, he said to himself: *Well, Maldoon do you still insist on continuing this experiment? Do you still wish to abolish identity and time and space as illusion-creating illusions?*

And he called back to himself, aloud:

'What do you mean? What do you *mean*?'

And he opened his eyes again and there were the bright ruins, sharp beneath the great, pale sun in the blue sky.

(Sun, sky, ruins+Maldoon=Maldoon−Maldoon.)

Now, slowly, he began to calm, his questions and his memories, for what they were worth, drifting apart.

He steadied himself on the ruins and walked towards a particularly large ash-pool. He stopped when he reached it. He stared down into it. He put his fingers to his lips and mused over the ash-pool.

He picked up a piece of brick and flung it down into the grey ash. When it reached the surface, the brick disappeared without disturbing the ash.

He took another brick and another and hurled them down. The same thing happened. The same thing didn't happen.

A shadow fell across him. He looked up and saw a tall building rising above him. It consisted of a huge shaft built of glass bricks with a series of platforms going up and up until at the top there was the last platform with a dome over it. A man stood there, beckoning to him.

He ran towards the tower, found he could spring on to the first platform and from that one to the next until he reached the platform covered by the dome.

A man similar to a frog was waiting for him.

'Look down there, Maldoon,' he said.

Maldoon looked out over the neat city spread below. Each block was of exactly the same dimensions, each one was square.

The man waved his reptilian hand. The light shone through it, grey as the ash.

'A country is like a woman,' said the man. 'Look down there. It *wants* to be subdued, wants to be bested by a strong man. I did it. I quieted the country's perturbation – and raped it!'

The frog-man looked self-satisfied.

'It's peaceful,' said Maldoon.

'The most peaceful country in the system,' the man-frog quipped. 'The most peaceful system in the country. Who are you, Maldoon?'

'Either you or me,' said Maldoon, forgetting his name.

'Jump, Maldoon,' said the man similar to a frog.
Maldoon merely stood there.
'Jump!'

He began to clamber around the ash-pool.
(Sun, sky, ruins+Maldoon)=(Maldoon−Maldoon)

His name was a throb in his head, merely a throb in his head. Mal-*doon*, Mal-*doon*, Mal-*doon*.

Had it ever been his name? Perhaps not. Perhaps it had always been – mal-*doon*, mal-*doon* – merely a throb in his head.

Yet, apart from the ruins and the light, there was nothing else to know.

He paused. Was that a memory? That, at the back there?

Out – mal-doon, mal-doon – out – mal-doon – concentrate, mal-doon.

The ruins appeared to blur for a moment and he stared at them sharply, suspiciously. They seemed to be folding themselves around him. No, he was folding himself around them. He flowed around them, over them, through them.

Maldoon! The cry from somewhere was imperious, desperate, ironic.

Yes, he thought, *which way*?

All or nothing, Maldoon, he cried to himself, *nothing or nothing, all or all!*

Out here is in here and it is infinite. He remembered, or was told, he could not tell.

(Infinity+Maldoon)=(Infinity)

With relief, he was glad to be back. Things were right again. He paused and sat on a piece of broken concrete which sprouted spliced hawsers and which changed to a mound of soft soil with reeds growing from it. Below him was the city – roofs, chimneys, church-spires, parks, cinemas, smoke drifting. Familiar, yet not what he wanted.

He got up from the mound and began to walk down the path towards the city, still only half-aware of who he was, why he was, what he was and how he was.

'Why do I tire myself out trying,' he thought. 'One day I shan't be able to exert enough will to pull myself back and they'll find me up here either raving or curled up in a neat little bundle.'

Yet he could not decide, still, which was true – the city below or the ruins.

'Are they both real?' he thought as he walked off the grass and on to the road leading into the city.

He sauntered along the road, passing under a railway bridge of thick girders and peeling green paint, turned a corner into a side-street which was full of the smoky smell of autumn. The houses were of red-brick and terraced with tiny gardens submerged beneath huge, overgrown hedges. Behind one of the hedges he heard children playing. He stopped and put his head round the hedge, watching them with their coloured bricks, building and pushing them down again.

When one of the children noticed him and looked up, he pulled his head back and walked on along the street.

But he was not to escape with impunity. The child cried 'It's him!' and followed him along the street with its companions chorusing rhythmically: 'Mad Maldoon! Mad Maldoon! Mad Maldoon – he's a loon!' and laughing at this old jest.

He pretended not to notice them.

They only followed him to the end of the street and he was grateful for this, at least. It was getting late. Dusk was falling over the houses. His footfalls echoed among the roofs, clattering hollowly from chimney pot to chimney pot.

Mad Maldoon, mad maldoon, madmaldoonmaldoonmaldoon.

Heart-beats joined in, maldoon, maldoon, head-beats, maldoon, maldoon and the houses were still there but superimposed on the ruins, the echoes swimming amongst their unreal chimney pots.

The dusk gave way to night, the night to light and slowly the houses vanished.

The bright ruins stretched away, never obscuring his view of the horizon. The blue, blue sky was above, and the sun which did not change its position.

The ash-pools, he avoided. The tumbling ruins, fixed and frozen in time and space, did not fall.

What caused the ruins?

He had completely forgotten.

There were just the ruins now, as the sky and the sun went out but the light remained. Just the sound of some unseen surf pounding at the last vestiges of his identity.

Mal-doon, mal-doon, mal-doon.

Ruins past, ruins present, ruins future.

He absorbed the ruins and they him. He and they went away for

ever, for now there was no horizon.
The mind could clothe the ruins, but now there was no mind.
Soon, there were no ruins.

The Golden Barge

A Fable

CHAPTER ONE

Right at the top of the city, in the centre, there was a cathedral where blind children wailed among lightless and forgotten galleries. Hopefully at first, in the Manor below, two lovers danced with puppets for partners and eventually became reconciled. In streets, men swaggered from café to café, drinking the while from bottles, pawning their clothes, piece by piece, in the appropriate departments of the wineshops. When morning came, the children still wailed and the lovers danced, but the men had gone home and Jephraim Tallow awoke, feeling the inside of his mouth with his fingers. There was no blood in his mouth as there had been for months past.

Jephraim Tallow went naked to his mirror and viewed his strange body – stranger now for the absence of a navel. The blood had gone and so had his navel. Tallow deliberated upon this discovery and then, frowning, returned to bed.

A number of hours later, Tallow awoke, put his hand into his mouth and found no blood, slid his large hand down his scrawny length and found no navel. He sighed and arose, donned his sackcloth clothes, opened the door of the hovel and looked out into the dark day full of mist. The mist was coming off the river, close by.

'I must investigate this phenomenon,' said Tallow, softly, so that his mother should not wake up. 'I have delayed too long. I should have enquired about . . . But now it is too late.' He cocked his big head, mused a moment, and closed the door behind him. Shivering slightly, he walked to the quayside, and sat down. Alone, he studied his reflection in the choppy water of a river which was so big that it took a lifetime to traverse. Above Tallow, and beyond him, white and silver clouds lay banked like pillows, softening the day. Tallow stared at the pale sun and his eyes were blank. Tallow was a travesty and an outcast, but, as luck would have it, was never at a loss for a word. Citizens who dwelt in the rotting city behind him were afraid of him.

Now, however, looking at the sun and then the river, dangling his abnormally long legs over the quayside, shifting his narrow buttocks on the cold stone, he began subtly to experience a mood. He narrowed his eyes and stared intently at the ripples of the river as he studied the reflection of Tallow, the man without a navel. Then he began to drag the new emotion from himself, nursing it up to his consciousness until, with an almost physical shock, he was curious. He wondered what lurked beneath the ominous surface of the river now that it was day. Unprecedented, the thought remained in his skull, drifting, seeking anchorage. Water . . . the depths and texture of it . . . had always vaguely disturbed him, but for the first time he wondered about it. It was the shock, of course. It is not every day a man wakes up to discover the loss of a navel.

The mist lay mysterious and chilly over the river; beautiful and peaceful in its calm movement, swirling and changing, metamorphosing into a hundred day-dream shapes. Tallow rose and impatiently strode the quay, peering into the mist. His heart beat rumbustiously against his thin-fleshed chest and he scratched nervously at the insect bites which scarred his tattered body. He looked to his right and his wandering eye was caught by a movement in the mist – a darker shadow which had a peculiar quality of solidity and stolidity. It was coming towards him seeming to move over, rather than through, the water. A ship would have swayed in the unquiet waters, but this shadow did not. It loomed larger out of the mist and Tallow screwed up his eyes, craning his neck the better to see the shape. He remembered a public holiday when he was small and his father, unburied then, promising him the sight of a witch-burning. He remembered the time because it was only that once before he had felt a tremble of anticipation in his dull body. He strained forward, his thin, pink tongue flickering around his long lips.

Then the mist eddied. Out of it, purposefully and with dignity, loomed a great golden barge, a barge which glittered with a light of its own. Tallow was astounded. He looked at the towering shape, agape. His tiny, self-contained world could not survive this second experience. He was no longer the integrated and impenetrable thing he had been, for he had not taken the golden barge into account before. He experienced a surge of new emotions. He became worried that the barge should not escape as it passed. It disappeared into the mist again. Tallow wondered if it might not have been a phantom, a trick of the imagination inspired by the changing mist-shapes. But be reconciled himself. He had no imagination.

He did not know from where the barge might have come. He could not guess its destination. He was quite certain that, once he caught up with it, the mystery of his missing navel would be solved. He scuttled along the quayside, hurrying towards the place where his small sloop was moored. It lay, dirty grey and brown, smelling of tar and fish, low in the greasy water which slapped against the silky stones of the quay. It lay as if expectant.

Tallow's mother appeared from the misty gloom of the alley which ran between warehouses towards the centre of the city. She moved diffidently and licked her mean lips, squinting at Tallow.

'Jephraim?'

'Yes, mother.'

Tallow answered absently, purely out of habit, as he struggled to untie the mooring line from the capstan.

'Where are you going?' Her voice was rasping, discordant even when she attempted to speak softly.

'Away, mother.' The knots on the line were firm and cemented by grease.

'Where, Jephraim?'

'I do not know.'

His mother coughed, like an actress taking her cue. It was a familiar cough which Tallow had never resented, but now he thought it unpleasant, he wanted to escape from it. Her old frail body shook and she looked at him through slitted eyes, hoping for sympathy. He gave her none; he had never given her any for he was incapable of sympathy. Reconciled for the millionth time, his mother clutched his arm and whined: 'You won't go? Not for ever, I mean? You won't leave me penniless?'

'Of course I shall have to go, mother.' Impatiently. 'It's the barge. Didn't you see it? My navel might be aboard. Mother, *you no longer exist.*'

But his mother had only understood the meaning of Tallow's first sentence. Big tears, disgusting and ludicrous, rolled down her seamed cheeks. She made a gobbling sound with her wet, naked mouth and Tallow decided that she stank of decrepitude. 'You need me son. What will you do, lacking me to look after you?'

Tallow considered her statement gravely, without resentment. Then after some moments, he realized: 'You need *me*, mother – you need me to need you. That is the truth.' He shook his head. 'In any case this is ridiculous. How can we exist together now?'

But the old hag had not been listening. She continued to sob, still seeking his non-existent sympathy. 'All I've done for you,' she moaned, 'all I've done.'

'You have done all you could, mother. There is nothing left to do.'

Tallow completely ignored his mother then. The line needed his full attention. Four feet of wide-mouthed, red-haired, grinning travesty of the human race, he did not squat down beside the capstan to untie the moorings; he folded down, like a spider. His long spindly legs, disproportionate to his body, bent in the middle so that his knees almost reached his ears and his thin fingers deftly began to unravel the knots of the slimy rope. With a jerk and a lurch, the sloop yawed away from the quay and sluggishly righted herself. Nimbly, Tallow leapt onto the dirty planks of the ship and groped for the rudder-bar. He found it and, drifting on the current of the river, moved into midstream. Leaving the rudder for a moment, he released the cords reefing the sail. The square canvas cracked down like a gun-shot and immediately the wind filled it.

Then he was following the barge down-river, the night-breeze in his favour. He heard his old mother's high-pitched voice screaming at him as mist obscured the city and finally the quay. He could not see her. In spite of himself he cried: 'Goodbye, mother!' behind him, and then wished that he had remained silent.

'Jephraim! Jephraim!' cawed Mrs Tallow. 'Where are you going?'

Tallow had to admit to himself that he did not know. He might realize his reasons later, but now the only thing to concentrate upon was steering a straight course after the barge.

Lighting his pipe with hands which trembled in time with his heart, he turned up his coat collar against the cold. Turned it up around his ears to muffle any sounds which might distract him.

CHAPTER TWO

Day broke.

Tallow had altogether lost sight of the golden barge. Once or twice during the night he had glimpsed it, only to see the mist engulf it once more. With no apparent means of propulsion, it was making stately and silent progress, always just ahead of Tallow's own small ship. Its calm objectivity inspired Tallow; never in his life before had he seen anything like it. The barge seemed to have a singleness of purpose as it ploughed on down the river, never stopping, never changing its speed – yet, always just ahead of him, sometimes lost in the mist, sometimes out of sight around a bend in the river. As he sweated to stay on course, Tallow knew that if he caught up with the barge, even if he followed where it led him, he too would realize what the purpose of his existence was. This was how he felt most of the time. Only occasionally did he find himself faltering, and then he would brush the doubts away. The barge *had* to be what he instinctively knew it to be. There was no turning back now.

But weariness was dragging at his muscles, making his eyes heavy. He would have to rest, soon, and also as he had left his home-city so hurriedly, he would need to take on provisions as soon as he came to a town.

Eventually the sun rose to its zenith, glancing off the water and making it shine like smashed glass, casting on to the river the shadows of the great trees and shrubs lining the bank. Tallow's vision was blinded by brilliant green and black and silver until eventually his eyelids closed; he did not have the energy to lift them again. His head fell against the wooden side of his ship, his legs sprawled amongst the dirty tackle and decaying fish baskets; his right hand was limp over the rudder-bar.

And so the boat drifted on the central tide of the river, drifted past a tall village, two black inns and an iron house; drifted until the sinking sun stained the waters scarlet, and changed the bright colours of the afternoon into more sombre tones which shifted from green into brown, eventually into grey, until all the world was grey and black as dusk came.

Owl-shapes hunted across the darkling, fast-streaming sky and the shrill screams of their prey at last impinged on Tallow's slumbering ears, waking him. He looked around, trying to remember where he was. His back ached and his shoulder throbbed. He painfully drew himself into a sitting position. The contours of the river bank were unfamiliar to him. With a shrug, he waggled the rudder-bar. His ship responded skittishly and this proof of his power over his craft helped him clarify his meandering thoughts. He marvelled at the length of time he had slept and how his ship had stayed more or less on course the whole while. He attempted to forget about his ravenous hunger and kept a sharp eye open for signs of a civilized settlement.

Sharp, vertical silhouettes in the distance soon stood out in contrast to the swaying outlines of the trees. He was approaching a town. Tallow sighed with pleasure and began to steer towards the bank. The trees became more and more sparse, until at last houses appeared among them, some on the very edge of the bank. The houses came closer together, eventually entirely replacing the willows and the poplars until the town was reached. Directly ahead of Tallow loomed a tall curved bridge. His trained eyes easily estimated its height, and he knew with certainty that he could sail under it without having to dismantle his mast. Under the bridge he went, into the deeper darkness for a few moments until he eventually broke out into an area of the river splashed by yellow light from lamps, which lined a small stone jetty. Tallow steered for the jetty, hailing a figure who stood upon it peering through the gloom.

'Hello!' shouted Tallow to the shape. 'Is there a berth handy for my sloop?'

'Aye,' responded a cautious voice. 'Aye – I think so.' There was silence as the man began to clamber down the steps which led from the jetty to the water. 'Who are you?'

'Jephraim Tallow. I'm a fisher and trader. Or was . . .' He appended his last sentence in an undertone. 'Where do I berth?'

'Over there.' The dim shape grew a horizontal appendage The man was pointing to an unoccupied stretch of the jetty wall. At intervals, iron rings were set into it. Expertly, Tallow steered his ship until it almost touched the wall, and he reached out to grasp one of the rings. He made his ship fast to two rings and eased himself on to the narrow ledge which led to the steps.

'I'll only be staying until tomorrow morning,' Tallow said as he neared the man. 'Is this a free harbour?'

'It is.'

Tallow could now make out the man. He was young and bearded. His eyes, caught in the glow of one of the lamps, looked wary, and he had put his head to one side as he stared at Tallow strutting towards him. Tallow stared up and back. 'How d'you do?' he enquired, letting himself grin in a friendly fashion. He stuck out a bony hand. 'Tallow at your service.'

'Hello, Mr Tallow,' slurred the bearded one, not taking the hand. 'It's a late time to be berthing your sloop, isn't it?'

'It is indeed.' Tallow sounded undaunted, but he was secretly annoyed that friendliness did not work on this wary eyed individual. 'I fell asleep, sir.'

'Aye? Well I suppose you'll be looking for an inn.'

'Very good of you to think of that. Where can you recommend?' The man made no move to return up the jetty steps.

'Cheap?'

'Yes – cheap,' assented Tallow, privately cursing the man. He smiled ingratiatingly. 'I'll be wanting to provision my ship, also.'

'Nowhere open, tonight.'

'I didn't expect there would be!' A querulous note crept into Tallow's previously assured voice. What a fool I've found myself, he thought. But he heard the note in his own voice and hastily corrected it. 'I'm sorry if I sound a little terse,' he smiled, 'but I've been on the river for twenty-four hours and I'm weary.'

'Follow me,' said the bearded one at last, turning and mounting the steps.

Tallow tripped behind him, glaring at his back.

He was led through a series of narrow alleys until eventually he saw ahead of him the lights of an inn. There was no sign over it, but beer advertisements were painted in ornate black lettering upon the windows. Among them was one which said 'Board'.

'This is the place,' Tallow's acquaintance said, and he strode on through the night, leaving Tallow no choice but to enter the building from which came the sounds of men drinking, glasses clattering, loud laughter and a babble of speech. He pushed open the door and walked in.

As he stalked up to the bar, men's heads turned to stare at him and quickly there was silence. It was a small inn, shadowy and overhot. A fire moved in the grate to Tallow's left, and three sides of the room were lined with wooden benches. A few chairs and tables were scattered about in the centre of the room, and every inch of seating space was occupied. The men were big-muscled, fleshy fishermen, with coarsened skin and faces flayed red by wind, water and sun. They clutched mugs of beer in their ham-sized hands and regarded Tallow. Most of them had hairy faces, long moustaches stained by beer and tobacco. Tallow continued on towards the bar, self-consciously pretending to ignore the silence and the stares. He approached the mottle-faced publican who was straining to pull a handle, siphoning beer into a pint tankard.

'Good evening,' Tallow smiled.

'Good evening, sir,' replied the publican, heaving at the handle. 'What can I do for you?' He was clean-shaven and his cheeks were brightly mottled.

Tallow's eyes barely came up to the counter. He felt uncomfortable among the beefy beer-swillers. They had resumed talking again, but not so loudly as before, neither were they laughing so heartily. However, encouraged, Tallow said:

'I want a room for the night, if you please, my friend.' He cursed himself. His voice had sounded condescending and haughty. Just the kind of voice men like these would resent. But he observed, with relief, that the publican only smiled and nodded his head. One or two of the fishermen laughed, that was all. Sometimes, Tallow reflected thankfully, his size was an asset.

'Ma!' The publican raised his voice to shout behind him. A dowdy woman appeared at the door behind the bar. She was thin and frail but she had large, kindly eyes. Tallow felt relieved, for here was someone he could master. Their eyes met and she smiled at him, like a mother.

'Ma,' repeated the publican. 'This gentleman requires a room.' The woman nodded, walking to the bar, lifted a hinged section and came out to confront Tallow. 'This way, sir,' she said.

'Much obliged, ma'am.' Tallow signed contentedly. He had been out of his element too long. Now he was back again. His step was jaunty as he followed her upstairs.

The room into which he was shown was practical. It had a bed and a washstand, plus a chest of drawers.

Tallow was satisfied. He said: 'The name's Jephraim Tallow, I'm on my way downriver. I've stopped off to pick up provisions and rest here for the night.'

'Pleased to meet you, Mr Tallow. We're Mr and Mrs Ollert. Have you travelled far?'

'Farther than usual for me, ma'am. I'm not sure what distance, for I fell asleep in my boat. Twenty-four hours' journey, anyway.' He hesitated. 'I'm following a ship. Perhaps you've seen it pass – or heard about it?'

She folded her arms in front of her and put her shoulders back. 'What kind of craft and what was her name?'

'I don't know her name, ma'am.' Tallow sat on the bed and began pulling off his boots. 'But she was painted – or burnished more likely – golden. No visible power and no sound of engines.' He was surprised to note a hardening of her eyes and her mouth setting in a grim line.

'No, Mr Tallow. We've seen no such ship pass. But if you'll take my advice, I wouldn't be following after her, anyway.'

She had not realized that her two statements contradicted each other. Tallow was astonished. Mrs Ollert hurried from the room. 'My husband will be up in a little while to see if there's anything you need,' she said as she left. The door closed with a thud and Tallow was left alone, listening to her footsteps patter away to be lost in the general noise drifting up from the bar-room. Shrugging, he took off his coat, his shirt and trousers, and finally, clothed only in his long underwear, pulled back the sheets and got into bed. There was a lamp above him. He left it on.

Half an hour later he was dozing. The fishermen had departed into the night soon after he had got into bed. He heard the stairs creak and heavy footsteps come towards his room. There was a knock on the door.

'Come in!' called Tallow, more loudly than was necessary. The door opened and Mr Ollert entered. He stood near the doorway.

'Sorry to disturb you, sir. Will you be wanting breakfast in the morning?'

'Yes please,' said Tallow. 'I'll be up early, for I want to be off as soon as possible.' There was silence. Mr Ollert remained where he was.

'The wife's said something to me,' he continued uncertainly. 'About a golden ship you're following.'

'That's right,' agreed Tallow. 'I am.' He was completely at a loss to explain the publican's manner.

Ollert took a step towards Tallow. 'I shouldn't, Mr Tallow. I really shouldn't,' he said hoarsely. 'You ain't the first, you know!'

Tallow sat up in his bed. 'What's it to do with you, anyway?' he cried.

'Nothing, sir – nothing.' Ollert's own voice had risen, but it was frightened, worried. 'But – others have gone after that bloody barge – and none of them have come back! For God's sake, sir – forget about it. It lures men to their deaths.'

If it had not been for Ollert's obvious sincerity, Tallow would have laughed aloud. He adjusted his emotions hastily; this melodrama could be relished. 'Rubbish, my friend,' he grinned. 'That ship won't kill me! What's wrong with it anyway?'

'I don't know, Mr Tallow, I'm sure. But it isn't the first time it's passed here. There was another man who claimed to have seen it – set off after it, he did, fifteen years ago. We never heard of him again – and he was the kind to keep in touch.'

'This is ridiculous,' laughed Tallow. 'There's nothing ominous in a man forgetting to "keep in touch" as you put it.'

He reached up to turn out the lamp. 'I'm sorry, Mr Ollert, but you can't convince me that your fear is well-founded. Goodnight.' He turned out the lamp, hissing angrily to himself as he brushed the hot glass of the lamp and burned his fingers.

Ollert left in silence.

Tallow found it difficult to understand exactly what Ollert had been getting at. But he wasn't going to allow the man to distract him. He knew the path towards his destiny – if he wished to live, then he must follow the barge.

CHAPTER THREE

Tallow was awakened by a loud thumping on his door. He shook his head, partly to clear it, partly in annoyance. It was morning. The sun shone brightly through the tiny window of the room.

'Who is it?' he mumbled. The thumping continued. 'Who is it?' he repeated loudly.

'Mr Ollert, sir. Time you was up, I believe.'

'Thanks, Mr Ollert,' called Tallow. He threw off the clothes and got out of bed. Stumbling over to the wash-stand, he poured water from the jug and splashed it over his head, drying himself on a rough towel which lay beside the basin. Then he dressed. His face was uncomfortably stubbly, but he had no razor so philosophically accepted the fact that he was growing a beard. He didn't like beards, he decided.

Feeling refreshed, he opened his door and walked along the landing until he reached the top of the stairs. He looked down the stairs and made out several figures standing around in the bar. He could only see their legs and torsos. Rather a lot of people about at this hour, he thought. Then he shrugged and went downstairs. Four tall men stood talking to Mr Ollert who was laying cutlery on three of the tables. Tallow heard Ollert say: 'Here he is now, gentlemen,' and then there was silence. Four heads swivelled to regard Tallow with eyes which were not unfriendly. Pretending not to notice them, Tallow nodded to Mr Ollert and sat down at one of the tables.

'Fine morning,' he remarked suddenly, startling the four men. They were all dressed identically, in green uniforms, with belts and boots. They had green caps in their hands. They were middle-aged men with bony faces and sunken, weary eyes.

'Yes,' said one of them. 'Certainly is.'

'Yes,' repeated his three comrades.

Tallow looked at the door, judging the distance. They were obviously here to see him; but why? As far as he knew, he had broken no laws. Were they policemen?

'These gents would like a word with you, sir,' Ollert said thoughtfully.

'Certainly,' said Tallow. 'What's the trouble?'

'No trouble, exactly, sir,' murmured the leader of the men, sitting down opposite Tallow. The way he used the phrase confirmed Tallow's suspicions that the man was an official. 'I'm Sergeant Vemmer – People's Protection League. These are constables Bunly, Arpit and Hemmison.' The three constables nodded as their names were mentioned. They looked somewhat embarrassed.

'We were wondering, sir, when you've finished your breakfast, whether you'd mind coming along to see Judge Wortmanlow? Mr

Ollert, here, thinks you might like a word with him.'

'What's all this about?' Tallow stared, bulging his eyes. 'I don't follow you.'

'It's about the golden ship, Mr Tallow.' The words came out of Ollert's mouth in a rush; he vomited them at Tallow. 'I told these gents. They'll be able to talk to you better than I could. Mr Tallow – it's for your own good. Just go along with them to see the Judge, sir. Take it calm, sir. They only want to talk.'

Tallow was baffled: 'What right have you got to tell me what to do? What right have any of you got? I won't go with you!'

'Please sir, please.' Ollert was wringing his hands. Tears trickled down his face. 'Please, please go with them. We don't want you to suffer!'

'*Suffer!* Suffer – what do you mean? What are you saying?' He stared wildly around him. The constables had softly surrounded him. There were expressions of pity on their grim faces.

'You see!' Ollert sobbed at the Sergeant. 'You see – he's not sane. I knew he wasn't.'

'It seems you're right, Mr Ollert,' said Sergeant Vemmer calmly. 'We'll take him along to see the Judge. He'll straighten him out. It's just a phase. We've had cases . . . like his before.'

He put a hand on Tallow's shoulder. Tallow shrugged it off, angry not only at them, but at his own impotence. The policemen towered two feet over his head.

'What are you doing?' he demanded. 'What have I done?' He ran, at last, for the door but Constable Arpit stepped forward and pinned his arms to his sides. He struggled hopelessly in the big man's grip. 'Stop it! Stop it!' he shrilled. 'You're madmen!'

Vemmer smiled pityingly. 'That's a joke,' he said.

Tallow kicked him in the chest as he was lifted bodily off the ground. Vemmer grunted, continuing to smile.

'That's not really civilized,' he said, 'but don't worry, you'll soon be better. Judge Wortmanlow will fix you up.'

Tears of anger sprang into Tallow's eyes as the constable's grip tightened. 'I don't know what you're talking about! Somebody tell me what I've done!'

'It's not what you've done exactly, Mr Tallow,' Vemmer remarked. 'It's what you might do. You might harm yourself. We don't like to let people harm themselves. It's our job to look after them – for their own good, of course.' The obvious sincerity of his tone nauseated Tallow. He subsided, allowing himself to be carried bodily from the inn.

It was horribly undignified, and his dignity was important to Tallow, as he was carted like a pig to market, along the winding streets of the town.

Eventually they came to a small grey house which bore the sign: *PROTECTOR OF SANITY – Judge Wortmanlow.*

He was hefted up the steps and pinioned while Vemmer rang the bell. A manservant, in tails and black tie, answered the door. The manservant was tall and angular; he had a head too small for his body. It rested on his long neck like a poppy on its stalk. For a moment, the manservant stared at Tallow pityingly.

'You'll be wanting to see His Worship,' whispered the manservant.

'Yes please,' assented Vemmer.

The manservant led the party through a hall which gleamed brown, full of polished wood; he knocked diffidently upon a door. A muffled vocal explosion sounded from behind the door. 'Sergeant Vemmer and party, Your Worship,' called the manservant. 'With a Case, sir.'

Tallow, throbbing in Constable Arpit's relentless embrace, felt a new surge of resentment. He didn't like being called a 'Case'. But there was nothing he could do. Perhaps the Judge – this Protector of Sanity – would be able to serve his function and protect him from the weird insanity of his captors. Tallow made an effort to control himself. He would have to make a good impression on the Judge.

They entered the Judge's office. Like the hall it was full of polished wood, stained dark brown. A large window, curtained by white netting, let in the morning sunshine. Brass candlesticks and wall-plaques gleamed around the walls. Two comfortable leather armchairs rested each side of a big blackened fire-place. It was a room which had been mellowed by years of use. Behind a large oak desk, placed in one corner of the room, sat the Judge. Behind him were shelves of large, legal books.

The Judge was an old delicate man with pale skin and a forehead which was corrugated into deep furrows. His long white hair hung over his face, his lips were pale and the only relief from the white and pink of his complexion were his eyes which were lost in dark shadow cast by his doming forehead which jutted out over the rest of his thin face like the brim of a hat. His claw-like hands rested on the table, appearing from the sleeves of a blue robe which covered his whole body up to his neck.

'Our Case, Your Worship,' said Sergeant Vemmer, removing his cap. The three constables did the same.

The Judge looked at Tallow.

'Do sit down, Mr –?'

'Tallow,' said Tallow. 'Jephraim Tallow.'

'Sit down, Mr Tallow.'

Tallow thought the Judge had a voice like soft cheese being grated.

The Judge turned to Vemmer who had taken up a position just behind the chair in which Tallow now seated himself.

'Why has this gentleman been brought here, Sergeant Vemmer?'

'For his own protection, sir.' Vemmer coughed. 'He says he saw a golden ship, sir. Means to follow it down-river until he finds it, sir.'

'I see,' said the Judge gravely. 'Obviously a genuine Case. Glad you haven't wasted my time, Sergeant. We must save him from himself.'

'But you haven't heard *my* story,' he cried bewilderedly.

'I've heard so many, my dear sir,' replied the Judge kindly. 'So many!' He sighed: 'Take Mr Tallow to the Home for Unfortunate Brethren, Sergeant. He should be better soon. Then we can allow him to go on his way – a better, more responsible human being.'

'But . . .' gabbled Tallow, 'but . . .?'

'It's for your own good,' said the Judge as the policeman escorted Tallow from the room. 'It's for your own good, my boy.'

Tallow was beginning to think that he was, indeed, mad – so many times had he heard that phrase repeated. Swamped with self-pity, he gave in at last, and, his feet dragging, walked dejectedly down the hall and out into the street where a large green van was waiting. Gold lettering on the side of the van informed him that it was the property of the PROTECTORS OF THE PEOPLE'S SANITY.

Tallow got into the van. It was dark inside, windowless. Ahead of him was a small aperture, through which he could see the driver. The other policemen were shadows around him.

The engine started with a roar and they were off, bumping and jumping to God knew where. Tallow put his aching head in his hands and began to sob. Too late to catch up with the barge, now.

The van sped onwards until eventually he heard its tyres crunch on gravel and he glimpsed a large house and green lawns through the driver's window. Where had they brought him? Obviously, the Home the Judge had mentioned.

The van stopped and one of the policemen opened its door. 'Here we are Mr Tallow, sir,' he said.

Tallow got up and walked towards the door, blinking in the sunlight. A huge grey house loomed above him. A stone house; a house with barred windows. A prison.

Surrounding him, the policemen led him up the steps of the house and through an open doorway. Looking back, Tallow saw that a high wall enclosed the grounds of the place. The grounds did not look like prison grounds, they were well-kept and had neat lawns and flower beds. But the strong doors and barred windows belied the lawns. Birds twittered outside. It was very peaceful. But Tallow knew his duty was to escape and attempt to catch up with the golden barge. He was led to a room where a circular man stood before a squat table.

There were bright pictures on the wall; it was a very cheerful room. The circular man, his body was round and his head was round, smiled cheerfully as Tallow and his escort entered. He had no real features. His tiny eyes and tiny nose were far too small for his balloon head and even his open, toothy mouth was small. He came towards Tallow, his hand outstretched.

'How d'e do, Mr Tallow,' he boomed. 'Heard you were coming to join us. We've fixed up a *nice* room for you.'

'Thanks,' said Tallow.

'We'll soon have you better Mr Tallow. I'm the Principal of the Home. You're a stranger to these parts, I understand?' He pulled on a bell rope. Somewhere in the bowels of the house there came a distant jangle.

'Yes – and I'd like to know what right you've got to keep me here.' Tallow's voice lacked its earlier anger.

A frown crossed the smooth brow of the governor. 'It's for your own good, you know, Mr Tallow,' he said.

Tallow felt sick.

A man in yellow overalls entered the room. He looked benign and happy. He smiled shyly at Tallow. A man of some sixty years, he had jet-black hair and a puckered, toothless mouth. He stood erect. Everything about him seemed to be a contradiction.

'This is Mr Tallow, Harold,' the Governor said. 'He'll be staying with us for a while. Look after him, will you?'

'Yes sir,' Harold smiled. 'Would you mind coming this way, Mr Tallow?'

Tallow shrugged and followed the old man out of the room. The Governor said something, but he didn't hear it. He looked back and saw that the big front door was closed. He was being led down a long scarlet-painted corridor, down some steps. Stout wooden doors were let into the corridor at intervals. Ahead of him a group of yellow-overalled warders were talking. As he passed. Tallow heard one say:

'I had a nightmare last night. I dreamed I went to work without any shoes on.'

The others heard this with gravity and smacked their lips sympathetically.

Harold led him to a door which stood open. Beyond the door was a small room, covered in striped wallpaper. Green and purple stripes clashed jarringly with curtains bearing large flower patterns. Tallow entered and heard the door close behind him.

'Make yourself at home, Mr Tallow,' Harold said, his voice creaking. 'Breakfast is at seven. I'll wake you then.'

Tallow would have said more, but another need arose. He looked under the bed and discovered what he was looking for.

When he had finished he undressed and got into bed. There was nothing else to do. His impotent impatience had waned for the moment. The bed faced the window and, as he lay his head on the soft pillow, a beam of sunshine struck him full in the face. Cursing, he turned over on his stomach and went to sleep.

At seven precisely, Harold shook Tallow awake.

'Up we get, Mr Tallow, sir.' He smiled toothlessly. 'Breakfast time, sir.'

Tallow swore at him and sat up. It was cold and he was naked. He got out of bed and began to don his clothes which, by this time, were dirty and tattered. Harold tutted and slapped himself on his left wrist with the palm of his right hand.

'Naughty me,' he said. 'Forgot.' He left the room, closing the door behind him. 'Get some,' he said.

Tallow hadn't wanted clothes, but now that they were coming he decided to wait for them. Soon Harold returned with a pair of white overalls. 'Here you are, sir,' he said apologetically. 'So sorry – very lax – should have remembered.'

Tallow put the overalls on. They were too big for him, but by rolling up legs and sleeves, he managed to adjust them to his own size. Harold then lathered Tallow's face and shaved him.

'Now we'll be off for our breakfast,' he said. 'This way, Mr Tallow. This way *please*, sir.'

With a snort, Tallow followed Harold once more through a maze of scarlet corridors. The place was abustle with the sounds of morning, clanks and cries, scuffling and water running. At last they came to a large bright yellow room wherein were seated, at long tables, about fifty white-overalled men. They were dull-eyed and did not look up as Tallow entered. Harold indicated a place at the end of one of the benches and rushed off, to return with a large bowl of porridge.

'Eat it up, sir,' he mumbled. 'Eat it up – it'll do you good, Mr Tallow.'

Tallow grunted surlily at the ancient warder, but he was hungry. He stuffed the porridge into his mouth by means of the wooden spoon provided. Harold, taking his place along the wall with some fifty other warders, looked on happily as Tallow ate. In the centre of the hall were Tallow's fellow prisoners. Around the walls stood their warders. The prisoners were eating like animals, snorting. Several were not eating at all but wept into their food. Their particular warders, looking hurt and baffled, shook their heads.

Tallow ate his food and drank the mug of milk which Harold provided for him. He finished just in time, for a whistle blew and all the prisoners rose, pushing the bench back with their legs. Tallow rose also and stood waiting for the next move. The prisoners were a dreadful lot, most of them unshaven, with long uncombed hair; most of them with bent, drooping shoulders.

The prisoners began to shuffle towards a door at the far end of the hall. Tallow followed. He had become used to following other people in the past couple of days.

The door led out into the garden Tallow had seen earlier. The prisoners began to shuffle around it, not looking up, simply staring at the ground. Their warders remained inside. Tallow felt that he was being watched and he looked about him. Behind him, standing on a balcony was the circular Governor. He waved to Tallow cheerfully.

Tallow made an obscene gesture with two fingers and turned his back on the Governor. He tapped on the shoulder of the man immediately in front of him. The man jumped jerkily, leaping off the ground with both feet. He quivered about on his heels and stared with huge round eyes at Tallow. Yet he didn't seem to be looking at Tallow, simply staring in his direction.

'Whaterwant?' asked the prisoner in a lifeless monotone.

'I was wondering, my friend, just why you are here?' enquired Tallow politely. 'What did they put you in here for?'

'I don't know,' said the man. 'I don't know. I don't know.'

Tallow persisted. 'You must know,' he went on. 'You must.'

'I forget,' said the prisoner, petulantly.

'Come now,' insisted Tallow. 'You must remember. Are you a madman? You look like one.'

The prisoner shrieked like a carrion bird. 'No! I'm not.'

Nonplussed, Tallow was beginning to regret the impulse which had driven him to begin the conversation.

'Then why are you here?' he said as calmly as he could, keeping a distance from the gibbering thing. 'Why are you here?'

The man subsided. 'Don't know,' he said dully. 'I liked music, once. They said it wasn't good for me.' He cocked his owl eyes at Tallow. 'Not good for me,' he repeated. 'Not good for my *neighbours.'*

Then, suddenly, as if triggered by this man's confession, the other prisoners wheeled round to face Tallow. They began to chant, one at a time, right down the line. But they weren't looking at Tallow. They were looking at the Governor on the balcony.

'I preferred women to men, but I – considered . . .'

'I invented a gun!'

'I loved!'

'I made my servants dress daily, in pink. In pink.'

'I feared my old father!'

'I threw myself into a well!'

The long list continued. Every one of them was guilty. Tallow was equally guilty. Now he knew it. Then there was a silence. They stared up at the Governor. Tallow also turned slowly, to look at him.

The Governor raised his hand. 'You were not doing what was good for you!' he said, as if accused himself. 'You're all madmen – insane! We're trying to help you!' He frowned to himself, mopping his forehead with a large yellow handkerchief. Then he smiled. 'You will all be better soon,' he promised.

The prisoners began to march around the grounds once more, eyes on the ground, feet dragging. Tallow shuddered and sat in the shade of the house, trying not to watch them.

In a few minutes another whistle-blast shrilled out and the prisoners began to troop back the way they had come. The Governor was still standing on the balcony, frowning to himself again. Tallow got into line and returned to the hall, thence to his own cell. Harold looked at him disapprovingly and shut the door behind him, sitting beside Tallow on the bed.

'I think you began that, sir,' he said, pursing his lips.

'What of it?' said Tallow. 'I didn't ask to come here.'

He picked up the chamber-pot, shiny and empty, and began to fiddle with it.

'I know you didn't, sir,' smiled Harold. 'And as you're new here, we can't blame you, of course. It's for your own good,' he said happily. 'It's for your own . . .'

Tallow smashed the old man's head with the chamber-pot. Blood and brains erupted outwards and upwards, staining the china. Calmly Tallow knew what he must do. He wrenched off his own overalls and stripped Harold's corpse. Then he put the yellow overalls on. They were not too large.

Then he walked out of the cell, still calm. He strolled slowly up to the front door of the Home and opened it. Two warders passed him, but they didn't stop him. He walked down the drive, smelling the scent of the flowers and new-cut grass, hearing his feet grinding the gravel of the path. A few yards away from him was a large iron gate, beside it a small lodge. An attendant stood outside, smoking a pipe.

Tallow heard himself say. 'Got to go into town. Be back in an hour or so.' He stared at the lodge-keeper as the man bent to unlock the gates with an enormous key. Then he was walking down the road, seeing the town in the distance and the river glinting beyond it. As soon as he was out of sight he began running, automatically, down the steep road towards the town.

The road was of concrete, neat and clean. On both sides of the road were tidy trees, swaying a little in gentle wind. The sky above was pale blue, speckled by white clouds which drifted aimlessly on the wind.

Tallow thought only of regaining the river. When he reached the outskirts of the town, he took a side-street, then another, still heading for the river. A few people turned to stare at him, but he ignored them, running, running until he came to a road which paralleled the river. On it were several sailing craft, some of them unattended. One, of a similar pattern to his own, lay moored to a timber pole, stuck in the bank. He jumped aboard and tore the mooring rope away from the pole. Then he guided the boat into the centre of the river once more and was away. He had escaped.

It was not until ten minutes later that he realized that he had killed a man. As he sped onwards into the late morning sun, he debated whether or not to turn back.

'It's for your own good.'

He stared ahead, not trusting his eyes. Then, clearly he saw the barge again. He still had time to catch up with it. He smiled.

'I killed him for his own good,' he said.

But even as he laughed, the memory of the blood-spattered chamber-pot came back to him. The crushed eggshell covered in brains and matted black hair. The groan with which the ancient had died, the old frail, naked corpse after he'd stripped it. It was clearer in his memory than when he had first witnessed it. Surely he hadn't really slain Harold?

There was something uncomfortable around the neck of the yellow overalls. He put his finger up to loosen the collar and felt stickiness. He drew his finger away again.

Congealed blood sat accusingly on his index finger. He was suddenly frightened, terror-stricken. He looked back. The city was no longer in sight. He looked ahead – he could no longer see the barge.

But it was in front of him, he knew. It had to be – he had seen it and recognized it.

Still, as he sailed on, he saw a battered head and narrow, naked shoulders. Bile rose in his throat even as he steered his boat after the golden barge and truth. The navel! Where was it?

CHAPTER FOUR

Day gave way to night, inevitably, for the fourth time since Tallow had begun his chase. He slept at the rudder trusting to his luck, and the next morning awoke to find himself soaked to the skin, but still on course. The yellow overalls he wore had not been meant for outdoor wear. He had not slept well, for his dreams had been scarlet dreams; but now that it was morning, he could forget. What was one man's life? How did a single murder matter when the golden barge moved surely onwards?

The rain sliced down out of a grey sky, lancing into the waters of the river, spattering over the canvas of the boat. And a wind was beginning to blow. Instead of willows, rhododendrons now lined the banks of the river. They were heavy with the fallen water, sinking beneath its sodden weight. The wind was rising and bending them into rustling nightmare beasts which reached out obscenely to tempt Tallow ashore. He laughed at them, and the wind filled his ship's sail, distending it until the mast creaked.

Suddenly, Tallow realised his danger; realised that he had no cause for laughter, for the wind was driving his vessel towards the luring beast bushes.

Frantically, he attempted to adjust the sail, but the rig was unfamiliar to him and in his panic he succeeded only in tangling it into a mess of knots. The wind blew stronger, bending the mast, swelling the sail like a cannibal's belly.

He tore at the knots until his fingers bled and his nails were broken shreds catching in the tackle. Then, as the wind increased, he had to concentrate on the rudder-bar in order to keep the boat on some kind of course. He saw that he was nearing a bend in the river, and saw two other things; a white flash against the dark-green, and the golden barge just ahead, looming tall. He had been so busy concentrating upon the sail, that he had not sighted his objective. He prayed that he could stay on course long enough to reach the barge and board her – but even as his ship gained furious speed, he came to the bend in the river and his ship lurched and shuddered to a halt – he had run aground on a hidden sand-bar.

Angry and screaming his disappointment to the wind and the rain, Tallow leapt out into the shallow water and attempted to shift the ship off the bar as rain smote him in the face and flayed his skin. His efforts were useless. In a second, the barge had disappeared from his sight and he had sunk to his knees in the water, sobbing in frustration.

The rain began to fall less heavily and the velocity of the wind dropped, but still Tallow remained on his knees, bowed in the swirling, dirty water, his hands above him, gripping the sides of his boat. The rain and wind subsided and eventually the sun dissected the clouds. The sun shone on the boat, on Tallow, on the river, on bushes and trees – and on a white house, five stories high, which gleamed like the newly-washed face of a child.

Tallow lifted red eyes and sighed. He tried once more to move the boat, but could not. He looked around him. He saw the house. He would need help. With a shrug he splashed, knee-deep through the water, to the bank, climbing up its damp, crumbling, root-riddled earth and cursing his luck.

Tallow, in some ways, was a fatalist. And his fatalism at last came to his rescue as ahead of him he saw a wall; a wall of red-brick, patched with black moss-growths. His mood changed almost instantly and he was once again his old, cold cocky self. For beyond that wall he could make out the head and shoulders of a woman. The barge could wait for a little while.

CHAPTER FIVE

She was a sharp-jawed, pout-lipped beauty and her eyes were green as scum. She wore a battered felt hat and stared at Tallow over the short stone wall which reached almost to her shoulder.

'Good God!' she gasped. *'A man!'* She smiled. One of her delightfully even teeth was stained brown. Two others were green, matching her eyes.

Tallow's senses for women had been dull and dormant for years. Women had never been attracted to him, nor he to them. But somehow he knew instinctively that he was going to form an attachment for this one. He savoured the knowledge. For the moment, hugging it to himself.

'Good morning, madam,' he said, straddling his legs and making a low, ungainly bow. This was not helped by his sodden condition. 'My sloop ran aground and I'm stranded.'

'Then you must stay with me,' she responded. 'That's my house, over there.' She stretched a rounded arm and pointed. Her fingers were long and delicate, terminating in purple-painted talons.

'A fine house it is, too, madam, by the looks of it.' Tallow swaggered towards the low wall.

'It is fine,' she said, 'but rather empty. I have only two servants.'

'Not enough.' Tallow frowned. 'Not enough.' His luck, he felt, was changing. He would find the barge again, sometime. He could always catch it up.

He vaulted the wall. This was a remarkable feat for one of his stature, and he achieved it with a delicacy and grace normally alien to him. He stood beside her. He looked at her from beneath half-closed lids. 'I would be grateful for a bed for the night,' he said. 'And help in the morning. My ship must be refloated.'

'I will arrange it,' she promised. She had mobile lips which moved smoothly around the words as she spoke. She was slim-waisted and full-hipped. Her bottom was round and firm beneath a skirt of yellow silk. Her large breasts pushed at the shining silk of a black blouse and the heels of her shoes were six inches long. She turned and headed for the house.

'Follow me,' she said.

Tallow followed, marvelling at the way she kept her balance on her high heels. Without them, he thought gleefully, she was only an inch or so taller than he. She led him through the garden of spear-like leaves, finally arriving at a sandy road which wound towards the house.

A two-wheeled carriage stood empty, drawn by a bored donkey. The woman's flesh was soft and itched at Tallow's finger tips as he helped her into the carriage, doing mental somersaults all the while. He grinned to himself as he got in beside her and took the reins.

'Gee up!' he shouted. The donkey sighed and moved forward at a tired walk.

Five minutes later Tallow tugged hard at the donkey's reins and brought the cart to a crunching halt on the gravel outside the house. A flight of solid stone steps led up to big timber doors which were half-open.

'My home,' the woman remarked unnecessarily. Tallow felt a disappointed shock at this inanity; but the feeling soon passed as it was replaced by his glee for his good fortune.

'Your home!' he yelled. 'Hurrah!' He didn't bother to mask his emotions any more. He bounced out of the carriage and helped her from it. Her legs were well-shaped and trim. She smiled and laughed and treated him to a gorgeous display of brown, green and white.

They climbed the steps together, leaping up them like ballet dancers, with their feet clattering in time. Her hand slipped into his as they pushed the door open and marched into the hall with rafters lost in gloom. It was a shadowy hall, hushed as a church. Dust flew in a single beam of sunlight which entered by way of the door. The door was apparently warped, for it did not shut properly. Dust swirled into Tallow's nostrils and he sneezed. She laughed delightfully.

'My name's Miranda,' she told him. 'What's yours?'

'Tallow,' he replied, his eyes watering and his nose still itching. 'Jephraim Tallow, at your service!'

'At my service!' She clapped her hands and the echoes reverberated around the hall. 'At my service!' She clapped and laughed until the hall resounded with the applause and laughter of a vast audience.

A voice like the last trump boomed and crashed into Tallow's startled eardrums. 'Do you require me, madam?'

Staring through the gloom, Tallow was surprised to see that the hollow drum-voice emanated from a bent and wizened ancient, clad in faded finery of gold and silver. A livery, tarnished and varnished with years of wear. Miranda answered the man, obviously one of the servants she had mentioned.

'Dinner, Yorchem!' she cried. 'Dinner for two!'

'Yes, madam.' With a swirl of dust, the bent one vanished through a barely discernable door.

'One of my servants,' whispered Miranda. 'The other one's his wife – *damn her*!' She cursed quite viciously – softly and sibilantly, like a snake spitting.

Tallow, knowing nothing of the place, wondered how an old woman could arouse such wrath in Miranda. But a thousand reasons swam into his head and he rejected them all. He was not a man to jump to conclusions. Conclusions were too final – they led to death.

She clutched his hand and led him through the hall to where wide oak stairs twisted upwards. 'Come, Jephraim,' she murmured, gay once more. 'Come my tender Tallow, and let us get you dressed!'

Tallow recovered his self-confidence and rushed like a rabbit up the stairway, his long legs stepping high. They polka'd hand in hand to the third floor of the vast dark house. Their hair, his red, hers black as jet, flew behind them and they laughed all the while, happily, insensitive to everything but themselves.

Up to the third floor they bounded and she led him to a door, one of a number, as solid as its fellows. He was slightly out of breath, for he was not used to climbing so many stairs. As she strained to turn the knob on the door, using both hands, bending her body and screwing up her face until eventually the door creaked open, he began to hiccup.

Meanwhile the wind, which had driven Tallow on to the sand bar, was howling around the golden barge as it pushed calmly onwards; northwards, to whatever victories or dooms awaited it.

'Jephraim,' whispered Miranda as he sat back in his chair, sipping brandy from a glass as big as his head.

'Mmmm?' he said, smiling foolishly. The meal had been liberally diluted with night-red wine.

'Jephraim – where are you from?' She leant forward across the small table. She had changed into a dress of dark blue which flowed off her smooth shoulders to cascade like a waterfall down her figure, flaring at the knees. She wore two rings on her left hand – sapphires and emeralds – and around her throat hung a thin chain of gold. Tallow's new emotions were rioting through him – and still a childish awe for his good fortune stuck in part of his mind, even as he stretched out a hand and groped for Miranda's taloned fingers. Pinpricks of excitement and anticipation were becoming almost too much to bear and his voice throbbed as he spoke, echoing his heartbeats.

'From a town many miles away,' he said, and this appeared to satisfy her.

'Where were you going, Jephraim?' This question was asked idly.

'I was – I am – following a golden ship which passed your house just before I ran aground. Didn't you see it?'

She laughed, and her laughter hurt him. 'Silly Tallow,' she cried. 'No such ship passed – I didn't see it and I was in the garden for hours – watching the river. I never miss the ships which sail by.'

'You missed this one,' he muttered, glaring into his glass.

'Your jokes are hard to understand, Jephraim,' she said more softly. 'But I'm sure I'll like them – when we know each other better.' Her voice dropped lower and lower until it was almost inaudible, but the timbre of it was enough to churn Tallow's thoughts into other channels almost immediately. Some of his self-assurance, so badly shattered recently, returned to him and he disentangled his hand from hers, folded his ten fingers around the brandy glass, lifted it, and poured the entire contents down his throat. He smacked his lips and gasped, then put the glass down with a bang, clattering the dirty cutlery.

He wiped his mouth on the back of his hand, the scarlet sleeve of his new corduroy jacket somewhat impeding his action, and looked around the small candle-lit room. It blurred. Pettishly he shook his head to clear it and, supporting himself with hands planted on the table, stood up.

'Miranda,' he slurred. 'I love you.'

'Good,' she purred. 'That makes it so much easier.'

Tallow was too drunk to wonder what it was which would be easier. He ignored the statement and rocked towards her. She stood up, slowly, carefully, and glided towards him. He gathered her in and kissed her throat. As she was standing up, he couldn't quite reach her mouth. Her breasts pushed against his chest and her arms slid up his back, one hand caressing the nape of his neck. The other hand moved startlingly down his back and around his hip.

'Ouch!' he moaned a moment later. 'That ring hurts!' She pouted, then smiled, and took her rings off. He wriggled in his tight, black velvet trousers and wished that he were naked.

'Shall we go to bed now?' she suggested at just the right moment.

'Yes,' agreed Tallow with certainty. 'Yes.'

She supported his reeling body as they left the room and made their way up the flight of stairs to her own bedroom.

CHAPTER SIX

A week throbbed by. A bedded week, wearing for Tallow, but delightful. Miranda's expert lessons had taught him, among other things, that he was a man. A man, to boot who had learned to please Miranda. The week had taught him something else. He had now a tighter rein on his emotions; could control both appetite and expression to a greater degree.

Tallow lay in bed beside a sleeping Miranda, attempting to shift the sheet which covered her. His eyes were as yet unsatiated by the sight of her lying naked and at his mercy. The truth was (even Tallow had to admit) that for the most part he was at her mercy.

But Miranda was a woman, and took only the right advantage of her superior position. Tallow remained in love with her, and was content. Her yielding and her occasional pleas were so much more worth it when they came. But weariness was fast making a wreck of Tallow the travesty. He slept longer, made love a trifle less violently (though with more skill) than on the first two nights of his stay. Miranda, on the other hand, could never be fully satisfied.

Even now, after ten hours of sleep, Tallow did not feel rested, but nonetheless, he was content. He felt happiness and sometimes sadness when Miranda outraged him, but the joy far outweighed the pain.

He had just laid bare her breasts, when she awoke. She blinked and then opened her eyes as widely as she could, looked at him, looked down and gently, tantalizingly, drew the sheet back towards her chin. Tallow grunted his disappointment, raised himself on one elbow, cushioning his head in his hand, and stared down at her.

'Good morning,' he said with mock hardness.

'Morning, Jephraim.' She smiled like a schoolgirl, stirring tenderness and desire in him. He flung himself upon her in a flurry of sheeting. She laughed, gasped, was silent for some seconds, and then kissed him.

'God,' she said. 'You're good.'

'Thanks,' he smiled maliciously. 'That was for last night.'

'I earned it, didn't I?' she said, staring into his eyes.

'You did.' He rolled over and sat up in bed.

'You need me, don't you?' she said softly, behind him.

'Yes,' he said, and then paused, thinking – he had answered the question too quickly. Before he had considered it, he had said, 'At least I think so.'

Her voice was still soft, unchanged. 'What do you mean – you think so?'

'Sorry,' he smiled, turning towards her and looking down at her. 'Sorry – I don't know what I meant.'

She frowned then and shifted in the bed. 'I don't either,' she said. 'I don't know what you mean. What did you mean?'

'I've told you,' he said, deciding that he was a fool. 'I don't know.'

She turned over on her side, towards the wall, away from him. 'Either you need me or you don't,' she said.

'That's not strictly true.' Tallow sighed. 'I can need you – and I can't. There are things to need at certain times. I need you sometimes.' I'm right, he thought – for it was clear to him now and it had never been so before.

She was silent.

'It's true, Miranda.' He knew he should stop, but he couldn't. 'Surely you see that it's true?'

She was silent.

'Love isn't everything!' he mumbled lamely, feeling uncertain and beaten.

'Isn't it?' Her voice was muffled, but cold.

'No!' he said, angrily, and got up. He pulled on his clothes and walked over to the window, viciously tearing back the curtains. It was raining outside.

He stomped from the room, on his way to the bathroom. He felt troubled and annoyed, but he couldn't analyse the feeling. He knew, somehow, that he was right; knew that he shouldn't have spoken to her as he had, but was glad, somehow, that he had done so. The floor was cold to his bare feet as he walked, and he could hear the rain beating to the ground and onto the roof. It was a drab day and fitting for his mood.

At breakfast she soon got over her former temper and soon, for the moment at least, they had forgotten their conflict.

'What shall we do today?' she said, putting down her coffee cup.

'Ride!' answered Tallow on the spur of the moment. 'Ride! That's what we'll do! You have some horses – I've seen them.'

'I have – but I didn't know you could ride.'

'I can't,' he grinned. 'I can't, my beauty, but I can learn!'

'Of course you can!' She was now in his mood. 'But what shall we do about the rain?'

'To hell with the rain – it can't affect us. Come, love – to horse!' He struck a theatrical pose and galloped from the breakfast-room. Laughing, she ran after him.

They rode all through the day, stopping sometimes to eat and to make love, when the sun shone. They rode, and after two uncertain hours, Tallow soon learned how to sit his mare and to guide her. He was still an amateur, but a fast learner. Since the night he had seen the barge he had been learning many things, quickly. Ideas rushed into his open, greedy mind and he gratefully absorbed them.

So they rode through the rain and the sunshine and they laughed and loved together, forgetful of anything else; Tallow with his tiny frame and long legs, perched high above the ground on a chestnut mare; Miranda, petite and voracious for his attention, sometimes gay, often enigmatic; Miranda the woman.

They rode for hours until at last they came to a stretch of the river upstream, which Tallow had passed a week earlier, but whilst asleep. They came to a hill and, breathless and excited, fell into one another's arms, dovetailed together, and sank onto the damp turf, careless and carefree.

'Your river,' whispered Miranda, some time later. 'I'll always think of it as yours, now. I used to think it was mine, but I know it isn't.'

Tallow was puzzled. He said: 'It's everyone's river – that's the beauty of it. Everyone's.'

'No,' she said. 'It's yours – I know.'

'It's not just mine, darling,' he said tenderly. 'Anyone can sail on it, bathe in it, drink from it. That's why it's there.'

'Perhaps,' she compromised at last. 'Perhaps it is, but I know what I shall always think.'

'One day I may make you a present of it, sweetheart,' he smiled, and he was right, though he didn't know it.

He stared at the river and then, just for a fleeting moment, he saw the golden barge, sailing calmly, as it always did, unruffled. He turned to her, pointing. 'There!' he cried excitedly. 'There – now you see I wasn't joking! The golden ship! I must have seen a mirage or something the last time – I passed it while I was asleep!' But when he looked again it had gone and Miranda was getting up, walking towards where they had tethered the horses.

'You always spoil things,' she said. 'You always say something to worry me.'

In silence, they rode away from the river. But Tallow was thinking of the barge – and was weighing his thoughts carefully.

Later that night, the rift unhealed, they sat in front of a fire, in the dining room, drinking. She was truculent, unapproachable; he was turbulent, wondering if, after all, the things he wanted were unattainable. So they sat, until there was a disturbance outside and Tallow went to the window to see what was happening. It was dark and he couldn't see much. The night was a confusion of laughter and screams, flickering torches and shifting shadows. Tallow saw that a drunken group was coming towards the house. As he felt then, he welcomed the interruption.

'Visitors,' he said.

'I don't want to see them.'

'Why not – we could have a party or something.'

'Shut up!' she pouted.

He sighed and went downstairs into the dark cold, draughty hall. By the time he reached it, people were thumping on the half-open door.

'Is anyone in?'

'Shelter, we beg thee, shelter!'

Laughter.

'Are you sure this house *belongs* to someone?' A woman's voice, this. Answered by another woman: 'Yes dear, I saw a light in an upstairs window.'

'Is anyone home?'

'We've got plenty of bottles!'

Laughter again.

Tallow pulled the door back and stood confronting the interlopers.

'Good evening,' he said, belligerently now.

'Good evening my dear sir, good evening to you!' A grinning corpulence, swathed in extravagant clothing, a cloak, knee-length boots, a top-hat, bearing a silver-worked cane, and bowing theatrically.

'Can I help you?' said Tallow, hoping that he couldn't.

'We're lost.' The man was drunk. He swayed towards Tallow and stared at him; his breath stinking of alcohol. 'We're lost and have nowhere to go! Can you put us up?'

'This isn't my house,' said Tallow stupidly. 'I'll see. You'd better come in anyway. How'd you get this far?'

'By boat – boats – lots of boats. Fun. Until we got lost, that is.'

'All right.' Tallow walked back up the stairs and rejoined Miranda. She was still sulking.

'Who is it?' she said petulantly. 'Tell 'em to go away and let's go to bed.'

'I agree, dearest.' Tallow's mood changed to its former state and his quick tongue babbled, though he didn't mean what he said. 'But we can't turn 'em away – they're lost. They can sleep here. Won't bother us, will they?'

'I suppose I'd better see them, Jephraim.' She got up, kissed him, and together, warmly, arm in arm, they went downstairs.

The revellers' torches were still burning, lighting up the dusty hall. As the fat leader saw Miranda and Tallow descending the stairs he leered at Miranda.

'The lady of the house!' he bawled to his friends, and they laughed uneasily; he was embarrassing them now. The noise in the dusty cavern of a hall became a zoo-like cacophony.

Miranda said politely, but without feeling: 'You may stay the night here, if you wish. We have plenty of beds.' She turned to go upstairs.

'Beds!'

The drunken mob took the word up gleefully, chanting it round the hall. *'Beds. Beds. Beds.'* After a short while the word became meaningless and they subsided into high-pitched laughter. Miranda and Tallow stood observing them. 'Let's have some light, Jephraim,' she said.

Obediently but reluctantly, he went over to the candles and put a taper to them. The hall erupted with light, dazzling the revellers. Again the giggling began. In the centre of the hall was a long table; chairs lined the walls. This was the first time Tallow had seen the room lighted. Grime was everywhere and the paint was peeling. Mildew had formed in patches on the ceiling and walls and the light only served to pick it out. Tallow shrugged and moved to return upstairs again, but Miranda put her hand on his arm. 'We'll stay for a short while,' she said.

I wish she'd make up her mind, he thought glumly, now regretting the impulse which had driven him to allow the people admission.

They were soft, these people, soft beyond Tallow's experience, pampered darlings to the last; slim, brittle-eyed women and fat blank-eyed men, bewilderedly running over the surface of life, content with their own fear-moulded values, foolish and fooling themselves that they were alive. Tallow could only pity them and hate them. Every second they remained they drove him into himself, retreating into the embracing depth of his own dark soul.

He continued to stare at them from out of his skull; continued to stare as bottles were piled on the table and Miranda was lost among the others, absorbed into their shallowness. Tallow was vaguely terrified then, but his mind refused to control his body and he stood on the stairs watching them, unable to leave or join them.

Clothes were flung in all directions and Tallow saw a blue dress and a black cape flutter outward together. Naked bellies wobbled and naked breasts bounced and white unhealthy flesh was a background for dark hair.

Tallow felt ill. At last his feet dragged him upwards back to the bedroom. His ego had been shattered; but the pain of his loss, of his humiliation, was greater. He lay on the bed, sobbing; thoughtless and emotionful, his whole world a timeless flood of self-pity.

He lay, his head throbbing and aching, for hours; eventually falling into a fitful slumber which lasted another hour. When eventually he awoke, he was calm. He knew that he had done wrong, had destroyed a part of himself in denying the barge for Miranda's love. He had delayed too long, and the barge should be followed, if there was still time. That was his aim, his goal, his function in life – to follow the barge and to go where it led him, irrespective of what other things distracted him.

He got a large woollen cloak from a cupboard and put it around his shoulders. Then he left, perturbed that he would have to leave through the hall.

When he reached it, he was astounded.

In the centre of the room was a pulsating pyramid of flesh; clean flesh and dirty flesh; soft flesh and rough flesh. It was ludicrous. There were limbs of all descriptions in most peculiar juxtaposition. A pair of pink buttocks seemed to spring an arm; noses lay upon legs, faces on torsos, breasts upon toes.

Such a scene might have disgusted Tallow; instead he was astounded, for the strangest sight of all was the arm which waved at the top of the throbbing human mountain. It clutched a coruscating wine glass.

The fingers were purple-painted talons, Miranda's fingers. Every so often the arm would disappear into the pile and the glass would return, less full, held like a triumphant torch, to its place above the pyramid. Tallow swallowed, his eyes wide. On tip-toe, his bitterness surging inside him once more, he circumnavigated the heap and pulled on the door.

'Goodnight, Miranda,' he called as he left.

The wine-glass hand waved. 'Good night Jephraim, see you later!' The voice was muffled and slurred, tinged with false gaiety which was not like Miranda at all; normally she was either happy or sad, never false in her feelings.

'No you won't, Miranda,' he called as he at last pulled the door open and fled into the rain-sodden night, blindly running down the sandy path, towards the river. Running from something which remained inside him, which he couldn't flee from, which was destroying him and which he was powerless to combat.

So Tallow fled.

CHAPTER SEVEN

The boat was still on the sand bar, half-full of rainwater. Tallow looked at it dispiritedly. Then, with a shrug, he took off his cloak and lowered his legs into the cold, murky water. He shivered, tensed and forced forward. The boat's timber felt good to his hands as he hoisted himself into it. He stared through the gloom, searching for the bailing pans. At last he found them and began bailing the water out.

When he had finished, he swung over the side again and slowly made his way round the boat, inspecting it as much as he could in the dim moonlight. Then he returned to the stern and put his shoulder to it, heaving. The vessel shifted slightly. He moved round to the port side and began rocking it, shifting some of the compressed sand.

Three hours later, the boat was afloat. Weary with his effort, he sank into it and lay on the wet boards, half-asleep. He eventually arose when he heard someone moving about on the shore. Levering himself upright, he looked over the side and saw Miranda standing there, framed against the moonlight, her hair ruffled by the wind, a man's dark cloak around her.

'Jephraim,' she said. 'I'm sorry – I don't know how it happened.'

Tallow, his heart heavy inside him, his mind dull, said: 'That's all right, Miranda. I'm going now anyway.'

'Because of – that?' She pointed back to the house.

'No,' he said slowly. 'At least, not *just* because of that. It helped.'

'There's nothing I can say, of course.' Her eyes were frank, her body slack.

'No – nothing. It had to come, Miranda. You could have followed the barge with me, once, perhaps, but not now – never. I'd have liked you with me, but you'll always regard the barge as a rival – won't you?'

'No!' she cried. 'Oh, no – I'll come with you – *please*!' She moved towards the water. 'There's still time – I'll try to see the barge as well. I will.'

'No,' he said. 'It's too late. I'm going alone. I love you, Miranda – but I know my destiny. You've lost your place in it. Perhaps it's my fault – perhaps not. I don't know.'

'Take me with you,' she repeated humbly. 'I'll do whatever you want.'

'No,' he said, shaking out the sail. 'Goodbye!'

But she flung herself into the water and grasped the side of the boat, pulling herself into it with desperate strength.

'Go back, Miranda!' he shouted, seeing his doom in her actions. 'Go back – go back! It's finished – you'll destroy me!'

She made her way towards him, flinging her bedraggled body at his feet in horrible humility. 'Take me!' she moaned.

The boat was now in midstream, making swiftly away from the sandbank.

'Oh, God, Miranda,' he sobbed. 'Don't make me – I *must* follow the barge.'

'I'll come, Jephraim, darling. I'll come with you.'

Tears were streaming down his face, he was breathing quickly, his brain in tumult, a dozen emotions clashing together making him powerless for any action save speech.

'You'll destroy me,' he said. 'You'll ruin me, my darling; my love.' He gave in suddenly, ashamed for her degradation. He sank down beside her, taking her damp, heaving body in his arms and sharing her grief.

And so, locked together in their fear and bewilderment, they slept.

Dawn was vicious; cloudless and bright. Tallow's eyes ached.

Miranda still remained in troubled slumber, but she was on the borderline of wakefulness.

Tallow was lost in introspection, and he could not see a real end to his mental conflict. He loved Miranda, but the barge beckoned. Without her encumbance he might yet find it. He had a responsibility towards her – could he deny that in order to achieve the destiny he felt was his? It was responsibility to himself or to her. There was no way out that he could think of.

He didn't know. The words clamoured endlessly in his head – indecision wracked him and sapped his strength.

He didn't know.

As she sighed and began to struggle towards consciousness, an overpowering feeling of pity for her welled up in him. Then he looked down-river where it stretched straight into the horizon.

Gold glimmered. Tallow acted. It was now or never.

He picked her up in his arms. She smiled in her sleep, loving him. He wrenched her away from him and hurled her outwards – hurled her into the river.

She screamed suddenly, in horror. She knew.

She threshed wildly in the water, calling his name, pleading with him, needing him, terrified of what his actions implied.

'I can't live without you!' The words, a cliché, ancient even to Tallow, had a meaning he had never realized. They were not empty words – they were desperate words, shouted with truth and honesty.

He sobbed, moaning for her to stop. 'It's got to *be*!' he kept saying. 'You'll destroy me.'

'Love! Jephraim! Oh, God – Jephraim – no, please – please – Jephraim.'

Her words were confused, her tone desperate. She loved him.

He clapped his hands to his ears, shutting out her cries. But his agony was still intense.

'My love . . .' he whimpered. 'My love . . .'

Soon he could no longer hear her voice. He looked back through eyes which were blurred. He stared at a dot in the water, far behind him. It was her head. He refused to look for long, afraid that he would see the head sink. Then he realized what he had done. But it was far too late. He retired once more within himself.

He sailed on, the barge still ahead of him, still in the distance, until at last his pain had dulled; his eyes fixed on the glittering ship, his mind was blank; he submerged his fear.

Tallow the destroyer, the bungler, the visionary; Tallow the travesty, sailed on, but once again the ship was lost and he could no longer see it.

A week passed and Miranda's misery, his own pain, became an emotion to be destroyed by his mind, once more coldly logical, dispassionate and ruthless. Heedless of his loss, he continued, until at last he came to a vast stone city.

Its featureless multi-storied buildings reared into the grey sky, squeezed together, the narrow gaps between them forming dark streets shielded eternally from the light. It stained the river bank, a blot on the landscape. But in it were shops which sold the food for which Tallow was desperate. After berthing just beyond the quayside, he walked towards the walled city.

At the main gateway to the city, Tallow paused. A man menaced him with a rifle. Upon the end of the gun was a long, slim bayonet, as grey as the sky. The man was heavy-featured, bumpy-bodied, coarse and uncouth.

'Halt!' he growled. 'Who are you?'

'Tallow.'

'So?'

'My name is Tallow – I am a traveller, passing through your city. I want supplies and hope to purchase them here.'

The man pondered upon this, still with bayonet pointed at Tallow. At last, after looking him over as if the little man were a piece of dubious meat, he stepped reluctantly away from the gate. 'Very well,' he said. 'Go on in. But watch your step, lad – do anything against the law and you'll be hung, drawn and quartered.'

Disconcerted and perturbed, Tallow walked into the city. It was quiet, like a mausoleum, hushed and still, as if deserted. But people shuffled through the streets. Mean people, wretched people, half-alive people in shawls and patched rags, grim, unshaven, unwashed, unhappy people who did not even look at Tallow as he passed by them on his way through the town. Eventually he was lost in the maze of streets.

A woman passed. She was thin-faced and had red lips painted on her sunken mouth; her glasses were round and rimless and her hair hung down her face like string. Over her shoulders was draped an old brown coat, beneath that a startlingly brilliant flowered dress. It was incredibly out of place.

Tallow, attracted by the colour, stopped her. She looked up at him, cringing, her eyes big beneath her glasses.

'Yes?' she whispered.

'Which way to the food shops?' enquired Tallow, not wasting politeness.

She pointed westwards, and shuffled onwards.

Eventually, Tallow reached a market-place, unlike most markets he had known. While it had bustle and noise, the bustle was somehow apathetic, the noise somehow muted – an undertone of whispers and corner-of-the-mouth comments. Only one voice was raised – and that was vibrant with emotion. Tallow heard a few of the words as he inspected fruit on a stall, conscious of the people's stares – corner-of-the-eye stares.

'Sin!' he heard, 'God . . . the worlds beyond . . . infinite . . . mercy . . . pity . . . together . . . love . . .' It was a voice with a message and, judging by the crowd around the unseen speaker, people were listening to the message.

Tallow bought fruit, vegetables and salt-meat, then he walked towards the crowd.

A man turned to look at Tallow as the little man stood on tip-toe, attempting to peer over the shoulders of the packed people. The man's eyes were bright, his manner nervous and enthusiastic.

'It's Glory Mesmers,' he whispered. 'He's preaching again. He's wonderful. But he'll be arrested if he isn't careful – he's been warned not to preach in the market.'

'Why?' asked Tallow.

'Because They say he's attempting to undermine Their Authority. He might be too, come to think of it. There don't seem to be any City Guards around at the moment. I hope They don't catch him – or us, listening to him.'

'Who're They?' whispered Tallow, puzzled and becoming warier all the time.

'Florum's men.' The fellow turned away, looking once more towards the centre of the circle. Tallow gathered that Florum was the ruler of this city.

'My friends, you know me well. I am not a man who hates. I feel only pity for Florum and his corrupt little underlings. I do not ask you to overthrow him or depose his government – all I ask is that you learn to live in harmony together. Forget your fears – your dislikes – and Florum will never be able to harm you!'

All very well, thought Tallow, but what if those Guards do turn up? He swivelled round, staring back into the market place. The preacher's voice certainly was sincere; there was no doubt that he believed what he said and, if the other man had been right, he had courage. The words meant little to Tallow, but he observed that the others were deeply impressed. Then he saw guards spreading out over the market place, coming towards the throng.

'Look out!' he yelled, before he knew it. 'Guards!'

Suddenly the rapt audience changed into a hundred frantic, frenzied, jostling fragments, fleeing in all directions. In seconds, only Tallow and the preacher were left – and the Guards. Mesmers, dressed in a simple blue robe, frayed at the edges, stood stock still, staring at them. Tallow acted.

'Come on!' he shouted, leaping forward and grabbing the white-haired man's arm. 'Come on – let's get away from here.' He hustled the preacher towards one of the many maze-like streets which wound from the market. He had almost to drag the preacher with him. Until, behind him, a gunshot blasted the hushed air; then the preacher began to run faster, but still reluctantly.

They ran on – boots clattering only a short distance away, shrill voices crying for them to halt.

'In here,' said Mesmers eventually, indicating a dark doorway. Tallow jumped inside. Mesmers opened the door and they entered a hall which was lightless.

'Thank you.' Mesmers' voice came out of the blackness as Tallow leaned against the wall, panting. 'You are a stranger here, are you not?'

'I am,' agreed Tallow, 'Tallow's the name.'

'Mesmers – Ophum Mesmers.'

'I heard you preaching back there. It – it sounded good.' Tallow was lying, he had hardly heard the preacher's words.

'Thank you again,' said Mesmers, and Tallow had the idea that the preacher was smiling. He heard Mesmers shuffle about. Eventually a candle was lighted and Tallow was amazed at the squalor of the room – not even in his home city had he seen such poverty and filth. He sat down on an upturned box. 'What do we do now?' he enquired.

'Hide for a bit,' Mesmers said practically; he looked round at Tallow, who was surprised to see that the teacher was far older than he had thought. He was incredibly ancient. His skin twisted like tree-bark up his face and his eyes were of sparkling blue, a blue which was pale, almost to greyness. They were humorous, wise and humane, zesty eyes which had found life good and worth the living. Glory Mesmers was a human being.

Tallow suddenly realized that he could love this man. He had never met anyone who made such a strange impression on him. He could serve him. There was wisdom in the preacher's old face – but it was not so much the wisdom which attracted Tallow – it was the deep knowledge he appeared to have. A knowledge of a basic thing – a knowledge of the truth – of God? He, thought Tallow, has found his barge. But how? If he stayed with him, he might discover how. It was necessary to remain.

The next few days were perilous days; days which astounded Tallow, for the atmosphere of suspicion and fear which dominated the entire city was like a sickness – a disease which spread, infecting Tallow.

He learned the art of sneaking, of shadow-hugging and of listening. Just as a herbivore's sensitive ears help protect it from the carnivore which hunts it, so were Tallow's ears his protection. Soon he could identify every sound in the stone jungle, for Tallow was a hunted foreigner and the police were after Mesmers, dead or alive.

Being a foreigner, and having physical characteristics both unusual and identifiable, Tallow could not even rely on sympathetic friends, other than Mesmers' small circle of allies. But he was close to the preacher, being his sense of fear, for Mesmers appeared unaware of his danger most of the time; either unaware or else unperturbed; it was hard to tell which.

Mesmers changed his headquarters several times a week, for informers were everywhere. Tallow attempted to convince him that he should leave the town – hide in the hills for a while and let the people come to the preacher. But Mesmers would not agree – he felt his duty, he said, and if he did not share the people's danger then he could not share their fears and hopes either. It was inarguable – but Tallow continued to argue. His respect and admiration for Mesmers had grown into a quiet thing and, for the first time since the sight of the golden barge, had, in effect, opened his eyes to the world around him; he knew peace. Like the city's atmosphere, Mesmers' enthusiasm for life, his faith in humanity, was catching.

It was the words of the preacher which worried Tallow. Words like God, Universal Brotherhood, Eternal Love, Good and Evil. These were all words which meant little to him. So it was not Mesmers' words which inspired him to action which had previously been alien to him. The very thought of risking his life for someone else would have shocked and dismayed him and even now he regretted his sacrifice in one way – though he could not define exactly why.

It was as if he had betrayed himself; betrayed his own character, for, basically, Tallow was still self-sufficient, selfish. He had loved and hated selfishly, with no ulterior motivation. He knew it, and was not ashamed. Why should he be? He had been complete.

But meeting Mesmers had destroyed his completeness, destroyed something of his cockiness. And he still feared the emotions which were growing inside him – even though the emotions were good, worthy. He could not help it – they were not Tallow's emotions, not the emotions of the Tallow that he had been all his life. Not the emotions of the Tallow he wished to be – they were too disturbing and distracting. They had already distracted him away from the barge and now they threatened to drive him to self-destruction. Sometimes he would be unable to sleep, the horror of what was happening to him would be so intense. Yet it took a few minutes in Mesmers' company to make him forget entirely his self-betrayal.

And so another decision loomed, but Tallow dared not admit it.

CHAPTER NINE

The room was hot, dark and full of the smoke and smell of burning oil-lamps. Some thirty people sat quietly on stools and chairs. At the front of the room, near the door, Glory Mesmers knelt, praying silently, unostentatiously. Eventually he arose and smiled welcome to those gathered in the room. Tallow sat at the other end of the room, idly staring at the dowdy backs and filthy hair of Mesmers' congregation. He was outside, not a part of them, and he resented their presence.

Mesmers' sermons bored Tallow, although it was obvious that the reaction of the audience was exactly the opposite. They would troop in with shifty eyes and bowed shoulders, not looking at one another, but when they left they would be standing straighter, smiling together with bright eyes. This was partly what Tallow resented – he hated this sharing. Although Mesmers' presence did much the same for him, he did not like to share his dark admiration. He was selfish.

Glory Mesmers began to speak slowly.

'How do most of you think of God?' he began. 'Is he a formless cloud of all-embracing love? A venerable white-haired ancient in the sky? A fiery sword of justice?'

Murmurs from the congregation. They did not appear to like the question. Tallow received a certain amount of satisfaction from this.

'He's all of those things,' said Mesmers, and the crowd relaxed. Tallow sneered to himself. Then Mesmers said: 'Shall I tell you how I see God? I see him in you – in myself – in Mr Tallow over there.'

Tallow was shocked and embarrassed. 'I see him in the walls of the room, in the lamps, in the smoke, in a day, in a cloudless sky, in a cloud, in a dog or a knife. I see him in all of these things because he *is* in all of them. They are him – he is them. God is nothing in particular – and he is everything. That is why our quarrels and our hates are wrong. Our job is to stick together – to love and respect everyone. Then, whatever Florum does to one of you, you will have the strength of all. Florum can fight hate with hate – but he cannot fight love. He cannot fight the strength you will have.'

Mesmers continued in this vein for another twenty minutes – answering questions, elaborating upon his theme, calm, friendly, persuasive, respectful of the opinions he heard. And as he talked, the tattered, dowdy people seemed to unite into a whole with Mesmers, becoming one entity, leaving a bored, resentful Tallow on the outside, still.

He waited impatiently for them to leave and then got up and walked over to Mesmers who was obviously deep in thought.

'Mr Mesmers,' he said respectfully; but Mesmers did not appear to hear him. 'Mr Mesmers.'

Mesmers remained in his reverie. Tallow stretched out an arm to touch the preacher on the shoulder, but then he changed his mind. He opened the door and looked out into the street. There was a man standing in the opposite doorway, looking at Tallow. He averted his eyes immediately and began to stroll off with studied calmness, down the street. Tallow knew that he was a spy for Florum, he could sense it in every movement of the man. He hastily closed the door, went over to Mesmers and shook him.

'What is is, Tallow?'

'Someone's been watching the house – must have seen the crowd leaving. He saw me. We must leave, quickly.'

Mesmers sighed. 'Very well – we'll get out by the back way.' As he spoke they heard a discreet tap on the outside door. Tallow again guessed that this was no member of Mesmers' congregation – it was an old trick of Florum's Guards. Thumping would alert anyone inside – a discreet tap would mean, they thought, a friend. Tallow knew better. He hurried Mesmers through the house, into the back streets. Soldiers were waiting at both ends of an alley.

His heart was pounding, his mouth dry and twitching. Tallow forced himself to think as panic seized him. He grabbed Mesmers roughly and threw him into a doorway, quickly following him. The door was locked, but rickety. Tallow shoved his puny body against it and it rocked. He kicked at it savagely, frantically, and it burst inwards. Then they were in a small, evil-smelling room occupied by an old man in a disgusting bed. A fire smoked in a grate and the old man looked up, eyes bright with fever. He coughed horribly and saliva dribbled down his chin.

'What's this?' he wheezed. 'Robbers? Looters? Is Florum deposed?'

'No – he seeks us – we're wanted men.' Tallow could not afford to waste words on this ancient. 'Where does that room lead?' He indicated a door.

'Ladder to upstairs – but . . .'

'Thanks,' panted Tallow, hustling Mesmers through the door, closing it once they were through. It was not locked. They heard the soldiers enter the room they had just vacated. The old man's voice was high with a note of fear, the soldiers' voices were grunts, impatient and angry.

'I don't know! I don't know! Please – stop it!' Thumps and threats, the old man's voice pleading, the only words they could hear clearly.

Mesmers made to go back into the room. 'I can't let him be ill-treated for my sake,' he whispered passionately, his eyes full of pain.

'Fool!' growled Tallow, 'you're more important than a dying old man. He's served a useful purpose for once – come on!' He grabbed Mesmers by his frayed robe and forced him up a ladder. But Mesmers, when they had reached a loft, still made to go back. Tallow hit him – smashed him on the side of the neck with a balled fist and the old man moaned, then lost consciousness. From somewhere downstairs there came a terrible, animal scream – like a pig in pain, changing suddenly to an atrocious gurgling; a bubbling moan.

Tallow shuddered and humped the old preacher on to his back as footfalls sounded beneath him and a red-smeared bayonet appeared in the loft's entrance. Up another ladder he went, struggling with the sprawling body of the preacher, stopping a moment to haul the ladder after him.

On and on – up and up, through a dark, squalid maze of tiny rooms. Sometimes he disturbed families, women and men, broods of children, huddled like nesting field-mice. He would scatter them in his wild flight, and all he would see would be white, frightened faces, stick-like arms, and shifting sacks which were bodies.

Every so often he would stop to remove a ladder, while the thumping of the soldiers would grow quieter and quieter, farther and farther away until he could no longer hear them. Then he paused for breath, taking the foul air of the building in with great racking sobs, his lungs feeling as if they had been seared by fire, his chest a heavy thing, full of dull, aching pain. His arms were weary from bearing

Mesmers' unconscious weight and his legs shook, threatening to collapse and leave him helpless.

But he let himself rest for only a couple of minutes before heaving the preacher up and climbing two more ladders. The final ladder took him on to the roof. He hauled the ladder after him, laid it carefully on the filthy stone and swung the cover of the manhole down, battening it with a half-rotten length of timber.

A low parapet surrounded the roof. He staggered over to it and looked down. It was a long drop, some eighty or a hundred feet to the street. Little dots had completely surrounded the building.

Tallow could not afford to waste time thinking too deeply. He had to keep acting. It was the only thing which would save Mesmers and himself. It was four or five feet to the next building. Tallow knew that he would not be able to jump the gap – especially with Mesmers' weight.

Then he remembered the ladder. It was about six feet long. He grasped it and swung it out over the gap. It bounced on the opposite parapet. He tested it as best he could by leaning outwards and pressing his weight on to it with his hands. It felt weak, but there was nothing for it but to risk the crossing.

Once again Mesmers, now beginning to moan, was heaved over his shoulder. Shakily he clambered onto the parapet, not daring to look down. Then he placed a foot on the ladder and ran across it. He had absolutely no recollection of the crossing. Only the first few steps outwards, then he was safe and hauling the ladder after him.

Four times he made crossings from building to building, with gaining confidence, but with no memory of the drop beneath him. Then, feeling sick and weary, he collapsed onto the greasy stone of a roof. His head was near Mesmers' head and the old man was groaning, his eyes flickering open, his old, delicate hands fluttering like white doves up to his head where Tallow had hit him.

Tallow looked at him. 'We're saved,' he whispered. 'I saved you.'

Mesmers' tone was chiding, almost angry. He said: 'At what expense, Tallow?' That was all. Then he was silent again. They remained like this for several hours until darkness came and they slept.

Tallow awoke just as the night was changing into the grey of morning. He stretched aching limbs and yawned. The cold morning air bit into his throat and lungs, reviving him. Mesmers was gone.

It took several seconds for Tallow to realize this. He was up in an instant, then, looking around the expanse of grey roof. Mesmers was not there, and the ladder remained where Tallow had dropped it the previous night.

But a manhole into the roof was open, like a fledgeling's mouth, agape in surprise, mimicking Tallow's own expression.

He went over to the hole and stared downwards. He could see nothing but blackness. Desperately he wriggled into the hole, hung by his hands and dropped, landing on bare boards. There was no one in the room. He hastily made for the door and tore it open. No one. This house was better designed than the one through which he had made his escape. A landing was outside and stairs led downwards. He ran for the stairs, leaping down them, heedless of the noise he was making. No one came out of doors to stare at him. The house might have been empty for all the notice that was taken of Tallow as he leaped desperately downwards.

He saw Mesmers' robe, now streaked with filth, disappearing out of the street door as he reached the last landing. Not daring to call, he ran after him, eventually catching him up as he turned a corner of the street.

'Why did you leave me, Mr Mesmers?' he gasped.

'I do not want you to sin for me again, Tallow,' replied the preacher without looking at the little man or slackening his pace.

'But you need me, sir – you need me. You'd be in Florum's prison if it wasn't for me.'

'I do not need you, Tallow – you have only succeeded in interfering.'

Tallow's mind was a whirlpool of desperate thoughts as he tried to understand the import of Mesmers' words.

'Then I need you,' he said craftily, and truthfully. 'I need you, sir. Don't leave me like this after all I've done to help you. Help me now, sir. Help me.'

'You have rejected the kind of help I can give you; you may stay with me, however, on condition that you listen to what I have to say. Stop interfering in my destiny.'

'But your destiny is mine.'

'It might have been,' said Mesmers, regret in his voice. 'It might well have been – once.'

'What have I done wrong – tell me and I'll make amends. I swear it.'

Mesmers stopped at a door. Tallow knew it was one of their places of refuge. He turned and contemplated Tallow, pity in his wise eyes.

'Your reasons for helping me have not been the right reasons. I have been responsible for the death of a man – because of you. I do not *need* you Tallow – our association will lead to further violence. More death – more unhappiness for these unhappy people. I offer them life – you could bring them nothing but pain and grief – your own pain, your own grief. Can't you see that?'

'No! You are unjust.'

'I have tried to be just – perhaps you are right. But I think not. Your sins are grey about you.'

'What sins? I have never sinned – I would know it if I had. I do not know it.'

Mesmers sighed and entered the house. Tallow followed him, clutching at his robe. 'I do not know it,' he repeated, 'so I have not sinned – have I? If what you said about every man knowing deep in himself that he has sinned is true – then I am innocent.' Tallow felt a tiny surge of triumph.

Mesmers closed the door and looked deeply into Tallow's eyes, the pity still in his gaze – a hopeless pity.

'If you do not know, then perhaps my faith is wrong – I hope not. But if you do not know – then all I have said is doubly true.'

Suddenly Tallow felt relieved and his attitude altered. His affection for Mesmers, this alien self-sacrifice, had been like chains on his legs for too long. Now he saw a way out of his dilemma. This was the turning point; he could be free again.

'Fool!' he sneered. 'Blind idiot! You are no visionary! You are nothing in this city, you waste your time upon others and they hate you for it. *You* are the person who matters – not the others, they are dragging you down with them – and I would have followed you. I have realized this at last, thank God.'

Mesmers stood in silence, his ancient face calm. Tallow raved on, submerging the feeling of insignificance which Mesmers' stare instilled in him; submerging the feelings in rage: 'You've denied your own destiny. I'll leave you – though I tried to save you. I have a purpose greater than yours!'

He wrenched the door open and went out into the street.

'Come back, Jephraim!' said Mesmers suddenly. 'You'll be caught and shot if you go out at this hour! Come back man. If you must go, wait until nightfall!'

But Tallow was heedless of the preacher's warning. He marched out towards the river, knowing that the barge would take weeks to catch up with. But it was his only hope.

Mesmers called again, urgently. Tallow ignored the cry. His destiny beckoned.

CHAPTER TEN

Soon, Tallow's calculating mind came once more to his aid as he realized his danger. He kept to back streets, following tortuous alleys to the river-side, uncertain of how he was going to get out of the city, for every gate was guarded.

He slunk onwards, his rage quiet and unreasonable within him. He was determined to get to the gates and then decide what to do when faced with the decision.

It took him two hours of pausing, hiding and scurrying before he could reach the city wall. Following it along, he finally came to a gate. Three Guards leant against the wall, wary and watchful. They had increased the number of soldiers – probably because of the chase of the previous day.

He shrunk back onto shadow as one of them turned to look in his direction. But he had not been quick enough.

'Hey! You! Come out of that alley and show yourself.' Tallow swallowed down the panic which rose inside him and ran hastily back the way he had come.

'I could swear it was the red-haired midget we're after!' he heard the Guard shout to his friends. 'Cript, come with me – there's a reward on his head!'

Now Tallow's only emotion was fear; it embraced him – dominated him – drove him recklessly away from the shouting Guards. He fled.

He fled for three days – ruthlessly hunted. He became a frightened animal, cowering and afraid; skulking in sewers, hiding in the houses of a few people he thought he could trust. But betrayal always sent him running again. Three days were spent in scuttling and skulking; they were weary days, for he dare not allow himself to succumb to sleep. Cocky, self-reliant, selfish Tallow learned what it was to depend on others – to trust a glib-tongued informer and discover that the man was leading soldiers to his hiding place. Soon Tallow forgot everything save his need to escape.

Then, one day, Mesmers found him.

'You are sick,' said Mesmers to the unshaven, shivering wretch who pleaded to him. 'You should have listened, my friend.'

'I'll listen now – I will. Save me – hide me – that's all I ask, sir. Save me – I should have listened. I've been pursued and shot at – I've been fooled and betrayed. You were right, Mr Mesmers – oh, you were right, sir. Hide me now – please.'

Mesmers frowned, hating what Tallow had become, hating what had made him the thing he now was. 'I will hide you until it is safe for you to leave,' he said. 'Then you will go away from here.'

'But suppose they catch me when I leave – they'll kill me. My blood'll pour out – I'll die. They'll torture me, sir, for you. They'll want to know where you are and they'll make me tell them. They will, sir – they will. Save me.' Tallow sobbed horribly, clawing at Mesmers' robe with a hand caked in filth.

'We'll see,' said Mesmers. 'But first you must rest.' Several young men, followers of the preacher, came forward at a signal and grasped Tallow, dragging him away from the old man.

'Put him to bed, my friends,' murmured Mesmers, looking at Tallow. 'Make him sleep. Later we'll attempt to smuggle him out. I owe him that.'

But it was not easy for Tallow to sleep. Mesmers or one of his followers remained always at Tallow's bedside, listening to the moans and screams as Tallow relived the three days of terror in his nightmares. Occasionally Tallow would wake up, shrieking and roaring and he had to be quietened. Silence was the order of the day of Florum's rule.

It was Mesmers with his quiet voice and persuasive manner who virtually hypnotised Tallow into a deep sleep; Mesmers who effected Tallow's cure and helped the little man recover some of his self-respect and assurance. Mesmers, against his better judgement, built a new Tallow after the pattern of the old – for he could not build an entirely new Tallow without new materials. He gave Tallow back his cockiness. He gave Tallow what had been taken away from him. And he knew that his gift was a seed – a seed which had nearly destroyed the man he was now saving. If Mesmers had not been an optimist, he would have despaired.

Soon, Tallow was grinning his old fool's grin, his wide-mouthed, sharp-toothed grin – his crocodile smile. He sat up in the bed – Mesmers' bed – and cocked his head at the preacher.

'Thank you,' he said, without gratitude. 'You certainly knew how to cure me, didn't you? The credit's square now. I saved you; you saved me. I'll be on my way as soon as I've rested a little more.'

Mesmers nodded sadly and got up. There were dark patches under his eyes which showed that he had slept even less than usual. He walked tiredly away from Tallow, and his shoulders drooped. 'I'll make sure you leave the town safely,' he sighed, 'but I shan't see you again, Mr Tallow.'

'Goodbye,' grinned Tallow, folding his arms behind his head and sinking back onto his pillows. 'I hope you make out!'

'Goodbye.' Mesmers left slowly and was soon gone. Tallow heard the outer door close.

Two days later an old woman in a shawl shuffled away from the house where Tallow had been resting. The old woman was Tallow.

In his disguise, Tallow hoped to reach the quayside and mingle with the crowd which gathered there every day to watch the ships come in. There, Mesmers' followers had said, he might be able to stow away on one of the foreign boats – or steal a boat if he could do so without too much risk.

The disguise was perfect. He acted his part perfectly, a battered basket on one arm, the other hand clutching his shawl about his head, hiding his face in shadow.

No one even glanced at him – there were so many poor old women in the city. When he reached the main street which led towards the quayside, he joined a slowly-moving crowd which was walking purposefully in the direction of the river. There was a fence cutting off the dock area from the rest of the city and the fence was guarded, but the crowd was allowed through. His heart thumping, Tallow passed a Guard he recognized, but the Guard was staring hard at a young girl, to his left, who walked behind her father. The Guard leered, all his thoughts concentrated, for the moment, on the girl. Tallow began to view things with more calm. So far, it had been easier to get to the quay than he had originally thought.

The tall ships came into sight and Tallow was instantly filled with longing. Each ship offered escape – and more. Each ship was a means of following the golden barge. Several small one-man boats of a type Tallow was familiar with, bobbed among the larger craft. One of those would be excellent.

He followed the crowd, coming to a standstill on one side of the quay. Men were busy loading and unloading goods to and from the many ships. But the place was still thick with sour-faced Guards, watchful Guards, distrustful of any sign which was other than normal.

Tallow relaxed and waited for his opportunity.

It came at last when there was a disturbance on the opposite side of the quay. Tallow could not make out what was causing it, but it held the Guards' attention. They swung menacing rifles towards it and Tallow heard rough voices demanding something. The Guards began to move in the direction of the noise. Tallow started running.

He ran for the river, hearing a yell behind him. A rifle-shot exploded quite close to him, but he kept running. Then Guards were converging from all directions, some lumbering to cut off his escape towards the water. He stared around him wildly, encircled by gleaming bayonets.

Then, desperately, he pointed towards the crowd – 'He's in there – Mesmers is in the crowd. He made me run out so that he could get away.' The Guards wavered, uncertain.

'It's true!' shouted Tallow. 'He'll get away. He's wanted dead or alive!'

Guns began to level on the crowd. Seeing their danger, the people attempted to draw back. A captain bawled an order: 'Stay where you are – nobody move.'

But the crowd was frightened now. They began to run, knocking one another aside in their haste.

'Fire! Fire!'

Gunshots cracked and two men fell.

'Stop!'

But the gunshots had served to turn the crowd into a panicking mass. They scattered in all directions over the quayside. The Guards fired blindly into them, attempting to stop the rush for the fence. The girl who had distracted the gate Guard's attention fell, screaming. Two boys leapt high and fell, kicking, to the ground, clutching their thighs, trying to stop the pain which flowed in their bodies.

Tallow ripped off his shawl, and turned towards the river. He dived in and struck out for a motor-boat moored nearby. Two of the Guards saw him. They aimed their guns at him. Bullets splattered around him in the water, but he reached the boat.

He hauled himself into the tiny cabin and started the motor. It roared. Zestfully the propeller churned the muddy waters of the river, driving the boat forward.

Tallow laughed at the helpless Guards and ducked as a bullet whistled by. Several soldiers ran for two larger boats moored together. Tallow increased speed and had soon left the quayside, laughing all the while in mad relief.

On the quayside, the people were still running – running towards the opposite end, where the original disturbance had came from. As if participating in a macabre game of hare-and-hounds, they left a trail of bleeding bodies in their wake. A smaller group, who had remained still, staring at Tallow, while the larger crowd had fled, made no move to run. The crowd reached them and engulfed them.

Two of the members of the group fell dead as bullets tore into the mass of flesh which screamed in panic. Some of them were climbing the fence now, many to be picked off by bullets. Bodies hung like dirty washing over the fence. Then the crowd stopped and looked fearfully back at the soldiers.

The captain shouted again: 'Stop, now! We wish to make an inspection. You have nothing to fear if you are innocent!' Cowed, the crowd subsided.

The captain and two lieutenants moved among the people, inspecting the bodies and the faces of the living.

One of the soldiers called to the captain.

'He was right, sir – look!'

He pulled a dark cloak away from an ancient, blue-robed man. A man with white hair and staring, humane eyes. A man with a pale face, with skin of twisted tree-bark, down which blood now coursed – a hundred miniature rivers of red, from head, from mouth and from two wounds in the body.

'It's Mesmers all right, sir. I've seen him several times, preaching in the market place. We've got him at last, sir.'

'Yes,' smiled the captain, like a shark. 'It's him. So our little friend didn't lie. Is the preacher still alive?'

'Yes, sir. I think so.' The lieutenant bent down beside the old man. His eyes flickered.

'I – was – wrong – I suppose,' gasped Mesmers. 'I should not – have – rebuilt – him. He – destroyed – me – as I – knew he would.'

'What's he talking about?'

'Don't know – probably about his little rat of a friend, sir. These people are all the same – betray anyone if they think they're saving themselves. Shouldn't be surprised if the little man was the red-haired midget who rescued Mesmers a few times in the last couple of weeks. Funny thing, that – saving him, then getting him killed.'

He stared down at Mesmers. The preacher stared back, glassily, soullessly. Mesmers was dead.

'What a bastard thing to do,' murmured the lieutenant, staring down-river. Tallow's boat had disappeared, but the two larger craft were giving chase, overweighted with men. 'What a bastard thing to do!'

'Come on, lieutenant,' said the captain impatiently, 'let's get the corpse to headquarters. There should be a nice little bit in this for all of us – you'll be able to buy your girlfriend that ring she wants, now.'

The young soldier smiled, cheering up at once: 'So I shall, sir,' he said. 'Hadn't thought of it.'

Two Guards hefted Mesmers' pitiful corpse between them and began to cart it off. The young lieutenant looked back once more down-river. 'Funny, that . . .' he said to himself, following his captain.

Meanwhile, a jaunty Tallow, unaware of the death of Mesmers, easily outdistanced the overloaded pursuing boats and looked happily ahead, hoping for a glimpse of the barge.

CHAPTER ELEVEN

Miranda didn't like the look of the captain, but she had no choice, his was the only ship available. She put her bag down at her feet and looked up at him. His eyes moved over her body, not meeting her eyes for some seconds. She pursed her lips.

'How far are you going down-river?' she asked.

'How far?' He rubbed his stubbly chin with one hand and scratched the back of his inhabited head with the other.

'How far are you going?'

'Two hundred miles, maybe, more or less.'

'Fair enough. Will this pay for it?' She displayed a bag of coin. 'It's gold.'

'Yes,' he said. She could tell by his eyes that it was more than enough.

'Of course I'll want a private cabin,' she added quickly.

'Of course,' he said tonelessly.

'Then I'll get on board,' she said in a hard voice, quite unlike her usual one. 'When do you cast off?'

'Four o'clock,' he replied. 'In an hour's time.'

'Thanks,' she said.

She had left her arrangements for as late as possible. The man she had obtained the money from might follow her and demand that she return. Not that she had been particularly unhappy with him; it was simply that he wasn't Tallow. Her search for, and pursuit of Tallow had become an obsession. She still loved him.

The cabin was bare of ornament, and small, though clean. A bunk was erected on the port side and a locker opposite it. That was all. The sailor who showed her the cabin said; 'I'll bring you hot water for washing every morning at eight, ma'am. You'll get your breakfast in your cabin at about eight-thirty, give or take a bit.'

'Thank you.' She smiled. The sailor was big and handsome. He looked at her shyly – the way she liked some men to look at her. 'The trip should be pleasant.'

'I hope so, ma'am,' he said.

'So do I.' She smiled again, looking at him through hinting eyes. She couldn't help it – it was habit with her. Anyway, she qualified, my love for Tallow isn't purely sexual, otherwise I wouldn't bother to do what I'm doing now. I'll follow him – but I certainly shan't bother to be faithful to the bastard. Her deep, aching longing for her deserter was eased a little by this thought. She smiled a third time: to herself.

Hers had been a long, hard journey. When she had eventually struggled ashore, she had had to walk miles to a town. There she had easily made friends, eventually winding up with the mayor. From him she had procured her fare down as far as the next town – for she had to leave quite suddenly when the mayoress discovered her husband's attachment.

And so she had gone on, getting her fare, moving when she could – or when she had to. And at last she had found a rich man and a ship travelling an appreciable distance. The two combined had been an excellent stroke of luck.

She still didn't know why she was following Tallow. He had treated her atrociously; but she knew he still loved her. Her ego had been shattered, that was all – and she was not altogether happy about her soaking and subsequent travelling. One part of her mind maliciously promised her that she would make Tallow cringe when she caught up with him. And she was going to catch up with him – it was necessary.

So she began to unpack her few belongings, waiting impatiently for the ship to leave the berth. If she knew her Tallow, he would not have got very far ahead.

CHAPTER TWELVE

Tallow had caught up with the barge. It was only about quarter of a mile distant. But the weather was bad. Wind howled around him and the river was choppy and dangerous at this wide stretch. The swirling water and wind did not affect the barge in the slightest. It went purposefully on – calm, implacable, imperturbable, moving down the river as if the water did not exist. The currents which so confused Tallow had absolutely no effect upon the steadily-moving golden ship. They did not shift it one inch from the path it steered in the very middle of the river. Tallow was not amazed or confused by this. He had come to expect it. Otherwise there would have been no point in following. He was excited, however, and annoyed at the sudden change in the weather, which had occurred just as he had sighted the barge again. It was always the same. Whenever he had a chance to catch up with it, something happened to divert him – man or nature. Was it his doom to follow it eternally – or was there a chance of it leading him to something? At that moment, for some reason, as he battled with the elements, it did not seem to matter at all.

A few days earlier, when he had left the city in such haste, he had been hard-pressed to elude the gunboats and river-bank patrols which searched for him, but now Florum's men had given up the chase.

Tallow regretted the fact that he had been responsible for a number of the citizens losing their lives, but he balanced this by telling himself that if he had been caught and tortured, he might have betrayed Mesmers and he still felt admiration for the preacher whilst abhoring his ideals.

What a companion on a voyage such as mine, he thought. This is his place, beside me, following the barge. But he had a nagging feeling in the back of his mind that perhaps Mesmers had already followed the barge – and discovered its ultimate destination. Hadn't the old preacher said something to that effect at some time? He thought so. But he couldn't remember the moment. Perhaps when he had been raving after his ordeal? No – it wasn't any good, he couldn't be certain.

But suppose the barge led him to those horrible acts of self-sacrifice of which Mesmers had been guilty? No – he had to be sure that the barge led a man to his personal destiny – depending on the man. If he, Tallow, was strong, as he was, then his destiny would be that much more certain, surely?

Tallow saw that his boat was being forced to one side of the river bank. Hastily, he corrected the course and plugged on after the barge which was swiftly outdistancing him.

He cursed and fumed, but it was no good; the barge, without increasing its speed, was making far better progress than he was.

Eventually it had disappeared from his sight once more and, for the moment, he gave up the chase. There would be only one thing to do – wait for better weather, and then attempt to make up for lost time.

He guided the boat over to the river bank and tied it up to a tree-trunk. The boat had been well-stocked with equipment and provisions, including a tent. He would pitch the tent on the shore and sleep, then he would continue in the morning.

Making sure that the boat was moored securely, he jumped onto the bank, throwing his tent in front of him. The ground was damp and squelched beneath his feet as he walked through the silent wood, water dripping from the branches, mingling with the rain and sweat on his face. It was peaceful in the woods, in contrast to the turbulent waters of the river. A good place to rest.

In a glade, shielded by trees, the ground had absorbed much of the water into itself – and the surface, protected by turf, made a better spot than most for pitching his tent. As he began to adjust the tent-poles and check the guy-ropes, he heard a peculiar wailing noise coming from a hillock a few yards away.

Curious, he went over to investigate and found a baby.

It was an ugly, skinny child, about two months old. It lay in a cot of woven twigs and sodden blankets covered it. Tallow bent down and removed the blankets, picked up the child and replaced the damp cloth with his cloak turned inside out. The baby ceased to wail and began to gurgle happily.

Tallow picked up the cot and took it over to where he had planned to pitch the tent. Leaving the child, he erected the tent and placed the cot inside.

He decided that the baby had probably been left out to starve by some woman who couldn't keep it. Well, it could wait until morning. He managed to feed it some milk and then got into his sleeping bag and slept, heedless, during the night, of the occasional wails from the baby.

Next morning he set off in the opposite direction from the river, intent on discovering the baby's owner. He reasoned that there must be some collection of cottages, or town, nearby.

He was right. Coming out of the wood on a morning which was sunny, bright and cloudless, he saw the smoke of chimneys some distance away to the west. The baby's cot was heavy in his arms, but he didn't want to be responsible for its death and knew from experience that people were usually soft enough to take a baby in. All he knew was that he wasn't.

As he got nearer to the village, he noticed that the fields surrounding it were barren. Trees were rotting and an evil smell pervaded the whole area. Occasionally he passed a dead animal, its stomach bloated and distended, flies crawling over it. Cattle, horses, sheep and pigs were scattered like seeds over the countryside. A few wild deer, rabbits and hares were also in presence, in the same condition as the domestic animals. It was these which were the cause of the vile odour.

Soon the putrid corpses were piled high by the road-side, the marks of some leprous plague on their rotting hides. And everywhere were flies. Big, fat flies, gorging on the foul remains. It was like a battlefield – which had had knightly mules and proud pigs as its participants, instead of men. The further Tallow went, the more he wanted to vomit as the number of corpses increased. Once or twice he saw a human corpse, bloated, putrid and bearing the signs of the same disease as the animals.

Tallow debated whether it was wise to continue. The plague which had killed so many was a thing to be avoided. But the child was not his responsibility. He could only go on – in his boat it would hamper his progress.

The grey thatch of cottages lay ahead and smoke hung over it, clinging like an obscene bat to the area which the village occupied. For a mile, it seemed, there were only varying shades of grey. The village was bereft of colour. The nearer Tallow came to the place, the louder became the crackling of fire, the more pungent the smell of burnt flesh.

He recalled the witch-burnings of his boyhood. Yes, the smell was familiar. But screams and laughter were not apparent. Obviously the witch was roasted, if, of course, witch it was who blazed.

Hovering on the outskirts of the village, shifting from one foot to the other, Tallow attempted to peer through the deathladen smoke, but it was impossible to make much out. He could see nothing but a flicker of fire and a few moving shapes in the murk. The sound of men walking and the grunt of human voices told him that the village was inhabited.

Reassured, he continued his way towards the fire. All around him rose the walls of cottages, menacing sentinels.

Then he saw them. Tattered skeletons moving near the fire, and then drawing back from it, like a tide. They flung burdens on to the fire.

Tallow shivered; the stench of death was everywhere, fouling the atmosphere. As he neared the skeleton figures, one turned and saw him. Tallow was nauseated, there seemed hardly a shred of flesh on the man – yet he lived. Blotches of green, mauve and yellow spattered their way over his face. Only his eyes were dark – staring out of holes in his skull.

'What do you want?' said the man hollowly.

'I have brought a child I found in the forest. It was abandoned.'

'Take it away – and leave while you can.'

'But I cannot keep it.'

'Neither can we.'

'Surely there's a woman here who'll take it in.'

'No.'

'There must be.'

'There is no woman who can spare food for a stranger-child.'

'Are you the head man of the village?'

'No.'

'Then I want to see him.'

'He is dead.'

'Did he die of the plague?'

'No. He starved to death.'

'If the baby remains with me, it will starve also. Surely you don't want that.'

'I can do nothing about it.'

Tallow jerked his way through the staring villagers, going up to a woman; she looked at him apathetically.

'Will you take the baby?'

'No.'

'Would you let a child starve?'

'My children have starved to death.'

'This one will take their place.'

'On the fire?'

Tallow looked desperately about him, ringed by dull skulls.

'Someone *must* take the baby!'

No answer.

'They *must*!'

The villagers turned away and began to throw more burdens on to the fire. Tallow saw that the burdens were corpses – flopping, skinny bodies.

'Where's the next village?'

A grey bone pointed westwards.

'Five miles.'

'Wretches – pitiless horrors! May the plague take you all!'

Then Tallow fled westwards, running hard, the cradle like a boulder in his arms. The skeletons watched him leave and one of them smiled – a gaping split in his head.

Tallow did not pause until a hill obscured the village and he could only see the slowly rising smoke above it. Then he stopped for a moment, before resuming his trek westwards with long striding steps.

He felt bile in his throat and his thoughts were constantly upon the safety of the boat he had left miles back at the riverbank.

He knew he had reached the next village. The smoke hovering over a valley told him where to find it.

It was a larger village, with a larger fire and even fewer of the living-dead. Fire blazed on some rooftops, and houses crumbled. Two stark-eyed horses sped by bearing fleshless naked riders who held torches in their talons and flung flame wherever they passed.

Apart from the thumping hooves and the sound of fire, there was silence. It was as if the smoke was a cloak, muffling most noise.

Tallow plucked the child from its blanket and flung the cot upon a blazing heap of bodies. Then, with less weight to carry, he backed out of the village and loped towards the hills. He was frantic and furious. His luck had left him.

The child woke up and began to wail. Tallow quieted it by the simplest method he knew. He put his hand over its mouth. Such noise seemed sacrilege.

He coughed and spat a vile taste from his throat. As he ran on, the two riders galloped past him, racing one another up the valley slopes. Torches still flared in their hands and their ribs tore through their pale hides.

Humped over their steeds, they reached the top of the hill and disappeared. Tallow stumbled after them, hearing his own voice crying to them, but he could not hear the words.

For the rest of the day, Tallow scoured the miles which lay eastwards and westwards, and everywhere he saw smoke, sometimes riders, but he avoided them wherever possible. He could not stop the baby's crying, and soon he was no longer aware of it.

Tortured and torn, Tallow grew aimless. His mind was chaotic, his loneliness, never previously sensed, a terrible thing. The world took on proportions of towering fear and creeping horror and he felt he must be in Hell as he staggered over the dreadful countryside, the baby clutched to his chest. The child was linked to him by disturbing ties and he could not now be rid of it. There was no one to help him – no mother, no Miranda, no Mesmers. He was alone, completely, and could see no way out of the circumstances he had effected.

He had denied his mother, his lover and his teacher and, lacking these, had taken a responsibility upon himself which he was incapable of accepting.

For the first time, the travesty became like one of his fellow human beings; a condition brought about by the combined influences of those he encountered on his trip down river. Again he experienced mental anguish and subjective emotion, but this time he did not fear it – he could not. It engulfed him.

Hemmed in by smoking villages and the horrors of famine and plague, he soon lost all sense of direction.

The hills were heaving mounds of green slime, waiting to smother him. The valleys were gaping maws waiting to gobble him. There was no escape, nowhere to hide. Nowhere to go.

Then the river flashed ahead. With a sob of thanks he ran towards it, reached it, wetted his aching head in it, embraced it; the child lying helpless beside him on the grass.

He ran upriver, anxiously scanning the bank for his boat. He found it where he'd left it. An old wizened man stood near it, regarding it through benevolent eyes. His face was shielded by a battered, broad-brimmed hat and he smiled amiably at Tallow as he approached. Seeing the man, Tallow was reminded of the baby he had left further down.

'A baby,' he said. 'Down there.' He pointed. The old man's benevolence and amiability, at close quarters, was the outward sign of his senility, for he only grinned and nodded at Tallow.

'Do you understand?' asked Tallow abruptly.

'Yeth,' replied the old man through a mouth devoid of teeth, wet and wrinkled.

'Will you look after it?'
'Yeth.' But he did not move.
'You're sure?'
'Yeth.'
Tallow boarded his boat and cast off. The man on the bank remained still, smiling at Tallow, his eyes dim and blank.
'You're sure?'
The wizened ancient had turned away.
'You're sure?' Tallow called after him, but he didn't hear the shout.
Tallow soulfully started the motor; it throbbed angrily, turning the propeller, churning the water.
In a few moments, he had gone past the wailing child and was on his way down-river again.

CHAPTER THIRTEEN

Tallow regarded the men bleakly, fatalistically.
It was two days since he had left the place of the smoking villages. He accepted the fact that he was to be delayed again and hoped that it would be for only a short time.
He had been waylaid by the ruffians as he rested on the bank beside the boat. They were bearded and garbed in the remnants of uniforms, originally of some neutral colour which had been obscured by grime. Their lean hands were moulded around guns – pistols and rifles.
'What do you want? I've nothing of value – and I need my boat,' said Tallow sadly.
'We want your boat,' answered the foremost, grinning a wolf's grin. 'And information.'
'I need my boat, and I have no information of use to you.'
'Where are you from?'
'Many towns up-river.'
'Where are you bound?'
'I don't know.'
'You don't know? You don't know where you're going? Then why are you so anxious to keep your boat?'
'I am following another ship. A great golden barge – perhaps you've seen it pass?'
'We've seen no craft of the sort you describe. *We* need your boat. Let's not have to shoot you. Join us or die.' He rattled off the last sentence in the same way as a hungry child rattles off grace.
'But –'
'It's your choice, friend. We've little time to waste.'

'I'll join you,' said Tallow hastily. 'But what am I joining?'

'Zhist's Army. The Free Fighters.'

Tallow whimpered under his breath. 'I'll join,' he said. 'I'll join any army of men fighting for freedom. Yes, indeed, the prospect arouses the old fire in my heart. What do you want me to do, comrade?'

The soldier smirked cynically at Tallow. 'Let us make use of your boat,' he said.

'Certainly,' assented Tallow. 'It is yours.'

'I know,' grinned the soldier. Then he said: 'You can help us load the crates.'

Tallow was escorted back into the bushes. Here were more men of the same stamp, sitting on long wooden boxes, like coarse coffins. They all had the appearance of carnivores which had been fed on fruit for months. They were lean, fox-featured and half-starved. Some of them got up as Tallow and the others entered the clearing.

'This the boatman?' growled one of them, jerking his thumb at Tallow.

'Yes – he's joined us. We'll have to have him vetted by Zhist, of course. But that'll be later. Meanwhile, he loads with us – and drives that boat.'

'Very well, let's get started.'

Tallow lifted one end of a crate and the speaker took the other. They staggered with it to the boat. The man made to heave it on, but Tallow stopped him.

'I'll supervise the stacking,' he said. 'You could capsize her by doing that.'

The soldier looked at his leader, questioningly. The leader nodded. Tallow skipped aboard and began to check the loading.

Soon the boat was low in the water, heavy with crates. The leader joined Tallow in the small cabin. 'Now,' he said, 'steer where I direct. It was lucky you came along. It would have taken days to have carted this lot overland. And we've no time to waste.'

It took hours – and Tallow was forced to guide his boat into a smaller stream which joined the main river. This wound for miles inland.

Then they disembarked and pushed their way through thick near-tropical vegetation. Tallow had soon lost all his sense of direction but somehow the leader of the ambushers – Niko – appeared to know exactly where he was going.

They broke out into a clearing as the sun set. Thick with tents and shanties, it was smeared with sprawled bodies and tiny camp-fires. A few men stood around talking. Slatternly women cooked over fires and everywhere guns were stacked against the sides of the makeshift shacks and tents.

'This way,' instructed Niko, leading Tallow towards a shack, larger than the rest, which occupied the centre of the clearing. He stopped and knocked on the side.

'Who is it?' The voice coming from the depths of the hut was low and vibrant, like a cat's purr.

'This is Niko. I've brought along a new recruit for you to have a look at – his name's Tallow. We commandeered his boat, Colonel Zhist.'

'Enter.'

The interior of the hut was dark and smelled predominantly of foul pipe-tobacco. When Tallow's eyes became accustomed to the darkness he saw a man only six inches taller than he. A short man with a thin fringe of beard, large brown eyes and a tight mouth dominated by an eagle's beak of a nose. His head was sharp and tapering, his body thin and wiry.

'Thanks, Niko, you can go,' said Zhist, nodding to his lieutenant. 'Tallow is a stranger here, is he not?' His voice was soft and precise.

'Yes, sir,' replied Niko as he got up and ducked out of the shack.

When Niko had left, Zhist signed for Tallow to squat down beside him. He was puffing on a large pipe. He waved a pouch of tobacco at Tallow who accepted it and stuffed his own pipe full of the thick, coarse stuff. He lit up, the smoke boiling into his throat. He coughed, his whole body shaking as the stuff reached his lungs.

'Not used to our forest blend, obviously,' smiled Zhist.

'No,' said Tallow, reassured by Zhist's friendly manner. 'What do you want to ask me about?'

'I want to find out whether you're a spy – whether you'll be useful to us. Whether you can be trusted.'

Tallow decided to risk frankness. 'I'm not a spy,' he said. 'I don't know whether I'll be useful to you and you can trust me not to betray any of your plans – but you cannot trust me to remain with you if I get a real chance to go on my way – I have an urgent mission.'

'Fair enough,' said Zhist. 'You owe us nothing. But let me tell you a little of what we're fighting for – then maybe you'll be more sympathetic to our cause.'

'Very well,' assented Tallow, 'but I warn you – much of what you say will be lost on me.'

'I'll risk that,' said Zhist gravely. 'We're outlaws – renegades – guerillas. A number of other names, according to where your sympathies lie. Seven years ago our ruler, Prince Gorlin, was deposed by the people. He wasn't a bad man – it was simply that he represented a system of government which was decadent, uneconomic, unjust and outdated. So we changed it, banished Gorlin and set up a new system of government temporarily controlled by the man who had led the revolution, General Damaiel Natcho. Is it inevitable, what happened? Natcho abused the trust the people had put in him. He imposed a more tyrannical rule upon the people than Gorlin's ministers had ever done and, since most of the army consisted of men who admired and respected Natcho, he managed to keep the people down. Many of them, me included, attempted to rouse our countrymen to overthrow him. This failed. A number of us were captured, shot – others, like me, fled to the woodlands. Since then we have been fighting Natcho when we could and slowly building up our own army. I am certain he doesn't know how well organized we are. Otherwise he might well have defeated us by a concerted attack at any time. We are a thorn in his side, but one which he has underestimated. Recently we raided an army arsenal and escaped with most of the guns stored there. We blew the place up afterwards and made it appear that the guns had been destroyed with the buildings. Now we are well-armed and are ready to attack Rimsho, our capital city, and depose Natcho.'

In his dirty cap and uniform, ragged of beard and of speech, Conrad Zhist had not much to inspire men to follow him. Not at first sight, anyway. As he crouched in the gloomy shack and murmured his plans and his reasons for making them to Tallow, then it became apparent why. Zhist was an orator; a natural orator with a gift for picking words which, in their very sounds, were keyed to the pitch of men's emotions. It was not his lucid choice of phrases which made him what he was – it was his onomatopoeic flare of rhetoric, the rough, inspiring music of his voice. Tallow soon found himself listening to the rhythms rather than to the sentences, his various emotions being triggered off by certain words and phrases which, combined, made him feel that the only thing in the world he wanted was a rifle – the only enemy Damaiel Natcho.

By the time Zhist had finished, Tallow was thinking of ways and means to help him, all his earlier urgency to reach the golden barge forgotten. Zhist had probably known this before he began talking, had relied on his talents to win Tallow as an ally.

Now Tallow was speaking, quickly, excitedly.

'With my boat, you will be able to keep in closer liason with many of your men. I will be able to steer it, and you can ride in it with me. We can travel up and down the rivers, gathering recruits. What do you say?'

'I like the idea,' smiled Zhist. 'You're ready to change what you said earlier, are you?'

'Yes,' said Tallow. 'Yes – you can trust me, Colonel. I'm your man.'

'Good.' Zhist sat back, puffing on his pipe with an air of satisfaction. 'I'll fix you up with quarters – and a gun.'

Tallow didn't like the sound of his having a gun. He had no experience of fire-arms, but he didn't object when Zhist took him outside, picked up a rifle and handed it to him.

'Know how to check the firing mechanism and ammunition?'

'No,' said Tallow.

'I'll get someone to show you. Hang on to that gun – and never lose sight of it. It's precious.'

'Thanks,' murmured Tallow uneasily.

Zhist took him over to one of the many camp-fires. Three men sprawling around it got up and saluted as he reached them.

'This is Jephraim Tallow,' Zhist said. 'I want you to show him the ropes. He'll be kipping with you boys. Show him how to use that rifle he's got.' He patted Tallow on the back and left the three soldiers staring at the little man with amusement and interest.

'That gun looks a bit big for you, mate.' The shortest of the soldiers, a man about five-foot-six, grinned.

'It is, my friend,' said Tallow, wary inside but seeming calm and self-possessed to the others. 'But the bullets do as much damage as anyone's.'

The three men laughed self-consciously. 'Well,' said the tallest, 'since Zhist seems to like you – welcome to our camp. I'll show you where our tent is.' Tallow turned his back on the other two and followed the man through a maze of fires and shacks to a large canvas tent. He stooped and entered. Inside it was littered with lengths of webbing, boots, haversacks, dirty plates and other equipment collected by encamped soldiers.

'Clear a space and put your gear on it,' said the soldier. 'My name's Jantor. Stay here, I'll get you a sleeping bag.'

'That's good of you,' said Tallow, 'thanks a lot.'

'Don't mention it,' smirked Tallow's future billet mate, and he crawled out of the opening.

Tallow looked distastefully at the rubbish cluttering the ground and with his boot kicked away much of the stuff which did not lie on untidy sleeping-bags, making an oblong clearing in the refuse. By the time he had finished, Jantor returned with a rolled-up sleeping bag under his arm and dumped it down with a grunt.

'Here you are,' he said. 'Get settled in and join us for a game of cards later, if you like. We'll be at the fire.'

'Thanks,' said Tallow. He couldn't reach the man – couldn't manoeuvre him. It was demoralizing. He decided not to join the card-game as he unrolled the bag, discovering as he did so, that at one end of it, where his head would be, a small mound he had thought would be useful as a pillow was, in fact an ant-hill.

Sighing, Tallow crawled into the bag and subsided into sleep.

Tallow remained in the camp three days, learning how to use a gun and meeting the men who were now his comrades-in-arms.

The revolutionaries were good men, every one of them – eyes perpetually bright in mud-grimed, bearded faces, their tattered uniforms kept together by leather straps bearing arms and ammunition. They were fighting mainly out of desperation. Originally they had talked politics and spoken high, idealistic phrases. Now they fought for their lives, their families – and they fought from habit; it kept them going. They would crawl through the forests on their bellies until it became second-nature to crawl, to keep a finger on a trigger, to talk in sparing whispers, to tread softly, carefully. And it was second nature for them to hate. They did that from habit, too – though they still had cause to hate – for Natcho had driven them out, destroyed their dreams. There was much that could be destroyed in men which they would accept, – dignity, love, loyalty – even their souls – but it was dangerous to kill dreams. Natcho would, said the men, soon realize that. In talks with Zhist, Tallow learned that the country controlled by Natcho was a nation of six million people. Next to it was a monarchy, larger but having fewer industries. It was mainly a rural country – lorded over by barons and dukes who, in turn, were lorded over by a king – a dull, stupid man who was controlled by his ministers. The ministers, the barons and the dukes all were envious of the industries of their neighbour and war had been frequent, down the centuries, between the two countries.

At the moment, Natcho was worried. The king, egged on by his ministers, was constantly raising his voice and shaking his first towards the other country, crying that the land had been overrun by peasants who knew nothing of rulership and that he, personally, would one day see fit to restore a monarchy to the vacant throne. He did not state which monarchy. War was imminent and Natcho had to spend much time parleying with ambassadors. In this way, also, was his strength weakened.

Zhist, however, realised that even were he and his followers successful in deposing Natcho, they would have to guard against attack.

The day came when all the revolutionaries were marshalled in one place – Zhist's main camp where Tallow was billeted. Tallow was visited by Zhist and asked to accompany the Colonel to his quarters.

Again Zhist offered tobacco to Tallow and Tallow accepted. He was feeling miserable. He had been unable to become friendly with his three comrades and they had constantly made remarks about his puny size and awkwardness. Zhist's request came to him as a relief and for the first time since he had arrived in the camp, he managed to relax a little.

'I've become bored, Colonel,' said Tallow. 'Is there something for me to do at last?'

'Yes,' replied Zhist, 'there is. I want you to take me down-river – to a place about a mile away from the capital. I have scouts there and spies who will tell me the latest news of Natcho's movements. Have your boat ready to leave in a quarter-of-an-hour. I'll join you there.'

Tallow got up quickly. 'Depend on me,' he sang as he ran out of the shack, towards the river.

They made the journey down-river safely, uneventfully, and on the bank were met by a party of soldiers, Niko amongst them, who swiftly helped them ashore.

'There's a carnival in the city,' said Niko, his mouth twitching. 'A red, blue and yellow affair with roundabouts and side shows. Haven't seen one since I was a kid!'

A carnival in Rimsho? What's Natcho's game?'

'I'd say he smelled trouble and has brought the carnival in to lull the people. The whole city's in confusion and everyone's going to the carnival. The sideshows are outside the suburbs – on the Big Green where we used to hold our sports.'

'I know it,' said Zhist laconically. 'This is a break for us. Many of us can join the crowds and assemble well inside the city. There are strangers in town – gypsies – so bearded face and wary walk won't be so noticeable.'

'You expect to be able to penetrate the city disguised as fair-folk?' said Tallow aghast. 'But how will you hide your guns?'

'We'll only take pistols,' Zhist told him. 'We'll get any rifles we need from members of Natcho's army.' He paused and slapped Tallow on the back. 'Tallow, my friend,' he sighed. 'You may not know it, but this is the opportunity I've needed. Fate is on our side today.'

'But what do you hope to achieve apart from your own suicide?' said Tallow.

'We'll be able to rouse the people. They are all sick of Natcho's rule. The carnival is a relief from it, true, but not enough to make them insensitive to years of oppression. Also, we'll be able to save innocent lives by warning those incapable of fighting to stay in their homes until peace is restored.'

'What do I do?' asked Tallow, dreading to hear the answer.

'You can guard the boat and do what you can in this area. When the city's won, I'll send for you. You may not know much of fighting, Tallow; but you've got a brain. And something else. Something, I think, which I once had and lost to some degree. I should hope that there'll be a place for you in civil administration when we get organized; that's if you want it, of course. We'll have to work fast – for Hyriom lurks at our borders even now, with loaded guns, eager for civil war and a weakened nation.'

Tallow breathed in relief. 'I'll wait here, then,' he smiled. 'Good luck'.

'Thanks,' said Zhist as he led his men back into the forest.

CHAPTER FOURTEEN

Miranda was surprised to see the bustle and commotion in the city. She had been warned by the captain of the ship that she might find it dull and restrictive. On the contrary, it appeared to be a city gone mad with colour and cacophony. Hurdy-gurdies blared out their brassy music, tradesmen called their wares, and stall-vendors bellowed the delights of their games and prizes.

'So this is Rimsho, is it?' She spoke to her escort, the young sailor, Cannfer. 'It must have changed a good deal since you put in here last.'

'It has, darling. Never thought I'd see it. The old bastard who used to control the city must be dead or deposed.' Cannfer stared over the thronged quayside. 'No!' he exclaimed, surprised. 'There's his picture – big as a house, pasted on that far wall. See it?' He pointed.

Miranda saw a painting of a handsome, grey-haired, military-looking man. 'Sexy,' she said.

Cannfer grinned. 'I'm jealous,' he said. 'Before I know it, you'll be after him!'

Miranda became serious. 'Remember what I told you,' she frowned. 'Remember – never get jealous. One day I may find my lover Jephraim again.'

Cannfer looked at the ground. 'I'll remember.'

Miranda took his hand. 'Come on,' she smiled. 'Let's join in the fun.'

Zhist, lurking in the shade of a red and black striped booth, saw Miranda and Cannfer disembark. He craned his head in order to see if others were coming ashore, but the girl and the sailor were the only ones.

Zhist had hoped that the entire crew of the ship would go ashore, then he and a few of his men might have sneaked aboard and stolen whatever arms there were. Although disappointed, he still regarded Miranda and her escort with interest. Always anxious for information, he decided that he would talk to them as soon as he could. As they mingled with the holiday-makers, he slipped from his hiding-place and followed them.

Tallow, for all his relief that he did not have to risk the dangers of the town, soon became bored with waiting. In his cabin was a flask of rum. Thoughts of boredom were quickly gone; all coherent thoughts, in fact, disappeared. Tallow finished the flask and collapsed, happily, to the ground. He lay with a seraphic smile on his ugly features, looking more like a contented crocodile than anything else.

He slept and dreamed of a dragon with a hundred eyes which moved relentlessly towards him. He was armed with a green sword which flashed with some slumbering power, which gave him strength and a mysterious grandeur. The dragon bore down on him. Behind it lurked huge-boled trees which had their topmost branches hidden by a dense layer of gleaming, deep-blue clouds. The trees were orange and yellow and the dragon was black with diamond eyes. Its red-fanged mouth was wide and a long tongue flickered out. It touched Tallow and the sword-power flowed through him, healing a wound the poisonous tongue had made. He hacked at the tongue and the thing flopped to the ground to wriggle away into the undergrowth.

Then, in his dream, the dragon swallowed Tallow. Breathed him in, down into the maw, down into the stomach which was lighted by torches of black-flame.

The sword was gone from Tallow's aching hand and he travelled downwards into the dragon with incredible velocity. So fast was he going that soon he could make out nothing but a blur on both sides and utter darkness ahead. He began to scream and then he woke up.

Zhist and Miranda stood over him. Miranda looked vaguely uncomfortable and Zhist frowned.

Tallow was certain that he was not awake; he believed that he had simply switched dreams. He lay on his back, waiting for something to happen.

Zhist grunted: 'I hadn't expected this, Tallow. I think that the lady here knows you.'

Tallow struggled to a sitting posture.

'Yes,' he said, eyeing Miranda warily. 'We have met.'

'I've found you, Jephraim,' said Miranda softly. 'I'm glad. I'm sorry if what happened was my fault. I forgive you.'

'Thanks,' Tallow winced as he got to his feet. His head felt delicate and his hands shook. 'How did you find me?'

'Colonel Zhist mentioned your name. We're going to help him with his revolution.'

'We?'

'Cannfer and I. Don't worry, darling, he knows about our relationship. I've told him not to be jealous.'

'Good,' lied Tallow, wondering how he could get out of this situation. 'How do you intend to help Colonel Zhist?'

'I'm going to seduce President Natcho, keep him busy while the Colonel takes the city.'

Tallow decided not to continue his questioning. 'I see,' he said after a while.

'Come on, Jephraim.' Zhist motioned tersely. 'We'll need your help. We're going back into the city. The revolution begins tonight. We want you and Miranda to berth in Rimsho and ask to see the President. Then you'll get a message to him that you have a girl for sale. Such deals are frequent under Natcho's regime.'

Tallow was in no position to resist. He said: 'Very well, Colonel, we'll get going now, shall we?'

'Yes,' replied Zhist. 'But don't let me down.'

'I shan't, Colonel,' said Tallow as he started the motor and helped Miranda aboard without meeting her eyes.

Neither Miranda nor Tallow attempted to begin a conversation and the journey to Rimsho was completed in silence. They berthed half-an-hour after leaving Zhist. Tallow hailed an urchin who chewed grubby candy-floss, dangling his legs over the oily water.

'You!' shouted Tallow. 'Tell one of the President's guards that I have a message for His Excellency.'

The boy blinked, then he scurried off. He soon reappeared, pointing Tallow out to a brown-uniformed soldier. The man came up to Tallow's boat and saluted politely.

'You have a message for President Natcho?'

'That's right,' said Tallow, assuming a crafty air, 'I have a personal letter for him.'

'I will have it delivered,' assured the soldier.

Tallow handed it to him. The soldier saluted again and strode off into the crowd.

Tallow and Miranda had to wait for another half-hour before the soldier returned.

'The President orders me to accompany you to his palace,' said the soldier, saluting again.

Tallow and Miranda disembarked from the boat and followed the man through the jostling populace of Rimsho.

Tallow did not like the faces of the people. Their grins were too fixed. Brittle smiles and uneasy laughter. Their eyes were glassy and bewildered. They had been too long under Natcho's heel to remember how to be happy. They could not see the enjoyment and freedom lasting; this festival was a respite, not an escape. Despair and darkness was behind them, oppression and fear ahead of them. Most of them were drunk; many of them were near to collapsing, but they carried on drinking, not daring to stop. They were pitiful, these people, but Tallow felt only contempt for them.

He felt uncomfortable and dazed. Very little of the happenings of the immediate past had affected his brain. He could not register what he felt – nor could he accept Miranda's presence. She was there and he knew he wasn't dreaming, yet he could not get close to her, could think of nothing to say. He wished that he were back on the wooded bank of the river – anywhere but in Rimsho with Miranda by his side. Soon they were walking in quieter streets – a larger bleak building ahead of them, squat dwellings on either side. On top of the big building was a flag which Tallow recognized as one which Zhist had described to him. It was green with a black falcon emblazoned upon it. Natcho's flag. They came to the end of the street and passed through guarded gates, mounting a long, wide flight of stone steps. A huge doorway was black and unwelcoming. They entered it and Miranda and Tallow were left in the centre of a vast corridor while the soldier showed some papers to a guard and talked with him for a few minutes. The soldier returned to them and motioned for them to precede him down the corridor. At the end of the corridor was another guard and the soldier once more showed his papers and held a short whispered conversation. The guard opened the big metal doors and said loudly:

'Corporal Blight and party.'

A gruff voice, softened by a slight echo, said: 'Enter.'

The soldier led Tallow and Miranda into a large hall devoid of ornament. It was a naked hall, furnished only by a big desk at the far end. At the desk sat a big man, older than the man whose portraits decorated the city but obviously President Natcho. He had small eyes and an upper lip which folded down over his lower lip. His moustache was grey and short, a military moustache. A fuzz of grey hair on his chin attempted to strengthen it and hide the folds of flesh beneath it but it only served to emphasize weakness and age. Natcho was dressed in a simple brown military uniform and wore a cap upon his grey head. Several medals adorned the right breast of his tunic and he sat with his hands folded in front of him, staring sternly at his visitors.

'You may leave us now, Blight,' he said.

Blight saluted, clicked his heels, wheeled sharply about and left the hall, closing the metal doors behind him.

'This is the girl?' Natcho enquired abstractedly, eyeing Miranda with a dispassionate appraisal which made her feel the need to vomit.

'Yes, your Excellency.'

'How much?'

'Thirty gold pieces,' recited Tallow, remembering the little Zhist had told him.

'Good. I'll give you a note to my secretary. He'll pay you your money. Is the girl clean?'

'Yes, Your Excellency.'

'She'd better be,' growled Natcho. On his desk was a bottle of brandy and a large glass. He poured brandy into the glass, drank it down in a gulp, winced and held his stomach with his left hand. His eyes had pain in them as he motioned Tallow to leave.

'The note, Your Excellency?'

The eyes were suddenly angry and Tallow regretted the insistence in his tone. Then the expression faded from the President's face and he opened a drawer and took out paper, pen and ink. He scribbled something down, folded the note and held it out. Tallow ran up to take it, then, with a peculiar glance at Miranda, walked swiftly past her and opened the doors.

Outside, he asked the guard: 'Where do I find the President's Secretary?'

'Upstairs,' replied the guard. 'First door on your right.'

Tallow scampered up the stairs the guard indicated and located the door. He knocked. A bored and languid voice drawled, 'Come in.'

Tallow entered the room. It was much smaller than the hall he had just left but almost as bare. Save for a filing cabinet which stood near a window overlooking a courtyard, and a desk and chair, it had no furnishings.

A bland-faced and elegant young man was sitting on the edge of the desk lighting a long-stemmed pipe. He raised an eyebrow when he saw Tallow and stared at the little man in affected amusement. 'What can I do for you – sir,' he said, insolently and indolently.

'Are you the President's Secretary?' Tallow was feeling increasingly uncomfortable.

'I am.'

'I have a note for you.'

The languid Secretary stretched out his hand and Tallow put the letter into it.

Placing his pipe carefully in a narrow oblong ash-tray, the Secretary dusted down his spotless uniform with delicate fingers and unfolded the note. He studied it for some moments, refolded it, placed it on his desk and put a heavy gold paperweight on top of it.

'I see,' he drawled mysteriously, looking Tallow up and down lazily. 'Wait here, will you?'

'Yes,' said Tallow, his fingers curling and anger flowing through him. He did not have to wait very long. Almost immediately the Secretary returned with two burly guards. He pointed at Tallow. 'Take him to the cell-block,' he commanded. 'Keep him there until you receive further orders.'

Tallow felt panic. 'What have I done?' he shouted, struggling between the two guards. 'Why are you arresting me?'

'President's orders, old boy,' smiled the Secretary sadly. 'That's what the note suggested – that you be arrested.'

'But why?'

'Don't ask me,' the Secretary answered wistfully as if Tallow had been granted a great honour which the Secretary coveted. 'You may discover that later.'

Tallow was pushed roughly into the corridor and borne through long corridors, down stairs, into another corridor lined with barred doors. One of these was opened and he was shoved into a concrete cell, windowless and dark. A light bulb illuminated the cell and the place was shadowless. A narrow wooden bench occupied one side of the cell.

For the second time, Tallow became a prisoner, only this time his gaolers made no secret of his status.

An hour later Miranda joined him in the cell. A guard laughed as he pushed her in and said something unintelligible.

'What happened?' said Tallow dully.

'Natcho knew something of our plan,' she said abstractedly, staring at the wall. 'He knew that you are in Zhist's employ, at least. Apparently he had a spy in Zhist's camp at the time you joined the rebels. The man obviously discovered little, for Zhist did not trust him, then.

But your description and the circumstances under which you joined Zhist were well known to Natcho. He intends to torture us in order to find out about Zhist's plans.'

'I felt that there was something wrong,' said Tallow moodily. 'I couldn't tell what, but I knew it. Has Natcho any idea of when the new revolution begins?'

'No – and he certainly doesn't expect it so soon. There may be a chance for us yet. We may be liberated before he begins his tortures.'

'I hope so,' said Tallow, feelingly. 'Though I doubt it. I am not a lucky man.'

'No.' Miranda considered this. 'You are not lucky. There is a doom about you, Jephraim and I cannot tell what it is – I wish I knew. Then I might help you.'

'I do not need anyone's help!' Tallow snorted. 'But I am weary of interference. I wish only to be left in peace to pursue my destiny in my own way. Too many people have interfered already – you most of all, for I welcomed your interference at first. I did not wish to dispose of you in the way I did – but I had to. For my sake mainly, but also for yours. There is no great happiness in my fate, Miranda. There is nothing but doom. But I shall welcome the doom when it comes. I would not wish to involve anyone else.'

'Suppose someone else wishes to become involved?' whispered Miranda softly.

'Then I will eventually destroy them. Not out of hate, you understand, but out of necessity. I do not wish to destroy – but it is a question of survival. I cannot be hampered. I still love you, Miranda, I think, but this does not alter the fact that I cannot take you with me. You have contributed much to my downfall. And I to yours, I suppose.'

'That cannot be rectified now, my love,' said Miranda, 'but can't we see that the future is better?'

'How can I tell? The future is unknown to me. I have staked my soul upon the future – and I cannot share what is ahead. My quest is for something so intangible that I cannot even feel it properly – let alone describe it. I seek for something I lack – yet the more I seek the more I lose of myself. Even those I have destroyed in some ways have, in turn, destroyed part of me – they have made my quest more and more difficult. I have only a faint hope that I can resume my journey. I must discover what I seek before I die, otherwise I am lost.'

'You need help,' said Miranda simply, with conviction. 'You need my help, Jephraim – and you need the help of men like Zhist.'

'No! I need no help but my own. I am tormented by those who

attempt to help me. I have never required their help – never asked it. I wish to be left alone. I wish for my own dark peace – not the black agony which comes with friendship and responsibility. I am forced too often to make decisions which should be unnecessary. I am not like other men – I am not greater than they are, neither am I smaller – I am apart from them and they try to make me like them. This can never be. Humanity does not admit Tallow into its ranks and Tallow has no ambition to join humanity. I am separate as I have always been. When I meet men I like, I conflict with them, ruin them as they ruin me. I have no place among you – and I need no friends or lovers for they only become my enemies, and I theirs. I cannot argue with them, I cannot fight them. Only men with something in common can conflict in this way. I have nothing to offer – and they can give me nothing.'

'You speak of a soul,' interjected Miranda. 'If you have a soul – then you have something in common with us. You have made these barriers because you fear us – you fear our humanity! You are fighting your destiny in refusing to see this. Every man's destiny is to become absorbed – to lose that which makes him an individual. When he dies, his body is absorbed into the earth – his soul into the myriad souls of the world. You are no different at this moment. Break this link if you like, Jephraim. Break it if you can – but it will mean your complete destruction! You seek for something on earth which most men find in death. Your quest is for death – not life.'

'You are *wrong* – utterly wrong! What I shall find will make death known to me – I shall not fear it. This is what makes me different – and apart from you and the rest.'

Tallow was trembling, dizzy; he sat down, hunched on the bench, his long fingers clasped together, his whole body tight.

'Where does the river lead?' he said to himself.

Miranda knew that he had not asked her the question, but in spite of this she replied: 'It leads to the sea – and all our souls are only the tiny drops from the sea.'

He did not hear her, nor did he wish to. He shut himself off from her and she knew that it was hopeless to continue.

They remained silent until the guards came for them several hours later. They had had no sign that the revolution had begun and Miranda was suddenly aware that it might have failed already. Until then, she had no thought of failure.

Eventually Tallow felt no more pain. Natcho's torturers were not subtle. They relied on the lash and the rack – and Miranda's screaming presence. They knew from previous experience that to torture a man's woman in front of him often loosened his tongue. But they did not know Tallow.

Miranda had been lashed and her body stretched until she had become a blind animal, a frenzied thing which bellowed for respite from the agony inflicted upon it and Tallow had sat watching – motionless, his eyes troubled but insensitive to her anguish; if he could hardly understand his own pain, how could he understand another's? Even when they had started on him – *lash, question, lash, question* – he had felt the pain in an abstract way, not fully knowing why he should suffer it. Only this had stopped him from answering the questions. It was not courage which had made him silent – he had not heard the questions. The Secretary's cool voice had become incorporated into the lash so that it was only part of it, like the swish before the sting.

His back was raw and his bones ached horribly. His body throbbed and he moaned in agony. Soon, he gasped when he moved, when the lash fell, but he gasped because he knew his body was in pain, though he no longer felt it.

At last the Secretary said wearily: 'Take them back to their cell. I did not realize that human beings could be so tenacious. They might as well be animals, unable to speak our tongue. All they can do is whine for mercy – and tell us nothing of what they know. They puzzle me.' He motioned distastefully to the guards and left the torture room. Then suddenly he was back again.

'On second thoughts,' he said, 'release them. And have them followed by our best tracker. They may lead us to a den of their fellows. The more we have in our net – the more chance we'll have of finding out about their plans.'

A guard with the face of a moose nodded and hauled Tallow and Miranda up. Both were naked and bleeding, their blood mingling, their breath in unison.

The moose grunted to another soldier who picked Miranda from the blood-spattered stone floor and flung her over his shoulder. The pair left the room by a different door, one which led downwards into a dark, unlighted tunnel. They tramped for two miles along this tunnel until, at last, they came to another door. This led out on to a part of the forest which crouched near the western wall of the city. The place had been fenced off. It was a burial ground. Open graves had been dug and filled with quick-lime. A few decaying corpses lay in the graves. The guards passed these and unlocked a small gate in the fence. They took the man and the woman some distance into the forest and dropped them to the ground, then they returned, introspectively picking droplets of dried blood off their uniforms.

Later, in grey twilight, Miranda recovered consciousness and pulled herself painfully into a sitting position. Tallow lay nearby; he had not yet awakened. Miranda crawled slowly towards him, every movement sending fresh spurts of agony through her ruined body.

Around her and above her the trees of the forest seemed to seethe with sentience – with malevolent life. They were the oldest, tallest trees she had ever seen, and their trunks twisted skywards to be lost to her vision. Tallow, face down in the moss, mumbled in quiet delirium. Miranda tenderly rolled him over and saw that his eyes were wide and blank, the irises small, the orbs rolling wildly.

A slight scuffling in the undergrowth behind her attracted her attention. She turned round and winced as the movement sent new pain through her. She stared into the gloom but could see nothing which could have caused the kind of sound she had heard. There was only blackness beyond the first circle of ancient trees.

She returned her attention to Tallow who now looked at her in puzzlement. 'Miranda?' he mouthed through lips which were puffed and blue.

'Don't worry, darling,' she said. 'It seems they have released us.'

'We're free?'

'Yes, love.'

'Why –?'

'Because we could not talk, I suppose. We must find water. Can you get up?'

Tallow rose to his feet and shrieked as the lash-wounds burned into him. 'God!' he swore. 'Why did they do this to us?'

'For information.'

'But we gave it to them didn't we – how did we bear this? I must have told them what they wanted.'

'You did not – and I don't know why. I knew little and said less – but my motives, I suppose, were loyalty. You have no loyalty, save to yourself.'

'You are right.' He cringed as he tried to walk. 'I cannot understand it. I must get back to my boat.'

'Not yet, love, not yet. We should find a stream first and bathe our wounds.'

She took his hands and slowly led him through the forest. Griff, the Tracker, lurking in the shadows of the big trees, craned his long neck and silently pecked his lips together. Griff had the sharp eyes of the bird of prey and he looked a little like the falcon which decorated Natcho's flag. Griff grinned to himself, there would be no difficulty in following these two for they could only travel slowly. The woods afforded all the cover he needed – more than enough. He slunk after the pair, silently; as softly as a carrion bird.

Then they vanished. Baffled, Griff increased his pace and began to run lightly through the forest. It was darker now, but his eyes could see in the dark. His sharp ears could no longer hear the sound of their movements; they had disappeared completely. Griff was not superstitious, he was not imaginative enough to fear the supernatural for he was unaware of its possible existence. One moment they had been in sight, the next they were gone. Griff found their tracks and, with his face close to thc ground, bent like a macabre ostrich, he traced the tracks until they, too, disappeared abruptly. Griff looked upwards into the trees and could not see them; he searched the ground around the last of the tracks and could find no tunnel or hollow into which they might have fallen.

Tallow and Miranda noticed nothing strange; they were both in too much pain to see that the forest was brighter and that the trees were of abnormal colours. Hand in hand, they searched for a river and finally found one, which was clear and pure. Thankfully, Miranda sank down beside the narrow stream and bathed her hands and head in it. Tallow collapsed beside her and lay, breathing heavily, on his stomach, his head pillowed by his claw-like hands.

The water soothed Miranda more than she had expected and it did the same for Tallow. After drinking of the stream they felt fitter and less weary. By now it was pitch dark and they could see little, not even the sky for it was obscured by a thick mesh of branches and leaves. They wandered on for a while, aimlessly, until they grew tired, a tiredness which was normal from lack of sleep, not the dreadful weariness of bodies which have borne torture. They slept and, upon awakening in the pale morning, were astounded at what they saw.

'Are we dead?' said Miranda, frowning at the orange-boled trees and the mauve leaves. 'Or have we travelled into fairyland?'

'We are not dead,' answered Tallow with confidence, 'or else I would know. And having had no experience of fairyland I cannot tell whether we are there or not, though I doubt it. Certainly the colourings of the vegetation are unusual, but there is probably a rational scientific explanation to the phenomenon. There is no law which says that bark should be brown and leaves green, is there? Or do we just expect them to be that way? We wouldn't be surprised if someone we knew who normally wore red clothing one day appeared in yellow clothes, so why should we be surprised by orange trunks and mauve leaves?'

'You are too logical, Jephraim,' said Miranda slowly. 'Far too logical to be human – if you really mean what you say. However, it's certainly reassuring to have your logic here. The place is very strange.'

'I'm glad that you grant me one thing I said yesterday,' grinned Tallow. 'You said I was far too logical to be human. I don't know about the logic – but you've agreed, without realizing it, that I'm not like the rest of humanity.'

'All the more reason for you to strive to be like us,' Miranda frowned. She got up and was surprised that the pain of the previous day was now only a dull ache. Tallow's back which had been red and raw was almost healed. 'There's magic or something here,' she said softly.

'Impossible!' Tallow exclaimed angrily. 'The river we bathed in could be full of natural salts which we'd just not heard of before. I'll believe in magic when I see someone stop the sun rotating.'

Miranda said nothing. She went up to one of the orange boles and examined it. Apart from its colour, it was the same as any other tree she had ever seen. 'I suppose we'd better get moving,' she said.

'All right,' agreed Tallow, also studying the tree. 'Which way?'

'Onwards, I suppose. If we go back we might well be captured again.' She took his hand and led him forward over short grass which was bright yellow and cool to their naked feet.

The forest was cool also, even though the sun had reached its zenith and was glaring down through parts of the foliage less thick than the rest. There was an air of timelessness about the place, of ancient calm. Tallow's logic could not explain the alien sensations which came to him, the smell of the forest which was not quite like any other smell he knew. The bird calls and the tiny golden birds which he saw from time to time were also unfamiliar.

'I wish I knew how long we were unconscious,' he said, 'perhaps we were taken to some foreign land – an island, possibly. I don't know why Natcho should go to that amount of trouble – but it looks as if that's what he did.'

'It's the only explanation,' agreed Miranda. 'But there's something – unearthly – about the place. Something so calm and peaceful that it would seem we were on another planet.'

'That's going a bit too far,' said Tallow. 'Almost like your idea that we're in fairyland!'

'I didn't mean that literally,' Miranda said petulantly. 'I only meant that it seemed like the fairyland I used to have described to me when I was a little girl.'

'That seems to fit into your impression.' Tallow smiled, pointing ahead. Miranda saw a vast domed building, magnificent in marble and blue mosaic. It stood in a clearing of yellow grass and the marble caught the sun, flashing like fire. Miranda sighed. '*We must* still be dreaming,' she said. 'There's nothing else to explain it.'

Both of them, in their own ways, were attempting to rationalize the place in which they found themselves. Both of them were trying to link it with things within their own experience. But it was virtually impossible.

They neared the domed construction and saw that it was supported by big marble columns set into a platform of milky jade. In the centre of the platform, a stairway of blue-stone curved upwards and disappeared into a circular aperture. There were wide windows set into the sides of the raised building but they could not see inside. There were no inhabitants visible and it would have seemed strange to the pair if there had been. They crossed the yellow glade and stepped onto the green platform. It was warm, as if it had been exposed to the sun. Their unshod feet were helpful in their progress towards the stairway; if they had been wearing shoes, they would have slipped on the smooth stone.

They reached the blue steps and mounted them, staring upwards, but they could still see nothing. They did not attempt to ask themselves why they were invading the building with such assurance; it seemed quite natural that they should do what they were doing. There was no alternative.

Inside was a cool, shadowy hall, a blend of soft darkness and bright sunlight which entered by the windows. The floor was pearl-pink and the ceiling deep scarlet. The hall reminded Miranda of a womb. 'It's wonderful,' she breathed. 'Magnificent!'

'Very pleasant,' commented Tallow. 'Certainly a change from the places I've been used to. I wonder who lives here.'

'We may find out if we remain much longer,' said Miranda. 'The owners of this place may resent us entering it.'

'Maybe,' Tallow said, 'but since there are no locks or even doors, I shouldn't be surprised if they aren't used to people coming in.'

'Probably you're right.'

Partially hidden by deep shadow was a small doorway and beyond it steps. Tallow looked questioningly at Miranda. 'Do we proceed in our exploration?'

'We might as well.'

They climbed the steps and found themselves in a smaller hall similar to the one beneath them. This hall, however, was furnished with twelve wide thrones placed in a semi-circle in the centre. Against the wall near the door were several chairs, upholstered in purple fabric. The thrones were of gold, decorated with fine silver, padded with white cloth. There was nothing barbaric or distasteful about the colours; they were quiet, blending with each other.

A door behind the thrones opened and a tall, fragile-looking man appeared, followed by others whose faces were almost identical. Only their robes were different in any noticeable way. Their faces were pale, almost white, their noses straight, their lips thin but not cruel. Their eyes were un-human – green-flecked eyes which stared into eternity with sad composure. The leader of the tall men looked at Tallow and Miranda. He nodded and waved a pale, long-fingered hand gracefully.

'Welcome,' he said. His voice was high and frail, like a woman's, but beautiful in his modulation. The other eleven men seated themselves in the thrones but the first man, who had spoken, remained standing. 'Sit down, please,' he said.

Tallow and Miranda sat down on two of the purple chairs.

'How did you come here?' enquired the man. 'Do you know?'

'No,' replied Tallow, 'we do not even know where we are.'

'I thought not – your people rarely come to us, except by accident.'

'Where are we?' asked Miranda as the man seated himself in the remaining throne.

'This is a place not *within* your own space-time continuum, yet *part* of it. There are strong links – though several dimensions separate us. Once our land was part of the earth you know, but in the dim past it became separated from the Mother Planet. Our bodies, unlike yours, are immortal. We choose this, but we are not bound to our flesh, as you are.'

'I don't understand,' frowned Tallow. 'What are you saying?'

'I have said what I can in the simplest terms understandable to you. If you do not know what I say then I can explain no further. We are called, by some of your people who know of us, guardians – though we guard nothing. We are warriors, if you like, fighting forces as alien to you as we are. We do not hate these forces, neither is there any material or ideological gain involved. We fight only to keep a balance of some kind.'

'All very well,' grunted Tallow. 'But what has this to do with us?'

'Not much,' admitted the man. 'You came here by accident. We will attempt to get you back to your own continuum as soon as possible. Meanwhile you may stay here – or explore the surrounding forest, just as you like. You will not be harmed.'

'Thanks,' said Tallow, staring at Miranda. But the girl refused to look at him, her eyes were on the tall speaker.

'Can't we remain here?' she begged.

'No, you can not. One day, perhaps, many of you will join us. But that will be on what you call the day of judgement – or Armageddon. When your people are ready, long deaths and lives in the future of your plane, then shall we all assemble here to fight the foes the guardians fight now. Then, if we win, the destiny of this universe will be settled and new seeds sown. If we lose – it means chaos and eventual destruction.'

'This is meaningless,' argued Tallow, 'you speak as if the world has united purpose. Surely every individual must discover his own destiny.'

'Certainly,' agreed the Guardian, smiling. 'I agree. But he must never lose his links with his fellows – otherwise he is destroyed. Or else, worse for him, he joins the ranks of those we fight.'

'You are demented, obviously!' Tallow sneered. 'You are decaying here while you fight your imaginary battles. When a man has discovered his eventual destiny, the meaning of his life, then he will need no one. He will be gloriously alone!'

'I respect your views,' smiled the Guardian, 'but if you fulfil your quest, then you will realize what you have missed. Then it will be too late to go back and live according to what you discover. It is always too late. You spend your lives chasing that which is within you and that which you can find in any other human being – but you will not look for it there – you must follow more glamorous paths – to waste your time in order to discover that you have wasted your time. I am glad that we are no longer like you – but I wish that it was lawful to help you. This, however, we may not do.

'You will be informed when you are to leave,' he ended abruptly. 'Now we must return to our fight.' He got up, bowed and, followed by the silent eleven, passed, once more, through the door.

'Come on, Miranda,' growled Tallow, taking her hand, 'let's get out of this decadent madhouse!'

Miranda went with him reluctantly and once again they walked over the cool yellow lawn and entered the forest. They wandered on and then they were out of the dark wood, standing on the shores of a sea. It was a grey, heaving, timeless sea, a mysterious sea which stretched into infinity. There could be no other shores beyond this rolling plain of water. No other lands or rivers or dark, cool woods, no other men or women or ships. It was a sea which led to nowhere.

Over this timeless ocean hovered a brooding ochre sun which cast moody shadows of black and green across the water, so that the whole scene seemed enclosed in a vast cavern, for the sky above was gnarled and black with ancient clouds. And all the while the doom-carried crash of breakers, the lonely, fated monotony of the ever-rearing white-topped waves; the sound which portended neither death nor life nor war nor peace – simply existence, shifting in harmony.

They could go no further. Tallow clutched Miranda's hand and moved towards the ocean, but Miranda held back. He looked at her, his whole ugly face swathed in black shadow and scarlet – his eyes puzzled. She tugged at his hand and tried to move back into the forest; he hesitated, keeping her between himself and the tall trees.

'Come, love.' He grinned his twisted grin. 'Let us bathe in this dark sea! At last we may find what we want.'

'No, Jephraim, let us return. I hate that ocean. I am sure it is what the guardians fight. Let us go back, Jephraim.'

But he pulled her on, relentlessly, towards the shifting waters. She broke free and ran back to the edge of the forest, calling to him like a sea-bird. 'Do not go, Jephraim! Do not perish!'

Tallow tried to continue his progress towards the ocean, but with Miranda gone, could not. He stood with one foot on the sand, as brown as dried blood, one foot on the yellow turf, undecided and afraid. 'Would you have me perish alone?' he jeered.

'That is what you said you wanted!'

'No! I did not say that – I will achieve my destiny alone – and it is not in my fate wholly to perish.'

'Then come back!'

The sea roared and tumbled, the sound of it increasing to a fury; daring Tallow to go on towards it, welcoming him with a wild temptation – offering him nothing but achievement – the achievement of death. He shivered and then he was running back towards the forest, feeling that the strange sea was pouring up the beach towards him. He looked back and saw that it had gone no further, that the breakers were less wild, the sea more calm. She gripped his hand with a frenzy of fear and hauled him towards her as if she had rescued him from a whirlpool. He clung to her and their bodies heaved in unison, locked and private. So they remained for a long time, while the sea called to Tallow and the wind was a cold caress on their flesh. But Tallow could no longer hear the sea and could only feel Miranda's warm body against him. In the bleak greyness of the alien shore, under a sun which gave no heat, their united bodies shone like a star in the night and once again Tallow knew the truth of companionship; a truth which he feared and hated while loving Miranda and all that she offered him. Even as they returned to the wood and lay down together by an orange tree-trunk on blue moss; even as he kissed her and spoke softly of his love, he was vaguely tormented and afraid of the consequences of his actions.

Hours later, Miranda said: 'I wonder if the revolution was successful.'

'I hope so,' he whispered, 'for if we are to go back, at least we have the chance of returning to friends.'

'Shall we see if the guardians are ready to send us back to Rimsho?' she suggested.

'Yes,' he said.

They began to retrace their way to the domed dwelling of the twelve fragile men. When they arrived, the man who had spoken to them previously awaited them.

'Walk on in that direction,' he commanded, 'and you will arrive at the place where you entered our land.'

They went by him silently, through the clearing into the forest. They passed the silver river and saw golden birds again. Some time later they came to a place where the light seemed to shimmer like heat-haze and when they were beyond it they found themselves in the forest which lay to the west of Rimsho. Looking back they perceived that the unearthly trees had disappeared and ordinary woodland stretched behind them.

Something out of place swung like a pendulum back and forth across the path they had trodden on the previous day. Nearing it, they looked up and saw that it was a man hanging. A long-necked hawk-like man whose name had been Griff. He had an expression of astonishment on his white, dead face, a look which had been there even before men had come to hang him.

'Something's been happening, anyway,' commented Tallow dryly. 'Either Natcho's quashed the rebellion and is hanging those he thinks are traitors – or else this is one of Natcho's men and Zhist's followers have hanged him.'

Miranda shivered. 'Let's go on,' she said, 'and find a gate.'

They found a gate, jubilantly guarded by a member of the Free Fighters. He grinned at Tallow and leered at Miranda so that they were suddenly conscious that they were naked.

'Where have you been?' chuckled the soldier, who recognized Tallow.

'Fairyland,' replied Tallow good-naturedly and went into the city leaving an astounded guard behind him.

At the first house they came to they knocked and borrowed a couple of blankets from the old woman who answered them.

The townsfolk were now really enjoying themselves, the fixed grins and glassy eyes had brightened and warmed. Zhist's soldiers were everywhere, taking advantage of the hero-worship lavished on them by the women of Rimsho. Tallow asked one of the soldiers where the Colonel might be found.

'Where else but in Natcho's old quarters?' laughed the man and turned once more to his bottle and his girl.

'Should have thought of that,' said Tallow as he and Miranda, in blanketed dignity, strode through the streets towards ex-President Natcho's palace.

CHAPTER FIFTEEN

'I'm afraid Cannfer was killed in the fighting,' said Zhist with regret. Tallow felt only slightly elated that there was one complication less. Zhist went on: 'As were many other brave men. He heard that you and Miranda were in trouble and was the first to reach the palace – he was shot down, of course. What happened to you two?'

'We were tortured and left for dead in the forest,' Tallow answered. 'We wandered in delirium for some time until we came to a stream. It has wonderful healing properties. Look, you can still see the marks of the lash. They are only scars now.' He slipped off his blanket to show Zhist unasked-for proof of his ordeal.

'Miraculous!' exclaimed Zhist. 'We must look for that river sometime. I suppose you've no idea where it was?'

'None,' said Tallow truthfully. 'I doubt if I could ever find it again.'

'Pity,' said Zhist. The food he had ordered earlier arrived and the three of them sat around the desk at which Natcho had first interviewed Tallow and Miranda. They began to eat ravenously, for this was the first food they had had for some time.

'Hyriom's rumbling again,' remarked Zhist, munching a roll. 'They're growling about the Rights of Kings or something – say that our country's been overrun by a revolutionary rabble. This is the excuse they've been waiting for. They're going to invade us any day now – and we've got to be ready for them!'

'Good luck,' said Tallow. He had just realized that Cannfer would have been more use alive. He could have taken Miranda off his hands. 'I hope you succeed. In the morning I must be off. I've stayed for too long.'

'You can't go, Tallow,' Zhist said, 'I'll need you here as my secretary.'

'But I have delayed for nearly a week – if I do not hurry I shall miss the barge altogether.'

'Forget about the barge, it can wait – follow me, instead. You'll be an honoured man in this city. And what about Miranda? Because of you she's been through hardship and finally torture. You can't desert her again?'

'He could,' said Miranda, resignedly. 'And probably he will.'

'You understand, though, don't you Miranda?' said Tallow hopefully. He felt trapped.

'No,' she said, 'I don't fully understand. I would have thought that you'd have remained – now. But I suppose you'll do what you want to do in spite of me – in spite of Colonel Zhist – in spite of everyone who's attempted to be your friend and help you.'

Tallow said doggedly: 'Miranda – I've told you. I don't need help or friendship. Help of your kind serves to hinder me – friends delay me. I cannot afford the responsibilities which friendship – even help – affords. I am a man apart – a lonely man. I enjoy my loneliness.'

'You're a strange bird, Tallow.' Zhist chewed his food moodily. 'A very strange bird. I can't make you out.'

'I don't want to be made out!' replied Tallow angrily. 'That's what I'm getting at.'

'Can't make you out,' repeated Zhist. 'You appear to have no loyalties but those to yourself. Yet you didn't betray me under torture. From what you've told me of your journey down-river, you've attempted to help several people – and instead, have succeeded in ruining them in some way. You're a murderer – yet you don't act like a murderer. You have no motives, that I can see, for murder. You're in love with Miranda – and she with you. Yet you deserted her and are preparing to do the same again. What makes you tick, Tallow?'

'My mind,' said Tallow, 'that's what makes me tick – not my heart. Most men are ruled by their hearts – they use their minds to rationalize what they feel. With me it's mind first – emotions second, if at all. I never knew what emotion was until I first saw the golden barge going through the river. In that case it was emotion of some sort first – a *feeling*, you'd say – mind much later – if at all. I still haven't worked out what the barge offers me. But I'm sure it offers a great deal more than friendship, love, honour. These things will destroy me

– make me one of the herd. I am not built for herd life. I can't exist among men – I haven't the mind, the physique, or the face. I don't enjoy the same things and I don't hate needlessly. I sometimes hate the things which interfere with me, but not for long. Miranda offers me comfort and peace of mind, satisfaction sexually, a lot of other things – but she cannot offer what the barge offers – whatever that is.'

'Perhaps she can, only you don't see it,' said Zhist.

'Don't argue with him,' said Miranda. 'Don't try – it gets you nowhere. I know.'

'It's not my fault,' Tallow said lamely. 'It's not my fault, is it?'

'I'm sure if you remain among men and understand them, let them understand you, you'll find what you're looking for,' Zhist persisted. 'You are the stuff of which idealists are made – the wrong kind. They follow their own personal star and attempt to make the world a better place – they wind up with the blood of millions on their hands – or their heads in nooses they've knotted themselves.'

'I don't know what you mean.'

'Listen,' said Zhist. 'These things which you – and a few others like you – want to find are right here. So many people go through life looking for something, trying to find it in money, in power, in sexual experience, even, occasionally, in painting, or music or writing. They don't know what they're looking for – yet something remote and unattainable seems to offer it. I'll tell you this – I offer it – Miranda offers it. That baby you found offered it. And you were too blind to know it! You're blinded by the glinting gold of the barge – seeking what you realize dimly as truth in something which doesn't involve responsibility of any kind. To find what you're looking for, Tallow, you must accept responsibility – accept friendship and love – even honour. They all involve responsibility. It is this process of *involvement* which teaches you the truth you struggle after!'

'Why should I become involved? Why? If it wasn't for you and Miranda, for people like you, I'd have reached the barge by now. Must I forever be plagued by people?'

'You are a man,' said Zhist simply. 'And a man has a soul – a life-force – call it what you like. There are millions of souls on this planet. Probably millions more in the universe. The very ground you tread has its own particular kind of soul – a sentience. We're all involved, Tallow. We can't escape the fact. We're all part of something huge. We're going forward Tallow. That's why I fought for the freedom of my people – it was my part in a far greater thing. That's why some men paint pictures – why some men go to war. You want something for yourself which all men should have. What will you do with your 'truth' once you've found it? What will it tell you – it will tell you what I have told you – will you deny it then?'

'Impossible! What I want has no relation to what you've said. If anything I want the opposite.'

'I can't convince you?'

'No.'

Zhist sighed and stared at Miranda with resignation. 'What do we do?' he said to her.

'Do? There's nothing we can do. I've tried to convince him – you have. Lots of other people have. We can only hope he gives up the chase and eventually comes back.'

'The chase will become more desperate as it progresses,' Zhist sighed. 'He won't come back.'

Tallow said: 'Look – I'll stay for a few more days – then I'll have to go.'

'Why are you relenting now – you said you were convinced that your quest was right?' Zhist got up and wriggled his shoulders, trying to instill vigour into his tired body.

'I'm not relenting. I shan't. But I'd like to rest for a short while and think. I'd like my boat checked over and plenty of rations aboard before I leave.'

'I'll see to it tonight,' promised Zhist. 'Meanwhile – in the hope that you'll stay – you're my personal aide. You and Miranda can have Natcho's old rooms.'

'Thanks,' said Tallow. He felt hemmed in – first the position, now Miranda. He had lost part of his battle already. He was frustrated and, at this stage, could see no chance of surcease from the conflict he hated. *They're almost as bad as the people who imprisoned me 'for my own good', he thought. So many bloody do-gooders harming me and getting themselves harmed in the process.*

'I hope you'll leave me alone, for a while at least,' he said.

'Certainly. I'll see you midday tomorrow if that's all right?'

Tallow nodded and left the hall. Miranda followed him, at a distance. She smiled at Zhist as she went out.

Tallow and Miranda slept together but neither of them felt like love-making. Tallow was too worried about his dilemma and Miranda troubled about the future. They did not sleep well and Tallow rose early, pulled on the clothes Zhist had obtained for him and walked out into the bright dawn streets of the capital.

There was no one about. Most of the inhabitants had obviously caroused late into the night and had only recently gone to bed.

Tallow's boots made a clatter on the cobbles and concrete of the city and the air was cool and clean to his lungs. The air, however, did not help him to clear his head of the thoughts which troubled him. He could not deny, though he wanted to, the fact that his conversations of the previous day had affected him. But, as far as he was concerned, there had been nothing constructive in the arguments of Miranda and of Zhist, all of which had followed a similar pattern and practically paraphrased one another. The arguments had served only to confuse and mystify him. He was as certain as ever that his path was the right one – he could not be deterred from it; but the inkling of other paths, equally as effective in their end, was causing him a great deal of consternation and more delays were imminent.

Torn bunting littered the deserted streets, flags were draped everywhere, over buildings, balconies, windows, lamp-posts. They flapped listlessly in the refreshing early-morning breeze. Rubbish of all kinds had collected in the gutters, where such existed; bottles of every kind, many smashed, the glittering glass scattered like diamonds over the streets, were in profusion. And then, Tallow saw the boy.

The child lay curled up amongst the rubbish, quite naturally. He did not look at all out of place; he was a piece of refuse himself with his ragged clothes and untidy hair. He slept, his face obscured by his crooked arm upon which his head rested. Without knowing just why, Tallow walked slowly over to the child and pushed at the frail body with the toe of his boot. The child stirred and sprang awake, glaring up at Tallow with hideous yellow eyes streaked with red lines. The eyes, like the large unwholesome nose, were too big for the rest of his thin wrinkling face. His neck was scrawny and reptilian, the skin dry and scabby like a discarded snakeskin. He looked exactly like a tortoise; even his hunched awkward body resembling the domed shell, his huge nose dominating his sloping, almost non-existent chin, his big eyes having the hard quality of a rheumy reptile. When he spoke, he hissed hoarsely, thickly, the voice uncouth and jarring.

'What have I done?'

'Nothing that I know of,' said Tallow. 'Why aren't you at home?'

'Haven't got one any more.'

Tallow nodded, silently, at a loss for anything to say in answer to this. He wondered why he had bothered to disturb the child and at the same time tried to guess his age. By his stature he was about nine or ten, the face could have been that of a new-born baby's; it could also have belonged to a grown man or a nonagenarian. There was no telling.

'Why are boxes always square?' enquired the boy suddenly.

'That's the easiest way to make them,' Tallow answered.

'Then why don't they make them in different shapes? It would be better.'

'Possibly,' said Tallow gravely, wanting to go. The tortoise-boy turned his ugly profile towards the sun and got up; he stood looking at the sun in silence. Tallow was fascinated by him – he had never realized that children could be so ugly; usually children's faces were neutral, occasionally pleasant or beautiful. The boy's whole face and body were repellent; particularly his yellow eyes which now moved to regard Tallow. Tallow stared back, unable to do otherwise. They stood there in the centre of the street, looking into one another's eyes. Tallow experienced a peculiar sense of affinity with the unattractive child and said, at last, against his will: 'We are outcasts, you and I.'

The boy's voice was distant, it had a thick, dreamy quality: 'Friends,' he said. 'Are we friends?'

'No. We are not friends. We could never be friends. Are dogs ever friends?'

'Dogs don't like me.'

'Neither do I,' said Tallow vaguely, trapped helplessly in the conversation. 'You are repellent.'

'Does that mean bad?'

'No.'

'Nobody likes me at all. My aunt said I have the evil-eye. I can see as well as she can. My mother turned me out when my new father came. I do not want to be liked but it is hard.'

'I know.'

'What shall I do? I am lost here. I don't know what to do. What shall I do?'

'Stay here. You are better off in a place you're used to. Things may get better when you're older.'

As they talked, their eyes continued to stare, locked as they contemplated one another warily as if they had met a perfect twin of themselves which they had never seen before. Yet there were differences. Tallow knew that this child was not sufficiently like himself to become a comrade, yet was too similar to be ignored. He had never suspected that there could be someone else so near to what he was. He wondered if there were others – other outcasts, misfits, aimless wanderers through existence. If so, why should they not be told of his barge – his aim?

'There is a barge sailing the river,' Tallow informed the boy. 'It is great and golden and is undisturbed by the tides which flow through the water, by the sun, or the wind. It moves with purpose. It is going somewhere and when it arrives, if you were there, it would help you. Would you follow it, given the chance?'

'No,' answered the boy calmly, 'why should I?'

'Because then you, also, would have purpose. The barge would help you, do you see?'

'I don't know what you mean. How can I be helped by some ship on the river? Will my aunt stop cursing me and my mother take me back if I see this ship? What good could it do for me?'

'You would know if I showed it to you. You would.'

'You are a man – I am a boy. That is not the same. We are different.'

'Only in age. One day I will show you the barge. Come with me when I leave and you will find what I have found.'

'But what good will it do me? What has this ship done for you?'

'Nothing, yet,' said Tallow sadly. 'Nothing yet. But it will. Do you know others like yourself?'

'My sister,' the boy said. 'She is ugly. My mother lets her stay. My aunt gives her food. I know you – you are ugly.'

'I don't mean others who look like you. Are there others who feel like you?'

'How do I feel?'

Tallow said carefully: 'You feel alone. Unwanted. Unneeded. You feel that you need no one.'

'Yes, that is how I feel. But I know of none like me. Should I?'

'No. I never did.'

Tallow felt dislocated, out of his depth and his element. He was frantically searching for a word which would act as a key – as a link; something to make the boy realize that he was no longer alone. Tallow wondered if he did, indeed, need someone, whether the boy needed anyone, whether they were not both better off alone. The boy demanded nothing of him, was obviously beginning to feel restless. Desperately, Tallow brayed: 'Come with me now. Come with me to the river.'

'Why?' persisted the tortoise child. Tallow grasped him and pinned his kicking limbs. He hoisted the boy in his arms and began to run. To his surprise, the boy did not shout, but he continued silently to kick and heave in Tallow's grasp. Tallow ran furiously and quickly down towards the river; he hoped that he would not be seen for this act might rank, however unwanted the boy was, as kidnapping.

Finally, he reached the river, unseen. His boat lay moored, half-full of the same kind of refuse which was spread through the streets. The whole river near the quay was full of bobbing bottles and wet, sluggish paper bunting. The corpse of a dog, swollen like a blown-up bladder, knocked against the side of his boat. He took a flying leap onto the deck and twisted the boy's arm so that he could not move without breaking it. Then he switched on the ignition and pulled open the throttle. The boat's engine began to chug into sluggish life, then roared with full volume and began to tug away, hampered by the mooring line. Tallow threw off the rope and guided the boat into the open river. He released the child.

'I can't swim,' The boy rubbed his bruised arm and looked back at the city.

'You don't need to. The boat will not sink.'

'Why are you doing this?'

'To help you,' Tallow replied and stopped himself saying 'it's for your own good'.

Surprisingly, the child began to cry. 'Take me back,' he sobbed. 'Take me back, please. You're frightening me. I don't want to go.'

'Listen,' Tallow hissed urgently. 'Listen to me you brat. What I'm doing will give you a meaning to your wretched life. I'm taking you with me for your sake – not because I want you with me. Do you understand that?'

'No! No! You're taking me away from my home. I can't swim, the water frightens me. We'll drown!'

'It would be better for you to drown than to exist as you will do in Rimsho. You'll be friendless there – you will do nothing of value. You will grow up, you will age – you will die. No one will know of your passing. This way, at least, I give you something to die for – a cause for living. Can't you realize this? Can't you? Ingrate!' Tallow calmed somewhat. 'When you have seen the golden barge,' he went on in a more consciously level tone, 'when you have seen it you will know that what I am saying is true. You will want to follow it, also, as I am doing. We will learn what few of those fools back in the city will ever have an inkling of. Stay silent now, for I must make speed; I have lost too much time.'

The boy subsided. His sobbing could still be heard above the throb of the engine as Tallow concentrated on the waters ahead.

Four days went by and Shoorom, the child, refused to eat more than the barest scraps required to keep him alive. He moaned in his sleep and was silent when awake. Tallow soon dismissed him from his thoughts and put all his energy into coaxing speed from his boat until, on the fourth day, the golden barge was jubilantly sighted. Tallow said nothing until the barge was much closer. As implacable as ever, it sailed on towards its mysterious destination. Then, when it lay ahead, dominating the entire river, he tapped the child on the shoulder. Shoorom started and turned his yellow eyes on Tallow.

'Yes?' he said, dispiritedly.

Tallow pointed at the barge and grinned. His face split into a wide gap. 'There!' he exclaimed. 'There's the barge, Shoorom. There it is!'

Shoorom looked unwillingly in the direction Tallow indicated. No new expression, as Tallow had expected, came into his eyes. He looked back, behind the boat and continued to stare at the water. Tallow was astounded at this anti-climax. 'Well?' he said, impatiently. 'What do you think of it?'

'Think of what?'

'The barge, of course, the golden barge! Wasn't I right?' Tallow could tell that the barge had made little impression and could not understand it; he had been certain that once Shoorom had seen the barge then he would admit that he, Tallow, had been right.

'What barge? I see only the river ahead and the river behind. I want to go home!'

'Look again,' cried Tallow desperately. 'Look again!' Dejectedly, the boy turned his head to stare, once more, ahead of him. He frowned and glared at the barge – and through it.

'What do you think of it?' Tallow said proudly, with the air of a man showing off a personal treasure.

'Please, Mr Tallow, let me go home. I can't see anything at all. You're mad. Don't hurt me any more. I want to go back.'

Tallow seized the boy's shoulders and roughly shook them. 'You're blind!' he screamed. 'Of course you can see it! Why are you tormenting me like this? You can see it – you must see it. I'm not mad – others have seen it. I'm not mad – others have told me. Stop tormenting me! Stop it! Stop it! Tell the truth, you brat – you wretch! Tell me you can see it!'

'Oh, I can't. I can't, Mr Tallow. Let me go home. Please!'

Tears popped from Tallow's eyes and rolled along his nose. He switched off the motor and sank down on to the deck, his large head in his huge hands. 'You're certain you can't see it?' he wept. 'You're sure?'

'Yes – I'd see it if I could. I tried to see it, honestly. But I can't. Can we go back now?'

'Why?'

'I want to go home.'

'I should throw you over the side. I thought you, if no one else, would see the barge. Am I really mad?'

'I don't know. Maybe only grown-ups can see the barge. Maybe children can't – just like children can see things grown-ups can't see. Don't throw me overboard!' The boy was shaking in terror.

'You want me to take you home?'

'Yes.'

'Why won't you see the barge? This is your last chance for life. I am offering you the chance of great secrets – of truth. Why don't you try and see it?' Tallow was pleading now.

'Oh, I have tried, Mr Tallow. I told you.'

'You think children can't see it – you may be right. But then, I always thought that children knew more about these things than adults. I was wrong.'

'Maybe children see things differently.'

'You want to go home? All right. I'll take you home. Why, I don't know, for you've shattered a dream – I should hate you. But,' he sighed, 'I'll take you back.'

Eight days after his sudden departure, Tallow reberthed in Rimsho. The quay was heavily guarded, but he was recognized and managed to get past the sentries with little difficulty. The boy scampered away from him and disappeared into a side-street. Tallow did not bother to stop him, or even bid him goodbye. He had long since lost interest in the boy and was glad to see him go. He wondered why he had taken the trouble to go all the way back to the city when he had been so near to the barge. He realized that he would have done such a thing only for the repellent child. Although his hopes had been shattered, he could not, after what he had done, desert Shoorom or drown him. The only thing he could have done was to take the boy back. Sullenly, disconsolately, Tallow wandered slowly towards the palace of the President.

When he got to the building, he reached his own apartments seeing no one but a few officials and soldiers. The place was full of rushing people and there was an air of urgency about the way they moved. Many carried papers or files – some had maps rolled under their arms. It was obvious that the expected attack by Hyriom was coming closer. In his apartments he found a note; it had had wine spilled on it and the stain was now dry. The note was addressed to him. Frowning, he opened it:

DEAR JEPHRAIM,

IF YOU DO RETURN – PLEASE STAY HERE UNTIL I COME

Miranda.

Frowning still, Tallow folded the note and put it in his pocket.

Curiosity made him remain in the apartment for two hours, then Miranda came in.

'Hello, Jephraim,' she smiled, kissing him quickly as if she had seen him only a few hours earlier. 'When did you get back?'

'Just now. What does your note mean?'

'Oh – that – I wrote it a week ago. Colonel Zhist wanted to see you. It was urgent – then. Where have you been?'

'For a trip on the river. I saw the barge again.'

This plainly astonished Miranda: 'Then why did you come back?'

'I'm not sure.'

'Was it to see me? Was it? Or did Zhist convince you to stay, after all? Oh, Jephraim, I do hope so. Are you going to stay now? I'm very happy!' She was radiant, as she had been once or twice in the months before when they had been together. He couldn't answer her. He dare not, for he could only have answered her truthfully, and that truth would have hurt her in her present mood. She so obviously wanted to be happy. He would wait until she was in a different frame of mind. Meanwhile he might just as well occupy his time doing what he could to help Zhist. It would save him the trouble of having to explain things and also would stop him having to think too much. He took her by her shoulders, stretched on tip-toe, and kissed her on the mouth; she returned his kiss eagerly, in her old insatiable manner.

Later, he asked her, 'Where's Zhist now?' She replied: 'In the main hall. War is imminent and Zhist's test is near. The people look to him to save them from conquest by the Hyriomians. If he succeeds, then he is their leader, un-questioned. If he fails, they will be a subject nation anyway, but their faith in Zhist as a leader will be broken – he will have no chance of rallying them. I hate to think what would happen.'

Tallow heard this dispassionately.

Soon, a hideous plan began to form in his brain and although part of him attempted to quell the idea, another part argued that with Zhist gone, he would have no reason for remaining in the city – no one to shatter his complacency – no one to delay him. He hoped that Zhist might somehow die – and that the war would give him cover. He would escape in the confusion and Miranda would think him dead. So, effectively, he could dispense with all that was hindering him and could continue his quest in absolute peace. All this he thought as he led Miranda to the bed and began to unbutton her blouse. A decision had to be made – and now, he thought, he had made it.

CHAPTER SIXTEEN

'Jephraim, I'm going to have a baby!' Miranda smiled into Tallow's eyes. 'It's yours.'

'Wonderful!' exclaimed Tallow half-heartedly. More complications were combining to weigh him down and hamper his progress. 'When is it due?'

'In four months.'

Tallow was at a loss for anything appropriate to say. In the last few days he had been steadily growing back to become his old introverted self. All around him people moved and spoke, were grim, laughed; but he was detached from them, like a man watching a cinema film.

Tallow could not believe that he was part of it all and was growing impatient. He had still no methods with which to put his plans into operation and so he concentrated upon looking for the right circumstances. Zhist now only spoke to him and saw him when it was absolutely necessary – Zhist could no longer reach him and even Miranda was beginning to show signs of discomfort. She was studiously cheerful, trying to convince herself that everything was going the way she wanted it. But it was difficult with a blank-eyed, monosyllabic Tallow to deal with, a Tallow who made love automatically and whispered hollow endearments into her ears at night.

'Are you pleased?' she asked.

'Yes, of course,' answered Tallow, wondering if he was ever going to escape from the traps he himself was making.

'Shall we have a boy or a girl?' she persisted, the gaiety in her voice becoming edged with strained uncertainty.

'Boy or girl. Fine.'

'Boy?'

'A boy. Fine.' Tallow knew that the war with Hyriom would not be put off much longer. A week or two at the most. He heard Miranda's voice again.

' . . . name him . . .'

'Name him?'

'Yes, what shall we call the boy?'

'Call him Accursed!' said Tallow with dull rage. 'Call him that if he's his father's son. Call him the Accursed and let him follow in his father's footsteps.' He left the room, leaving Miranda wide-eyed behind him, tears beginning to form in the green depths.

She did not attempt to follow him. She remained standing in the room, her arms limp at her sides, hurt and troubled, her self-made dreams crumbling as she fought the madness she knew was inevitable.

The madness which must come eventually to her and for which she must wait; she could no longer fight it. Her weapons were gone.

Tallow wandered the frenzied streets of Rimsho as the city prepared for war. He knew that a certain inn near the outskirts of the city was the headquarters of subversive politicos. This information had reached him in his capacity as Zhist's secretary and it had gone no further, for the men who plotted Zhist's downfall, whatever their reasons, would be useful in Tallow's scheme.

It was impossible now, simply to flee the city as he had fled before, from other cities. He could not have done it. He had to have a reason for leaving, something he had never had before – other than the necessity of following the barge. He was doing his best to manufacture a reason. He realized this dimly, but dare not analyse why. To do that would result in further indecision. Whatever force it was which drove Tallow, it was at last beyond his control and he steadfastly followed a decision which would result in doom and dark betrayal. He could not help himself. He knew now that he had always realized this. It was too late to change it. Too late to do anything but tread the road he had chosen, for to step off it would mean chuckling, screaming chaos and that he must fight if his barge were to lead him to the knowledge that he desired. Toleration was now no longer one of his traits. His own schemes had not been tolerated – so he was learning that tolerance was an alien thing to most men and their intolerance could only be fought with that very weapon. Tallow let his decision to live and let live sink away from him and he resolved, with grim anger, to pay those who had driven him to the decision. To pay them with a sample of their own philosophy. His thoughts confused, his body sluggishly obeying the message of his chaotic brain, he moved doggedly onwards towards the inn, uncertain what he would do there but sure that any events would prove useful to his dimly conceived plans, whatever happened.

The inn seemed an unlikely haven for political plotters. It was a big place, with a hotel and restaurant attached, surrounded by lawns of neat turf. Tallow remembered its name, The Black Inn. It was a fashionable rendezvous for the rich of Rimsho. The plotters probably reckoned that the customers of the Black Inn were thought above suspicion.

As Tallow entered the main room of the Inn, he was hailed by several groups of people who shouted good-naturedly and beckoned him. He smiled back, politely, knowing that their shouts were false and their beckonings those of men and women who thought that to have his ear was almost the same as having Zhist as a personal friend.

It was difficult for the little man to realize that he was in Rimsho an important figure. He reckoned that it was not going to be easy to contact the plotters who would think him the last man capable of betraying the Colonel.

With a mental shrug, Tallow went over to join one of the groups.

Mr Slorm, owner of the prosperous Black Inn, was puzzled. He had seen Tallow enter and had recognized him, though Zhist's secretary had never been to the inn before. Mr Slorm was also worried, for he was a royalist. His business had been even better while there had been a monarch ruling the land. He was honest with himself and admitted his reasons. Upstairs, in one of the hotel rooms, other royalists plotted. And Tallow was downstairs. Had they been betrayed? Slorm tugged abstractedly at his long moustache which lay like drooping wings beneath his snout-like nose. His heavy eyebrows drew sharply together to form a single line over his deep-set eyes and he sucked thoughtfully on his few remaining teeth. Why was Tallow here?

Slorm was used to having many of his questions left unanswered. It was his nature to accept the situation as it came – although he would have preferred a monarchy he would never have troubled to alter the situation if he had not been approached by Largek and his friends. General Largek was one of the few military men who had served the exiled king and survived Natcho's regime. Now the General saw a chance to restore the monarchy. Slorm welcomed the chance and had risked letting the General use his hotel as his meeting-place. Beyond that, Slorm was not prepared to go. And Tallow's presence here might mean nothing – or it could mean the end of his, Slorm's prosperity.

Slorm decided to warn the General.

Tallow knew that Slorm was a royalist, and, when he saw the innkeeper run hastily up the stairs leading to the hotel apartments, he decided to follow. With a mumbled apology to his companions, he left the group and pursued the innkeeper silently. He saw him knock hastily on a door and enter. Tallow leapt after him on his long legs and reached the door as it closed. He bent and listened. He could hear nothing beyond a few hysterical murmurings from Slorm and the calmer grunt of the man to whom Slorm spoke.

Tallow delicately took hold of the door handle and risking his life and his hopes, danced into the room shutting the door behind him and leaning against it with an insane grin on his face.

'Gentlemen,' smiled Tallow, bowing. 'Your servant!'

Tallow had drunk three large glasses of wine and these influenced him. He was not drunk in the sense in which most men become drunk. Tallow was drunk in his own unique manner and now cared not a damn for anything, including himself. And this is not how most men become drunk, nor why. Tallow noted the looks of astonishment on the faces of the assembled plotters; he noted the look with delight and warmth, and he recognized General Largek.

'Good evening, General,' he laughed. 'Good evening, to you, sir. Good evening. Very pleased to see you here.'

'What do you want, Mr Tallow?' said Slorm nervously.

'Why are you here, sir?' demanded the General with a hastily assumed air of indignation. 'Is there not a place in Rimsho where men can meet privately if they choose?'

'Of course there is, General. Of course there is a place. The Black Inn it is called and it's a den of royalists.'

The General cursed and reached for his holstered revolver. But Tallow raised an arm. 'Please – General – the dramatics are wasted, sir. Wasted. To shoot me would defeat your own aims.'

'What do you mean, sir?'

'I mean that I'm willing to help you!'

'Why? You are Zhist's right-hand-man.'

'Both right and left, my dear General,' corrected Tallow. 'He has no other. And so the right-hand knows rather well what the left-hand is doing. Luckily Zhist is unaware of the movements of either. You are safe – I shall not betray you. I have had the chance. Otherwise, why would I be here tonight?'

'Mr Tallow, what's your game?'

'My game is your game, sir. Your game – up to a point. I've told you I'll help you. Only Zhist himself, could help you more than I!' Tallow was enjoying himself in his own drunken manner. He let the words babble out in a half-mocking flow.

'You are here to help us?' The General sounded disbelieving

'Exactly, sir.'

'Why – is this a trap? Some plan to get us out into the open? Why should you help us? We've heard of you, Mr Tallow – we know you're cunning. You keep yourself to yourself and there are some who say you're the power behind Zhist.'

This misapprehension amused Tallow and he laughed for several minutes, collapsing at last into a sitting position, with his back to the door. It was surprising, for this was the first time he'd heard the idea voiced. Still, it would not do to correct the General. If he thought that Tallow ruled Rimsho – so much the better for Tallow's plans.

'That's as may be.' He tittered again, unable to control the reaction. 'And perhaps you're right. The fact is that I'm willing to aid you. I don't care what you do. But Zhist must be got rid of. Exiled, preferably.'

'Do it yourself. Why don't you engineer it yourself?'

'I need a good excuse. Couldn't manage it. Too many of the army people are on his side. I need you, gentlemen – and you need me.'

'True.'

'Very true. I'll give you an excuse for rousing a mob against Zhist – you'll do the rest. Do you agree?'

'Conditionally,' said the Colonel warily, unable to make Tallow's mood out. Seeing the look in the General's old eyes, Tallow began to laugh again. He chuckled uncontrollably and got up to plump himself down in a big armchair, from which the General had recently risen.

'What conditions?' he managed to gasp, as the chair engulfed him.

'How do we know we can trust you?'

'Well, you don't – you don't, General. And at this moment I don't know why you should. The thing is – I need your help – you need mine.'

'That line of reasoning certainly appeals to me, Mr Tallow. If you had said that you were a royalist, I doubt whether I should ever have believed you.'

'I wouldn't have believed myself, General. Anyway, I never wanted to get involved with the revolution. Zhist blackmailed me into joining his men in the first place.'

'Yes, I've heard that story. But why did you remain with him?'

Tallow decided that a lie he had prepared might appeal to General Largek. He said: 'My – um – wife turned up unexpectedly. She fell in love with Zhist. I remained to attempt to take her with me. She would not go. If Zhist dies – or has to go away, I shall be able to convince her of her mistake in thinking she's in love with him.'

'Ah,' said the General knowingly. 'Ah – jealously, eh, Mr Tallow? Now I see . . .'

Tallow simulated a look of discomfort. 'But we'll talk about that no more, General,' he muttered. 'Could you raise a mob?'

'I think so – but I dislike the idea.'

'You have to use the methods of the enemy,' said Tallow with conviction. 'I'll make Zhist unpopular in certain quarters – you raise the mob. The rest will follow. Do you understand?'

'Perfectly.'

'Fine,' chuckled Tallow, laughing again at the seriousness of the General's demeanour. 'Fine, my friends.' He got up and bowed to the mystified civilians and army officers. Some of them bowed back.

Tallow scampered from the room delightedly. 'I shall keep in touch through Mr Slorm,' he called as he paced jauntily along the corridor and down the steps towards the main bar.

Blithely he ignored the chatter of welcome as he passed the groups on his way out. He waved a hand in uncertain salute and bounced towards the door.

Remembering the distance he had walked to get to the Black Inn, he decided to test his power. 'Can anyone give me a lift?' he shouted suddenly.

A dozen voices chorused their willingness to aid him home. He selected the loudest and, with the man following him, pushed open the doors and went out into the night.

The man was big and beefy in the crested coat of a banker. He talked all the time and Tallow heard enough of his babble to interject a polite nod occasionally. The carriage was a four-seater affair, driven by a single coachman who commanded a pair of horses. The banker was obviously trying to get Tallow interested in a project which would see him and Tallow well set up for funds and the country rather the worse off. But Tallow, when he had made sense of the man's conversation, put on an expression of shocked horror, mumbled words like 'treason' and 'shot' which successfully drove the man into a frightened silence for a while. He had just begun to beg Tallow to keep the proposition dark when the carriage stopped outside the palace. Tallow disembarked, thanked the banker, treated him to a steely glare and hopped into the palace by way of a side-door.

Awakening the next morning with a dull headache and a return to his introverted, brooding mood, Tallow managed to get up without disturbing the pale-faced, tense Miranda and pull on his official uniform.

He had formed a plan as he slept, and he knew how he could aid Largek and his friends and also start the events which should, if his plan worked, lead to his own freedom. It would have to be done very quickly.

Zhist, as was usual, had already risen and was in his office staring at maps, and worrying.

'Good morning,' said Tallow with a worthy simulation of the previous night's cheerfulness. 'How are you?'

Zhist answered with considerable surprise: 'Good morning, Tallow. You're feeling better?'

'I am Colonel.'

'That's a relief. I haven't been able to make you out these past days.'

'Sorry, I've been worried.'

'So I gathered. Where did you go last night, by the way?'

Hoping that Zhist did not suspect him Tallow answered truthfully. 'To the Black Inn – I'd had news of plotters – royalists. I investigated the information and found the "royalists" to be three or four harmless old men. They won't be any trouble – to arrest them would create unnecessary disruptions for us. Their friends might object and we would only succeed in feeding the propaganda fires of the monarchists.'

'True,' Zhist nodded.

'But I discovered something far graver,' said Tallow slowly. 'I discovered that some twenty of your officers are planning to desert to the enemy.'

Zhist's eyes showed his surprise for a moment, then he said calmly, with a hard undercurrent to his voice: 'How did you find this out?'

'From the royalists themselves. I pretended to be sympathetic to their cause and they gave me the names of the army officers they hope will aid them. Of course, they will be worse off if Hyriom wins the war – and they'll never get their king back. But the poor old fools don't realize this. I think the news calls for strong – and quick – measures.'

'You're right! But – you're certain that the information was correct?'

'Yes – I checked. You'll be surprised when you learn who some of the men are.'

'Who are they?' said Zhist dully.

Tallow recited a list of names, being careful to name fifteen or so of the most untrustworthy men in the army and about five of Zhist's more dependable – and highly popular – officers. When he had finished, he said: 'This is what's been worrying me for the past few days. I'd heard rumours – but that's all. What the royalists said last night confirmed the reports.'

'Any ideas what we should do?' said Zhist brokenly. 'I wouldn't have believed it of some of the men you mention.'

'Nor I,' agreed Tallow with veracity. 'But the facts are there.'

'We'd better round up those officers and hear their stories. See to it, will you, Tallow? With war so close we can't afford to risk allowing traitors to go free. It will make the men – and many of the citizens – restless, but we'll have to do it.'

'I'll see to it,' promised Tallow, and left Zhist to his maps.

He made his way to his own office and there wrote down the ranks and names of the men he had mentioned. Every one of them, as far as he knew, was wholly innocent of treason or anything else. An orderly entered the room in answer to a bell Tallow rang. Tallow put the sheet of paper into an envelope, sealed it and handed it to the orderly.

'Give this to Commander Partoc,' he said. 'Make sure he gets it and no one else.' Commander Partoc was head of the Military Police.

'Yes sir,' The orderly saluted and left.

Tallow sat back in his chair. He felt nothing – not even satisfaction. But part of his plan was already put into action. He could see no reason why the rest should not work. For a few hours he had to wait. Patiently, Tallow waited.

Barely two hours after he had sent the message to Commander Partoc, the orderly reappeared. He saluted and handed a sealed dispatch to Tallow. Tallow signed for the orderly to leave and opened the letter.

It stated that the twenty men had been arrested and that two had resisted. Bluntly the letter said that the men were restless and did not like the sudden swoop. It was signed by Partoc.

Tallow rang the bell and the orderly re-entered. 'Ask Commander Partoc to come to my office,' he said.

A quarter-of-an-hour later, Commander Partoc stood before Tallow. Tallow said: 'Those officers you arrested. Colonel Zhist wants them shot.'

'The men won't like it, sir.'

'Have them shot, Commander. I don't like it either – but we all have to obey orders.'

'Very well, sir.' The Commander saluted smartly and, grim and grey of face, left the office.

An hour passed and the Commander returned. Twenty men had died by gunfire. Tallow nodded. 'Good,' he said. 'Very efficient, Commander. I'll mention this to Colonel Zhist. It took courage to carry out that order.'

'Thank you, sir.'

Another hour went by and the orderly reported to Tallow. 'Half the army's on the verge of mutiny, sir, over today's executions.'

'I see,' said Tallow, gravely writing. He sealed another envelope and handed it to the orderly. 'Take this to Mr Slorm at the Black Inn. Do you know it?'

'Yes, sir.'

The orderly disappeared and Tallow sat back to wait. This time he waited four hours and he heard the mob in the streets outside the palace, just as Zhist sent for him.

Zhist was angry and worried. He strode about his huge office with huge strides. He turned sharply as Tallow entered and pointed a blunt figure at him. 'Did you order those men shot?' he accused.

'Yes, Colonel, I did,' said Tallow smugly He was certain now that Zhist was doomed. 'I thought it would be best. It was clean and swift.'

'Too bloody clean and swift – now half the city's up in arms against me. You've done more damage than those twenty men might have done between them!'

'I'm sorry, Colonel. I did what was best – for me.'

'You did what was best. The country's finished now, because of that stupid order. Without faith in their leader they'll never rally to fight the enemy!' There was rage and horror in his voice. 'All I've struggled for will be over in a few days – because of you!' He had not heard Tallow's last words, obviously.

'So what!' spat Tallow. 'Does it matter?'

'You did this *deliberately*?' There was disbelief in Zhist's voice. 'You *planned* this?'

'Yes.'

'You knew that I'd be blamed for it?'

'Yes.'

'Why, Tallow?' Now Zhist's tone was pleading; there were real tears in his eyes, whether of rage or of sorrow Tallow did not know. 'Why did you betray *me*?'

'I owe you no loyalty – you said so yourself.'

'But you did not owe me *this*!'

'I did – though you'll never realize why. I tried to reason with you. In a way you brought this upon yourself.'

'What do you mean?'

'I can't explain again.' Tallow had not realized that this interview would be so difficult. He found himself attempting to justify his actions. What was it about this fanatical little army officer which aroused unwanted emotions in him?

'But if you hated me enough to do this – what about all the innocent people who will suffer?'

'Damn the people. They don't matter. It doesn't matter if they die now or in a few years.'

'It is not their lives I'm worried about. It's their freedom – the freedom of their children. Don't you realize that? They have a right to freedom. They have a right to be individuals.'

'Who gave them those rights?'

'I was going to give them the rights.'

'Did they ask for them – did they ask you for them? Did they?'

'No – but they wanted them.'

'Did they? They wanted food, air and sex – that's all they wanted. You decided – and men like you decided – that they wanted these amorphous rights. It was you who interfered – not I.'

'Tallow – every man has a right to live as he wants to.'

'Exactly. All you are doing is making him live another way. You are not letting him live as he wants to. A man lives as he *needs* to live.'

'Your arguments are unimportant. How am I going to stop them doing something they'll regret?'

'Your actions are unimportant. They already regret deposing the king – Natcho – they'll regret deposing you when they have a conquerer sitting on Hyriom's throne!'

Zhist shook his head and turned his back on Tallow.

'I can't understand you, Tallow. I can't. I tried to help you.'

'You've tried to help too many people, Colonel Zhist. Far too many people. Outside you'll hear their thanks.'

The mob was roaring. Storming at the gates of the palace. A few sentries put up a half-hearted resistance but it was obvious that they were struggling between their duty and their sympathy.

'You said you wanted a tolerant regime,' Tallow went on. 'And your whole premise is based on intolerance. Intolerance of Natcho – intolerance of a political system That's how this started – you were intolerant of a fairly harmless system. You said it was harmless yourself – you said its fault was that it was "outdated". Toleration is fine – if everybody practises it, as I hoped to practise it. As I practised it once. Non-interference, call it what you like. If you want your Harmonious Utopia – you can't be a politician. You must learn to be wholly tolerant and hope that it works – little by little, that way. You can't *enforce* tolerance, Colonel!'

'But I *loved* these people.'

'I have never loved nor hated them, Colonel. I haven't the capacity for love or hate. Colonel – I have only just realized that I am more *of* these people than you are. I represent the "mass", Colonel. I don't *want* to be helped. I just want to lead my life without interference, wherever possible. You decided to help me. Was it your love of me that made you make that decision?'

'No – oh, I don't know what it was. I'm not a bad man, Tallow. I don't deserve this betrayal.'

'You're not a bad man, Zhist, I agree. But you deserve this – and more. I believe you or Miranda said that I regard people as "Them" not "Us". I agreed with you, I think. Now I don't agree so much – I think I'm more of "Us" than you or anyone else who accused me. I'm "Us" because I don't think of it. I'm "Us" because I don't attempt to help anyone. I'm an individual, certainly. Just as everyone who composes the "mass" is an individual until the politicians and the mystics and the do-gooders get to work on them. They're individuals because they don't stop and think "I'm an individual". Find a man, however, who admits to being one of the "mass". Find him, Colonel, and I might concede you have a small point – your point will be that you have an ability to mould a man's mind. I think I do hate you, Colonel, in my own way – because of what you represent – not because of what you are.'

'You're wrong, too, Tallow. You know you're wrong.' Zhist had collapsed over his desk. The mob was swarming in the square outside now, they had passed through the gates.

'I may be – but I don't think so, Colonel.'

'Tallow – you forget your duties. I concede that you may have no rights – but you have duties – and those duties should breed rights eventually. That's probably where they begin – as duties – but eventually they turn into rights. You have duties to your fellow human beings. You have responsibilities. By your very philosophy of non-interference you may harm countless people. If you try to help them, instead, you won't hurt them so much. I don't think I am as much a villain as you, Tallow.'

'But where does it end, Colonel? Where is the line between helping the few and helping the many? Where do you leave off recognizing your "duties" and where do you start imposing new ones? Where does it end?'

Zhist sighed a deep sigh. He said: 'Perhaps you're right. Maybe that sums up the whole problem of life and philosophy – "Where does it end?" – I think we're both extremists, Tallow. We've gone in two directions – and both are the right ones – up to a point. Extremes are dangerous – and extremists are unhappy men – aren't we, Tallow? But is there a right direction which will not take us too far – or are there so many directions that we cannot choose? There are so many directions, Tallow.'

'There are,' agreed Tallow, 'but I have found the true one.' His voice faltered as he spoke and he fought off the nagging doubts which were invading his mind once more.

'But we can't stop this little turn of events now, Colonel,' he said hurriedly. 'Maybe I want to – maybe I don't – but I started the course – I made the turn. I must go with it to the end. You realize that?'

'I realize it. The same thing goes for me. If I hadn't forced you –

and I suppose I did force you – to join me, I wouldn't be betrayed by you, now. We all start a wheel, Tallow. We start it turning and we must spin with it while we live. I am becoming a fatalist, my friend – as I think you are, too.'

'Maybe.' Tallow smiled viciously. 'But I'm winning on this particular turn and I'll stay this way as long as I can.' He regretted the pettiness of his words as he spoke them, but he followed them up with a pettier action. He was caught up in it now. He drew his revolver from his holster and pointed it at the Colonel.

'You are my prisoner, Colonel.'

Zhist shrugged. 'So be it,' he smiled painfully. 'I'll not bother you. Will you kill me – or let me live?'

'Which do you prefer?'

'I think I'd rather live. I'd like time to think about our conversation – and events which caused it. I'm not afraid of that,' he finished defiantly.

'I'll try and see that you're exiled,' promised Tallow, and meant it.

'Imprison me, if you like. I shan't mind.'

'We'll see.'

Three soldiers burst into the room. They carried rifles. They were mutineers. Tallow said quickly: 'The Colonel is my prisoner – take him to the cells. Do not harm him.'

The three men looked at each other.

'Do as I say,' ordered Tallow, 'I'm in command for the moment. You can lose nothing by arresting him.'

'The people want his blood, Mr Tallow. They want to lynch him!'

'What will they achieve by that? They've lynched so many people since the revolution.'

'They want him, sir.'

Tallow turned to look at Zhist. The Colonel shrugged once more. Tallow said: 'Very well – let them have him.' He did not meet Zhist's eyes again. He put his pistol back in its holster and the three soldiers grabbed Zhist and hustled him out of the room. The Colonel still had his lithe, animal vitality even as he walked away. He did not speak to Tallow but though he may have accepted the position fatalistically his body had not – it still had its energy, its power. Tallow felt a brief pang of sorrow and then the men disappeared and he closed the big doors behind them. He went to the window. The mob seethed – a grey mindless mass of protoplasm with only one thought now – Zhist's death. Largek and his men had done well – he had never thought them such good mob orators. It was Tallow's turn to sigh and he felt weary – he had none of Zhist's vitality.

Miranda came into the room. She was furious.

'What have you done?' she hissed. 'What have you done now, Jephraim? Is this how you repay Zhist – with treachery? I thought you'd changed! And now you do this!' Her face was disgusting in its rage. Her voice was hysterical and her whole body tensed with a fury she could not express in words. She reached out and slapped his face. She kept on slapping it but he hardly felt it. He just stood looking out of the window until eventually she stopped. She followed his gaze. The mob had Zhist. They had ripped most of his clothing away so that he was incongrously clad in tattered underclothes and his boots. He was bleeding but still conscious. A rope went over a gargoyle which stuck out from the wall. A noose.

'No!' screamed Miranda. 'No! They can't do it!'

Tallow laughed – an unpleasant sound devoid of humour. 'They're doing it,' he said.

'Why did you let them?'

'I had no choice.'

Now they had placed the noose over Zhist's neck. Men began to tug on the other end of the rope, hoisting the dangling figure up. The body twisted about for long seconds and then the boots clicked together three times in a military salute. Zhist said farewell and died. He hung there jerking, his face twisted, distorted by the constricting rope, his body stiff, soldierly to the last.

Miranda began to sob.

Tallow wished that he had managed to dispose of Miranda before his plans were put into operation. But it was too late now. He noticed that she was fatter; that her stomach appeared to have swollen. For the first time he fully realized that she was pregnant – with his child. 'My love child' he thought cynically, bitterly. 'What shall I do?' Suddenly he was sorry that he had done what he had – he regretted it. And then Miranda spoke again.

'I pity you, Jephraim Tallow,' she sobbed. 'I pity you – and I hate you.'

'Don't hate me, sweetheart,' Tallow said tenderly. 'But at this moment I need your pity – and your help. I've never asked for help before – never. Now I need it.'

She shrugged his hand away. 'It's too late, Jephraim,' she said. 'Far too late. Only a day ago I might have helped you. But a day ago you refused my help. It's no good – you must take help when it's offered, or not expect it at all. I'm only human, Jephraim, unlike you.'

'I'm human now, Miranda. Help me.'

'Too late,' she repeated and turned away.

Tallow felt as if he was swimming out of a deep pool and the pool was composed of all the emotions he had feared. He seemed to reach the top and his head cleared and he reached for his pistol. Once more he was calm.

'Thank you for that, Miranda,' he said gratefully. 'You saved me with those words. But you have destroyed yourself.' She turned, suddenly fearful.

'No, Jephraim!' she screamed, seeing the pistol, knowing his intent.

'No! You would not. You loved me – I loved you. No, Jephraim!'

He squeezed the trigger of the gun. It exploded several times before she collapsed. He did not look at her body. He dared not look. He was surrounded by corpses. Hemmed in by gigantic corpses which mocked him and accused him. Their accusations he could fight – but not their mockery.

Now he was uncertain what to do. He could flee – yet still he did not want to. Why? He could think of no logical reason. The corpses alone were enough to make him go. Instead, his feet moving automatically, he went to the big windows which led to the balcony. He opened them.

Before he realized it, he was speaking to the people.

'My friends,' he shouted. 'Colonel Zhist is dead – the tyrant we served is destroyed. But our freedom is still at stake. Even now we are threatened by war – and if the enemy wins – we shall be a subject people. It will take centuries to throw off the yoke, once gained. We cannot fight the invaders – but let us give them nothing when they come! Blow up your factories and seek refuge in the woods and hills. Our only hope is to go far away and found new homes for our children. It is not entirely the fault of our leaders that we live this way. It is the fault of our cities – our society – our circumstances. Our greed is our downfall. Make a new start – or you will end your days in misery.'

The wave of derisive laughter which wafted up to him was agony in Tallow's ears. He turned and fled. Now, his thoughts were at last only for his boat – and the golden barge.

CHAPTER SEVENTEEN

Now Tallow progresses down the river. His thoughts are chaotic, his actions confused. He feels like a cripple. He sobs sometimes and moans. At other times he laughs. He is frenzied but does not work with speed for his arms and legs are slow in obeying his mental impulses. He jumps about in his boat like a clowning fool. Nothing is harmonious. He is the antithesis of all the golden barge represents. Now the original yearning is gone – or is altered. It has been replaced by a frantic necessity. What the barge represents is no longer important. What it might offer is a question which no longer disturbs Tallow's pitiful mind. Now it is *habit*, sheer, unalterable habit which drives the wretch on. For something has rubbed off on our hero – he has ceased to be uninfluenced and this cessation contributes to his downfall. Plain, blunt, devious, blind, ridiculous Tallow does not even have his questionable faith any longer. He has lost it and strives ludicrously, in his madness, to find it again. He hopes that sight of the barge will bring a return to his earlier state of mind. But too much has happened and even in his weakness Tallow has become weaker. He has lost his dreams, cannot even remember what they felt like, he only knows that they were preferable to the mental situation in which he has found himself at last.

On he sails, and no longer bothers to ask '*Why?*'

Swirling echoes in his skull mock him. He still sees corpses, this little tragic figure. We can only laugh at him – and feel sympathy. Are we, also, among the mockers? We have followed his progress. Seriously? Facetiously? Cynically? With boredom? Troubled? Happily? How have we followed this idiot's progress? This blind man's caperings? This visionary's struggle? Poor Tallow. He has attempted too much, perhaps?

Tallow sails desperately on in chaotic frenzy. The wind fills the sails of the craft he has picked at random from the quayside. It is a very different ship to the little *Gorgon* in which he first set sail.

The wind in his face is balm to him, it soothes his poor, strained nerves. He realizes that his teeth are tightly clenched together and deliberately, with the first coherent thought he has had since Miranda's death, he relaxes his muscles and parts his lips, breathing in the fresh, clean river air. His body aches and he has no idea how much time has passed since he resumed his disrupted journey. He cannot be bothered even to look upwards at the sun which glares down. All around him he sees only a misty haze of greenery and the shimmer of the silver water ahead of him.

His lungs are heavy in his body, his chest feels constricted and his head aches horribly. He mutters to himself sometimes and the words are meaningless mumblings, scrambled words without theme or construction. And tears glisten down his red face to fall upon his distorted nose and his wide mouth with lips set in a maniac's chilling grin.

Wretched and insane, Tallow keeps his long-fingered right hand upon the rudder-bar of his ship and guides it automatically, sailing through the golden mornings and the bleak, black nights, passing towns, villages, cities, farms, and mansions and not seeing them, nor realizing that they pass and, in his own way, Tallow sleeps and eventually the fever of fear leaves him and one morning he looks around and knows where he is and what he follows.

Rain is falling steadily, with angry vigour, and the skies are grey and sombre. The rain rivets into the river, stirring the water so that it swirls with increased energy about the boat.

And now Tallow falls forward. He collapses to the bottom of his craft and lies in dirty water, his breath coming in racking gasps, the water gurgling around his mouth, his starved, pinched features. He attempts to lift himself up out of the water. He succeeds at last in hoisting his weary body over a seat. Then he vomits liquid out of his stomach and consciousness leaves him.

Now a city lies ahead of Tallow's boat. It is a quiet city, a peaceful city of marble and mosaic, of green strips of turf and of stately people. But Tallow does not see the city, for he is still unconscious. His boat drifts on the river, at the mercy of a current which plays with it, whirling it around and rocking it. A tall man, in simple clothes which flow over his body, sees the boat and points it out, silently, to his companion, a woman of his own age with greying hair and a calm face. She looks at him for a moment and they speak. Then they turn quickly back and walk swiftly towards a large building on the quayside.

A few moments later men erupt from the building and run with long, easy strides down to where a boat is moored. It is a rowing boat, without sails or motor and it is slim with a high tapering prow. They climb into the boat and row in the direction of Tallow's craft which, by this time, is almost past the city.

Deftly, they manoeuvre their own boat until they can touch Tallow's vessel. They attach lines to it and begin to tow it back to shore. They speak rarely and then only when it is necessary. They are a strange, silent people, apparently self-possessed and attuned to each other.

The shore is soon reached and the men gently take Tallow's gangling body in their arms and, with him cradled thus, place him upon a wheeled stretcher which awaits them. They push the stretcher towards a tall tower which stretches higher than the other buildings.

An hour later, on a bed, surrounded by puzzled people, Tallow wakes up and sees his rescuers.

He is unable to understand the circumstances and he is disorientated. The people surrounding him are silent and their eyes are sympathetic. One of them, the man who first saw Tallow, says:

'Do you wish us to help you?'

'No,' replies Tallow, automatically.

'Then you may rest here until you feel like continuing. Or you may stay if you wish to.'

'Where am I?'

'The City of Melibone,' the man answers. He looks at his companions, but they cannot help him, they do not feel there is anything they can do.

'Where is that?'

'Fifty miles inland from the Sea.'

'The Sea – it is so close. I had not realized. Tell me –' Tallow struggles up in his bed, his eyes intense, 'Have you seen a barge pass? A golden barge?'

'Many times. Do you seek it?'

'Yes.'

'You are not the first.'

'So I believe.'

The man is helpless. He cannot communicate with Tallow – cannot find the words which will warn him and which will not change his mind for him. At last, after an internal struggle with himself, he remains silent. By this time, Tallow's mind is wandering again and he, too, is attempting to tell the man something.

'I have seen sunsets and the stars. I have seen gay water and dancing birds, pirouetting through the air.' Although he talks on and on, Tallow does not communicate either. He wants to tell these people something, but he is unable to do so. No words come to him. 'I have seen all these things in a year; never before.'

The people around the bed are indistinct, their eyes stare, perturbed, at Tallow, at each other. They stare all the time and Tallow wants to tell them that which he cannot voice. He babbles on.

The people, also, are worried. Their code, an alien, almost inhuman code, forbids them to interfere in any man's destiny. But they are kindly people – they want to help him. They hope that Tallow will elect to stay with them. But they realize that this is unlikely.

'I am alone – yet surrounded – I am no individual. I am a blind man who has seen – a deaf man who has heard – but I am still dumb – as dumb as I have ever been. Why should this be? Is this the fate of every man – or is it my individual fate? Even the visions are not clear any more – the sounds are indistinct. Must I end my days in silence and darkness, when I desired – expected – light and words which were true? Too many questions. All down the river there have been too many. If only I had stayed on course. But am I to blame? No. Yes. I am both – and so are they. Oh, God, – where am I?'

Tallow's mind has been overwhelmed by thoughts filtering from the depths. Feelings – emotions – previously untapped, unexplored, unanalysed, surge up now and his brain cannot control them, for it has never known of their presence.

The people file out of the room, leaving Tallow alone, raving still.

'Why? Does a dog suffer this way? No – it is the suffering of a child. A child grown up too quickly – too suddenly to assimilate the data – too proud to heed the warnings of others. But were the others right – any of them? I was angry in that first town – they took away my individual rights – and now I know there are no individual rights – only duties. Perhaps if I had stayed – no – no. But what of Miranda – could my yearnings have been satisfied – found fruition through my life with her – through the child which I gave her? Perhaps. That was better. And Zhist – could he have helped me? No. Miranda, Miranda – why did I kill her? Why? And Mesmers – perhaps – perhaps Mesmers? Mesmers and Miranda – they could have helped, if I had asked for the right things. But they only had certain things with which to help me. They did not offer all I required. Or did they? Uncertainty – it is horrible. Is it death I see ahead? Or is there still a chance in the barge? It is all I have now – I need it more than I ever needed it. Perhaps this is why I have been through all this? But must there be a reason? Too many questions – no answers. I am incapable of justifying my actions. Damn them! They have done this to me. They should have realized I was different. Or am I so different? Every thought brings a new question. I think there is still a chance if I can reach the barge in time. I must rest here, but only for a short while. Then I must continue. There is nothing *left* to do but follow the barge. Nothing.'

Tallow's self-asked questions follow, repetitively. He desperately seeks an answer – one answer. But none comes. His sense of aloneness pervades his whole being; once again he is dependent entirely upon himself – but he is not so self-contained or self-reliant as he was. He has destroyed – and he has been destroyed. All that was strong in him – good or bad, whatever it was – all this confidence has gone now, crumbled out of him, leaving him only his weakness and a dream of regaining his lost strength.

Perhaps he has tried too hard – or not hard enough? He doesn't know. Indecision – the old indecision – has returned and it has been made more terrible because it is now abstract. He has nothing concrete to grasp.

For hours the questions still come and he seeks to shut up his mind, to forget the past and his hopes for the future. He is dreadfully frightened – his fear, perhaps, is the one tangible thing in his existence. But its very tangibility horrifies him and he would rather have it that nothing was tangible – nothing at all. In that way he might escape. More days pass.

He spends his time eating and sleeping. His waking hours spent in desperately attempting to assimilate his confused thoughts; his sleeping hours plagued by nightmares in which he sees the mocking, swinging, flowing corpses of those he has destroyed. Eventually he is physically fit again and he is taken to his boat and luck is wished upon him by the people of Melibone. They stand staring after him as he sets sail, dazedly, down the river.

CHAPTER EIGHTEEN

It was not long after he had left Melibone that Tallow glimpsed the golden barge again.

His sense of relief was something which thrilled through his body and he speedily laid on sail in an attempt to catch up with the vessel. But a bend in the river, then another, obscured all sight of it. Tallow, for the first time in weeks, felt reassured and was certain that he would sight it again.

Then, to his miserable disappointment, he rounded a bend to discover that the river forked in two directions and the barge was gone. Which way?

The long island which lay like a basking crocodile in the centre of the river was in contrast to the leafy shrubbery which thronged both banks. It had been settled. Without any apparent plan, buildings were scattered upon it for as far as Tallow could see. Very few trees grew there. The dwellings were hope to Tallow – it was just conceivable that someone had seen the barge pass and could tell him which direction it had taken. His previous experiences had taught him to expect little; to expect the possibility that no one had seen the barge; but it was his only melancholy hope and he had to try to interrogate the islanders, at least. He could think of no other course of action.

The island did not have a real quayside to which Tallow could moor his boat, only jetties scattered haphazardly around its shores. Selecting one which appeared to be of stronger construction than the rest, Tallow tied up his craft and climbed up the wooden ladder which led to the top of the jetty. A few curious children stopped, gathered and stared at him, one or two adults gave him a look as they passed, but none approached him. There was no apparent order to the collection of buildings and what streets there were appeared to be nothing more than tracks winding tortuously among the houses.

Tallow tried to speak to the children first, but they just laughed at him and ran away to disappear behind the single-storey hovels which lay nearest the river-bank. The adults either did not hear him, see him, or more likely, did not choose to recognize his presence.

Eventually, one old man stopped reluctantly as Tallow planted himself in front of him and bellowed a question in his ear. 'Have you seen a boat pass this way?'

The question seemed to have more effect on the old man than it should have had. He looked startled and confused.

'May have done,' he said at last, warily.

'What do you mean, "may have done"? The boat is of gleaming gold and follows a straight course, never varying, putting in at no ports. Have you seen such a ship?'

'May have done – now I must go.' The old man pushed past Tallow and continued his progress, but Tallow walked beside him, angrily repeating his questions.

'I must know – which direction did it take?'

'Don't remember – it was more than two years ago I saw it – and thirty years before then. I've seen the bloody thing twice and don't want to see it again.'

'Which way did it go?'

'Never seen – and that's the truth. I followed it this far, thirty years ago – then I lost it. It frightens me, it does. Ask old Roothen – he'll tell you about that barge. I know it's a ghost ship.'

Tallow did not attempt to stop the ancient as he tottered on his way. Old Roothen – what was the significance of that statement? he wondered.

He stumbled along, between the houses, with no idea where he was going. At dusk, he was almost a mile inland and had reached a place lighted by torches. It was a fairly large space devoid of buildings and in this space were gathered a number of people. Men, women and children sat on the ground or stood in groups, talking. The women were cooking over fires and the men had plates of food in their hands, or wooden beakers of drink. The gathering seemed to be some kind of celebration, for the people were laughing happily, enjoying themselves. Tallow walked up to one group.

He tapped a man on the shoulder. The man turned; he was white-haired and young with a thin, rat-like face. He said: 'What do you want?'

Tallow asked him: 'Have you – or any of your friends – seen a golden barge pass recently?'

The man belched in Tallow's face and turned back to his companions. He chuckled nastily. 'This stranger wants to know about the fool's ship.' The men laughed derisively, nervously, and looked at Tallow who stood there, uncertain of himself, hating them. One of them grinned crookedly. 'Old Roothen will tell you about the ship, mate. He's been telling us what we already know for the last forty years and he'd like a new audience. We followed the bloody thing, same as him – but he says his case is different. I suppose you've come to tell us to go after it with you. If you have – you'd better find Roothen. We've got families to think of now. If he's not too drunk, you'll get a good story out of Roothen. He'll tell you.'

'Where can I find him?'

'Follow your nose – you'll smell him.'

'You don't know?'

'No – don't care, either. If your story's the same as his, I pity you. But don't tell it to us.'

'I wouldn't,' retorted Tallow, walking away.

He attempted to approach other groups, and received facetious replies. Soon, against his will, he was the centre of attraction and most of the hundred or so people in the gathering were staring at him.

'Who's that little man?'

'Some madman – trying to say the ship's real. We'd all still be following it if it was real. We were lucky enough to get out in time. Must be some river-madness that effects 'em. Why should this deranged idiot try and make us crazy too? You can't talk to him, though, not in a state like that – let's get him out of here!'

'What's he bothering us for?'

'That's what I'd like to know!'

'Coming here – spoiling our party. I knew it was going to be a bad day since I got up.'

'Always was the trouble . . .'

'Think they can come here and . . .'

'Bothering us . . .'

'Why . . .?'

'What . . .?'

'Who . . .?'

'How . . .?'

Tallow's self-control broke: 'Morons! You all went after the barge at some time. You didn't have the courage to continue or the will to go back against the current – so you're afraid when someone else comes along who has guts enough to take a risk. You think I'm mad – well I'll tell you something – I'd rather be mad than stagnating here like you!'

Someone tittered. A stone came hurtling out of the blackness beyond the firelight. It caught Tallow a stinging blow on the wrist.

'Run away!'

'I'm going –' Tallow ran, concerned for his own safety. He had experience of crowds before, when he was a child among children. They had resented him then, and he had not known why. He still could not guess at any logical reason – but he had learned by his early experience. He could not stop them by shouting at them – he could only run.

He ran through the night, away from the torch-glare, and he pitied himself.

He lost his bearings and could not find the shore again so he sat down, panting, beside the first tree he came to, a big oak. No houses had been built near it. He sat with his back against the bole and wondered how he was going to find the mysterious old man the villagers had mentioned. Did Roothen really know something? Tallow wondered. He'd find out if he met the old man.

Dare he sleep – or should he go on, find his boat and make his own decision about which fork of the river he should take? As he pondered the problem, he heard a wheezing voice singing, seemingly from out of the sky. He looked upwards. There must be a man in the tree, he thought.

'Hello there, youngster. You're a sailor by the looks of you. Where you going?'

Tallow still could not see anyone. 'Hello,' he said cautiously, peering up into the branches. 'I'm going down-river.'

'Which fork are you taking?' This question was followed by a cracked, senile laugh.

'Not sure.'

'Come up and join me!' There was a rustle of movement in the branches above and something fell down out of the air and struck Tallow on the right shoulder. He gasped and swore. He investigated the object and found it to be a rope-ladder leading upwards. With a shrug, he began climbing.

The ladder terminated about half-way up the tall tree and hung from a platform, crudely constructed, but strong and firm. Tallow pulled himself upwards, on to the platform and, through the darkness made out the pale face of an ancient, wrinkled man who grinned at him with a crooked mouth and eyes which hinted at strange madness.

'Who are you?' Tallow enquired.

'Roothen – old Roothen. I'm insane, you know – so the fools tell me. But I'm not insane – no more than you are.'

'You're following the barge – or you know something about it?'

'What barge?' The question came cautiously, in a whisper like the rustle of dead leaves.

'The golden barge. Someone told me you'd seen it.'

'Oh, I have – yes indeed. I've seen it. I followed it for three hundred long miles down-river.' The old man was grizzling wretchedly and sickening Tallow. 'I followed it, young fellow. Yes I did.'

'Why did you stop here, then?'

'Why did you – why did the others?'

'I wasn't sure which fork to take.'

'Neither was I, my friend, and neither were they.'

'But – they say you've been here for thirty years. Is that true?'

'Thirty? Yes – it might have been thirty. It might have been more for all I know. Some have been here longer.'

'Didn't you think of taking a chance – didn't you decide which fork?'

'Decide!' The cackle rose higher and died away like a sigh of wind. 'Decide! I've been trying to decide for thirty years. Which fork – which fork – which fork? You know what it'll mean to take the wrong one? I'll miss the barge forever.'

'Why? Couldn't you come back and try the other one?'

'Would there be time? Have any of those who went on ever come back?'

'There would have been if you hadn't waited thirty years. Why have you waited so long? The others may have found the barge.'

'I've waited in the hope that I'd see the barge again and would know which way it went. I'm down by the bank most nights when I'm not too drunk. I drink a lot – I don't know why. I'll see her when she comes. She's elusive is that one – I've thought myself miles behind her and then I've been laying-to in port and seen her pass me by. I've missed her for days – weeks – and found her again as if she'd only been an hour ahead of me. What do you make of that? I've been delayed and held prisoner – but I've gone on – sometimes with blood on my hands. But I've always seen the barge – just ahead – just ahead, but never close enough to board and rip the secrets out of her.

Why do you seek her, lad? She hasn't passed this way unless it was last night or a fortnight ago.' Roothen ignored the second part of Tallow's question – he had no answer.

'It was last night that she passed, Roothen. I know because I followed her this far and lost her again.'

'No!'

'Yes,' said Tallow, almost delightedly. He felt nothing but contempt for the old man.

'Oh – you're lying to me. Torturing me. You're lying. Say you're lying, lad.' The old man sobbed pitifully and Tallow heard him gulping at some liquid. 'You are lying, aren't you?' He spoke anxiously.

'No,' said Tallow, 'I'm not lying.'

The gulping noise again and a pitiful whining moan was all Tallow heard from Roothen.

'You deserve this,' he said. 'You deserve all of it – you don't deserve your dreams or your memories. You're a coward and a fool. You're as bad as the others – only you suffer different delusions.'

'Don't say that!'

'It's true.'

'No it isn't – I know it isn't. There's still time. I'm not that old.'

'Are you young enough even to manoeuvre a boat?'

'Of course!'

'Are you!'

'Yes – yes! Of course I am. Take me with you, lad, and I'll show you. We'll risk it. We'll risk it, together. We're comrades, lad. We know something the others don't.'

'We know nothing – we only know about something.'

'Yes, but we'll know soon, won't we?' The old man moved forward, tottering towards Tallow. He clutched at Tallow's clothing and breathed foul liquor fumes into his face. 'Take me with you, lad.' He was pleading, whining, and Tallow was disgusted.

'Why? Do you deserve a chance? I'm strong enough to go on, my friend. Nothing will stop me from risking the rest of the river. I'll find the barge – and maybe I'll come back and tell you what it was. Shall I do that?'

The old man wasn't angered by Tallow's words. He continued to beg to be taken along, but Tallow shook the feeble hands off his coat.

'I've lost a lot, old Roothen – I've lost more than most men and I've lost my strength. I'm weak, Roothen, but not so weak that I can't continue, to find what I want.'

'What do you want?'

'I'll know when I reach the barge. Where the barge leads me, I'll follow, until I'll know every secret that's ever worried me. I'll know the answer to every question which has ever come to plague me!' Even as he spoke, doubts were nagging in Tallow's mind, but he fought them down.

'Don't torture me, lad! Don't do that – take me along. I'll do my bit and we'll discover the knowledge together. I had a wife – I had a family – I had money. I've forsaken them all to follow the barge – and now I'm stuck here. You'd have pity on me – for I'm like you.'

'No you're not.'

'I am, lad. I am. There aren't many who've seen the barge – even fewer with the courage to follow it. We had the *courage*.'

'Curiosity,' said Tallow. 'It was curiosity to begin with not courage. And our vision is suspect. Why should it be the best and only way? What secrets did we leave behind us? A man can discover his "truths" by following many paths. I've found that. I've found that out too late – so I'm left with one path. A lonely path. I could have found what I wanted by remaining in most of the places I stayed at. I think this is why the barge leads men on – most of us, anyway. It leads us only a short distance, to show us something. But we don't realize that until it's too late to alter things. Finally, there's nothing to do but follow the barge on to the end and hope that it will lead you to an explanation of why you follow it. Why did you follow the barge? Why did I? Perhaps those who've settled here are right, after all.'

'We followed the barge because we knew it had the truth. It was the only way.'

Tallow looked up at the dark sky – at the small stars. He spoke distantly. 'Were you as selfish as I was?'

'No – not selfish. I – I – just knew that there was a greater destiny offered to me if I followed it. I *knew* this, lad – I *knew* it!' The old man's feet scraped on the wooden planking.

'So I thought once, also.'

'But it's true – don't let yourself think that it's not. It's true.'

'Perhaps. It's all we have left.' Tallow's disgust and his anger had calmed now, and he hardly realized the other man's presence. It was as if he were speaking to himself again, as he had done so frequently in the immediate past. 'I must take the chance – or I'll end my days like you – fighting madness with a bottle.'

'That's a cruel thing to say to an old man, lad.'

'It's the truth.'

'What of it?'

'Doesn't it matter that you're a drunken old dotard when you could have known the secret of life itself?'

'Yes – it matters; when I think of it.'

'Then that truth should matter.'

'I suppose it should. Go on, lad. Go on without me, I don't care. Probably you'll only get yourself killed. I'll have *life* anyway. How do we know that the barge is anything more than an illusion? Water plays funny tricks when the light's on it. It could be a sailor's madness – like these folk tell me. Couldn't it? A lot of people should know better than one.'

'Do you believe that?' insisted Tallow, who was not sure what to believe.

'I don't know.'

'So you rot here in your uncertainty. You might know whether you've wasted your life entirely, or not, if you followed the barge to the sea. You might find some kind of explanation.'

'That's right – I might. So why not take me with you?'

'We've destroyed too much – you and I. I'm afraid we'd destroy one another.'

'How? We'd help one another.'

'Would we?'

'Of course. Look – we're both after the same thing. One of us could sail and the other sleep. That way we could keep going indefinitely.'

'It's no good, Roothen. No good at all. I'm going. And don't try to stop me – I've killed too many people to worry overmuch about your death on my hands. Anyway – you're as good as dead!'

'You bastard!'

Tallow began to climb down the rope ladder. Palsied hands above him attempted to shake the ladder but the old man hadn't the strength to dislodge Tallow. He landed on the ground and set off again, in the hope of reaching at least one bank, which he could follow round and so find the place where he had moored his boat.

The streets were unlit and the few people who were abroad did not even notice him. He felt slightly scared but not too worried. The villagers would, by this time, have found other diversions. He eventually came to a river bank, got his bearings and trudged along until he came to the jetty. Soon he was in his boat, once more, and attempting to decide which fork to take.

He decided at last to leave it to the current. He took the boat out and waited. Soon he was sailing down on the stream of water bearing towards the left-hand fork.

The water flowed swiftly and smoothly, almost with the same sureness of purpose as the golden barge. Tallow decided that if he was wrong and this was not the correct fork, then he would sail up-river again and take the other fork. But time, he felt, was beginning to run out at last. The old sense of urgency returned and he hoped desperately that he was on the right course.

CHAPTER NINETEEN

This is the last stretch of the long, winding river. The river which runs from an unknown source down to an unknown sea. Imperturbable, it cannot be changed; only the banks change and the things on the banks. It is the life source of the cities and towns and villages which throng the banks – and it brings death. It brings hope and it destroys dreams. On it sail Tallow and a golden barge. We see it from above, see all its countless misty miles. We float over it and see only Tallow's boat; even we cannot see the barge at this moment.

Tallow struggles onwards and the water rushes ominously, gurgling and frothing; a sound which drowns all other sounds. But overlying this water-sound is a calm silence which speaks of great empty spaces and an eternity of peace. Tallow senses it – yet he is not insensitive of the state of the water, which predicts catastrophe. Tallow knows what the troubled waters signify. He knows but he cannot do anything. He is helpless – unable to fight that which he knows is inevitable. Faster and faster the water rushes until it is a torrent dragging the unwilling boat with it.

At last Tallow's fears are realized and he sees ahead of him dark wet rocks, splashed by white spume, sharp, like the teeth of a yawning dragon. Rapids are ahead of Tallow; dangerous, deadly rapid – uncompromising in their stagnant power. Frenziedly, the little voyager grasps for the boat-hook which lies along the length of the ship. He lays it across the sides and grips the rudder-bar with hands that are white and which tremble with the tension he is experiencing.

Still the peaceful silence overlying the boiling, hurtling waters. Still the sense of solitude – of destiny.

Tallow acts. The first rocks rush past him and he is safe for the moment. There is the throbbing roar of the torrent in his ears. With marvellous dexterity, using his only innate skill, he steers the boat expertly through the rapids, his right hand on the rudder bar. With his left hand he deftly wields the pole, pushing the boat away from the closest rocks.

It is over. The rocks of the rapids are past him, and he sweats, trembles, moans softly. Now he knows he cannot turn back. His chance is gone. If he has not followed the correct course – then he is doomed. He cannot even return to the haphazard village where the river forks. He is completely alone at last, with no one to trouble him. He has what he desired.

The boat rides the water like a prancing horse, jubilantly dancing as if it has a will of its own. It rocks Tallow as it surges down towards the sea – swifter and swifter until at last Tallow cries out.

'Too late, my fine boat – too late to go back. Too late to dare – too late to destroy. It is finished now – for better or worse, it is finished. I am at the mercy of you – of the river – and of whatever fate awaits me at the river's end.

'Too late for my mother, Miranda and Mesmers. Too late for the power I could have had – the riches – the woman – the knowledge. Too late for peace of mind. I have it now – I have my lonely solitude!'

He looks down into the river which murkily mirrors his face. He sees, in horror, an older man – too old! He sees lines on the face which a greater passage of time should have brought. Pain in the eyes where, a year before, no pain was – only blank incomprehension.

Tallow is a man fighting madness with stone-wall methods. He is clinging to his last vestiges of pseudo-sanity – blocking any ideas or concepts which can shatter his terrible illusion. He is desperately trying to convince himself of something – but he can find no conviction which appeals to him. Every idea which comes to him, now, he rejects. He shouts to himself above the crash of water. He yells sentences and phrases – hurls them into the implacable silence.

'Free – I am free. Free at last to pursue the barge. I have gained much in my journey – now my yearnings shall be satisfied. I shall yearn no longer, for I have paid all prices! There is nothing left to pay. I have nothing else! I am free!'

The boat twists and turns, racing down the river towards the sea. Tallow laughs in a hideous imitation of joy. He throws away the boat-hook and releases his grip on the rudder. He stands up in the bobbing boat, and he spreads his arms wide, looking upwards and around him – calling, calling. Calling until the shout is all on one note – a chant which soon becomes meaningless – the words lost in his surging emotions.

And now he looks forward, suddenly. He cocks his head on one side in the old manner and he screws up his eyes to peer ahead. His eyes widen, slowly; they widen and his lips part. He stumbles towards the prow of the boat, but the river whirls it around. He moves jerkily, attempting to keep in sight that which he has seen. It is the barge, the golden barge – larger than at any time since he first saw it. He feels he can almost touch it. Like a miming clown he reaches out towards it, but the boat turns again. Desperately, he strives to keep it in sight and part of his mind regrets the impulse which made him throw away the boat-hook. He cries out – pleading – frantic.

'Save me – save me. You have made me what I am! Save me – have mercy! I am here.'

The barge is sentient. Tallow knows that. It is alive and needs no crew. How can the barge help him? He realizes that it has no arms to drag him aboard, no hands to reach out to rescue him. How can it help him? Tallow knows that he will never get aboard.

'Help me! You have led me to sorrow and madness – you have made me kill. I have even killed myself for you. I have made every sacrifice. I have made the sacrifice of blood, of misery and of terror. What other dark horrors would you have me experience before you will take me to you? Take me now – I have paid your price!'

It is obvious to Tallow that there has been no price needed. That his quest has been useless – unless he follows the barge to the end. He must continue to follow. He must. It is too early. There has been no price asked but tenacity of purpose. Still implacable, the barge courses on, unsullied by the water which derisively plays with Tallow's boat. His vessel is caught in a miniature whirlpool which spins it round and round while the barge continues on course, without variance of speed or direction.

Automatically, Tallow continues to call to it and he is reminded, against his will, of Miranda's shouts from the river, after he had thrown her overboard.

But a strange elation fills him and with a wrench on the rudder, he turns the ship out of the whirlpool's embrace and, battling the currents, sails swiftly in the golden barge's wake. It shimmers ahead of him, tantalizingly, seemingly omniscient. Is it God? Tallow asks himself as, with mounting jubilance, he hounds the barge. Is it God who taunts me so? He is still irrational – but with an irrationality born out of his impatient elation – not his previous morbid, rambling yearnings.

Faster and faster flows the current. Faster – down towards the sea. Now Tallow hears the surge of the surf on an unseen shore – he sees, beyond the barge, a vast expanse of water, greater than any he has imagined. And his elation diminishes as doubt encompasses him. His fear of water – the old fear which he had of the river – his fear of depth – these fears grip him in a hideous embrace. Can he dare the ocean? But what lies at the river-mouth? Surely the barge will go no further? It is at the estuary that he will find his goal. He must.

As it nears the sea, the current becomes calmer, slower and the river widens. The barge keeps directly in the centre of the river. Continues onwards without pausing. Tallow shouts after it, the fear returning.

'No – don't betray me! Don't! Stay – come back. Not the sea. No, not the sea!' If the barge is aware of Tallow's presence, it makes no sign. On it goes, past the last land and out on to the ocean.

Tallow still follows – his sails bellying with the wind of the sea. His boat veers and scuds onwards, still in the wake of the glorious barge. As it sails over the ocean, which Tallow has not yet reached, a new iridescence radiates from it. It seems to swell to gigantic proportions; it is even larger than before. Tallow chokes in frustration and great tears well in his red-rimmed eyes. A huge salty drop careers along his nose and hangs there. More tears course down his face; they glisten in his stubbly beard. Onwards drives the golden barge – onwards towards the horizon. It is surrounded by massive depths of water on all sides. Mysterious ocean – more frightening than the dark sea which tempted Tallow on the day of Zhist's revolt. What is the ocean? Tallow wonders. Dare he cross it and follow the barge? But what will he find out there? Death? Or knowledge? Are they synonymous? Tallow does not know.

'I must decide, Now! I must decide. The sea is so great. My boat is tiny and I am even smaller. Dare I take the risk? Am I right? Is the barge what I believed it to be? Is it? If only I had a way of telling. If only it would show me some sign – then I would know – then I might follow it. But suppose I have been wrong? Suppose I have followed a dream of my own designing? No! Impossible! It cannot be true. It must not be true. I will not allow it to be true. The idea is false – for I know what the barge offers. I know it intuitively – deep in my ruined soul. Soul? It is my mind which is ruined. Mine was not great enough to take the strain. Or was it too small? Should I have taken the middle path? Succumbed to Miranda's temptation – to Mesmers – to Zhist? To the prison even? I know now that in any of these I might have found what I yearned for. But I demanded rights – and reasons – and tolerance. The human mind was never tolerant – or rarely so. Mine was not – though I thought it was, at one time. Intolerance breeds intolerance. There can be no unity – no harmony. We are all fragments, drifting after goals which half the time, perhaps all the time, do not exist. They are our hopes – our reassurances – some explanation for meaningless yearnings. There are only responsibilities

– duties. If only we could talk to one another in words which mean the same things! Where is our end? Must we forever follow the golden barges? Must we forever drift down nameless rivers to nameless goals? To oceans which we dare not sail? Unable to share our boats, however hard we try? I wish I knew. Too many rivers – too many currents – too many tides. I am finished.'

The boat slowly moves to a halt at the point where the river becomes the sea. It will need Tallow's guidance to sail it further. But Tallow makes no move.

Tallow sinks to his knees and his last defence against insanity breaks. He hears his own voice, clearly chanting a litany of madness: 'Mother – gone. Murder! Miranda – gone! Blasphemy. Betrayal. Mesmers – gone. Destroyer!' His voice shouts on, listing his crimes as he sees them. He hears the sound of the voice but will not listen, knowing that to do so will engulf him in a final madness. A dreadful, black madness. He clasps his hands to his ears and sobs. The voice stops.

He grins triumphantly and stands up in the dangerously rocking boat, an old man, prematurely aged. A rotten husk. But he twists his lips in a smile and his crafty head jerks to one side.

'I know the truth,' he says. 'I know it. And I don't need the barge. It was not courage I lacked to follow it. I need the barge no longer. It has taught me what I wanted to know. I have no longings, now – no yearnings. I am free of them, at last. Yes, Tallow triumphs, finally. And the barge has served its purpose.'

A small, almost imperceptible voice within him keeps saying, *You are wrong. You are lying.* But he will not hear it – he rejects it. He will not listen. He dare not.

He stares in hopeless uncertainty as the barge reaches the horizon, still visible, still golden and gleaming, and disappears.

The Deep Fix

ONE

Quickening sounds in the early dusk. Beat of hearts, surge of blood.

Seward turned his head on the bed and looked towards the window. They were coming again. He raised his drug-wasted body and lowered his feet to the floor. He felt nausea sweep up and through him. Dizzily, he stumbled towards the window, parted the blind and stared out over the white ruins.

The sea splashed far away, down by the harbour, and the mob was again rushing through the broken streets towards the Research Lab. They were raggedly dressed and raggedly organized, their faces were thin and contorted with madness, but they were numerous.

Seward decided to activate the Towers once more. He walked shakily to the steel-lined room on his left. He reached out a grey, trembling hand and flicked down three switches on a bank of hundreds. Lights blinked on the board above the switches. Seward walked over to the monitor-computer and spoke to it. His voice was harsh, tired and cracking.

'GREEN 9/7–O Frequency. RED 8/5–B Frequency.' He didn't bother with the other Towers. Two were enough to deal with the mob outside. Two wouldn't harm anybody too badly.

He walked back into the other room and parted the blind again. He saw the mob pause and look towards the roof where the Towers GREEN 9/7 and RED 8/5 were already beginning to spin. Once their gaze had been fixed on the Towers, they couldn't get it away. A few saw their companions look up and these automatically shut their eyes and dropped to the ground. But the others were now held completely rigid.

One by one, then many at a time, those who stared at the Towers began to jerk and thresh, eyes rolling, foaming at the mouth, screaming (he heard their screams faintly) – exhibiting every sign of an advanced epileptic fit.

Seward leaned against the wall feeling sick. Outside, those who'd escaped were crawling round and inching down the street on their bellies. Then, eyes averted from the Towers, they rose to their feet and began to run away through the ruins.

'Saved again,' he thought bitterly.

What was the point? Could he bring himself to go on activating the Towers every time? Wouldn't there come a day when he would let the mob get into the laboratory, search him out, kill him, smash his equipment? He deserved it, after all. The world was in ruins because of him, because of the Towers and the other Hallucinomats which he'd perfected. The mob wanted its revenge. It was fair.

Yet, while he lived, there might be a way of saving something from the wreckage he had made of mankind's minds. The mobs were not seriously hurt by the Towers. It had been the other machines which had created the real damage. Machines like the Paramats, Schizomats, Engramoscopes, even Michelson's Stroboscope Type 8. A range of instruments which had been designed to help the world and had, instead, virtually destroyed civilization.

The memory was all too clear. He wished it wasn't. Having lost track of time almost from the beginning of the disaster, he had no idea how long this had been going on. A year, maybe? His life had become divided into two sections: drug-stimulated working-period; exhausted, troubled, tranquillized sleeping-period. Sometimes, when the mobs saw the inactive Towers and charged towards the laboratory, he had to protect himself. He had learned to sense the coming of a mob. They never came individually. Mob hysteria had become the universal condition of mankind – for all except Seward who had created it.

Hallucinomatics, neural stimulators, mechanical psychosimulatory devices, hallucinogenic drugs and machines, all had been developed to perfection at the Hampton Research Laboratory under the brilliant direction of Prof. Lee W. Seward (33), psychophysicist extraordinary, one of the youngest pioneers in the field of hallucinogenic research.

Better for the world if he hadn't been, thought Seward wearily as he lowered his worn-out body into the chair and stared at the table full of notebooks and loose sheets of paper on which he'd been working ever since the result of Experiment Restoration.

Experiment Restoration. A fine name. Fine ideals to inspire it. Fine brains to make it. But something had gone wrong.

Originally developed to help in the work of curing mental disorders of all kinds, whether slight or extreme, the Hallucinomats had been an extension on the old hallucinogenic drugs such as Co2, Mescalin and Lysergic Acid derivatives. Their immediate ancestor was the stroboscope and machines like it. The stroboscope, spinning rapidly, flashing brightly coloured patterns into the eyes of a subject, often inducing epilepsy or a similar disorder; the research of Burroughs and his followers into the early types of crude hallucinomats, had all helped to contribute to a better understanding of mental disorders.

But, as research continued, so did the incidence of mental illness rise rapidly throughout the world.

The Hampton Research Laboratory and others like it were formed to combat that rise with what had hitherto been considered near-useless experiments in the field of Hallucinomatics. Seward who had been stressing the potential importance of his chosen field since university, came into his own. He was made Director of the Hampton Lab.

People had earlier thought of Seward as a crank and of the hallucinomats as being at best toys and at worse 'madness machines,' irresponsibly created by a madman.

But psychiatrists specially trained to work with them, had found them invaluable aids to their studies of mental disorders. It had become possible for a trained psychiatrist to induce in himself a temporary state of mental abnormality by use of these machines. Thus he was better able to understand and help his patients. By different methods – light, sound-waves, simulated brain-waves, and so on – the machines created the symptoms of dozens of basic abnormalities and thousands of permutations. They became an essential part of modern psychiatry.

The result: hundreds and hundreds of patients, hitherto virtually incurable, had been cured completely.

But the birth-rate was rising even faster than had been predicted in the middle part of the century. And mental illness rose faster than the birth-rate. Hundreds of cases could be cured. But there were millions to be cured. There was no mass-treatment for mental illness.

Not yet.

Work at the Hampton Research Lab became a frantic race to get ahead of the increase. Nobody slept much as, in the great big world outside, individual victims of mental illness turned into groups of – the world had only recently forgotten the old word and now remembered it again – *maniacs.*

An overcrowded, over-pressured world, living on its nerves, cracked up.

The majority of people, of course, did not succumb to total madness. But those who did became a terrible problem.

Governments, threatened by anarchy, were forced to re-institute the cruel, old laws in order to combat the threat. All over the world prisons, hospitals, mental homes, institutions of many kinds, all were turned into Bedlams. This hardly solved the problem. Soon, if the rise continued, the sane would be in a minority.

A dark tide of madness, far worse even than that which had swept Europe in the Middle Ages, threatened to submerge civilization.

Work at the Hampton Research Laboratory speeded up and speeded up – and members of the team began to crack. Not all these cases were noticeable to the over-worked men who remained sane. They were too busy with their frantic experiments.

Only Lee Seward and a small group of assistants kept going, making increasing use of stimulant-drugs and depressant-drugs to do so.

But, now that Seward thought back, they had not been sane, they had not remained cool and efficient any more than the others. They had seemed to, that was all. Perhaps the drugs had deceived them.

The fact was, they had panicked – though the signs of panic had been hidden, even to themselves, under the disciplined guise of sober thinking.

Their work on tranquillizing machines had not kept up with their perfection of stimulatory devices. This was because they had had to study the reasons for mental abnormalities before they could begin to devise machines for curing them.

Soon, they decided, the whole world would be mad, well before they could perfect their tranquilomatic machines. They could see no way of speeding up this work any more.

Seward was the first to put it to his team. He remembered his words.

'Gentlemen, as you know, our work on hallucinomats for the actual *curing* of mental disorders is going too slowly. There is no sign of our perfecting such machines in the near future. I have an alternative proposal.'

The alternative proposal had been Experiment Restoration. The title, now Seward thought about it, had been euphemistic. It should have been called Experiment Diversion. The existing hallucinomats would be set up throughout the world and used to induce *passive* disorders in the minds of the greater part of the human race. The co-operation of national governments and World Council was sought and given. The machines were set up secretly at key points all over the globe.

*

They began to 'send' the depressive symptoms of various disorders. They worked. People became quiet and passive. A large number went into catatonic states. Others – a great many others, who were potentially inclined to melancholia, manic-depression, certain kinds of schizophrenia – committed suicide. Rivers became clogged with corpses, roads awash with the blood and flesh of those who'd thrown themselves in front of cars. Every time a plane or rocket was seen in the sky, people expected to see at least one body come falling from it. Often, whole cargoes of people were killed by the suicide of a captain, driver or pilot of a vehicle.

Even Seward had not suspected the extent of the potential suicides. He was shocked. So was his team.

So were the World Council and the national governments. They told Seward and his team to turn off their machines and reverse the damage they had done, as much as possible.

Seward had warned them of the possible result of doing this. He had been ignored. His machines had been confiscated and the World Council had put untrained or ill-trained operators on them. This was one of the last acts of the World Council. It was one of the last rational – however ill-judged – acts the world knew.

The real disaster had come about when the bungling operators that the World Council had chosen set the hallucinomats to send the full effects of the conditions they'd originally been designed to produce. The operators may have been fools – they were probably mad themselves to do what they did. Seward couldn't know. Most of them had been killed by bands of psychopathic murderers who killed their victims by the hundreds in weird and horrible rites which seemed to mirror those of pre-history – or those of the insane South American cultures before the Spaniards.

Chaos had come swiftly – the chaos that now existed.

Seward and his three remaining assistants had protected themselves the only way they could, by erecting the stroboscopic Towers on the roof of the laboratory building. This kept the mobs off. But it did not help their consciences. One by one Seward's assistants had committed suicide.

Only Seward, keeping himself alive on a series of ever-more-potent drugs, somehow retained his sanity. And, he thought ironically, this sanity was only comparative.

A hypodermic syringe lay on the table and beside it a small bottle marked M-A 19 – Mescalin-Andrenol Nineteen – a drug hitherto only tested on animals, never on human beings. But all the other drugs he had used to keep himself going had either run out or now had poor effects. The M-A 19 was his last hope of being able to continue his work on the tranquilomats he needed to perfect and thus rectify his mistake in the only way he could.

As he reached for the bottle and the hypodermic, he thought coolly that, now he looked back, the whole world had been suffering from insanity well before he had even considered Experiment Restoration. The decision to make the experiment had been just another symptom of the world-disease. Something like it would have happened sooner or later, whether by natural or artificial means. It wasn't really his fault. He had been nothing much more than fate's tool.

But logic didn't help. In a way it *was* his fault. By now, with an efficient team, he might have been able to have constructed a few experimental tranquilomats, at least.

'Now I've got to do it alone,' he thought as he pulled up his trouser leg and sought a vein he could use in his clammy, grey flesh. He had long since given up dabbing the area with anaesthetic. He found a blue vein, depressed the plunger of the needle and sat back in his chair to await results.

TWO

They came suddenly and were drastic.

His brain and body exploded in a torrent of mingled ecstasy and pain which surged through him. Waves of pale light flickered. Rich darkness followed. He rode a ferris-wheel of erupting sensations and emotions. He fell down a never-ending slope of obsidian rock surrounded by clouds of green, purple, yellow, black. The rock vanished, but he continued to fall.

Then there was the smell of disease and corruption in his nostrils, but even that passed and he was standing up.

World of phosphorescence drifting like golden spheres into black night. Green, blue, red explosions. Towers rotate slowly. Towers Advance. Towers Recede. Advance, Recede. Vanish.

Flickering world of phosphorescent tears falling into the timeless, spaceless wastes of Nowhere. World of Misery. World of Antagonism. World of Guilt. Guilt – guilt – guilt . . .

World of hateful wonder.

Heart throbbing, mind thudding, body shuddering as M-A 19 flowed up the infinity of the spine. Shot into back-brain, shot into mid-brain, shot into fore-brain.

EXPLOSION ALL CENTRES!

No-mind – No-body – No-where.

Dying waves of light danced out of his eyes and away through the dark world. Everything was dying. Cells, sinews, nerves, synapses – all crumbling. Tears of light, fading, fading.

Brilliant rockets streaking into the sky, exploding all together and sending their multicoloured globes of light – balls on a Xmas Tree – balls on a great tree – x-mass – drifting slowly earthwards.

Ahead of him was a tall, blocky building constructed of huge chunks of yellowed granite, like a fortress. Black mist swirled around it and across the bleak, horizonless nightscape.

This was no normal hallucinatory experience. Seward felt the ground under his feet, the warm air on his face, the half-familiar smells. He had no doubt that he had entered another world.

But where was it? How had he got here?

Who had brought him here?

The answer might lie in the fortress ahead. He began to walk towards it. Gravity seemed lighter, for he walked with greater ease than normal and was soon standing looking up at the huge green metallic door. He bunched his fist and rapped on it.

Echoes boomed through numerous corridors and were absorbed in the heart of the fortress.

Seward waited as the door was slowly opened.

A man who so closely resembled the Laughing Cavalier of the painting that he must have modelled his beard and clothes on it, bowed slightly and said:

'Welcome home, Professor Seward. We've been expecting you.'

The bizarrely dressed man stepped aside and allowed him to pass into a dark corridor.

'Expecting me,' said Seward. 'How?'

The Cavalier replied good-humouredly: 'That's not for me to explain. Here we go – through this door and up this corridor.' He opened the door and turned into another corridor and Seward followed him.

They opened innumerable doors and walked along innumerable corridors.

The complexities of the corridors seemed somehow familiar to Seward. He felt disturbed by them, but the possibility of an explanation overrode his qualms and he willingly followed the Laughing Cavalier deeper and deeper into the fortress, through the twists and turns until they arrived at a door which was probably very close to the centre of the fortress.

The Cavalier knocked confidently on the door, but spoke deferentially. 'Professor Seward is here at last, sir.'

A light, cultured voice said from the other side of the door: 'Good. Send him in.'

This door opened so slowly that it seemed to Seward that he was watching a film slowed-down to a fraction of its proper speed. When it had opened sufficiently to let him enter, he went into the room beyond. The Cavalier didn't follow him.

It only occurred to him then that he might be in some kind of mental institution, which would explain the fortress-like nature of the building and the man dressed up like the Laughing Cavalier. But, if so, how had he got here – unless he had collapsed and order had been restored sufficiently for someone to have come and collected him. No, the idea was weak.

The room he entered was full of rich, dark colours. Satin screens and hangings obscured much of it. The ceiling was not visible. Neither was the source of the rather dim light. In the centre of the room stood a dais, raised perhaps a foot from the floor. On the dais was an old leather armchair.

In the armchair sat a naked man with a cool, blue skin.

He stood up as Seward entered. He smiled charmingly and stepped off the dais, advancing towards Seward with his right hand extended.

'Good to see you, old boy!' he said heartily.

Dazed, Seward clasped the offered hand and felt his whole arm tingle as if it had had a mild electric shock. The man's strange flesh was firm, but seemed to itch under Seward's palm.

The man was short – little over five feet tall. His eyebrows met in the centre and his shiny black hair grew to a widow's peak.

Also, he had no navel.

'I'm glad you could get here, Seward,' he said, walking back to his dais and sitting in the armchair. He rested his head in one hand, his elbow on the arm of the chair.

Seward did not like to appear ungracious, but he was worried and mystified. 'I don't know where this place is,' he said. 'I don't even know how I got here – unless . . .'

'Ah, yes – the drug. M-A 19, isn't it? That helped, doubtless. We've been trying to get in touch with you for ages, old boy.'

'I've got work to do – back there,' Seward said obsessionally. 'I'm sorry, but I want to get back as soon as I can. What do you want?'

The Man Without A Navel sighed. 'I'm sorry, too, Seward. But we can't let you go yet. There's something I'd like to ask you – a favour. That was why we were hoping you'd come.'

'What's your problem?' Seward's sense of unreality, never very strong here for, in spite of the world's bizarre appearance, it seemed familiar, was growing weaker. If he could help the man and get back to continue his research, he would.

'Well,' smiled the Man Without A Navel, 'it's really your problem as much as ours. You see,' he shrugged diffidently, 'we want your world destroyed.'

'What!' Now something was clear, at last. This man and his kind did belong to another world – whether in space, time, or different dimensions – and they were enemies of Earth. 'You can't expect me to help you do that!' He laughed. 'You *are* joking.'

The Man Without A Navel shook his head seriously. 'Afraid not, old boy.'

'That's why you want me here – you've seen the chaos in the world and you want to take advantage of it – you want me to be a – a fifth columnist.'

'Ah, you remember the old term, eh? Yes, I suppose that is what I mean. I want you to be our agent. Those machines of yours could be modified to make those who are left turn against each other even more than at present. Eh?'

'You must be very stupid if you think I'll do that,' Seward said tiredly. 'I can't help you. I'm trying to help *them*.' Was he trapped here for good? He said weakly: 'You've got to let me go back.'

'Not as easy as that, old boy. I – and my friends – want to enter your world, but we can't until you've pumped up your machines to such a pitch that the entire world is maddened and destroys itself, d'you see?'

'Certainly,' exclaimed Seward. 'But I'm having no part of it!'

Again the Man Without A Navel smiled, slowly. 'You'll weaken soon enough, old boy.'

'Don't be so sure,' Seward said defiantly. 'I've had plenty of chances of giving up – back there. I could have weakened. But I didn't.'

'Ah, but you've forgotten the new factor, Seward.'

'What's that?'

'The M-A 19.'

'What do you mean?'

'You'll know soon enough.'

'Look – I want to get out of this place. You can't keep me – there's no point – I won't agree to your plan. Where is this world, anyway?'

'Knowing that depends on you, old boy,' the man's tone was mocking. 'Entirely on you. A lot depends on you, Seward.'

'I know.'

The Man Without A Navel lifted his head and called: 'Brother Sebastian, are you available?' He glanced back at Seward with an ironical smile. 'Brother Sebastian may be of some help.'

Seward saw the wall-hangings on the other side of the room move. Then, from behind a screen on which was painted a weird, surrealistic scene, a tall, cowled figure emerged, face in shadow, hands folded in sleeves. A monk.

'Yes, sir,' said the monk in a cold, malicious voice.

'Brother Sebastian, Professor Seward here is not quite as ready to comply with our wishes as we had hoped. Can you influence him in any way?'

'Possibly, sir.' Now the tone held a note of anticipation.

'Good. Professor Seward, will you go with Brother Sebastian?'

'No.' Seward had thought the room contained only one door – the one he'd entered through. But now there was a chance of there being more doors – other than the one through which the cowled monk had come. The two men didn't seem to hear his negative reply. They remained where they were, not moving. 'No,' he said again, his voice rising. 'What right have you to do this?'

'Rights? A strange question.' The monk chuckled to himself. It was a sound like ice tumbling into a cold glass.

'Yes – rights. You must have some sort of organization here. Therefore you must have a ruler – or government. I demand to be taken to someone in authority.'

'But I am in authority here, old boy,' purred the blue-skinned man. 'And – in a sense – so are you. If you agreed with my suggestion, you could hold tremendous power. Tremendous.'

'I don't want to discuss that again.' Seward began to walk towards the wall-hangings. They merely watched him – the monk with his face in shadow – the Man Without A Navel with a supercilious smile on his thin lips. He walked around a screen, parted the hangings – and there they were on the other side. He went through the hangings. This was some carefully planned trick – an illusion – deliberately intended to confuse him. He was used to such methods, even though he didn't understand how they'd worked this one. He said: 'Clever – but tricks of this kind won't make me weaken.'

'What on earth d'you mean, Seward, old man? Now, I wonder if you'll accompany Brother Sebastian here. I have an awful lot of work to catch up on.'

'All right,' Seward said. 'All right, I will.' Perhaps on the way to wherever the monk was going, he would find an opportunity to escape.

The monk turned and Seward followed him. He did not look at the Man Without A Navel as he passed his ridiculous dais, with its ridiculous leather armchair.

They passed through a narrow doorway behind a curtain and were once again in the complex series of passages. The tall monk – now he was close to him, Seward estimated his height at about six feet, seven inches – seemed to flow along in front of him. He began to dawdle. The monk didn't look back. Seward increased the distance between them. Still, the monk didn't appear to notice.

Seward turned and ran.

They had met nobody on their journey through the corridors. He hoped he could find a door leading out of the fortress before someone spotted him. There was no cry from behind him.

But as he ran, the passages got darker and darker until he was careering through pitch blackness, sweating, panting and beginning to panic. He kept blundering into damp walls and running on.

It was only much later that he began to realize he was running in a circle that was getting tighter and tighter until he was doing little more than spin round, like a top. He stopped, then.

These people evidently had more powers than he had suspected. Possibly they had some means of shifting the position of the corridor walls, following his movements by means of hidden TV cameras or something like them. Simply because there were no visible signs of an advanced technology didn't mean that they did not possess one. They obviously did. How else could they have got him from his own world to this?

He took a pace forward. Did he sense the walls drawing back? He wasn't sure. The whole thing reminded him vaguely of *The Pit and The Pendulum.*

He strode forward a number of paces and saw a light ahead of him. He walked towards it, turned into a dimly-lit corridor.

The monk was waiting for him.

'We missed each other, Professor Seward. I see you managed to precede me.' The monk's face was still invisible, secret in its cowl. As secret as his cold mocking, malevolent voice. 'We are almost there, now,' said the monk.

Seward stepped towards him, hoping to see his face, but it was impossible. The monk glided past him. 'Follow me, please.'

For the moment, until he could work out how the fortress worked, Seward decided to accompany the monk.

They came to a heavy, iron-studded door – quite unlike any of the other doors.

They walked into a low-ceilinged chamber. It was very hot. Smoke hung in the still air of the room. It poured from a glowing brazier at the extreme end. Two men stood by the brazier.

One of them was a thin man with a huge, bulging stomach over which his long, narrow hands were folded. He had a shaggy mane of dirty white hair, his cheeks were sunken and his nose extremely long and extremely pointed. He seemed toothless and his puckered lips were shaped in a senseless smile – like the smile of a madman Seward had once had to experiment on. He wore a stained white jacket buttoned over his grotesque paunch. On his legs were loose khaki trousers.

His companion was also thin, though lacking the stomach. He was taller and had the face of a mournful bloodhound, with sparse, highly-greased, black hair that covered his bony head like a skull-cap. He stared into the brazier, not looking up as Brother Sebastian led Seward into the room and closed the door.

The thin man with the stomach, however, pranced forward, his hands, still clasped on his paunch, and bowed to them both.

'Work for us, Brother Sebastian?' he said, nodding at Seward.

'We require a straightforward "Yes,"' Brother Sebastian said. 'You have merely to ask the question "Will You?" If he replies "No," you are to continue. If he replies "Yes," you are to cease and inform me immediately.'

'Very well, Brother. Rely on us.'

'I hope I can.' The monk chuckled again. 'You are now in the charge of these men, professor. If you decide you want to help us, after all, you have only to say "Yes." Is that clear?'

Seward began to tremble with horror. He had suddenly realized what this place was.

'Now look here,' he said. 'You can't . . .'

He walked towards the monk who had turned and was opening the door. He grasped the man's shoulder. His hand seemed to clutch a delicate, bird-like structure. 'Hey! I don't think you're a man at all. What *are* you?'

'A man or a mouse,' chuckled the monk as the two grotesque creatures leapt forward suddenly and twisted Seward's arms behind him. Seward kicked back at them with his heels, squirmed in their grasp, but he might have been held by steel bands. He shouted incoherently at the monk as he shut the door behind him with a whisk of his habit.

The pair flung him on to the damp, hot stones of the floor. It smelt awful. He rolled over and sat up. They stood over him. The hound-faced man had his arms folded. The thin man with the stomach had his long hands on his paunch again. They seemed to rest there whenever he was not actually using them. It was the latter who smiled with his twisting, puckered lips, cocking his head to one side.

'What do *you* think, Mr Morl?' he asked his companion.

'I don't know, Mr Hand. After you.' The hound-faced man spoke in a melancholy whisper.

'I would suggest Treatment H. Simple to operate, less work for us, a tried and trusty operation which works with most and will probably work with this gentleman.'

Seward scrambled up and tried to push past them, making for the door. Again they seized him expertly and dragged him back. He felt the rough touch of rope on his wrists and the pain as a knot was tightened. He shouted, more in anger than agony, more in terror than either.

They were going to torture him. He knew it.

When they had tied his hands, they took the rope and tied his ankles. They twisted the rope up around his calves and under his legs. They made a halter of the rest and looped it over his neck so that he had to bend almost double if he was not to strangle.

Then they sat him on a chair.

Mr Hand removed his hands from his paunch, reached up above Seward's head and turned on the tap.

The first drop of water fell directly on the centre of his head some five minutes later.

Twenty-seven drops of water later, Seward was raving and screaming. Yet every time he tried to jerk his head away, the halter threatened to strangle him and the jolly Mr Hand and the mournful Mr Morl were there to straighten him up again.

Thirty drops of water after that, Seward's brain began to throb and he opened his eyes to see that the chamber had vanished.

In its place was a huge comet, a fireball dominating the sky, rushing directly towards him. He backed away from it and there were no more ropes on his hands or feet. He was free.

He began to run. He leapt into the air and stayed there. He was swimming through the air.

Ecstasy ran up his spine like a flickering fire, touched his back-brain, touched his mid-brain, touched his fore-brain.

EXPLOSION ALL CENTRES!

He was standing one flower among many, in a bed of tall lupins and roses which waved in a gentle wind. He pulled his roots free and began to walk.

He walked into the Lab Control Room.

Everything was normal except that gravity seemed a little heavy. Everything was as he'd left it.

He saw that he had left the Towers rotating. He went into the room he used as a bedroom and workroom. He parted the blind and looked out into the night. There was a big, full moon hanging in the deep, blue sky over the ruins of Hampton. He saw its light reflected in the far-away sea. A few bodies still lay prone near the lab. He went back into the Control Room and switched off the towers.

Returning to the bedroom he looked at the card-table he had his notes on. They were undisturbed. Neatly, side by side near a large, tattered notebook, lay a half-full ampoule of M-A 19 and a hypodermic syringe. He picked up the ampoule and threw it in a corner. It did not break but rolled around on the floor for a few seconds.

He sat down.

His whole body ached.

He picked up a sheaf of his more recent notes. He wrote everything down that came into his head on the subject of tranquilomats; it helped him think better and made sure that his drugged mind and body did not hamper him as much as they might have done if he had simply relied on his memory.

He looked at his wrists. They carried the marks of the rope. Evidently the transition from the other world to his own involved leaving anything in the other world behind. He was glad. If he hadn't, he'd have had a hell of a job getting himself untied.

He tried hard to forget the questions flooding through his mind. Where had he been? Who were the people? What did they really want? How far could they keep a check on him? How did the M-A 19 work to aid his transport into the other world? Could they get at him here?

He decided they couldn't get at him, otherwise they might have tried earlier. Somehow it was the M-A 19 in his brain which allowed them to get hold of him. Well, that was simple – no more M-A 19.

With a feeling of relief, he forced himself to concentrate on his notes.

Out of the confusion, something seemed to be developing, but he had to work at great speed – greater speed than previously, perhaps, for he daren't use the M-A 19 again and there was nothing else left of much good.

His brain cleared as he once again got interested in his notes. He worked for two hours, making fresh notes, equations, checking his knowledge against the stack of earlier research notes by the wall near his camp bed.

Dawn was coming as he realized suddenly that he was suffering from thirst. His throat was bone dry, as were his mouth and lips. He got up and his legs felt weak. He staggered, almost knocking over the chair. With a great effort he righted it and, leaning for support on the bed, got himself to the hand-basin. It was filled by a tank near the roof and he had used it sparsely. But this time he didn't care. He stuck his head under the tap and drank the stale water greedily. It did no good. His whole body now seemed cold, his skin tight, his heart thumping heavily against his ribs. His head was aching horribly and his breathing increased.

He went and lay down on the bed, hoping the feeling would leave him.

It got worse. He needed something to cure himself.

What? he asked.

M-A 19, he answered.

NO!

But – Yes, yes, yes. All he needed was a small shot of the drug and he would be all right. He knew it.

And with knowing that, he realized something else.

He was hooked.

The drug was habit-forming.

THREE

He found the half-full M-A 19 ampoule under the bed where it had rolled. He found the needle on the table where he had left it, buried under his notes. He found a vein in his forearm and shot himself full. There was no thought to Seward's action. There was just the craving and the chance of satisfying that craving.

The M-A 19 began to swim leisurely through his veins, drifting up his spine –

It hit his brain with a powerful explosion.

He was walking through a world of phosphorescent rain, leaping over large purple rocks that welcomed his feet, drew them down towards them. All was agony and startling Now.

No-time, no-space, just the throbbing voice in the air above him. It was talking to him.

DOOM, Seward. DOOM, Seward. DOOM, Seward.

'Seward is doomed!' he laughed. 'Seward is betrayed!'

Towers Advance. Towers Recede. Towers Rotate At Normal Speed.

Carnival Aktion. All Carnivals To Explode.

Up into the back-brain, into the mid-brain, on to the fore-brain.

EXPLOSION ALL CENTRES!

He was back in the torture-chamber, though standing up. In the corner near the brazier the grotesque pair were muttering to one another. Mr Hand darted him an angry glance, his lips drawn over his gums in an expression of outrage.

'Hello, Seward,' said the Man Without A Navel behind him. 'So you're back.'

'Back,' said Seward heavily. 'What more do you want?'

'Only your All, Seward, old man. I remember a time in Dartford before the war . . .'

'Which war?'

'Your war, Seward. You were too young to share any other. You don't remember *that* war. You weren't born. Leave it to those who *do*, Seward.'

Seward turned. 'My war?' He looked with disgust at the Man Without A Navel; at his reptilian blue skin and his warm-cold, dark-light, good-evil eyes. At his small yet well-formed body.

The Man Without A Navel smiled. '*Our* war, then, old man. I won't quibble.'

'You made me do it. I think that somehow you made me suggest Experiment Restoration!'

'I said we won't quibble, Seward,' said the man in an authoritative tone. Then, more conversationally: 'I remember a time in Dartford before the war, when you sat in your armchair – one rather like mine – at your brother-in-law's house. Remember what you said, old man?'

Seward remembered well. 'If,' he quoted, 'if I had a button and could press it and destroy the entire universe and myself with it, I would. For no reason other than boredom.'

'Very good, Seward. You have an excellent memory.'

'Is that all you're going on? Something I said out of frustration because nobody was recognizing my work?' He paused as he realized something else. 'You know all about me, don't you?' he said bitterly. There seemed to be nothing he didn't know. On the other hand Seward knew nothing of the man. Nothing of this world. Nothing of where it was in space and time. It was a world of insanity, of bizarre contrasts. '*How* do you know all this?'

'Inside information, Seward, old boy.'

'You're mad!'

The Man Without A Navel returned to his earlier topic. 'Are you bored now, Seward?'

'Bored? No. Tired, yes.'

'Bored, no – tired, yes. Very good, Seward. You got here later than expected. What kept you?' The man laughed.

'I kept me. I held off taking the M-A 19 for as long as I could.'

'But you came to us in the end, eh? Good man, Seward.'

'You knew the M-A 19 was habit-forming? You knew I'd have to take it, come back here?'

'Naturally.'

He said pleadingly: 'Let me go for God's sake! You've made me. Made me . . .'

'Your dearest wish almost come true, Seward. Isn't that what you wanted? I made you come close to destroying the world? Is that it?'

'So you *did* somehow influence Experiment Restoration!'

'It's possible. But you haven't done very well either way. The world is in shambles. You can't reverse that. Kill it off. Let's start fresh, Seward. Forget your experiments with the tranquilomats and help us.'

'No.'

The Man Without A Navel shrugged. 'We'll see, old boy.'

He looked at the mumbling men in the corner. 'Morl – Hand – take Professor Seward to his room. I don't want any mistakes this time. I'm going to take him out of your hands. Obviously we need subtler minds put on the problem.'

The pair came forward and grabbed Seward. The Man Without A Navel opened the door and they went through it first, forcing Seward ahead of them.

He was too demoralized to resist much, this time. Demoralized by the fact that he was hooked on M-A 19. What did the junkies call it? The

Habit. He had The Habit. Demoralized by his inability to understand the whereabouts or nature of the world he was on. Demoralized by the fact that the Man Without A Navel seemed to know everything about his personal life on Earth. Demoralized that he had fallen into the man's trap. Who had developed M-A 19? He couldn't remember. Perhaps the Man Without A Navel had planted it? He supposed it might be possible.

He was pushed along another series of corridors, arrived at another door. The Man Without A Navel came up behind them and unlocked the door.

Seward was shoved into the room. It was narrow and low – coffin-like.

'We'll be sending someone along to see you in a little while, Seward,' said the man lightly. The door was slammed.

Seward lay in pitch blackness.

He began to sob.

Later, he heard a noise outside. A stealthy noise of creeping feet. He shuddered. What was the torture going to be this time?

He heard a scraping and a muffled rattle. The door opened.

Against the light from the passage, Seward saw the man clearly. He was a big, fat negro in a grey suit. He wore a flowing, rainbow-coloured tie. He was grinning.

Seward liked the man instinctively. But he no longer trusted his instinct. 'What do you want?' he said suspiciously.

The huge negro raised his finger to his lips. 'Ssshh,' he whispered. 'I'm going to try and get you out of here.'

'An old Secret Police trick on my world,' said Seward. 'I'm not falling for that.'

'It's no trick, son. Even if it is, what can you lose?'

'Nothing.' Seward got up.

The big man put his arm around Seward's shoulders. Seward felt comfortable in the grip, though normally he disliked such gestures.

'Now, son, we go real quietly and we go as fast as we can. Come on.'

Softly, the big man began to tiptoe along the corridor. Seward was sure that TV cameras, or whatever they were, were following him, that the Man Without A Navel, the monk, the two torturers, the Laughing Cavalier, were all waiting somewhere to seize him.

But, very quickly, the negro had reached a small wooden door and was drawing a bolt. He patted Seward's shoulder and held the door open for him. 'Through you go, son. Make for the red car.'

It was morning. In the sky hung a golden sun, twice the size of Earth's. There was a vast expanse of lifeless rock in all directions, broken only by a white road which stretched into the distance. On the road, close to Seward, was parked a car something like a Cadillac. It was fire-red and bore the registration plates YOU OOO. Whoever these people were, Seward decided, they were originally from Earth – all except the Man Without A Navel, perhaps. Possibly this was his world and the others had been brought from Earth, like him.

He walked towards the car. The air was cold and fresh. He stood by the convertible and looked back. The negro was running over the rock towards him. He dashed round the car and got into the driver's seat. Seward got in beside him.

The negro started the car, put it into gear and shoved his foot down hard on the accelerator pedal. The car jerked away and had reached top speed in seconds.

At the wheel, the negro relaxed. 'Glad that went smoothly. I didn't expect to get away with it so easily, son. You're Seward, aren't you?'

'Yes. You seem to be as well-informed as the others.'

'I guess so.' The negro took a pack of cigarettes from his shirt pocket. 'Smoke?'

'No thanks,' said Seward. 'That's one habit I don't have.'

The negro looked back over his shoulder. The expanse of rock seemed never-ending, though in the distance the fortress was disappearing. He flipped a cigarette out of the pack and put it between his lips. He unclipped the car's lighter and put it to the tip of the cigarette. He inhaled and put the lighter back. The cigarette between his lips, he returned his other hand to the wheel.

He said: 'They were going to send the Vampire to you. It's lucky I reached you in time.'

'It could be,' said Seward. 'Who are you? What part do you play in this?'

'Let's just say I'm a friend of yours and an enemy of your enemies. The name's Farlowe.'

'Well, I trust you, Farlowe – though God knows why.'

Farlowe grinned. 'Why not? I don't want your world destroyed any more than you do. It doesn't much matter, I guess, but if there's a chance of restoring it, then you ought to try.'

'Then you're from my world originally, is that it?'

'In a manner of speaking, son,' said Farlowe.

Very much later, the rock gave way to pleasant, flat countryside with trees, fields and little cottages peaceful under the vast sky. In the distance, Seward saw herds of cattle and sheep, the occasional horse. It reminded him of the countryside of his childhood, all clear and fresh and sharp with the clarity that only a child's eye can bring to a scene before it is obscured and tainted by the impressions of adulthood. Soon the flat country was behind them and they were going through an area of low, green hills, the huge sun flooding the scene with its soft, golden light. There were no clouds in the pale blue sky.

The big car sped smoothly along and Seward in the comfortable companionship of Farlowe, began to relax a little. He felt almost happy, would have felt happy if it had not been for the nagging knowledge that somehow he had to get back and continue his work. It was not merely a question of restoring sanity to the world, now – he had also to thwart whatever plans were in the mind of The Man Without A Navel.

After a long silence, Seward asked a direct question. 'Farlowe, where is this world? What are we doing here?'

Farlowe's answer was vague. He stared ahead at the road. 'Don't ask me that, son. I don't rightly know.'

'But you live here.'

'So do you.'

'No – I only come here when – when . . .'

'When what?'

But Seward couldn't raise the courage to admit about the drug to Farlowe. Instead he said: 'Does M-A 19 mean anything to you?'

'Nope.'

So Farlowe hadn't come here because of the drug. Seward said: 'But you said you were from my world originally.'

'Only in a manner of speaking.' Farlowe changed gears as the road curved steeply up a hill. It rose gently above the idyllic countryside below.

Seward changed his line of questioning. 'Isn't there any sort of organization here – no government. What's the name of this country?'

Farlowe shrugged. 'It's just a place – no government. The people in the fortress run most things. Everybody's scared of them.'

'I don't blame them. Who's the Vampire you mentioned?'

'He works for the Man.'

'What is he?'

'Why – a vampire, naturally,' said Farlowe in surprise.

The sun had started to set and the whole countryside was bathed in red-gold light. The car continued to climb the long hill.

Farlowe said: 'I'm taking you to some friends. You ought to be fairly safe there. Then maybe we can work out a way of getting you back.'

Seward felt better. At least Farlowe had given him some direct information.

As the car reached the top of the hill and began to descend Seward got a view of an odd and disturbing sight. The sun was like a flat, round, red disc – yet only half of it was above the horizon. *The line of the horizon evenly intersected the sun's disc!* It was some sort of mirage – yet so convincing that Seward looked away, staring instead at the black smoke which he could now see rolling across the valley below. He said nothing to Farlowe.

'How much further?' he asked later as the car came to the bottom of the hill. Black night had come, moonless, and the car's headlights blazed.

'A long way yet, I'm afraid, son,' said Farlowe. 'You cold?'

'No.'

'We'll be hitting a few signs of civilization soon. You tired?'

'No – why?'

'We could put up at a motel or something. I guess we could eat anyway.'

Ahead, Seward saw a few lights. He couldn't make out where they came from. Farlowe began to slow down. 'We'll risk it,' he said. He pulled in towards the lights and Seward saw that it was a line of fuel pumps. Behind the pumps was a single storey building, very long and built entirely of timber by the look of it. Farlowe drove in between the pumps and the building. A man in overalls, the top half of his face shadowed by the peak of his cap, came into sight. Farlowe got out of the car with a signal to Seward to do the same. The negro handed his keys to the attendant. 'Fill her full and give her a quick check.'

Could this be Earth, Seward wondered. Earth in the future – or possibly an Earth of a different space-time continuum. That was the likeliest explanation for this unlikely world. The contrast between recognizable, everyday things and the grotesqueries of the fortress was strange – yet it could be explained easily if these people had contact with his world. That would explain how they had things like cars and fuel stations and no apparent organization necessary for producing them. Somehow, perhaps, they just – *stole* them?

He followed Farlowe into the long building. He could see through the wide windows that it was some kind of restaurant. There was a long, clean counter and a few people seated at tables at the far end. All had their backs to him.

He and Farlowe sat down on stools. Close to them was the largest pin-table Seward had ever seen. Its lights were flashing and its balls were clattering, though there was no one operating it. The coloured lights flashed series of numbers at him until his eyes lost focus and he had to turn away.

A woman was standing behind the counter now. Most of her face was covered by a yashmak.

'What do you want to eat, son?' said Farlowe, turning to him.

'Oh, anything.'

Farlowe ordered sandwiches and coffee. When the woman had gone to get their order, Seward whispered: 'Why's she wearing that thing?'

Farlowe pointed at a sign Seward hadn't noticed before. It read THE HAREM HAVEN. 'It's their gimmick,' said Farlowe.

Seward looked back at the pin-table. The lights had stopped flashing, the balls had stopped clattering. But above it suddenly appeared a huge pair of disembodied eyes. He gasped.

Distantly, he heard his name being repeated over and over again. 'Seward. Seward. Seward. Seward . . .'

He couldn't tell where the voice was coming from. He glanced up at the ceiling. Not from there. The voice stopped. He looked back at the pin-table. The eyes had vanished. His panic returned. He got off his stool.

'I'll wait for you in the car, Farlowe.'

Farlowe looked surprised. 'What's the matter, son?'

'Nothing – it's okay – I'll wait in the car.'

Farlowe shrugged.

Seward went out into the night. The attendant had gone but the car was waiting for him. He opened the door and climbed in.

What did the eyes mean? Were the people from the fortress following him in some way. Suddenly an explanation for most of the questions bothering him sprang into his mind. Of course – telepathy. They were probably telepaths. That was how they knew so much about him. That could be how they knew of his world and could influence events there – they might never go there in person. This comforted him a little, though he realized that getting out of this situation was going to be even more difficult than he'd thought.

He looked through the windows and saw Farlowe's big body perched on its stool. The other people in the café were still sitting with their backs to him. He realized that there was something familiar about them.

He saw Farlowe get up and walk towards the door. He came out and got into the car, slamming the door after him. He leaned back in his seat and handed Seward a sandwich. 'You seem worked up, son,' he said. 'You'd better eat this.'

Seward took the sandwich. He was staring at the backs of the other customers again. He frowned.

Farlowe started the car and they moved towards the road. Then Seward realized who the men reminded him of. He craned his head back in the hope of seeing their faces, but it was too late. They had reminded him of his dead assistants – the men who'd committed suicide.

They roared through dimly-seen towns – all towers and angles. There seemed to be nobody about. Dawn came up and they still sped on. Seward realized that Farlowe must have a tremendous vitality, for he didn't seem to tire at all. Also, perhaps, he was motivated by a desire to get as far away from the fortress as possible.

They stopped twice to re-fuel and Farlowe bought more sandwiches and coffee which they had as they drove.

In the late afternoon Farlowe said: 'Almost there.'

They passed through a pleasant village. It was somehow alien, although very similar to a small English village. It had an oddly foreign look which was hard to place. Farlowe pulled in at what seemed to be the gates of a large public park. He looked up at the sun. 'Just made it,' he said. 'Wait in the park – someone will come to collect you.'

'You're leaving me?'

'Yes. I don't think they know where you are. They'll look but, with luck, they won't look around here. Out you get, son. Into the park.'

'Who do I wait for?'

'You'll know her when she comes.'

'Her?' He got out and closed the door. He stood on the pavement watching as, with a cheerful wave, Farlowe drove off. He felt a tremendous sense of loss then, as if his only hope had been taken away.

Gloomily, he turned and walked through the park gates.

FOUR

As he walked between low hedges along a gravel path, he realized that this park, like so many things in this world, contrasted with the village it served. It was completely familiar just like a park on his own world.

It was like a grey, hazy winter's afternoon, with the brittle, interwoven skeletons of trees black and sharp against the cold sky. Birds perched on trees and bushes, or flew noisily into the silent air.

Evergreens crowded upon the leaf-strewn grass. Cry of sparrows. Peacocks, necks craned forward, dived towards scattered bread. Silver birch, larch, elm, monkey-puzzle trees, and swaying white ferns, each one like an ostrich feather stuck in the earth. A huge, ancient, nameless trunk from which, at the top, grew an expanse of soft, yellow fungus; the trunk itself looking like a Gothic cliff, full of caves and dark windows. A grey and brown pigeon perched motionless on the slender branches of a young birch. Peacock chicks the size of hens pecked with concentration at the grass.

Mellow, nostalgic smell of winter; distant sounds of children playing; lost black dog looking for master; red disc of sun in the cool, darkening sky. The light was sharp and yet soft, peaceful. A path led into the distance towards a flight of wide stone steps, at the top of which was the curving entrance to an arbour, browns, blacks and yellows of sapless branches and fading leaves.

From the arbour a girl appeared and began to descend the steps with quick, graceful movements. She stopped when she reached the path. She looked at him. She had long, blonde hair and wore a white dress with a full skirt. She was about seventeen.

The peace of the park was suddenly interrupted by children rushing from nowhere towards the peacocks, laughing and shouting. Some of the boys saw the tree trunk and made for it. Others stood looking upwards at the sun as it sank in the cold air. They seemed not to see either Seward or the girl. Seward looked at her. Did he recognize her? It wasn't possible. Yet she, too, gave him a look of recognition, smiled shyly at him and ran towards him. She reached him, stood on tiptoe and gave him a light kiss on the cheek.

'Hello, Lee.'

'Hello. Have you come to find me?'

'I've been looking for you a long time.'

'Farlowe sent a message ahead?'

She took his hand. 'Come on. Where have you been, Lee?'

This was a question he couldn't answer. He let her lead him back up the steps, through the arbour. Between the branches he glanced a garden and a pool. 'Come on,' she said. 'Let's see what's for dinner. Mother's looking forward to meeting you.'

He no longer questioned how these strange people all seemed to know his name. It was still possible that all of them were taking part in the conspiracy against him.

At the end of the arbour was a house, several storeys high. It was a pleasant house with a blue and white door. She led him up the path and into a hallway. It was shining with dark polished wood and brass plates on the walls. From a room at the end he smelled spicy cooking. She went first and opened the door at the end. 'Mother – Lee Seward's here. Can we come in?'

'Of course.' The voice was warm, husky, full of humour. They went into the room and Seward saw a woman of about forty, very well preserved, tall, large-boned with a fine-featured face and smiling mouth. Her eyes also smiled. Her sleeves were rolled up and she put the lid back on a pan on the stove.

'How do you do, Professor Seward. Mr Farlowe's told us about you. You're in trouble, I hear.'

'How do you do, Mrs –'

'Call me Martha. Has Sally introduced herself?'

'No,' Sally laughed. 'I forgot. I'm Sally, Lee.'

Her mother gave a mock frown. 'I suppose you've been calling our guest by his first name, as usual. Do you mind, professor?'

'Not at all.' He was thinking how attractive they both were, in their different ways. The young, fresh girl and her warm, intelligent mother. He had always enjoyed the company of women, but never so much, he realized, as now. They seemed to complement one another. In their presence he felt safe, at ease. Now he realized why Farlowe had chosen them to hide him. Whatever the facts, he would *feel* safe here.

Martha was saying: 'Dinner won't be long.'

'It smells good.'

'Probably smells better than it tastes,' she laughed. 'Go into the lounge with Sally. Sally, fix Professor Seward a drink.'

'Call me Lee,' said Seward, a little uncomfortably. He had never cared much for his first name. He preferred his middle name, William, but not many others did.

'Come on, Lee,' she took his hand and led him out of the kitchen. 'We'll see what there is.' They went into a small, well-lighted lounge. The furniture, like the whole house, had a look that was half-familiar, half-alien – obviously the product of a slightly different race. Perhaps they deliberately imitated Earth culture, without quite succeeding. Sally still gripped his hand. Her hand was warm and her skin smooth.

He made to drop it but, involuntarily, squeezed it gently before she took it away to deal with the drink. She gave him another shy smile. He felt that she was as attracted to him as he to her. 'What's it going to be?' she asked him.

'Oh, anything,' he said, sitting down on a comfortable sofa. She poured him a dry martini and brought it over. Then she sat demurely down beside him and watched him drink it. Her eyes sparkled with a mixture of sauciness and innocence which he found extremely appealing. He looked around the room.

'How did Farlowe get his message to you?' he said.

'He came the other day. Said he was going to try and get into the fortress and help you. Farlowe's always flitting about. I think the people at the fortress have a price on his head or something. It's exciting isn't it?'

'You can say that again,' Seward said feelingly.

'Why are they after you?'

'They want me to help them destroy the world I come from. Do you know anything about it?'

'Earth, isn't it?'

'Yes.' Was he going to get some straightforward answers at last?

'I know it's very closely connected with ours and that some of us want to escape from here and go to your world.'

'Why?' he asked eagerly.

She shook her head. Her long, fine hair waved with the motion. 'I don't really know. Something about their being trapped here – something like that. Farlowe said something about you being a "key" to their release. They can only do what they want to do with your agreement.'

'But I could agree and then break my word!'

'I don't think you could – but honestly, I don't know any more. I've probably got it wrong. Do you like me, Lee?'

He was startled by the directness of her question. 'Yes,' he said, 'very much.'

'Farlowe said you would. Good, isn't it?'

'Why – yes. Farlowe knows a lot.'

'That's why he works against *them*.'

Martha came in. 'Almost ready,' she smiled. 'I think I'll have a quick one before I start serving. How are you feeling Lee, after your ride?'

'Fine,' he said, 'fine.' He had never been in a position like this one – with two women both of whom were extremely attractive for almost opposite reasons.

'We were discussing why the people at the fortress wanted my help,' he said, turning the conversation back the way he felt it ought to go if he was ever going to get off this world and back to his own and his work.

'Farlowe said something about it.'

'Yes, Sally told me. Does Farlowe belong to some sort of underground organization?'

'Underground? Why, yes, in a way he does.'

'Aren't they strong enough to fight the Man Without A Navel and his friends?'

'Farlowe says they're strong enough, but divided over what should be done and how.'

'I see. That's fairly common amongst such groups, I believe.'

'Yes.'

'What part do you play?'

'None, really. Farlowe asked me to put you up – that's all.' She sipped her drink, her eyes smiling directly into his. He drained his glass.

'Shall we eat?' she said. 'Sally, take Lee in to the dining-room.'

The girl got up and, somewhat possessively Seward thought, linked her arm in his. Her young body against his was distracting. He felt a little warm. She took him in. The table was laid for supper. Three chairs and three places. The sun had set and candles burned on the table in brass candelabras. She unlinked her arm and pulled out one of the chairs.

'You sit here, Lee – at the head of the table.' She grinned. Then she leaned forward as he sat down. 'Hope mummy isn't boring you.'

He was surprised. 'Why should she?'

Martha came in with three covered dishes on a tray. 'This may not have turned out quite right, Lee. Never does when you're trying hard.'

'I'm sure it'll be fine,' he smiled. The two women sat down one either side of him. Martha served him. It was some sort of goulash with vegetables. He took his napkin and put it on his lap.

As they began to eat, Martha said: 'How is it?'

'Fine,' he said. It was very good. Apart from the feeling that some kind of rivalry for his attentions existed between mother and daughter the air of normality in the house was comforting. Here, he might be able to do some constructive thinking about his predicament.

When the meal was over, Martha said: 'It's time for bed, Sally. Say good night to Lee.'

She pouted. 'Oh, it's not fair.'

'Yes it is,' she said firmly. 'You can see Lee in the morning. He's had a long journey.'

'All right.' She smiled at Seward. 'Sleep well, Lee.'

'I think I will,' he said.

Martha chuckled after Sally had gone. 'Would you like a drink before you go to bed?' She spoke softly.

'Love one,' he said.

They went into the other room. He sat down on the sofa as she mixed the drinks. She brought them over and sat down next to him as her daughter had done earlier.

'Tell me everything that's been happening. It sounds so exciting.'

He knew at once he could tell her all he wanted to, that she would listen and be sympathetic. 'It's terrifying, really,' he began, half-apologetically. He began to talk, beginning with what had happened on Earth. She listened.

'I even wondered if this was a dream-world – a figment of my imagination,' he finished, 'but I had to reject that when I went back to my own. I had rope marks on my wrists – my hair was soaking wet. You don't get that in a dream!'

'I hope not,' she smiled. 'We're different here, Lee, obviously. Our life doesn't have the – the *shape* that yours has. We haven't much direction, no real desires. We just – well – *exist*. It's as if we're waiting for something to happen. As if –' she paused and seemed to be looking down deep into herself. 'Put it this way – Farlowe thinks you're the key figure in some development that's happening here. Supposing – supposing we were some kind of – of experiment . . .'

'Experiment? How do you mean?'

'Well, from what you say, the people at the fortress have an advanced science that we don't know about. Supposing our parents, say, had been kidnapped from your world and – made to think – what's the word –'

'Conditioned?'

'Yes, conditioned to think they were natives of this world. We'd have grown up knowing nothing different. Maybe the Man Without A Navel is a member of an alien race – a scientist of some kind in charge of the experiment.'

'But why should they make such a complicated experiment?'

'So they could study us, I suppose.'

Seward marvelled at her deductive powers. She had come to a much firmer theory than he had. But then he thought, she might subconsciously *know* the truth. Everyone knew much more than they knew, as it were. For instance, it was pretty certain that the secret of the tranquilomat was locked somewhere down in his unconscious if only he could get at it. Her explanation was logical and worth thinking about.

'You may be right,' he said. 'If so, it's something to go on. But it doesn't stop my reliance on the drug – or the fact that the Man and his helpers are probably telepathic and are at this moment looking for me.'

She nodded. 'Could there be an *antidote* for the drug?'

'Unlikely. Drugs like that don't really need antidotes – they're not like poisons. There must be some way of getting at the people in the fortress – some way of putting a stop to their plans. What about an organized revolution? What has Farlowe tried to do?'

'Nothing much. The people aren't easy to organize. We haven't much to do with one another. Farlowe was probably hoping you could help – think of something he hasn't. Maybe one of those machines you mentioned would work against the fortress people?'

'No, I don't think so. Anyway, the hallucinomats are too big to move from one place to another by hand – let alone from one world to another.'

'And you haven't been able to build a tranquilomat yet?'

'No – we have a lot of experimental machines lying around at the lab – they're fairly small – but it's a question of modifying them – that's what I'm trying to do at the moment. If I could make one that works it would solve part of my problem – it would save my world and perhaps even save yours, if you *are* in a state of conditioning.'

'It sounds reasonable,' she dropped her eyes and looked at her drink. She held the glass balanced on her knees which were pressed closely together, nearly touching him. 'But,' she said, 'they're going to catch you sooner or later. They're very powerful. They're sure to catch you. Then they'll make you agree to their idea.'

'Why are you so certain?'

'I know them.'

He let that go. She said: 'Another drink?' and got up.

'Yes please.' He got up, too, and extended his glass, then went closer to her. She put bottle and glass on the table and looked into his face. There was compassion, mystery, tenderness in her large, dark eyes. He smelled her perfume, warm, pleasant. He put his arms around her and kissed her. 'My room,' she said. They went upstairs.

Later that night, feeling strangely revitalized, he left the bed and the sleeping Martha and went and stood beside the window overlooking the silent park. He felt cold and he picked up his shirt and trousers, put them on. He sighed. He felt his mind clear and his body relax. He must work out a way of travelling from this world to his own at will – that might put a stop to the plans of the Man Without A Navel.

He turned guiltily as he heard the door open. Sally was standing there. She wore a long, white, flowing nightdress.

'Lee! I came to tell mummy – what are you doing in here?' Her eyes were horrified, accusing him. Martha sat up suddenly.

'Sally – what's the matter!'

Lee stepped forward. 'Listen, Sally. Don't –'

Sally shrugged, but tears had come to her eyes. 'I thought you wanted *me*! Now I know – I shouldn't have brought you here. Farlowe said –'

'What did Farlowe say?'

'He said you'd want to marry me!'

'But that's ridiculous. How could he say that? I'm a stranger here. You were to hide me from the fortress people, that's all.'

But she had only picked up one word. 'Ridiculous. Yes, I suppose it is, when my own mother . . .'

'Sally – you'd better go to bed. We'll discuss it in the morning,' said Martha softly. 'What was it you came in about?'

Sally laughed theatrically. 'It doesn't matter now.' She slammed the door.

Seward looked at Martha. 'I'm sorry, Martha.'

'It wasn't your fault – or mine. Sally's romantic and young.'

'And jealous,' Seward sat down on the bed. The feeling of comfort, of companionship, of bringing some order out of chaos – it had all faded. 'Look, Martha, I can't stay here.'

'You're running away?'

'If you like – but – well – the two of you – I'm in the middle.'

'I guessed that. No you'd better stay. We'll work something out.'

'Okay.' He got up, sighing heavily. 'I think I'll go for a walk in the park – it may help me to think. I'd just reached the stage where I was getting somewhere. Thanks for that, anyway, Martha.'

She smiled. 'Don't worry, Lee. I'll have everything running smoothly again by tomorrow.'

He didn't doubt it. She was a remarkable woman.

He put on his socks and shoes, opened the door and went out on to the landing. Moonlight entered through a tall, slender window at the end. He went down the two flights of stairs and out of the front door.

He turned into the lane and entered the arbour. In the cool of the night, he once again was able to begin some constructive thinking.

While he was on this world, he would not waste his time, he would keep trying to discover the necessary modifications to make the tranquilomats workable.

He wandered through the arbour, keeping any thoughts of the two women out of his mind. He turned into another section of the arbour he hadn't noticed before. The turnings became numerous but he was scarcely aware of them. It was probably some sort of child's maze.

He paused as he came to a bench. He sat down and folded his arms in front of him, concentrating on his problem.

Much later he heard a sound to his right and looked up.

A man he didn't know was standing there, grinning at him.

Seward noticed at once that the man had overlong canines, that he smelt of damp earth and decay. He wore a black, poloneck pullover and black, stained trousers. His face was waxen and very pale.

'I've been looking for you for ages, Professor Seward,' said the Vampire.

FIVE

Seward got up and faced the horrible creature. The Vampire continued to smile. He didn't move. Seward felt revulsion.

'It's been a long journey,' said the Vampire in a sibilant voice like the sound of a frigid wind blowing through dead boughs. 'I had intended to visit you at the fortress, but when I got to your room you had left. I was disappointed.'

'Doubtless,' said Seward. 'Well, you've had a wasted journey. I'm not going back there until I'm ready.'

'That doesn't interest me.'

'What does?' Seward tried to stop himself from trembling.

The Vampire put his hands into his pockets. 'Only you.'

'Get away from here. You're outnumbered – I have friends.' But he knew that his tone was completely unconvincing.

The Vampire hissed his amusement. 'They can't do much, Seward.'

'What are you – some sort of android made to frighten people?'

'No.' The Vampire took a pace forward.

Suddenly he stopped as a voice came faintly from somewhere in the maze.

'Lee! Lee! Where are you?'

It was Sally's voice.

'Stay away, Sally!' Lee called.

'But I was going to warn you. I saw the Vampire from the window. He's somewhere in the park.'

'I know. Go home!'

'I'm sorry about the scene, Lee. I wanted to apologize. It was childish.'

'It doesn't matter.' He looked at the Vampire. He was standing in a relaxed position, hands in pockets, smiling. 'Go home, Sally!'

'She won't, you know,' whispered the Vampire.

Her voice was closer. 'Lee, I must talk to you.'

He screamed: 'Sally – the Vampire's here. Go home. Warn your mother, not me. Get some help if you can – but go home!'

Now he saw her enter the part of the maze he was in. She gasped as she saw them. He was between her and the Vampire.

'Sally – do what I told you.'

But the Vampire's cold eyes widened and he took one hand out of his pocket and crooked a finger. 'Come here, Sally.'

She began to walk forward.

He turned to the Vampire. 'What do you want?'

'Only a little blood – yours, perhaps – or the young lady's.'

'Damn you. Get away. Go back, Sally.' She didn't seem to hear him.

He daren't touch the cold body, the earth-damp clothes. He stepped directly between the girl and the Vampire.

He felt sick, but he reached out his hands and shoved at the creature's body. Flesh yielded, but bone did not. The Vampire held his ground, smiling, staring beyond Seward at the girl.

Seward shoved again and suddenly the creature's arms clamped around him and the grinning, fanged face darted towards his. The thing's breath disgusted him. He struggled, but could not break the Vampire's grasp.

A cold mouth touched his neck. He yelled and kicked. He felt a tiny pricking against his throat. Sally screamed. He heard her turn and run and felt a fraction of relief.

He punched with both fists as hard as he could into the creature's solar plexus. It worked. The Vampire groaned and let go. Seward was disgusted to see that its fangs dripped with blood.

His blood.

Now rage helped him. He chopped at the Vampire's throat. It gasped, tottered, and fell in a sprawl of loose limbs to the ground.

Panting, Seward kicked it in the head. It didn't move.

He bent down and rolled the Vampire over. As far as he could tell it was dead. He tried to remember what he'd read about legendary vampires. Not much. Something about a stake through its heart. Well, that was out.

But the thought that struck him most was that he had fought one of the fortress people – and had won. It was possible to beat them!

He walked purposefully through the maze. It wasn't as tortuous as he'd supposed. Soon he emerged at the arbour entrance near the house. He saw Sally and Martha running towards him. Behind them, another figure lumbered. Farlowe. He had got here fast.

'Seward,' he shouted. 'They said the Vampire had got you!'

'I got him,' said Seward as they came up and stopped.

'What?'

'I beat him.'

'But – that's impossible.'

Seward shrugged. He felt elated. 'Evidently, it's possible,' he said. 'I knocked him out. He seems to be dead – but I suppose you never know with vampires.'

Farlowe was astonished. 'I believe you,' he said, 'but it's fantastic. How did you do it?'

'I got frightened and then angry,' said Seward simply. 'Maybe you've been over-awed by these people too long.'

'It seems like it,' Farlowe admitted. 'Let's go and have a look at him. Sally and Martha had better stay behind.'

Seward led him back through the maze. The Vampire was still where he'd fallen. Farlowe touched the corpse with his foot.

'That's the Vampire all right.' He grinned. 'I knew we had a winner in you, son. What are you going to do now?'

'I'm going straight back to the fortress and get this worked out once and for all. Martha gave me an idea yesterday evening and she may well be right. I'm going to try and find out anyway.'

'Better not be over-confident, son.'

'Better than being over-cautious.'

'Maybe,' Farlowe agreed doubtfully. 'What's this idea Martha gave you?'

'It's really her idea, complete. Let her explain. She's an intelligent woman – and she's bothered to think about this problem from scratch. I'd advise you to do the same.'

'I'll hear what it is, first. Let's deal with the Vampire and then get back to the house.'

'I'll leave the Vampire to you. I want to use your car.'

'Why?'

'To go back to the fortress.'

'Don't be a fool. Wait until we've got some help.'

'I can't wait that long, Farlowe. I've got other work to do back on my own world.'

'Okay,' Farlowe shrugged.

Farlowe faded.

The maze began to fade.

Explosions in the brain.

Vertigo.

Sickness.

His head ached and he could not breathe. He yelled, but he had no voice. Multicoloured explosions in front of his eyes. He was whirling round and round, spinning rapidly. Then he felt a new surface dragging at his feet. He closed his eyes and stumbled against something. He fell on to something soft.

It was his camp bed. He was back in his laboratory.

Seward wasted no time wondering what had happened. He knew more or less. Possibly his encounter with the Vampire had sent him back – the exertion or – of course – the creature had drawn some of his blood. Maybe that was it. He felt the pricking sensation, still. He went to the mirror near the wash-stand. He could just see the little marks in his neck. Further proof that wherever that world was it was as real as the one he was in now.

He went to the table and picked up his notes, then walked into the other room. In one section was a long bench. On it, in various stages of dismantling, were the machines that he had been working on, the tranquilomats that somehow just didn't work. He picked up one of the smallest and checked its batteries, its lenses and its sonic agitator. The idea with this one was to use a combination of light and sound to agitate certain dormant cells in the brain. Long since, psychophysicists had realized that mental abnormality had a chemical as well as a mental cause. Just as a patient with a psychosomatic illness produced all the biological symptoms of whatever disease he thought he had, so did chemistry play a part in brain disorders. Whether the change in the brain cells came first or afterwards they weren't sure. But the fact was that the cells could be agitated and the mind, by a mixture of hypnosis and conditioning, could be made to work normally. But it was a long step from knowing this and being able to use the information in the construction of tranquilomats.

Seward began to work on the machine. He felt he was on the right track, at least.

But how long could he keep going before his need for the drug destroyed his will?

He kept going some five hours before his withdrawal symptoms got the better of him.

He staggered towards one of the drug-drawers and fumbled out an ampoule of M-A 19. He staggered into his bedroom and reached for the needle on the table.

He filled the syringe. He filled his veins. He filled his brain with a series of explosions which blew him clean out of his own world into the other.

Fire flew up his spine. Ignited back-brain, ignited mid-brain, ignited fore-brain. Ignited all centres.

EXPLOSION ALL CENTRES.

This time the transition was brief. He was standing in the part of the maze where he'd been when he'd left. The Vampire's corpse was gone. Farlowe had gone, also. He experienced a feeling of acute frustration that he couldn't continue with his work on KLTM-8 – the tranquilomat he'd been modifying when his craving for the M-A 19 took over.

But there was something to do here, too.

He left the maze and walked towards the house. It was dawn and very cold. Farlowe's car was parked there. He noticed the licence number. It seemed different. It now said YOU 009. Maybe he'd mistaken the last digit for a zero last time he'd looked.

The door was ajar. Farlowe and Martha were standing in the hall.

They looked surprised when he walked in.

'I thought the Vampire was peculiar, son,' said Farlowe. 'But yours was the best vanishing act I've ever seen.'

'Martha will explain that, too,' Seward said, not looking at her. 'Has she told you her theory?'

'Yes, it sounds feasible.' He spoke slowly, looking at the floor. He looked up. 'We got rid of the Vampire. Burned him up. He burns well.'

'That's one out of the way, at least,' said Seward. 'How many others are there at the fortress?'

Farlowe shook his head. 'Not sure. How many did you see?'

'The Man Without A Navel, a character called Brother Sebastian who wears a cowl and probably isn't human either, two pleasant gentlemen called Mr Morl and Mr Hand – and a man in fancy dress whose name I don't know.'

'There are one or two more,' Farlowe said. 'But it's not their numbers we've got to worry about – it's their power!'

'I think maybe it's over-rated,' Seward said.

'You may be right, son.'

'I'm going to find out.'

'You still want my car?'

'Yes. If you want to follow up behind with whatever help you can gather, do that.'

'I will.' Farlowe glanced at Martha. 'What do you think, Martha?'

'I think he may succeed,' she said. 'Good luck, Lee.' She smiled at him in a way that made him want to stay.

'Right,' said Seward. 'I'm going. Hope to see you there.'

'I may be wrong, Lee,' she said warningly. 'It was only an idea.'

'It's the best one I've heard. Goodbye.'

He went out of the house and climbed into the car.

SIX

The road was white, the sky was blue, the car was red and the countryside was green. Yet there was less clarity about the scenery than Seward remembered. Perhaps it was because he no longer had the relaxing company of Farlowe, because his mind was working furiously and his emotions at full blast.

Whoever had designed the set-up on this world had done it well, but had missed certain details. Seward realized that one of the 'alien' aspects of the world was that everything was just a little too new. Even Farlowe's car looked as if it had just been driven off the production line.

By the early afternoon he was beginning to feel tired and some of his original impetus had flagged. He decided to move in to the side of the road and rest for a short time, stretch his legs. He stopped the car and got out.

He walked over to the other side of the road. It was on a hillside and he could look down over a wide, shallow valley. A river gleamed in the distance, there were cottages and livestock in the fields. He couldn't see the horizon. Far away he saw a great bank of reddish-looking clouds that seemed to swirl and seethe like a restless ocean. For all the *signs* of habitation, the countryside had taken on a desolate quality as if it had been abandoned. He could not believe that there were people living in the cottages and tending the livestock. The whole thing looked like the set for a film. Or a play – a complicated play devised by the Man Without A Navel and his friends – a play in which the fate of a world – possibly two worlds – was at stake.

How soon would the play resolve itself? he wondered, as he turned back towards the car.

A woman was standing by the car. She must have come down the hill while he was looking at the valley. She had long, jet black hair and big, dark eyes. Her skin was tanned dark gold. She had full, extraordinarily sensuous lips. She wore a well-tailored red suit, a black blouse, black shoes and black handbag. She looked rather sheepish. She raised her head to look at him and as she did so a lock of her black hair fell over her eyes. She brushed it back.

'Hello,' she said. 'Am I lucky!'

'Are you?'

'I hope so. I didn't expect to find a car on the road. You haven't broken down have you?' She asked this last question anxiously.

'No,' he said. 'I stopped for a rest. How did you get here?'

She pointed up the hill. 'There's a little track up there – a cattle-track, I suppose. My car skidded and went into a tree. It's a wreck.'

'I'll have a look at it for you.'

She shook her head. 'There's no point – it's a write-off. Can you give me a lift?'

'Where are you going?' he said unwillingly.

'Well, it's about sixty miles that way,' she pointed in the direction he was going. 'A small town.'

It wouldn't take long to drive sixty miles on a road as clear as this with no apparent speed-limit. He scratched his head doubtfully. The woman was a diversion he hadn't expected and, in a way, resented. But she was very attractive. He couldn't refuse her. He hadn't seen any cart-tracks leading off the road. This, as far as he knew, was the only one, but it was possible he hadn't noticed since he didn't know this world. Also, he decided, the woman evidently wasn't involved in the struggle between the fortress people and Farlowe's friends. She was probably just one of the conditioned, living out her life completely unaware of where she was and why. He might be able to get some information out of her.

'Get in,' he said.

'Oh, thanks.' She got in, seeming rather deliberately to show him a lot of leg. He opened his door and slid under the wheel. She sat uncomfortably close to him. He started the engine and moved the car out on to the road again.

'I'm a stranger here,' he began conversationally. 'What about you?'

'Not me – I've lived hereabouts all my life. Where do you come from – stranger?'

He smiled. 'A long way away.'

'Are they all as good looking as you?' It was trite, but it worked. He felt flattered.

'Not any more,' he said. That was true. Maniacs never looked very good. But this wasn't the way he wanted the conversation to go, however nice the direction. He said: 'You're not very heavily populated around here. I haven't seen another car, or another person for that matter, since I set off this morning.'

'It does get boring,' she said. She smiled at him. That and her full body, her musky scent and her closeness, made him breathe more heavily than he would have liked. One thing about this world – the women were considerably less inhibited than on his own. It was a difference in population, perhaps. In an overcrowded world your social behaviour must be more rigid, out of necessity.

He kept his hands firmly on the wheel and his eyes on the road, convinced that if he didn't he'd lose control of himself and the car. The result might be a sort of femme fatality. His attraction towards Sally and Martha had not been wholly sexual. Yet he had never felt such purely animal attraction that this woman radiated. Maybe, he decided, she didn't know it. He glanced at her. There again, maybe she did.

It said a lot for the woman if she could take his mind so completely off his various problems.

'My name's Magdalen,' she smiled. 'A bit of a mouthful. What's yours?'

It was a relief to find someone here who didn't already know his name. He rejected the unliked Lee and said: 'Bill – Bill Ward.'

'Short and sweet,' she said. 'Not like mine.'

He grunted vaguely, consciously fighting the emotions rising in him. There was a word for them. A simple word – short and sweet – lust. He rather liked it. He'd been somewhat repressed on his home world and had kept a tight censorship on his feelings. Here it was obviously different.

A little later, he gave in. He stopped the car and kissed her. He was surprised at the ease with which he did it. He forgot about the tranquilomats, about the M-A 19, about the fortress. He forgot about everything except her, and that was maybe why he did what he did.

It was as if he was drawn into yet another world – a private world where only he and she had any existence. An enclosed world consisting only of their desire and their need to satisfy it.

Afterwards he felt gloomy, regretful and guilty. He started the car savagely. He knew he shouldn't blame her, but he did. He'd wasted time. Minutes were valuable, even seconds. He'd wasted hours.

Beside him she took a headscarf from her bag and tied it over her hair. 'You're in a hurry.'

He pressed the accelerator as far down as he could.

'What's the problem?' she shouted as the engine thudded noisily.

'I've wasted too much time already. I'll drop you off wherever it is you want.'

'Oh, fine. Just one of those things, eh?'

'I suppose so. It was my fault, I shouldn't have picked you up in the first place.'

She laughed. It wasn't a nice laugh. It was a mocking laugh and it seemed to punch him in the stomach.

'Okay,' he said, 'okay.'

He switched on the headlamps as dusk became night. There was no milometer on the dashboard so he didn't know how far they'd travelled, but he was sure it was more than sixty miles.

'Where is this town?' he said.

'Not much further.' Her voice softened. 'I'm sorry, Lee. But what *is* the matter?'

Something was wrong. He couldn't place it. He put it down to his own anger.

'You may not know it,' he said, 'but I suspect that nearly all the people living here are being deceived. Do you know the fortress?'

'You mean that big building on the rock wastes?'

'That's it. Well, there's a group of people there who are duping you and the rest in some way. They want to destroy practically the whole of the human race by a particularly nasty method – and they want me to do it for them.'

'What's that?'

Briefly, he explained.

Again she laughed. 'By the sound of it, you're a fool to fight this Man Without A Navel and his friends. You ought to throw in your lot with them. You could be top man.'

'Aren't you angry?' he said in surprise. 'Don't you believe me?'

'Certainly. I just don't share your attitude. I don't understand you turning down a chance when it's offered. I'd take it. As I said, you could be top man.'

'I've already been top man,' he said, 'in a manner of speaking. On my own world. I don't want that kind of responsibiliy. All I want to do is save something from the mess I've made of civilization.'

'You're a fool, Lee.'

That was it. She shouldn't have known him as Lee but as Bill, the name he'd introduced himself by. He stopped the car suddenly and looked at her suspiciously. The truth was dawning on him and it made him feel sick at himself that he could have fallen for her trap.

'You're working for him, aren't you. The Man?'

'You seem to be exhibiting all the symptoms of persecution mania, Seward. You need a good psychiatrist.' She spoke coolly and reached into her handbag. 'I don't feel safe with you.'

'It's mutual,' he said. 'Get out of the car.'

'No,' she said quietly. 'I think we'll go all the way to the fortress together.' She put both hands into her bag. They came out with two things. One was a half bottle of brandy.

The other was a gun.

'Evidently my delay tactics weren't effective enough,' she mocked. 'I thought they might not be, so I brought these. Get out, yourself, Seward.'

'You're going to kill me?'

'Maybe.'

'But that isn't what The Man wants, is it?'

She shrugged, waving the gun.

Trembling with anger at his own gullibility and impotence, he got out. He couldn't think clearly.

She got out, too, keeping him covered. 'You're a clever man, Seward. You've worked out a lot.'

'There are others here who know what I know.'

'What do they know?'

'They know about the set-up – about the conditioning.'

She came round the car towards him, shaking her head. Still keeping him covered, she put the brandy bottle down on the seat.

He went for the gun.

He acted instinctively, in the knowledge that this was his only chance. He heard the gun go off, but he was forcing her wrist back. He slammed it down on the side of the car. She yelled and dropped it. Then he did what he had never thought he could do. He hit her, a short, sharp jab under the chin. She crumpled.

He stood over her, trembling. Then he took her headscarf and tied her limp hands behind her. He dragged her up and dumped her in the back of the car. He leant down and found the gun. He put it in his pocket.

Then he got into the driving seat, still trembling. He felt something hard under him. It was the brandy bottle. It was what he needed. He unscrewed the cap and took a long drink.

His brain began to explode even as he reached for the ignition.

It seemed to crackle and flare like burning timber. He grabbed the door handle. Maybe if he walked around . . .

He felt his knees buckle as his feet touched the ground. He strained to keep himself upright. He forced himself to move round the car. When he reached the bonnet, the headlamps blared at him, blinded him.

They began to blink rapidly into his eyes. He tried to raise his hands and cover his eyes. He fell sideways, the light still blinking. He felt nausea sweep up and through him. He saw the car's licence plate in front of him.

YOU 099

YOU 100

YOU 101

He put out a hand to touch the plate. It seemed normal. Yet the digits were clocking up like the numbers on an adding machine.

Again his brain exploded. A slow, leisurely explosion that subsided and brought a delicious feeling of well-being.

Green clouds like boiled jade, scent of chrysanthemums. Swaying lilies. Bright lines of black and white in front of his eyes. He shut them and opened them again. He was looking up at the blind in his bedroom.

As soon as he realized he was back, Seward jumped off the bed and made for the bench where he'd left the half-finished tranquilomat. He remembered something, felt for the gun he'd taken off the girl. It wasn't there.

But he felt the taste of the brandy in his mouth. Maybe it was as simple as that, he thought. Maybe all he needed to get back was alcohol.

There was sure to be some alcohol in the lab. He searched through cupboards and drawers until he found some in a jar. He filled a vial and corked it. He took off his shirt and taped the vial under his armpit – that way he might be able to transport it from his world to the other one.

Then he got down to work.

Lenses were reassembled, checked. New filters went in and old ones came out. He adjusted the resonators and amplifiers. He was re-charging the battery which powered the transistorized circuits, when he sensed the mob outside. He left the little machine on the bench and went to the control board. He flicked three switches down and then, on impulse, flicked them off again. He went back to the bench and unplugged the charger. He took the machine to the window. He drew the blind up.

It was a smaller mob than usual. Evidently some of them had learned their lesson and were now avoiding the laboratory.

Far away, behind them, the sun glinted on a calm sea. He opened the window.

There was one good way of testing his tranquilomat. He rested it on the sill and switched it to ATTRACT. That was the first necessary stage, to hold the mob's attention. A faint, pleasant humming began to come from the machine. Seward knew that specially shaped and coloured lenses were whirling at the front. The mob looked up towards it, but only those in the centre of the group were held. The others dived away, hiding their eyes.

Seward felt his body tightening, growing cold. Part of him began to scream for the M-A 19. He clung to the machine's carrying handles. He turned a dial from Zero to 50. There were 100 units marked on the indicator. The machine was now sending at half-strength. Seward consoled himself that if anything went wrong he could not do any more harm to their ruined minds. It wasn't much of a consolation.

He quickly saw that the combined simulated brainwaves, sonic vibrations and light patterns were having some effect on their minds. But what was the effect going to be? They were certainly responding. Their bodies were relaxing, their faces were no longer twisted with insanity. But was the tranquilomat actually doing any constructive good – what it had been designed to do? He upped the output to 75 degrees.

His hand began to tremble. His mouth and throat were tight and dry. He couldn't keep going. He stepped back. His stomach ached. His bones ached. His eyes felt puffy. He began to move towards the machine again. But he couldn't make it. He moved towards the half-full ampoule of M-A 19 on the table. He filled the blunt hypodermic. He found a vein. He was weeping as the explosions hit his brain.

SEVEN

This time it was different.

He saw an army of machines advancing towards him. An army of malevolent hallucinomats. He tried to run, but a thousand electrodes were clamped to his body and he could not move. From nowhere, needles, entered his veins. Voices shouted SEWARD! SEWARD! SEWARD! The hallucinomats advanced, shrilling, blinking, buzzing – *laughing*. The machines were laughing at him.

SEWARD!

Now he saw Farlowe's car's registration plate.

YOU 110

YOU 111

YOU 119

SEWARD!

YOU!

SEWARD!

His brain was being squeezed. It was contracting, contracting. The voices became distant, the machines began to recede. When they had vanished he saw he was standing in a circular room in the centre of which was a low dais. On the dais was a chair. In the chair was the Man Without A Navel. He smiled at Seward.

'Welcome back, old boy,' he said.

Brother Sebastian and the woman, Magdalen, stood close to the dais. Magdalen's smile was cool and merciless, seeming to anticipate some new torture that the Man and Brother Sebastian had devised.

But Seward was jubilant. He was sure his little tranquilomat had got results.

'I think I've done it,' he said quietly. 'I think I've built a workable tranquilomat – and, in a way, it's thanks to you. I had to speed my work up to beat you – and I did it!'

They seemed unimpressed.

'Congratulations, Seward,' smiled the Man Without A Navel. 'But this doesn't alter the situation, you know. Just because you *have* an antidote doesn't mean we have to use it.'

Seward reached inside his shirt and felt for the vial taped under his arm. It had gone. Some of his confidence went with the discovery.

Magdalen smiled. 'It was kind of you to drink the drugged brandy.'

He put his hands in his jacket pocket.

The gun was back there. He grinned.

'What's he smiling at?' Magdalen said nervously.

'I don't know. It doesn't matter. Brother Sebastian, I believe you have finished work on your version of Seward's hypnomat?'

'I have,' said the sighing, cold voice.

'Let's have it in. It is a pity we didn't have it earlier. It would have saved us time – and Seward all his efforts.'

The curtains behind them parted and Mr Hand, Mr Morl and the Laughing Cavalier wheeled in a huge, bizarre machine that seemed to have a casing of highly-polished gold, silver and platinum. There were two sets of lenses in its domed, head-like top. They looked like eyes staring at Seward.

Was this a conditioning machine like the ones they'd probably used on the human populace? Seward thought it was likely. If they got him with that, he'd be finished. He pulled the gun out of his pocket. He aimed it at the right-hand lens and pulled the trigger.

The gun roared and kicked in his hand, but no bullet left the muzzle. Instead there came a stream of small, brightly coloured globes, something like those used in the attraction device on the tranquilomat. They sped towards the machine, struck it, exploded. The machine buckled and shrilled. It steamed and two discs, like lids, fell across the lenses. The machine rocked backwards and fell over.

The six figures began to converge on him, angrily.

Suddenly, on his left, he saw Farlowe, Martha and Sally step from behind a screen.

'Help me!' he cried to them.

'We can't!' Farlowe yelled. 'Use your initiative, son!'

'Initiative?' He looked down at the gun. The figures were coming closer. The Man Without A Navel smiled slowly. Brother Sebastian tittered. Magdalen gave a low, mocking laugh that seemed – strangely – to be a criticism of his sexual prowess. Mr Morl and Mr Hand retained their mournful and cheerful expressions respectively. The Laughing Cavalier flung back his head and – laughed. All around them the screens, which had been little more than head-high were lengthening, widening, stretching up and up.

He glanced back. The screens were growing.

He pulled the trigger of the gun. Again it bucked, again it roared – and from the muzzle came a stream of metallic-grey particles which grew into huge flowers. The flowers burst into flame and formed a wall between him and the six.

He peered around him, looking for Farlowe and the others. He couldn't find them. He heard Farlowe's shout: 'Good luck, son!' He heard Martha and Sally crying goodbye. 'Don't go!' he yelled.

Then he realized he was alone. And the six were beginning to advance again – malevolent, vengeful.

Around him the screens, covered in weird designs that curled and swirled, ever-changing, were beginning to topple inwards. In a moment he would be crushed.

Again he heard his name being called. SEWARD! SEWARD!

Was it Martha's voice? He thought so.

'I'm coming,' he shouted, and pulled the trigger again.

The Man Without A Navel, Magdalen, Brother Sebastian, the Laughing Cavalier, Mr Hand and Mr Morl – all screamed in unison and began to back away from him as the gun's muzzle spouted a stream of white fluid which floated into the air.

Still the screens were falling, slowly, slowly.

The white fluid formed a net of millions of delicate strands. It drifted over the heads of the six. It began to descend. They looked up and screamed again.

'Don't, Seward,' begged the Man Without A Navel. 'Don't, old man – I'll make it worth your while.'

Seward watched as the net engulfed them. They struggled and cried and begged.

It did not surprise him much when they began to shrink.

No! *They* weren't shrinking – he was growing. He was growing over the toppling screens. He saw them fold inwards. He looked down and the screens were like cards folding neatly over the six little figures struggling in the white net. Then, as the screens folded down, the figures were no longer in sight. It got lighter. The screens rolled themselves into a ball.

The ball began to take on a new shape.

It changed colour. And then, there it was – a perfectly formed human skull.

Slowly, horrifyingly, the skull began to gather flesh and blood and muscles to itself. The stuff flowed over it. Features began to appear. Soon, in a state of frantic terror, Seward recognized the face.

It was his own.

His own face, its eyes wide, its lips parted. A tired, stunned, horrified face.

He was back in the laboratory. And he was staring into a mirror.

He stumbled away from the mirror. He saw he wasn't holding a gun in his hand but a hypodermic needle. He looked round the room.

The tranquilomat was still on the window-sill. He went to the window. There, quietly talking among the ruins below, was a group of sane men and women. They were still in rags, still gaunt. But they were sane. That was evident. They were saner than they had ever been before.

He called down to them, but they didn't hear him.

Time for that later, he thought. He sat on the bed, feeling dazed and relieved. He dropped the needle to the floor, certain he wouldn't need to use it again.

It was incredible, but he thought he knew where he had been. The final image of his face in the mirror had given him the last clue.

He had been inside his own mind. The M-A 19 was merely a hallucinogenic after all. A powerful one, evidently, if it could give him the illusion of rope-marks on his wrists, bites on his neck and the rest.

He had escaped into a dream world.

Then he wondered – but why? What good had it done?

He got up and went towards the mirror again.

Then he heard the voice. Martha's voice.

SEWARD! SEWARD! Seward, listen to me!

No, he thought desperately. No, it can't be starting again. There's no need for it.

He ran into the laboratory, closing the door behind him, locking it. He stood there, trembling, waiting for the withdrawal symptoms. They didn't come.

Instead he saw the walls of the laboratory, the silent computers and meters and dials, begin to blur. A light flashed on above his head. The dead banks of instruments suddenly came alive. He sat down in a big chrome, padded chair which had originally been used for the treating of test-subjects.

His gaze was caught by a whirling stroboscope that had appeared from nowhere. Coloured images began to form in front of his eyes. He struggled to get up but he couldn't.

YOU 121

YOU 122

YOU 123

Then the first letter changed to a V.

VOU 127

SEWARD!

His eyelids fell heavily over his eyes.

'Professor Seward.' It was Martha's voice. It spoke to someone else. 'We may be lucky, Tom. Turn down the volume.'

He opened his eyes.

'Martha.'

The woman smiled. She was dressed in a white coat and was leaning over the chair. She looked very tired. 'I'm not – Martha – Professor Seward. I'm Doctor Kalin. Remember?'

'Doctor Kalin, of course.'

His body felt weaker than it had ever felt before. He leaned back in the big chair and sighed. Now he was remembering.

It had been his decision to make the experiment. It had seemed to be the only way of speeding up work on the development of the tranquilomats. He knew that the secret of a workable machine was imbedded in the deepest level of his unconscious mind. But, however much he tried – hypnosis, symbol-association, word-association – he couldn't get at it.

There was only one way he could think of – a dangerous experiment for him – an experiment which might not work at all. He would be given a deep-conditioning, made to believe that he had brought disaster to the world and must remedy it by devising a tranquilomat. Things were pretty critical in the world outside, but they weren't as bad as they had conditioned him to believe. Work on the tranquilomats *was* falling behind – but there had been no widespread disaster, *yet*. It was bound to come unless they could devise some means of mass-cure for the thousands of neurotics and victims of insanity. An antidote for the results of mass-tension.

So, simply, they conditioned him to think his efforts had destroyed civilization. He must devise a working tranquilomat. They had turned the problem from an intellectual one into a personal one.

The conditioning had apparently worked.

He looked around the laboratory at his assistants. They were all alive, healthy, a bit tired, a bit strained, but they looked relieved.

'How long have I been under?' he asked.

'About fourteen hours. That's twelve hours since the experiment went wrong.'

'Went wrong?'

'Why, yes,' said Dcotor Kalin in surprise. 'Nothing was happening. We tried to bring you round – we tried every darned machine and drug in the place – nothing worked. We expected catatonia. At least we've managed to save you. We'll just have to go on using the ordinary methods of research, I suppose.' Her voice was tired, disappointed.

Seward frowned. But he *had* got the results. He knew exactly how to construct a working tranquilomat. He thought back.

'Of course,' he said. 'I was only conditioned to believe that the world was in ruins and I had done it. There was nothing about –

about – the *other* world.'

'What other world?' Macpherson, his Chief Assistant asked the question.

Seward told them. He told them about the Man Without A Navel, the fortress, the corridors, the tortures, the landscapes seen from Farlowe's car, the park, the maze, the Vampire, Magdalen . . . He told them how, in what he now called Condition A, he had believed himself hooked on a drug called M-A 19.

'But we don't have a drug called M-A 19,' said Doctor Kalin.

'I know that now. But I didn't know that and it didn't matter. I would have found something to have made the journey into – the other world – a world existing only in my skull. Call it Condition B, if you like – or Condition X, maybe. The unknown. I found a fairly logical means of making myself *believe* I was entering another world. That was M-A 19. By inventing symbolic characters who were trying to stop me, I made myself work harder. Unconsciously I knew that Condition A was going wrong – so I escaped into Condition B in order to put right the damage. By acting out the drama I was able to clear my mind of its confusion. I had, as I suspected, the secret of the tranquilomat somewhere down there all the time. Condition A failed to release that secret – Condition B succeeded. I can build you a workable tranquilomat, don't worry.'

'Well,' Macpherson grinned. 'I've been told to use my imagination in the past – but you *really* used yours!'

'That was the idea, wasn't it? We'd decided it was no good just using drugs to keep us going. We decided to use our drugs and hallucinomats directly, to condition me to believe that what we feared will happen, *had* happened.'

'I'm glad we didn't manage to bring you back to normality, in that case,' Doctor Kalin smiled. 'You've had a series of classic – if more complicated than usual – nightmares. The Man Without A Navel, as you call him, and his "allies" symbolized the elements in you that were holding you back from the truth – diverting you. By "defeating" the Man, you defeated those elements.'

'It was a hell of a way to get results,' Seward grinned. 'But I got them. It was probably the only way. Now we can produce as many tranquilomats as we need. The problem's over. I've – in all modesty –' he grinned, 'saved the world before it needed saving. It's just as well.'

'What about your "helpers", though,' said Doctor Kalin helping him from the chair. He glanced into her intelligent, mature face. He had always liked her.

'Maybe,' he smiled, as he walked towards the bench where the experimental tranquilomats were laid out, 'maybe there was quite a bit of wish-fulfilment mixed up in it as well.'

'It's funny how you didn't realize that it wasn't real, isn't it?' said Macpherson behind him.

'Why is it funny?' he turned to look at Macpherson's long, worn face. 'Who knows what's real, Macpherson? This world? That world? Any other world? I don't feel so adamant about this one, do you?'

'Well . . .' Macpherson said doubtfully. 'I mean, you're a trained psychiatrist as well as everything else. You'd think you'd recognize your own symbolic characters?'

'I suppose it's possible.' Macpherson had missed his point. 'All the same,' he added. 'I wouldn't mind going back there some day. I'd quite enjoy the exploration. And I liked some of the people. Even though they were probably wish-fulfilment figures. Farlowe – father – it's possible.' He glanced up as his eye fell on a meter. It consisted of a series of code-letters and three digits. VOU 128 it said now. There was Farlowe's number-plate. His mind had turned the V into a Y, He'd probably discover plenty of other symbols around, which he'd turned into something else in the other world. He still couldn't think of it as a dream world. It had seemed so real. For him, it was still real.

'What about the woman – Martha?' Doctor Kalin said. 'You called *me* Martha as you were waking up.'

'We'll let that one go for the time being,' he grinned. 'Come on, we've still got a lot of work to do.'

The Real Life Mr Newman

(Adventures of the Dead Astronaut)

I

The London fog was lifting. In Charing Cross Gardens black skeletons of trees became visible and Newman could now make out the shadowy buildings beyond them. As the fog dispersed he got up from the bench. He did not welcome the change in the weather.

He seemed to be the only person about. What time was it?

London was still silent as he swung his huge body, swaddled in its thick, tan overcoat, towards the Embankment, plodded through the gates of the Gardens and out into the main road. Running across the road he noticed the stationary bus and wondering briefly why the passengers sat so still. Then he leaned on the Embankment wall and peered down into the river.

He thought for a moment that the Thames, too, was petrified. But he had been mistaken. It was moving, very sluggishly; alive with bobbing refuse, stained with oil. Turning his head to his right, Newman saw the ugly railway bridge, rusted steel and peeling green paint, a suburban train clanking across it. On his left marked by its orange lights was white Waterloo Bridge, curving over the water like a graceful sea-beast. And across the river, marked only by patches of light breaking through the fog, was the Festival Hall. Newman turned and put his back against the wall, staring across the road at the entrance to Embankment Underground Station. He was disappointed. He had expected the fog to last much longer. He was never afraid in the fog.

Near the Underground entrance a few vague shapes moved. Grey figures emerged from the fog and became black silhouettes in the light of the station foyer.

He crossed the road in a lumbering run, skipped hastily on to the pavement, as a hooting taxi narrowly missed him, and rushed into the lobby. He paused, fumbling in his coat for change. He put his money into a machine, took his ticket from the slot and walked slowly to the barrier. The attendant ignored him as he went through.

*

He had gone past the barrier and was about to step on to the downward escalator when he paused and began to tremble. He could not calm the trembling which rapidly became violent.

For a few seconds he fought to conquer his fear, but it was hopeless. He could not take a single step towards the escalator. It was well lit; he could see to the bottom where a short tunnel led to the platform. The layout of the station was familiar to him. There was no danger. But he could go no further. He turned and stumbled back through the barrier, out of the station by its other entrance and up Villiers Street, still dark and silent, towards Trafalgar Square.

As the fog dispersed Newman's peace of mind evaporated. He now felt troubled, persecuted. He ran faster when he reached the Strand and turned towards Trafalgar Square.

He stopped dead again at what he thought he saw.

Nelson's Column had grown to gigantic size, seeming to fill the whole square with its grimy masonry, stretching above him into the remnants of the rising fog. He shut his eyes and rubbed them – for him, a normal habit. When he opened them again the column had grown even larger. He raced down the Strand away from it, colliding with several people.

Now the rest of the buildings began to increase in size. Even passers-by seemed larger. Vast walls of concrete towered higher and higher – no longer buildings, but sheer, cave-studded sides of immense black cliffs. He charged on through canyons that appeared to fold in upon him. Blurs of light – red, blue, green, orange – darted like fire-flies before his eyes. There were noises; distant roars and shrieks. He felt the sensation of blows on his body, and everywhere the smell of iodine and almonds. Vibrating lines attacked his face, veering off as he raised his pale hands against them. His lungs were filled with a million tiny, stabbing icicles, his stomach was hollow, painful; his legs liquid, without bone or muscle.

The solid, thrumming note of a drum filled his skull – the sound of his maddened pulse as his heart sought to free itself from its restraining flesh and ribs. His breathing was a series of huge gasps – he could not get enough of the thin air. Booted feet ached, thighs and groin throbbed; hands waved on bruised arms – hands like peeled sticks waving in a high wind.

As a boy in England and later in Virginia, where his mother had gone with her American husband, Newman had admired trees more than anything else. He liked them green and golden and rustling in summer; he liked them stark and black and brittle in winter. He rarely broke a branch or stripped a twig of its bark or its leaves. He liked sometimes to climb them in summer, particularly when climbing helped him breathe in their sweetness and look down at a surging sea of foliage. But most of the time he had liked simply to walk among their trunks or lie in their shade, his back to the grass. He had resented it if he had been called away from the woods, where he would have drowned among trees if it had been possible.

'Alexander!' his mother used to call in her half-English accent. 'Are you there?'

'Come on, Al!' The good-natured voice of his stepfather, slightly embarrassed by the authority over her child which marrying Alexander's mother had given him.

Usually Alexander would come when called. He was an obedient child. But sometimes he would hide, or creep deeper into the woods that went on without end at the back of the house. He had fancied sometimes that the house stood on the edge of civilization – beyond it, endless forests without houses or human beings. He didn't need to populate this forest of his imagination; the forest was enough.

He had been a cheerful boy, lonely by choice. He had mixed well enough at school, sometimes playing with the neighbourhood children. He had been personable and clever, though he absorbed knowledge intuitively rather than consciously. Exams would release facts he did not know he knew. Blindly and amiably, he followed his stepfather into the Air Force when he left college – he had majored in physics – and became an efficient, mildly-liked officer. He was one of the men selected to go up in a space capsule when the Special Space Project got under way.

Col. Alexander Newman, USAF, ran blindly through the transformed streets of a terrifying London. Since his flight was silent, he was cursed rather than restrained by the people he bumped into. He did not look very different from a commuter late for his train. He ran down the Strand, past Aldwych, where cars braked as he crossed their paths, up Fleet Street until, exhausted, he stopped, drained of adrenalin. The aural and visual sensations diminished and disappeared. His physical sensations remained. His mouth was dry and he was wet with sweat.

He looked up at the *Daily Express* building. It had the appearance of a monstrous, Edwardian public lavatory and wash-house, covered in shiny tiles. He knew then that he was in Fleet Street. He had not come particularly far, but could not remember how he had got here. He guessed something like this had happened several times already. He looked at his watch. It had stopped. He pulled up his coat collar, wiping the sweat from his face. No-one seemed to be looking at him, so he decided that his behaviour had not been too abnormal. He hailed a taxi, climbed in and gave the address.

A towering, glowering, twisted London went past as the driver took him towards Notting Hill. Nothing looked man-made. Everything had the appearance of a strange, natural landscape – canyons and crags, grey and black, with dim lights gleaming here and there. Asymmetrical and organic it had an air of being as yet only partly formed, waiting for a shape that would be given it. The shape, Newman felt, would not be that of the London he knew.

The sense of menace increased as the taxi sped on and he controlled his urge to tell the driver to stop.

Above all, Newman thought, it was bleak; it was a waste-land. It had never been alive.

Yet there was life there – life in it, like the maggots in a corpse. Life in the tall, brooding cliffs, hollowed by a million burrows. Life full of misery and disease and hopeless repetition of senseless actions. Life neurotic. Nothing could make it worse than it was, and only total destruction, perhaps, could improve it.

Part of one of the burrows was his; in the miserable slum he would once have recognized as, North Kensington, which apart from being a shade of two darker was now little different from anywhere else.

The taxi stopped. Newman paid, looking up at the distorted face of the immense cliff and trying to remember which entrance at the base he should crawl through to find his burrow.

Habit guided him. He clambered up obsidian slopes to enter the cave-mouth.

It was dark and smelled of damp and old age. A switch clicked beneath his hand but the place remained dark. He headed upwards, climbing slowly, gripping a balustrade he felt rather than saw.

At last he reached his room. Turning on the light, he reeled, for the walls appeared to be at odd angles, and there were too many surfaces. He made out the gas fire and the ring and the meter, the divan bed, the chest of drawers and the cane-seated chair.

He knew he paid thirty shillings a week for the room and he had lived in it for seven weeks since checking out of a nearby American servicemen's club where he had stayed for a week-end. He had told the club that he was going on to Italy. Perhaps they were looking for him there.

As an astronaut, Newman was a hero and on indefinite leave for having circled Mars umpteen times with his co-pilot, who had died. A steel capsule, cluttered with noisy instruments and his space-suited body lying in a semi-horizontal position.

He had had to work hard to get permission to travel around incognito. He had skipped his shadow when he had left the club. He had grown a full beard and let his hair grow longer. He wore dark glasses. His accent was American, but especially unnoticed in the area where he'd chosen to live. Here, nothing about him was particularly peculiar.

Not even his madness, he thought. He was undoubtedly mad, he supposed. For some reason he had the feeling that he was observing things as they actually were. His vision had distorted everything since his return from space, and yet the suspicion persisted that, when landing, he had seen everything clearly for the first time.

Yet the London out there was a madman's London – a dark dream, an ultra-subjective impression and not, as he had sometimes supposed, a super-objective impression.

He staggered towards the bed. Tomorrow he must go out and try to find someone who could help him but would not betray him to the U.S. authorities, who were looking for him. Perhaps others were looking for him, too?

Was all this hallucination? he wondered. Or was it absolute reality – not the apparent reality of conscious life but the reality of the unconscious, the reality responsible for effecting events and controlling society? Was he seeing it as well as sensing it? Or had his senses turned themselves in such a way that images appeared to his conscious mind exactly as they did to his unconscious?

Taking off his overcoat, he lay down on the bed and slept. The London he dreamed of was the London he had passed through in the taxi.

2

It is possible that Alexander Newman was mad, but when he woke up next morning it was with a feeling of tranquility. Outside, the sun had risen, its pale light reflected on the huge, crooked cliffs that had been the buildings of London. This morning they looked solid and permanent. Newman no longer doubted their reality.

He got off the bed and made his way across the angular room to the gas fire. He lit that and the gas ring and filled a large kettle with water from the tap. When it had boiled he washed himself and felt even more relaxed.

Having breakfasted on milk and cereal, he dressed and went down the twisted stairs and out into the street, now a gleaming ribbon reminiscent of frozen lava running between the cliffs. A few people passed, their faces quite blank. When he accidentally knocked into one, the man did not seem to notice. When Newman apologized, the man did not hear him.

They were like zombies, Newman thought. Like marionettes.

Though the buildings had changed, the general plan of the city had not, and Newman headed towards the Bayswater Road, walking up the narrow, winding gully that had been Portobello Road. He hardly noticed the girl who walked past him dressed in a farthingale – returning home, possibly, from a late fancy dress party.

Before he reached the end of the street he heard the clang of metal on metal and wondered where the sound came from. Until now he had not realized that the silence had been so complete. He turned into a court, smelling fire and hot steel, and there, in a workshop like a blacksmith's forge, a little man hammered at a beautifully engraved breast-plate from a suit of armour. The man was engrossed in this and Newman watched as he hammered, expertly turning the breast-plate on the anvil with a pair of tongs held in his left hand. The burnished steel shone and glinted in the red light from the fire that burned in the wide grate to the left of the workshop. The armour was covered in small, intricate designs of flowers, crosses and little figures in pastoral settings. It was the design for a lady's sampler rather than for a suit of armour, and the combination of the delicate, embroidery-like design and the martial nature of the thing seemed odd to Newman.

Evidently satisfied at last, the old man straightened up to become almost as tall as Newman. His shoulders were stooped and his face had a pink, healthy appearance. He wore glasses and his hair, like his old-fashioned moustache, was thick and white. He gave Newman a genial nod and began to strip off the heavy leather gloves he had worn when working the breast-plate. His apron was also leather, and he now wiped his hands down it to get rid of the sweat.

'Good morning,' Newman said. 'I don't know anyone like you worked around here.'

'You didn't?' The old man smiled. 'Good morning. You aren't a customer, by the look of you.'

'How can you tell?'

'I can tell a man who needs armour.'

'You're an armourer?'

'That's my trade.'

'But surely no one wears armour these days. Only a few ceremonial regiments maybe. Do they employ you?'

The old man shrugged. 'Anyone may employ me. Many do. I restore old armour and I make new armour – armour of all kinds, you know. My name is Schweitzer.'

'Mine's Newman, Mr Schweitzer. How do you do?'

'How do you do? Would you like a cup of tea? My wife should have one ready.'

'Thanks.'

Newman followed the old man through the workshop and entered a dark room behind it – a parlour. It contained a solid table covered with a thick, tasselled tablecloth with a rich, Indian design in purple and gold. An earthenware teapot in a knitted cosy stood on it, steam curling from the spout. There was a small window with dark, velvet curtains and heavy net; a dresser in dark oak held crockery primarily of willow-pattern. Mr Schweitzer indicated one of two leather armchairs and Newman sat down while Mr Schweitzer poured the tea into two large mugs.

When they were both sitting, Mr Schweitzer said: 'You seem to have a problem, Mr Newman. Can I help?'

'I don't think so,' Newman said. 'I have been confused for some time now, ever since I returned to Earth, but this morning I feel calm. I've a feeling of detachment. You know, of peace – certainty, if you like.'

'A very valuable feeling. If all were like you I should be out of work.' Mr Schweitzer smiled and sipped his tea.

'I don't follow you,' Newman said.

'I make armour of many sorts, Mr Newman. Many sorts.' Mr Schweitzer stretched his arm towards the table and put down his cup. 'Would you like to see some of the armour I make?'

Newman admitted that he was curious and the old man led him from the parlour, up a narrow staircase and into a storeroom, very neatly arranged. Here were shelves and racks bearing a strange assortment of things. There were cards full of pairs of sun-glasses, hats with veils, helmets with visors, a suit of city clothes – black coat, pin-stripe trousers, bowler hat, briefcase and umbrella – on a dummy. There were masks, plain and embroidered and fashioned into grotesque faces; there were Chinese fans, suits of armour from every period of history and every age; there were costumes – crinolines in brown and black, broadcloth suits in black. There were no bright colours among the suits and dresses.

'This is only one section of my stock of armour,' Mr Schweitzer told him. 'Call them travelling caves, portable fortresses. But my main stock cannot really be seen.'

Puzzled, Newman asked what it was.

'I trade in tangible intangibles, if you like.' Schweitzer smiled. 'Intangibles that have tangible effects, to be more precise.' He went to a bureau and pulled out a drawer full of books. Taking them from the drawer, he spread them before Newman. They were religious books. A Bible, a Koran, the Vestas – all kinds of works by religious thinkers, including modern works.

'I don't understand,' said Newman. 'This is armour?'

'The most lasting kind, Mr Newman. It is the armour of *ideas* and of *ritual*. Mental armour to shut out those other ideas . . .'

'Those are?'

'The ideas we fear, that we refuse to investigate unless swathed in armour. What if there were no purpose to existence, Mr Newman, other than to exist?'

Newman shrugged. 'What of it? That idea does not disturb me.'

'I told you I did not think you were a customer of mine. You have the manner of a man who has retreated so far that he has circled right back to the thing he fears – approaching it from the rear, as it were, and finding it not so fearsome as he felt. But that is an unfair judgement. I do not know you.'

'You may be right or you may be wrong,' Newman answered carelessly. 'Even now it occurs to me that I may be totally insane and that you are a figment of my imaginings.'

'What of it? Am I not as real as anything you have known in the past?'

'More so, in many ways.'

'Well, then?'

Newman nodded. 'I see your point. But could not all this – that transformed city out there, this shop, yourself – could they not be a monstrous suit of armour I have constructed for myself?'

'I am an armourer. I have been in the trade for longer than I would like to say. I know a customer when I see one. You are no customer for me.'

'Already you give me reassurance.' Newman smiled. 'You comfort me with your words – you ease my mind.'

'If you say so. There is a difference between self-confidence and self-deception.'

'Fair enough.' Newman paced around the storeroom, looking at everything. Now that Schweitzer had mentioned it, he could see that it was armour – all of it. It disturbed him that people should go to such lengths to embellish it, to put all their arts and skills into producing it.

There were more books, also – books of attractive, comforting philosophy.

'Antidotes, do you see, Mr Newman. My job is not to effect cures.'

'Just the diving suits,' Newman said, picking up a heavy diver's helmet. 'So that the depths can be visited but never really explored. And you sell all these?'

'I do not sell them, Mr Newman. Call me a philanthropist. I give them away.' Schweitzer moved towards another door. 'This way.'

In the next room were large, old-fashioned bottles of the kind once used for keeping sweets. Newman stared at some of the labels. They read: *Cynicism* (J); *Hatred* (M); *Idealism* (R5); *Despair* (12). And so on.

'All armour?' Newman asked.

'Just so. Like the knight who wore that breast-plate you saw me working earlier, people lumber around in their heavy suits and their actions becoming cruder, their movements more sluggish, the longer they wear them. But what can one do? Needs must when the devil drives . . .'

'And what is the devil, Mr Schweitzer?'

'Fear. Let us go back to the parlour and see if the tea is still hot enough for a second cup.'

While they sat drinking their tea in silence, Newman thought a little about the things he had seen in Mr Schweitzer's storerooms. A short time later, the door from the workshop opened and a girl came in. She was very tall and beautiful, wearing no make-up and with long, dark hair framing her face. She wore an ankle-length dress of crimson and both hands held leashes. At the end of one leash was a lyre-bird, very tame and confident, and on the other a peacock with its tail at its peak of splendour, sweeping the ground behind it as it walked beside the girl.

'Good morning, Mr Schweitzer,' she said with a friendly smile. 'Is it all right to pop in?'

'Of course, Fanny.'

Newman got up.

'This is Miss Fanny Patrick,' Schweitzer said. 'Mr Newman.'

The girl transferred one leash to her left hand and shook hands, giving him the same open smile she had given Schweitzer. 'How do you do, Mr Newman?'

For the first time it struck Newman, not very seriously, that he might have died and entered some previously unimagined heaven or hell – or, more likely, purgatory – since his experiences so far had not affected him particularly strongly in any direction. Fanny Patrick, however, could have come from a dream, for she appeared to be his ideal woman.

He even liked her choice of pets.

'You're not a Londoner, Mr Newman,' she was saying.

'I was born here,' he said. 'But I went to the States as a kid. I was a space-pilot. I came back to Europe because' – he laughed self-deprecatingly – 'because I was looking for some roots, I guess.'

'Roots, eh?' She raised an eyebrow. 'Geographical?'

'That's what I thought. It all sounds so phoney. Psychological, maybe.'

'Have you found them?'

'I'm not sure. Almost, perhaps.'

'That's fine. I'm lunching up the road. Why don't you join me?'

'I'd like to.'

'I'd really come to ask Mr Schweitzer if he felt like an early lunch out,' she said, turning to the old man. 'What do you say, Mr Schweitzer?'

'No, thank you.' Mr Schweitzer smiled. 'I've some work to get on with. I'm being kept pretty busy at the moment. I'll see you again, Mr Newman.'

Newman and the girl said goodbye and left through the workshop. The sun was bright and the sky cloudless as they sauntered up the canyon towards a café with a striped awning that jutted out from the cliff-wall on their right. They sat down at one of the tables under the awning and an old, black-clad waiter took their order with a nod of greeting to Fanny Patrick.

'What's your first name?' she asked as they waited for their food.

'Alexander.'

'Well, there are so few of us here that we tend to get on first-name terms right away. Is that all right by you?'

'Suits me.' Newman smiled 'Ah, I feel as though I'm on holiday.'

'You've just got in, have you?'

'I don't quite follow you.'

She smiled. 'I mean, things have changed recently. Your surroundings – that sort of thing.' She watched as her two birds, which she had freed from their leashes, ran among the tables pecking at scraps of food.

'That's right.'

'It happened to me. I was in a mental hospital for quite a while. Then, one day, everything seemed to sort itself out. The images, that I'd kept glimpsing, suddenly solidified, if you know what I mean. And here I was. I like it here.'

A thought struck Newman. 'Do you ever get the feeling you should be *doing* something here?'

She shook her head. 'I just take it easy,' she said. 'There's nothing to do – unless you're someone like Mr Schweitzer, working for the outside people.'

'Who are they?'

'Almost everybody,' she said. 'Look, you see that young man walking this way.'

Newman looked and saw him. He was fair-haired, sallow, and his face was somehow tight yet devoid of expression. He walked mechanically, like the people Newman had seen earlier. The other noticeable thing about him was that he was dressed in Edwardian clothes.

Fanny Patrick got up and walked towards the young man. She shouted 'Good morning,' but he didn't seem to hear her. She walked alongside him, peering into his face, tapping him gently on the shoulder. A suggestion of vague irritation crossed his brow but he walked on without looking at her. She shrugged, spread her hands and came back to the table.

The young man turned a corner and was gone.

'That's the outside people for you, Alexander,' she said as she sat down. 'Now do you know what I mean?'

'I suppose so. What makes them like that?'

'Oh, too many things.'

The lunch came. Newman had ordered schnitzel and noodles; Fanny had a Steak Diane.

'Those people are still living in the world we knew, is that it?' Newman suggested.

'I suppose it is,' she said. 'They go in and out of houses, along streets, buy things in shops that are still there as far as they're concerned. Yet we can see that they're not. Two kinds of reality, you see – co-existing. It still comes down to the question, if you care to ask it and worry about it: Is it the minority or the majority who are really insane? Or are all insane?'

3

Drinking coffee after lunch, Fanny Patrick glanced at her watch.

'I'm sailing for Paris this afternoon,' she said. 'Mustn't miss the ship.'

'Paris.' Newman was disappointed. 'So you're going away.'

'Why don't you come, too?' she suggested with a quick smile. 'You'd enjoy the voyage. And you've nothing else on, I gather.'

'No,' he said. 'I haven't. But I don't have much money with me and I'd need clothes . . .' He'd already made up his mind to go if he could.

'Don't worry about either. We don't use money. There's so few of us and we've everything we need. You can get some clothes there.'

'All right,' He grinned. 'I'll come.'

'Good. We'll pop-back to my place; get my bag, make sure the birds are looked after. That was one reason for calling on Mr S – his wife usually takes care of them for me while I'm away. Then we'll be off.'

They left the restaurant and walked round the corner to where a pale section of cliff, like a sandstone butte, stood alone. This was her house. Inside it was spacious, with white walls and red carpets, the furniture of light wood and upholstered in blue. He waited for her in a room which looked out over a landscaped garden with a fountain in the middle. She wasn't long. She came into the room with her bag in her hand, the lyre-bird and the peacock running behind her.

He took the bag.

'I've got a dog-cart ready at the side of the house,' she said.

He followed her out to where a scarlet and gold dog-cart, with a palomino pony between its shafts, was waiting for them. She climbed into the seat and lifted the placid birds into the back. Newman got up beside her. She jiggled the reins and the pony moved off.

After they'd left the birds with the pale, pleasant-voiced Mr Schweitzer, Fanny headed East.

'Where's the boat docked?' he asked.

'Port o'London,' she said. 'Sailing with the next tide.'

London, in spite of its transformation, still seemed brooding and repressive as they made their way through it, but the sun was bright and their mood was good. They passed a few cars, with marionettes at their wheels, and two old people cycling along, the man in plus-fours, the woman in a long, divided skirt. They waved to them cheerfully.

'Not outside people,' Newman said, holding on to his seat as the cart gathered speed.

'No, I suppose not. The trouble is, of course, that not so many people of our age seem to get through. They're mostly children or elderly, and the children don't stay long. It's a shame, isn't it?'

'Yes, it is. What about people born here?'

'Children born here are usually taken from their parents after a while. They go outside. Some stay – not many. It's one of the big tragedies – one of the main sacrifices of people who live here.'

'It's strange when you think of it,' Newman said as they left the canyon that had been Oxford Street and entered another which was High Holborn. 'There are traffic jams and jostling crowds here, yet we can't see them and they can't see us. Yet we both exist – we're both solid and real.'

'I've often wondered about it,' she said. 'Are we ghosts? Or do we have an existence in both worlds, just as so many of the outside people do? Perhaps we're corpses lying somewhere in the out-world, eh?'

'I don't like the idea. I can't believe it.'

'Neither can I. There's no need to look for explanations, really. Look at that!' She pointed as a man in wig and clothes of the mid-eighteenth century was carried past in a sedan chair by two automata wearing twentieth century clothes. 'Have you noticed how time is so mixed up? This is still the twentieth century in most respects, but some people speak and dress like people from as far back as the sixteenth. And here and there you meet people who seem to be from a short way into the future.'

'It is surprising,' Newman agreed. 'It's as if time has sorted itself out into zones where, perhaps, the true mood or event is shown – not in the sequence, or apparent sequence, of the history we knew, but into . . . well, zones of *influence*, if you like. You know those historians who divide history up into the Age of this and the Age of that. Maybe all the people in this world are from an Age where a particular psychological mood prevailed, dating from around the Renaissance in this case.'

'Psychic time zones.' She smiled. 'Where the nature of the psyche changes very slightly – perhaps even a lot – from zone to zone.'

Newman laughed. 'Something like that. It all sounds a bit queer.' It was odd, he thought, how a conversation like this would not have come at all naturally to him in his other life, yet here it seemed normal.

The pony trotted on through Stepney. The cliffs were blacker and gloomier than ever, with an atmosphere of decay and menace about them. Newman half-expected ghoulish, flying creatures to come flapping and squawking from their eyries, and to see mis-shapen troglodytes scuttling into cave-mouths, hurling poison-tipped flint spears before disappearing. The sound of the pony's hooves echoed hollowly and Fanny seemed to sense the mood, for she gave the animal its head. It galloped along, and soon the docks were in sight.

The docks were grim and grey, with jagged cliffs stretching along one side and the black river on the other. But the single ship floating at anchor there was in positive contrast to its surroundings. She was a great white clipper ship, her beams bound in bright brass, shining like gold; her sails, as pale as her paint, loose on her four tall masts.

Etched in gold letters on her side was the name, *White Lass*. The dog-cart trundled onto the dockside beside the clipper's main gangplank. An Asiatic sailor, dressed in trim blue jacket and trousers, called to them from the rail.

'Hurry aboard, there – we're sailing within the next five minutes.'

They climbed down and walked up the gangplank, Fanny leading the way, Newman behind carrying her bag.

A man in a merchant captain's uniform from around the turn of the century, a clipboard under one arm, came towards them along the deck. He gave them a cheerful salute. He was middle-aged, weather-tanned, and with an imperial beard. His nose was strong and aquiline, his mouth firm and sensitive.

'Good afternoon, captain.' Fanny smiled. 'Can you take another passenger? This is Mr Alexander Newman.'

'Good afternoon, Miss Patrick – Mr Newman. Yes, we've plenty of room aboard. You're welcome, sir.'

He spoke with a faint foreign accent; a deep voice with a permanent note of warm irony.

'This is Captain Conrad,' said Fanny, introducing them. Newman shook hands with him.

'The cabin next to yours is empty,' Conrad said. 'I think it will suit Mr Newman, Miss Patrick. You'll excuse me while I get back to work – we're sailing almost at once.' He beckoned a white-coated steward who had just emerged from below deck. 'Will you put Mr Newman in the cabin next to Miss Patrick's, please?'

The steward took Fanny's bag from Newman and led them back the way he had come, down a short companionway into a passage which had six doors leading off it, three on each side.

'This is the passenger section,' Fanny explained. 'The ship is mainly a cargo vessel.'

The steward opened one door and took the bag in. Fanny and Newman followed. The cabin was comfortable, with a wide bunk against one bulkhead, a large porthole, washing facilities, a writing desk and a cane chair bolted to the deck under the port-hole and a heavier armchair opposite them.

The steward took Newman out of this cabin and into the one next to it. This was furnished similarly.

'Will that be all, sir?' asked the steward.

'Yes, thanks.'

The steward left.

Fanny sauntered into Newman's cabin. 'Not bad, eh?' she said. 'She's a beautiful ship. You'll realize that most of all when we're on the open sea.'

Newman heard shouts above them, felt the ship list very slightly, then right herself.

'They've cast off,' Fanny said excitedly. 'Come on. Let's go up on deck.'

The sails billowed and the ship was soon moving rapidly down river, speeding past the cliffs that were warehouses and rotting buildings, towards open countryside and then the sea.

They joined the captain on the poop deck. He was leaning on a rail and staring down the long river. He looked up with a smile. 'Cabins all right?'

'Couldn't be better,' said Newman.

'Good.'

Newman noticed the silence of the ship as it sailed – just the faint creaking of the rigging. The perpetual noise and smell of even the best steamers was noticeably absent and it seemed a shame to Newman that the clippers, which could match many steamships for speed and capacity, had been abandoned. The slender ship slipped through the water of the river so smoothly that it was almost impossible to tell that they were moving, save for the scenery going past on both sides. Newman saw the helmsman in the wheelhouse behind him, guiding the clipper down the winding strip of water. A bell sounded. Sailors ran about tidying the ship, making lines fast, checking the sails and fastening hatches. The ship was bright, clean and trim, yet with an air of sturdiness about her. She was a fine-looking ship, but it was evident that she could stand hard work, too.

They reached the sea as evening came, the cold, watery flats of the Thames mouth racing by in the waning light; the reeds waving, making the land a parody of the sea.

Now at sea, they left the deck to join the captain in his cabin for supper.

As they ate, Newman said: 'This is rather a long way of getting to Paris, isn't it, captain? Normally ships bound for France leave Dover, I thought.'

The captain smiled. 'Outside, they do, Mr Newman. But here there are so few ships, and we suit outselves. It is a longer voyage, but we use the rivers as much as we can. On this trip, for instance, we shall be going all the way to Paris, up the Seine. It is longer but simpler, since there are difficulties in getting overland transportation for our cargo and passengers sometimes.'

'I can understand now.' Newman smiled. 'It is a nice way to travel.'

'I agree,' Fanny said. 'We'll cross the sea at night and by morning should have reached the mouth of the Seine. Here, it is possible for ships of this size to sail the big rivers.'

In the morning, Newman was awakened by a knock on his door. He called, 'Come in,' and Fanny entered with some clothes in her arms. There was a pair of jeans and a white shirt, a black, roll-neck jumper and some underwear.

'Captain Conrad managed to sort these out for you,' she said. 'Will they do? I think they'll fit.'

'That's good of him,' Newman replied. 'They'll be fine.'

'I'll see you on deck for breakfast in about half-an-hour,' she said as she left.

Newman got up. There was warm water in the taps of the wash-basin and he washed himself all over before drying off and climbing into the clothes Fanny had left. They were a good fit, the waist of the jeans being a little loose, but a broad leather belt answered that problem.

On deck, a small table and two chairs had been set out. Coffee and rolls were on it and Fanny was pouring herself a cup of coffee as he sat down.

The sea was bright blue and the sun exceptionally warm. There was a light wind, sufficient to refresh him and fill the sails of the clipper. Ahead he could see the coast. Captain Conrad called from the poop. 'Good morning, you two. Sleep well?'

'Very well,' Newman shouted amiably back. 'And thanks for the clothes, captain.'

'Join me as soon as you've finished breakfast,' Conrad disappeared.

The food was good and the coffee delicious. Completing breakfast, they climbed up to the captain's bridge. Conrad handed Fanny his field-glasses and she peered through them towards the coast.

'You can just see the mouth of the river.' Conrad pointed.

Fanny passed the glasses to Newman, who now saw the river mouth clearly, the tide swirling amongst sandbanks.

'It looks difficult to negotiate.' He returned the glasses to Conrad.

'Not when you know it well.' The captain frowned.

'How long have you been sailing this route?' Newman asked.

'A long time, I should think, Mr Newman. It is difficult to judge the passing of time in this world. The days are of the same duration, but few people bother to count them. The seasons are the same; the tides are the same. Nature does not change, and neither do men and women in this world. They make few attempts to change nature and nature makes few attempts to change them. Time means little here.'

'You can't remember when you arrived?'

'About 1912, I should say.'

'And you were the same age then as you are now?'

'I suppose so. I am like a kind of Flying Dutchman, eh?' Conrad laughed. 'Except I am very happy with my situation.'

'You feel no regret – no boredom?'

'I don't think so. I was once a man of action. I played my part in the world, as you did. But not any more. Perhaps I should feel uncomfortable about the kind of life I lead now, but I don't.'

'But you play a part in this world. What is this world?'

'It is the real world as seen by the inner mind, Mr Newman. The real world as seen by the outer mind is the one you left. In my opinion the inner mind is the true mirror of human history. It is the inner mind that creates the ideas that produce the great events, the outer mind translates them into action – deals with the details, you might say. Yet when the outer mind tries to interpret these events that it has helped produce, it always fails. It always finds anomalies, puzzles – while to the inner mind everything is clear. That is the irony of it.'

'The outer mind needs the inner mind, then?'

'They are complementary. We know which governs what, but the important thing is which controls the individual. Most people pay too little attention to the inner mind, allowing their judgements to be swayed by the apparent logic of the outer mind.'

'But aren't we just as guilty, obeying the inner mind too completely?'

'Perhaps. I only know what I prefer to do.'

Newman was in a quandary for the first time since he had come here.

'Has this world no future, then?' he asked. 'No future of its own?'

'Apparently not. A few things change from time to time, depending on where you are, but there is no progress in the terms of the outer mind. It's strange, really, for only the inner mind is unaffected by the passing of time – or affected very little, at least. Yet only the inner mind can predict, in general ways, the future as it is likely to be. It can plot a rough course; it can even judge which winds are likely to change, and when. But it does not care. That is left to the outer mind, for the outer mind produces the actions after the inner mind has supplied the original impulse.'

'Then should there not be a balance?' said Newman.

'Ideally, Mr Newman. But this is not an ideal world. We are lucky, the few of us here, to have the choice.'

The Seine flowed through rich countryside which was picturesque even for the season. It was entirely rural, with no towns sighted until Paris came in view.

Newman had expected something similar to London, but he had been wrong.

Paris was a city of coloured crystal, a dazzling piece of gigantic yet delicate jewellery from which light blazed. Newman was delighted. 'Magnificent!' he said to Fanny, who stood beside him by the rail of the main deck. 'I never imagined anything so beautiful. It's like a heavenly city.' He laughed. 'Will Saint Peter let us in, do you think?'

She smiled back, tucking her arm in his. 'I don't think there'll be much difficulty, Alexander.'

The *White Lass* sailed into Paris a short while later, her whole deck alive with the light from the city, the water sparkling with a thousand reflected colours. Tall poplars grew along the banks of the river and the buildings were not the bleak cliffs of London but great structures of multi-coloured crystal, with tall spires and turrets and domes.

They docked. Fanny and Newman thanked Captain Conrad and disembarked.

'They love glory, the French.' Fanny grinned as they walked through the avenues while the city seemed almost to sing with colour and light. 'This city is like so much of their music – delightful yet, you suspect, insubstantial. Romantic, rather grandiose, beautiful but artificial. Yet, like their philosophy and their art,' she smiled, pretending to shade her eyes, 'it is dazzling.'

'You seem to have a great affection for the French.'

'So I have. They treat serious things lightly and light things seriously. This makes them amusing and, to the Anglo-Saxon, refreshing. Take existentialism. What other race could make a profound philosophy of the obvious?'

4

The crystal city was entrancing. They wandered through it hand in hand as Fanny showed Newman the sights.

Although the faceted structures were not recognizable as any buildings Newman had ever known, they had the grace and inspiration of great architecture. Yet, like London's black stone cliffs, they seemed natural phenomena rather than man-made. They were, at least in one sense, man-made, for, like London, they represented an ideal of a city. Newman wondered what it was about the average Londoner that he should desire his cave dwellings and gloomy abysses to a city like Paris, alive with colour and light. The broad avenues were tree-lined and there were a few more people about than there had been in London, though the marionette population from the 'outside' were still in evidence.

Having lunched inside one of the crystal buildings – all gilt, plush and big mirrors, with waiters in the white aprons and black suits of the '90s – Newman and Fanny wandered out until they came to a wide square full of topiary animals and birds, cathedrals and famous figures from French history, all exquisitely cut from the shrubs. In miniature lakes, fountains of ormolu and precious metals, marble and delicately painted enamel, played water coloured like rainbows. Some distance away from a small pavilion, its little roof of red, white and blue stripes, its supports of gilded iron, twisted like barley sugar sticks, bunting looped between them, came music.

A string quartet with a French horn player, their music on stands in front of them were playing Mozart's E flat Quintet for French horn and strings, its wit and humanity at once blending and contrasting with the surroundings.

The performers were dressed in the clothes of Mozart's time: fine silk coats, embroidered waistcoats, lace-trimmed shirts and elaborate wigs. They might have been performing for the last of the Bourbons at Versailles.

A few people, one or two dressed like the performers but most of them in different styles of the twentieth century, stood around the pavilion listening to the music. Newman and Fanny joined them.

When the piece was finished the performers stood up and bowed as the listeners applauded. They had played magnificently. They stepped down from the pavilion and began to chat with the others. Newman had expected to hear them talking in the flowery speech of eighteenth century France. Instead, he was astonished at their accents, which were evidently American.

Newman approached the horn player. 'Are you from the States?' he asked in English.

'Sure, man.' The horn player nodded. 'But we'd better talk French here, if it's okay with you. These guys don't like anything else.'

'You played very well,' Newman said in French. 'That was the best Mozart chamber music I ever heard.'

'Good of you to say so. They seem to like our way of playing too. Excuse me.' The horn player pointed across the park to where a Renault had drawn up. The driver was waving to them. 'We've got another engagement. Hope to see you again.'

The musicians, their instruments and music under their arms, walked through the park to the car, climbed in and the car drove away.

At length, almost everyone else had gone, apart from three men, who stopped to chat with Fanny. One of them was dressed in the elaborate clothes of the eighteenth century; another wore the heavy, respectably high-crowned hat, frock-coat and dark trousers of the Second Empire, while the third had on black, tight-fitting trousers, a black pullover and a black beret on his thick hair. A cigarette hung from his lower lip. He looked a caricature of an *apache*.

'I think I prefer Debussy,' the man in the bright silk coat was saying. 'There is something just a trifle *heavy*, even in Mozart.'

'I can't say I agree,' Fanny replied with a smile. 'This is my friend, Alexander Newman. He's an American, too.'

'Delighted,' said the three men as they shook hands with Newman.

'What did you think of your cousins' performance?' asked the man in the top hat.

'Brilliant,' said Newman. 'No doubt about it.'

'Mmm, perhaps. Myself, I felt it was rather insufficiently restrained.'

'You would think that, Berger,' said the man in the beret, slapping him on the back. 'Restraint in all things for you, eh?'

'Just so, M. Alfred.'

'I wonder if M. Sol agrees,' Berger said, turning to the man in the eighteenth century finery. 'What do you think, Sol? Not restrained enough for you – the performance?'

'It was too restrained. A little more flair was called for, I felt,' Sol replied with a faint smile.

They could have been brothers. Their complexions were dark, their lower lips protuberant, their noses large, their eye-lids heavy and expression deliberately controlled. With an exchange of clothes they might have been the same man.

'Ah, well.' Alfred smiled. 'Enough of this. Let's have some wine at my place. Will you join us, madamoiselle, monsieur.'

'Certainly,' said Fanny, 'if you'll have us.'

'Come, then.'

They all followed Alfred from the park and up an avenue, in through a door of rosé glass into a passageway lined with gilt-framed mirrors that were a little fly-specked and their gilt rather faded.

A quaint lift-cage of rococo ironwork took them up several stories and then they were in Alfred's room. It was lit by a large skylight that almost covered one wall and the roof. A mattress lay against the far wall, its blankets untidy. On it lay a girl staring blankly upwards. A table was covered with pages of manuscript and books. Several bottles of wine stood on it.

'Oh, Alfred!' Berger said, pointing at the girl. 'How could you do that?'

Newman thought Berger was shocked at finding a woman in Alfred's room, but then he noticed that the girl had the dazed, set expression of an 'outsider'.

'Why not?' Alfred said lightly. 'After all, we can manipulate them sometimes if we wish to. Yesterday I wished to. And what will she know about it?'

'It is not done to disturb these people,' Mr Sol said. 'You know that, Alfred. Who do you think you are to justify this? How would you justify it? With the logic of a de Sade?'

Alfred shrugged. 'I'll get rid of her, then. Take care of the wine, will you, Sol?' He stooped, lifted the girl in his arms and carried her out.

Sol gave them all wine and, when Alfred returned, handed him a glass.

The atmosphere was strained for a while, but the wine helped to restore everyone to better spirits.

'Is this your first visit to Paris, M. Newman?' Berger asked. He had taken off his top hat and placed it on a chair beside him.

'The first under these conditions,' Newman replied. 'I'm impressed. In London I was convinced that the images that reached the . . . the "inner mind", were wholly depressing. I was wrong. Paris is a miracle.'

'And what do you think of France in general?'

'I have only been here a few hours.'

'But the French,' M. Sol said, waving a hand at the window as if the French were waiting outside to hear Newman's judgement. 'The

French. You must have an opinion of us. Everyone has.'

'Just as we have an opinion of everyone,' said Alfred with a smile.

Rising to the occasion, Newman said: 'I find the French charming, the architecture breathtaking and the public transport bewildering. The museums are magnificent, the exhibits on the whole, mediocre. The French are absolutely courteous – and absolutely ill-mannered.'

'Never "absolute"!' whispered M. Sol in mock horror. 'Never that!'

'What do you mean?'

Fanny laughed. 'Yes, what do you mean, M. Sol?'

'The Frenchman knows of the absolute, madamoiselle, but he despises it,' Alfred interjected.

'Exactly,' said Sol. 'It is the curse of the French that they will go to extremes. We declare a republic and then worship an emperor. We have been doing it for nearly two hundred years. Republic, emperor – republic, emperor. Sometimes we call them by different names. Yet the Frenchman claims to avoid extremes and never to approach the absolute. But we are a nation of enthusiasts. When an idea fires us we put all we have into it. When it bores us we abandon it. We are not sufficiently obsessive to stick at one thing for long. Our ambitions are short-lived. We have become afraid of excess, m'sieu. M. Berger, as you noticed this afternoon, distrusts any hint of it. Yet give him a mission for a day or so and he would show you what excess really meant!' Sol laughed.

'Nonsense,' said Berger, looking embarrassed.

Alfred laughed, too. Drunkenly. He swayed around the room, refilling everyone's glass. He kept blinking.

'Do not drink so much,' Berger said to him. 'You will go back.'

'My will is too strong.' Alfred bellowed as he fell on to his mattress.

'We shall see,' Berger murmured.

Newman began to feel uncomfortable. He looked at Fanny, trying to see if she were ready to leave, but she made no sign. She seemed to be enjoying herself.

Alfred shook his head dazedly. 'I am an intellectual,' he said. 'I am the life-blood of France.'

'Nonsense,' Berger said. 'It is the intellectuals who have ruined France. It is the bourgeoisie who have tried to sustain her.'

'It is the aristocrats who have managed to,' Sol put in. 'Every time France flounders she finds a new élite. The Bourbons, Napoleon, de Gaulle and so on . . . What else do you expect of a paternalistic nation? It must be so.'

Alfred rose, staggered to his desk, opened a drawer and took out a revolver. 'And so must this be so!' He shouted and waved the gun.

'Not these days, surely,' Sol murmured sardonically.

Fanny got up. 'M. Alfred, is the gun loaded?'

'It is, ma'amoiselle,' he said with a drunken bow. He pointed it at his head. She reached out hastily to take it, but he staggered back, his arm falling. Again he began to blink rapidly. His other hand went to his temple and squeezed it. 'Ah! You are right, Berger. I must stop drinking.'

'Why do you do it – this drinking to excess?' Berger seemed perturbed and worried for his friend. 'And the girl. Why are you so irresponsible about your own fate and everyone else's?'

'Curiosity,' Sol remarked. 'Isn't that so, Alfred? Curiosity?'

'Yes, yes.' Alfred wandered back to the mattress.

'He is not merely content to be in this ideal world,' Sol said, turning to Newman and Fanny. 'He must investigate it always – test it. He ruins what could be a perfectly good and long life. Can you believe it?'

Newman felt some sympathy with Alfred. He was the first man he had met here who seemed to be dissatisfied with the "inner world".

'There could be something in what he is trying to do,' Newman suggested. 'Living here is like a perpetual holiday. There's nothing to do when you get here. It's nice for a while, but . . .'

'But then you want to start spoiling it,' Berger said heatedly. 'Others have tried without success. Most of them have died or gone back. Think of that! Dying and leaving heaven!'

'Be content,' Sol said. 'Relax and be content. It is this contentedness which should mark us from the others "outside".'

'It makes us superior?' Newman asked.

'Of course it does. Have you something against superiority?'

'I don't believe it.'

'Do not try to pursue your American ideal of equality here, my friend,' Sol mocked.

'Surely,' Newman said, 'the only difference between us and them is that we recognize and control the inner mind? But those out there still possess inner minds – and they still represent a force to be reckoned with, for they can take action. What sort of action can be taken here that will affect the destiny of mankind?'

'Mankind has no destiny but to exist.' Alfred had risen from the mattress again, the revolver still in his hand. 'All that the inner mind is, is a survival mechanism that controls his actions, makes them fit the pattern of the universe, though this is not always observable in the outer world. The inner mind makes him behave in accordance with the laws of nature, though his outer mind would attempt to thwart those laws and thus destroy him. The inner mind is in tune with the rhythm of the spheres, gentlemen. As individuals we are nothing and as a race we simply exist. That is our only purpose. Why should we seek another? The inner mind does not seek another. We do not seek another here.'

'And if one cannot believe it?' Newman enquired.

'Then you have no business being here!' Sol stood up. 'He is right. You know he is right.'

'He is right, Alexander,' said Fanny. 'I'm sure of it.'

'So am I,' Newman said. 'And I suspect anything I'm so sure of. I think of Mr Schweitzer's armour.'

'You are in a worse position than Alfred,' Berger said with a sidelong glance at Sol. He winked.

There was a shot. Alfred was falling, the gun clattering to the floor, his eyes staring as he pitched forward.

'The fool,' Sol said casually. 'He has denied his purpose. He has thwarted his destiny. He has ceased to exist!'

Fanny began to sob and Newman tried to comfort her.

M. Sol sighed. 'What do we do now, Berger? This is upsetting. I feel a trifle uncomfortable. What does one do in such a time of crisis?'

Berger began to take off his jacket. 'Change clothes, M. Sol. It is all there is to do.'

Beside the corpse of Alfred, the two men began to strip off their clothes and trade them. Soon Sol was dressed in Berger's frock-coat, trousers and top hat, and Berger wore Sol's silks and lace. Newman was horrified by the charade and watched speechlessly as Fanny sobbed on and the pair left the room.

'Let's get away from here, Alexander,' Fanny said a little later. 'Poor M. Alfred. It was so unexpected.'

Newman helped her out to the lift. As they descended, he said. 'Do you want to leave Paris altogether, then?'

'Don't you?'

'I wouldn't mind.'

'I have a car near here. We can leave right away.'

'Where shall we go?'

'I don't care. Just drive.'

The car was a big, old Citroen limousine. Newman found it easy to handle. He drove through the streets of the crystal city, Fanny staring blankly ahead.

Soon they were in the countryside, heading north.

5

Newman drove for more than a day along a wide, straight road that went on and on between flat fields. He did not know where it led, and he did not care. He was trying to think and finding thinking difficult.

It was on the second day of living off raw vegetables found in the fields and sleeping in the car that they saw a van ahead of them, driving in the same direction.

By this time Fanny had cheered up a little. When she saw the van she brightened even more.

'Alexander! It's Mr Schweitzer's van. I wonder where he's going.'

Relieved at the prospect of seeing a familiar face, Newman accelerated, passing the van with a wave as he saw Mr Schweitzer in the cabin.

Looking a trifle puzzled Schweitzer smiled and pulled into the side of the road.

Newman backed the Citroen up to the van and helped Fanny out. They reached the van as Mr Schweitzer climbed down.

'What are you two doing here?' he asked. 'I thought you'd gone to Paris.'

'We decided to leave,' Newman told him. He described what had happened.

Schweitzer shook his head and pursed his lips, sighing.

'Yes, yes. That sometimes does happen. They shun my wares there, you know, but they need them, really . . .'

'They need something,' said Fanny earnestly.

'Where does this road lead?' Newman asked. 'We've no idea.'

'It leads to Berlin, Mr Newman. I don't think you want to go there.'

'Why not?'

'It's an unpleasant place at the best of times. A strange place. My biggest single customer, you know. Why don't you turn round – go back to Paris or take a side road to Amsterdam or Hamburg and see if you can find a ship to get you to London?'

'I'm curious now,' Newman smiled. 'I think I'd like the experience of Berlin, Mr Schweitzer.'

'I suppose it can do you little harm, Mr Newman. Very well. If you'd like to keep pace with my old van, we'll travel together.'

They followed the road for the rest of the day and at night camped beside it. Mr Schweitzer was well equipped with a primus stove and provisions. They ate well for the first time since they had left Paris.

They slept in the tent Mr Schweitzer lent them and at dawn were on the road again.

A few hours later they saw Berlin.

A vast wall surrounded the city and it was really this they sighted. Berlin itself was completely hidden by the wall.

Its black, basalt sides were high and smooth and small gateways led through from the roads.

As they neared it, Newman could make out figures high above on the top of the wall. The figures were encased in full medieval armour with sub-machine guns cradled in their arms.

'Here the whole city is populated by those who see with the inner eye,' Schweitzer explained. 'But what their inner eye sees – its terrible ideal . . . Oh dear! This Berlin – it is the City of Fear. Such a strange people – so perceptive yet so terrified. They warp their perceptions even as they find them. A dreadful mix-up, I'm afraid.'

The guards seemed to recognize Schweitzer's van, for the doors of the gateway swung open and they passed through into the city.

Berlin was smaller than London in every respect, but what Newman had not noticed was that the whole city had a roof, stretching from wall to wall. The roof was of heavy, smoked glass, or something similar, and it let in little light.

Many of the buildings looked like huge, round boulders with tiny entrances, just about big enough for a man to crawl through.

The streets, like the tunnels of some stone maze, were full. Lumbering horses bore the great, clumsy weight of armoured men, while others, on the pavements, wore masks or heavy hoods to hide their faces.

Unable to negotiate the narrow streets, the van was forced to stop in a small square.

They got out. A man in a 1914–18 flying suit, with fur jacket, boots and gauntlets, but wearing a Gothic helmet on his head, the visor covering his face, walked towards Schweitzer, hand held out.

When he spoke in German, a language which Newman understood only imperfectly, his voice was an echo in the helmet. After shaking hands with the man, Schweitzer introduced Newman and Fanny as English.

'Herr von Richthofen, eh?' Newman said. 'Any relation to the Baron?'

Von Richthofen shrugged. 'We don't use those titles in our Germany, Herr Newman. Would you like to come back to my house for some refreshment?'

The house was one of a number of boulders on the far side of the square. Stooping through the small doorway they entered. Inside it was, if anything, gloomier than outside. A few torches illuminated a fairly large hall and a fire glimmered in a grate. A stone staircase led upwards and von Richthofen climbed it until they entered a smaller, slightly more hospitable room, heated by some sort of steam apparatus. Newman sat down on a wet chair, coughing as the hot, damp air entered his lungs. The place was like a Turkish bath and there was a faint smell of salt.

'Some food will be brought to us,' von Richthofen said. 'Well, Herr Schweitzer, what have you got this time? Heavier stuff than last, I hope. The fashions change so rapidly and now one must wear an even thicker plate than ever if one is to fit in.' He reached up and lifted off his ornate steel helmet. The face revealed was of a man of about thirty-five – handsome, self-indulgent, faintly cynical.

'That's better,' he said. 'Only in here do I feel comfortable with it off.'

Newman looked around. There were no windows in the room. It seemed very strange to him and he could not imagine why people should choose to live in such places.

The food arrived. Dull, German food – sausages, sauerkraut, bread, but good coffee.

When they had eaten, von Richthofen leant back in his wooden armchair.

'Have you just come from England, Herr Newman?'

'I was in Paris first.'

'A wonderful city. Very romantic. You liked it?'

'In general. It seems strange that you should like it, Herr von Richthofen, when your own taste in architecture is so different.'

'Aha! So very different, eh? But *secure*, do you see, Herr Newman? Strong, invincible, able to withstand anything.'

Newman was puzzled. 'But why should it be? Are you expecting trouble? Who'd attack you?'

'Better safe than sorry, eh?'

Newman, the damp having penetrated his clothing, shifted uncomfortably on his chair. 'I suppose so.'

Von Richthofen seemed to notice his discomfort. He laughed. 'You get used to that. Oh, we know all about freedom and beautiful surroundings making beautiful minds. All that sort of thing. But we have made a conscious sacrifice. A study of history will show you that a race which holds firmly together, building heavy walls, survives longer than one which lives in idyllic surroundings. Look at Greece. Compare it with Rome. You see what I mean?'

Newman did not. He thought von Richthofen was misguided. He could see no logic in what the man was saying.

'I should have thought that here, in the inner world, you would not need such walls or such ideas. Your walls are built because you fear something – something which you do not know exists. Living in this world, you surely realize this?'

'We realize that you are probably right. But there is a possibility that you are wrong. It is that possibility we prepare for, Herr Newman. The Berliner is capable of mental detachment more than anyone.

'But you use this detachment to escape, it seems to me,' Newman said. 'Some people read adventure stories. You invent complicated systems of metaphysics. And you achieve the same end. You leave reality.'

'Is not our reality the same as yours – on the inner or the outer plane?'

'It borders on it. But is your fortified city "realistic" in this world? Is your fashion for wearing heavier armour "realistic"? Surely these are totally subjective things. I find it very difficult to understand how these things, so typical of the outer world, can exist in the inner world. I remember reading of some Crusaders once who went across the desert to fight a battle They refused to dispense with their armour, in spite of crippling heat and utter weariness. They rode for days, until all sense of reality was driven from them. Finally, harried all the way by Saracens, they reached their battle-ground and were trapped and massacred. If only they had taken their armour off to cross the desert they would have done so at greater speed and arrived fresh. Because of their *need* for their armour – which *reason* told them they did not need – they perished. Their armour killed them, in fact.'

Von Richthofen pursed his lips ironically. 'A nice little moral tale, Herr Newman. But we are different. We see things in a far bigger way. We do not just take the world view – we take the universal view.'

'How does that bear on what we're discussing?'

'It has every bearing. Every bearing.'

Von Richthofen got up. 'I would like some time to show you what

Athens has become.'

'I've never been to Athens,' Fanny put in. 'What has it become?'

Von Richthofen put his hand to his chin. 'You want to know? Very well, I will fly you there myself. Tomorrow. When we have seen what Mr Schweitzer has to offer us. How would you like that?'

Newman was willing to take any opportunity to leave Berlin as speedily as possible. 'Suits me,' he said. 'I'd like to go to Greece. It's one of my favourite countries.'

'Is it, Herr Newman? Is it? Good.'

6

Von Richthofen's plane was very modern. It lay on an airfield outside the walls of Berlin. It resembled an American Phantom fighter-bomber in almost every detail. On its wings and fuselage, however, were painted large swastikas.

'They are just for old times' sake,' von Richthofen said with a laugh as he led them up to the plane. They were all dressed in pressure suits. They had just said goodbye to Mr Schweitzer. 'A joke, you know,' Richthofen added. 'I feel no embarrassment these days. Do you?'

Newman said nothing. He helped Fanny into the big cockpit, wider than a Phantom's. It could take three – two in the front and one just behind. Expertly, he settled himself into his own seat. He had flown similar aircraft before he began training for space.

Von Richthofen started the engine and at length the plane began to move off down the long runway. They were quickly airborne and von Richthofen, for Fanny's sake, kept them down to just over the speed of sound.

They flashed through the peaceful sky at four thousand feet, heading south-east for Greece.

They landed on a long airstrip just outside Athens. There were none of the usual airport buildings, just the tarmac with grassy slopes on either side.

Newman was surprised to see that Athens was not the modern city but the ancient one transformed. Graceful villas, widely spaced, surrounded tree-lined squares. Here and there were larger buildings, like the Parthenon and the Acropolis. Most of the people wore togas or linen jerkins tied loosely at the waist. The women wore the flowing robes that Newman had previously only seen represented on statues, paintings or bas reliefs. But there were several who wore the clothes of other periods, including Newman's own.

The sun was warm and the mood of the city leisurely. A few people waved cheerfully to them, but most were gathered in little groups, lazing in the sun, drinking wine and eating fruit and talking all the time. The hum of conversation filled the city.

'It hasn't been changed,' Newman said to von Richthofen. 'Why is that?'

'There has been no need, my friend. This Athens is the Athens of the Golden Age, altered in only minor details. Here the idea and the actuality are one. Here, the inner mind and the outer mind merged to produce an idea. It happens rarely. The cities you have seen so far – London, Paris, Berlin – are transformed because the idea the builders had of them was never fulfilled in actuality. Only an approximation was produced. Not so with the Athenians. It took later ages to spoil the ideal city – later events. But events have not altogether changed the Greeks as they changed us Northerners. Time has not "moved on" so much.' Von Richthofen laughed unpleasantly. 'But they are not strong, Herr Newman – Fraulein Patrick.'

'They don't need to be *strong*,' Fanny said in bewilderment, putting her arm through Newman's. 'What have they to fear here?'

'Only the inconsistent – only some arbitary action disobeying the fundamental laws of existence. We of the inner world all recognize these laws, I believe.'

'And they are?' Fanny said.

'Simple. That nature follows a pattern – a simple cycle of birth, death and rebirth. Everything obeys this law, from the tiniest particles to the suns and galaxies of the infinite universe. But, basically, everything remains the same – everything is consistent, fixed forever according to the pattern.'

'It simply exists, is that it?' Newman said, remembering the words of the late M. Alfred. 'It had no purpose but to exist.'

'Exactly. So your Parisians exist in their crystal city, in their still somewhat artificial way. Here, in Athens people exist in a simpler, more natural way. This is right, you say; this is proper. This obeys the law of the universe.'

'Fair enough,' said Fanny. 'But what are you driving at?'

'I am trying to tell you what we Berliners protect ourselves against in this perfect inner world, Fraulein Patrick. All you have seen here so far – apart from our Berlin – have accepted that to live without fear, without protection and suspicion, is *moral* – that is, it accords with the true pattern of existence.'

'Okay,' said Newman. 'What about it?'

'Have you never considered that detachment of the kind we have might recognize that law, might understand the essential morality of our Greek friends here – but decide coolly, out of pure whim, *to disobey the law and live immorally?* A man or a group of men might decide to "throw a spanner in the works", *ja*! Out of boredom, perhaps – out of despair or out of curiosity? We are ultimately bound by the law, Herr Newman, but that does not stop us from *consciously* disobeying it. To recognize the invulnerable and eternal law is not automatically to obey it. Do you see? We are conscious, reasoning beings – we can *decide* to disobey.'

'But what point would there be in doing that?' Fanny asked, bemused. 'In the outer world the law is broken all the time – insensately, out of fear and greed and bewilderment. That's understandable. But here, who would break the law?'

'You ask what point is there in doing such a thing.' Von Richthofen smiled. 'But there again what point is there in existence? None. To make one's mark, however small, one can only behave illogically in an ultimately logical universe. Who are the great myth figures of our history? Disrupters all! Even where they preached the law they succeeded in producing more chaos than had existed before they came. Here, in this inner world, we are all equal. Supposing a man achieved this plan and refused to accept what he found. Suppose he deliberately offended against the law of the universe. What then?'

'This is the possibility you fear in Berlin?' Newman said quietly. 'This?'

'Why should we not fear it in Berlin? Haven't we sufficient cause to do so? Is not our history full of the servants of chaos?'

'And of order, too. Your composers, your poets, your novelists –'

'Just so. We have the ability, as I told you, to *see* – but there are those amongst us who are not content with seeing – they wish to take action in a world that denies action, other than those necessary for existence alone, and demands the *status quo*.'

'You sound like one yourself.' Newman smiled half-heartedly.

Von Richthofen shrugged. 'I am not the stuff of the anti-Christ,' he said. 'I only try to illustrate what Berlin still fears; detachment, vision, knowledge do not bring an automatic absence of danger.'

'You mean that what people say in the outer world – that if everyone could achieve detachment, control over emotion, everything would be better? You mean that's not necessarily true?' said Fanny.

'Why should it be?'

'Why, indeed . . .' Newman agreed. 'But you serve no good to yourselves or others by wrapping yourselves in stone and metal, and hiding.'

Richthofen smiled. 'It is our duty. We obey the universal, fundamental law.'

'How?' Newman asked.

'We exist – and we see to it that we continue to exist. But enough of this. I came here not only to tell you what I meant, but to illustrate my point.' He took something from the pocket of his flying suit. Then he threw back his arm and flung the object towards the Parthenon. 'Witness,' he said. 'The arbitary action.'

He must have thrown a grenade.

The Parthenon blew up, bodies were scattered, many torn to pieces. Greeks came hurrying on to the scene, absolutely shocked, almost incapable of action. Slowly, a few began to go to the aid of the wounded.

Newman and Fanny were horrified. 'Murder . . .' whispered Newman.

'Murder, yes. Call it what you will. Suppose such a man as myself came to Berlin. He would do little harm.'

Von Richthofen turned around with a crooked smile on his face and began to walk casually away from the destruction. Nobody tried to stop him.

'I'm returning to Berlin now,' he said. 'Do you want to come? You'll be welcome.'

'I'll take my chances,' Newman said grimly, his mind reeling. 'What about you, Fanny?'

'Me, too,' she said.

Around them, Athens was fading and soon all they could see was the ruin of the Parthenon. The airfield had gone; so had von Richthofen and his jet.

'We're back,' Fanny said faintly. 'Aren't we, Alexander?'

'I think so.'

'What do we do now?'

'We've got to do something,' he said. 'I suppose.' They walked away from the ruin of the Parthenon towards that other Athens.

Good-bye, Miranda

Good-bye, Miranda.

Good-bye, Miranda.

Miranda.

He swerved and swooped over the grey water like a seabird. He was quite mad.

Good-bye, Miranda.

His crying laugh was ugly against the sounds of the sea. It held far too much pain for any listeners to sympathize with it. They could only react against that sound, try to stop it, quickly. But they couldn't catch him. Nicholas could fly.

Miranda!

'I wish I had a gun, Miranda.'

'Would you kill him, father?'

'Sure I would. Kill him dead. Why's he do it?'

'He's mad, father. If I got you a gun, would you kill him?'

'Sure I would, dead. I can't stand it. He's tormenting us deliberate.'

'I loved him.'

'I know you did – once. But that don't give him the excuse to come wailing round here. Just like a banshee. Just like one.'

'It's love, father – love turned to madness. He *ought* to be shot. It's what he wants, I think.'

'It's what I want, anyhow.'

They stayed in the little house on the headland. They wouldn't go out. But he'd been outside for two days and nights, now. The flying madman. Well, he shouldn't have told them about that – levitation – should've kept it to himself. A man needn't know. But if he does, then he's got to do something about it. He couldn't have his daugher marrying – a spook.

Now look what had happened. He'd found them, at last. Miranda had said he would.

By God, if only he had a gun . . .

Please come out and say good-bye to me, Miranda.

He was on the roof again.

It's only me – Nicholas.

By the chimney, shouting in that high voice, just like a bird's.

Say good-bye to me, Miranda.

She was covering her ears. Her face bunched up in the terrible pain his voice made on her nerves. It was physical pain. 'Stop him, father!'

'How can I stop him? If I had a gun I'd shoot him dead.'

'We've got to get a gun.'

'Where? Where can we get one?'

'You'll have to go to the village.'

'Not with him out there.'

Oh, Miranda. Just good-bye.

'Good-bye, good-bye, good-bye! Go away, Nicholas! Go *away*! Please!'

'He's doing it deliberate. My God, he'll have us mad, too. I'll go down to the village tomorrow. I'll risk it. Three days. My God!'

Miranda!

'Tomorrow,' he said. 'Tomorrow, I'll definitely go.'

'You said that yesterday.'

'Well, I'll go tomorrow. Doesn't he sleep?'

Miranda! Good-bye.

She leapt at her father, her pale hands tearing. 'Go, father. Get the gun! The gun! The gun!'

'Tomorrow.' He struggled with her. 'Stop that. I said I'd go tomorrow and I will.' His yellow fingers gripped her. 'Stop that, now, Miranda!'

'The gun!'

'Go *away, Nicholas!*'

Her breathing was a thin noise. She was dirty, her face was lined and the knife was still in her hand. Her father's blood dripped on to her father's corpse.

Just good-bye, Miranda. That's all. I love you.

Her thin body shuddered.

She walked towards the door, each step carefully made. She reached for the bolt and the brown sleeve fell down her bruised arm. She pulled back the bolt.

'Go *away, Nicholas!*'

She heard his voice among the torn clouds. *Miranda!*

The air was sharp, as sharp as his voice.

She looked up, over the roof of the house and glimpsed his mad body darting, gliding. She heard the passing of his body above her and saw it wheeling over the sea, heard the voice, shrill, agonized: *Good-bye, Miranda.* She became aware of the heart pushing at her flesh, beneath her breast. She gripped the knife.

Miranda!

'Oh . . .' she said as the knife pierced her and she began to fall, first against the swinging door, then back, dropping with a flat sound on the stones of the floor.

When he came back, he saw that the light was swirling around outside the door, released from the house and dissipating into the night. He landed beside the door but was too physically weak to walk so had to glide into the house and see the corpses.

He was puzzled. His dark, thin, ravaged face moved with the effort of thought, but thought was now beyond him.

Miranda?

He shook his head slowly, but it was no good.

His body moved backwards out of the door, a foot above the ground.

Good-bye, Miranda.

He flew away, but he was still calling, and strangely there was no sorrow in the cry.

Islands

Schmeling came back into the half-light of his sitting room and placed his graceful, bulky body into the armchair opposite mine.

'Sorry to have left you so abruptly,' he said, in reference to the phone call which had taken him from the room.

'You seem excited,' I said, noting the look of jubilation in his eyes.

'I am,' he said. 'Indeed, I am.'

I had to leave it at that, for he didn't seem prepared to talk about it.

He seemed to dismiss whatever he was thinking about and gave me a quick smile. 'Well, how are things in sociological circles?'

'Going in circles for me at present,' I said good-humouredly. 'I've a particularly interesting case right now. By all the evidence – environment, family background, I.Q., and so on – he should fit neatly into a certain broad category. But he doesn't. He shows, in his thinking and behaviour, all the classic symptoms of an under-privileged slum child from a split home – whereas, in fact, his background is almost the opposite.'

Schmeling appeared only mildly interested in my work, yet he caught hold of something I said and it set him off on another track.

'So? You really think that all these superficial influences have a deep effect on an individual?'

'Normally, yes. And I don't consider them superficial. They can have a deep and lasting significance for a person.'

He smiled patronizingly. 'I consider so-called inherited traits also superficial – not to say non-existent.'

'It astounds me!' I said lightly. Schmeling seemed about to indulge in one of his conversational exercises where he would take a dogmatic stand on a point about which he had little serious interest. Such an exercise was often entertaining and I prepared to join in his mood by taking an equally dogmatic stand against him.

Schmeling waved his hand. 'We talk of heredity as a fact and we talk of mutual experience as a fact. Yet how much experience *is* shared?'

'All of it,' I said immediately.

Schmeling's large, aquiline head nodded thoughtfully, and then he glanced at me with undue seriousness. 'People find it easy to ascribe a pattern to the human psyche, for there are many such superficial similarities between men. I believe, however, that we'd rather accept a pattern that explains things comfortably, than attempt to grasp the idea of the infinite variety and complexity of human experience. A variety limited only to the number of individuals existing on the world. And I contend that each man is, mentally and physically, a total individual – unique.'

'There is no such thing as an individual,' I pointed out. 'There are minor superficial differences in behaviour, that is all.'

'I say there are minor superficial similarities which we have come to accept as constituting the *total* human psyche. There are depths, my friend, which haven't begun to be explored. And also,' he said, with a note of slight triumph in his voice, 'how would you explain the increase, during this century, in advanced schizophrenia? No two schizophrenics are alike.'

'That's debatable,' I said.

Schmeling grimaced. 'And I have heard you call yourself an individualist!'

'So I am – within certain limitations,' I said, a trifle overwarmly.

'You *are* an individual,' he replied, leaning back in his chair and sticking his feet before the fire. I could see he was beginning to enjoy the argument, which meant he was fairly certain of winning it.

'You are, indeed,' he emphasized. 'The very impossibility of our ever fully communicating with one another proves that conclusively. How much time is an elephant?'

'Eh?'

'Can you answer?'

'The question is nonsense!'

'To you, perhaps, but not to people who see time in terms of mass – and many do. Recent experiments have shown that the question receives as many answers as there are individuals asked it. These are many other pointers to prove my case – the people who see Sunday as a particular colour whereas others see it as a line of particular length – everything seen with the *mind*'s eye, heard with the *mind*'s ear, inhaled with the *mind*'s nose, touched with the *mind*'s touch, tasted with the *mind*'s palate means something entirely different to everyone! That, I contend, is where reality lies – in the *mind*'s senses, where we experience what we want to experience – not what we are told to!'

'This conversation still leads nowhere,' I said. 'Abstract questions regarding man's nature can only produce abstract answers.'

'True,' he eyed me triumphantly, as if he had deliberately provoked me into an admission, 'but when a concrete solution appears, it has the effect of making the problem concrete also. Do you agree?'

'Yes.'

'Well, I received concrete proof, not long ago, of the *fact* that each man does exist as an individual – totally, irreversibly – that, although environment and "heredity" act upon him from birth, they act to make him appear a non-individual. You see the difference? He begins as a *whole* individual but superficial influences force him not to be, do you see?'

'You would say that society imposes a pattern on the individual which we regard as inherent but you see as superficial. I think I follow you. Your extreme example would be the suburbanite who conforms rigorously, I suppose?'

'More tragic examples could be made – the Zeitgeist dominating Germany in the thirties, for instance.' He paused, seeming to consider his native country which he had left so many years before. 'A German word,' he mused, 'to describe the German Disease – the need to inflict patterns and generalizations on every aspect of human existence. The insidious Freud must have found German a ready-made language for his doctrines. A language with so many words which are, in reality, unspecific, leads to the kind of unspecific thinking I find so abhorrent.'

He shrugged and nodded. 'But the suburban man is a fair example.'

He got up. His large, vital body tensed in the manner of an actor about to deliver an oratory, but instead of speaking immediately, he left me in suspense while he helped himself to some of his horrible herbal tobacco from a box on the sideboard. When the deed was done, the metal-stemmed pipe alight and the sweet smoke, so much less pleasant than ordinary tobacco, invading my nostrils, he resumed his seat by the fire.

'And perhaps the schizophrenic psychopath – the rebel without a cause – is the extreme example of the individual who experiences the obvious wrongness of this conformism and reacts against it violently.'

'A million suburbanites can't be wrong,' I said ironically, and he smiled around the clenched pipe.

'A single psychopath can't be wrong, either. A single psychopath, according to his own little universe, is absolutely right, absolutely justified in taking any course of action he chooses – simply because *he* chooses it!'

'But unfortunately, this attitude works to produce anarchy,' I said.

'If he doesn't conform to a certain degree, his actions interfere with other people's actions producing either chaos if he is successful, or else further curtailment of his liberty. I'm right.'

'To a degree you're right,' he nodded. 'But if everyone accepted the individual's right to be an individual and the tyranny of conformism were lifted, perhaps we could give a greater dignity to existence – and still work together in the manner of individuals aiding individuals . . .'

'We're coming close to talking politics,' I warned him with a smile, adding: 'Or religion – the two unprovables.'

'Both attract psychopaths, at any rate. Witness the fact that both religious and political movements are notoriously inclined to break into almost as many splinter-groups as there are individuals comprising them.'

'All facts,' I agreed. 'But you said you'd received concrete proof that all men are unequal!'

'I did not – as far as "equality" enters into this argument, I would say I had proved that all men *are* equal, in that all men are different and existing,' he paused dramatically, and I envied him, his poise, his resonant voice, 'existing in *physically* different universes!'

'Oh, come now . . .'

'Time and space are relative. And the time and space of the individual are relative to that of other individuals. But they are not the *same*. I have proof that every man exists in his own space-time continuum as well as in the larger one we all share. Why is it that for one man an hour passes slowly and for another it passes rapidly?'

'His state of mind at the time he's experiencing the hour's passage, surely?'

'His state of mind – exactly. He imposes his own time sense on the time he is *told* is the right one.'

'What of this assertion of proof?' I said, feeling the conversation to be losing its dynamic.

'Very well,' he said, glancing at his watch. He shifted in his chair and began in the manner of a story-teller, choosing all his phrases with care. I also settled myself, expecting to be entertained, for Schmeling is a good talker who only requires an attentive audience to bring forth his skill.

A few months ago (he said in his deep, faintly-accented voice) I was enjoying a leisurely day at my Harley Street surgery, dispensing sympathy and disguised aspirin to the elderly women who finance my private research, when my hag of a receptionist entered in haste, a rare feat for one of her age. My clients resent young receptionists.

'Mrs Thornton is in the waiting room,' she croaked.

'But she has no appointment,' I said in irritation. These women are either hypochondriacs or else incurable. I choose them with care since both involve me in little real work.

Mrs Thornton was a little of both – an incurable hypochondriac, an otherwise charming woman in late middle-age, very rich and still vivacious whenever she took time off from her self-induced spells of migraine. Yes, she was, indeed, very rich, and also I quite liked her. Therefore, after a moment's deliberation, I told my receptionist to keep her waiting for a while and then show her in.

In a practice like mine it does not do to answer a patient's surprise visit immediately. If they conclude you are at the beck and call of every Tom, Dick, or Harry, they feel unimpressed by your skill as a doctor.

So, finally, Mrs Thornton was shown in, all delicious fur and a trifle too much expensive perfume. Her face was skilfully made-up and her tinted grey hair beautifully arranged. But I noted that she was distraught, glimpsed the smallest smear of mascara in the corner of her right eye.

She, the poised Mrs Thornton, appeared to have been crying in public.

I rose and indicated a chair for her to sit in. She sat on its edge.

'You seem to be in pain, Mrs Thornton,' I said solicitously, feeling that she had wished a particularly bad migraine upon herself.

'Not physical, Doctor Schmeling,' said she, 'but doubtless the emotional pain I am suffering will result in another migraine.'

Again I felt irritated.

My patients have a tendency to bring their emotional problems to me and expect me to treat them. Mind you, a receptive ear is usually sufficient, and a soft and ambiguous word of consolation. So, I prepared myself to hear her out, making a mental note to append this consultation on to another bill in the near future.

'Now calm yourself,' I said in the gruff and kindly voice which at once commands the impression of professional integrity and human warmth.

'Tell me the trouble, before you ask me to clear it up.'

She smiled a small smile of thanks, responding beautifully to the emotional cues I was feeding her.

'It is my nephew, doctor, who is in trouble, not I.'

'He is ill?'

I have a dislike of treating male patients since there is a greater chance of them penetrating my façade, so necessary if I am to be allowed to continue my private work. Yet I prepared myself for the worst, since Mrs Thornton's contribution was that much larger than my other patients.

'Not physically,' Mrs Thornton gave me the melting look of one who confides in a friend and expects help.

'Mentally,' I hinted, with just the right tactful emphasis.

She nodded mutely.

'But, my dear Mrs Thornton, you must understand that I am not a psychologist – I am a simple physician . . .' I was, of course, lying since although I am qualified as a physician, my work in fact centres upon understanding the psychological quirks of my clientele.

'I know, I know,' she said eagerly, 'but you are so *understanding*, doctor, in my own case. You realize that migraine is caused by *mental* and *nervous* and *emotional* stresses, so I thought . . .'

I controlled the tendency to smile. All migraine sufferers are inclined to ascribe non-physical causes to their condition, when, as often as not, a simple physical act of bending down or eating the wrong food is the cause of that admittedly exacting complaint.

Instead, I nodded sternly and kindly. 'True, true, true,' muttered I in the mystical manner of so many psychiatrists – hinting at things which only the fully enlightened disciple of Freud might learn. There is no doubt about it. They are the new priesthood.

'Then – for my sake, doctor – come and see him. Try to help him. And I beg you to use discretion in this matter – a public scandal would result if . . .'

'Of course,' I said conspiratorially, 'and if I cannot help him I can recommend an extremely discreet friend – a specialist in mental disorders – a wonderful man, I assure you, of undoubted brilliance and integrity.'

But it was I whom she wanted. I prepared myself to act out a particularly long part. Have you noticed how people act, quite unconsciously, in set ranges of expression and emotion which fit particular categories – Sympathetic, Righteous Indignation, Bewildered Grief and so on, when in fact beneath the surface, though they do not for a moment admit it to themselves, they feel nothing of what they express on the surface? Gestures, gestures – bolstering up the inane meaninglessness of modern life. And thanks to modern communications, we are assured, more and more, of the Right Way To Feel In A Given Situation. Comforting – certainly, comforting. Good God, we are like water-beetles skating the slimy surface which covers the clear, pure water below. And, worse, we contribute to the extent and thickness of the slime, piling it higher and higher until, with any luck, we shall sink down with its weight to the bottom. What do you think will happen then? Madness? But I digress.

Mrs Thornton's town house lay in a quiet Belgravian Square. I drove her there myself, leaving a note to my receptionist to re-arrange the rest of the day's appointments.

Two marble columns fronted the main entrance and we went through the heavy oak door into a chill and imposing hallway, also of the same barren marble. We gave our street clothes to an attractive little maid and Mrs Thornton asked her where Mr Davenport was.

'In the study, ma'am,' the maid replied with a worried glance at me.

'Would you tell him that I have brought Doctor Schmeling and should like to see him in the drawing room?'

We entered the large, light drawing room which was fashionably furnished in a slightly Victorian manner. A heavy secretaire had been converted into a cocktail cabinet and from this Mrs Thornton offered me a drink. I accepted a dry sherry and stood sipping it while we awaited Nicholas Davenport. Mrs Thornton moved nervously about the room for a moment before sitting down on the arm of a chair.

Nicholas entered, pale, disconsolate, defiant. A black-haired youth of a distinctly wild appearance, shaking me too firmly by the hand as we were introduced and going immediately to the cabinet and pouring himself a drink. I expected him to disclaim need of a doctor, but instead he turned, still with a defiant look in his eye, and said 'I hope to God you can do something about this, doctor.' The defiance, it seemed, was permanent and directed at the world in general rather than any single individual.

'Perhaps I can,' I said, eyeing him a little warily, wondering what he would make of me. 'Would you care to tell me your trouble?'

'Troubles,' he said, taking a romantic stance by the curtains.

This, I decided with enjoyment, was to be a play of high drama. But, at that moment, I underestimated Davenport. I was to learn that he was a good actor, in the sense you know me to mean, but, for some reason, had hopelessly garbled his lines, lost his cues – or at least imposed his own lines and cues upon a play which resented them and was discomforted by them. My first hint of this came very soon after Mrs Thornton had tactfully left the room and he and I stood facing one another across its length, drinks in hand in the manner of duelists about to stand and fire.

'Doctor Schmeling, you are not, I understand, a psychologist?'

'No, I am a physician. I have a certain private bent towards psychology, though. However, if you wish to consult a qualified man . . .'

'No, no – I'm sorry, but I'm afraid a man not fully conversant with – mental disorders – might dismiss what I tell him as nonsense.'

Curious, I shook my head. 'That won't happen,' I told him, 'but I may be forced to recommend a specialist if I do not feel competent to deal with your case.'

'Fair enough,' he said. 'I am having illusions.'

I restrained an urge to discourse philosophically on the meaning of the word and instead raised my eyebrows. 'What kind of illusions, Mr Davenport?'

'Many kinds. Illusions of complete physical detachment, where my mind looks down on my body and observes it with clinical objectivity. Illusions of size where I am sometimes so small as to be a pin-prick in the vastness of infinite space and at the same time am so huge as to dwarf the universe. Illusions of hearing voices speaking phrases I might not hear for days later, or should have heard days before; illusions where a place is familiar though I have never before visited it – *déjà vu*, I believe it is called – illusions where a place I have known for years, this house for instance, becomes suddenly unfamiliar as if I am seeing it for the first time. Those are a few – just a very few, doctor.'

I frowned thoughtfully. The illusions he had mentioned were, in fact, all of a kind. They were what we call 'hypnagogic images' – the illusions experienced while falling asleep – the illusions between being awake and being asleep, between sleeping and dreaming. I have read that these illusions closely resemble those induced by mescaline and the like.

'We are all subject to illusions of this kind,' I said reluctantly, disappointed that his complaint was so undramatic after all. 'I myself sometimes get them.'

'Ah, yes,' he nodded rapidly, '*sometimes*. Sometimes, doctor. But do you get them all the time? Are you forced, as I am forced now, to exercise a rigid and deliberate control upon yourself, to force yourself to behave normally, to converse reasonably and logically, to walk a few yards to a shop to buy a newspaper, to consciously exert tremendous concentration if you are to see that newspaper in your hands and read it?'

'No, of course not.' I felt excited then.

'Of course not.' His pale face tautened and he drew his lips tight and wetted them and continued. 'Some time ago, under circumstances mildly resembling those I have described, I came across the source of a much used quotation. A poem by John Donne – that glib fool and mystic – "No man is an island" – you remember it, of course, with its preaching pantheistic nonsense. Well, I am an island, doctor – cut off from my fellow men most of the time by seas more uncrossable than the vastness of intergalactic space – I am an island existing in my *own* space, my *own* time – in fact, in my own universe which has little contact with the universe around it!'

You must understand that at this time, though interested, I was not convinced, as now, of what is literally physical individuality. I was at a loss for something to say for a moment. I could only mouth a trade-phrase.

'And when did you begin to experience all this?' I asked him.

'Some years ago,' he said impatiently. 'At first, as you pointed out, only between wakefulness and sleeping, then between sleeping and waking, then they continued through the morning, then all day and all night. I am not insane, doctor. I know I am not. But I shall soon go mad with the strain of keeping myself anchored to reality.'

'Do something for me, now,' I told him. 'Let loose your grip so that I can, as it were, observe the symptoms as I would an ordinary medical case.'

'Let loose . . . doctor, I am even unsure that I could regain it if I did.' He seemed to think for a moment and then looked up at me, the defiance fading from his eyes to be replaced by the startling look of pleading which I have seen in the dying man afraid of death. 'If it means you will be able to cure me, I'll do it.'

'I cannot guarantee that until I have seen what it is,' I said, almost as intense as he.

'Then, by God, see!'

His face muscles seemed to relax to such an extent that his whole face appeared to lengthen. He staggered and I helped him into a deep armchair.

'I have told you, aunt, I have no wish to see a psychiatrist,' he said. His aunt, of course, was not in the room. Was he reliving the discussion which had led to Mrs Thornton consulting me?

Then I stepped back as he rose from the chair and began a peculiar and disturbing pantomime. I have seen similar scenes in cases of extreme shock where the patient re-enacts the phase leading up to traumatic experience again and again. Yet there was something odd even about this.

His lips were forming sentences, but I could not hear what he said. Then he went through the motions of taking off all his clothes, although his real clothes remained on his body. Then he seated himself.

He seated himself firmly upon thin air!

Astonished, not to say frightened, I rushed towards him and gripped him, sank to one knee and felt the air beneath him, saw that his feet were slightly lifted from the ground.

Then his arms moved and his head lolled upon his chest as if he had become unconscious.

I could not stand there and watch any longer, but seized him and shook him begging him to wake up.

His eyes opened and he stared about him, but seemed not to see me.

'Doctor,' he said, 'I believe you have done it.' But he stared beyond me and to my left, addressing some unseen image of myself, perhaps.

Before I entirely lost my own grip, I again grasped his shoulders and spoke urgently into his ear.

'Davenport – Davenport – it is Doctor Schmeling – you are in the drawing room of your aunt's house. Can you hear me? Can you understand?'

Slowly his pale face turned and his body trembled in my hands. Once again the muscles stiffened as he stared, with difficulty, at me.

'I understand you. I remember. But what did I do? There seems to be no memory of . . .'

'Listen,' I said urgently. 'I want you to come with me and visit a close friend of mine – a physicist named King – this is not a case for psychologists or physicians, I am sure. We will go to see him now – will you come?'

'Will he help me?'

'If anyone can, King will help you,' I promised wildly.

'Very well.'

I told Mrs Thornton some vague story of needing to examine her nephew at my surgery and bundled him into my car, driving across London and out beyond Greenwich to the Special Research Institute of which King is the director.

Soon we were in King's office and had told him everything I knew. Then he listened to Davenport's story.

'You were right to come here,' he said. 'And I'm grateful, Schmeling, for you know we are currently doing research into the different degrees of physical awareness. We have several psychologists working with us, of course, and together we may be able to help Mr Davenport as well as,' he smiled at me, 'gaining some valuable information from any experiments we may have to instigate in order to find a cure.'

'So I'm to be a guinea-pig, is that it?' Davenport said bitterly.

'Yes,' King replied, 'but you must remember that the more we learn about your – um – affliction, the easier will be the task of helping you to readjust to reality.'

Soon afterwards it was arranged with Mrs Thornton that Nicholas Davenport should remain at the Research Institute until such a time as he was cured. We promised utmost secrecy and indeed were pleased to have it, since Davenport's condition was so astounding that any hint of it reaching the hungry ears of the sensational press would bring us untold irritation from journalists and cranks.

Time passed until, between them, King and his team had constructed a machine – a beautiful specimen – capable of recording Davenport's experiences while he underwent his illusions and of pulling him back, to some degree at least, to reality.

The data mounted, was sorted and investigated, until slowly we came close to arriving at certain conclusions regarding the nature of Davenport's problem.

Not only did Davenport dwell in a private universe, scarcely related to our commonly-shared time and space, but, if left entirely within it we observed it taking a definite course and shape so that, to himself, his existence had logical progression through both time and space. His past, present, and future experiences were arranged in a perfectly orderly manner save for one thing – his past experiences sometimes existed in our future and his present or future experiences often existed in our past.

Now, up to this point, we had investigated only Nicholas Davenport and it was possible that he was a freak, that no others like him existed. But we had to put this to the test – and I volunteered to be the control. By this time, their experiments with the first machine had enabled them to create another which might, if it worked according to the principle they had devised, have the effect of flinging me into what we were beginning to call 'the permanent hypnagogic state.'

The machine was a masterpiece, producing in the human metabolism the controllable effects of certain drugs like mescalin, lysergic acid or andrenolutin, by exercising a direct electronic control on both mind and blood-stream.

Whatever happened, I was assured of some interesting personal experiences.

I seated myself in a chair while the machine was focused upon my body. A recording device, of the kind I have mentioned, was also present.

The tests began.

The illusions were quite clear – in fact considerably sharper than most every-day experiences – they involved voice, pictures, actions, smells, and my sense of touch as well as certain mildly ecstatic emotional states which could turn swiftly to mildly depressed states. But then, this jumble began to sort itself out, the impressions and illusions began to form a definite pattern until I felt I was living an ordered life, scarcely different from the one I normally followed, save that I seemed to *know* better what it was all about, seemed, if you like, more at home in it.

Now, I learned later, I was released from my chair and allowed to wander around and was then confronted by Davenport in a similar state.

I saw him quite clearly, yet sensed absolutely no involvement with him, had no desire to approach him or interfere verbally or physically with his personal existence. However, after a time, he approached me and said politely:

'So you are free, too, Doctor Schmeling. Doubtless we were deliberately brought together in some way, but if we are allowed to continue in this state I look forward to communicating with you in some period when the time and space of the universe are favourable to another meeting – perhaps we have met already, in your past and my future?'

'Not yet,' I replied.

You see the new state of our existence? Without being directly involved, we were living in what were virtually wholly separate private universes. The nature of time had changed – or at least we had changed in relation to its nature – and it was quite possible for one individual to remember a meeting which had not yet taken place for another individual! We were free! Absolutely free and living what, I am convinced, is man's real and natural existence. Whatever freak occurrence on Earth ever set us off on the wrong road, I do not know. But now the truth was entirely clear. The fumblings of mystics, philosophers, and scientists towards this revelation had been forestalled by the world at large for centuries.

We conducted similar tests on large groups. King was as excited as I. We made no attempt to 'cure' Davenport and, once he understood what had happened to him, what must have happened to the thousands of poor 'schizophrenics' and 'victims of insanity' locked up all over the world, he accepted his condition as being normal – and our conditions as being abnormal.

Watching the experiments on the large groups, we saw Paradise – we saw Heaven, my friend – bands of angels living a peaceful and ordered personal existence – freed from the chains of so-called conformity, from the position of actors playing parts in a bad play, to real men performing real actions with meaning and absolute relevance to their personal existence. More – this state precludes any interference with the lives of their fellows.

It is what politicians have been shouting about for years and never achieving.

Thanks to young Nicholas Davenport, we have achieved the release of mankind from the slavery of togetherness. The tribe will go, the nation will go – there will be only independent men and women.

Schmeling leaned towards me, his heavy, aquiline head jutting forward, his large, square-tipped fingers spread upon the woven material of the armchair.

'Freedom,' he repeated. 'True Freedom!'

But I did not share his exultation. I was, in fact, horrified by the idea. It was impossible, to begin with. But the concept alone – the irresponsible concept – was enough to make me angry. I controlled myself as best I could.

'A good yarn, Schmeling,' I tried to smile. 'You were at your best. But really, man, the very idea of such an existence is appalling to an intelligent man. Society as we understand it would crumble – without organization we cannot have civilization – we could not have buildings, or railways or even newspapers.'

'But we could have books – books that one man produces lovingly upon his own press!'

'How many books? And how would they be distributed? How would he get his ink, his type, his spare parts for his press? Who would read them, anyway?'

'What do you mean?'

'Have animals any desire to read books, Schmeling?'

'That is irrelevant!'

'Oh, no – because the state you are holding up as desirable is an animal existence, don't you see?'

'Your vision is limited,' he said, seeming deliberately to relax in his chair. 'The kind of communication I speak of needs no books, anyway. It is a state of ecstasy, man – heaven on earth. It is what we have been promised for years!'

'Very well, you need no books. But man does not live by books alone – he lives by bread, too!'

'The individual finds the vitamins he needs by – well, by a kind of instinct I can't explain.'

I laughed openly at this naive statement from a learned physician.

'I'm sorry, Schmeling, but our conversation is fast becoming ridiculous. I became too involved in your tale. Let's forget about all this talk of "perfect states" and "transcendental experience" before we wind up like two old Indian priests quarrelling in a monastery.'

But he did not respond to my desire to drop the subject before the argument became bitter and threatened our friendship.

'No,' he insisted. 'Look at it this way – you're a humane and liberal man, are you not? You give the individual a right to holding his own ideas so long as they do not harmfully interfere with another individual.'

I nodded without really listening, for I was bored with the argument.

'Ideas are large or small according to the individual,' he continued. 'You'd agree that if we criticize his ideas according to our own scale, we are wronging that man?'

'Yes.'

'Just as it is possible that an infinite number of things occupy the same space as our planet, having space and time as we have but otherwise existing in a different set of dimensions, so I know that every human being has "dimensions" individual to him. There are many instances where common dimensions are shared, but because this is true we have no business to conclude that therefore *all* dimensions are shared! Therefore you must concede that Man's right to be an individual is as much a physical necessity as it is a philosophical necessity. That to accept the shared dimensions as the only important or "real" ones and to reject those individual *to* the individual as "unnatural" or "wrong" is to deny a *physical truth*!'

'Come now, Schmeling. You have become too caught up in your speculation and yarn-spinning to continue with all this. Calm down, fill your pipe, and I'll be off in a moment or two. I never, I must admit, expected to hear a man of your intellect and common-sense talking so wildly. What you have postulated is total anarchy – an abhorrent state for any thinking creature. Thank God it is not so.'

I glanced with curiosity at Schmeling who had completely relaxed and was filling his pipe as I'd suggested. He chuckled to himself, as if over a private joke.

'You see I am right.' I smiled, rising.

'You'll see that I am right.' he chuckled.

'What do you mean?'

'Why, my dear chap, we have built several such machines of the kind I described. Large ones. They are set up at strategic points the world over. Within a few hours, we shall be flooding the planet with their effect – and real life will begin for man – the New Era – the era of salvation!'

I could take no more.

Shocked and disturbed at seeing so fine a mind behaving so childishly, I returned home. But I could not rid myself of a half-conviction that he had been speaking the truth all along.

I am home now and sitting in my study these write to notes analyse was in it whatever my fostered that conviction order . . .

3: Some Reminiscences of the 3rd Word War

Casablanca

An Episode in the Third World War

'We are betrayed by what is false within.'
George Meredith

Beyond the deserted huts and artificial pools, far out to sea, like a cold wall around our world, a mist had formed. I saw an oil tanker moving through it, coming away from the Gulf, while on the harbour and the unkempt flat roofs, where TV dishes were raised like broken shields, a thin drizzle settled. I turned from the window but found no warmth in the room.

'Well, darling, you told me so! Panos is a complete bastard.' She advanced on me, put her hand on my arm, her head against my shoulder. 'Forgive me?' Her lips anticipated the pleasure of my assent.

Again I resisted the ritual. The effort was considerable. 'I'm tired of what you do,' I said. 'I'm going to leave you.'

'Sweetie!' Her disbelief was observably turning to fury at the prospect of being denied her usual blessing. I wondered if she had always loathed me and if every betrayal I had so far accepted had been from fear of that one terrible truth.

'Faithless . . .' I began, but moralizing was beyond me. I had known her from the beginning. Any pain she caused was of my own seeking. I felt disgust. I stepped back from the balcony. 'We have to separate, Nadja.'

'That doesn't suit me.' She controlled herself. 'I need you.'

'I've nothing left to give. I'm exhausted.'

'I've been selfish. I didn't think.' But she gave up this approach almost at once, retrieving her dignity and her sense of perspective at the same time. She laughed. I had confirmed her view of the world. Her golden skin glowed like metal and her eyes were ancient stones.

'I'm going,' I said. 'I'm in an hotel on Rue de la Radiance du Sol. We'll be in contact, eh? I shan't want the flat immediately.' I was tempted to touch her hair for the last time; hair as delicate and as coarse as her love-making, as black as her most secret despair.

I turned my back on her. I turned my back on Africa. She went past me and stood on the balcony, deliberately re-entering my field of vision. She let the moisture settle in her hands, combing it into her hair, spreading Casablanca's oily atmosphere over her face, arms and shoulders and cleansing whatever vestiges of sin she imagined to be still visible on her body.

I wish that she had not made an awful sort of choking noise when I left.

My chief met me in the Travel Bureau, which was closed for the afternoon, its plate glass staring on to an almost deserted Boulevard Emile Zola, where a few cars moved in the brightening afternoon light. He was a thin man with a moustache modelled on Georgian lines, I would guess, so he looked like a wolfish caricature of Stalin, something he was unconscious of and would have been horrified to know. His name was Yagolovski. He had been born in Riga and was of that new breed of traditionalist who emerged from the Gorbachev period. We sat together in the empty chairs watching a video of the Barbados beaches reflected in the shop's window. 'You've made your plans?' he asked.

'She and I are finished.'

'And you're happy with that?' Yagolovski became avuncular with approval. 'You're a strong one. Good boy!'

I had not suffered such praise for many years.

All this happened some time ago, before I took up my last post in England and during that prolonged 'phoney' period prior to the outbreak of the World War. After my spell in Athens and before I settled in London, I was working in Casablanca. Most people will tell you that Casablanca is not the real Morocco but she remains my favourite. She was big, even in those days, with a population of around seven million, much of it in shanty towns, had few remarkable features and even her Medina was sleazy in the way of the most industrial ports. The tourist trade, primarily dependent on the Bogart myth, had established holiday villages along the somewhat bleak and dangerous beaches, a series of bathing lagoons and some restaurants with names like *Villa Tahiti* and, of course, *Café Americaine*, which looked even grubbier in the foul weather which blew so frequently off the Atlantic.

The years of rain, following the drought of the 70s and 80s, were, of course, to Morocco's benefit and helped establish her as one of Africa's richest nations, but during my time in Casablanca most people were worried about what the wet weather would do to their vacation business.

If the rain had no serious effect on the port traffic and the factories, it was a relief for the people living in the countless shanties, since it cut down Casa's smog, the equal to Los Angeles', and made the city a little healthier. For a while local entrepreneurs had managed to sell copied Burberry trenchcoats to tourists determined to milk at least a little romance from a city having more in common with the reality of Liverpool than the fantasy of Hollywood.

As usual I was working as an art dealer, specializing chiefly in North African antiquities, and had been established in the name of Erich Volker, a Czech emigré, in the old harbour quarter's Rue Sour el Djedid, a street becoming fashionable amongst successful Moroccan bohemians, chiefly painters and photographers.

'Women are grief,' said Yagolovski. 'You should know that.' Out of deference to me he did not light the cigarette between his fingers. I was making one of my attempts to stop smoking. 'You're lucky this job came up.' Even in his sympathetic mood he reminded me of a jocular Stalin about to betray some old comrade. 'It will take you away from Casablanca. And, when you return, never fear – she'll have discovered some new supporter.' He cleared his throat and picked up a file. 'They're ten a penny.'

I welcomed his remarks. I did not need comfort at that stage. I was glad to be going.

'You like Marrakech, don't you?'

'For a holiday. Is that my destination?'

'Initially. You'll be staying at the Mamounia. It's well-known, of course.'

The Mamounia had remained Morocco's most famous hotel for half a century and, like similar legendary hotels across the world, had never quite lost its romance or failed to disappoint, very slightly, those who had imagined for years how they might get there. I preferred the smaller hotels in the Medina, or the Es Saadi, where the French show-people went and which could offer an equally magnificent view of the High Atlas. But at least I had never been to the Mamounia with Nadja. 'It was Churchill's favourite.' I looked out past the reflected waves and consciously took control of myself. 'He painted in their gardens. And I think de Gaulle, Roosevelt went there. Possibly Stalin. John Foster Dulles. And of course all those emirs and kings from the other side of Suez. It sounds as if I'm to hob-nob with a better class of people.'

When I looked at him Yagolovski was grinning. 'Just a richer class. No Saudi princes or Gulf sultans, I'm afraid.' He outlined the first part of my assignment, which was to make contact with an Algerian agent who would book into the Mamounia as an Egyptian businessman.

Although officially Morocco was no longer at war with Algeria, who had apparently given up ambitions in the old Spanish Sahara and withdrawn support for the Polisario guerillas, there was still a great deal of political activity under the surface, much of it, of course, in relation to Libya and Algeria's frustration at having no Atlantic seaboard. For that reason we continued to maintain a department in Casablanca and another in Algiers.

'I suppose you want me to leave tomorrow,' I said.

Raising his unlit cigarette to his heavy moustache Yagolovski chuckled as he shook his head. 'Tonight,' he said. 'You meet your Egyptian businessman in the morning. But, believe me, this should take your mind off your troubles.'

The Marrakech plane was full of pale tourists going on to Agadir whose beaches were golden and whose hotels were high and white. A town destroyed by God, they said of the earthquake, restored by Man and populated by Satan. I think Satan was a euphemism for Europe. The nearest thing I had seen to even a simple *djin* in that Moroccan Miami Beach was a German holiday-maker creeping out before dawn to lay claim to a pool-chair with his towel. The place consisted entirely of hotels, restaurants and tourist shops and was, I thought, an unfortunate vision of Morocco's future.

My own country was also eager for hard currency in those days, so I sympathized with Moroccan policies, even as I regretted the signs of standardization which threatened to place a Laura Ashley and a McDonald's in every identical shopping mall from Moscow to Melbourne. Marrakech had kept so much of her character through her position in one of the country's richest agricultural areas while the Berbers in particular did not so much resist the evils of capitalism as ignore those aspects of it they did not need.

It was not in my nature to express judgements, but I would have been happy if the tourist industry had confined itself to North Africa's Atlantic coast.

The journey was short. By the time we landed at Minar Airport I was thinking of nothing but Nadja and already, of course, weakening. Walking from the plane to the embarkation building I put on my wide-brimmed Panama and drew a deep breath of the relaxing heat, turning my face to a heaven which had something of that dark, moistureless desert blue of skies beyond the High Atlas. The soldiers on duty smoked and chatted, showing us only casual interest. I remembered what I had liked about Marrakech and why I feared her attraction. Of all Maghrebi cities, she possessed the greatest love of pleasure, a carelessness, a good humour, that reminded me of Cairo. The French had never been very secure in Marrakech. Her easy-going confidence derived, I think, from her once superior position as the centre of a great Berber Empire from the Pyrenees to the Sahara, successfully resisting all would-be outside conquerors. I suppose Casablanca's cautious cynicism, developed in the service of a dozen masters, was preferable to me.

After suffering the irritating passport and customs rituals which refused to distinguish residents from visitors, I found a taxi to take me to the Mamounia. I chatted in French with a driver who assumed me to be a tourist and recommended a variety of relatives for whatever goods or services I might require. I did not reveal any knowledge of Arabic. It is my habit to seem unfamiliar with languages. People have a way of revealing much more if they think you have only a word or two of their native tongue.

As we drove along the broad red avenues of the Menara quarter of the new town, I remembered how Nadja and I had wandered these streets when we were first together. Now I felt more pain than I had imagined possible. I wondered if this were an important job or if my chief, knowing that it was in my interest to stay away from Casablanca as long as possible, had done me a favour. He, like all his kind, possessed a fatherly and sometimes unwelcome concern about the private lives of his officers. It is in the tradition of our Service and goes back long before the Revolution.

For my part, I should have been unhappy without that concern. 'Follow the rules and enjoy the love of the Father,' as the priests used to say in our little town. My mother was fond of the phrase and would repeat it sometimes like a litany. My own father's rules were inviolable but I could not say he loved any of us.

I grew up in the shadow of Stalin and, even though he was dead by the time I could read, the old habits lived on. It makes us slow to take decisions sometimes, even now. But that is often no bad thing.

A case in point was our decision to remain in the Maghreb when almost everyone else removed their agencies altogether, usually leaving one officer at their consulate. An American friend of mine, who had guessed my job as I had guessed his, was amused by it. 'You Russians keep as many staff in warm countries as you can possibly justify. I don't blame you, with your hideous climate, but it's a standing joke amongst most intelligence crews. Your chiefs want to be sure of a few days of sunshine every year.' I was reminded of all the engineers, military experts and technicians volunteering for work in, for instance, Libya, and how Afghanistan with her awful winters had proved such a disappointment to certain colleagues.

We drove through broad streets cooled by tall palms, flanked by red-brown walls, by wrought-iron which gave glimpses of villas decorated with bright tile and pastel lime-wash, with vibrant trailing flowers and vines, lush shrubs and trees, the New City, which we used to call the French City, lying outside the walls of the Medina. The Mamounia was almost as famous a landmark as the tall, elegant outline of the Katoubia Mosque, the Mosque of the Booksellers, where from the surrounding shops, it was again possible to buy exquisitely printed editions of Ibn Rushd's Aristotle commentaries, al-Khwarizmi's mathematical treatises, as well as any number of editions of the Qu'ran. Unlike the Mosque, however, the Mamounia, lying just within the high crenellated walls of the Medina at the Djedid Gate, had changed to meet changing times. My suitcase was taken from the taxi by a man dressed for a touring production of *The Desert Song* who carried it into a foyer half reproduction deco, half the interior of Los Angeles' *Dar Maghreb* restaurant.

I was a little shocked and at the same time amused. The place was a vulgar Arabian Nights fantasy, an authentic extension of Hollywood. I reflected that as Morocco grew richer she resembled California in all her ways. Perhaps this was the logic of wealth? Perhaps our notions of value and culture and human dignity were old-fashioned? Certainly nobody suffered in modern Marrakech as when the Caids held power.

I went to sleep in a bed whose canopy of red silk, whose massive purple pillows and yellow sheets would have put to shame the ostentation of a Turkish pasha and in the morning was served, on a tray of rosewood, silver and mother-of-pearl, coffee and croissants the rival of anything I had tasted in Paris. I showered in a black and silver stall almost the size of the flat I had been born in, then shaved and dressed, started down to the pool to keep my appointment, seemingly a casual meeting, in the shade of some palms flanking the hotel garden.

I remembered when Nadja and I had stayed at a little hotel just outside the Medina and seen the dawn rising in a pale mist of pink and blue: the palms and eucalyptus dark green against the red walls of the city. From some shuttered shop came the resonant lute and drum music of Rouicha Mohemed while elsewhere Azzahia sang of metaphysical love to inspire images of birds, animals and flowers as vivid as any picture. This was the perfect life of Marrakech or, at least, a perfect moment, a pause before the day began. The smell of sweet mint tea joined the aroma of baking bread and woodsmoke. She had told me how much she loved me and how she would always love me and I had had her again, as the sounds of the city rose around us like a symphony.

There were already a few Americans and Germans around the pool, distinguished from one another only by the tone of their tanning agents. My man stood smoking under an orange tree, apparently fascinated by the brilliant pinks of a bougainvillaea. He was tall and handsome, reminding me of an Egyptian film-star I saw frequently on billboards in Casablanca. About thirty-five, with dark, sardonic eyes, carefully groomed black curly hair and moustache, he wore a grey silk suit which had not been bought this side of the Italian Riviera. His name, even his cover name, was unknown to me, but we had a rather childish conversation code for mutual identification.

'A beautiful morning,' I said.

'Like the first morning in Paradise.' He smiled. 'Have you been in Marrakech long?' He purred his words like a Cairene.

'A matter of hours. I live in Casablanca. I have a business there.' I replied in French.

We walked away from the pool. On the other side of the hotel wall came sounds of the city's ordinary commerce, the muezzin, a radio playing Rai hits.

I yawned. 'I'm still a little sleepy. I arrived late last night. The mountains are magnificent from my room.'

'Unfortunately I have only a concourse. You're in business in Morocco? That's interesting.'

'I deal in antiques.'

'Quite a coincidence,' he murmured in what was virtually an aside to the tree. 'I sell cotton. I'm at present in Esna but my home's in Alexandria. You know Egypt, I suppose?'

'Fairly well. I do very little buying there now.'

'The export restrictions on that sort of thing are pretty much total. And if they're not there, it's clear what you buy is a fake!'

We talked a little longer, then shook hands and agreed to meet before lunch. At about noon, in a horse-drawn taxi, we toured the city's pink sandstone walls which served, among other things, to protect the Medina from fierce winter sandstorms.

My contact smoked constantly. Eventually I accepted his offered Marlboro and, with a sense of considerable relief, lit it. I felt I gave my liberty up to a familiar and not unkind master. I had always understood the basic meaning of Islam, which was 'Surrender'. The Egyptian's name was Tewfik al-Boulekh, he said. We used English, of which our driver had only a few words.

'You'll be wanting to interview the boy?' He tossed a dirham coin towards the group of shouting children now running beside our carriage. Some scrambled for the money while others kept pace with us. I admired their stamina. *'M'sieu!'* they called. *'Un dirham! Un dirham!'* I was reminded of an English friend telling me how he had pursued American jeeps during the Second World War pleading for gum. Across the road men used materials and methods unaltered for a thousand years to rebuild the walls. The red mud blended with older remains of houses and stables. 'The Maghreb is so much cleaner than Egypt.'

'I know very little.' I thought it wise not to admit my complete ignorance. 'Is he here in Marrakech?'

'No, no.' He turned his head as our driver reined in suddenly to begin a passionate argument with a man whose donkey was almost hidden by a huge bundle of newly-picked mint. Clutching at his brown-and-white-striped djellabah in a gesture that was as obscene as it was obscure, the Berber further enraged our cabman and brought another donkey-owner into the argument while passengers boarding a nearby bus, on to which one man was forcing two sheep he had just bought, turned with interest to witness the argument concerning the first donkey's absolute refusal to move from the tarmac to the strip of hardened mud beside it and so give the taxi a clear passage. Meanwhile we were joined by a score of astonishingly lovely Marrekshi children asking us for stylos and money. I ignored them until we were on the move again then threw them a cheap ballpoint and some small change.

Al-Boulekh continued: 'The boy was born in France but his papers are absolutely authentic. There can be no question of his lineage.'

'Are his ancestors well-known?'

The Egyptian laughed heartily. 'Oh, indeed!'

'Provenance is so important in my walk of life,' I said.

He dropped his voice. 'There is no question that our young friend is a direct descendant of the Prophet. If anything his blood better than any ruling Fatimid.'

I hid my surprise and cursed my chief for not warning me of the fantastic nature of the assignment. I regarded the Algerian agent with increased suspicion. Was I to be involved in some bizarre kidnapping? Even during my early days with the Service such schemes had fallen out of fashion.

We went together to Djemaa al-Fna. The great central square of Marrakech was crowded as always with every kind of produce, with entertainers, with tourists. It always reminded me, I told my companion, of London's Portobello Road. There were spice-sellers and food-stalls, fruit and vegetables, pots and pans, and two great handcart displays of every type of Japanese digital time-piece. The modern goods were offered side by side with rugs pottery and tools in use since the city's foundation when William the Conqueror was making London his capital.

We sat at a table outside the *Café de France*. I had the *simple* and my Algerian-Egyptian had the *filtre*.

'You know where we are going tomorrow?' he asked.

'I believe I am to travel to the other side of the mountains.' I gestured with my cup at the distant peaks.

'We have to be pretty cautious at this moment.' Chiefly because I had no cigarettes myself I refused his offered Marlboro.

After lunch, we walked through the souk and then went to see the Majorelle Gardens, the *Bou Saf Saf*, whose entrance was in a little side-street in the Gueliz district not far from the Doukkala Gate. As usual the botanical gardens were almost deserted and I was immediately captured by their peacefulness. I am always impressed by the Arab appreciation of zones of tranquillity, little bits of paradise on earth, though this particular garden was the creation of a French painter.

'There's nothing like this in Cairo now.' Al-Boulekh was impressed. 'People have to go out to the pyramids if they want some space. That city should be a warning to us.'

I told him Cairo was one of my favourite cities. Given her thirty million inhabitants, she was a splendid example of how people of disparate religions and politics could survive together, however tenuously.

This did not suit his own views. Changing the subject, he said he had known a Volker in Munich who ran a little private toy museum there, near the open market. Was I a relative? I told him I was not German but had been born near Prague and emigrated with my parents in the 1950s. He accepted this lie as readily as he accepted any other story from me. He had that way of Mediterranean and African peoples, who seem to judge you not by the accuracy but by the quality of your accounts. For his benefit I next invented a trek across no-man's-land, guards shooting at us, my little sister being killed.

'Yet now you work again for the Russians?' He introduced a sudden reality into our exchange.

I laughed aloud and he joined me; just, I decided, for the relief of it. Since we demanded no superficial logic of our ancient myths and legends, why should we demand it of our modern ones?

We paused beside a mosaic fountain, under great feathery branches of trees which had covered the Earth before the first fish crawled to land and filled its lungs.

'There's an economic crisis coming here.' He blew smoke towards a sky so blue and still it might have been painted by a New York pop artist. 'Until now King Hassan has been able to control the Left. But with the population explosion, with the collapse of their European markets, with a restless and newly-educated and largely unemployable middle-class, with the Libyan trouble, the situation will soon become volatile, wouldn't you say?'

I agreed his projection had some basis in truth, though privately I believed Morocco could solve her problems and maintain a stability already making her one of the most progressive countries in Africa.

'The Left on its own has no one to lead a successful coup. We've nobody left in the UNFP. And anyway all the attempted coups have come from the Right. The Left needs a good alternative to Hassan. His sons won't do, of course. Hassan can't last very much longer. It's at that point we have the chance to win the country over.'

'You expect us to co-operate with you in financing a revolution?' I was incredulous.

'It wouldn't amount to anything hugely disruptive. Not with the cards we have to play.'

'I thought your people had stopped supporting the Polisarios?' The guerrillas of the old Spanish Sahara had been neutralized in their bid for an independent nation controlling the phosphate mines which gave Morocco so much of its hard currency.

'You know the pressure we were under.' He began to walk down one of the brick paths towards a group of sinuous plants whose brilliant, spiky blossoms suggested they had been brought from the continental interior. 'We expected the United States to reduce her aid. Instead she increased it. For a while she was almost as generous to Morocco as she was to Israel. Yet somehow Hassan kept faith with everyone. Largely because of his importance to Islam. There are not many like him left.' He meant, I assumed, that Hassan was a descendant of the Prophet's daughter, Fatima, which many accepted as the purest of all royal bloodlines. 'His survival has proved to many Islamic leaders, even those directly opposed to his policies, that he is Allah's chosen. Well, you know that. His *baraka* has never been more evident.'

This was European logic, of which I was always suspicious if presented by an Arab, yet again I was bound to agree with him. The word, distinctly Arabic, had a wealth of meaning – a mixture of status, *charisma, chuztpah*, glamour and good fortune which, in a world whose rulers, even socialist presidents, were regarded as God's representatives as well as the State's, was of crucial significance now that the fundamentalists gained so much power. My chief always complained how our Moscow people refused to understand that to Moslems, even our own Moslems, politics and religion were synonymous.

'The problem,' my companion continued, 'has never been how to overthrow Hassan, but who will replace him.'

Again I agreed. Sentimentally, of course, I could see no possible point in replacing Hassan, who had proved himself since 1976 (when, leading his people into the desert, he had peacefully occupied the Spanish Sahara) a brilliant politician. His esteem in the country and throughout the world had never been higher. Moroccan troops had fought bravely beside Syrians in the Golan Heights while at the same time Hassan had encouraged Jews to return to his country, displaying that tolerance for other faiths which his greatest ancestors had exercised throughout their long rule in Africa and Europe. He had demonstrated ethical and pragmatic judgement at least equal to Sadat's and any hint of our interfering with his rule would lose us authority throughout the world.

I wondered why my chief, who knew my admiration for Hassan, had given me this task. Hassan was everything great that Stalin could have been. But Stalin was a failed priest, ever unable to placate his own ghosts or reconcile his past with a future for which he had relinquished his place in heaven. Self-sacrifice is always borne with greater dignity if that sacrifice is proved of value.

The Egyptian again revealed his obsession. 'This boy has Almohad, Fatimid and Abbasid blood. By showing increased support to orthodoxy he could win unprecedented influence through the entire Islamic world. It might be truly united for the first time in history!'

'Under whom?' I asked. He did not reply.

We walked back from the gardens and visited some of the shopping streets of the French Quarter. He paused in the Place du 16 Novembre outside a motorbike showroom. Staring through the display window al-Boulekh was surprised by a poster on which three Japanese women in one-piece bathing suits advertised a new Kawasaki.

'Doesn't it occur to you how behind the times we are in this profession?' I said. 'The Japanese concern themselves with commercial espionage, with the empire of the market place. It makes a great deal of sense.'

He was predictably disapproving. 'It certainly does, if you've something to sell. These days Moscow has very little people want. You relied on exporting an ideal.'

'But that's a bit obsolete now. These days we're trying for the consumer market. We're out of practice.'

He was dismissive. 'If the war doesn't escalate, you'll do it, I'm sure. You still have a low paid and extremely well-disciplined workforce.'

I found myself unamused by his irony. I remained suspicious of Arab socialists. I was more comfortable with traditional power-seekers.

We returned to the Mamounia and I went to my room, having agreed to see him for dinner. On impulse I put through a call to Casablanca but was told that there was no reply. Trying to avoid thinking of Nadja, I watched a James Cagney movie on television, *Yankee Doodle Dandy* dubbed into French with Arabic sub-titles. Eventually I turned the TV off and listened to the radio news. As usual England was justifying some piece of American gunboat diplomacy to her EEC allies while Israel accused Syria of arming the Jews for Palestine guerrillas recently allied to the PLO. South Africa's invasion of Mozambique and Libya's "border dispute" with Tunisia seemed to be taking place unopposed.

These familiar reports were almost comforting. When the Folklorique performances followed I was irritated and found a Tunisian discussion on the changing face of France. Maghrebis share that complicated fascination with their former rulers which Indians have with the British. Not everyone benefits from colonialism and there are many losses in the name of Western progress, but I cannot dismiss all imperialist expansion as harmful. I was raised in a tradition, old-fashioned in the non-Communist world almost before I was born, and it is still hard for me not to take a paternalist view of what was once the Third World, especially since paternalism prevails there. We Russians understand and accept the nature of power rather more readily than the ambivalent English, for instance, or those who inherited and developed their particular brand of imperialism, the Americans.

Until I was on the edge of sleep I gave no thought to what al-Boulekh had told me. The Egyptian's story seemed the fantastic concoction of some distant intelligence agency without enough real business. According to the Algerians I was to meet a young man whose Sharifian lineage, just on one strand alone, went back to the 17th century Alouite sultans of Marrakech. With such potent blood, the Egyptian claimed, Hassan and his family could be deposed and a regime more closely aligned to the socialist world be installed in Rabat. To me the scheme, even if the boys' ancestry were perfect, was so pointless and reminiscent of a foolish 19th century Ottoman plot, that I was hardly able to stop scoffing at it on the spot. Yet the Egyptian revealed himself as being closely involved with and committed to the scheme. Doubtless he had supplementary ambitions.

'Wait until you meet him,' he had said. 'You'll be won over.'

I had my orders. I had no choice. The next morning we were to drive over the High Atlas to a small town on the edge of the Sahara which had been colonized by Club Med and was primarily patronized by middle-class French people in their late thirties. In 1928 Ouarzazate had been a Foreign Legion garrison town on the site of an old kasbah and was more than once attacked by various bands of determined irregulars, who refused to accept European protection and were still not completely pacified at the outbreak of the Second World War.

At that time Route P31 over the Tizi 'n' Tichka Pass to the Draa Valley was, after the first few miles, somewhat bleak, rising about 8,000 feet amongst peaks still snow-capped and frequently as barren as those parts of the Lake District where as an exchange student in the 1960s I used to hike. Until spring, when wild flowers make them vibrant, they are unremarkable mountains, dotted with ruined kasbahs from which local chieftains, controlling the caravan routes and trails, had raided as successfully as the Scottish robber barons in the Highlands.

Obviously familiar with the range, my companion drove our Avis Renault at headlong speed around the mountain roads, his horn frequently in use, occasionally missing a collision with a truck or a tourist bus. The radio was turned up to full volume. *'Too tired to make it, too tired to fight about it,'* sang al-Boulekh with the Eagles. As we descended towards the Draa we followed the river, the Oued Imini, south-east through shale slopes and grey-black rock occasionally brightened by a little foliage, a narrow strip of cultivated land, a small goat herd or a dusty, broken tower.

For twenty years Old Ouarzazate, the provincial capital, had been the location of so many Hollywood films that it immediately struck a romantic chord. The low, pleasant houses, the crenellated walls, the half-ruined kasbah, the palm-trees and oases where nomads came to trade, were familiar to anyone who ever saw *Lawrence of Arabia*. The reality confirmed the fantasy so thoroughly it seemed they were the same.

Al-Boulekh told me a little of his work with the Polisario guerrillas. Until recently he said they had camped not a hundred miles from here. The Algerians were too cautious to involve directly any of their own people, so the contact officers had been, like al-Boulekh, from friendly Arab countries or else were disaffected Berbers, sometimes Moroccan Touaregs considering a career move. Pressured by us, the Americans and the Arab League, Algeria had agreed to stop even her indirect Polisario support. That war drained everyone and had only strategic results for the Polisarios. Ironically, Morocco was at one time forced to put more men and money into that particular field than the French spent maintaining power over the whole Maghreb.

Al-Boulekh was tired by the drive and wanted a drink. I suggested stopping at a little place called *Zitoun*, the Olive Grove, but he shook his head.

'It's hard now to find a public bar in Ouarzazate. *Zitoun* doesn't sell alcohol. For a while, you know, Club Med had the monopoly. Did you ever try to get a beer in Moulay Idris?'

'That's hardly a good example. It's a holy town.'

He shrugged. Like so many younger Arabs he equated drinking with modernity. He would no more patronize a café which did not sell liquor than he would sit and listen to the love-songs of Oum Kal Thoum, the classical Egyptian singer I admired. He only listened to American pop, he had said, like Dire Straits. So he preferred, I replied, to hear middle-aged millionaires from San Luis Obispo wailing their contempt for microwaves and colour televisions? There had been a familiar note of puritanism in his voice, echoing writers I had known who dismissed narrative, or painters who loathed anything remotely figurative: an attitude which in Europe had seemed radically progressive twenty years earlier but which I nowadays found embarrassing. We had entered a more conservative phase of our cultural history and I was consoled by it. But at least he had revealed something of his moral view and I felt pleasantly satisfied by this, as if I had mysteriously gained an advantage in an unfamiliar game.

Near the old Glaovi Kasbah we found a pleasant restaurant with rooftop seats looking down on to Ouarzazate's ever-expanding main street, where stalls now sold trinkets, handicrafts and Pakistani brass-work to tourists. In the uncompromising near-desert heat German automobiles manoeuvred for space with donkeys, bicycles, horsemen and ancient trucks whose gaudy decoration was reminiscent of the nomad tents we had passed coming in. Once a detachment of smart Moroccan soldiers marched by. I almost mistook them for paras. Their presence surprised me.

'Is the Sahara trouble starting up again?' I asked as I sipped my Valgrave.

'Who knows?' He had stretched out his long legs and was as relaxed as the hopeful cats who sat politely around us.

'You, possibly?' I was sardonic. I guessed he had high ambitions.

'Oh, we're nothing but intermediaries. You understand that. Messenger boys at best. Even you, M. Volker, in spite of your rank.'

I was mildly amused by this display of knowledge. I had no information about him, but someone had shown him a dossier on me.

'I'm a simple antique dealer,' I said. 'A Czech emigré.'

'I had forgotten.' It seemed a genuine apology.

When he had finished his beer we drove to the Club Med buildings. The great kasbah-style walls looked as if they might have resisted the whole of Abd el-Krim's 1920s tribal army. Had it not been for some kind of special pass displayed by al-Boulekh, I think we could have found it impossible to reach the reception area.

The place was decorated in French-Moorish, a rather unhappy combination of two splendid aesthetics, and we were greeted by a pretty young Berber woman stylish in Parisian casuals. Her name was R'Kia and she was the Customer Relations Liaison Officer. She had been told to expect us. Normally, she said, visits from relatives were discouraged by the Club. She was charming. She was sure we could understand why these rules existed.

I told her I too was a great believer in rules, and she was winningly grateful. She led us around the pool where near-naked women stretched themselves on loungers and their men played water-football or lay reading paperback spy thrillers, through an archway, up a short stair until we stood outside a bright blue door on which she tapped.

During the pause I said: 'You have a world of your own here.' We were all speaking French.

'Yes. You never need to leave, if you don't want to. Everything is provided.' She called through the door. 'M. Maquin. Your uncle and his friend are here.'

The door was opened by a handsome boy of about twenty dressed in shorts and grey silk beach shirt. He was below middle height but had the physique of a body-builder. He shook hands, greeting us in an educated Parisian accent. I guessed that French was his first language. It was immediately obvious why al-Boulekh was convinced and why our Odessa office had given credence to the scheme. The boy radiated *baraka*.

Alain Makhainy knew nothing of my people's involvement and, I would guess, had not been told of any historic destiny planned for him by whatever Algerian Secret Service department had concocted this Ruritanian scheme to replace him at the head of the Moroccan state. Al-Boulekh had described his vision of a shining new monarch coming out of the desert at the head of an Algerian-Soviet equipped army to unite the Maghreb, including Libya, into one powerful nation. Wild as the plan was, many people in those days of flux would have given it credence. Myths of hope were in short supply. It was not the most bizarre plan invented by the world's intelligence agencies, nor the most dangerous. Indeed, in retrospect, it has for me a certain innocence. At that time, however, in a very different climate, I was utterly sceptical.

Makhainy took us to a bar with a wide balcony looking out over the battlements to palms and a shallow stream. When I tried to pay for our drinks he laughed and gave the waiter some coloured beads from his pocket. 'This is the only currency we're allowed here.'

The boy believed he was to be interviewed for a sensitive job representing one of the main international banks where his lineage would stand him in unusually good stead with Arab clients.

I questioned him about his parents, who were both second-generation Parisians. His grandfather had come from Lebanon and his grandmother from Sinai. During the War they had lived in Casablanca. His maternal grandparents were both Palestinian Arabs who had emigrated to Lyons after 1947. He had birth-certificates, family photographs, documents of every kind from half-a-dozen French and Arab authorities, including references to his ancestors in a variety of Islamic historical texts. His paternal grandfather was the son of a mutual ancestor of the Moroccan Sultans. They had been a distinguished family of Islamic judges and scholars. In France, as merchants, they had experienced great wealth for a while. I was in no doubt about his bloodlines, neither was I surprised by his family's recent past. Not everyone desires to be a prince or even an eminent holy man. 'My parents are French citizens,' he said. 'My father was a socialist.'

'And you?' I asked casually.

He shrugged. 'I am a child of my age. I need a well-paid job which will make the best use of my talents.'

'You are fluent in Arabic?' I asked in that language.

'A bit rusty,' he told me. 'But practice should take care of that. Eh, m'sieu?' He offered me a wonderful smile. I think he had the measure of his own gifts.

The Egyptian and I stayed overnight at a local *fonduk*, rather like one of those pensions you used to find in provincial France, and which had the same air of fly-blown cosiness. We each had a single iron-framed bed and the Turkish toilet facilities were on the floor below.

Al-Boulekh was elated by what he was certain had been a successful encounter. 'Isn't he perfect?' He had removed his European clothes and sat on his bed's edge wearing a blue and white Alexandrian gelabea.

'He's certainly convincing and he has personality.' I carefully folded my clothes and sat them on the tiled floor. 'Let's hope he does well at the doctor's examination.'

He frowned from where he lay with a book supported by his pillows. 'A doctor? What for?'

'Oh, it's one of our rules,' I said. 'You know what bureaucracies are like. Moscow will want it.'

'He doesn't look the type to have a heart attack.' Then he smiled. 'I know. You're worried about AIDS. I'm sure he's fundamentally heterosexual.'

I said nothing to this. Neither did I tell him how much I had liked the young man and, unusually for me, did not wish him to be destroyed by what I considered an already doomed adventure. Algeria had taken the wrong lessons from us. Times and methods were changing rapidly. At that stage we were hoping to avert what the Americans called 'a major conflict'.

'And he can always brush up his Arabic,' said al-Boulekh.

Next morning we returned to Marrakech. The Egyptian was exceptionally friendly on the journey back and even turned off the radio at my request, whereupon he outlined the great benefits of the Maghreb's unification. 'What Hassan did for Morocco, Hamed – his original name – will do for the whole of North Africa. Imagine! A unified socialist Arab alliance the length and breadth of the Mediterranean from the Atlantic to the Red Sea. And what an example for the rest of Africa! Within a couple of generations they could form a bloc as powerful as Europe!' Was this naivete a display for my benefit?

I envied him, I said, his old-fashioned optimism. In my own country Lenin's great ideal was giving way to Lenin's equally great pragmatism and it was fashionable to describe how Stalin had lost the way, that Lenin had foreseen what could go wrong and thus had introduced the New Economic Policy which, essentially, most well-established socialist states were now reproducing. There is sometimes nothing worse than being taken for the representative of an ideal – or even a sexual preference – one has discarded in the light of experience.

In Marrakech I tried to phone my flat from the airport while I waited for the delayed plane but my operator was unable, he said, to make the connection, though I insisted I had heard the number ring. I had decided to try one last time to come to an agreement with Nadja and felt urgently she should know.

The plane eventually came in from Agadir. It was packed with sun-reddened tourists wearing locally-bought straw hats, Rose Sarkissian shirts covered in rhinestones and gilded cowboy emblems, and cheaply-made kaftans. I found a seat on the smoking side of the plane. Moroccans had solved the problem of non-smoking accommodation by simply dividing the plane down the middle. Halfway to Casablanca I bought a packet of English cigarettes from the stewardess but did not light one until I was outside the airport waiting for my car.

I went straight to the office and gave my report to my chief.

'You seem unimpressed,' he said. It was still raining heavily. The water poured like mercury down the plate glass. 'This is a little awkward for me.'

'He's a very personable young man. Simply tell him he has to have a medical before we can give him a firm answer.'

'You're not normally so assertive.' Without comment he accepted a Silk Cut from my packet. 'Very well. I'll tell Odessa. And they'll tell Moscow. And we'll hear in a month. You think the scheme's crazy, don't you?'

'And you?'

I expected no reply.

He shrugged. 'Otherwise, you'd say he was what he claims?'

'I think claims are being made for him. All he wants is an easy, well-paid job. But yes – he's kosher.' And I smiled as I picked up my bag. 'I think the Algerians are trying to get back into the game. He's all they have at present.'

He was equally amused. 'Very romantic, Erich. Just like the Great Game, eh?' Typical of his years, he was a keen reader of Kipling and Jack London. 'More like a plot from the turn of the century. Don't you feel nostalgic? Like a character in John Buchan. Or one of those old Alexander Korda movies?'

'Our destinies are just as determined by mythology as were our ancestors'. I used to be frightened by the idea.'

'That girl of yours, by the way, has a new gentleman friend. A Tunisian sardine wholesaler. Named Hafid. You'll be at your hotel?'

'My flat. I have some stuff there I want.'

He said nothing as he watched me leave. I enjoyed the walk through the rain to the taxi stand. The car took me along the seafront with its closed-down bars and abandoned night-clubs, its waterlogged beach umbrellas and torn red-, white- and blue-striped awnings, its drunks in their filthy European suits, its desolate whores. I was sure the boy would be found to be uncircumcized. An uncircumcized Moslem is a contradiction in terms. If he did not know Arabic well, he did not know the Qu'ran and therefore had no prospect of a crown by that route. Without our support, he was not the slightest threat to Hassan or his sons, all of whom were thoroughly educated in Islam. The Egyptian clearly had some sort of financial stake in this scheme.

The taxi dropped me off outside the whitewashed walls of my building. When I pressed the code on the electronic lock there was some trouble with it and I could not get in. I shivered as I put my finger to my own bell and was answered by Nadja's voice.

'It's Volker,' I said. 'I'm back from Marrakech.'

After a short pause she pushed the button to admit me. I walked up the stairs, obscurely thinking I should give her a little time before I reached the door, but she had opened it and was waiting for me as I walked in. Her clothes were unfamiliar. She wore a tight red skirt and a gold blouse. Her make-up had created a stranger. She was already established in her newest role.

'I'm leaving in the morning,' she told me. There were a few boxes and suitcases packed. 'I shan't take much.'

'Perhaps you'll let the concierge have my keys,' I said.

'Of course,' she said. 'You look tired. Your trip didn't do you much good.'

'Oh, I enjoyed myself, I think. A little.' I turned to go. 'The department knows about your Tunisian. You'll be careful, I hope. No mistakes. Nothing about me.'

She took my warning without expression and then kissed me gravely. 'For a while,' she said, 'I thought I had worked a miracle. I convinced myself I had brought the dead to life.'

My answering smile appeared to disturb her.

Going to Canada

I was ordered to Canada; that pie-dish of privilege and broken promises: to Toronto. My chief was uncomprehending when I showed disappointment. 'Canada! Everybody wants to go there.'

'I have stayed in Toronto before,' I told him.

He knew. He became suspicious, so I said that I had been joking. I chuckled to confirm this. His old, Great Russian face, moulded by the imposition of a dozen conflicting tyrannies, made a little mad smile. 'You are to look up Belko, an emigré. He is the only Belko in the phone book.'

Very well, Victor Andreyevitch.' I accepted the colourful paper wallet of tickets and money. This supply was an unusual one. My 'front' normally allowed me to be self-supporting. I work as an antique-dealer in the Portobello Road.

'Belko knows why you are meeting him. He will tell you what you have to know. It concerns some American planes, I gather.'

I shook hands and descended the green-carpeted stairs into the rain of East London.

During our Civil War many pretended to be Bolsheviks in order to terrorise local communities. After the war these people had continued as commissars. It had been their class which had gradually ousted most of the original Marxists. Stalin became their leader and examplar. My father had been a member of that embryonic aristocracy.

Like the order it had replaced, our aristocracy had been founded on banditry and maintained by orthodox piety. I was a younger son without much of a patrimony. Previously I might have gone into the priesthood or the army. I went into the modern combination of both, the KGB. The KGB was a far more conventional and congenial profession than most Westerners imagine. There I enjoyed myself first as a minor bureaucrat in a Moscow department, later as a special officer on one of our passenger ships plying between Leningrad and New York, Odessa and Sydney. Later still I became a plant in London where until recently I lived for twelve relatively uneventful years. I flattered myself that my background and character suited me to the role of a seedy near-alcoholic dealer in old furniture and over-priced bric-a-brac. It was believed that I was a Polish expatriate and indeed I had taken the name and British passport of just such an emigré; he had returned voluntarily to Poland on a whim and had sold his old identity to us in a perfectly amiable arrangement. We eased his way with the Cracow authorities who granted him new papers and found him a flat and a job.

In spite of changing regimes my own life had remained relatively untroubled. My name in London was Tomas Dobrowsky. For my private amusement I preferred the name of Tom Conrad. It was this name, in thirties 'modern' lettering, which adorned my shop. I paid taxes, VAT, and owned a TV licence. Although I had no particular desire to maintain my part forever, I enjoyed it for its complete lack of anxiety and the corresponding sense of security it gave me. Now that I was to return briefly to the real world, I should have to seek a fresh *context*.

A Russian citizen requires a *context*, because his conditioning makes him a permanent child. Anything will do. Therefore the *context* is often simple slavery. Even I, of Jewish Ukrainian extraction (through my grandmother), need that sense of boundaries. It is probably no coincidence that Kropotkin, founder of modern anarchism, was a Russian: his defiant views are directly opposed to our needs, which are on the whole of an authoritarian nature.

My father had been a naval petty officer. Later he became 'commissar' of a small town in Belorussia. He had eleven other deserting sailors with him when he had arrived in early 1918. They represented themselves as Bolsheviks. He had worn a leather jacket with two Mauser pistols in his belt and he had rarely taken off his sailor's peaked cap. Somehow the Civil War did not touch the town much, so the gang made the most of its time.

My father took five young girls from the local gymnasium for himself and gave the rest to his men. He instructed the girls in every debauchery. When the Civil War ended and it became obvious who had won, my father did not do away with the girls (as he might well have – it was common practice) but made them read to him from the works of Marx and Engels, from Lenin's writings, *Pravda* and *Izhvestia* until he and they were all familiar with the new dogma. Then he formed his thugs into the nucleus of the local Party, sent four of the girls (now fully-fledged Komsomol leaders) back to the gymnasium as teachers and married Vera Vladimirovna, my mother.

In time he was praised for his example to the community and was awarded a medal by the State. During the famines of the next few years he and my mother were never hungry. During the purges they never seemed to be in danger. They had two children, a boy and a girl.

In 1936 my father went off on Party business and in 1938 I was born. The young writer who begat me was subsequently sent to a camp and died. I had long considered myself the secret guardian of his blood. My father was in most respects a realist. He preferred to accept me as his own rather than risk the scandal of his name being associated with that of the writer. My older sister was killed in the War. My older brother became a hero during the Siege of Stalingrad. He ran a large power-plant near Smolensk on the Dnieper. He was a self-satisfied, right-thinking man.

'A little pain,' my mother used to say to her friends, 'makes good girls of us all.'

My father trained his girls to kiss his feet, his legs, his private parts, his arse. My mother was more wholehearted at this than her rivals, which is how he came to pick her as his wife. Again, she behaved in a Russian way. She was dutiful in all things, but, when his authority was absent, she became irresponsible. The Russian soul is a masochist's wounds. It is a frightening, self-indulgent, monumentally sentimental relinquishing of individual responsibility: it is schizophrenic. More than elsewhere, personal suffering is equated with virtue.

My grandmother was apparently raped by a young Jew and my mother was the result. The Jew was killed shortly afterwards, in a general pogrom resulting from the affair. That was in Ekaterinaslav province in the last years of the nineteenth century. My grandmother never would say for certain that it had been rape. I remember her winking at me when the word was mentioned. My great-uncle, the surviving brother of the dead man, told me that after the Revolution some Red Cossacks came to his shtetl. He was mortally afraid, of course, and would have done anything to stay alive. A Cossack named Konkoff billeted himself in my great-uncle's house. My great-uncle was mindless with terror, grovelling before the Cossack, ready to lick the soles off his boots at the first demand. Instead, Konkoff had laughed at him, offered him some rations, pulled him upright, patted him on the back and called him 'comrade'. My great-uncle realized that the revolution had actually changed things. He was no longer a detested animal. He had become a Cossack's pet Jew.

In Russia, in those days before the present War, there had been a resurgence of Nationalism, encouraged by the State. Because of the absence of real democratic power, many had turned (as they did under Tsarism) to Pan-Slavism. A direct consequence of this movement was anti-Semitism, also blessed unofficially by the State, and a spirit amongst our élite which, while not so unequivocally anti-Semitic, was reminiscent of the Black Hundreds or the Legion of the Archangel Michael, the early 20th century pogromists. It was obvious that the State equated radicalism with intellectual Jewish troublemakers. The State therefore encouraged – through the simple prejudices of its cunning but not considerably intelligent leaders – a movement in no way dissimilar to that which had followed the troubles of 1905, when Jewish socialists had been scapegoats for everything. Stalin had eliminated virtually the entire Jewish element of the Party, of course, by 1935.

When I was young it had been fashionable to scoff at the trappings of Nationalism – at folk costumes, at peasant blouses and so on. Outside of cultural exhibitions and performances these things were a sign of old-fashioned romanticism. They were not considered progressive. When I returned to Russia briefly in 1980 young people were walking the streets looking as if they had stepped out of a performance of *Prince Igor*. Even some of the younger leaders would on occasions be photographed in Cossack costume. Anti-Semitic books and paintings, even songs, received official patronage. The authoritarian republic had at last, in sixty years, managed to resemble in detail the autocracy it had replaced. Soon there would be no clear differences save that poverty and sickness had been abolished in the Slavic regions of the Union.

These benefits had been gained by relinquishing dignity and liberty, and the nobler forms of idealism which had given the early Revolution its rhetoric and its impetus. There were no longer any private arts. Everything had been sacrificed to formalized ceremonies similar to Church ritual or other primitive affirmations of superstition. The Soviet Union had codified and sanctified this terrifying impulse of human beings to shout reassuring lies to one another while standing with eyes tight shut on the brink of a chasm of reality. The State pretended that it was impossible (or at very least immoral) for such a chasm to exist. Soviet bureaucracy, too, formalized human failing and gave it shape and respectability; it did not merely accept this failing: it exalted it. I was as conditioned as anyone to believe that our lobotomizing methods of ordering the human condition were the most sensible. I had found all these aspects of Soviet life comforting and reassuring. I did not have the character necessary for the enjoyment of personal freedom.

Like the Celts, Russians have no ethical system as such, merely a philosophy of life based firmly on the dignity of pain, on fear of the unknown and suspicion of anything we cannot at once recognize. That is why Bolshevism was so attractive an ideology to many peasants who identified it with a benevolently modified Church and Monarchy and for a time believed that Lenin intended to restore the Tsar to his throne; it is why it was so quickly adapted to Russian needs and Russian methods. I do not disapprove of the government of the Soviet Union. I accept it as a necessity. In 1930, as a result of the bourgeois Revolution headed by Kerenski, and the Revolution initiated by the bourgeois Lenin, women and children were starving to death all over Russia. Stalin was at heart an Orthodox peasant. He and other Orthodox peasants saved Russia from the monster released upon the nation by foolish, middle-class idealists. In doing so he punished the Communists who had brought about the disaster; the intellectuals and fanatics who were truly to blame for our misfortunes.

Stalin took on the great burden and responsibilities of a Tsar and all his ministers. Stalin knew that History would revile him and that his followers would become cynical and cruel. He countered their cynicism and cruelty with the only weapon he was able to use: terror. He became mad. He was himself not a cynic. He made factories efficient. He gave us our industry, our education, our health service. He made homes clean and sanitary. He killed millions for the sake of all those other millions who would otherwise have perished. He made it possible for us to round, eventually, on Hitler and drive him back to Germany. He returned to us the security of our Empire. And when he died we destroyed his memory. He knew that we would and I believe that he understood that this would have to happen. He was a realist; but he possessed an Orthodox conscience and his conscience made him mad. I am a realist happily born of an age which countered and adapted Christianity and that is doubtless what continues to make me such a good and reliable employee of the Russian State.

Because of the increasingly strict controls applied to those who wished to travel to and from Canada, it was necessary for me to go to my doctor for a medical certificate. I used a fashionable private doctor in South Kensington who was quick to prescribe the drugs I required. In his waiting-room I found three young women wearing the elaborate and violent make-up and costume then favoured by the British demi-monde. They were whispering together in a peculiar way common only to whores and nuns, full of sudden shifts of volume and tone and oblique reference, glances and gestures, so I only heard snatches of their conversation.

'I was doing this job, you know – straight . . . At the club. He said he wanted me to work for him – you know – so I said I wouldn't – he said to go out with him – but I wouldn't – he was a funny guy, you know – he gave me this –' A bandaged arm was held up. It was a soft arm in a soft dress. 'He had a bottle, you know – they called the cops – they're prosecuting – his lawyer phoned me and offered me thirty thousand to settle out of court . . .'

'Settle,' advised one of the other girls.

'I would,' said the second.

'But my lawyer says we can get fifty.'

'Settle for thirty.'

'He gave me seventeen stitches.' All this was relayed in a neutral, almost self-satisfied tone. 'What you doing here, anyway?'

'I just came with her,' said the prettiest. 'It's about her pills.'

'I came to get my slimming pills changed. Those others make me feel really sick, you know.'

'What! Durophets?'

'Yeah. They make me feel terrible.'

'What you going to ask him for? Terranin?'

'They're what I use,' said her friend.

'They're much better,' agreed the wounded whore. 'You're looking different,' she told the girl's friend. 'I wouldn't have recognized you. You're looking terrible.'

They all laughed.

'Did you know what happened to Mary?' She put her mouth close to the girl's ear and began to whisper rapidly.

The doctor's receptionist opened the door. 'You can go in now, Miss Williams.'

' . . . all over the bed,' finished Miss Williams, rising and following the receptionist.

When she had gone the other two began to discuss her in a disinterested fashion, as if they followed some unconscious habit. Neither, it emerged, believed that thirty thousand pounds had been offered. 'More like three,' said one. They, too, were not at all outraged by the event. Most whores are frightened of any demonstration of passion, which is why they choose masters who treat them coldly. I had for a short while been in charge of a whore-house in Greece and had learned how to deal with the girls who were conditioned to confuse love with fear. If they were afraid of their master they thought they loved him. Because they were not afraid of their clients they could not love them and in the main felt contempt for them. But it was self-contempt they actually felt. I remembered with some dismay the singlemindedness of such girls who pursued persecution and exploitation as an anodyne, as their customers often pursued sexual sensation; who learned to purchase the favours of their employers with the very money they received from the hire of their own bodies. My spell as a whore-master had been the only time I had tasted direct power and it had taken every ounce of self-discipline to administer; it was a relief to become what I now was.

Miss Williams rejoined her friends. 'I'm going to have it photographed this afternoon,' she told them, pulling down her sleeve.

The two girls went in to the doctor. They came out. All three left together.

I was next in the surgery. The doctor smiled at me. 'More trouble?'

I shook my head.

'The penicillin worked?'

'Yes.'

'It's funny that. Acts like a shot on you, won't touch me. Well, what's the trouble?' He spoke rapidly in a high-pitched voice. He was a Jew.

'None. I just need a certificate to say I'm not suffering from anything a Canadian's likely to catch.'

He laughed. 'That depends on you, doesn't it?' He was already reaching for his pad of forms. 'Canada, eh? Lucky you.'

He filled in the form swiftly and handed it to me. 'Going for long?'

'I don't think so,' I said.

'Business?'

'Believe it or not, we're buying our antiques from North America these days.' It was true.

'No! Really?' He was amused. He stood up as I stood up. He leaned across his desk to shake hands. 'Well, good luck. Enjoy yourself.'

'I will.'

I left his surgery and began to walk up Kensington Church Street, passing the three girls who were waiting on the kerb for a taxi. One of them looked very much like the girl who had given me the disease. I wondered if she would recognize me as I went by. But she was too deep in conversation to notice, even though I walked to within an inch or two of her shoulder, close enough to identify her heavy perfume.

*

The morning of the day I was due to take the overnight plane from Gatwick (it was a budget flight) I read the news of a border clash between China and India, but I did not give it too much attention. The Russo-Indian Pact had been signed the previous year, in Simla, and I believed that the Chinese would take the pact seriously. By the afternoon the radio news reported Moscow's warnings to Peking. When I left for Gatwick on the train from Victoria, I bought an evening paper. I had begun to consider the possibility of war between Russia and China. The evening news was vague and told me no more than had the radio news. On the plane, which took off on schedule, I watched a Walt Disney film about two teenage girls who seemed to be twins.

I reached Toronto at eleven o'clock in the evening, local time, took a taxi to a downtown hotel and turned on the television to discover that Confederation troops and tanks were invading China while Indian forces, with some British and American divisions already stationed there, were moving towards the Chinese border. A newsflash brought the information that both CIS and EC countries had lent their support to India and that China and her allies were expected to capitulate very soon.

Early the next day I found myself in a pleasant suburban street of tall, Victorian wooden houses, birch-trees and maples and soft lawns, ringing the bell of my contact, Mr Belko. An angry girl, a pudgy seventeen, came to the door. She was wearing a blue dressing gown.

'Mr Belko is expecting me,' I told her.

She was triumphant. 'Mr Belko left an hour ago.'

'Where did he go? Would you mind?'

'To the airport. Hadn't you heard? It's World War Three!'

For a moment I was amused by the inevitability of her remark; the assumption, moreover, of the inevitable event.

'You look beat,' she said. 'Are you a diplomat?'

'Not really.'

She grew to feeling guilty. 'Come in and have some coffee.'

'I accept. Thank you.'

Her mother was at breakfast in the large, modern kitchen. 'Dubrowski,' I said, removing my hat. 'I am so sorry . . .'

'Vassily's left. Janet told you?'

'Yes.' I unbuttoned my overcoat. Janet took it. I thanked her. I sat down at the table. I was brought a cup of that Western coffee which smells so good but does not taste of anything. I drank it.

'Was it important?' asked Janet's mother.

'Well . . .'

'To do with the crisis?'

I was not sure. I waved a palm.

'Well,' said Janet's mother, 'you're lucky to be here, that's all I can say.'

'You think there will be a full-scale war?' I accepted sugar from the young girl's hands.

'Let them fight it out,' said Janet's mother. 'Get it over with.'

'It will involve Canada.'

Janet's mother buttered some toast. 'Not directly.'

'Are you Ukrainian, too?' said Janet.

'Too?'

'We're Ukrainians.' Janet sat down beside me. I became aware of her warmth. 'Or at least momma and poppa are.'

I looked at the woman in the housecoat with her dyed red hair, her make-up, her American way of slouching against the table. I wondered if I were not enduring some kind of complicated test.

'I came over in 1947,' said Janet's mother. 'From England. We'd been deported during the German occupation and when the allies arrived we managed to get to England. Fedya was born here. Are you Ukrainian?'

I began to laugh a little. It was a feeble titter, but it was the first spontaneous expression of emotion I had had in years. 'Yes,' I said. 'I am.'

'We haven't really stayed in touch much,' said Janet's mother, 'with the Community here, you know. Janet's been to some meetings. She sees more of the old people than we do. She's a Nationalist, aren't you, dear?'

'Convinced,' said Janet.

'Canadian,' I asked, 'or Ukrainian?' I was genuinely confused.

Janet took this well. She put youthful fingers on my sleeve. 'Both,' she said.

When I returned to my hotel I found a note telling me to go to our embassy. At the embassy I was ordered to fly direct to Moscow on the next Aeroflot flight. There I would be briefed about my new role. By the time I reached Moscow, Allied troops were already withdrawing from China and an agreement was being negotiated in the United Nations. I was given a Ukrainian passport and told to return to London.

My brief stay in Moscow had made me homesick. I would have been grateful for a holiday in the country for a week or two. I have yet to have my dream fulfilled. A month after I got back, the real War broke and I, in common with so many others, began to taste the euphoria of Armageddon.

Leaving Pasadena

I was asked by the woman why I had no pity. She sat on the floor, her elbow resting upon a couch, her head in her hand. She had not wept. Her anguish had tempered her eyes: they glittered with unvoiced needs. I could not touch her. I could not insult her with my compassion. I told her that pity was an inappropriate emotion. Our world was burning and there was no time for anything but rapid action. Africa and Australia were already gone. The clouds and the contamination were a matter of anxiety to those who survived. She told me, in slow, over-controlled syllables, that she was probably dying. She needed love, she said. I told her she should find someone, therefore, whose needs matched her own. My first loyalty was to my unit. I could not reach my hand to her. Any gesture would have been cruel.

The other two women came into the room. One had my bag. 'You still don't know where you're going?' said the blonde, Julia. Her fashionably garish cosmetics appeared to give her face the lustre and texture of porcelain.

I turned my back and walked into the hallway. 'Not yet.'

Julia said: 'I'll try to look after her.'

As I got to the front door of the apartment, the brown-haired woman, Honour, said: 'You pious bastard.' She wore no make-up. Her face was as pale as Julia's.

I accepted her accusation. I had at that moment nothing left but piety and I would not dignify it with words. I nodded, shook hands with them both. I heard her mumbling some despairing question from the room, then I had walked down the white steps of the Pasadena condominium, crossed the courtyard with its silenced fountain, its poised cherubs, brilliant in the sun, and entered the car which had been sent to collect me. I was leaving California. That was all I had been told.

My chief had a rented house in Long Beach, near the marina. We drove to it through avenues of gigantic palms until we reached the almost deserted freeway. Vehicles kept well apart, considering the others warily. Only government people had official driving permits;

anyone else could be psychotic or a criminal.

Long Beach was still populated. There were even people sailing their yachts into the harbour. The Pacific threat seemed to bother the people only as much as they had been bothered by the threat of earthquakes. The houses were low and calm, divided by shrubs and trees, with neat grass. I saw a man riding a pony across his lawn. He waved sardonically at the car. Groups of women stared at the limousine with expressions of contempt. We found my chief's house. The chauffeur went to tell him we were there. He came out immediately.

As he stopped to join me, the chief said: 'You look bad. You should sleep more.'

I told him, dutifully, about the woman. He was sympathetic. 'There's a war on. It's how it is in War.' Naturally, I agreed with him. 'We are fighting for their good, after all,' he added.

We drove to a military airfield. Both Soviet and U.S. planes were there. We went immediately to our Ilyushin, and had scarcely settled in the uncomfortable seats before we took off.

My chief handed me a passport. It had my real name and a recent photograph. 'You're officially with the liaision staff, at last,' he said. 'It means you can report either to the Americans or to us. Nothing will be kept back. Matters are too urgent now.' I expressed appropriate surprise.

I looked down on Los Angeles; its beaches, its fantasies. It was like setting aside a favourite story as a child. We headed inland over mountains, going East.

'The Third World War has already been fought,' said my chief, 'in the third world, as the Americans call it. Why else would they call it that? This is actually the Fifth World War.'

'What was the Fourth?' I asked.

'It was fought in the country of the soul.'

I laughed. I had forgotten his sentimentality. 'Who won?'

'Nobody. It merely prepared us for this.'

There were clouds beneath us. It seemed to become calm as the altitude encouraged deafness. I could hardly hear his next remark: 'It has sharpened our wits and deadened our emotional responses. War is a great relief, eh? A completely false sense of objectivity. The strain to remain grown-up is too much for most of us.'

It was familiar stuff from him. I unfastened my seat-belt and walked clumsily along the plane to where a Cossack sergeant served at a small bar. I ordered some of the Finnish vodka we had recently acquired. I drank the glass down and returned to my place. Four high-ranking officers in tropical uniforms were arguing in the seats behind me. One of them was of the opinion that we should begin full-scale rocket attacks on major Chinese cities. The others were for caution. The bombing had, after all, been stopped. Most of the civilized countries were still unharmed.

My chief began coughing. It was that dry noise usually associated with smoke inhalation. He recovered himself and in answer to my concerned expression told me that he was probably getting a cold. 'We should be in Washington soon. All this travelling about is bad for the constitution.' He shrugged. 'But life is never easy. Even in wartime.'

An official car met us at the airport. It bore the arms of the President. We passed the monstrous neo-classical buildings which celebrated that naive 18th century rationalism we all now regretted and from which we seemed to be suffering at present. We arrived at a modern block of government offices. In the elevator my chief told me not to show surprise at whatever we discussed. He believed that we were thought to know more than we had actually been told.

A bland, smooth-faced man in a light-coloured suit introduced himself as Mansfield and offered us deep, black chairs. He asked us about our journey, about California, and told us of the people living along the West Coast. 'People learn to identify their homes with their security. When something like this happens . . . Well, we all know about the Jews refusing to leave Germany.'

'Your newspapers contradict themselves,' said my chief. He smiled. 'They say there is little to fear.'

'True.' Mansfield offered us Lucky Strike cigarettes which we accepted. My chief coughed a little before he took a light.

'We think you'll have more success in Venezuela.'

Mansfield returned the lighter to his desk. 'They are suspicious of our motives, naturally.'

'And not of ours?' My chief continued to smile.

'They could believe your arguments better. They are not too sure if the alliance will maintain itself. You might be able to persuade them.'

'Possibly.'

'They can't stay neutral much longer.'

'Why not?'

'Because someone will attack them.'

'Then perhaps we should wait until that happens. It would be easier to liberate them, eh?'

'We need their oil. This freeze of theirs is pointless. It does nobody any good.'

'And why do you want us to go?'
'The Russians?'
'No.' My chief waved a hand at me. 'Us.'
'We have to contact their intelligence first. After that the politicians can sort things out.'
'You've made arrangements?'
'Yes. It was thought best not to meet in Caracas. You'll go to Maracaibo. It's where the oil is, anyway. Most of their oil people want to sell. We're not certain of the attitudes you'll find, but we understand that there is a lot of pressure from that side.'
'You have material for us?'
Mansfield lifted a folder from his desk and showed it to us.
Although my chief seemed to be taking the meeting seriously, I began to wonder at the vagueness of its content. I suspected that our going to Maracaibo would have no effect at all. We were going because it was something to do.

I resisted an urge, when we reached our hotel in Maracaibo, to telephone the woman and ask how she was. It would do her no good, I decided, for her to hear from me. I knew that, in other circumstances, I would have loved her. She had done me several favours in the course of my work, so I was also grateful to her. The sense of gratitude was the only indulgence I allowed myself.
My chief walked through the connecting door into my room. He rubbed his eyebrows. 'I have a meeting with a member of their intelligence. A colonel. But it is to be a one to one thing. You're free to do what you like this evening. I have the name of a house.'
'Thank you.' I wrote down the address he gave me.
'It will do you good,' he said. He was sympathetic. 'And one of us might as well enjoy the pleasures of the town. I hear the whores are of a high quality.'
'I am much obliged to you.' I would go, I thought, only because I had no wish to stay in my room the whole time. His giving me leave confirmed my suspicion that there was no real reason for us being in Maracaibo.
The town, with its skyscrapers and remnants of Spanish-style architecture, was well-lit and relatively clean. I had once been told that 'Venezuela is the future'. They had been experimenting with different energy sources, using their oil income to develop systems which would not be much dependant on oil. But Maracaibo seemed very little different, save that the lake itself, full of machinery and rigging, occasionally gave off mysterious puffs of flame which would illuminate

buildings and create uncertain shadows. There was a stink of oil about the place. As I walked, local map in hand, to the address my chief had given me I saw one of their airships, built by a British firm at Cardington, sail into the darkness beyond the city. Venezuela had been perhaps the last country to associate romance with practical engineering.

I reached the house. It was large and fairly luxurious. The decor was comfortable and lush in the manner of some of the more grandiose family restaurants I had visited in Pasadena. There was a pianist playing similar music to his American counterpart. There was a bar. I sat down and ordered a Scotch. I was approached by a pretty hostess who wore a blonde wig. Her skin was dark and her smile was wide and seemed genuine. In English she said that she thought she had seen me there before. I told her that this was only my second visit to Maracaibo. She asked if I were Swedish. I said that I was Russian. She kissed me and said that she loved Russian people, that they knew how to enjoy themselves. 'Lots of vodka,' she said. But I was drinking Scotch; was I an emigré? I said, from habit, that I was. Her name was Anna. Her father, she said, had been born in South London. Did I know London? Very well, I said. I had lived there for some years. Anna wondered if Brixton were like Maracaibo. I said there were some similarities. We look for formaliarity in the most unlikely circumstances before we accept what is strange to us. It is as true of travellers as it is of lovers.

Anna brought a girl for me. She had fine black hair tied back from her face; a white dress with a great deal of lace. She looked about sixteen. Her make-up was subtle. She pretended to be shy. I found her appealing. Her name was Maria, she told me. She spoke excellent English with an American accent. I bought her a drink, expecting to go to her room, but she said she would like to take me home, if that suited me. I decided against caution. She led me outside and we drove in a taxi to a street of what seemed to be quiet, middle-class apartment buildings. We climbed two flights of stairs. She opened a well-polished wooden door with her key and we entered an apartment full of quality furniture in subdued good taste. I began to suspect I had been picked up by a schoolgirl and that this was her parents' home. But the way she moved in it, getting me another Scotch, switching on the overhead fan, taking my jacket, convinced me that she was the mistress of the place. Moreover, I knew that she was actually older than sixteen; that she cultivated the appearance of a teenager. I began to experience a reluctance to go to bed with her. Against my will I remembered the woman in Pasadena. I forced myself towards that belief that all women were, after all, the same, that it satisfied them to give themselves up to a man. The whore, at least, would make money from her instincts. The woman in Pasadena came by nothing but pain. We went into the bedroom and undressed. In the large and comfortable white bed I eventually confessed that I was in no haste to make love to her. I had been unable to adjust my mood. I asked her why she had shaved her pubic hair. She said that it increased her own pleasure and besides many men found it irresistible. She began to tell me her story. She had been, she said, in love with the man who introduced her to prostitution. Evidently she was still obsessed by him, because it required no great expression of interest from me for her to tell me the whole story. It was familiar enough. What she said, of course, was couched in the usual sort of sentimentality and romanticism. She mentioned love a great deal and her knowledge that, although he did not say so, he really loved her and cared for her and it was only right, because she loved him, that he should be allowed to be the way he was. He had many other girls, including, I gathered, a wife. Initially Maria had, in the manner of despairing women, attempted to make of herself an improved piece of capital: she had dyed her hair, shaved her pubis, painted her face and nails. The girl-whore is always highly valued wherever one goes in the world. I gathered that while the man had appreciated the gesture he had told her that he intended to continue seeing other women. All this was depressing, for I was never particularly interested in economics. I found myself moralizing a trifle. I told her that maturity and self-possession were in the end more attractive qualities to me. They guaranteed me a certain kind of freedom based on mutually accepted responsibility. She did not understand a word, of course. I added that a woman's attempts to use a man as her context were thoroughly understood by me. I had my loyalties. But, like most men, I was not able to be either a woman's nation or her cause. Maria made some attempt to rouse me and then fell back. She said that it was her bad luck to pick up a bore. She had thought I would be interesting. She added that she did not feel she could charge me much. I was amused. I got up and telephoned the hotel. The chief had not yet returned. I said that I would stay longer in that case. She said that she would enjoy my company, but I would have to be more entertaining. Eventually I achieved a reasonable state of mind and made love to her. She was soft, yielding and foul-mouthed. She was able to bring me to a more than satisfactory orgasm. As I left, she insisted that I telephone her the next day if I could. I agreed that I would if it were at all possible.

My chief was jovial when we breakfasted together in his room. 'We have at least a week here,' he said. 'There are subtleties. These people are worse than the Arabs.'

I reported the girl. He shrugged. 'You have nothing to reveal. Even if it is some kind of strategy, they would be wasting their time.'

I had the impression that he had brought me here on holiday. In the outside world, the news was not good. A bomb had landed somewhere in India and no-one was absolutely certain where it had come from. No major city had been hit. This was not acceptable warfare, said my chief. War was supposed to cut down on ambiguities.

I telephoned the girl from the breakfast table. I arranged to see her for lunch.

We ate in a smart restaurant at the top of a modern tower. There was mist on the lake and Maracaibo was covered in pale gold light. She wore a red suit with a matching hat. She was gentle and obviously amused by what she saw as my stiffness. She had a way of making me relax. Naturally, I resisted falling too much under her spell.

After lunch, she took us to a quay. Several men in tattered nautical clothes called to her. She spoke to one of them and then we had climbed down into a small, elegant motorboat. She started the engine, took the wheel, and we rode out into the mist.

I asked her what her man thought of all this. She became gay. 'He doesn't care.'

'But you are making no money.'

'It's not really like that,' she said. 'He's kind, you know. Or can be.'

The whole episode had the character of a lull in a singularly bad storm. I could not entirely rid my mind of the knowledge of the woman in Pasadena, but I could think of no better way of spending my time. Maria steered the boat inexpertly past a series of oil derricks which stood in the water like stranded and decapitated giraffes. A breeze began to part the mist. I had the impression of distant mountains.

She stopped the engine and we embraced. She suggested that we fuck. 'It's always been an ambition of mine,' she said.

I did my best, but the boat was uncomfortable and my body was too tired. I eventually brought her to orgasm with my mouth. She seemed more than contented. After a while she got up and returned to the wheel. 'You look happier,' she said. 'So do you,' I replied. I was hard put not to feel affection for her. But that sense of affection did me no good because it recalled the woman in Pasadena. I began to tell her a joke about the War. Some Chinese commandos had entered what they thought was Indian territory and completely destroyed one of their own bases. She became serious. 'Will the War reach Venezuela?'

'Almost certainly,' I said. 'Unless a few people come to their senses. But there has been no true catharsis yet.'

She asked me what I meant. I said: 'No orgasm, eh?'

'My God,' she said.

On the quay, we agreed to meet at the same spot that evening. 'I want to show you the lake at night.' She looked up suddenly and pointed. There was a soft sound of engines. It was another airship, white and painted with the Venezuelan military colours. Reassessed technology was to have been the salvation of the world. Now this country would be lucky if it escaped complete destruction. I said nothing of this to Maria.

When I was first ordered to work abroad I felt I was going into exile. The territory was unfamiliar, offering dangers I could not anticipate. I saw Maria to her taxi and walked back to my hotel. For some reason I was reminded, perhaps by a sign or a face on the street, of the strange suburb-ghetto of Watts, where everyone lived better than almost anyone in the Soviet Union. It had amused me to go there. They had food stamps: the young have never known a breadline. One had hoped to match America. Before the War, we were only a short distance behind on the road to discontented capitalism. Beyond that was anarchy, which cannot appeal to me, although I know it was supposed to have been our goal.

I bought a Polish-language newspaper. It was over a week old and I could barely understand the references. The newspaper was published in New York. But I enjoyed the feel of the print. I read it as I lay in my bath. My chief telephoned. He sounded drunk. It occurred to me that he, too, believed himself to be on vacation. He told me that I was free for the evening.

Maria had two friends with her when I arrived at the quay. They were both some years older than she and wore the sort of heavy 'forties make-up which had been fashionable a few years previously in the West. Their cotton dresses, one pink and one yellow, followed the same style, as did their hair. They wore very strong perfume and looked like versions of Rita Hayworth. They were far more self-conscious than Maria. She said they spoke little English and apologized for bringing them along. Her explanation was vague, consisting mainly of shrugs and raised brows. I made no objection. I was content to enjoy the close presence of so much femininity.

Once again, Maria drove us out into the twilight. The water seemed to brighten as it became blacker. The two older women sat together behind Maria and myself. They produced some Mexican Tequila and passed the bottle. Soon we were all fairly drunk. When Maria stopped the boat in the middle of the lake again, we all rolled together in one another's arms. I realized that this was part of Maria's plan. Another fantasy she wished to experience. I allowed the women to have their way with me, although I was not of much use to them. It gave me considerable pleasure to watch them making love. Maria took no part in this, but observed and directed, giggling the whole time. The unreality was disarming. The situation was no stranger than the situation in the world at large. It seemed that I moved from one dream to another and that this dream, given the cheerfulness of everyone involved, was preferable to the rest. I knew now that Maria felt safe with me, because I controlled my emotions so thoroughly and because I was a stranger. I knew that I was proving of help to her and this made me happy. I thought of warning her that in seeking catharsis through her sexuality she could lose touch with the source of her feelings, lose her lovers, lose her bearings, but it did not seem to matter. With the War threatening to become more widespread our futures were all so thoroughly in doubt that we might as well enjoy what we could of the present.

Several days and nights passed. Each time we met, Maria would propose another sexual escapade and I would agree. My own curiosity was satisfied, as was my impulse to believe myself of use to someone. My chief continued to be drunk and wave me on, even when I reported exactly what was happening. As I grew to know her better I believed that she was desperately anxious to become a woman, to escape the form of security in which she now found herself. Her need for instantaneous maturity, her greedy reaching for experience, however painful, was in itself childish. She had indulged herself and been indulged for so long that her means of achieving liberty were crude and often graceless. And yet liberty, maturity might gradually come to her, earned through trauma and that feminine willingness to find fulfillment in despair. There was no doubt that her activities, her attitudes, disguised a considerable amount of despair and emotional confusion. I wondered if I were not exploiting her, even though superficially she seemed to be exploiting me. We were, I determined, merely making reasonble use of one another's time. And in the meanwhile, I recalled, there was the figure of her protector, Ramirez. He presumably knew what was happening, just as my chief knew. I began to feel a certain fondness for him, a certain gratitude. I told Maria that I should like to meet him. This did not appeal to her, but she said she would let him know what I had said. I told her that I would let her know when I was leaving, so that the meeting, if it occurred, could be on my last night. I also warned her that I might be forced to leave suddenly. She said that she had guessed this. On one level, I realized, I was asking her to give up the only power she had. I made some drunken remarks about people who surround themselves with ambiguity in order to maintain their course. They are eventually trapped by the conditions they have created, become confused and begin to question almost every aspect of their own judgement. I felt a certain amount of self-disgust after this statement. I had no business offering Maria a moral education. But political habits are hard to lose.

Puzzled, she told me that she thought Ramirez meant security for her. Yet she knew that she had no desire to marry him. She would not be happy if, tomorrow, he came to her and offered her his all. We laughed together at this. Women marry for security, I remarked, while men often marry merely for the promise of regular sex. The man is inclined to keep his side of the marriage bargain because it is fairly clear. But the woman, having no idea of what the bargain was, is baffled when the man complains.

'Are all marriages like that?' she asked. She had doubtless had many customers who had verified this. I said no, not all. I knew of several very satisfactory marriages. By and large, however, in countries where political or religious orthodoxy held sway, sexual relationships became extremely confused. Again I had lost her. I became bored with my own simplifications. As we made love, I found myself desperately yearning for the woman in Pasadena.

Maria began to speak more and more of Ramirez. I was now a confessor. From what she said I formed an opinion of him. He was tight-fisted but had made his caution and lack of generosity into a creed so that it sometimes seemed he was expressing self-discipline and neutrality, whereas he was actually indulging himself absolutely. As a result he had begun to fail in business (her flat was threatened), partly through an inability to risk capital, partly through the loss of nerve which comes when security is equated with material goods and well-being. His was a typical dilemma of the middle-class, but she had no way of knowing that since she had spent most of her life in a working class or bohemian environment. This materialism extended into his sex-life, as is so frequently the case: he hoped to get something for nothing if he could (his life was a series of deals) but expected a good return on any expenditure. He was attractive, boyish and emotionally somewhat naive. These qualities appealed, needless to say, to many women, not all of them childless. He was easily understood and fairly easy to manipulate. Moreover, the woman had some sense of control over the relationship, for such men can also be, on certain levels, highly impressionable: they are nearly all ego. However, his inability, ultimately, to accept responsibility either for himself or others, made him a frustrating partner and his relationships were inclined to deteriorate after a period in which some reform had been attempted on him and he had become resentful. We are changed only by circumstance, never by will alone. She had, for her part, she said, accepted him gladly for what he was. He was better than most, and more interesting. He was not a fool. Neither am I, I found myself saying. She shook her head. 'No. You are a big fool. It is why I'm fond of you.' I was astonished.

News came from my chief early that morning that we were due to return to the United States the next day. I saw Maria for lunch and said that I should like to see Ramirez. She made me swear that I was leaving and then arranged to meet later at the quay.

From the quayside we went to a nearby bar. It was an ordinary place, dark and a little seamy. Maria knew many of the regulars particularly the women, whom she kissed. Ramirez arrived. He wore a good suit of dark blue cloth and I was surprised that he was bearded and had spectacles. He shook hands. His flesh was a little soft and his grasp feminine. He said that he was not sure why he had come, except 'I can resist no request from Maria'. We had several strong drinks. We took the motor boat out into the lake. It was a warm night. He removed his jacket but not his waistcoat and asked me if I sniffed cocaine. I said that I did. As he prepared the drug on a small hand-mirror he informed me that he was Maria's master and allowed her sometimes, as in this case, to play with other men: I should go away now or I might find myself the subject of either blackmail or violence. I was amused when I realized that Maria was deceiving him. I decided to play her game as best I could. I told him that I had run whores in Greece and that I knew he did not possess the character of a true ponce. He was not insulted. We took the cocaine. It was of the best quality. I complimented him. 'You understand me, however,' he said. I did not reply until we returned to the harbour. When we were out of the boat and standing together, Maria on my right, Ramirez beside the open door of his car, I threatened him with death. I told him that I was an agent of the KGB. He became nervous, made no comment, got into his car and left. Maria, on the way home, was disturbed. She asked me what she was going to do. I told her that she was free to take a number of choices. She said she needed money. I gave her some. We stayed together in her flat through the rest of that night and in the morning drove the boat onto the lake again. When Maracaibo disappeared and we seemed alone in the middle of the still, blue water, she took out a small packet of cocaine and, steadying her thin body against a seat, carefully cut two lines on her compact mirror. I took the first, through an American ten dollar bill. She paused before sniffing half the line into one nostril, half into the other. She smiled at me, weary and intimate. 'Well?'

'You'll go back to Ramirez?'

'Not if I can stay at an hotel.'

'And if you stay at an hotel?'

'I can earn some money. Could you help me get to America?'

'At present? You're safer here.'

'But could you?'

'Only on terms I do not wish to make. I repeat, you're better off here.'

'Really?'

'Believe me.'

Her dark eyes looked away into the lake. 'The future is no better than the past.'

I guessed that within a week she would be back with Ramirez; within a year she would be free of him. I started the engine and headed towards the reality of the rigs and refineries. I told Maria that I knew she would survive, if there were any luck in the world at all. She had none of that self-involved sexuality which contains in it a peculiar coldness: the more it is indulged, the more the coldness grows. One meets libertines whose lives are devoted to sex and yet who have gradually lost any sexual generosity. Certain women are the same. They cease to celebrate and come more and more to control. It is the inevitable progress of rationalized romance, as I knew well.

In the hotel my chief notified me suddenly that he was dying. He wanted me, eventually, to go to Kiev as liaison officer with a Cossack regiment. 'I think it's the best I can offer you,' he said. He added that his will-power had failed him. I asked him if he were suffering from radiation poisoning. He said that he was. He would be returning to Long Beach for a short while, but I could stay in Washington if I wished. I would be allowed some leave. I could not begin to guess at the manipulation and persuasion he had exerted in order to gain us both so much time, but I was grateful to him and indicated as much. I had decided, I said, to return to Pasadena.

'Good,' he said. 'We can take the same plane.'

I decided not to telephone ahead but went directly from Burbank airport to Pasadena. Los Angeles was quieter than ever, though there was now some evidence of desertion and vandalism. Most of the cars on the freeways were police vehicles. As I drove my rented Toyota towards the richer suburbs I was stopped twice and had my papers checked. Now, in the current situation, it had become an advantage in America to possess a Soviet passport and KGB identification.

I drove off the freeway onto South Orange. The wide, palm-shaded streets seemed without texture or density after Maracaibo. A thin dream. Pasadena was a geometrical kindergarten vision of security. Only downtown, amongst the bricks and stones of the original settlement, and at the railroad station, was there a sense of complexity at all, and that was the complexity of any small American rural town. I yearned for Europe, for London and its mysterious, claustrophobic streets.

I parked in the communal garages, took my bag from the back seat and walked along the neat crazy-paving to the end block of the condominium. Like so much Los Angeles building it was less than ten years old and beginning to show signs of decay beneath the glaring white glaze. I walked up the steps, glad of the shade, and rang the bell on the right of the double doors. I stopped and picked up a folded newspaper, surprised that there were still deliveries. Julia's voice came from the other side of the doors. I said who it was. She seemed delighted. 'You came back. This is wonderful. She's been in a bad way.' I felt as if, unknowingly, I had reaffirmed Julia's faith in the entire human race. Some of us have such a terrible desire for a decent world that we will clutch at the tiniest strand of evidence for its existence and reject all other proof to the contrary. Julia looked tired. Her hair was disordered.

I unbuttoned my light raincoat and handed it to her. I pushed my suitcase under a small table which sat against the wall of the entrance hall.

'Honour went back to Flagstaff,' said Julia. She looked rueful. 'Just as well. She didn't think a lot of you.'

'I enjoyed her candour,' I said.

The woman knew I had arrived but she continued to sit at the easel we had erected together in the large front room. Light fell on a half-finished landscape, on her thinning, ash-blonde hair, on her pastel skin. She was more delicate, more beautiful, yet still I checked myself against the sensation of love for her.

'Why are you here?' She spoke in a low voice. She began to turn, resisting hope, looking at me as if I might wound her afresh. 'The War isn't over.'

I gestured with the newspaper. 'Apparently not.'

'This is too much,' she said.

I told her that I had decided to take a leave. Nobody but my chief knew where I was and he had made up some story about my need to go underground with a group of radical pacifists.

'Your people won't believe that.'

'Our structure is so rigid it can be resisted only by the most audacious means,' I said, 'and then often very successfully. It is probably one of the few advantages of orthodoxy.'

'You're full of bullshit, as ever,' she said. 'You can't do what you did to me a second time. I'd kill myself.'

I moved close to her so that my chest was on a level with her lovely head. We did not embrace. She did not look as grey or as drawn as she had when she had first been given confirmation of her illness. As she looked up at me I was impressed with her gentle beauty. She was at once noble and pathetic. Her eyes began to fill with tears. One fell. She apologized. I told her there was no need. I touched her shoulder, her cheek. She began to speak my name several times, holding tightly to my hand.

'You don't look well,' she said. 'You were afraid you would go crazy, weren't you?'

'I am not going to go mad,' I told her. 'I often wish that I could. This state of control is a kind of madness, isn't it? Perhaps more profoundly insane that any other kind. But it has none of the appeal of irresponsibility, of giving up any sense of others, which the classic lunatic experiences.' I laughed. 'So it has no advantages.'

'What about your duty?'

'To the War?'

'Or your cause, or whatever.'

'Excellent excuses.'

'What's more important?'

I drew a breath. 'I don't know. Affection?'

'You've changed your mind. Your rationale. Your logic.'

'I had to simplify.'

'Now?'

'I am defeated. I can no longer maintain it. Things remain as perplexing as ever.'

'What are you saying?'

I shrugged. 'Love conquers all?'

'Not you!' She shook her head.

'I do not know,' I said, 'what the truth is. It has been my duty to lie and to counter lies. Duty allows this, demands it. The only other truth for me is the truth of my feelings, my cravings, and senses. Anything else is hypocrisy, self-deception. At best it is a sentimental rationale. We are all moved by self-interest.'

'But sometimes self-interest takes on a broader form,' she said. 'And that is when we become human. Why are you here?'

'To see you. To be with you.'

'We'll lie down,' she said. 'We'll go to bed.'

The bed was very large. The place had belonged to her parents. Now they were in Iowa where they believed themselves to be safer. We undressed and I took her in my arms. We kissed. Her body was warm and still strong. We did not make love, but talked, as we always had. I told her that I did not know the meaning of love and that what had brought me back to her was a sense that the alternatives were less tolerable to me. I told her that a mixture of sentimentality and power politics had been the nearest substitute for love I had been able to afford in my circumstances. Altruism was a luxury. She said that she believed it a necessity. Without altruism there was no virtue in human existence, therefore if one rejected it one also rejected the only rationale for the race's continuation. Could that be why I was now on leave from the War?

I praised her for her fine fundamentalism and said that I regretted my inability to live according to such principles. She told me that it was not difficult: one did not take extra responsibility – one relinquished power and in doing that one also relinquished guilt. The very idea, I told her humorously, was terrifying to the Russian soul. Without guilt there was no movement at all! She shook her head at what she called my cynicism, my self-contempt. I said that I preferred to think I had my own measure.

I got out of bed and went into the hall. From my bag I took a pendant I had bought for her in Maracaibo. I came back and presented it to her. She looked at it and thanked me bleakly. She set it aside. 'You'll never be free, then?' she said. 'I believe not,' I said. It was too late for that.

She rose and put on a robe, walking with her hands folded beneath her breasts into the room she used as a studio. 'Love and art wither without freedom.' She stared at a half-finished portrait stacked against the wall. I seemed much older in the picture. 'I suppose so,' I said. But I was in the business of politics which, by definition, was opposed both to lovers and to artists. They were factors which always would over-complicate the game and cause enormous frustrations in those of us who preferred, by temperament, to simplify the world as much as possible.

'You've always found my reasoning stupidly romantic, haven't you?' she said. She discredited my intelligence, I said. We lived in a world of power and manipulation. Currently political decisions (I took her hand) decided if we should live or die – if we should love or create art. My realism, I said, was limited to the situation; hers was appropriate to her life as an artist and as an individual who must continue to hope. 'But I am dying,' she said. 'I have no need for hope.' She smiled as she completed the sentence. She turned away with a shrug which had much of her old gaiety in it. She ran her hands over the frames of the canvases. 'I wish my life to have had some point, of course.'

I could not answer her, yet suddenly I was lost in her again, as I had been during the early days of our affair. I went towards her and I embraced her. I kissed her. She recognized my emotion at once. She responded. There was a great generosity in her, a kindness. I could not at the moment bear to think of its leaving the world. But I should have a memory of it, I thought.

I told her that I admired her tendency to ascribe altruistic motives to me, to all other people. But most of us were far too selfish. We had to survive in a cynical world. She said that she had to believe in self-sufficiency and altruism was the only way by which we could, with any meaning, survive at all. One had to keep one's eye on the world as it was and somehow learn to trust oneself to maintain tolerance and hope. I said her courage was greater than mine. She acknowledged this. She said that a woman found it necessary to discover courage if she were to make any sense of her life as an individual. 'But you pursued me,' I said gently. 'I love you,' she said. 'I want you for myself and will do everything I can to keep you.'

'I cannot change.'

'I would not wish it.'

'You have won me.'

'Well,' she said, 'I have won something of you and for the time being am content. Have I won it honourably do you think? Did you return simply out of pity?'

'I was drawn here, to you. I have no reservations.'

'You don't feel trapped?'

'On the contrary.'

'You'll stay here?'

'Until you die.'

'It might be – I might ask you to kill me when the worst begins.'

'I know.'

'Could you?'

'I suspect you were attracted to me because you knew that I could.'

She became relieved. The tension between us vanished completely. She smiled at me and took my hand again: in love with her executioner.

Crossing Into Cambodia

I

I approached and Savitsky, Commander of the Sixth Division, got up. As usual I was impressed by his gigantic, perfect body. Yet he seemed unconscious either of his power or of his elegance. Although not obliged to do so, I almost saluted him. He stretched an arm towards me. I put the papers into his gloved hand. 'These were the last messages we received,' I said. The loose sleeve of his Cossack cherkesska slipped back to reveal a battle-strengthened forearm, brown and glowing. I compared his skin to my own. For all that I had ridden with the Sixth for five months, I was still pale; still possessed, I thought, of an intellectual's hands. Evening light fell through the jungle foliage and a few parrots shrieked their last goodnight. Mosquitoes were gathering in the shadows, whirling in tight-woven patterns, like a frightened mob. The jungle smelled of rot. Yakovlev, somewhere, began to play a sad accordion tune.

The Vietnamese spy we had caught spoke calmly from the other side of Savitsky's camp table. 'I think I should like to be away from here before nightfall. Will you keep your word, sir, if I tell you what I know?'

Savitsky looked back and I saw the prisoner for the first time (though his presence was of course well known to the camp). His wrists and ankles were pinned to the ground with bayonets but he was otherwise unhurt.

Savitsky drew in his breath and continued to study the documents I had brought him. Our radio was now useless. 'He seems to be confirming what these say.' He tapped the second sheet. 'An attack tonight.'

The temple on the other side of the clearing came to life within. Pale light rippled on greenish, half-ruined stonework. Some of our men must have lit a fire there. I heard noises of delight and some complaints from the women who had been with the spy. One began to shout in that peculiar, irritating high-pitched half-wail they all use when they are trying to appeal to us. For a moment Savitsky and I had a bond in our disgust. I felt flattered. Savitsky made an impatient gesture, as if of embarrassment. He turned his handsome face and looked gravely down at the peasant. 'Does it matter to you? You've lost a great deal of blood.'

'I do not think I am dying.'

Savitsky nodded. He was economical in everything, even his cruelties. He had been prepared to tear the man apart with horses, but he knew that he would tire two already over-worked beasts. He picked up his cap from the camp table and put it thoughtfully on his head. From the deserted huts came the smell of our horses as the wind reversed its direction. I drew my borrowed burka about me. I was the only one in our unit to bother to wear it, for I felt the cold as soon as the sun was down.

'Will you show me on the map where they intend to ambush us?'

'Yes,' said the peasant. 'Then you can send a man to spy on their camp. He will confirm what I say.'

I stood to one side while these two professionals conducted their business. Savitsky strode over to the spy and very quickly, like a man plucking a hen, drew the bayonets out and threw them on the ground. With some gentleness, he helped the peasant to his feet and sat him down in the leather campaign chair he had carried with him on our long ride from Danang, where we had disembarked off the troop-ship which had brought us from Vladivostock.

'I'll get some rags to stop him bleeding,' I said.

'Good idea,' confirmed Savitsky. 'We don't want the stuff all over the maps. You'd better be in on this, anyway.'

As the liaison officer, it was my duty to know what was happening. That is why I am able to tell this story. My whole inclination was to return to my billet where two miserable ancients cowered and sang at me whenever I entered or left but where at least I had a small barrier between me and the casual day-to-day terrors of the campaign. But, illiterate and obtuse though these horsemen were, they had accurate instincts and could tell immediately if I betrayed any sign of fear. Perhaps, I thought, it is because they are all so used to disguising their own fears. Yet bravery was a habit with them and I yearned to catch it. I had ridden with them in more than a dozen encounters, helping to drive the Cambodians back into their own country. Each time I had seen men and horses blown to pieces, torn apart, burned alive. I had come to exist on the smell of blood and gun-powder as if it were a substitute for air and food – I identified it with the smell of Life itself – yet I had still failed to achieve that strangely passive sense of inner calm my comrades all, to a greater or lesser degree, displayed.

Only in action did they seem possessed in any way by the outer world, although they still worked with efficient ferocity, killing as quickly as possible with lance, sabre or carbine and, with ghastly humanity, never leaving a wounded man of their own or the enemy's without his throat cut or a bullet in his brain. I was thankful that these, my traditional foes, were now allies for I could not have resisted them had they turned against me.

I bound the peasant's slender wrists and ankles. He was like a child. He said: 'I knew there were no arteries cut.' I nodded at him. 'You're the political officer, aren't you?' He spoke almost sympathetically.

'Liaison,' I said.

He was satisfied by my reply, as if I had confirmed his opinion. He added: 'I suppose it's the leather coat. Almost a uniform.'

I smiled. 'A sign of class difference, you think?'

His eyes were suddenly drowned with pain and he staggered, but recovered to finish what he had evidently planned to say: 'You Russians are natural bourgeoisie. It's not your fault. It's your turn.'

Savitsky was too tired to respond with anything more than a small smile. I felt that he agreed with the peasant and that these two excluded me, felt superior to me. I knew anger, then. Tightening the last rag on his left wrist, I made the spy wince. Satisfied that my honour was avenged I cast an eye over the map. 'Here we are,' I said. We were on the very edge of Cambodia. A small river, easily forded, formed the border. We had heard it just before we had entered this village. Scouts confirmed that it lay no more than half a verst to the west. The stream on the far side of the village, behind the temple, was a tributary.

'You give your word you won't kill me,' said the Vietnamese.

'Yes,' said Savitsky. He was beyond joking. We all were. It had been ages since any of us had been anything but direct with one another, save for the conventional jests which were merely part of the general noise of the squadron, like the jangling of harness. And he was beyond lying, except where it was absolutely necessary. His threats were as unqualified as his promises.

'They are here.' The spy indicated a town. He began to shiver. He was wearing only torn shorts. 'And some of them are here, because they think you might use the bridge rather than the ford.'

'And the attacking force for tonight?'

'Based here.' A point on our side of the river.

Savitsky shouted. 'Pavlichenko.'

From the Division Commander's own tent, young Pavlichenko,

capless, with ruffled fair hair and a look of restrained disappointment, emerged. 'Comrade?'

'Get a horse and ride with this man for half-an-hour the way we came today. Ride as fast as you can, then leave him and return to camp.'

Pavlichenko ran towards the huts where the horses were stabled. Savitsky had believed the spy and was not bothering to check his information. 'We can't attack them,' he murmured. 'We'll have to wait until they come to us. It's better.' The flap of Savitsky's tent was now open. I glanced through and to my surprise saw a Eurasian girl of about fourteen. She had her feet in a bucket of water. She smiled at me. I looked away.

Savitsky said: 'He's washing her for me. Pavlichenko's an expert.'

'My wife and daughters?' said the spy.

'They'll have to remain now. What can I do?' Savitsky shrugged in the direction of the temple. 'You should have spoken earlier.'

The Vietnamese accepted this and, when Pavlichenko returned with the horse, leading it and running as if he wished to get the job over with in the fastest possible time, he allowed the young Cossack to lift him onto the saddle.

'Take your rifle,' Savitsky told Pavlichenko. 'We're expecting an attack.'

Pavlichenko dashed for his own tent, the small one close to Savitsky's. The horse, as thoroughly trained as the men who rode him, stood awkwardly but quietly beneath his nervous load. The spy clutched the saddle pommel, the mane, his bare feet angled towards the mount's neck. He stared ahead of him into the night. His wife and daughter had stopped their appalling wailing but I thought I could hear the occasional feminine grunt from the temple. The flames had become more animated. His other daughter, her feet still in the bucket, held her arms tightly under her chest and her curious eyes looked without rancour at her father, then at the Division Commander, then, finally, at me. Savitsky spoke. 'You're the intellectual. She doesn't know Russian. Tell her that her father will be safe. She can join him tomorrow.'

'My Vietnamese might not be up to that.'

'Use English or French, then.' He began to tidy his maps, calling over Kreshenko, who was in charge of the guard.

I entered the tent and was shocked by her little smile. She had a peculiar smell to her – like old tea and cooked rice. I knew my Vietnamese was too limited so I asked her if she spoke French. She was of the wrong generation. 'Amerikanski,' she told me. I relayed

Savitsky's message. She said: 'So I am the price of the old bastard's freedom.'

'Not at all.' I reassured her. 'He told us what we wanted. It was just bad luck for you that he used you three for cover.'

She laughed. 'Nuts! It was me got him to do it. With my sister. Tao's boyfriend works for the Cambodians.' She added: 'They seemed to be winning at the time.'

Savitsky entered the tent and zipped it up from the bottom. He used a single, graceful movement. For all that he was bone-weary, he moved with the unconscious fluidity of an acrobat. He lit one of his foul-smelling papyrosi and sat heavily on the camp bed beside the girl.

'She speaks English,' I said. 'She's a half-caste. Look.'

He loosened his collar. 'Could you ask her if she's clean, comrade?'

'I doubt it,' I said. I repeated what she had told me.

He nodded. 'Well, ask her if she'll be a good girl and use her mouth. I just want to get on with it. I expect she does, too.'

I relayed the D.C.'s message.

I'll bite his cock off if I get the chance,' said the girl.

Outside in the night the horse began to move away. I explained what she had said.

'I wonder, comrade,' Savitsky said, 'if you would oblige me by holding the lady's head.' He began to undo the belt of his trousers, pulling up his elaborately embroidered shirt.

The girl's feet became noisy in the water and the bucket overturned. In my leather jacket, my burka, with my automatic pistol at her right ear, I restrained the girl until Savitsky had finished with her. He began to take off his boots. 'Would you care for her, yourself?'

I shook my head and escorted the girl from the tent. She was walking in that familiar stiff way women have after they have been raped. I asked her if she was hungry. She agreed that she was. I took her to my billet. The old couple found some more rice and I watched her eat it.

Later that night she moved towards me from where she had been lying more or less at my feet. I thought I was being attacked and shot her in the stomach. Knowing what my comrades would think of me if I tried to keep her alive (it would be a matter of hours) I shot her in the head to put her out of her misery. As luck would have it, these shots woke the camp and when the Khmer soldiers attacked a few moments later we were ready for them and killed a great many before the rest ran back into the jungle. Most of these soldiers were younger than the girl.

In the morning, to save any embarrasment, the remaining women were chased out of the camp in the direction taken by the patriarch. The old couple had disappeared and I assumed that they would not return or, if they did, that they would bury the girl, so I left her where I had shot her. A silver ring she wore would compensate them for their trouble. There was very little food remaining in the village, but what there was we ate for our breakfast or packed into our saddle-bags. Then, mounting up, we followed the almost preternaturally handsome Savitsky back into the jungle, heading for the river.

2

When our scout did not return after we had heard a long burst of machine-gun fire, we guessed that he had found at least part of the enemy ambush and that the spy had not lied to us, so we decided to cross the river at a less convenient spot where, with luck, no enemy would be waiting.

The river was swift but had none of the force of Russian rivers and Pavlichenko was sent across with a rope which he tied to a tree-trunk. Then we entered the water and began to swim our horses across. Those who had lost the canvas covers for their carbines kept them high in the air, holding the rope with one hand and guiding their horses with legs and with reins which they gripped in their teeth. I was more or less in the middle, with half the division behind me and half beginning to assemble on dry land on the other side, when Cambodian aircraft sighted us and began an attack dive. The aircraft were in poor repair, borrowed from half-a-dozen other countries, and their guns, aiming equipment and, I suspect, their pilots, were in worse condition, but they killed seven of our men as we let go of the ropes, slipped out of our saddles, and swam beside our horses, making for the far bank, while those still on dry land behind us went to cover where they could. A couple of machine-gun carts were turned on the attacking planes, but these were of little use. The peculiar assortment of weapons used against us – tracers, two rockets, a few napalm canisters which struck the water and sank (only one opened and burned but the mixture was quickly carried off by the current) and then they were flying back to base somewhere in Cambodia's interior – indicated that they had very little conventional armament left. This was true of most of the participants at this stage, which is why our cavalry had proved so effective. But they had bought some time for their ground-troops who were now coming in.

In virtual silence, any shouts drowned by the rushing of the river, we crossed to the enemy bank and set up a defensive position, using the machine-gun carts which were last to come across on ropes. The Cambodians hit us from two sides – moving in from their original ambush positions – but we were able to return their fire effectively, even using the anti-tank weapons and the mortar which, hitherto, we had tended to consider useless weight. They used arrows, blow-darts, automatic rifles, pistols and a flame-thrower which only worked for a few seconds and did us no harm. The Cossacks were not happy with this sort of warfare and as soon as there was a lull we had mounted up, packed the gear in the carts, and with sabres drawn were howling into the Khmer Stalinists (as we had been instructed to term them). Leaving them scattered and useless, we found a bit of concrete road along which we could gallop for a while. We slowed to a trot and then to a walk. The pavement was potholed and only slightly less dangerous than the jungle floor. The jungle was behind us now and seemed to have been a screen hiding the devastation ahead. The landscape was virtually flat, as if it had been bombed clean of contours, with a few broken buildings, the occasional blackened tree, and ash drifted across the road, coming sometimes up to our horses' knees. The ash was stirred by a light wind. We had witnessed scenes like it before, but never on such a scale. The almost colourless nature of the landscape was emphasized by the unrelieved brilliance of the blue sky overhead. The sun had become very hot.

Once we saw two tanks on the horizon, but they did not challenge us. We continued until early afternoon when we came to the remains of some sort of modern power installation and we made camp in the shelter of its walls. The ash got into our food and we drank more of our water than was sensible. We were all covered in the grey stuff by this time.

'We're like corpses,' said Savitsky. He resembled an heroic statue of the sort which used to be in almost every public square in the Soviet Union. 'Where are we going to find anything to eat in this?'

'It's like the end of the world,' I said.

'Have you tried the radio again?'

I shook my head. 'It isn't worth it. Napalm eats through wiring faster than it eats through you.'

He accepted this and with a naked finger began to clean off the inner rims of the goggles he (like most of us) wore as protection against sun, rain and dust. 'I could do with some orders,' he said.

'We were instructed to move into the enemy's territory. That's what we're doing.'

'Where, we were told, we would link up with American and Australian mounted units. Those fools can't ride. I don't know why they ever thought of putting them on horses. Cowboys!'

I saw no point in repeating an already stale argument. It was true, however, that the Western cavalry divisions found it hard to match our efficient savagery. I had been amused, too, when they had married us briefly with a couple of Mongolian squadrons. The Mongols had not ridden to war in decades and had become something of a laughing stock with their ancient enemies, the Cossacks. Savitsky believed that we were the last great horsemen. Actually, he did not include me; for I was a very poor rider and not a Cossack, anyway. He thought it was our destiny to survive the War and begin a new and braver civilization: 'Free from the influence of women and Jews'. He recalled the great days of the Zaporozhian Sech, from which women had been forbidden. Even amongst the Sixth he was regarded as something of a conservative. He continued to be admired more than his opinions.

When the men had watered our horses and replaced the water bags in the cart, Savitsky and I spread the map on a piece of concrete and found our position with the help of the compass and sextant (there were no signs or landmarks). 'I wonder what has happened to Angkor,' I said. It was where we were supposed to meet other units, including the Canadians to whom, in the months to come, I was to be attached (I was to discover later that they had been in our rear all along).

'You think it's like this?' Savitsky gestured. His noble eyes began to frown. 'I mean, comrade, would you say it was worth our while making for Angkor now?'

'We have our orders,' I said. 'We've no choice. We're expected.'

Savitsky blew dust from his mouth and scratched his head. 'There's about half our division left. We could do with reinforcements. Mind you, I'm glad we can see a bit of sky at last.' We had all felt claustrophobic in the jungle.

'What is it, anyway, this Angkor? Their capital?' he asked me.

'Their Stalingrad, maybe.'

Savitsky understood. 'Oh, it has an importance to their morale. It's not strategic?'

'I haven't been told about its strategic value.'

Savitsky, as usual, withdrew into his diplomatic silence, indicating that he did not believe me and thought that I had been instructed to secrecy. 'We'd best push on,' he said. 'We've a long way to go, eh?'

After we had mounted up, Savitsky and I rode side by side for a while, along the remains of the concrete road. We were some way ahead of the long column, with its riders, its baggage-waggons, and its Makhno-style machine-gun carts. We were sitting targets for any planes and, because there was no cover, Savitsky and his men casually ignored the danger. I had learned not to show my nervousness but I was not at that moment sure how well hidden it was.

'We are the only vital force in Cambodia,' said the Division Commander with a beatific smile. 'Everything else is dead. How these yellow bastards must hate one another.' He was impressed, perhaps admiring.

'Who's to say?' I ventured. 'We don't know who else has been fighting. There isn't a nation now that's not in the War.'

'And not one that's not on its last legs. Even Switzerland.' Savitsky gave a superior snort. 'But what an inheritance for us!'

I became convinced that, quietly, he was going insane.

3

We came across an armoured car in a hollow, just off the road. One of our scouts had heard the crew's moans. As Savitsky and I rode up, the scout was covering the uniformed Khmers with his carbine, but they were too far gone to offer us any harm.

'What's wrong with 'em?' Savitsky asked the scout.

The scout did not know. 'Disease,' he said. 'Or starvation. They're not wounded.'

We got off our horses and slid down into the crater. The car was undamaged. It appeared to have rolled gently into the dust and become stuck. I slipped into the driving seat and tried to start the engine, but it was dead. Savitsky had kicked one of the wriggling Khmers in the genitals but the man did not seem to notice the pain much, though he clutched himself, almost as if he entered into the spirit of a ritual. Savitsky was saying 'Soldiers. Soldiers', over and over again. It was one of the few Vietnamese words he knew. He pointed in different directions, looking with disgust on the worn-out men. 'You'd better question them,' he said to me.

They understood my English, but refused to speak it. I tried them in French. 'What happened to your machine?'

The man Savitsky had kicked continued to lie on his face, his arms stretched along the ashy ground towards us. I felt he wanted to touch us: to steal our vitality. I felt sick as I put the heel of my boot on his hand. One of his comrades said: 'There's no secret to it. We ran out of essence.' He pointed to the armoured car. 'We ran out of essence.'

'You're a long way from your base.'

'Our base is gone. There's no essence anywhere.'

I believed him and told Savitsky who was only too ready to accept this simple explanation.

As usual, I was expected to dispatch the prisoners. I reached for my holster, but Savitsky, with rare sympathy, stayed my movement. 'Go and see what's in that can,' he said, pointing. As I waded towards the punctured metal, three shots came from the Division Commander's revolver. I wondered at his mercy. Continuing with this small farce, I looked at the can, held it up, shook it, and threw it back into the dust. 'Empty,' I said.

Savitsky was climbing the crater towards his horse. As I scrambled behind him he said: 'It's the Devil's world. Do you think we should give ourselves up to Him?'

I was astonished by this unusual cynicism.

He got into his saddle. Unconsciously, he assumed the pose, often seen in films and pictures, of the noble revolutionary horseman – his head lifted, his palm shielding his eyes as he peered towards the West.

'We seem to have wound up killing Tatars again,' he said with a smile as I got clumsily onto my horse. 'Do you believe in all this history, comrade?'

'I've always considered the theory of precedent absolutely infantile,' I said.

'What's that?'

I began to explain, but he was already spurring forward, shouting to his men.

4

On the third day we had passed through the ash-desert and our horses could at last crop at some grass on the crest of a line of low hills which looked down on glinting, misty paddy-fields. Savitsky, his field-glasses to his eyes, was relieved. 'A village,' he said. 'Thank god. We'll be able to get some provisions.'

'And some exercise,' said Pavlichenko behind him. The boy laughed, pushing his cap back on his head and wiping grimy sweat from his brow. 'Shall I go down there, comrade?' Savitsky agreed, telling Pavlichenko to take two others with him. We watched the Cossacks ride down the hill and begin cautiously to wade their horses through the young rice. The sky possessed a greenish tinge here, as if it reflected the fields. It looked like the Black Sea lagoons at midsummer. A smell of foliage, almost shocking in its unfamiliarity, floated up to us. Savitsky was intent on watching the movements of his men, who had unslung their carbines and dismounted as they reached the village. With reins looped on their arms they moved slowly in, firing a few experimental rounds at the huts. One of them took a dummy grenade from his saddle-bag and threw it into a nearby doorway. Peasants, already starving to the point of death it seemed, ran out. The young Cossacks ignored them, looking for soldiers. When they were satisfied that the village was clear of traps, they waved us in. The peasants began to gather together at the centre of the village. Evidently they were used to this sort of operation.

While our men made their thorough search I was again called upon to perform my duty and question the inhabitants. These, it emerged, were almost all intellectuals, part of an old Khmer Rouge re-education programme (virtually a sentence of death by forced labour). It was easier to speak to them but harder to understand their complicated answers. In the end I gave up and, made impatient by the whining appeals of the wretches, ignored them. They knew nothing of use to us. Our men were disappointed in their expectations. There were only old people in the village. In the end they took the least aged of the women off and had them in what had once been some sort of administration hut. I wondered at their energy. It occurred to me that this was something they expected of one another and that they would lose face if they did not perform the necessary actions. Eventually, when we had eaten what we could find, I returned to questioning two of the old men. They were at least antagonistic to the Cambodian troops and were glad to tell us anything they could. However, it seemed there had been no large movements in the area. The occasional plane or helicopter had gone over a few days earlier. These were probably part of the flight which had attacked us at the river. I asked if they had any news of Angkor, but there was no radio here and they expected us to know more than they did. I pointed towards the purple hills on the other side of the valley. 'What's over there?'

They told me that as far as they knew it was another valley, similar to this but larger. The hills looked steeper and were wooded. It would be a difficult climb for us unless there was a road. I got out the map. There was a road indicated. I pointed to it. One of the old men nodded. Yes, he thought that road was still there, for it led, eventually, to this village. He showed me where the path was. It was rutted where, some time earlier, heavy vehicles had been driven along it. It disappeared into dark, green, twittering jungle. All the jungle meant to me now was mosquitoes and a certain amount of cover from attacking planes.

Careless of leeches and insects, the best part of the division was taking the chance of a bath in the stream which fed the paddy-fields. I could not bring myself to strip in the company of these healthy men. I decided to remain dirty until I had the chance of some sort of privacy.

'I want the men to rest,' said Savitsky. 'Have you any objection to our camping here for the rest of today and tonight?'

'It's a good idea,' I said. I sought out a hut, evicted the occupants, and went almost immediately to sleep.

In the morning I was awakened by a trooper who brought me a metal mug full of the most delicately scented tea. I was astonished and accepted it with some amusement. 'There's loads of it here,' he said. 'It's all they've got!'

I sipped the tea. I was still in my uniform, with the burka on the ground beneath me and my leather jacket folded for a pillow. The hut was completely bare. I was used to noticing a few personal possessions and began to wonder if they had hidden their stuff when they had seen us coming. Then I remembered that they were from the towns and had been brought here forcibly. Perhaps now, I thought, the war would pass them by and they would know peace, even happiness, for a bit. I was scratching my ear and stretching when Savitsky came in, looking grim. 'We've found a damned burial ground,' he said. 'Hundreds of bodies in a pit. I think they must be the original inhabitants. And one or two soldiers – at least, they were in uniform.'

'You want me to ask what they are?'

'No! I just want to get away. God knows what they've been doing to one another. They're a filthy race. All grovelling and secret killing. They've no guts.'

'No soldiers, either,' I said. 'Not really. They've been preyed on by bandits for centuries. Bandits are pretty nearly the only sort of soldiers they've ever known. So the ones who want to be soldiers emulate them. Those who don't want to be soldiers treat the ones who do as they've always treated bandits. They are conciliatory until they get a chance to turn the tables.'

He was impressed by this. He rubbed at a freshly-shaven chin. He looked years younger, though he still had the monumental appearance of a god. 'Thieves, you mean. They have the mentality of thieves, their soldiers?'

'Aren't the Cossacks thieves?'

'That's foraging.' He was not angry. Very little I said could ever anger him because he had no respect for my opinions. I was the necessary political officer, his only link with the higher, distant authority of the Kremlin, but he did not have to respect my ideas any more than he respected those which came to him from Moscow. What he respected there was the power and the fact that in some way Russia was mystically represented in our leaders. 'We leave in ten minutes,' he said.

I noticed that Pavlichenko had polished his boots for him.

By that afternoon, after we had crossed the entire valley on an excellent dirt road through the jungle and had reached the top of the next range of hills, I had a pain in my stomach. Savitsky noticed me holding my hands against my groin and said laconically, 'I wish the doctor hadn't been killed. Do you think it's typhus?' Naturally, it was what I had suspected.

'I think it's just the tea and the rice and the other stuff. Maybe mixing with all the dust we've swallowed.' He looked paler than usual. 'I've got it, too. So have half the others. Oh, shit!'

It was hard to tell, in that jungle at that time of day, if you had a fever. I decided to put the problem out of my mind as much as possible until sunset when it would become cooler.

The road began to show signs of damage and by the time we were over the hill and looking down on the other side we were confronting scenery if anything more desolate than that which we had passed through on the previous three days. It was a grey desert, scarred by the broken road and bomb-craters. Beyond this and coming towards us was a wall of dark dust; unmistakably an army on the move. Savitsky automatically relaxed in his saddle and turned back to see our men moving slowly up the wooded hill. 'I think they must be heading this way.' Savitsky cocked his head to one side. 'What's that?'

It was a distant shriek. Then a whole squadron of planes was coming in low. We could see their crudely-painted Khmer Rouge markings, their battered fuselages. The men began to scatter off the road, but the planes ignored us. They went zooming by, seeming to be fleeing rather than attacking. I looked at the sky, but nothing followed them.

We took our field-glasses from their cases and adjusted them. In the dust I saw a mass of barefoot infantry bearing rifles with fixed bayonets. There were also trucks, a few tanks, some private cars, bicycles, motor-bikes, ox-carts, hand-carts, civilians with bundles. It was an orgy of defeated soldiers and refugees.

'I think we've missed the action.' Savitsky was furious. 'We were beaten to it, eh? And by Australians, probably!'

My impulse to shrug was checked. 'Damn!' I said a little weakly.

This caused Savitsky to laugh at me. 'You're relieved. Admit it!'

I knew that I dare not share his laughter, lest it become hysterical and turn to tears, so I missed a moment of possible comradeship. 'What shall we do?' I asked. 'Go round them?'

'It would be easy enough to go through them. Finish them off. It would stop them destroying this valley, at least.' He did not, by his tone, much care.

The men were assembling behind us. Savitsky informed them of the nature of the rabble ahead of us. He put his field-glasses to his eyes again and said to me: 'Infantry, too. Quite a lot. Coming on faster.'

I looked. The barefoot soldiers were apparently pushing their way through the refugees to get ahead of them.

'Maybe the planes radioed back,' said Savitsky. 'Well, it's something to fight.'

'I think we should go round,' I said. 'We should save our strength. We don't know what's waiting for us at Angkor.'

'It's miles away yet.'

'Our instructions were to avoid any conflict we could,' I reminded him.

He sighed. 'This is Satan's own country.' He was about to give the order which would comply with my suggestion when, from the direction of Angkor Wat, the sky burst into white fire. The horses reared and whinnyed. Some of our men yelled and flung their arms over their eyes. We were all temporarily blinded. Then the dust below seemed to grow denser and denser. We watched in fascination as the dark wall became taller, rushing upon us and howling like a million dying voices. We were struck by the ash and forced onto our knees, then onto our bellies, yanking our frightened horses down with us as best we could. The stuff stung my face and hands and even those parts of my body protected by heavy clothing. Larger pieces of stone rattled against my goggles.

When the wind had passed and we began to stand erect, the sky was still very bright. I was astonished that my field glasses were intact. I put them up to my burning eyes and peered through swirling ash at the Cambodians. The army was running along the road towards us, as terrified animals flee a forest-fire. I knew now what the planes had been escaping. Our Cossacks were in some confusion, but were already regrouping, shouting amongst themselves. A number of horses were still shying and whickering but by and large we were all calm again.

'Well, comrade,' said Savitsky with a sort of mad satisfaction, 'what do we do now? Wasn't that Angkor Wat, where we're supposed to meet our allies?'

I was silent. The mushroom cloud on the horizon was growing. It had the hazy outlines of a gigantic, spreading cedar tree, as if all at once that wasteland of ash had become promiscuously fertile. An aura of bloody red seemed to surround it, like a silhouette in the sunset. The strong, artificial wind was still blowing in our direction. I wiped dust from my goggles and lowered them back over my eyes. Savitsky gave the order for our men to mount. 'Those bastards down there are in our way,' he said. 'We're going to charge them.'

'What?' I could not believe him.

'When in doubt,' he told me, 'attack.'

'You're not scared of the enemy,' I said, 'but there's the radiation.'

'I don't know anything about radiation.' He turned in his saddle to watch his men. When they were ready he drew his sabre. They imitated him. I had no sabre to draw.

I was horrified. I pulled my horse away from the road. 'Division Commander Savitsky, we're duty-bound to conserve . . .'

'We're duty-bound to make for Angkor,' he said. 'And that's what we're doing.' His perfect body poised itself in the saddle. He raised his sabre.

'It's not like ordinary dying,' I began. But he gave the order to trot forward. There was a rictus of terrifying glee on each mouth. The light from the sky was reflected in every eye.

I moved with them. I had become used to the security of numbers and I could not face their disapproval. But gradually they went ahead of me until I was in the rear. By this time we were almost at the bottom of the hill and cantering towards the mushroom cloud which was now shot through with all kinds of dark, swirling colours. It had become like a threatening hand, while the wind-borne ash stung our bodies and drew blood on the flanks of our mounts.

Yakovlev, just ahead of me, unstrapped his accordion and began to play some familiar Cossack battle-song. Soon they were all singing. Their pace gradually increased. The noise of the accordion died but their song was so loud now it seemed to fill the whole world. They reached full gallop, charging upon that appalling outline, the quintessential symbol of our doom, as their ancestors might have charged the very gates of Hell. They were swift, dark shapes in the dust. The song became a savage, defiant roar.

My first impulse was to charge with them. But then I had turned my horse and was trotting back towards the valley and the border, praying that, if I ever got to safety, I would not be too badly contaminated.

(In homage to Isaac Babel, 1894–1941?)

Mars

The wandering earth herself may be
Only a sudden flaming word,
In clanging space a moment heard,
Troubling the endless reverie.
W. B. Yeats
The Song of the Happy Shepherd

Hesitating at the edge of the beautiful ghost town Morgan watched red rust run like a river over a smashed Cerum screen. From below came the uncertain vibration of some abandoned atmosphere plant, its echo murmuring through endless catacombs where the majority of Martians preferred to survive. Only a few like Morgan chose to live beneath the pale wash of the planet's pastel skies and breathe dusty air smelling of licorice, lilac and the sweet old Earth of childhood.

Morgan was sixteen when the community congregated within pink brick Gothic arches to watch an accelerator picture bloom on the viewing wall. Earth, then Neptune, had quietly vanished from the solar system. 'A great experiment.' Gran had seemed regretful. Scientists who had issued warnings of just such dramatic results were vindicated, but since the colonies were self-sufficient it merely meant the end of innocence, not of civilization. This was to be a period of forgetting.

Mars had already developed a consciously introspective culture. To them the idea of Earth's departure was more interesting than the fact. Symbolism offered at once a larger and less involving reality.

Morgan reached through the thin, fast-flowing dust to pick up an old paperback lying on the fused clay beneath. It was obsolete and the expensive machines to play it belonged only to collectors, but the cover was interesting. Even after so much exposure the holograms were garish, crude, ungraduated. A figure in a red-and-purple smock threatened another with some sort of weapon and the calligraphy was so complicated it was almost impossible for Morgan, trained on the spare alphabets once fashionable in Morocco, to decipher. It was clearly from Earth. Had the whole planet been so loud? To Morgan's ears much of the music had the same unsubtle quality; it was brutal, almost alarming, though some Martians thought it vivid, possessed of a primitive vitality they had lost.

'We're too cultured for our own good,' Wren had said the other day. 'It's Mars. At this rate we'll go the way of the other civilizations.'

Mars has seen at least nine major cultures thrive and fade. The youngest had lived in the deepest caverns of all before dying out as peacefully and as mysteriously as all the rest. 'Mars was never meant to support life. Mars represents the tranquillity of death. Perhaps you should have gone to Venus while you had the chance?'

Once, aged eleven, Morgan had visited Venus and found the elegant landscaping, the elaborately geometrical gardens, the tastefully arranged forests, far too classical. Because her surface had hardly been worth altering, Mars remained much as she had been when the first Earth settlers arrived, her limitless deserts and worn mountains, her craters and her shallow valleys relieved only by occasional bands of low vegetation marking the existence of subterranean rivers and oceans serving those twilight countries whose original architecture had been so carefully adapted and utilized by the latest Martians. At least two previous civilizations had been humanoid and one of them had certainly been a colonizing culture, either from another system or possibly even marooned here from another spacetime. There was a theory that Mars herself had not originally been part of this system. Fragments of old machines suggested attempts to use the whole planet as a means of transportation. The remains of what were evidently spaceships could have brought visitors to Mars or had perhaps been built in a failed attempt to leave the planet. Only one culture – the huge four-armed tusked bipeds – had apparently succeeded in travelling on.

'They come to Mars to die,' Wren had said. 'Or they leave. We have no intention of leaving. Mars lets us grow old gracefully.'

Nothing in Morgan could easily resist the idea. Few babies had ever been born on Mars and in spite of all efforts fewer still had reached healthy adulthood. Regenerations maintained the race.

'Mars rejects children.' Wren's voice had contained a certain depth of satisfaction. 'She rejects everything which isn't already mature. She's a planet for people who've grown tired not of life but of exploration. You, Morgan, are in an uneasy position here, for you were almost an adult when you arrived and you never expected to stay. Do you miss your parents?'

Morgan's grandparents had always seemed much closer. They had settled on Mars as part of a scheme offered on Earth to encourage early retirement, but their parents had been born here to the first real settlers who built the surface towns and the Cerum screens.

'Mars has no secrets from those who love her.' Wren had smiled and, in a gesture of sad regret, caressed Morgan's hand.

But Morgan loved Mars. Possibly Morgan's love contained too much passion for the planet to bear. Mars's mysteries were everywhere and were part of her fascination. Morgan enjoyed curiosity for its own sake and was rarely disappointed by unanswered questions.

The paperback replaced in the river bed, Morgan moved towards ochre walls; some old public buildings in the Second Arabian style. Adding water to Martian clay produced a cement as strong as stone. The cheapness of their materials had always allowed the Martians more fanciful and elaborate structures than the Venusians or Ganymedians. Dust could be moulded into baroque splendour and some mock-Versailles raised from the desert in days. It never rained on Mars so only the action of the winds affected these fantastical towns whose architecture recorded the history of Earth's finest periods. Impossible to combine with tints, the towns were the same pale oranges, yellows, browns, pinks and rusty reds as their surroundings, the subtle skies which never quite formed clouds. Attempts to vary the colours by raising holograms and even 2D billboards, by using the picture facilities of the Cerum screens whenever possible, had produced tones too bright for eyes grown accustomed to subtler shades and before their exodus to reinhabit the prehistoric cities few Martians had desired anything but the planet's familiar spectrum. On arriving, Morgan, at first unable to distinguish easily between colours, had thought the place sinister. Even the people had a faded quality, their voices like whisperings in a graveyard. Though they were robust enough, it had been easy to believe in grandparents over two hundred years old.

Morgan's grandparents' generation still tended to call the planet 'Pacifica', from the first colonial advertisements. While it bore a closer relationship to the landscapes, the name was hollow to Morgan. Mars had not been associated in anyone's mind with a Roman war god for centuries. What had been 'martial' to Morgan's ancestors meant almost its opposite now. To Morgan the word Mars had always been a synonym for peace.

Profoundly opposed to any return to the surface, for weeks Morgan's grandparents had spoken of nothing but the danger. Cheap generators and equipment from Earth factories were no longer available to maintain meteor beams or control dust-storms. Morgan and the others had tried to explain how these unpredictable elements were part of the reason for going back.

Familiar with defeat but not reconciled to it, Morgan had on that occasion persevered, eventually winning the agreement of the community. A year ago twenty-eight people, mostly of Morgan's generation, had set themselves up in Egg City, close to the Little Crack, a dust-river which coursed without interruption across half the planet before joining Main Run near the equator.

Used to solitary lives, the majority gradually went their separate ways until only Morgan and Wren were left in Egg. Faad was furthest away, on the Back Line, some three thousand kilometres from Egg. Faad had travelled on an ancient dust-coaster brought from underground. They were dangerous, inclined to capsize, but you could ride the dust-tides down the deep cracks and cover an enormous distance. Faad had the whole of Whistler to live in. This was the most elaborately fanciful of all Martian cities, with replicas of almost every monumental building Earth had ever raised, from the Taj Mahal to the Empire State to the Gibraltar Berber Mosque, though the location let the winds erode them into extraordinary versions of their originals.

Morgan had not lost any love for the underworld's beauty, the great plumes of atmosphere rising from the hydros in the morning, and shafts of sunlight cutting down from a mile above to strike water which glowed like copper; the pewter caverns, the carved gold-green stalactites whose disturbingly alien faces bore expressions of unguessable sorrow. Or was it sorrow at all? What did humanity really know of any alien entity? Once it was realized that dead aliens offered no threat they were forgotten by everyone save a few academics, as if people refused to consider the implications, the fact that not one race, no matter how perfectly adapted, had continued to exist on Mars for more than eleven or twelve millennia?

Along the banks of frozen rivers and lakes, wonderfully symmetrical structures had been erected, side by side with crazily angular buildings, clearly the productions of two different races who at one time had shared the planet equably. One race had been humanoid, the other avarian but flightless.

An earlier species resembling fine-featured Oriental cats had left statues to themselves all over Mars and Morgan had become almost as familiar with their culture as with Earth's. Their celebrations had all seemed to concern enormous failures. They seemed a race addicted to defeat. Morgan believed in the power of habit, of rituals maintaining patterns of behaviour which had long since lost their psychic or practical usefulness. Humans were the same, especially around power or powerlessness. For millennia, when gender had been a class definition, half the race had seemed addicted to power and half to powerlessness, producing profound philosophies and art forms, religions and sciences out of their addictions.

To Morgan much of what those ancestors had valued seemed trivial or debased and it was only possible to hold faint distaste for so barbaric a past. With Earth's disappearance had gone the reminders of their shame, while the reminders of their glories lived on as magnificent Martian ghosts.

If Earth had contained the descendants of those addicted to power, then Mars sheltered a people who made a virtue of powerlessness; this remained the element in Martian culture which caused Morgan greatest unease. There was no nobility in surviving for the sake of surviving – unless a virus or an amoeba were instrinsically noble – but neither was there any particular moral purity in reconciling oneself to extinction.

Sometimes Wren said that every single piece of architecture on the planet was nothing more than an elaborate tombstone. Wren's ideas were easily understood when, alone, you looked out across red dunes towards eroded cliffs and a sky turned to smoky yellow streaked with orange; but they were too easy, Morgan had decided. Mars was not dead and her people were not dying. It would be a million years before anyone needed to consider the notion.

Morgan got back on the brog and hovered a few feet above the surface before moving forward. There was a good chance of reaching Egg before twilight, though there was no urgency. Any of the old cities were capable of giving temporary shelter. Morgan's vehicle offered electronic intimacies as it calculated distances and speeds, warming the cabin to compensate for Mars's slow, wonderful sunset. Wren waited in Egg and Morgan was nervous of returning, wary of a new relationship which, no matter how perfect, might interfere with this abiding love-affair with Mars, this sense of coming to know profoundly the identity of an entire planet, the nature of her history, the qualities which made her unique among the planets.

Already Wren had introduced a note of scepticism. 'You're not exploring Mars. You're exploring yourself, Morgan. That's surely all anyone does? That's what Mars makes you do. That's what Mars gives you. And in turn you learn how to explore and understand others. You're the youngest of us but I always trusted you, most of all, to realize that.'

'Mars isn't me,' Morgan had said. 'I'm not greatly interested in myself.'

This statement was so contrary to fundamental Martian belief that Wren's only possible response had been laughter. 'Your Mars is you!' Then Wren had dropped the subject. Wren was in love with Morgan, whose pale skin and black hair were strikingly similar to Wren's own. It was the epitome of the Martian ideal of beauty.

Morgan's fascination with Wren had something to do with narcissism but was also a wish to retain emotional contact with another human being, as if that in itself were some sort of safety-line. Aware of Wren's stronger infatuation, Morgan knew it did not matter if a day or two went by before returning to Egg. Wren would almost certainly be waiting. Martians were not encouraged to form intense relationships. Wren would probably expect no more of Morgan and it was not for Morgan to speculate about and respond to Wren's possible or unstated feelings.

Deliberately slowing the brog, Morgan rode beside a line of ridges that were probably an old crater rim. The sun continued its tranquil descent. Delighted by the almost imperceptible alternation of shades, Morgan next reordered the magnetics to let the vehicle drift off towards Rose de la Paix where once spaceships had come and gone in such numbers.

Just before dark, when the main constellations shone a greenish blue in the depths of the sky, Morgan reached the old port's outskirts, surprised to see that someone had changed its familiar silhouette. Morgan was sure a new building had been added since Faad had driven them here when Isutep and Katchga left for Venus.

Finding a cocoon-bay, Morgan prepared for the night, welcoming the positive security and comfort of the coffin-shaped survival box. In the morning it would be interesting to investigate the new additon to Rose, perhaps one of those random sculptures erected by the Caziz siblings, Mars's leading artists and a constant source of irritation to the underworlders.

An hour or so after dawn Morgan watched fragile sunlight fragment into red and gold bands layering the horizon like geological strata. There was, indeed, an addition to the port, sitting half on a launch-disc which shone like polished lead, a massive thing of ornate brass curves, silver loops and sinuously interwoven tubes seemingly partly metallic and partly organic, its function impossible to guess. But it was clearly not by the Cazizes. There were no materials like it on Mars. Morgan decided it must surely be a vessel, its occupants recognizing a spaceship port. Was this the vanguard of the next wave of colonists?

The vessel's colours had now become predominantly greens and dark rich blues, with some glittering reds and almost jarring metal pinks. Morgan could not look at it for any length of time without developing a mild headache. Searching amongst the miscellaneous stuff in the back of the brog, Morgan found an antiglare mask and put this on. The ship now appeared to shift very slowly back and forth through the spectrum, an unexpected effect which gradually stabilized. After some minutes there was a kind of flickering passage across part of the lower latticework of the ship and two indistinct figures stood almost gingerly on the gleaming disc.

Morgan eventually realized they were moving. They were bipeds, chunky in outline but at the same time ethereal. A further flicker in the air and heads were revealed. To Morgan the creatures, almost without necks, with flat features and dramatically deepset eyes, were not immediately attractive. When one of them spoke, it was like a distantly heard harp, the notes drawn out and indistinct, yet Morgan understood a few words. '. . . *unpeace . . . targettable . . . apologisation . . . unfamiliarian . . . intraspaced . . . relationates . . . upset-forthuns . . . plastmuritum . . .*'

Clearly the aliens had learned from Earth broadcasts, for this was spaceship patois and technonlex, which Morgan could speak a little. Replying in the same mixture, Morgan asked them if they had travelled far. They did not understand initially, but after several attempts, lasting almost until noon, they responded, each word drawn out so that it took them hours to deliver their information.

They had come intraspacially and picked up the megaflow which brought them most of the way. Believing themselves in danger, they needed, Morgan thought they said, to contact a shipcontroller so they could be buried.

Were they pursued? Morgan asked, and it was almost dark before he began to understand their reply. Probably not. They were being cautious and wanted to hide their ship. There had been home planet 'beleaguerments'. Considerable 'unpeace'. The newcomers seemed chiefly concerned for the safety of their fellows. They seemed to be advance scouts or else were already the sole survivors of some catastrophe. They referred sometimes in technonlex and sometimes in English to a place called Erdorig or Three. When Morgan asked them the name of their planet they hesitated until just before dawn the next day and then said 'Earth', which Morgan thought a fairly useless piece of translation.

Morgan tried to explain the need to sleep and eventually simply returned to the cocoon for a few hours. On Morgan's coming back to the disc they reappeared before him, ready to continue. Morgan was bewildered by their mixture of terrible urgency and unreal tranquillity. The way the aliens spoke and moved perhaps reflected a radical difference in the texture of their home space. They would pause sometimes for quarter-of-an-hour between words, clearly from need and habit, not because they were seeking the appropriate phrase. Morgan wondered if in their language silences of a particular kind were in fact a form of communication. Their exchange could still take over an hour and still prove meaningless. Morgan maintained this intercourse for almost two more days with little sleep before deciding that Wren must be brought here. Wren was better qualified to continue the dialogue, having a background in semantics and anthropology.

Privately joking that the journey from Rose to Egg and back could probably be completed before the aliens finished their next observation, Morgan assured them they were welcome and that he went to seek others who might help them better. Morgan raced the brog back to Egg, the red dust shrieking and spiralling as it reacted to the vehicle's overtaxed magnetics.

As usual, only Wren was in Egg, sitting in the main square on the steps of a sandstone Los Angeles City Hall watching old newscasts. As Morgan drove in Wren folded the viewer and smiled. 'I knew you'd be late. It's all right.'

Before Wren spoke Morgan had been full of the event, but now felt a great reluctance to say anything at all, let alone the half-lie which emerged. 'I was delayed in Rose.'

'Something happening?' Clearly Wren was torn between relief at seeing Morgan and irritation for having been made to speculate.

'Nothing really.' Climbing down from the brog, Morgan took a rag and began removing a layer of bronze-brown dust from the side. 'I'm glad you weren't disturbed.'

'I'm a Martian. We're never disturbed.'

Morgan failed to detect Wren's irony and instead looked back towards Rose. 'There's a new ship on one of the launch discs.'

'Going to Venus? From Venus?'

'Alien. From sideways I'd guess. They're not quite in focus, if you know what I mean. I've been with them most of the time. I can't find out what they're here for. They speak a form of technonlex, bits of other Earth languages, ship's patois.'

'Two days and they haven't told you why they're here?' Wren began to walk towards the slender triple towers where they always stayed when in Egg City. 'Not what I'd call communication, Morgan.

What are they hiding?'

'They seem to fade out – physically, I mean. Then they'll become so solid and immovable I think they're turning into statues before my eyes. You'd have to see it, Wren.'

Wren paused, the anger and frustration dissipating. 'What?'

'It's the oddest thing I've ever experienced. It's as if they're fluctuating between maximum stability and maximum entropy. They probably have means of controlling the space they occupy. They're very nearly human. Superficially.'

'Remember Faad's joke?' Wren was sceptical.

'This isn't like Faad's joke. It's very easy to tell. These people are frightened. Or angry. I don't know.'

'Frightened of you?'

'Maybe. Perhaps of something they've left behind. You should come out to Rose, Wren. You know all those versions of technonlex. You're trained for this. It might be the only real chance you ever get to make use of that prolonged education.'

In a newly-relaxed face Wren's smile was beautiful. It was their running game. Wren came striding back to embrace Morgan who beamed with the pleasure of reconciliation. 'I can't be everything you'd like, Wren. But I love you.'

'Yes,' said Wren. 'That's what makes it painful. We're fools, we Martians. Is all of this imposed? Is it just the stupid, useless rationalizations of the early settlers? Shouldn't we be trying to change how we look at things? I was considering all that stuff we talked about the other day . . .'

Already Wren was moving the conversation towards abstraction. Morgan could see this typically Martian trait objectively, but Wren was almost entirely unaware of it.

'This is a real event, Wren. These people seem desperate. Do you want to help them?'

'Why not? Can the brog stand a return trip?'

'We'll take the spare. I got careless. Do you need anything?'

'Some food. Some reference stuff. You fetch the brog and I'll be ready.'

Suddenly enjoying Wren's companionship, Morgan drove them back directly towards Egg, sailing up over smaller obstacles, gracefully curving around cliffs.

'You seem happy,' said Wren. 'I mean happier. Is it the excitement?'

'I like doing things with you, Wren, better than I like having conversations. People talk too much for me.'

'That's Mars.' Wren again unconsciously refused any reason for action or change. 'Good old Mars. She does that.'

'Well, these people might need something more than talk.' Morgan grinned at this. 'If there's time.'

'You're goony today.' Wren enjoyed Morgan's mood, sitting closer and offering an affectionate hug. 'You're like a kid. I suppose you are our kid, really. What can we offer the visitors? Or are you just being rhetorical?'

'Help.' Morgan shrugged, keeping an eye firmly on the forward terrain, for the automatics were off in order to achieve greater speed. 'I think that's why they're here.'

'They're not would-be colonists, then? I thought everyone wanted to settle on Mars. Have you ever wondered why such a barren place is so attractive to so many different races?'

'You're sliding off the point again, Wren.'

Wren was amiably baffled. 'I didn't know there was one. They're emissaries? Are they?'

'That's why I need you, Wren.'

Clearly flattered by this, Wren settled more comfortably in the seat. 'I like a good problem.'

'We might have to start solving this one as rapidly as possible.'

'I'll try not to disappoint you, Morgan.' Head shaking in amusement, Wren studied the copper-coloured mossy South Dales in the distance. The light caught a sheen of tiny stems so that the entire landscape resembled a vast jewelled snake warming its body beneath the sun. 'Oh, this is so good, Morgan. Don't you love Mars?'

Soon Morgan saw Rose coming up on the horizon: fractured skyscrapers, rusted geometries of disused instruments and signals, eroded control towers, domes the colour of pale chocolate and bleached strawberries, ruined customs buildings, a silted quarantine enclosure and, beyond, the Art Hazardos splendours of the Mannaheim Apartments, raised in the days before the fashion for imitation became the ruling aesthetic and gave Martian cities their characteristic appearance of bizarre monuments to a lost planet.

'Awful,' said Wren without thinking. Like most Martians, Wren believed any style not previously seen on Earth was vulgar and simply lacking in any beauty. To Morgan the buildings were only hard to read, almost like the spaceship which now came into view and made Wren exclaim noisily about its oddness. 'This is stranger than anything we have already. They won't shoot me or anything, will they?'

The two aliens had not moved very far from their original spot. Currently they were so utterly solid, standing firmly on the faintly reflective disc, that almost everything surrounding them seemed a little unreal.

'Well, first things first,' said Wren, raising a hand in a sign which no real logic accepted as a universal gesture of peace. Yet the salute was eventually answered, awkwardly, as if the aliens were trying to recall forgotten briefings. Their stolid, ugly faces stared with considerable alertness from massive hairless heads wearing some kind of transparent, protective covering, possibly a membrane or thin bone. 'Could you tell me your names? I'm Wren. This is Morgan.'

Morgan felt foolish for not having considered this simple first step. Yet the aliens were bewildered until Wren, growing a little more sober, tried a whole series of technonlex versions. The process was as slow as it had been earlier, but at last Wren turned to Morgan with some information. 'They're Directed Beings from the Pastoral Choice, they say, and are called Sendes-endes-Ah and Luuk Shenpehr, as far as I can tell. Directed Beings, I think, are people who choose physical work and the Pastoral Choice is probably the nearest thing to a country – a province, maybe. What are they? Farm labourers? There'll be a long way to go before we have a true notion of how they live. But that's all we need for the moment.' Wren had become unusually engaged. 'Now I'll try to find out a bit more as to why they came here.'

A little disturbed by Wren's brusque, almost proprietorial tone, Morgan knew a protective pang. 'They must be exhausted. Should we offer them food?'

Wren shrugged, as if finding this question unnecessary, but nonetheless addressed the aliens and after less than twenty minutes discovered that they had taken nourishment while Morgan was away. 'I think I embarrassed them.' Wren grinned. There was, indeed, a great deal of fading in and out and both aliens had changed from pasty white to a kind of lime green. Now they resumed their solidity and original colouring.

Unhappy with the anthropologist's lighthearted attitude to the aliens, Morgan felt Wren should display more respect. But the aliens were almost certainly unaware of any nuances and Wren was making far greater progress with them. By the following morning the aliens retired to their spaceship while Wren and Morgan, occupying some old crew's quarters not far away, had pieced together a large part of the basic story.

'They were coming back.' Wren frowned. 'They're sure of that. They've said it every possible way. They were coming back, hoping to find help or escape. They seem to be saying they're Martians,

Morgan. Yet there's nothing like them anywhere on Mars. Were they the original inhabitants, so long ago no trace remains?' Wren looked out at the ship. 'Their own planet, which either has no name or a name which sounds very much like Earth, is no longer inhabitable. A new species has attacked? Possibly a disease? Their knowledge of technonlex is excellent but it's a version I've never come across. There are gaps, in other words. They want to hide their ship. We should humour them in that, I think.'

'Humour them?' Again Morgan was unhappy with Wren's choice of phrase.

'Respect their wishes, then. Don't those pads lower into the ground? They'll have to make a more precise landing, though. They're funny-looking creatures. Old, old people would be my guess. I asked how many inhabitants of their race were left on the planet and they said twelve. But it might have have been twelve hundred, twelve thousand – technonlex won't do it, so far. We'll have to consult with the community. I told them. They seem a worthy enough pair, if a bit boring and ugly.' Wren laughed. 'Sorry, Morgan. But have you considered this could be a clever trick on their part. What if they're the conquering bully-boys?'

They looked up and saw the air flush with a yellowish red, then the spaceship grew insubstantial for a few seconds. When it regained its solidity it stood dead-centre on the disc. Emerging again, the two aliens settled themselves in front of Wren and Morgan, ready for the next day's conversation. The first thing they did was repeat, rapidly in their terms, that the ship must be hidden.

'We'll need permission from the rest.' Wren was clearly impressed. 'You'd better go and ask, Morgan. Find your grandparents. I'll carry on here.'

Though reluctant to leave and even more reluctant to confront the underworlders, Morgan responded to the urgency and took the brog over to Rose's nearest shaft-gate, driving down into the cool half-light of the hollow world below.

When Morgan returned, having once again earned some subtle kind of disapproval for a failure, as the underworlders saw it, of courtesy, Wren was sitting on the ground with hands in the air and looking at one of the aliens who, perhaps aggressively, brandished what might have been a weapon.

Obviously afraid, Wren looked back at Morgan. 'I made a serious gaff, Morgan. I've asked them not to shoot me, but I'm not sure their technonlex has a word for mercy.' Wren's mouth was dry. 'We made some progress. Maybe too much. They're from Earth, Morgan. Old

Earth which went off with Neptune, sideways through the multiverse – not deliberately, you'll recall – and now they're a million or two years in our future. Well, you know more about physics than I do.' Wren was talking from panic rather than enthusiasm. 'These are the descendants of our original ancestors. They *were* "coming back" – not to their home planet but to their home star-system. They knew about Mars. Morgan, they were coming home to die! I was right. Everyone comes to Mars to die! Even me, it seems.'

Frowning, Morgan stared uncertainly from what appeared to be the weapon in Luuk Shenpehr's hands to the seated, frightened Wren. 'To live,' said Morgan firmly. 'They're here because they're trying to find a way to survive. Surely that's more logical? How did you offend them, Wren?'

'Maybe I got a bit noisy when I realized the truth. Obviously their space-time is now radically different to this one and that explains their apparent slowness and the occasional insubstantiality – which incidentally they seem in the process of correcting . . .' Wren paused. 'Don't let them shoot me, Morgan. They like you.'

'They said that?'

'They're not pointing a gun at you.' This irritating tendency to trivialize even in such circumstances almost made Morgan want to abandon Wren to whatever fate was in store.

'But they were looking for help.' Morgan did not want to believe in any reverse.

'The interpretations are tricky. They say they're seeking transformation – resolution? – this is their technonlex, maybe hundreds of years ahead of ours, maybe more.'

Earth unpeace . . . Sendes-endes-Ah spoke again in a voice like the distant song of a harp, but stronger, less hesitant. Still Morgan could only understand the one phrase. Was it some kind of ultimatum?

'They won't respond to me.' Wren was shaking now. 'Please intercede.'

'They're not being attacked?' Morgan's voice was faint.

'They are being "pushed down", they said. Another force is simply occupying their planet as if they don't exist. Morgan!'

Morgan moved cautiously forward. Behind the alien ship the Martian sun had risen like an angel's armour, proclaiming some unspecific glory. The old, red hills began to pulse. The smell of orange blossom crystals sweetened the thin air and made it magical.

'But, Wren, you haven't explained how you angered them.'

'Perhaps I was facetious. I couldn't believe they hadn't resisted the invaders. They say they're fewer than twelve now.' Wren took deep breaths, trying to control panic. 'A civil war? Oh, Morgan.' The gun moved in Luuk Shenpehr's hand. The risen sun made it blossom with sudden colour. Then, in a second of inspiration, Morgan stepped forward and took it from the alien. There was no resistance.

Shaking with relief, Wren stood up, while Morgan held the thing to the light. Wren began to smile sheepishly, but Morgan's features had grown profoundly sad. Morgan understood the object's function.

'I think you saved my life.' Wren was anxious to fill in the silence.

Morgan's head moved in a tiny gesture of contradiction.

Stretching towards the blazing, complicated thing, Wren asked: 'How does it fire?'

'It doesn't,' said Morgan, sighting along it. 'It can't.' There were no moving parts.

'It's clearly a gun. I've seen stuff like it in paperbacks.'

Morgan turned the object this way and that to let the sun's rays play on its awkward curves and peculiar angles, this icon, perhaps created in desperation from insubstantial data on a race's long dead past. 'It's not a gun, Wren.'

The dust blew for a moment around their legs while from the Northern Shafts the Martians, masked against the light, were emerging, moving hesitantly towards their Earthling cousins. At last Morgan handed the object to a still baffled Wren.

'It's only the memory of a gun.'

The Frozen Cardinal

MOLDAVIA. S. POLE. 1/7/17

Dear Gerry,

I got your last, finally. Hope this reaches you in less than a year. The supply planes are all robots now and are supposed to give a faster service. Did I tell you we were being sent to look over the southern pole? Well, we're here. Below zero temperatures, of course, and at present we're gaining altitude all the time. At least we don't have to wear breathing equipment yet. The Moldavian poles have about twice the volume of ice as those of Earth, but they're melting. As we thought, we found the planet at the end of its ice-age. I know how you hate statistics and you know what a bore I can be, so I won't go into the details. To tell you the truth, it's a relief not to be logging and measuring.

It's when I write to you that I find it almost impossible to believe how far away Earth is. I frequently have a peculiar sense of closeness to the home planet, even though we are light years from it. Sometimes I think Earth will appear in the sky at 'dawn' and a rocket will come to take me to you. Are you lying to me, Gerry? Are you really still waiting? I love you so much. Yet my reason cautions me. I can't believe in your fidelity. I don't mean to make you impatient but I miss you desperately sometimes and I'm sure you know how strange people get in these conditions. I joined the expedition, after all, to give you time by yourself, to reconsider our relationship. But when I got your letter I was overjoyed. And, of course, I wish I'd never signed up for Moldavia. Still, only another six months to go now, and another six months home. I'm glad your mother recovered from her accident. This time next year we'll be spending all my ill-gotten gains in the Seychelles. It's what keeps me going.

We're perfectly safe in our icesuits, of course, but we get terribly tired. We're ascending a series of gigantic ice terraces which seem to go on forever. It takes a day to cross from one terrace to the wall of the next, then another day or so to climb the wall and move the equipment up. The small sun is visible throughout an entire cycle of the planet at this time of year, but the 'day', when both suns are visible, is only about three hours. Then everything's very bright, of course, unless it's snowing or there's a thick cloud-cover, and we have to protect our eyes. We use the brightest hours for sleeping. It's almost impossible to do anything else. The vehicles are reliable, but slow. If we make any real speed we have to wait a consequently longer interval until they can be re-charged. Obviously, we re-charge during the bright hours, so it all works out reasonably well. It's a strangely orderly planet, Gerry: everything in its place. Those creatures I told you about were not as intelligent as we had hoped. Their resemblance to spiders is remarkable, though, even to spinning enormous webs around their nests; chiefly, it seemed to us, for decoration. They ate the rations we offered and suffered no apparent ill-effects, which means that the planet could probably be opat-gen in a matter of years. That would be a laugh on Galtman. Were you serious, by the way, in your letter? You couldn't leave your USSA even to go to Canada when we were together! You wouldn't care for this ice. The plains and jungles we explored last year feel almost deserted, as if they were once inhabited by a race which left no mark whatsoever. We found no evidence of intelligent inhabitants, no large animals, though we detected some weirdly-shaped skeletons in caves below the surface. We were told not to excavate, to leave that to the follow-up team. This is routine official work; there's no romance in it for me. I didn't expect there would be, but I hadn't really allowed for the boredom, for the irritation one begins to feel with one's colleagues. I'm so glad you wrote to say you still love me. I joined to find myself, to let you get on with your life. I hope we both will be more stable when we meet again.

The gennard is warmed up and I'm being signalled, so I'll close this for the time being. We're about to ascend another wall, and that means only one of us can skit to see to the hoist, while the others go up the hard way on the lines. Helander's the leader on this particular op. I must say he's considerably easier going than old IP whom you'll probably have seen on the news by now, showing off his eggs. But the river itself is astonishing, completely encircling the planet; fresh water and Moldavia's only equivalent to our oceans, at least until this ice age is really over!

8/7/17 'Dawn'

A few lines before I fall asleep. It's been a hard one today. Trouble with the hoists. Routine stuff, but it doesn't help morale when it's this cold. I was dangling about nine hundred metres up, with about another thousand to go, for a good hour, with nothing to do but listen to Fisch's curses in my helmet, interspersed with the occasional reassurance. You're helpless in a situation like that! And then, when we did all get to the top and started off again across the terrace (the ninth!) we came almost immediately to an enormous crevasse which must be half-a-kilometre across! So here we are on the edge. We can go round or we can do a horizontal skit. We'll decide that in the 'evening'. I have the irrational feeling that this whole section could split off suddenly and engulf us in the biggest landslide a human being ever witnessed. It's silly to think like that. In relationship to this astonishing staircase we are lighter than midges. Until I got your last letter I wouldn't have cared. I'd have been excited by the idea. But now, of course, I've got something to live for. It's peculiar, isn't it, how that makes cowards of the best of us?

9/7/17

Partridge is down in the crevasse at this moment. He thinks we can bridge, but wants to make sure. Also our instruments have picked up something odd, so we're duty-bound to investigate. The rest of us are hanging around, quite glad of the chance to do nothing. Fedin is playing his music and Simons and Russell are fooling about on the edge, kicking a ration-pack about, with the crevasse as the goal. You can hardly make out the other side. Partridge just said he's come across something odd imbedded in the north wall. He says the colours of the ice are beautiful, all dark greens and blues, but this, he says, is red. 'There shouldn't be anything red down here!' He says it's probably rock but it resembles an artefact. Maybe there have been explorers here before us, or even inhabitants. If so, they must have been here relatively recently, because these ice-steps are not all that old, especially at the depth Partridge has reached. Mind you, it wouldn't be the first practical joke he's played since we arrived.

Later

Partridge is up. When he pushed back his visor he looked pale and said he thought he was crazy. Fedin gave him a check-up immediately. There are no extraordinary signs of fatigue. Partridge says the outline he saw in the ice seemed to be a human figure. The instruments all suggest it is animal matter, though of course there are no life-functions. 'Even if it's an artefact,' said Partridge, 'it hasn't got any business being there.' He shuddered. 'It seemed to be looking at me. A direct, searching stare. I got frightened.' Partridge isn't very imaginative, so we were all impressed. 'Are we going to get it out of there?' asked Russell. 'Or do we just record it for the follow-up team, as we did with those skeletons?' Helander was uncertain. He's as curious as the rest of us. 'I'll take a look for myself,' he said. He went down, said something under his breath which none of us could catch in our helmets, then gave the order to be hoisted up again. 'It's a Roman Catholic cardinal,' he said. 'The hat, the robes, everything. Making a benediction!' He frowned. 'We're going to have to send back on this and await instructions.'

Fedin laughed. 'We'll be recalled immediately. Everyone's warned of the hallucinations. We'll be hospitalized back at base for months while the bureaucrats try to work out why we went mad.'

'You'd better have a look,' said Helander. 'I want you to go down one by one and tell me what you see.'

Partridge was squatting on his haunches, drinking something hot. He was trembling all over. He seemed to be sweating. 'This is ridiculous,' he said, more than once.

Three others are ahead of me, then it's my turn. I feel perfectly sane, Gerry. Everything else seems normal – as normal as it can be. And if this team has a failing it is that it isn't very prone to speculation or visual hallucinations. I've never been with a duller bunch of fact-gatherers. Maybe that's why we're all more scared than we should be. No expedition from Earth could ever have been to Moldavia before. Certainly nobody would have buried a Roman Catholic cardinal in the ice. There is no explanation, however wild, which fits. We're all great rationalists on this team. Not a hint of mysticism or even poetry among us. The drugs see to that if our temperaments don't!

Russell's coming up. He's swearing, too. Chang goes down. Then it's my turn. Then Simons'. Then Fisch. I wish you were here, Gerry. With your intelligence you could probably think of something. We certainly can't. I'd better start kitting up. More when I come up. To tell you the absolute truth I'm none too happy about going down!

Later

Well, I've been down. It's dark. The blues and greens glow as if they give off an energy of their own, although it's only reflections. The wall is smooth and opaque. About four metres down and about half a metre back into the ice of the face you can see him. He's tall, about fifty-five, very handsome, clean-shaven and he's looking directly out at you. His eyes seem sad but not at all malevolent. Indeed,

I'd say he seemed kind. There's something noble about him. His clothes are scarlet and fall in folds which suggest he became frozen while standing naturally in the spot he stands in now. He couldn't, therefore, have been dropped, or the clothing would be disturbed. There's no logic to it, Gerry. His right hand is raised and he's making some sort of Christian sign. You know I'm not too hot on anthropology. Helander's the expert.

His expression seems to be one of forgiveness. It's quite overwhelming. You almost find your heart going out to him while at the same time you can't help thinking you're somehow responsible for his being there! Six light years from Earth on a planet which was only catalogued three years ago and which we are supposedly the first human beings to explore. Nowhere we have been has anyone discovered a shred of evidence that man or anything resembling man ever explored other planets. You know as well as I do that the only signs of intelligent life anyone has found have been negligible and certainly we have never had a hint that any other creature is capable of space-travel. Yet here is a man dressed in a costume which, at its latest possible date, is from the twentieth century.

I tried to stare him down. I don't know why. Eventually I told them to lift me up. While Simons went down, I waited on the edge, sipping ade and trying to stop shaking. I don't know why all of us were so badly affected. We've been in danger often enough (I wrote to you about the lavender swamps) and there isn't anyone on the team who hasn't got a sense of humour. Nobody's been able to raise a laugh yet. Helander tried, but it was so forced that we felt sorry for him. When Simons came up he was in exactly the same state as me. I handed him the rest of my ade and then returned to my biv to write this. We're to have a conference in about ten minutes. We haven't decided whether to send back information yet or not. Our curiosity will probably get the better of us. We have no specific orders on the question, but we're pretty sure we'll get a hands off if we report now. The big skeletons were one thing. This is quite another. And yet we know in our hearts that we should leave well alone.

'Dawn'

The conference is over. It went on for hours. Now we've all decided to sleep on it. Helander and Partridge have been down for another look and have set up a carver in case we decided to go ahead. It will be easy enough to do. Feeling very tired. Have the notion that if we disturb the cardinal we'll do something cataclysmic. Maybe the whole planet will dissolve around us. Maybe this enormous mountain will crumble to nothing. Helander says that what he would like to do is send back on the cardinal but say that he is already carving, since our instruments suggest the crevasse is unstable and could close. There's no way it could close in the next week! But it would be a good enough excuse. You might never get this letter, Gerry. For all we're told personal mail is uninspected I don't trust them entirely. Do you think I should? Or if someone else is reading this, do they think I should have trusted to the law? His face is in my mind's eye as I write. So tranquil. So sad. I'm taking a couple of deegs, so will write more tomorrow.

10/7/17

Helander has carved. The whole damned thing is standing in the centre of the camp now, like a memorial. A big square block of ice with the cardinal peering out of it. We've all walked round and round the thing. There's no question that the figure is human. Helander wanted to begin thawing right away, but bowed to Simons, who doesn't want to risk the thing deteriorating. Soon he's going to vacuum-cocoon it. Simons is cursing himself for not bringing more of his archaeological gear along with him. He expected nothing like this, and our experience up to now has shown that Moldavia doesn't *have* any archaeology worth mentioning. We're all convinced it was a living creature. I even feel he may still be alive, the way he looks at me. We're all very jittery, but our sense of humour has come back and we make bad jokes about the cardinal really being Jesus Christ or Mahomet or somebody. Helander accuses us of religious illiteracy. He's the only one with any real knowledge of all that stuff. He is behaving oddly. He snapped at Russell a little while ago, telling him he wasn't showing proper reverence.

Russell apologized. He said he hadn't realized Helander was superstitious. Helander has sent back, saying what he's done and telling them he's about to thaw. A *fait accompli*. Fisch is unhappy. He and Partridge feel we should replace the cardinal and get on with 'our original business'. The rest of us argue that this *is* our original business. We are an exploration team. 'It's follow-up work,' said Fisch. 'I'm anxious to see what's at the top of this bloody great staircase.' Partridge replied: 'A bloody great Vatican, if you reason it through on the evidence we have.' That's the trouble with the kind of logic we go in for, Gerry. Well, we'll all be heroes when we get back to Earth, I suppose. Or we'll be disgraced, depending on what happens next. There's not a lot that can happen to me. This isn't my career, the way it is for the others. I'll be only too happy to be fired, since I intend to resign as soon as I'm home. Then it's the Seychelles for us, my dear. I hope you haven't changed your mind. I wish you were here. I feel the need to share what's going on – and I can think of nobody better to share it than you. Oh, God, I love you so much, Gerry. More, I know, than you'll ever love me; but I can bear anything except separation. I was reconciled to that separation until you wrote your last letter. I hope the company is giving you the yellow route now. You deserve it. With a clean run through to Maracaibo there will be no stopping the old gaucho, eh? But those experiments are risky, I'm told. So don't go too far. I think I know you well enough to be pretty certain you won't take unnecessary risks. I wish I could reach out now and touch your lovely, soft skin, your fine fair hair. I must stop this. It's doing things to me which even the blunn can't control! I'm going out for another walk around our frozen friend.

Later

Well, he's thawed. And it is human. Flesh and blood, Gerry, and no sign of deterioration. A man even taller than Helander. His clothes are all authentic, according to the expert. He's even wearing a pair of old-fashioned cotton underpants. No protective clothing. No sign of having had food with him. No sign of transport. And our instruments have been scouring a wider and wider area. We have the little beeps on automatic, using far more energy than they should. The probes go everywhere. Helander says that this is important. If we can find a vehicle or a trace of habitation, then at least we'll have the beginnings of an answer. He wants something to send back now, of course. We've had an acknowledgement and a hold-off signal. There's not much to hold-off from, currently. The cardinal stands in the middle of the camp, his right arm raised in benediction, his eyes as calm and sad and resigned as ever. He continues to make us jumpy. But there are no more jokes, really, except that we sometimes call him 'padre'. Helander says all expeditions had one in the old days: a kind of psych-medic, like Fedin. Fedin says he thinks the uniform a bit unsuitable for the conditions. It's astonishing how we grow used to something as unbelievable as this. We look up at the monstrous ice-steps ahead of us, the vast gulf behind us, at an alien sky with two suns in it; we know that we are millions upon millions of miles from Earth, across the vacuum of interstellar space, and realize we are sharing our camp with a corpse dressed in the costume of the sixteenth century and we're beginning to take it all for granted . . . I suppose it says something for human resilience. But we're all still uncomfortable. Maybe there's only so much our brains can take. I wish I was sitting on a stool beside you at the Amset having a beer. But things are so strange to me now that *that* idea is hard to accept. This has become normality. The probes bring in nothing. We're using every instrument we've got. Nothing. We're going to have to ask for the reserve stuff at base and get them to send something to the top. I'd like to be pulled back, I think, and yet I remain fascinated. Maybe you'll be able to tell me if I sound mad. I don't feel mad. Nobody is behaving badly. We're all under control, I think. Only Helander seems profoundly affected. He spends most of his time staring into the cardinal's face, touching it.

Later

Helander says the skin feels warm. He asked me to tell him if I agreed. I stripped off a glove and touched the fingers. They certainly feel warm, but that could just be the effect of sun. Nevertheless, the arm hasn't moved, neither have the eyes. There's no breathing. He stares at us tenderly, blessing us, forgiving us. I'm beginning to resent him. What have I done that he should forgive me? I now agree with those who want to put him back. I suppose we can't. We've been told to sit tight and wait for base to send someone up. It will take a while before they come.

11/7/17

Russell woke me up. I kitted up fast and went out. Helander was kneeling in front of the cardinal and seemed to be mumbling to himself. He refused to move when we tried to get him to stand up. 'He's weeping,' he said. 'He's weeping.'

There did seem to be moisture on the skin. Then, even as we watched, blood began to trickle out of both eyes and run down the cheeks. The cardinal was weeping tears of blood, Gerry!

'Evidently the action of the atmosphere,' said Fedin, when we raised him. 'We might have to refreeze him, I think.'

The cardinal's expression hadn't changed. Helander became impatient and told us to go away. He said he was communicating with the cardinal. Fedin sedated him and got him back to his biv. We heard his voice, even in sleep, mumbling and groaning. Once, he screamed. Fedin pumped some more stuff into him, then. He's quiet now.

Later

We've had word that base is on its way. About time, too, for me. I'm feeling increasingly scared.

'Dusk'

I crawled out of my biv thinking that Helander was crying again or that Fedin was playing his music. The little, pale sun was high in the sky, the big one was setting. There was a reddish glow on the ice. Everything seemed red, in fact. I couldn't see too clearly, but the cardinal was still standing there, a dark silhouette. And the sounds were coming from him. He was singing, Gerry. There was no one else up. I stood in front of the cardinal. His lips were moving. Some sort of chant. His eyes weren't looking at me any longer. They were raised. Someone came to stand beside me. It was Helander. He was a bit woozy, but his face was ecstatic. He began to join in the song. Their singing seemed to fill the sky, the planet, the whole damned universe. The music made me cry, Gerry. I have never heard a more beautiful voice. Helander turned to me once. 'Join in,' he said. 'Join in.' But I couldn't because I didn't know the words. 'It's Latin,' said Helander. It was like a bloody choir. I found myself lifting my head like a dog. There were resonances in my throat. I began to howl. But it wasn't howling. It was chanting, the same as the cardinal. No words. Just music. It was the most exquisite music I have ever heard in my life. I became aware that the others were with me, standing in a semi-circle, and they were singing too. And we were so full of joy, Gerry. We were all weeping. It was incredible. Then the sun had set and the music gradually faded and we stood looking at one another, totally exhausted, grinning like coyotes, feeling complete fools. And the cardinal was looking at us again, with that same sweet tolerance. Helander was kneeling in front of him and mumbling, but we couldn't hear the words. Eventually, after he'd been on the ice for an hour, Fedin decided to sedate him. 'He'll be dead at this rate, if I don't.'

Later

We've just finished putting the cardinal back in the crevasse, Gerry. I can still hear that music in my head. I wish there was some way I could play you the recordings we've made, but doubtless you'll hear them in time, around when you get this letter. Base hasn't arrived yet. Helander said he was going to let it be their responsibility. I'm hoping we'll be relieved for those medical tests we were afraid of at first. I want to get away from here. I'm terrified, Gerry. I keep wanting to climb into the crevasse and ask the cardinal to sing for me again. I have never known such absolute release, such total happiness, as when I sang in harmony with him. What do you think it is? Maybe it's all hallucination. Someone will know. Twice I've stood on the edge, peering down. You can't see him from here, of course. And you can't see the bottom. I haven't the courage to descend the lines.

I want to jump. I would jump, I think, if I could get the chance just once more to sing with him. I keep thinking of eternity. For the first time in my life I have a glimmering of what it means.

Oh, Gerry, I hope it isn't an illusion. I hope you'll be able to hear that voice on the tapes and know what I felt when the frozen cardinal sang. I love you Gerry. I want to give you so much. I wish I could give you what I have been given. I wish I could sing for you the way the cardinal sang. There isn't one of us who hasn't been weeping. Fedin keeps trying to be rational. He says we are more exhausted than we know, that the drugs we take have side-effects which couldn't be predicted. We look up into the sky from time to time, waiting for base to reach us. I wish you were here, Gerry. But I can't possibly regret now that I made the decision I made. I love you, Gerry. I love you all.

Peace on Earth

(with Barrington Bayley)

The *Trans-Galactos* came to a dead stop half a light year from the G-star. Within, its two occupants debated.

They were human, in the sense that they were the descendants of what had been human two million years ago and they still retained the bipedal, bimanual form. But they were lean and tall, with elongated faces, unhappy eyes and high brows which slanted sharply back. Their lank hair hung flaxen below their shoulders.

Most important, they were immortal.

At the moment, they were both feeling very uncertain of themselves. Fra-Thala held the Book in his hand as if it were a measure of reassurance. Bulk stared miserably at the G-star, Sol.

'We've got to try,' Fta-Thala said. 'We've got to. We can't let anything go by without trying.'

'Try what? We don't even know what to look for.'

'At least we can land and – look. Just look. It might be there – whatever it is.'

Bulik continued to gaze at the star. He did not move.

'Go on,' Fra-Thala told him. 'Why don't you engage the ship's drive? It's the third planet.'

'I don't know,' Bulik said slowly, almost whispering. 'I think – I'm *scared*.'

They were both silent for several seconds. They stared with strange fascination at Sol, a matter-of-fact, insignificant sun. Then Fra-Thala blanked out the viewport and the spell was lessened. The comforting walls of the ship were all about them.

'So you feel it too,' he said.

'Fear?'

'Yes.' Bulik's loosely jointed form paced the room. 'But why?' he demanded. 'We weren't afraid when we looked for it on Stulek Bal. We weren't afraid when someone told us it was in the Lesser Magellanic, or when we asked the Iddians for it. Why are we afraid now?'

Fra-Thala held up the black-bound Book. 'Perhaps because this says Earth is where it really is.'

'Why should that scare us?'
The other shrugged.

After a while, Bulik reluctantly made some computations. He looked again at Sol. Then he engaged the drive and the *Trans-Galactos* flashed to the region of the outermost planet, converted to interplanetary drive, and moved more slowly towards the Earth. Soon the ship was flooded with sunlight, which became gentle and diffused as they sank into the atmosphere of the third world, settling on to a vast arid plain.

The two men studied the landscape through the viewports. For five hundred years they had searched the galaxy until they had become gaunt with obsession. They had taken to gazing around them in a haunted way, as if the desperation of their quest had driven them into a misery and despair from which no force in the universe could rescue them.

And they were quite alone in their search. The *Trans-Galactos* was probably the only interstellar ship in the galaxy; they had built it themselves from ancient specifications. The rest of humanity lived placidly, aimlessly and immortally deep within the atmospheres of the settled planets. They had lost all meaning to life.

It was a meaning to life that Bulik and Fra-Thala sought. On the other side of the galaxy they had acquired the Book, written long ago by one of the greatest of all men, Aber Juillard, and real hope for the first time presented itself. They did not know how long ago the book had been written, for it was made from imperishable material, but they knew it was about as old as the oldest man living, for among his other accomplishments, Juillard had also given mankind immortality. It had taken many years of research to discover that he had refused the gift himself and was no longer available.

Juillard had also foreseen that one day men would lose something from their lives, and had written of it in the Book. He had not stated exactly what it would be, and the passages referring to it were obscure, but it would seem to be something of immeasurable value. Fra-Thala had become filled with excitement when he read the sentence: 'Those who wish to regain that precious thing that mankind loses should visit the planet Earth, the birthplace of the species, and there they shall find it.

Now he stared at the endless plain and felt hope sink again. He saw soft yellow dust strewn from here to the horizon, seeped in light from the low sun. The scene had such a delicate beauty as made him think of the meadows of his native world. Meadows of dust . . .

But nowhere was there any clue that might lead them to the unnamed object of their search.

A deep, moaning sigh escaped from Bulik. 'It's no use!' he cried. 'What is there here? Nothing. It's a dead world. Nothing lives. Nothing.' He took the Book from his companion and read once again from the place they had marked. 'This tells us nothing. He doesn't even mention anything specific. Perhaps it doesn't mean anything specific. Perhaps he was just being poetic.'

'Even we can't say what we're looking for,' Fra-Thala pointed out. 'All we have is this terrible feeling inside us; this feeling of something missing. The passage in the book seems to be the same sort of thing.'

He turned away from the viewport. The only label he could give it, he thought, was a desire for peace. Peace of mind, peace from the constant biting knowledge of something *gone*. There were centuries of life behind him: ahead was an eternity of trash, meaningless acts, futile existence.

Unless he could find this peace, this value that had vanished from the human mind.

'Well,' he said, 'let's look.'

'Look? Where?' Bulik gestured to the waste outside the ship. 'You can see everything from here.'

'The Book –'

'The Book!' Bulik had lost all faith. He prowled the room, head bent, his cloak falling limply about him. 'We've done what the Book said. We have come to Earth. And where are we? What have we found? Nothing. Juillard was being fanciful, I tell you!'

'No. He was too great for that. He had the finest understanding of human mentality of any creature before or since – he produced immortality, remember, on a purely mental level by adjusting the cortical control of physiological processes. I can't believe that he would write those words without good reason.'

He glanced again at the viewport. 'You're right, there's nothing in this desert. But the Earth's a fair-sized planet and it was well populated once. Let's move over the horizon until we find something.'

Bulik frowned, then moved to the control panel.

After a few moments the ship lifted twenty feet from the surface and travelled in the direction of the sun. As an afterthought he activated the detector to show the presence of refined metals.

This last action paid off. They travelled about a hundred miles without any change in the ochre desert before the indicator flashed.

Bulik put the ship into a slow circle, seeking the object of response.

It was a thick, flat cylindrical building, standing solidly on the desert floor and throwing off the cold light of afternoon as it must have done for countless thousands of years: it was so long since there had been living things on Sol's third planet that the air itself had become unbreathable.

'If could be anything,' Bulik said, 'but let's get out there and see. I hope there's a way in.'

There was. Fra-Thala walked nearly the full circumference, the boots of his light-weight atmosphere suit scuffing up dust, before he found it; a simple sliding door, its bearings cunningly protected against abrasion and time. The building gave the impression of having been built to endure.

When they got inside and switched on their torches, Bulik snorted with disappointment. 'Why, it's just a bookvault. I've seen them a hundred times.'

They wandered around for several minutes, without real interest. It was common practice for a community to leave samples and records of its culture when it abandoned a region and there was no reason to suppose there was anything special about this one, or about the society it represented.

Or was there? Fra-Thala awoke to the situation with a start. Since Earth was the original planet, the vault might contain traces of the most primeval periods, back before spaceflight. That in itself was rather unremarkable, but the Book . . .

With slightly more alertness, he took up a few of the volumes from their cases. He was pleased to find that although some of the languages and symbolisms were very ancient he was acquainted with most of them. An immortal has time to learn most things sooner or later. But after a little study his interest waned again. There was nothing he would not have expected, or that he might not have encountered on a thousand worlds.

Bulik was ambling moodily throughout the extent of the vault. Now he came up to Fra-Thala to see what he was doing. 'Do you think – do you think it *might* be here after all? Should we examine every one of these books, because the secret of it might be written here somewhere?' He seemed pathetically dismayed.

'No, I don't think so. Juillard wouldn't be so tedious, I'm sure of that. This is just an ordinary culture vault.'

Bulik considered, nodded and looked relieved. 'I suppose you're right. Let's get out of here. It makes me feel irritable. I could do with some sleep.'

Fra-Thala remembered that he also had not slept for a considerable time. Carelessly replacing the books in their cases he followed his companion, stumbling towards the block of pale-gold light that came from the open door.

Outside, he found that he had forgotten to replace one book. Mildly curious, he looked at the obsolescent script imprinted on the cover: *The Thousand and One Nights*. He flicked through it, stopped at a page and read:

'. . . *and he and the King and his father-in-law and their family resided in the most happy state and in the practice of good deeds, until they were visited by the terminator of delights, and the separator of companions.*'

He stared at the sentence blankly for a short time, and shuddered. Life, to an immortal, was most carefully guarded, and the loss of it was looked on with the greatest horror. The very suggestion of death would make a man look frantically about him for a source of danger.

Letting the book drop from his hand into the dust, he trudged wearily towards the *Trans-Galactos*.

A few hours later, Fra-Thala awoke to the realization that uneasiness had not left him since they had made the stop far beyond Pluto. It had stayed with him through the sleeping period, producing restless dreams.

He had dreamed that he was back on his home world before he had met Bulik and their twin frustrations had flared into life on contact. In the dream, it was as if he could see millions of years ahead of time. The people of the town where he was born had stared at him with stupefied eyes, stultified, gaping, grey with decay because they had lived for so long without the thing that would make them completely human. On waking he felt no horror but lay with his eyes closed, going over the details of the nightmare and letting his detached intellect extract the full sense from it. It would not take millions of years, he thought; it would only take thousands. It might have begun already.

It might happen to him, and to Bulik, unless they found the answer in time. He tried to examine his own mind, to find out what it was that was worrying him about this planet; but the question receded further and further from him as he approached it.

He rose from the sleeping couch, rinsed his face with ice-cold water and combed out his long hair where he had been lying on it. Usually when he woke he ate, but now food seemed like sacrilege to him.

Night had come and gone, and it was early morning. He looked at the small G-star which was pouring its perpetual energy over the landscape.

Fra-Thala shook his head. The terrible idea came to him that perhaps humanity was already too far gone to retrieve the precious item it had lost, like a corpse already on the road to decomposition. Perhaps he and Bulik would wander for centuries about the galaxy, never achieving their purpose, until the purpose became submerged in an inertia of mindless meandering.

With that thought in his head he seated himself at the control panels, his glazed eyes falling automatically on the multitude of meters. He blinked apathetically – then stood, suddenly vitalized with intelligence.

'Bulik! Here!'

Bulik continued to sleep. Impatiently he strode over to the couch and shook him roughly awake, dragged him over to the panels. Bulik shielded his eyes as the sharp sunlight fell on them.

'Look!' Fra-Thala said, pointing. 'The detector shows another energy converter on the planet. It must be another ship!'

Adjusting his eyes to the light, Bulik read the meter. There could be no mistake: nothing had the same composition of materials as an energy converter. 'From the look of it,' he stated, 'the converter has ceased functioning as an energy source. Probably an abandoned ship, or a derelict. It must have been here all the time and we never thought to check.'

'Shall we go and see it?'

Bulik shrugged. 'If you like. I don't suppose there'll be much to learn.'

He moved the *Trans-Galactos* a few miles for a triangulation fix and located the converter at a place somewhere around what was currently midday. As he geared the drive for the transplanetary hop, the yellow waste swayed beneath them and Sol rose swiftly into the sky. But the living quarters of the ship, with their own independent gravitation, were a closed system: it was as if the Earth moved and the room stayed still. Not even the sound of the air rushing over the exterior surface penetrated its calm. It might have been a staid dwelling on some garden world.

The sight of the other ship, when they found it, verified the opinion that it had lain motionless for a considerable time. Dust, blown by vagrant thin winds, had piled up on one side of it: the entire length of the vessel had bellied a few feet into the desert.

They went outside to inspect the ship, and Fra-Thala ran his gloved hand along the smooth metal. It was impossible to tell by appearance whether it had been built ten years ago or ten thousand, since the materials were of the permanent kind produced by molecular impaction: its position, however, and the fact that its power source had died, suggested an age of several millennia.

Bulik tried to open the airlock. It did not respond. 'As I thought,' he said. 'The ship's completely without power.' As he applied the emergency power pack to the external leads, the lock door slid aside with a whine, and they were able to step inside a vessel patterned largely after their own. FraThala began to feel a kinship with the owners, for the chances were that they came from his section of the galaxy.

They opened the door to the living quarters. Yellow light streamed through dusty viewports into a room in perfect condition, and without trace of an occupant.

Several minutes still elspased before Fra-Thala reached the quite obvious conclusion that this ship had landed long after the Earth's population had vanished, and then the owner had vanished also. The realization came as a shock. 'Bulik!' Fra-Thala fought against a great sense of panic. 'Bulik! What happened to the man?'

For a moment Bulik was unable to answer. His face was colourless. 'There couldn't have been . . . *danger.*'

'But where *is* he?'

Bulik shook his head.

Fra-Thala felt his nagging undercurrent of fear mount to a momentary climax of desperation. It was like being told that the spacecraft in which he was travelling was caught in a magnetic storm which would not fail to sweep it into a white-hot star. He peered about him for some clue.

He found one thing. A book, bound in black. A copy of Juillard's Book.

Amazed he snatched it up. It was identical to his own, the same edition. 'So there are others,' he murmured. 'Others with the same yearning. They obtained the Book – and they too followed its instructions.'

'Were others,' corrected Bulik. 'They're not here any more.'

'But what happened? Perhaps they found it.' Like a dynamo rising to its full speed he suddenly became full of excitement. 'Perhaps they found what they wanted – the secret of life!'

'Then why did they desert the ship?'

He fingered the imperishable volume, not knowing the answer. Eventually he said: 'Who knows what the secret of life brings? Perhaps they no longer needed the ship.'

His companion was not impressed. 'That sounds rather fanciful. A more prosaic theory would suit me better.'

Fra-Thala was prepared to admit that he was allowing his imagination free play. The bewilderment of their discoveries had released him into uninhibited dreams: for never before had they met companions in their search, apart from the sentiments expressed by the long-dead Aber Juillard.

And never before, in mankind's thinly-spread but supercautious society, had they heard of men who disappeared without a trace. An immortal life was far too precious a thing to take chances with.

'Listen,' he urged, 'there's a lead here – there's something to learn. There must be – the circumstances are too unusual. We must follow it up!'

'How?' Bulik had been searching the chamber for further information. He found none, except that there were two sleeping couches, indicating that the expedition consisted of a corresponding number. 'This ship was abandoned ages ago.'

Fra-Thala shook his head. 'You can always manage to dampen my enthusiasm, Bulik.'

A few minutes later they gave up and decided to go back to their own vessel. Fra-Thala still retained a feeling of unrest: and as they crossed the few yards between ships he lifted his head and surveyed the land. Through the thin material of his atmosphere suit he felt an insubstantial cold wind press against him, a wind that had swept the full length of the plain, down from those hills in the distance, and perhaps halfway across the face of the planet. Something in him stirred.

'You know,' he said, 'we haven't really carried out Juillard's instructions. Not yet.'

'What do you mean?'

'Juillard said to go to Earth. Well, we've landed here, that's all. We've spent about twenty minutes in all outside our ship, and the rest of the time we've cowered inside it. We should get to know what it feels like to be on Earth, walk about on the ground, explore by foot.'

He could see Bulik hesitating. 'All right,' the man admitted at last, 'perhaps you've got something. Perhaps that is what he meant. Let's do it.'

For both of them the act took a tremendous effort of will. Drawing strength from one another, they set out towards the hills which undulated on the horizon. Fra-Thala felt strangely light-headed and he sensed that his companion did too. After half a mile he turned to look back at the two starships, and his fear mounted again, without reason, like an animal bolting from a sudden noise. Yet he did not question what he hoped to find in the hills: he had a childlike compulsion to obey Juillard, and this was how he thought it should be done. Nervously they advanced together over the dead, brightly shining expanse.

By mid-afternoon they had gained the hills. There was not much difference: the ground still consisted of yellow dust lain on solid bedrock, but in places the stone was revealed and glittered as if showing its strength. Fra-Thala walked away up a gently rising slope and swivelled his eyes about. His attention was easily caught by the one item of interest.

His lungs snatched air in nausea and shock some seconds before the logical part of his mind recognized the object. It was the remains of a skeleton.

He ran over to it, frantically motioning Bulik to follow. 'The poor fellow! What can have happened? He – he *died*.'

He uttered the word in a tone of utter horror. He had never seen a deceased human before.

The man's atmosphere suit was lying some yards away. For some reason which Fra-Thala could not possibly guess at, he had seen fit to crawl out of it before dying – indeed, he could hardly have hoped to survive the act. Bulik inspected the suit: the perishable components had disintegrated, and the rest couldn't tell him much. 'Well,' he said, 'now we know why the ship's empty.'

Fra-Thala pointed out slowly: 'Our ship's empty, now.'

In an instant he became terribly afraid. 'Let's get back,' he urged. 'Quick. Now!'

Bulik did not need to voice his agreement. Striding rapidly, they fled in the direction of the *Trans-Galactos*. For no particular reason Fra-Thala glanced at his airmeter. He froze.

'Bulik . . . how's your air?'

His companion checked his own supply, and moaned in fright. 'Nearly gone!'

'Mine, too . . .' Incredulously, he glared at the meter. He couldn't begin to understand. 'How could we have been so careless! I never heard of anyone being so stupid . . .'

His voice trailed off, paralysed by the magnitude of the disaster. He thought of running for it, but simultaneously there came the realization that they just would not reach the ship in time.

He squatted down in the dust, shaking his head. He could not believe that their forgetting to renew the air supply was pure accident; men didn't make mistakes like that any more than they forgot to breathe. Men never took chances on their lives.

Yet he was to die. Soon.

His brain refused to carry the meditation any further. Alarmed that he could accept the idea of death, he tried to shake himself into action, made a tremendous effort to grasp the situation entirely . . .

And then he knew why he was going to die.

Looking up, he saw that Bulik had found the answer as well. Wordlessly they communicated their twin discoveries.

What was it that in primeval times had given form and significance to a human being's existence? A thing is worthwhile only because of the possibility of its removal: the factor was death. Fra-Thala remembered the story he had taken from the book-vault, and realized that the King and his family could not have lived happily had they been immortal.

'Bulik,' he said in surprise, 'so that was why we were afraid. Death is what we fear most of all – and death is what we were seeking. Juillard knew of the consequences of never-ending life. So he left a way out for those who are sensitive enough to desire it. That's why we were careless about our air supply: it was a subconscious suggestion implanted along with the immortality equations.'

The other nodded. Then they both hunched silently on the ground, breathing the oxygen remaining in their packs. Fra-Thala died shortly afterwards, but the intervening few seconds of his life were charged with meaning.

The End

The Mountain

The last two men alive came out of the Lapp tent they had just raided for provisions.

'She's been here before us,' said Nilsson. 'It looks like she got the best of what there was.'

Hallner shrugged. He had eaten so little for so long that food no longer held any great importance for him.

He looked about him. Lapp *kata* wigwams of wood and hides were spread around the immediate area of dry ground. Valuable skins had been left out to cure, reindeer horns to bleach, the doors unfastened so that anyone might enter the deserted homes.

Hallner rather regretted the passing of the Lapps. They had had no part in the catastrophe, no interest in wars or violence or competition. Yet they had been herded to the shelters with everyone else. And, like everyone else, they had perished either by direct bombing, radiation poisoning or asphyxiation.

He and Nilsson had been in a forgotten meteorological station close to the Norwegian border. When they finally repaired their radio, the worst was over. Fall-out had by this time finished off the tribesmen in Indonesian jungles, the workers in remote districts of China, the hill-billies in the Rockies, the crofters in Scotland. Only freak weather conditions, which had been part of their reason for visiting the station earlier in the year, had so far prevented the lethal rain from falling in this area of Swedish Lappland.

They had known themselves, perhaps instinctively, to be the last two human beings alive, until Nilsson found the girl's tracks coming from the south and heading north. Who she was, how she'd escaped, they couldn't guess, but they had changed their direction from north-east to north and begun to follow. Two days later they had found the Lapp camp.

Now they stared ahead of them at the range of ancient mountains. It was three a.m., but the sun still hung a bloody spread on the horizon for it was summer – the six-week summer of the Arctic when the sun never fully set, when the snows of the mountains melted and ran down to form the rivers, lakes and marshes of the lowlands where only the occasional Lapp camp, or the muddy scar of a broad reindeer path, told of the presence of the few men who lived here during the winter months.

Suddenly, as he looked away from the range, the camp aroused some emotion akin to pity in Hallner's mind. He remembered the despair of the dying man who had told them, on his radio, what had happened to the world.

Nilsson had entered another hut and came out shaking a packet of raisins. 'Just what we need,' he said.

'Good,' said Hallner, and he sighed inaudibly. The clean, orderly nature of the little primitive village was spoiled for him by the sight he had witnessed earlier at the stream which ran through the camp. There had been simple drinking cups of clay or bone side by side with an aluminium dish and an empty Chase and Sanborne coffee jar, a cheap plastic plate and a broken toy car.

'Shall we go?' Nilsson said, and began to make his way out of the camp.

Not without certain trepidation, Hallner followed behind his friend who marched towards the mountains without looking back or even from side to side.

Nilsson had a goal and, rather than sit down, brood and die when the inescapable finally happened, Hallner was prepared to go along with him on this quest for the girl.

And, he admitted, there was a faint chance that if the winds continued to favour them, they might have a chance of life. In which case there was a logical reason for Nilsson's obsessional tracking of the woman.

His friend was impatient of his wish to walk slowly and savour the atmosphere of the country which seemed so detached and removed, uninvolved with him, disdainful. That there were things which had no emotional relationship with him, had given him a slight surprise at first, and even now he walked the marshy ground with a feeling of abusing privacy, of destroying the sanctity of a place where there was so little hint of humanity; where men had been rare and had not been numerous or frequent enough visitors to have left the aura of their passing behind them.

So it was with a certain shock that he later observed the print of small rubber soles on the flat mud near a river.

'She's still ahead of us,' said Nilsson, pleased at this sign, 'and not so very far ahead. Little more than a day. We're catching up.'

Suddenly, he realized that he was displeased by the presence of the bootprints, almost resentful of Nilsson's recognition of their being there when, alone, he might have ignored them. He reflected that Nilsson's complete acceptance of the sex of the boots' wearer was entirely founded on his own wishes.

The river poured down towards the flat lake on their left, clear, bright melted snow from the mountains. Brown, sun-dried rocks stood out of it, irregularly spaced, irregularly contoured, affording them a means of crossing the swift waters.

There were many such rivers, running down the slopes of the foothills like silver veins to fill the lakes and spread them further over the marshland. There were hills on the plateau where trees crowded together, fir and silver birch, like survivors of a flood jostling for a place on the high ground. There were ridges which sometimes hid sight of the tall mountains in front of them, green with grass and reeds, studded with gorse.

He had never been so far into mountain country before and this range was one of the oldest in the world; there were no sharp peaks as in the Alps. These were worn and solid and they had lived through eons of change and metamorphosis to have earned their right to solitude, to permanency.

Snow still spattered their sides like galaxies against the grey green moss and rock. Snow-fields softened their lines.

Nilsson was already crossing the river, jumping nimbly from rock to rock, his film-star's profile sometimes silhouetted against the clear, sharp sky, the pack on his back like Christian's load in the *Pilgrim's Progress*. Hallner smiled to himself. Only indirectly was Nilsson heading for salvation.

Now he followed.

He balanced himself in his flat, leather-soled boots and sprang from the first rock to the second, righted his balance again and sprang to the next. The river boiled around the rocks, rushing towards the lake, to lose itself in the larger waters. He jumped again, slipped and was up to his knees in the ice-cold torrent. He raised his small knapsack over his head and, careless now, did not bother to clamber back to the rocks, but pushed on, waist-deep, through the freezing river. He came gasping to the bank and was helped to dry land by Nilsson who shook his head and laughed.

'You're hopeless!'

'It's all right,' he said, 'the sun will dry me out soon.'

But both had walked a considerable distance and both were tiring. The sun had now risen, round and hazy red in the pale, cold sky, but it was still difficult to gauge the passage of the hours. This, also, added to the detached air of timelessness which the mountains and the plateaux possessed. There was no night – only a slight alteration in the quality of the day. And although the heat was ninety degrees fahrenheit, the sky still looked cold, for it took more than the brief six weeks of summer to change the character of this wintry Jotunheim.

He thought of Jotunheim, the Land of Giants, and understood the better the myths of his ancestors with their accent on man's impermanency – the mortality of their very gods, their bleak worship of the forces of nature. Only here could he appreciate that the life span of the world itself might be infinite, but the life span of its denizens was necessarily subject to inevitable metamorphosis and eventual death. And, as he thought, his impression of the country changed so that instead of the feeling of invading sanctified ground, he felt as if a privilege had been granted him and he had been allowed, for a few moments of his short life, to experience eternity.

The mountains themselves might crumble in time, the planet cease to exist, but that it would be reincarnated he was certain. And this gave him humility and hope for his own life and, for the first time, he began to think that he might have a purpose in continuing to live, after all.

He did not dwell on the idea, since there was no need to.

They came with relief to a dry place where they lighted a fire and cooked the last of their bacon in their strong metal frying pan. They ate their food and cleaned the pan with ashes from the fire, and he took it down to the nearest river and rinsed it, stooping to drink a little, not too much, since he had learned from his mistake earlier, for the water could be like a drug so that one craved to drink more and more until exhausted.

He realized, vaguely, that they had to keep as fit as possible. For one of them to come to harm could mean danger for them both. But the thought meant little. There was no sense of danger here.

He slept and, before he fell in to a deep, dreamless sleep, he had a peculiar impression of being at once vast and tiny. His eyes closed, his body relaxed, he felt so big that the atoms of his body, in relation to the universe, hardly had existence, that the universe had become an unobservable electron, present but unseen. And yet, intratemporally, he had the impression that he was as small as an electron so that he existed in a gulf, a vacuum containing no matter whatsoever.

A mystic, perhaps, would have taken this for some holy experience, but he could do no more than accept it, feeling no need to interpret it. Then he slept.

*

Next morning, Nilsson showed him a map he had found in the village.

'That's where she's going,' he said, pointing at a mountain in the distance. 'It's the highest in this section and the second highest in the entire range. Wonder why she'd want to climb a mountain?'

Hallner shook his head.

Nilsson frowned. 'You're in a funny mood. Think you won't have a chance with the girl?' When Hallner didn't answer, Nilsson said impatiently, 'Maybe she's got some idea that she's safer on top of a mountain. With luck, we'll find out soon. Ready to go?'

Hallner nodded.

They moved on in silence.

The range was discernibly closer, now, and Hallner could look at individual mountains. Although looming over the others, the one they headed for looked squat, solid, somehow older than the rest, even.

For a while they were forced to concentrate on the ground immediately in front of them, for it had become little more than thick mud which oozed over their boots and threatened to pull them down, to join, perhaps, the remains of prehistoric saurians which lay many feet below.

Nilsson said little and Hallner was glad that no demands were made on him.

It was as if the edge of the world lay beyond the last ragged pile of mountains, or as if they had left Earth and were in a concave saucer surrounded by mountains, containing only the trees and the lakes, marshes and hills.

He had the feeling that this place was so inviolable, so invulnerable, miles from the habitation of men so that for the first time he fully realized that men had ceased to exist along with their artifacts. It was as if they had never really existed at all or that their spell of dominance had appeared and disappeared in practically the same moment of time.

But now, for the first time since he had heard the hysterical voice on the radio, he felt some stirring of his old feeling return as he stared at the great mountain, heavy and huge against the ice-blue sky. But it was transformed. Ambition had become the summit, reward the silence, the peace that waited at the peak. Curiosity was the desire to discover the cause of a freakish colouring half-way up the mountain and fear did not exist for in these enigmatic mountains there was no uncertainty. A vast, wall-less womb with the infinite sky curving above and the richly-coloured scenery, blues, whites, browns and greens, surrounding them, complete, cutting them off from even the sight of the ruined outside world.

It was a snow-splashed paradise, where well-fed wolves left the carcasses of their prey to lap at the pure water of the rivers. A wilderness replete with life, with lemming, reindeer, wolverine, wolf and even bear, with lakes swarming with fresh-water herring and the air a silent gulf above them to set off the smack of a hawk's wing. Night could not fall and so the potential dangers of savage wild-life, which could not be felt in the vastness of a world where there was room for everything, could never be realized.

Occasionally, they would discover a slain reindeer, bones dull and white, its hide tattered and perishing, and they would feel no horror, no emotion at all, for although its obvious killer, the wolverine, was a cruel beast, destroying often for the sake of destroying, the wolverine was not aware of its crime and therefore it was no crime at all.

Everything here was self-sufficient, moulded by fate, by circumstance, but since it did not analyse, since it accepted itself and its conditions without question, it was therefore more complete than the men who walked and stumbled across its uncompromising terrain.

At length they came to the sloping, grass-covered roots of the mountain and he trembled with emotion to see it rising so high above him, the grass fading, parting to reveal the tumbled rock and the rock vanishing higher up beneath banks of snow.

'She will have taken the easiest face,' Nilsson decided, looking at the map he had found in the camp. 'It will mean crossing two snow-fields.'

They rested on the last of the grass. And he looked down over the country through which they had passed, unable to talk or describe his feelings. It possessed no horizon, for mountains were on all sides, and within the mountains he saw rivers and lakes, tree-covered hills, all of which had taken on fresh, brighter colourings, the lakes reflecting the red of the sun and the blue of the sky and giving them subtly different qualities.

He was glad they were taking the easiest face for he felt no need, here, to test or to temper himself.

For a while he felt complete with the country, ready to climb upwards because he would rather do so and, because the view from the peak would also be different, add, perhaps to the fullness of his experience.

He realized, as they got up, that this was not what Nilsson was feeling. Hallner had almost forgotten about the girl.

They began to climb. It was tiring, but not difficult for initially the slope was gradual, less than forty-five degrees. They came to the first snow-field which was slightly below them, climbed downwards carefully, but with relief.

Nilsson had taken a stick from the Lapp camp. He took a step forward, pressing the stick into the snow ahead of him, took another step, pressed the stick down again.

Hallner followed, treading cautiously in his friend's footsteps, little pieces of frozen snow falling into his boots. He knew that Nilsson was trying to judge the snow-field's thickness. Below it a deep river coursed and he thought he heard its musical rushing beneath his feet. He noted, also, that his feet now felt frozen and uncomfortable.

Very slowly they crossed the snow-field and at length, after a long time, they were safely across and sat down to rest for a while, preparing for the steeper climb ahead.

Nilsson eased his pack off his shoulders and leaned against it, staring back at the field.

'No tracks,' he mused. 'Perhaps she crossed further down.'

'Perhaps she didn't come here after all.' Hallner spoke with effort. He was not really interested.

'Don't be a fool.' Nilsson rose and hefted his pack on to his back again.

They climbed over the sharp rocks separating the two snowfields and once again underwent the danger of crossing the second field.

Hallner sat down to rest again, but Nilsson climbed on. After a few moments, Hallner followed and saw that Nilsson had stopped and was frowning at the folded map in his hand.

When he reached Nilsson he saw that the mountain now curved upwards around a deep, wide indentation. Across this, a similar curve went up towards the summit. It looked a decidedly easier climb than the one which faced them.

Nilsson swore.

'The damned map's misled us – or else the position of the fields has altered. We've climbed the wrong face.'

'Should we go back down again?' Hallner asked uninterestedly.

'No – there's not much difference – we'd have still lost a lot of time.'

Where the two curves joined, there was a ridge high above them which would take them across to the face which they should have climbed. This was getting close to the peak, so that in fact, there would be no advantage even when they reached the other side.

'No wonder we missed her tracks,' Nilsson said pettishly. 'She'll be at the summit by now.'

'How do you know she climbed this mountain?' Hallner wondered why he had not considered this earlier.

Nilsson waved the map. 'You don't think Lapps need these? No – *she* left it behind.'

'Oh . . .' Hallner stared down at the raw, tumbling rocks which formed an almost sheer drop beneath his feet.

'No more resting,' Nilsson said. 'We've got a lot of time to make up.'

He followed behind Nilsson who foolishly expended his energy in swift, savage ascents and was showing obvious signs of exhaustion before they ever reached the ridge.

Unperturbed by the changed situation, Hallner climbed after him, slowly and steadily. The ascent was taking longer, was more difficult and he, also, was tired, but he possessed no sense of despair.

Panting, Nilsson waited for him on a rock close to the ridge, which formed a narrow strip of jumbled rocks slanting upwards towards the peak. On one side of it was an almost sheer drop going down more than a hundred feet, and on the other the rocky sides sloped steeply down to be submerged in a dazzling expanse of faintly creaking ice – a glacier.

'I'm going to have to leave you behind if you don't move faster,' Nilsson panted.

Hallner put his head slightly on one side and peered up the mountain. Silently, he pointed.

'God! Everything's against us, today,' Nilsson kicked at a loose piece of rock and sent it out into space. It curved and plummeted down, but they could not see or hear it fall.

The mist, which Hallner had noted, came rolling swiftly towards them, obscuring the other peaks, boiling in across the range.

'Will it affect us?' Hallner asked.

'It's sure to!'

'How long will it stay?'

'A few minutes or several hours, it's impossible to tell. If we stay where we are we could very well freeze to death. If we go on there's a chance of reaching the summit and getting above it. Willing to risk it?'

This last remark was a sneering challenge.

'Why yes, of course,' Hallner said.

Now that the fact had been mentioned, he noted for the first time that he was cold. But the coldness was not uncomfortable.

They had no ropes, no climbing equipment of any kind, and even his boots were flat-soled city boots. As the mist poured in, its grey, shifting mass limiting vision almost utterly at times, they climbed on, keeping together by shouts.

'Once, he could hardly see at all, reached a rock, felt about it with his boot, put his weight on the rock, slipped, clung to the rock and felt both feet go sliding free in space just as the mist parted momentarily to show him the creaking glacier far below him. And something else – a black, spread-out shadow blemishing the pure expanse of ice.

He scrabbled at the rock with his toes, trying to swing himself back to the main part of the ridge, got an insecure toehold and flung himself sideways to the comparative safety of the narrow causeway. He breathed quickly and shallowly and shook with reaction. Then he arose and continued on up the slanting ridge.

A while later, when the main thickness of the mist had rolled past and now lay above the glacier, he saw that they had crossed the ridge and were on the other side without his having realized it.

He could now see Nilsson climbing with obvious difficulty towards what he had called the 'false summit'. The real summit could not be seen, was hidden by the other, but there was now only another hundred feet to climb.

They rested on the false summit, unable to see much that was below them for, although the mist was thinner, it was thick enough to hide most of the surrounding mountains. Sometimes it would part so that they could see fragments of mountains, patches of distant lakes, but little else.

Hallner looked at Nilsson. The other man's handsome face had taken on a set, obstinate look. One hand was bleeding badly.

'Are you all right?' Hallner nodded his head towards the bleeding hand.

'Yes!'

Hallner lost interest since it was evident he could not help Nilsson in his present mood.

He noted that the mist had penetrated his thin jacket and his whole body was damp and chilled. His own hands were torn and grazed and his body was bruised, aching, but he was still not discomfited. He allowed Nilsson to start off first and then forced himself on the last stage of the climb.

By the time he reached the snowless summit, the air was bright, the mist had disappeared and the sun shone in the clear sky.

He flung himself down close to Nilsson who was again peering at his map.

He lay panting, sprawled awkwardly on the rock and stared out over the world.

There was nothing to say. The scene itself, although magnificent, was not what stopped him from talking, stopped his mind from reasoning, as if time had come to a standstill, as if the passage of the planet through space had been halted. He existed, like a monument, petrified, unreasoning, absorbing. He drank in eternity.

Why hadn't the dead human race realized this? It was only necessary to exist, not to be trying constantly to prove you existed when the fact was plain.

Plain to him, he realized, because he had climbed a mountain. This knowledge was his reward. He had not received any ability to think with greater clarity, or a vision to reveal the secret of the universe, or an experience of ecstasy. He had been given, by himself, by his own action, insensate peace, the infinite tranquillity of *existing*.

Nilsson's harsh, disappointed tones invaded this peace.

'I could have sworn she would climb up here. Maybe she did. Maybe we were too late and she's gone back down again?'

Hallner remembered the mark he had seen on the glacier. Now he knew what it had been.

'I saw something back on the ridge,' he said. 'On the glacier. A human figure, I think.'

'What? Why didn't you tell me?'

'I don't know.'

'Was she alive? Think of the importance of this – if she is alive we can start the human race all over again. What's the matter with you, Hallner? Have you gone crazy with shock or something? *Was she alive?*'

'Perhaps – I don't know.'

'You don't –' Nilsson snarled in disbelief and began scrabbling back the way he had come.

'You heartless bastard! Supposing she's hurt – injured!'

Hallner watched Nilsson go cursing and stumbling, sometimes falling, on his over-rapid descent of the mountain. He saw him rip off his pack and fling it aside, nearly staggering over the ridge as he began to climb down it.

Hallner thought dispassionately that Nilsson would kill himself if he continued so heedlessly.

Then he returned his gaze to the distant lakes and trees below him.

He lay on the peak of the mountain, sharing its existence. He was immobile, he did not even blink as he took in the view. It seemed that he was part of the rock, part of the mountain itself.

A little later there came an aching yell which died away into the silence. But Hallner did not hear it.

The Time Dweller

Dusk had come to the universe, albeit the small universe inhabited by Man. The sun of Earth had dimmed, the moon had retreated and salt clogged the sluggish oceans, filled the rivers that toiled slowly between white, crystalline banks, beneath darkened, moody skies that slumbered in eternal evening.

Of course, in the sun's long life this stage was merely one interlude. In perhaps a few thousand years, it would flare to full splendour again. But for the meantime it kept its light in close rein, grumbling in its mighty depths and preparing itself for the next step in its evolution.

It had taken time in its fading and those few creatures who had remained on its planets had managed to adapt. Among them was Man, indefatigable; undeserving, really, considering the lengths he had gone to, in previous epochs, to dispose of himself. But here he was, in his small universe consisting of one planet without even the satellite which had slid away into space long since and, in its passing, left legends on his lips.

Brown clouds, brown light, brown rocks and brown ocean flecked with white. A pale rider on a pale beast thumping along the shore, the dry taste of ocean salt in his mouth, the stink of a dead oozer in his nostrils.

His name was the Scar-faced Brooder, son of the Sleepy-eyed Smiler, his father and the Pinch-cheeked Worrier, his mother. The seal-beast he rode was called Urge. Its glossy coat was still sleek with the salt-rain that had recently ceased, its snout pointed eagerly forward and its two strong leg-fins thwacked the encrusted shore as it galloped along, dragging its razor-edged tail with scant effort. The Scar-faced Brooder was supported on his steed's sloping back by a built-up saddle of polished silicon that flashed whenever it reflected the salt-patches studding the ground like worn teeth. In his hand, held at its butt by a stirrup grip, was his long gun, the piercer with an everlasting ruby as its life. He was dressed in sealskin dyed in sombre rust-red and dark yellow.

*

Behind him, the Scar-faced Brooder heard the sound of another rider, one whom he had tried to avoid since morning.

Now, as evening quietly flowed brown and misty into black night, she still followed. He turned his calm face to look, his mouth tight and white as the scar which rose from its corner to follow his left cheek-bone. She was in the distance, still, but gaining.

He increased his speed.

Brown clouds boiled low like foam across the dark sand of the flat, and their seals slapped loudly over the damp shore as she neared him.

He came to a pool of salt-thick water and Urge splashed into it. It was warm. Still she followed him, even into the water, so that he turned his steed and waited, half-trembling, until she rode up, a tall, well-formed woman with light brown hair long and loose in the breeze.

'Dearest Tall Laugher,' he told his sister, 'for me there is no amusement in this game.'

Frowning, she smiled.

He pressed his point, disturbed, his calm face earnest in the fading brown light that was all the clouds would let pass.

'I wish to ride alone.'

'Where would you go, alone, when together we might be carried to more exotic adventure?'

He paused, unwilling and unable to answer.

'Will you come back?'

'I would prefer not to.'

A cold, silent wind began to buffet them as it came in suddenly from the sea. Urge moved nervously.

'You fear what the Chronarch might do?'

'The Chronarch has no love for me – but neither has he hatred. He would prefer me gone from Lanjis Liho, to cross the great salt plains of the west and seek my fortune in the land of fronds. He would not trust me with a small part of the Future, as you know, nor give a fraction of the Past into my safekeeping. I go to shape my own destiny!'

'So – you sulk!' she cried as the wind began to mewl. 'You sulk because the Chronarch delegates no honours. Meanwhile, your loving sister aches and is miserable.'

'Marry the Big-brained Boaster! He has trust of Past and Future both!'

He forced his restless seal-beast through the thick water and into the night. As it moved, he reached into the saddle sheath and took out his torch to light his way. He depressed its grip and it blazed out, illuminating the surrounding beach for several yards around. Turning, he saw her for a moment in the circle of light, motionless, her eyes aghast as if he had betrayed her.

Oh, I am lonely now, he thought, as the wind blew cold and strong against his body.

He headed inland, over the salt-rocks, towards the west. He rode all night until his eyes were heavy with tiredness, but still he rode, away from Lanjis Liho where Chronarch, Lord of Time, ruled past and present and watched the future come, away from family, home and city, his heart racked with the strain of the breaking, his mind fevered fire and his body all stiff from the demands he made of it.

Into the night, into the west, with his torch burning in his saddle and loyal Urge responding to his affectionate whispering. To the west, until dawn came slowly up from behind him and covered the barren land with soft light.

A little further through the morning he heard a sound as of cloth flapping in the wind and when he turned his head he saw a green tent pitched beside a shallow crevasse, its front flap dancing. He readied his long piercer and halted Urge.

Drawn out, perhaps, by the noise of the seal-beast's movement, a man's head poked from the tent like a tortoise emerging from the recesses of its shell. He had a beak of a nose and a fish-like pecker of a mouth, his large eyes were heavy-lidded and a tight-fitting hood hid hair and neck.

'Aha,' said the Scar-faced Brooder in recognition.

'Hmm,' said the Hooknosed Wanderer, also recognizing the mounted man confronting him. 'You are some distance from Lanjis Liho. Where are you bound?'

'For the land of fronds.'

He resheathed his piercer and clambered down from the high saddle. He passed the tent, its occupant's head craning round to follow him and stared into the crevasse. It had been widened and deepened by human tools, revealing pieces of ancient wreckage. 'What's this?'

'Nothing but the remains of a crashed spaceship,' replied the Hooknosed Wanderer in such obvious disappointment that he could not have been lying. 'My metal diviner found it and I had hoped for a capsule with books or film.'

'There were never many of those. I'd say they had all been gathered by now.'

'That's my belief, too, but one hopes. Have you breakfasted?'

'No. Thank you.'

*

The hooded head withdrew into the tent and a thin hand held back the flap. The Scar-faced Brooder bent and entered the cluttered tent. There was a great deal of equipment therein; the Hooknosed Wanderer's livelihood, for he sustained himself by bartering some of the objects he found with his metal diviner and other instruments.

'Apparently, you have no riding animal,' said the Scar-faced Brooder as he sat down and crossed his legs between a soft bundle and an angular statuette of steel and concrete.

'It was necessary to abandon her when my water was exhausted and I could find none to replace it. That is why I was heading for the sea. I am exceedingly thirsty, am suffering from salt-deficiency since I have no liking for the salt which grows in these parts.'

'I have plenty in my saddle barrel,' he said. 'Help yourself – good salt water, slightly diluted with fresh, if that suits your taste.' He leant back on the bundle as the Wanderer, nodding sharply, scrambled up, clasping a canteen and left the tent.

He returned smiling. 'Thanks. I can last for several days, now.' He pushed aside his clutter of antiques, discovering a small stove. He activated it, placed a pan on top and began frying the leg-fish he had trapped recently.

'Which city was your destination, Brooder? Only two are in easy reach from here – and both lie still many leagues hence. Is it Barbart or Piorha?'

'Barbart in the land of fronds, I think, for I should like to see green vegetation instead of grey or brown. And the ancient places thereabouts have, I must admit, romantic connotations for me. I should like to go and wallow in racial memory, sense the danger of uncontrolled Past, insignificant Present and random Future . . .'

'Some feel it as that,' the Wanderer smiled, shuffling the leg-fish on to plates. 'Especially those from Lanjis Liho where the Chronarchy holds sway. But remember, much will be in your mind. You may see Barbart and the land of fronds, but its significance will be decided by you, not by it. Try to do as I do – make no judgments or descriptions of this world of ours. Do that, and it will treat you better.'

'Your words seem wise, Wanderer, but I have no precedents by which to judge them. Perhaps when I have placed some of the Future in the Past, I will know.'

'You seem tired,' said the Wanderer when they were finished eating, 'would you like to sleep?'

'I would. Thanks.' And while the Hooknosed Wanderer went about his business, the Brooder slept.

*

He rose in the mellow afternoon, roused Urge who had taken advantage of his master's slumber to rest also, and wished the Wanderer goodbye.

'May your blood stay thick,' said the Wanderer formally, 'and your mind remain open.'

He rode away and by dusk had come to the moss which was primarily grey and brown, but tinted in places with patches of light green. He took out his torch and fixed it in its saddle bracket, unwilling to sleep at night because of the potential danger of predatory life.

Once the light from his torch showed him a school of oozers, moving at right angles to his path. They were far inland for their kind, these great white slug-creatures that raised their heads to observe him. He felt he could hear them sniffing at his body salt as perhaps their leech ancestors had sniffed out the blood of his own forefathers. Urge, without prompting, increased his speed.

As he left them, he felt that the oozers represented the true native of Earth now. Man's place was no longer easy to define, but it seemed that he had been superseded. By remaining alive on the salt-heavy Earth he was outstaying his welcome. If there was another home for Man, it did not lie here but in some other region; perhaps not even the region of space at all but in dimensions where natural evolution could not affect him.

Brooding, as was his bent, he continued to ride for Barbart and, by the following day, had reached the delicate frond forests that waved golden green in the soft sunlight, all silence and sweet scent. Urge's bounding gait became almost merry as they fled over the cushions of moss between the shaded spaces left by the web-thin fronds waving and flowing in the gusts of air which occasionally swept the forest.

He dismounted soon and lay back on a bank of comfortable moss, breathing the scented breeze in luxurious self-indulgence. His mind began to receive disjointed images, he heard his sister's voice, the sonorous tones of the Chronarch denying him a function in the House of Time – a function which he had expected as of right, for had not his grand-uncle been the previous Chronarch? He saw the twisting many dimensioned Tower of Time, that wonder-work of an ancient architect with its colours and strange, moving angles and curves. And then he slept.

When he awoke it was night and Urge was hooting at him to wake. He got up sleepily and hauled himself into the saddle, settled himself, reached for his torch and adjusting it rode through what seemed to be a network of black and stirring threads that were the fronds seen in the cold torchlight.

The next morning he could see the low-roofed houses of Barbart lying in a valley walled by gentle hills. High above the roofs, a great contrivance of burnished brass glowered like rich red gold. He speculated momentarily upon its function.

Now a road became evident, a hard track winding among the moss dunes and leading towards the city. As he followed it he heard the muffled thud of a rider approaching and, somewhat wary for he knew little of Barbart or its inhabitants, reined in Urge, his piercer ready.

Riding towards him on a heavy old walrus came a young man, long-haired and pleasant-featured in a jerkin of light blue that matched his eyes. He stopped the walrus and looked quizzically at the Scar-faced Brooder.

'Stranger,' he said cheerfully, 'it is a pleasant morning.'

'Yes it is – and a pleasant land you dwell in. Is that city Barbart?'

'Barbart, certainly. There's none other hereabouts. From where are you?'

'From Lanjis Liho by the sea.'

'I had the inkling that men from Lanjis Liho never travelled far.'

'I am the first. My name is the Scar-faced Brooder.'

'Mine is Domm and I welcome you to Barbart. I would escort you there save for the fact that I have a mission from my mother to seek herbs among the fronds. I am already late, I fear. What time is it?'

'Time? Why the present, of course.'

'Ha! Ha! But the hour – what is that?'

'What is "the hour"?' asked the Brooder, greatly puzzled.

'That's my question.'

'I am afraid your local vernacular is beyond me,' said the Brooder politely, but nonplussed. The lad's question had been strange to begin with, but now it had become incomprehensible.

'No matter,' Domm decided with a smile. 'I have heard you people of Lanjis Liho have some peculiar customs. I will not delay you. Follow the road and you should be in Barbart in less than an hour.'

'Hour' – the word again. Was it some division of the league used here? He gave up wondering and wished the youth 'thick blood' as he rode on.

The mosaiced buildings of Barbart were built in orderly geometric patterns about the central quadrangle in which lay the towering machine of burnished brass with its ridges and knobs and curlicues. Set in the centre of the machine was a great round plaque, divided into twelve units with each unit of twelve divided into a further five units. From the centre arose two pointers, one shorter than the other and the Scar-faced Brooder saw them move slowly. As he rode through Barbart, he noticed that facsimilies of this object were everywhere and he judged, at last, that it was some holy object or heraldic device.

Barbart seemed a pleasant place, though with a somewhat restless atmosphere epitomized by the frantic market-place where men and women rushed from stall to stall shouting at one another, tugging at bales of bright cloth, fingering salt-free fruits and vegetables, pawing meats and confectionaries amid the constant babble of the vendors crying their wares.

Enjoying the scene, the Scar-faced Brooder led his seal-beast through the square and discovered a tavern in one of the side plazas. The plaza itself contained a small fountain in its centre and benches and tables had been placed close by outside the tavern. The Brooder seated himself upon one of these and gave his order to the fat girl who came to ask it.

'Beer?' she said, folding her plump, brown arms over her red bodice. 'We have only a little and it is expensive. The fermented peach juice is cheaper.'

'Then bring me that,' he said pleasantly and turned to watch the thin fountain water, noting that it smelt of brine hardly at all.

Hearing, perhaps, a strange accent, a man emerged from the shadowy doorway of the tavern and, tankard in hand, stood looking down at the Scar-faced Brooder, an amiable expression on his face.

'Where are you from, traveller?' he asked.

The Brooder told him and the Barbartian seemed surprised. He seated himself on another bench.

'You are the second visitor from strange parts we have had here in a week. The other was an emissary from Moon. They have changed much, those Moonites, you know. Tall, they are, and thin as a frond with aesthetic faces. They dress in cloth of metal. He told us he had sailed space for many weeks to reach us . . .'

At this second reference to the unfamiliar word 'week', the Brooder turned his head to look at the Barbartian. 'Forgive me,' he said, 'but as a stranger I am curious at certain words I have heard here. What would you mean by "week" exactly?'

'Why – a week – seven days – what else?'

The Brooder laughed apologetically. 'There you are, you see. Another word – days. What is a days?'

The Barbartian scratched his head, a wry expression on his face. He was a middle-aged man with a slight stoop, dressed in a robe of yellow cloth. He put down his tankard and raised his hand. 'Come with me and I will do my best to show you.'

'That would please me greatly,' said the Brooder gratefully. He finished his wine and called for the girl. When she appeared he asked her to take care of his steed and to make him up a bed since he would be staying through the next darkness.

The Barbartian introduced himself as Mokof, took the Brooder's arm and led him through the series of squares, triangles and circles formed by the buildings, to come at length to the great central plaza and stare up at the pulsing, monstrous machine of burnished bronze.

'This machine supplies the city with its life,' Mokof informed him. 'And also regulates our lives.' He pointed at the disc which the Brooder had noted earlier. 'Do you know what that is, my friend?'

'No. I am afraid I do not. Could you explain?'

'It's a *clock*. It measures the hours of the day,' he broke off, noting the Brooder's puzzlement. 'That is to say it measures time.'

'Ah! I am with you at last. But a strange device, surely, for it cannot measure a great deal of time with that little circular dial. How does it note the flow . . .?'

'We call a period of sunlight "day" and a period of darkness "night." We divide each into twelve hours –'

'Then the period of sunlight and the period of darkness are equal? I had thought . . .'

'No, we call them equal for convenience, since they vary. The twelve divisions are called hours. When the hands reach twelve, they begin to count around again . . .'

'Fantastic!' the Brooder was astounded. 'You mean you recycle the same period of time round and round again. A marvellous idea. Wonderful! I had not thought it possible.'

'Not exactly,' Mokof said patiently. 'However, the hours are divided into sixty units. These are called minutes. The minutes are also divided into sixty units, each unit is called a second. The seconds are . . .'

'Stop! Stop! I am confounded, bewildered, dazzled! How do you control the flow of time that you can thus manipulate it at will? You must tell me. The Chronarch in Lanjis Liho would be overawed to learn of your discoveries!'

'You fail to understand, my friend. We do not *control* time. If anything, it controls us. We simply measure it.'

'You don't control . . . but if that's so why –?' The Brooder broke off, unable to see the logic of the Barbartian's words.

'You tell me you recycle a given period of time which you divided into twelve. And yet you then tell me you recycle a shorter period and then an even shorter period. It would soon become apparent if this were true, for you would be performing the same action over and over again and I see you are not. Or, if you were using the same time without being in its power, the sun would cease to move across the sky and I see it still moves. Given that you can release yourself from the influence of time, why am I not conscious of it since that instrument,' he pointed at the *clock*, 'exerts its influence over the entire city. Or, again, if it is a natural talent, why are we in Lanjis Liho so busily concerned with categorizing and investigating our researches into the flow if you have mastered it so completely?'

A broad smile crossed the face of Mokof. He shook his head. 'I told you – we have no mastery over it. The instrument merely tells us what time it is.'

'That is ridiculous,' the Brooder said, dazed. His brain fought to retain its sanity. 'There is only the present. Your words are illogical!'

Mokof stared at his face in concern. 'Are you unwell?'

'I'm well enough. Thank you for the trouble you have taken, I will return to the tavern now, before I lose all hold of sanity!'

The clutter in his head was too much. Mokof made a statement and then denied it in the same breath. He decided he would cogitate it over a meal.

When he reached the tavern he found the door closed and no amount of banging could get those inside to open it. He noticed that his saddle and saddle-bags were resting outside and he knew he had some food in one of the bags, so he sat the bench and began to munch on a large hunk of bread.

Suddenly, from above him, he heard a cry and looking up he saw an old woman's head regarding him from a top-storey window.

'Ah!' she cried. 'Aah! What are you doing?'

'Why, eating this piece of bread, madame,' he said in surprise.

'Filthy!' she shrieked. 'Filthy, immoral pig!'

'Really, I fail to –'

'Watch! Watch!' the old woman cried from the window.

Very swiftly, three armed men came running into the plaza. They screwed up their faces in disgust when they saw the Scarfaced Brooder.

'A disgusting exhibitionist as well as a pervert!' said the leader.

They seized the startled Brooder.

'What's happening?' he gasped. 'What have I done?'

'Ask the judge,' snarled one of his captors and they hauled him towards the central plaza and took him to a tall house which appeared to be their headquarters.

There he was flung into a cell and they went away.

An overdressed youth in the next cell said with a grin: 'Greetings, stranger. What's your offence?'

'I have no idea,' said the Brooder. 'I merely sat down to have my lunch when, all at once . . .'

'Your lunch? But it is not lunch-time for another ten minutes!'

'Lunch-time. You mean you set aside a special period to *eat* – oh, this is too much for me.'

The overdressed youth drew away from the bars and went to the other side of his cell, his nose wrinkling in disgust. 'Ugh – you deserve the maximum penalty for a crime like that!'

Sadly puzzled, the Brooder sat down on his bench, completely mystified and hopeless. Evidently the strange customs of these people were connected with their *clock* which seemed to be a virtual deity to them. If the hands did not point to a certain figure when you did something, then that act became an offence. He wondered what the maximum penalty would be.

Very much later, the guards came to him and made him walk through a series of corridors and into a room where a man in a long purple gown wearing a metallic mask was seated at a carved table. The guards made the Brooder sit before the man and then they went and stood by the door.

The masked man said in a sonorous voice: 'You have been accused of eating outside the proper hour and of doing it in a public place for all to see. A serious charge. What is your defence?'

'Only that I am a stranger and do not understand your customs,' said the Brooder.

'A poor excuse. Where are you from?'

'From Lanjis Liho by the sea.'

'I have heard rumours of the immoralities practised there. You will learn that you cannot bring your filthy habits to another city and hope to continue with them. I will be lenient with you, however and sentence you to one year in the antique mines.'

'But it is unjust!'

'Unjust, is it? Watch your tongue or I will extend the sentence!'

Depressed and without hope, the Brooder allowed the guards to take him back to his cell.

The night passed and morning came and then the guards arrived. 'Get up,' said the leader, 'the judge wishes to see you again!'

'Does he intend to increase my sentence, after all?'

'Ask him.'

The judge was tapping his desk nervously as the Brooder and his guards entered.

'You know of machines in Lanjis Liho, do you not? You have some strange ones I've heard. Do you wish to be released?'

'I wish to be released, of course. Yes, we know something of machines, but . . .'

'Our Great Regulator is out of control. I would not be surprised if your crime did not provide the shock which caused it to behave erratically. Something has gone wrong with its life core and we may have to evacuate Barbart if it cannot be adjusted. We have forgotten our old knowledge of machines. If you adjust the Great Regulator, we shall let you go. Without it, we do not know when to sleep, eat or perform any of our other functions. We shall go mad if we lose its guidance!'

Scarcely understanding the rest of the judge's statement, the Brooder heard only the fact that he was to be released if he mended their machine. On the other hand, he had left Lanjis Liho for the very reason that the Chronarch would not give him trust of any instruments. He had little experience, yet, if it meant his release, he would try.

When he arrived again in the central plaza, he noted that the machine of burnished bronze – the Great Regulator, they called it – was making a peculiar grumbling noise and shaking mightily. Around it, trembling in unison, stood a dozen old men, waving their hands.

'Here is the man from Lanjis Liho!' called the guard. They looked anxiously at the Scar-faced Brooder.

'The life-core. It must certainly be the life-core,' said an ancient, tugging at his jerkin.

'Let me see,' said the Scar-faced Brooder, not at all sure that he could be of help.

They wound off several of the machine's outer plates and he stared through thick glass and looked at the luminous life-core. He had seen them before and knew a little about them. He knew enough, certainly, to understand that this should not be glowing bright purple and showering particles with such constancy.

He knew, suddenly, that in an exceedingly short space of time – one of these people's 'minutes', perhaps – the life-core would reach a critical state, it would swell and burst from its confines and its radiation would destroy everything living. But, he ignored their shouts as he became lost in the problem, he would need considerably longer than that if he was to deal with it.

Soon, he realized helplessly, they would all be dead.

He turned to tell them this, and then it struck him. Why could not he, as he had guessed these citizens capable of, *recycle* that moment, personally?

Since the previous day, his mind had been trying to see the logic in what Mokof had told him and, using parts of things the Chronarch had told him, he had constructed an idea of what the process must be like.

Experimentally, he eased himself *backwards* in time. Yes, it worked. The core was now as he had first seen it.

He had never thought of doing this before, but now he saw that it was easy, requiring merely a degree of concentration. He was grateful for the Barbartians, with their weird time device, for giving him the idea.

All he had to do was to remember what the Chronarch had taught him about the nature of time – how it constantly and imperceptibly to ordinary beings re-formed its constituents to give it the apparently forward movement which affected, so broadly, the organization of matter.

Shifting himself into the time-area he had occupied a short while before, he began to study the temporal co-ordinates of the life-core. He could think of no physical means of stopping it, but if he could, in some manner, lock it in time, it would then cease to be a danger. But he would still have to work speedily, since, sooner or later, the temporal structure would fail to hold and he would sweep onwards, losing time continuously, until he was brought to the moment when the life-core began to spread its radiation.

Again and again he let himself drift up almost to the ultimate moment, shifting himself backwards, losing a few grains of time with every shift.

Then, at last, he understood the temporal construction of the core, With an effort of will he reduced the temporal co-ordinates to zero. It could not progress through time. It was frozen and no longer a danger.

He fell back into his normal time-stream, his body wet with sweat. They crowded about him, questioning in shrill, excited voices.

'What have you done? What have you done? Are we safe?'

'You are safe,' he said.

They seized him, thanking him with generous words, his earlier crime forgotten. 'You must be rewarded.'

But he scarcely heard them, as they bore him back to the judge, for he was brooding on what he had just accomplished.

As a man might step backwards to regain lost ground, he had stepped backwards to regain lost time. He had his reward. He was most grateful to these people now, for with their weird ideas about time, they had shown him that it was possible to exist at will in a point in time – just as it was possible to exist in a point in space. It was, he realized, merely a matter of *knowing* such a thing was possible. Then it became easy.

The judge had doffed his mask and smiled his gratitude. 'The wise men tell me that you worked a miracle. They saw your body flickering like a candle flame, disappearing and appearing constantly. How did you achieve this?'

He spread his hands: 'It was extraordinarily simple. Until I came to Barbart and saw the thing you call *clock*, I did not realize the possibilities of moving through time as I could move through space. It seemed to me that since you appeared capable of recycling the same period of time, I could do likewise. This I did. Then I studied the life-core and saw that, by manipulation of its time structure, I could fix it in a certain point, thus arresting its progress. So simple – and yet it might never have occurred to me if I had not come here.'

The judge passed a hand over his puzzled eyes. 'Ah . . .' he said.

'And now,' the Brooder said cheerfully, 'I thank you for your hospitality. I intend to leave Barbart immediately, since I shall obviously never understand your customs. I return to Lanjis Liho to tell the Chronarch of my discoveries. Farewell.'

He left the court-room, crossed the plaza through crowds of grateful citizens, and was soon saddling Urge and riding away from Barbart in the land of fronds.

Two days later he came upon the Hooknosed Wanderer grubbing in a ditch he had just dug.

'Greetings, Wanderer,' he called from the saddle.

The Wanderer looked up, wiping salty earth from his face.

'Oh, 'tis you, Brooder. I thought you had decided to journey to the land of fronds.'

'I did. I went to Barbart and there –' briefly the Brooder explained what had happened.

'Aha,' nodded the Wanderer. 'So the Chronarch is educating his people well, after all. I frankly considered what he was doing impossible. But you have proved me wrong.'

'What do you mean?'

'I think I can tell you. Come into my tent and drink some wine.'

'Willingly,' the Brooder said, dismounting.

From a plastic flask, the Wanderer poured wine into two cut-glass goblets.

'Lanjis Liho,' he said, 'was founded in ancient times as an experimental village where new-born children were taken and educated according to the teachings of a certain philosopher called Rashin. Rashin regarded people's attitude towards Time as being imposed on their consciousness by their method of recording and measuring it – by the state of mind which said "the past is the past and cannot be changed," "we cannot know what the future holds" and so forth. Our minds, he decided, were biased and while we continued to think in this way we should never be free of the shackles of time. It was, he felt, the most necessary shackle to cast off. He said, for instance that when the temperature becomes too hot, a man devises a means of keeping himself cool. When it rains he enters a shelter or devises a shelter he can transport with him. If he comes to a river, he builds a bridge, or if to the sea – a boat. Physical difficulties of a certain intensity can be overcome in a physical way. But what if the difficulties intensify to the degree where physical means can no longer work against them?'

The Brooder shrugged. 'We perish – or find some means other than physical to combat them.'

'Exactly. Rashin said that if Time moves too swiftly for a man to accomplish what he desires he accepts the fact passively. Rashin thought that with re-education Man might rid himself of his preconception and take as easily to adjusting Time to his requirements as he adjusts nature. A non-physical means you see.'

'I think I understand a little of what you mean,' said the Scar-faced Brooder. 'But why is it necessary, I wonder?' The question was rhetorical, but the Wanderer chose to answer.

'On this world,' he said, 'we must admit it, Man is an anachronism. He has adapted to a degree but not sufficiently to the point where he could sustain himself without artifice. The planet has never been particularly suitable for him, of course, but it has never been so inhospitable as now.

'The Chronarchy, as I have said, is a conscious experiment. Time and Matter are both ideas. Matter makes a more immediate impression on Man, but Time's effects are longer lasting. Therefore the Chronarchy, down the ages, has sought to educate its people into thinking of Time in a similar way as they think of Matter. In this way it has been possible to produce a science of time, like the science of physics. But it has only been possible to study time until now – not manipulate it.

'We may soon master Time as we once mastered the atom. And our mastery will give us far greater freedom than did our nuclear science. Time may be explored as our ancestors explored space. Your descendants, Scar-faced Brooder, shall be heir to continents of time as we have continents of space. They shall travel about in time, the old view of Past, Present and Future abolished. Even now you regard these in an entirely different light – merely as convenient classifications for the study of Time.'

'That is true,' he nodded, 'I had never considered them anything else. But now I am unsure what to do, for I fled to Barbart originally to settle and forget Lanjis Liho where I went unhonoured.'

The Wanderer smiled a little. 'I do not think you will go unhonoured now, my friend,' he said.

The Brooder saw the point and smiled also. 'Perhaps not,' he agreed.

The Wanderer sipped his wine. 'Your journeyings in space are all but ended, anyway. For space is becoming increasingly hostile to Man and will soon refuse to sustain him, however much he adapts physically. You and your like must enter the new dimensions you've discovered and dwell there. Go back to Lanjis Liho of your birth and tell the Chronarch what you did in Barbart, *show* him what you did and he will welcome you. Your reason for leaving no longer exists. You are the first of the Time Dwellers and I salute you as the salvation of mankind.' The Wanderer drained his glass.

Somewhat overwhelmed by this speech, the Brooder bade the Wanderer farewell and thick blood, left the tent and climbed upon the back of Urge.

The Wanderer stood beside the tent, smiling at him. 'One day you must tell me how you did it,' he said.

'It is such a simple thing – you just live through the same period of time instead of different ones. Perhaps this is just the start and soon I will be able to explore further abroad – or is the word "a-time"? But now I will be off for I'm impatient to tell my news to the Chronarch!'

The Wanderer watched him ride away, feeling a trifle as the last dinosaur must have felt so many millions of years before.

Once again, the Scar-faced Brooder rode along the seashore staring over the sluggish waves at the brown sky beyond.

Salt shone everywhere across the land, perhaps heralding an age where crystalline life-forms would develop in conditions absolutely unsuitable for animal life as he knew it.

Yes, the period when Man must change his environment radically had come, if Man were to survive at all.

The Earth would cease to support him soon, the sun cease to warm him. He had the choice of living for a while in artificial conditions such as the Moonites already did, or of completely changing his environment – from a physical one to a temporal one!

Definitely, the latter was the better choice. As the sky darkened over the sea, he took out his torch, depressed the handle and sent a great blaze of light spreading across the inhospitable Earth.

The first of the Time Dwellers goaded his seal-beast into a faster pace, impatient to tell the Chronarch his welcome news, impatient to begin the exploration of a new environment.

Escape from Evening

On Moon it was white like ice. An endless series of blocks and spikes, like an ancient cubist painting. But white; glaring, though the sun was almost dead, a red featureless disc in the dark sky.

In his artificial cavern, full of synthetic, meaningless things that contained no mythology or mood, Pepin Hunchback bent over his book so that the tears from his eyes fell upon the plastic pages and lay there glistening.

Of all the things that the glass cavern contained – pumps and pipes and flinching dials – only Pepin had warmth. His twisted body was a-throb with life and large emotions. His imagination was alive and active as each word in the book sparked off great chords of yearning within him. His narrow face, utterly pale save for the bright black eyes, was intense. His clumsy hands moved to turn the pages. He was dressed, as were all his fellow Moonites, in cloth-of-metal which, with a helmet fitted to its hauberk, protected his life from an impossibility – the threat of the System collapsing.

The System was Moon's imitation of life. It aped an older Earth than that which now existed far away, barely visible in space. It aped its plants and its animals and its elements – for the System was Moon's artificial ecology. Moon was a planet of goodish size – had been for centuries since it had ceased to be Earth's satellite and had drifted into the asteroids and attracted many of them to itself.

And Pepin hated the System for what it was. Pepin was a throwback, unsuited to his present Time or Space. Pepin's life was not the System, for with just that he would have died. It was his imagination, his sorrow and his ambition, fed by his few old books.

He read the familiar pages and realized again that the intellect had triumphed over the spirit, and both had conquered emotion. The men of Moon, at least, had become as barren as their accident of a planet.

Pepin knew much of Earth as his people's traders had described it. Knew that it was changing and was no longer as it was when his books were written. Yet still he yearned to go there and see if he could find some trace of what he needed – though he would only know what he needed when he found it.

For some time he had planned to visit Earth and his people were willing that he should go, if he did not return, for he discomfited them. His name – his true name – was on the list, close to the top. Soon a ship would be ready for him. His true name was P Karr.

Now he thought of the ship and decided to go to the list. He went to the list infrequently for in his atavism he was superstitious and believed completely that the more he looked at it, the less chance there would be of his name being at the top.

Pepin jerked his body off his stool and slammed the book shut. On the hushed world of Moon, he made as much noise as he could.

He limped, more evidently high-shouldered now that he was moving, towards the door section of his dome. He took down his helmet and fitted it on to his shoulders, activated the door section, and crossed the sharp, bright ground covering the distance between himself and the city. By choice, and to the relief of his people, he lived outside the city.

On the surface, there was little to see of the city. Merely a storey or two, perhaps three in places. All the prominences were square and transparent, to absorb as much energy from the waning sun as possible.

Another door section in one of the buildings opened to him and he went inside, hardly realizing that he had left the surface. He entered a funnel containing a disc-shaped platform and the platform began to fall downwards, slowing as it reached the bottom.

Here the light was completely artificial and the walls were of metal – plain, undecorated tubes twice the height of a tall, thin Moonite. Pepin was not typical of his race.

He limped along this tube for a short distance, until the floor began to move. He let it carry him through the labyrinthine intestines of the city until he came to the hall he wanted.

The hall was quite unpopulated until Pepin entered. It had a domed ceiling and was covered by screens, charts, indicators, conveying every item of information which a citizen might require to know in the day-to-day life of the city. Pepin went to the list, craning his head to look at it. He started at the bottom and followed the list of names up.

His name was at the top. He must go immediately to Ship Controller and apply for his ship. If he did not, his name would go back to the bottom, according to regulations.

As he turned to leave the hall, another Moonite entered. His helmet was flung back, lying against his shoulder blades. His golden hair was long and his thin face smiled.

This was G Nak, the greatest of the trader-pilots, and he did not need to look at the list, for he had a permanent ship of his own. The population of Moon was small, and G Nak knew Pepin as well as anyone.

He stopped sharply, arms akimbo, and contemplated the list.

'So you journey to Earth, P Karr. You will find it decadent and unpleasant. Take plenty of food – you will not like their salty grub.'

'Thank you,' bobbed Pepin as he left.

As if mutated by their constant contact with the mother planet, only the ships of Moon had character. They were burnished and patterned with fancifully wrought images. Ancient animals prowled along their hulls, gargoyles glowered from indentations created by heavily moulded figures of famous men, tentacled hands curled themselves over the curves like the arms of wrecked sailors clinging to spars, or else like the protective hands of a she-baboon about her young. The ships were so heavily decorated that in the light they looked like frozen lava, all lumps and gulleys in obsidian or brass.

Pepin, luggage on back, paused before he put foot on the short, moving ramp which would deliver him to the entrance of his allotted ship. He allowed himself time to study the raised images, then stepped upon the ramp and was whisked up to the airlock which opened for him.

The inside of the ship was very cramped and consisted mainly of cargo space. The cargo, which would go with Pepin and be delivered to an Earth-city called Barbart, was already stowed. Pepin lowered himself on to the couch where he would spend the journey. After Pepin and cargo had been delivered, the ship would return, as it had left, automatically.

A whisper of noise, hushed like all Moon sounds, warned him that the ship was about to take off. He braced himself; felt no sensation as the ship rose on course for Earth.

The bright ship sped through the soft darks of weary space, a bold spark intruding the blackness. It flickered along its path until at length Pepin's screen picked up the growing globe of Earth – brown, yellow and white, turning slowly in the scant warmth of the dormant sun.

The planet seemed vaguely unreal, perhaps because it was imperfectly focused on the screen, yet the stuff of space seemed to drift through it as if the planet's very fabric was worn thin. Pepin felt the hard metal rocket would not stop when it reached Earth, but tear through it easily and continue on into empty space where more vital stars pulsed. At one time, Pepin knew, the universe had been even thicker with bright stars, and even his own sun had possessed more than the three planets that now circled it.

Silently, the ship went into orbit, easing itself by stages into the atmosphere, down through the clear, purple sky, down into the brown cloud-banks that hung close to the ground, through the clouds until it had levelled out again and moved with decreasing speed across sluggish seas and wastes of dark yellow, brown and black, studded by great white patches of salt. Much further inland, grey moss became apparent, and later the waving light green of the fragile fronds that marked what Earth's inhabitants called the Land of Fronds. In the Land of Fronds were two principal cities, two towns and a village. Barbart, the trading port between Moon and Earth, lay in a gentle valley. The hills were covered in fronds that from above seemed like a rolling sea – more sea-like than the salt-heavy waters far to the east.

Barbart was laid out precisely, in quadrangles, triangles and star-shaped plazas. The roofs of the low houses were of dark green and brick-brown, yet seemed brightly coloured compared with their surroundings. The ship passed over the huge red-gold machine which rose high above the other buildings. This, Pepin knew, was called the Great Regulator and supplied necessary power to the city. Behind the Great Regulator, in the city's central plaza, was a cradlepad ready for his ship. It hovered and then dropped down on to the cradlepad.

Pepin shivered suddenly and did not rise immediately but watched his screen as people began to enter the plaza, moving speedily towards the ship.

Barbart was the city most like those he had read about in his books. It was considerably smaller than the Golden Age cities had been and resembled best a medieval Italian city. From the ground, even the frond-covered hills might be a forest of oaks and elms if they were not looked at closely. Also Pepin knew that the folk of Barbart were quite similar to the ancient folk of Earth. Yet he could not convince himself, though he tried, that he had returned to the Earth of his books. For one thing the light was fainter, the air darker, the drifting brown clouds unlike any that had existed in Earth's past. Pepin was not as disappointed as he expected. Whatever deficiencies existed here, at least the planet was *natural* and Pepin placed much value on the naturalness of things.

The airlock had opened and the Barbartians grouped themselves outside it, waiting for the pilot to appear.

Pepin took up his luggage from beside the couch, swung his well-shaped legs to the floor and limped out of the cabin and through the airlock.

The heavy, brine-laden air half-choked him. The smell of salt was so marked that he felt faintly sick. He swung his helmet up so that it enclosed his head. He turned on his emergency oxygen supply, deciding to give himself time to adjust.

The merchants of Barbart stood around the ramp leading from the cradlepad. They looked at him eagerly.

'May we inspect the cargo, Pilot?' enquired a heavy-shouldered man with broad cheek-bones and a flaking skin half-invisible beneath his thick, black beard. He wore a quilted coat, belted at his chest. This was a rusty black. A white stock was tied at his throat and he wore baggy yellow trousers tucked into furry boots.

Pepin looked at him, wanting to greet him in some manner that would convey the pleasure he felt at seeing a human being of heavy build, with muscles and flaws on his skin.

'Pilot?' said the merchant.

Pepin began to limp slowly down the ramp. He stood aside to let the bulky merchant move up it and duck his head to enter the airlock. Three others followed him, glancing rather quizzically at the silent Moonite.

A man smaller than Pepin with the narrow face of a reptile, dressed in dull red and black, sidled up clutching a handwritten list. Fascinated, Pepin looked at it, not understanding the words. He would like to have taken off his gauntlets and fingered the parchment, but he would wait for a little.

'Pilot? When do you return?'

Pepin smiled. 'I do not return. I have come to live here.'

The man was startled. He took the parchment back and turned his head, did not see what he looked for and gazed up the ramp towards the open airlock.

'Then be welcome,' he said absently, still not looking at Pepin. He excused himself and walked with short, rapid steps back to the warehouse at the side of the plaza.

Pepin waited until the merchant and his friends reappeared. They looked satisfied and were nodding to one another. The black-bearded merchant bustled down the ramp and slapped Pepin's arm.

'I admit it,' he grinned, 'a very generous cargo. We have the best of this month's bargain I think. Gold and alcohol for our fertilizers. May I begin unloading?'

'As you wish,' Pepin said courteously, wondering at this man who could delight in receiving such useless things in return for valuable fertilizers.

'You are new,' said the merchant, taking Pepin's arm and leading him towards the warehouse where the other man had gone. 'What do you think of our city?'

'It is wonderful,' sighed Pepin. 'I admire it. I should like to live here.'

'Ha! Ha! With all those marvels and comforts in Moon you have. You'd miss them after a while, Pilot. And every year we hear of cities dying, populations shrinking, fewer children than ever being born. No, I envy you Moonites with your safety and stability – you don't have to worry about the future, for you can plan efficiently. But we here can make no plans – we merely hope that things will not alter too much in our own lifetimes.'

'At least you are part of the natural order, sir,' Pepin said hesitantly. 'You might adapt further as the Earth changes.'

The merchant laughed again. 'No – we of Earth will all be dead. We accept this, now. The human race has had a long run. No one would have expected us to last this time, but soon the point will be reached where we can adapt no longer. It is already happening in less fortunate areas. Man is dying out on Earth. Yet while you have your System, that is not possible on Moon.'

'But our System is artificial – your planet is natural.'

They reached the warehouse. Men were already folding back the heavy doors. The casks of fertilizer were stacked in a cool, dark corner of the place. The man with the reptile face glanced at Pepin as he counted the casks.

'There is the matter of the pilot's gift,' said the merchant. 'The traditional gift of gratitude to the man who brings the cargo safely to us. Is there anything we have which you desire?'

Traditionally, the pilot asked for a small token gift of no great value and Pepin knew what was expected of him.

'You mine antiques in Barbart I believe?' he said politely.

'Yes. It provides employment for our criminals. Forty cities have stood where Barbart now stands.'

Pepin smiled with pleasure. Such history!

'I am fond of books,' he said.

'Books?' The merchant frowned. 'Why, yes, we have a stack of those somewhere. Have the folk of Moon taken to reading? Ha! ha!'

'You do not read them yourselves?'

'A lost art, Pilot. Those ancient languages are impossible. We have no scholars in Barbart, save for our elders – and their wisdom comes from here,' he tapped his head, 'not from any books. We've little use for the old knowledge – it was a knowledge suitable for a younger Earth.'

Though Pepin understood, he felt a pang of sorrow and disappointment. Intellectually he had known that the folk of Earth would not be like his idealized picture of them, yet emotionally he could not accept this.

'Then I would like some books,' he said.

'As many as your ship has room for when our cargo's loaded!' promised the merchant. 'What language do you read in? I'll let you sort them out for yourself.'

'I read in all the ancient tongues,' said Pepin proudly. His fellows thought his a useless skill and it probably was, but he did not care.

He added: 'And there is no need to load them. I shall not be returning with the ship. That will go back to Moon automatically.'

'You'll not be –? Are you then to be some sort of permanent representative of Moon on Earth?'

'No. I wish to live on Earth as one of her folk.'

The merchant scratched his nose. 'Aha, I see. Aha . . .'

'Is there reason why I should not be welcome?'

'Oh, no – no – I was merely astonished that you should elect to stay with us. I gather you Moonites regard us as primitives, doomed to die with the planet.' His tone was now mildly resentful. 'Your regulations admitting no one of Earth to Moon have been strict for centuries. No Earth-man has visited Moon, even. You have your stability to consider, of course. But why should you *elect* to suffer the discomforts of our wasted planet?'

'You will note,' said Pepin carefully, 'that I am not like other Moonites. I am, I suppose, some sort of romantic throwback – or it may be that my original difference has fostered mental differences, I do not know. However, I alone amongst my race have an admiration for Earth and the folk of Earth. I have a yearning for the past whereas my people look always to the future – a future which they are pledged to keep stable and as much like the present as possible.'

'I see . . .' The merchant folded his arms. 'Well, you are welcome to stay here as a guest – until you wish to return to Moon.'

'I never wish to return.'

'My friend,' the merchant smiled. 'You will wish to return soon enough. Spend a month with us – a year – but I warrant you'll stay no longer.'

He paused before saying: 'You'll find plenty of signs of the past here – for the past is all we have. There is no future for Earth.'

*

The clock, centrepiece of the Great Regulator, had measured off six weeks before Pepin Hunchback became restless and frustrated by the uncaring ignorance of the Barbartians. The citizens were pleasant enough and treated him well considering their covert antipathy towards the Moonites. But he made no friends and found no sympathizers.

He rejoiced in those books which were not techincal manuals or technical fiction. He enjoyed the poetry and the legends and the history books and the adventure stories. But there were fewer than he had expected and did not last him long.

He lived in a room at an Inn. He grew used to the heavy, briny air and the dull colours, he began to enjoy the gloom which shadowed the Earth, for it mirrored something of his own mood. He would go for walks over the hills and watch the heavy brown clouds course towards him from the horizon, smell the sweetish scent of the frond forests, climb the crumbling rocks that stood against the purple sky, worn by the wind and scoured by the salt.

Unlike Moon, this planet still lived, still held surprises in the sudden winds that blew its surface, the odd animals which crawled over it.

Pepin was afraid only of the animals, for these had become truly alien. The principal life-form other than man was the oozer – a giant leech which normally prowled the bleak sea shores but which was being seen increasingly further inland. If Man's time was ending, then the time of the oozer was beginning. As Man died out, the oozer multiplied. They moved in schools varying from a dozen to a hundred, depending on the species – they grew from two feet to ten feet long. Some were black, some brown, some yellow – but the most disgusting was the white variety which was also the largest and most ferocious, a great grub of a thing capable of fast speeds, able to outdistance a running man and bring him down. When this happened, the oozer, like its leech ancestor, fed off the blood only and left the body drained and dry.

Pepin saw a school moving through a glade once as he sat on a rock staring down into the frond forest.

'The new tenants,' he said aloud, after he'd conquered his nausea, 'are arriving – and the Earth ignores Man. She is not hostile, she is not friendly. She no longer supports him. She has forgotten him. Now she fosters new children.'

Pepin was given to talking to himself. It was the only time when words came easily – when he was alone.

*

Pepin tried to talk with Kop, the merchant and his fellow residents at the Inn, but though they were polite enough, his questions, his statements and his arguments made them frown and puzzle and excuse themselves early.

One fellow resident, a mild-mannered and friendly man called Mokof, middle-aged with a slight stoop, made greater attempts to understand Pepin, but was incapable, rather than unwilling, of helping him.

'With your talk of the past and philosophy, you would be happier in that odd city of Lanjis Liho by the sea,' he said pleasantly one day as they sat outside the Inn, tankards at their sides, watching the fountain play in the plaza.

Pepin had heard Lanjis Liho mentioned, but had been so curious about other matters, that he had not asked of the city before. Now he raised one fair, near-invisible eyebrow.

'I once knew a man from Lanjis Liho,' Mokof continued in answer. 'He had a strange name which I forget – it was similar to your last name in type. He had a scar on his face. Got into trouble by eating his food at the wrong time, saved himself by fixing the Great Regulator for us. We know nothing of these machines these days. He believed that he could travel in Time, though I saw little evidence of this while he was here. All the folk of Lanjis Liho are like him, I hear – bizarre, if you follow me – they know nothing of clocks, for instance, have no means of measuring the hours. Their ruler is called Chronarch and he lives in a palace called the House of Time, though only an oozer knows why they should emphasize Time when they can't even *tell* it.'

Mokof could tell Pepin very little more that was not merely opinion or speculation, but Lanjis Liho by the sea sounded an interesting place. Also Pepin was attracted by the words 'time travel' – for his true wish was to return to Earth's past.

During the seventh week of his stay in Barbart, he decided to journey eastwards towards Lanjis Liho by the sea.

Pepin Hunchback set off on foot for Lanjis Liho. Mokof in particular tried to dissuade him – it was a long journey and the land was dangerous with oozers. He could easily lose his direction without a good steed.

But he had tried to ride the seal-beasts which were the mounts of most Earthmen. These creatures, with their strongly muscled forefins and razor-sharp tails, were reliable and fairly fast. They had built-up saddles of silicon to give the rider a straight seat. Part of their equipment also included a long gun, called a piercer, which fired a ray from its ruby core, and a torch fed by batteries which supplied the traveller with light in the moonless, near-starless night.

Pepin Hunchback took a torch and balanced a piercer over his shoulder. He liked the feeling both gave him. But he did not trust himself to a seal-beast.

He left in the dark morning, with food and a flask in the pack on his back, still dressed in his cloth-of-metal suit.

The citizens of Barbart, like those of Moon, were not regretful when he had gone. He had disturbed them when they believed they had conquered all disturbances within themselves. For seven weeks he had interrupted their purpose and the purpose they wished to transmit to any children they might have.

That purpose was to die peacefully and generously on an Earth which no longer desired their presence.

Pepin was disappointed as he limped away from Barbart in the Land of Fronds. He had expected to find dynamic vitality on Earth – people prepared for change, but not for death. Somewhere on the planet – possibly in Lanjis Liho by the sea – he would find heroes. From what Mokof had hinted, he might even find a means of travelling into the past. This is what he wanted most, but he had never expected to achieve it.

The moss of the frond forests was springy and helped his walking, but by evening it was beginning to give way to hard, brown earth over which dust scurried. Ahead of him, ominous in the waning light, was a barren plain, cracked and almost featureless. Here and there chunks of rock stood up. He selected one as his goal, realizing, even as night fell, cold and pitch dark, that to sleep would be to risk his life. Oozers, he had been told, only slept when they had fed – and there was little to feed on save Man.

He depressed the grip of his torch and its light illuminated a distance of a few yards round him. He continued to walk, warm enough in his suit. As he walked, his mind became almost blank. He was so weary that he could not tell how long he had marched by the degrees of weariness. But when a silhouette of rock became apparent in the torch-light, he stopped, took off his pack, leant his back against the rock and slid down it. He did not care about the oozers and he was fortunate because no oozers scented his blood and came to care about him.

Dawn came dark brown, the muddy clouds streaming across the sky, blocking out much of the sun's dim light. Pepin opened his pack and took out the flask of specially distilled fresh water. He could not drink the salt-water which the folk of Earth drank. They, in turn, had adapted to the extent where they could not bear to drink fresh water. He took two tablets from a box and swallowed them. Having breakfasted, he heaved his aching body up, adjusted the pack on his back, slung the torch into its sheath at his side, shouldered the piercer and looked about him.

In the west, the frond forests were out of sight and the plain looked as endless in that direction as it did in the other. Yet the plain to the east was now further broken by low hills and many more rocks.

He set off eastwards. *In the east, he reflected, our ancestors believed Paradise lay. Perhaps I will find my Paradise in the east.*

If Paradise existed, and Pepin was entitled to enter, he came very close to entering two days later as he collapsed descending a salt-encrusted hill and rolled many feet down it, knocking himself unconscious.

As it was, the Hooknosed Wanderer saved him from this chance of Paradise.

The Hooknosed Wanderer was a burrower, a gossiper, a quester after secrets. Amongst all the Earth folk he was perhaps the only aimless nomad. No one knew his origin, no one thought to ask. He was as familiar in Barbart as he was in Lanjis Liho. His knowledge of Earth, past and present, was extensive, but few ever availed themselves of it. He was a short man with a huge nose, receding, chin, and a close-fitting hood and jerkin which made him resemble a beaked turtle.

He saw the fallen tangle that was Pepin Hunchback at much the same time as the school of oozers scented Pepin's blood.

He was riding a big, fat seal-beast and leading another on which was heaped a preposterous burden of rolled fabric, digging equipment, a small stove, angular bundles – in fact the Hooknosed Wanderer's entire household tied precariously to the seal-beast's back. The seal-beast seemed mildly pleased with itself that it was capable of carrying this load.

In the Hooknosed Wanderer's right hand, borne like a lance resting in a special grip on his stirrup, was his piercer. He saw Pepin, he saw the oozers.

He rode closer, raised his piercer, pressed the charger and then the trigger-stud. The concentrated light was scarcely visible, but it bit into the oozer school instantaneously. They were of the black variety. The Hooknosed Wanderer moved the piercer about very gradually and burned every oozer to death. It gave him satisfaction.

Then he rode up to where Pepin lay and looked down at him. Pepin was not badly hurt, he was even beginning to stir on the ground. The Hooknosed Wanderer saw that he was a Moonite by his dress. He wondered where Pepin had got the piercer and torch which lay near him.

He dismounted and helped the Moonite to his feet. Pepin rubbed his head and looked rather nervously at the Hooknosed Wanderer.

'I fell down,' he said.

'Just so,' said the Hooknosed Wanderer. 'Where is your spaceship? Has it crashed nearby?'

'I have no spaceship,' Pepin explained, 'I was journeying from Barbart, where I landed some seven weeks ago, to Lanjis Liho, which I am told lies close to the shores of the sea.'

'You were foolish to go on foot,' said the Wanderer. 'It is still a long way.'

He continued eagerly: 'But you must guest with me and we will talk about Moon. I should be happy to add to my knowledge.'

Pepin's head was aching. He was glad that this odd stranger had come upon him. He agreed willingly and even tried to help the Wanderer raise his tent.

When the tent was finally erected and the Wanderer's goods distributed about it, Pepin and he went inside.

The Wanderer offered him leg-fish and salt-water, but Pepin refused politely and swallowed his own food.

Then he told the Wanderer of his coming from Moon to Earth, of his stay in Barbart, of his frustration and disappointment, and of his ambition. The Wanderer listened, asking questions that showed he was more interested in Moon than Pepin.

Listlessly, Pepin replied to these questions and then asked one of his own.

'What do you know of Lanjis Liho, sir?'

'Everything but the most recent events,' said the Wanderer with a smile. 'Lanjis Liho is very ancient and has its origin in an experimental village where a philosopher tried to educate people to regard Time as they regard Matter – something that can be moved through, manipulated and so on. From this, the Chronarchy was formed and it became traditional in Lanjis Liho to investigate Time and little else. Perhaps by mutation, perhaps by the awakening of some power we have always possessed, a race of people exist in Lanjis Liho who can *move themselves through Time*!

'I had the good fortune to know the young man who first discovered this talent within himself and trained others in its use. A man called the Scar-faced Brooder – he is the present Chronarch.'

'He can travel into the past?'

'And future, so I hear. Once the chronopathic talent is released in Man, he can move through Time at will.'

'But the past,' said Pepin excitedly. 'We can journey back to Earth's Golden Age and not worry about natural death or artificial living. We can *do* things!'

'Um,' said the Wanderer. 'I share your love for the past, Pepin Hunchback – my tent is full of antiques I have excavated – but is it possible to return to the past? Would not that act change the future – for there is no record in our history of me from the future settling in the past?'

Pepin nodded. 'It is a mystery – yet surely *one* man, who did not admit he was from the future, could settle in the past?'

The Hooknosed Wanderer smiled. 'I see what you mean.'

'I realize now,' said Pepin seriously, 'that I have little in common with either my own people or the folk of Earth. My only hope is to return to the past where I shall find the things I need to exist fully. I am a man out of my time.'

'You are not the first. Earth's ancient history is full of such men.'

'But I shall be the first, perhaps able to find the Age which most suits him.'

'Perhaps,' said the Hooknosed Wanderer dubiously. 'But your wishes are scarcely constructive.'

'Are they not? What, then, has this Earth to offer mankind? We on Moon live an artificial life, turning year by year into machines less perfect than those which support us. And you here accept death passively – are only concerned with the business of facing extinction "well"! My race will not be human within a century – yours will not exist. Are we to perish? Are the values of humanity to perish – have the strivings of the last million years been pointless? Is there no escape from Earth's evening? I will not accept that!'

'You are not logical, my friend,' smiled the Wanderer. 'You take the least positive line of all – by refusing to face the future – by your desire to return to the past. How will that benefit the rest of us?'

Pepin clutched his head. 'Ah,' he murmured. 'Ah . . .'

The Hooknosed Wanderer continued. 'I have no wish to survive the evening. You have seen something of the horrors which will multiply as Earth's evening turns to night.'

Pepin did not reply. He had become inarticulate with emotion.

The Hooknosed Wanderer took him outside and pointed into the east. 'That way lies Lanjis Liho and her chronopaths,' he said. 'I pity you, Pepin, for I think you will find no solution to your problem –

and it *is* your problem, not humanity's.'

Pepin limped from weariness as well as deformity. He limped along a beach. It was morning and the dull, red sun was rising slowly from the sea as he moved down the dark shore towards Lanjis Liho. It was cold.

Grey-brown mist hung over the sea and drifted towards the bleak landscape that was dominated by the solid black outline of cliffs to his right. The brown beach glistened with patches of hard salt and the salt-sluggish sea was motionless, for there was no longer a nearby moon to move it.

Pepin still considered his conversation with the strange Wanderer. Was this the end of Earth, or merely one phase in a cycle? Night must come – but would it be followed by a new day? If so, then perhaps the future was attractive. Yet the Earth had slowly destroyed the greater part of the human race. Would the rest die before the new morning?

Suddenly, Pepin slipped into a pool of thick water. He floundered in the clinging stuff, dragging himself back by clutching a spur of hardened salt, but the salt wouldn't bear his weight and he fell into the pool again. Finally he crawled back to dry land. Everything was crumbling or changing.

He continued along the shore more carefully. Leg-fish scuttled away as he approached. They sought the deeper shadow of the crags of rock which rose from the beach like jagged teeth, corroded by wind-borne salt. They hid and were silent and the whole shore was quiet. Pepin Hunchback found no peace of mind here, but the solitude seemed to absorb his tangled thoughts and eased his brain a little.

The disc of the sun took a long time to rise above the horizon, and brought little light with it, and even less warmth. He paused and turned to stare over the sea which changed from black to brown as the sun came up. He sighed and looked at the sun which caught his face in its dull glow and stained it a deep pink, bringing a look of radiance to his native pallor.

Later, he heard a sound which he first took to be the squawking of fighting leg-fish. Then he recognized it as a human voice. Without moving his head, he listened more intently.

Then he turned.

A tiny figure sat a seal on the cliff above. Jutting upwards from it like a lance was the barrel of a long piercer. The figure was half-shadowed by the ruin of an ancient watch-tower and, as he looked, jerked at the reins impatiently, disappeared into the whole shadow and was gone.

Pepin frowned and wondered if this could be an enemy. He readied his own piercer.

Now the rider had descended the cliff and was nearing him. He heard the distant thwack of the beast's fins against the damp beach. He levelled the gun.

The rider was a woman. A woman from out of his books.

She was tall, long-legged, with the collar of her seal-leather jacket raised to frame her sharp-jawed face. Her brown hair drifted over it and flew behind. One hand, protected by a loose-fitting glove, clutched the pommel of her high, silicon saddle. The other held her beast's reins. Her wide, full-lipped mouth seemed pursed by the cold, for she held it tight.

Then her seal entered a deep pool of sluggish water and began swimming through it with great difficulty. The strong smell of the brine-thick liquid came to his awareness then and he saw her as a woman out of mythology – a mermaid astride a seal. Yet, she frightened him. She was unexpected.

Was she from Lanjis Liho? It was likely. And were they all like her?

Now, as she reached firm ground again, she began to laugh in rhythm with the seal's movement. It was rich, delightful laughter, but as she came towards him, the heavy drops of water rolling slowly from her mount, his stomach contracted in panic. He backed away a few paces.

At this moment she seemed to personify the bleak insanity of the dying planet.

She halted her beast close to him. She lowered her chin and opened her grey-green eyes. She still smiled.

'Stranger, you are from Moon by your garb. Are you lost?'

He put the piercer over his shoulder. 'No. I seek Lanjis Liho.'

She pointed backwards up the beach. 'You are close to our city. I am Tall Laugher, sister to the Scar-faced Brooder, Chronarch of the City of Time. I will take you there.'

'I am Pepin Hunchback, without kin or rank.'

'Climb up on my seal-beast's back, hang on to my saddle and we will soon be in Lanjis Liho.'

He obeyed her, clinging desperately to the slippery silicon as she wheeled the seal about and sped back the way she had come.

She called to him once or twice on the journey up the salty beach, but he could not make out the sense.

It had begun to rain a little before they reached Lanjis Liho.

*

Built upon a huge and heavy cliff, the city was smaller even than Barbart, but its houses were tower-like-slim and ancient with conical roofs and small windows. Lanjis Liho was dominated by the Tower of Time which rose from a building called, according to Tall Laugher's shouted description, the Hall of Time, palace of the Chronarch.

Both Hall and Tower were impressive, though puzzling. Their design was an impossibility of curves and angles, bright colours bordering on the indefinable, and creating an emotion in Pepin similar to the emotion created in him by pictures of Gothic architecture – though whereas Gothic took the mind soaring upwards, this took the mind in all directions.

The pale sun shone down on the city streets and the salt-rain fell, washing the gleaming salt deposits off the walls and roofs and leaving fresh ones. The drops even fell between the blades and domes of the Hall and Tower of Time.

There were few people in the streets, and yet there seemed to be an air of activity about the city – almost as if the people were preparing to abandon it.

Although quite similar in their various types to the folk of Barbart, these people seemed livelier – eager.

Pepin wondered if he had arrived at a festival time, as Tall Laugher reined in her beast on the corner of a narrow street.

He clambered down, his bones throbbing. She also dismounted and pointed at the nearest house. 'This is where I live. Since you claimed no rank, I gather you have come here as a visitor and not as an official emissary from Moon. What do you seek in Lanjis Liho?'

'Transport to the past,' he said at once.

She paused. 'Why should you want that?'

'I have nothing in common with the present.'

She looked at him through her cool, intelligent eyes. Then she smiled. 'There is nothing in the past that would attract you.'

'Let me decide.'

'Very well,' she shrugged, 'but how do you propose to find the past?'

'I,' his momentary confidence disappeared, 'I had hoped for your help.'

'You will have to speak with the Chronarch.'

'When?'

She looked at him, frowning slightly. She did not seem unsympathetic. 'Come,' she said, 'we will go to the Hall of Time now.'

As Pepin followed the girl, walking quickly to keep up with her long strides, he wondered if perhaps the people of Lanjis Liho were bent on keeping the secrets of Time to themselves.

Though they glanced at him curiously as they passed him, the citizens did not pause. The mood of hurried activity seemed even stronger as they reached the spiralling steps which led upwards to the great gates of the Hall.

The guards did not challenge them as they entered an echoing corridor, the tall walls of which were decorated with peculiar cryptographs inlaid in silver, bronze and platinum.

Ahead of them were double-doors of yellow gold. Tall Laugher pushed against these and they entered a large, oblong wall with a high ceiling. At the far end, on a dais, was a seated man talking to a couple of others who turned as Tall Laugher and Pepin Hunchback entered.

The seated man smiled calmly as he saw Tall Laugher. He murmured to the other two who left by a door at the side of the dais. The man's pale face bore a scar running from the left corner of his mouth along his cheek-bone. His black hair swept from a widow's peak to his wide shoulders. He wore clothes that did not suit him – evidently the clothes of his office. His shirt was of yellow cloth and his cravat, knotted high at his chin, was black. He wore a long-sleeved jacket of quilted blue velvet and breeches of wine-red. His feet were shod in black slippers.

The hall itself was strange. At regular intervals the walls were set alternately with symbolic mosaics and computers. Behind the seated man, close to the far wall, which was blank, was a metal bench bearing the ancient tools of alchemy. They seemed in bizarre contrast to the rest of the hall.

'Well, Tall Laugher,' said the man, 'who is this visitor?'

'He is from Moon, Brooder – and seeks to journey into the past!'

The Scar-faced Brooder, Chronarch of Lanjis Liho, laughed and then, looking sharply at Pepin, stopped.

Pepin said eagerly: 'I have heard that you can travel in Time at will. This is true?'

'Yes,' said the Brooder, 'but . . .'

'Do you plan to go backward or forward?'

The Scar-faced Brooder seemed nonplussed. 'Forward, I suppose – but what makes you think you have the ability for travelling in Time?'

'Ability?'

'It is a special skill – only the folk of Lanjis Liho possess it.'

'Have you no *machines*?' Pepin demanded, his spirits sinking.

'We do not *need* machines. Our skill is natural.'

'But I must return to the past – I *must*!' Pepin limped towards the dais, ignoring the restraining hand of the Tall Laugher. 'You want no one else to share your chance of escape! You must know much about Time – you must know how to help me return to the past!'

'It would do you no good if you went back.'

'How do you know?'

'We know,' said the Chronarch bleakly. 'My friend, give up this obsession. There is nothing we can do for you in Lanjis Liho.'

'You are lying!' Pepin changed his tone and said more levelly: 'I beg you to help me. I – I need the past as others need air to survive!'

'You speak from ignorance.'

'What do you mean?'

'I mean that the secrets of Time are more complex than you believe.' The Chronarch stood up. 'Now I must leave you. I have a mission in the future.'

He frowned, as if concentrating – and vanished.

Pepin was startled. 'Where has he gone?'

'Into the future – to join others of our folk. He will return soon, I hope. Come, Pepin Hunchback, I will take you to my house and let you eat and rest there. After that, if you'll accept my advice, you had best arrange to go back to Moon.'

'You must be able to construct a machine!' he shouted. 'There must be a way! I must return!'

'Return?' she said, raising an eyebrow. 'Return? How can you return to somewhere you have never been? Come.' She led the way out of the hall.

Pepin Hunchback had calmed down by the time he had eaten a little of the salty food in Tall Laugher's house. They sat in a small room with a bay window which overlooked the street. He sat on one side of a table, she on the other. He did not speak. His mood had become apathetic. She seemed sympathetic and he was attracted to her for the qualities which he had first noted on the beach, and for her warm womanliness, but his despair was greater. He stared at the table, his twisted body bent over it, his hands stretched out in front of him.

'Your yearning, Pepin Hunchback, is not for the past as it was,' she was saying softly. 'It is for a world that never existed – a Paradise, a Golden Age. Men have always spoken of such a time in history – but such an idyllic world is a yearning for childhood, not the past, for lost innocence. It is childhood we wish to return to.'

He looked up and smiled bitterly. 'My childhood was not idyllic,' he said. 'I was a mistake. My birth was an accident. I had no friends, no peace of mind.'

'You had your wonderment, your illusion, your hopes. Even if you could return to Earth's past – you would not be happy.'

'Earth's present is decadent. Here the decadence is part of the process of evolution, on Moon it is artificial, that is all. Earth's past was never truly decadent.'

'One cannot recapture the past.'

'An old saying – yet your ability disproves that.'

'You do not know, Pepin Hunchback,' she said almost sadly. 'Even if you used the ship, you could not . . .?'

'Ship?'

'A Time craft, an earlier, cruder experiment we abandoned. We have no need of such devices now.'

'It still exists?'

'Yes – it stands behind the Hall of Time,' she spoke vaguely, her thoughts on something else.

Afraid that she would soon guess what was in his mind, Pepin changed the subject.

'Maybe you are right, Tall Laugher. Old Earth has none to love her any longer – her appearance does not inspire love. If I am the last who loves Earth, then I should stay with her.' Part of him meant what he said, he realized. The words had come spontaneously, he had never considered this before.

She had only half-heard his words. She gave him a slightly startled look as he spoke. She rose from the table. 'I will show you to your room,' she said. 'You need sleep.'

He pretended to agree and followed her out. There would be no sleep now. He must seize his opportunity. Outside, in the fading light of evening, lay a Time craft. Soon, perhaps, he could return to the past, to security, to a green, golden Earth, leaving this tired ball of salt forever!

There was enough light coming from the houses to show him the way through the twisting streets to the Tower of Time. He was unobserved as he circled around the great building, searching for the ship which Tall Laugher had said was there.

At last, half-seen in shadows, he noticed a shape lying in a small square at the back of the Tower.

Resting in davits was a ship of cold, blue metal. It could only be the Time craft. It was large enough to contain three or four men. Several other machines stood nearby, showing signs of neglect. Pepin limped cautiously forward until he stood by the ship. He touched it. It swayed slightly and the davits squealed. Pepin tried to steady it, looking nervously around him, but no one had noticed. The ship was roughly egg-shaped, with a small airlock in its side. Running his hand over it, Pepin found a stud which he pressed. The outer door slid open.

With considerable difficulty, Pepin managed to heave himself into the violently swinging ship. The noise of the squealing davits was ghastly. He shut the door and crouched in the utter blackness of the interior as it swayed back and forth.

It was likely that a light-stud was near the door. His searching hand found a projection and hesitated. Then, risking the possibility that it was not for the light, he pressed it.

The light came on. It was a bluish, mellow light, but it served adequately to show the interior of the ship. There were no seats and most of the machinery seemed hidden behind squat casings. At the centre of the ship was a column on which was set, at hand height, four controls. The ship was still swaying as Pepin went over to the controls and inspected them. His life on Moon had made him very familiar with all kinds of machinery, and he noted that the system of measurement was the same. The largest dial was in the middle. A division on the right was marked with a minus sign and on the left with a plus sign – obviously indicating past and future. Yet Pepin had expected such a control to be marked off with dates. There were none. Instead there were figures – units from one to ten. One trip, however, was all he would need in order to equate these numbers with the actual period of time they measured.

Another dial seemed to indicate speed. A switch was marked 'Emergency Return' and another, mysteriously, 'Megaflow Tuner'.

Now all Pepin had to discover was whether the ship was still powered.

He limped over to another bank of instruments. There was a lever set into it. At the moment the indicator on its handle said OFF. His heart beating rapidly, Pepin pushed the lever down. A light flashed on the indicator and now it read ON. An almost inaudible humming came from the bank of instruments as needles swung and screens gleamed. Pepin returned to the column and put his large hand on the central dial. It moved easily to the right. He left it at – 3.

The ship no longer swung on its davits. There was no sensation of speed, but the banks of instruments began to click and whirr noisily and Pepin felt suddenly dizzy.

The ship was moving backwards in Time.

Soon, he would be in the past at last!

Perhaps it was something to do with the ship's motion, the eruptions of colour which blossomed and faded on the screens, or the weird sounds of the instruments that made Pepin become almost hysterical. He began to laugh with joy. He had succeeded! His ambition was close to fruition!

At last the sounds died down, the sensation of sickness left him, the ship no longer seemed to move.

Pepin trembled as he raised his helmet and set it over his head. He knew enough to realize that the air of an earlier Earth would probably be too rich for him at first. This action saved his life.

He went to the door and pressed the stud to open it. The door moved backwards slowly and Pepin stepped into the airlock. The door closed. Pepin opened the outer door.

He looked out at absolutely nothing.

A lightless void lay around the ship. No stars, no planets – nothing at all.

Where was he? Had the ship's instruments been faulty? Had he been borne into an area of space so far away from any material body?

He felt vertigo seize him, backed into the airlock for as far as he could go, frightened that the vacuum would suck him into itself. He closed the outer door and returned to the ship.

In panic he went to the control column and again twisted the dial. This time to – 8. Again the screens filled with colour, again lights blinked and needles swung, again he felt sick. Again the ship came to a stop.

More cautiously, he opened the inner door, closed it, opened the outer door.

Nothing.

Shouting inarticulately, he hurried back into the ship and turned the dial to – 10. The same sensations. Another stop.

And outside was the same featureless pit of empty space.

There was only one thing left to do to test the ship. Set the dial for the future and see what lay there. If it was the same, he could switch to Emergency Return.

He swung the dial right round to + 2.

The humming rose to a shrill. Lightning exploded on the screens, the needles sped around the dials and Pepin flung himself to the floor in panic as his head began to ache horribly. The ship seemed to be tossed from side to side and yet he remained in the same position on the floor.

At last the ship came to a halt. He got up slowly, passed through the airlock.

He saw *everything.*

He saw gold-flecked bands of blue spiralling away into infinity. He saw streamers of cerise and violet light. He saw heaving mountains of black and green. He saw clouds of orange and purple. Shapes formed and melted. It seemed he was a giant at one moment and a midget at the next. His mind was not equipped to take in so much.

Quickly, he shut the airlock.

What had he seen? A vision of chaos? The sight seemed to him to have been metaphysical rather than physical. But what had it signified? It had been the very opposite of the vacuum – it had been space filled with everything imaginable, or the components of everything. The ship could not be a Time craft after all, but a vessel for journeying – where? Another dimension? An alternate universe? But why the plus and minus signs on the controls? Why had Tall Laugher called this a Time ship? Had he been tricked?

He pushed back his helmet and wiped the sweat from his face. His eyes felt sore and his headache was worse. He was incapable of logical thought.

He was tempted to turn the dial marked 'Emergency Return', but there was still the mysterious dial marked 'Megaflow Tuner'. Filled with hysterical recklessness, he turned it and was flung back as the ship jerked into normal motion. On the screens he saw a little of what he had observed outside.

All kinds of images appeared and disappeared. Once human figures – like golden shadows – were seen for a moment. His eyes fixed insanely on the screens, Pepin Hunchback could only stare.

Much, much later, he fell back to the floor. He had fainted.

At the sound of Tall Laugher's voice, he opened his eyes. His initial question was scarcely original, but it was the thing he most needed to know.

'Where am I?' he said, looking up at her.

'On the Megaflow,' she replied. 'You are a fool, Pepin Hunchback. The Brooder and I have had a considerable amount of difficulty locating you. It is a wonder you are not insane.'

'I think I am. How did you get here?'

'We travelled up the Megaflow after you. But your speed was so great we wasted a great deal of energy catching you. I see from the instruments that you went into the past. Were you satisfied?'

He got up slowly. 'Was that – that vacuum the *past*?'

'Yes.'

'But it was not Earth's past?'

'It is the only past there is.' She was at the controls, manipulating them. He turned his head and saw the Chronarch standing, head bowed, at the back of the ship.

He looked up and pursed his lips at Pepin.

'I attempted to explain – but I knew you would not believe me. It is a pity that you know the truth, for it will not console you, my friend.'

'What *truth*?'

The Scar-faced Brooder sighed. He spread his hands. 'The only truth there is. The past is nothing but limbo – the future is what you have observed – chaos, save for the Megaflow.'

'You mean Earth only has existence in the *present*?'

'As far as we are concerned, yes.' The Brooder folded his arms across his chest. 'It means little to us of Lanjis Liho – but I knew how it would affect you. We are Time Dwellers, you see – you are still a Space Dweller. Your mind is not adjusted to understand and exist in the dimensions of Time-without-space.'

'Time without space is an impossibility!' Pepin shouted.

The Brooder grimaced. 'Is it? Then what do you think of the future – of the Megaflow? Admittedly something exists here, but it is not the stuff of space as you would understand it. It is – well, the physical manifestation of Time-without-space.' He sighed as he noted Pepin's expression. 'You will never properly understand, my friend.'

Tall Laugher spoke. 'We are nearly at Present, Brooder.'

'I will explain further when we return to Earth,' said the Chronarch kindly. 'You have my sympathy, Pepin Hunchback.'

In the Hall of Time, the Scar-faced Brooder walked up to his dais and lowered himself into his chair. 'Sit down, Pepin,' he said, indicating the edge of the dais. Dazedly, Pepin obeyed.

'What do you think of the past?' said the Chronarch ironically, as Tall Laugher joined them. Pepin looked up at her and then at her brother. He shook his head.

Tall Laugher put her hand on his shoulder. 'Poor Pepin . . .'

He did not have enough emotion left to feel anything at this. He rubbed his face and stared at the floor. His eyes were full of tears.

'Do you want the Chronarch to explain, Pepin?' she asked. Looking into her face, he saw that she, too, seemed extraordinarily sad. Somehow she could understand his hopelessness. If only she were normal, he thought, and we had met in different circumstances. Even here, life would be more than bearable with her. He had never seen such a look of sympathy directed at him before. She was repeating her question. He nodded.

'At first we were as astonished as you at the true nature of Time,' said the Chronarch. 'But, of course, it was much easier for us to accept it. We are capable of moving through Time as others move through space. Time is now our natural element. We have adapted in a peculiar way – we are able to journey into the past or future merely by an effort of will. We have reached the stage where we no longer need space to exist. In Time-with-space our physical requirements are manifold and increasingly hard to meet on this changing planet. But in Time-without-space these physical requirements no longer exist.'

'Brooder,' put in Tall Laugher, 'I do not think he is interested in us. Tell him why he found only limbo in the past.'

'Yes,' said Pepin, turning to stare at the Chronarch. 'Tell me.'

'I'll try. Imagine Time as a straight line along which the physical universe is moving. At a certain point on that line the physical universe exists. But if we move away from the present, backward or forward, what do we find?'

Again Pepin shook his head.

'We find what you found – for by leaving the present, we also leave the physical universe. You see, Pepin, when we leave our native Time stream, we move into others which are, in relation to us, *above* Time. There is a central stream along which our universe moves – we call this the Megaflow. As it moves it absorbs the stuff of Time – absorbs the chronons, as we call them, but leaves nothing behind. Chronons constitute the future – they are infinite. The reason you found nothing in the past is because, in a sense, space *eats* the chronons but cannot replace them.'

'You mean Earth absorbs this – this temporal energy but emits none herself – like a beast prowling through Time gobbling it up but excreting nothing.' Pepin spoke with a faint return of interest. 'Yes, I understand.'

The Chronarch leaned back. 'So when you came to me asking to return to the past, I almost told you this, but you would not have believed me. You did not want to. You cannot return to Earth's past because, simply, it no longer exists. Neither is there a future in terms of space, only in terms of the chronon-constituted Megaflow and its offshoots. We have managed to move ourselves where we wish, individually absorbing the chronons we need. Thus, the human race will continue – possibly we shall be immortal, ranging the continents of

Time at will, exploring, acquiring knowledge which will be useful to us.'

'While the rest of us die or turn into little better than machines,' said Pepin flatly.

'Yes.'

'Now I have no hope at all,' said Pepin, rising. He limped up to Tall Laugher. 'When do you leave for good?'

'Shortly.'

'I thank you for your sympathy and courtesy,' he said.

He left them standing silently in the Hall of Time.

Pepin walked along the beach, still moving towards the east, away from Lanjis Liho by the sea. The morning was a brown shroud covering the endlessness of sluggish sea and salt-frosted land, illuminated by a dying sun, blown by a cold wind.

Ah, he thought, *this is a morning for tears and self-contempt. Loneliness sits upon me like a great oozer with its mouth at my throat, sucking me dry of optimism. If only I could give myself up to this pitiless morning, let it engulf me, freeze me, toss me on its frigid wind and sink me in its slow-yielding sea, to lose sight of sun and sky, such as they are, and return to Mother Earth's ever-greedy womb . . .*

Oh, this alien Earth!

And yet he did not envy the Time Dwellers. Like the Moonites, they were renouncing their humanity. At least he still had his.

He turned as he heard his name called – a thin cry like that of an ancient seabird.

Tall Laugher was riding towards him, waving to him. She rode beneath the brown and heaving sky, her back straight and a smile on her lips and for some reason it seemed to him that she was riding to him out of the past, as when he had first seen her, a goddess from an age of mythology.

The red disc of the sun glowed behind her and again he noticed the strong smell of brine.

He waited by the edge of the thick, salt sea and, as he waited, he knew that his journey had been worth while.

Waiting for the End of Time . . .

Chill winds blew over Tanet-tur-Taac and the salt stink of the sea was in Suron's nostrils through all the night and all the day because the waters were rising as the moon sank down.

Chill winds shredded the clouds above Tanet and sometimes they brought snow and sometimes they brought hot rain and sometimes they merely made waves on the sea.

His long hair floating in the wind, Suron-riel-J'ryec stared up at the moon and beyond it to Kadel Star which had once been so far away from Tanet, last world on the Rim. There were many large stars in the sky now and soon they and their planets would be one huge body. Tanet, too, would soon be part of that body.

From where he stood on the city's tallest tower Suron could see the distant mountains and now he altered his vision to bring some particular area into sharper perspective. He was sure he had seen something moving there again. But the wind was stirring the snow on the slopes. Perhaps that had been all he had seen.

Suron looked behind him at the slender towers of the city which was called Rion-va-mëy – Inevitable Hope – a city which was also a machine. Suron had built Rion-va-mëy and he had named the city-machine which had been designed to make Tanet a world completely independent of its sun, to shift it away from the pull of the Mass before it became too strong, to cross intergalactic space and find a galaxy still in equilibrium. That was why they had chosen this stark Rim world for their experiment, because it was the last habitable world on the edge of the galaxy.

And the galaxy was doomed to undergo a monstrous change in which nothing would remain as it had been.

The galaxy was condensing.

They had known it would since their scientists had come to understand the nature of the huge, dark bodies which lay at the centre of the galaxy. Megaquasars with a mass so great that even photons could not escape them, they had begun to increase their mass with every body which entered their gravitational field.

And now the entire galaxy lay within that field and each sun and its satellites were inexorably being drawn in as the megaquasars consolidated into a single mass so vast that no real name could be invented for it. To most who referred to it at all it was just the Mass.

Suron watched the sky again as the day grew swiftly darker. His scheme had failed as it became clear that it was too late. Rion-va-mëy was the most sophisticated machine mankind had ever invented. Capable of providing a complete artificial environment, of shifting a planet as easily as a spacecraft, it could never be used for its original purpose. All it could do now was help Tanet to avert the inevitable collision for a few extra days.

It hardly functioned as a city now, for most of its citizens had departed when they realized Suron's scheme had failed. They had hoped to reach their home worlds before they were swallowed by their suns which would, in turn, be swallowed by larger suns before the Mass swallowed the whole.

Suron had remained, for Tanet was his world now. He loved it. And the one who loved Suron stayed with him.

The process had been gradual at first. A few thousand years ago it had scarcely been noticeable. A thousand years ago it had become plain what was happening. A hundred years ago half the suns and planets in the galaxy had been absorbed by the Mass and now the suns and planets of the Rim were moving towards each other.

A few more days, thought Suron, and we shall be on that last inward journey. And in less than a year, if the scientists' theories were correct, the Mass would collapse under the weight of its own gravitation and the entropic process would begin again. New stars, new planets, a new cycle.

Would the cycle repeat itself? Suron wondered. Was the galaxy programmed to form and re-form for eternity? Would mankind be reborn and recreate its history for perhaps the millionth time?

From the top of the tallest tower, his pale body exposed to the elements he savoured, Suron watched the waters. They had already reached some of the more distant structures. Again he looked at the Moon which now dominated the sky. It was a little closer than it had been yesterday, just as Tanet was a little closer to her sun, just as the stars gathered into a slightly tighter grouping.

Not long, he thought.

The short night passed. The sky's colour changed from deep blue to violet to a pale green and the clouds raced away over the horizon and were gone. The sun loomed over the horizon and Suron instantly felt its heat.

There was a whisper of sound behind Suron.

'So it was all for nothing.'

Mis'rn-bur-Sen placed a gentle hand on Suron's arm. 'The sun is closer, Suron.'

Suron turned and smiled at his husband.

'I dreamed, last night, of mankind. What was all for nothing?'

Mis'rn walked to the balustrade. Like Suron's, his skin was transparent and revealed the veins and organs of his hermaphroditic body. His pale hair waved in the warm wind.

'All the strife and the misery and the death. All the efforts of those who aspired to help mankind attain the tranquillity and security which we gained so recently. All wasted, Suron. Mankind has been cheated. At the moment of its triumph over its condition – over mortality, over its environment – nature still plays her jokes, still manages to find a way to destroy us.'

Suron smiled. 'A somewhat anthropomorphic view of the universe. Is it not enough to know that mankind did, eventually, triumph – did attain what the ancients called "a state of grace"? Is not the affection which you and I have something of a reward for all those millennia of struggle?'

Mis'rn bowed his head. 'Perhaps.'

The tower trembled. The sky darkened as new clouds came sweeping over the horizon. The roar of the sea drowned the sound of the wind. Suron put the tip of one long finger on the balustrade and drew a sign.

The bite of the wind and the bellowing of the sea were shut out as a field of energy formed an invisible dome over the tower. In the new silence Suron and Mis'rn stared into each other's large eyes.

'But our children are dead,' said Mis'rn at length.

Each had borne the other's child simultaneously some fifty years earlier. Both children had remained on the planet where they had been born and both now had been consumed.

Suron had accepted this fact without bitterness but Mis'rn, whose temperament was complementary to Suron's, still grieved.

And that was why Suron comforted his husband now. Wordlessly he expressed his sympathy and wordlessly Mis'rn communicated his gratitude. The tower shook again.

'What was your dream of mankind?' Mis'rn asked.

'I do not remember the images, merely the mood. I stood here and I dreamed and then I awakened and, Mis'rn, I was happy.'

'You have shared that with me. I wish that I could have such a dream. But my dreams, when they come, are all of conflict and disaster.'

Suron pointed to the mountains. 'After my dream I thought I saw something moving on the slopes yonder. Perhaps it was part of the dream.'

'I think so. We are the last two to remain on Tanet. And there are no beasts here. Our ancestors saw to that.'

'And yet I had an impulse to go to the mountains – to see.'

'It is too dangerous, Suron. All the city's energy is being used to resist the pull of our sun and to keep our moon from falling into us. If you left its environs it could not protect you.'

'I know.'

Suron took Mis'rn's hand and whispered a sound.

They were transported into the heart of the tower, to a room of soft, ever-changing light which beamed nourishment into their systems. Then they made sweet, tender love – scarcely touching each other as they moved about the room in a graceful ballet of emotion.

And the tower trembled once more and the light flickered for an instant before resuming its transformations.

Mis'rn paused in his dance and Suron saw that there were the traces of a forgotten emotion beginning to emerge on his face. The emotion was fear.

'We must accept this, Mis'rn,' he said. 'We named this city Inevitable Hope because it was inevitable that we should hope. But now that hope is lost, we must accept it.'

'I cannot,' Mis'rn murmured. 'Suron, I cannot.'

Suron crossed the room and embraced him. 'Put yourself into sleep,' he suggested. 'Cut off the objective world entirely. It might heal you.'

'I have not done that since childhood.'

'But do it now, Mis'rn. Sleep helped our ancestors in this way when they could not tolerate the implications of reality. That was why they slept.'

'I will try.'

Suron traced a particular sign on the wall of light and the air in the centre of the room shivered and whispered and a couch appeared.

Mis'rn went to the couch and lay down, staring up at Suron.

'Close your eyes,' Suron said, and Mis'rn closed them. 'I will come and wake you,' Suron promised.

And Suron returned to the top of the tower, blinking in the intense light. He caused the dome to darken so that he could peer out at the landscape.

The snow had melted on the mountains. The sea moved moodily around the lower towers. The monstrous sun marched across the sky.

Suron focused his eyes so that the mountain slope seemed to come closer. Carefully he inspected each yellow rock, each deep black shadow and fissure. But only the shadows moved as the sun sailed steadily on.

But then, as Suron shifted his gaze to the upper slopes, he saw a shadow which moved in the opposite direction and then disappeared behind one of the large fangs of rock which a recent earth tremor had split from the main body of the mountain.

There was, after all, a living creature out there. A man?

Suron was sure that no man could survive in the heat unless he had protective clothing.

A visitor, then, from one of the inner worlds?

Impossible. No spaceship could survive the immense gravitational forces which now existed in space. And there was no matter receiver still operating on Tanet-tur-Taac.

Suron wondered if the creature had come from a near-by galaxy.

He reached a decision. Still staring at the slope, he waited patiently for the evening.

It was now never completely dark on Tanet, but when the sun had reached the farther horizon and the moon had begun to heave its monstrous bulk over the tops of the mountains and the sky turned to deep blue and the stars once again made their appearance, Suron left Rion-va-mëy, city-machine of Inevitable Hope.

On his naked back he wore a light force-field pack which would protect him against the elements and propel him over the rocks.

Drifting a few inches above the ground, he flew against the wind as clouds thickened and obscured the sky, bringing the first snow of the evening.

Suron increased his body temperature to counter the cold and when the snow flakes fell on his naked shoulders they melted immediately.

Behind him the city had changed colour. It was now a peculiar shade of orange. Suron knew that its resources were almost exhausted. The sea covered more of the towers and those towers which remained had begun to sway and to shake again.

Suron reached the foothills of the mountains and began to ascend.

The sky turned to a rich purple and the wind slashed the clouds so that the moon could be seen again. It was even closer. Suron almost felt he could reach up and touch it. It dominated the landscape.

Peering ahead he thought he saw the moving shadow, near the summit of the mountain. He increased his speed.

*

He reached the summit. The wind was so strong now that he was forced to use more power in order to stop himself being hurled from his position. The moon seemed to threaten to crush him, seemed to fill the entire sky.

An anthropoid quadruped emerged from behind a rock just below him. It was clinging to the slope, its hairy body rimed with snow, its fur flattened by the wind. It looked at him from its intelligent eyes and Suron recognized it.

He gasped.

The anthropoid moved its head and stared at him warily. It opened its mouth and spoke but the wind's yell swamped the words.

Suron moved down the slope towards the creature.

The alien retreated and disappeared. Suron saw that the rock hid a fissure in the slope – a cave.

Without hesitating, Suron entered the cave.

Light came. The cave was artificial. It was a room – possibly one of a series of rooms – and its contents had largely been smashed or thrown about by the tremors. On its four legs the creature stalked across the room, skirting the litter, and seated itself upon an oddly shaped chair. Gravely it regarded Suron.

'I thought your species extinct,' Suron said. Then he frowned. 'Do you understand my tongue?'

The reply was clear, firm, musical. 'I understand it. My species was – extinguished. It was destroyed by your species a long time ago.'

'I did not know that,' said Suron.

'There was vegetation and beauty. There was peace. Ages ago your folk came with fire and burned all the beauty away, killed all my race save me. I hid, far underground. Then your folk went away. I could never discover why they destroyed our world.'

'How came you to learn our language?'

'A traveller.' The creature gestured with one of its hands and Suron saw a skull. It was the skull of a pre-hermaphroditic man. It must have been centuries old.

'You killed him?'

'He died. We were friends, I think.'

'Did he not know why your planet was burned?'

'He spoke of a war. He said this world had probably been a potential tactical position – something of that sort. He said that if they had known of us they might not have burned the planet but they assumed that creatures which walk on four legs are not "intelligent" – whatever that had to do with it.'

'My ancestors once made distinctions between beings who reasoned like them and beings of a less questioning disposition.'

'Those who were content were destroyed.'

'It has been put thus. But you survived all these years.'

'Yes – in order to die, it seems, with those who robbed me of my happiness. Is this catastrophe another of your actions?'

'I do not think so. I am called Suron-riel-J'ryec.'

'I am Mollei Coyshkaery. Then what has caused this?'

Suron explained.

The anthropoidal creature seemed amused. 'So none win. What happened to us now happens to you.'

'With one difference. There will be none to remember mankind when it is gone.'

'It is all it deserved.'

The cavern shuddered.

'I suppose it is.'

'You are not like my friend.' Mollei indicated the skull. 'You are calmer – you look different.'

'Our race had begun to evolve into an altogether dissimilar species. As you are, we were almost immortal. We had no conflict among ourselves, no enemies to threaten us. We spent our time in adapting to what you see before you. We would have changed further, but . . .' Suron paused. 'And we had learned the habit of love,' he said. 'We had forgotten the habit of hate.'

'I have not yet learned to hate,' said Mollei. 'And now it is too late.'

'I am sorry.'

'You think it good to hate?'

'I think it good to know all feelings.' Suron's gaze was drawn back to the skull.

Mollei brushed melted snow from his fur. His expression was contemplative. 'There used to be music,' he said. 'I have heard no music for so long.'

'Perhaps you will hear it again?'

'What do you mean?'

'Some think that the galaxy undergoes a perpetual cycle of birth, death and rebirth – that its history is repeated over and over again with only minor differences.'

'But that means I will know the pain again. Your words bring no comfort, Suron-riel-J'ryec.'

Suron sighed. 'I admit that the conception is also terrifying.'

'You seem unmoved by what is about to happen.'

'It is inevitable, Mollei Coyshkaery.'

The cavern tilted. In spite of his force field Suron was hurled to the far wall. Objects slithered with him. The skull struck the wall and shattered. Mollei tried to save himself but was flung down and lay just below Suron, shouting in pain, trying to rise. Rock fell from the ceiling. There was a mighty roaring everywhere as the cavern continued to shake. Then it was still.

Suron lowered himself to the angle of floor and wall where Mollei lay. There was misery in the alien's eyes. Some of his bones were evidently broken.

'That was the worst,' Mollei murmured. 'What caused it, I wonder . . .'

'The moon has fallen at last. Some distance from us, I would think.'

'What does that mean?'

'It means that in a short while your planet will be drawn into its sun almost at the same moment that the sun joins other stars. We are all moving towards the centre, Mollei. A few hours after we are dead there will be a single mass comprising what was once our galaxy. After that, it is believed, the mass will explode and the galaxy will begin again.'

'Death comes quickly,' gasped the alien, 'but life takes such a long time to form . . .'

'Will you come with me to Rion-va-mëy, my city?' Suron asked. 'There is the means, there, to ease your pain.'

'I am dying,' said Mollei. 'Let me die alone.'

'Very well.'

Suron sought the entrance to the cave, but it had been blocked when the moon had fallen. He went back to the dying alien. 'I am trapped, it appears.'

Mollei raised himself on his elbow and pointed to a doorway. 'There are several other exits. One of them may still not be blocked.'

'Thank you.'

'Good-bye, Suron-riel-J'ryec.'

'Good-bye.'

Suron knew that the power was beginning to fail in his pack. He drifted through the dark doorway and widened his eyes so that he could see into the murk of the next room. There were pictures here and artefacts of all kinds. He realized that Mollei had used the cave system as a museum – a monument to his slain race. Suron experienced what he thought might be guilt.

He made his way through several similar chambers, pausing only to stare at a very ancient relief which seemed to indicate that Mollei's people had once had indigenous enemies – it was a scene of warfare. The ape creatures were triumphantly driving away some kind of similarly armed epicene people.

And then he saw a rent in the roof and light was coming through.

Suron increased the power and moved up to the ceiling, passing through the crack and out on to the surface of the planet.

He gasped as the light struck his eyes and he covered them with his hands. He knew that there was little power left in his pack but he increased the strength of the field still further and shut out the burning heat and the light as much as he could.

He looked down the mountain and away to the sea.

The sea was boiling. Clouds of steam swirled around what was left of Rion-va-mëy. Huge black fissures split the mountain. As fast as he dared, he began to descend.

The screen around his body faltered. Suron knew he would die if it failed altogether – die more painfully and much quicker than ever his ancestors with their thicker skins would have died.

He drifted over a new-formed crevasse and even as he moved the far side began to lean away as it grew wider and wider. A monstrous roaring filled his ears. The whole planet shook.

With a sense of increasing panic he at last reached the far side.

One of the towers fell and then another swayed and toppled. Suron knew that the machine had failed at last.

The sky grew still brighter and it seemed that the heat would blister his skin. The surface of the distant sea was now bubbling and he could hear the hiss of its waters as they were turned to vapour.

Again the screen faltered and Suron's feet brushed the burning rocks.

The tallest tower still stood, but it was some distance away. He saw one of the great power bands which had girdled the planet bend and then snap as a steel wire might snap when cut. The several sections were flung high into the air, vibrating and twisting and then collapsing. Another tower fell into the boiling sea.

Suron felt faint. His vision became misty. He knew he would die very soon, before he could get back to the room where Mis'rn lay asleep.

There was chaos all about him. A terrifying confusion of flying rock and whirling steam.

He could no longer see Rion-va-mëy. Perhaps the city of Inevitable Hope had disappeared completely.

The sun grew even larger. Suron cried out in pain.

Then, still drifting, he fainted.

*

'Suron!'

It was a little cooler. He opened his eyes and looked into those of Mis'rn-bur-Sen. His were anxious eyes.

'Suron. You live!'

'Yes, I live. But I should be dead.'

'I awoke and looked for you. I knew you had gone, then, to the mountain. I took a boat and searched for you, finding you senseless. I brought you back to our tower.'

'It still stands, then?'

'It will stand for only a little longer. I have diverted all the remaining power to it.'

'I thought you asleep, my husband.'

'Something woke me – the moon falling, I suppose, or a sense of your danger. Perhaps both. I dreamed deep dreams, Suron – of mankind.'

'And they troubled you?' Suron rose from the couch and tried to stand on the swaying floor. The walls no longer shifted with a variety of colours. They were a pale green.

'They comforted me, Suron. It is better to die loving mankind than hating it.'

Suron nodded. 'Mollei will be dead by now.'

'Mollei?'

'I met a creature in the mountain, Mis'rn. The last indigenous inhabitant of Tanet-tur-Taac. Our ancestors destroyed his race with fire. They destroyed all the vegetation on the planet. He survived for centuries and yet he never knew hatred – only distress and puzzlement. He did not know why we killed his people.'

'Did you know?'

'I know only that mankind killed many such races as it spread through the galaxy.'

'And now you hate mankind?'

'No. But I understand his bewilderment. For now mankind is destroyed. We are probably the last still living. And soon we shall be dead.'

'But we are destroyed by unthinking nature.'

'And was not that the force which slew the people of this planet?'

'We slew them.'

'Yes. But perhaps we only think we think. We use our thoughts to justify actions which we should perform nonetheless . . .'

Mis'rn nodded. He moved to one of the two couches and lay down upon it. 'It is true that we conquered nothing,' he said. 'And now we are conquered.'

'We conquered ourselves. And having achieved that, we now die.'

'You think that was the purpose of our existence?'

'I have never thought our existence had a "purpose". And yet our ancestors believed something of the sort, that we were born to learn to love, that having done so we should be reunited with the universe.'

Mis'rn closed his eyes. 'Will you let in some of the light, Suron, so that we may see this world once more.'

Suron touched the wall and drew a sign. The outer wall became opaque and then transparent and the blinding light flew into the room. Heat came with it but this time they welcomed it.

Suron took his place on his couch and lay down. He reached out and touched Mis'rn's hand.

'And now we sleep,' he said. And, in love, they slept.

Then Suron and Mis'rn dreamed of mankind.

They dreamed of all it had striven to be, of all it had achieved, of all its failures. And it was a dream of love.

They dreamed of the stars and the planets of their galaxy and of those who had left the planet Earth so many millennia before, who had explored and destroyed and brutalized themselves because they thought that knowledge brought love and tranquillity.

And it seemed that they dreamed the whole history of the galaxy from its birth to its death, that they witnessed the formation of each star and each planet, that they lived the life of each individual creature which had come into existence on those planets.

And in their dreams they came to realize that Time was a meaningless idea just as Death meant nothing and Identity meant little.

And, as they dreamed, the last tower burned and Tanet-tur-Taac fell into the roaring heart of its sun. Then this sun joined Kadel Star and a hundred other suns rushed together to form a single fiery globe.

It was the last fire which, momentarily, burned in the darkness. Then it, too, fell into the Mass.

And there was only blackness where a galaxy had been.

But already something was starting to happen to the Mass as it began to implode under its own vast weight.

Perhaps Suron and Mis'rn, or something which had been them, continued to dream, at least until the moment when cracks of light began to reappear and the galaxy began to be reborn, as Suron and Mis'rn, an eternity later, might also be reborn.

For Time meant nothing and Death meant nothing and Identity meant only a little.

And Somewhere Else

The Stone Thing

A Tale of Strange Parts

Out of the dark places; out of the howling mists; out of the lands without sun; out of Ghonorea came tall Catharz, with the moody sword Oakslayer in his right hand, the cursed spear Bloodlicker in his left hand, the evil bow Deathsinger on his back together with his quiver of fearful rune-fletched arrows, Heartseeker, Goregreedy, Soulsnatcher, Orphanmaker, Eyeblinder, Sorrowsower, Beanslicer, and several others.

Where his right eye should have been there was a jewel of slumbering scarlet whose colour sometimes shifted to smouldering blue, and in the place of his left eye was a many-faceted crystal, which pulsed as if possessed of independent life. Where Catharz had once had a right hand, now a thing of iron, wood and carved amethyst sat upon his stump; nine-fingered, alien, cut by Catharz from the creature who had sliced off his own hand. Catharz' left hand was at first merely gauntleted, but when one looked further it could be observed that the gauntlet was in fact a many-jointed limb of silver, gold and lapis lazuli, but as Catharz rode by, those who saw him pass remarked not on the murmuring sword in his right hand, not on the whispering spear in his left hand, not on the whining bow upon his back or the grumbling arrows in the quiver; neither did they remark on his right eye of slumbering scarlet, his left eye of pulsing crystal, his nine-fingered right hand, his shining metallic left hand; they saw only the fearful foot of Cwlwwymwn which throbbed in the stirrup at his mount's right flank.

The foot of the Aching God, Cwlwwymwn Rootripper, whose ambition upon the old and weary Earth had been to make widows of all wives; Cwlwwymwn the Striker, whose awful feet had trampled whole cities when men had first made cities; Cwlwwymwn of the Last Ones, Last of the Last Ones, who had been driven back to his island domain on the edge of the world, beyond the Western Ice, and who now came limping after Catharz screaming out for vengeance, demanding the return of his foot, sliced from his leg by Oakslayer so that Catharz might walk again and continue upon his doom-laden quest, bearing weapons which were not his protection but his burden, seeking consolation for the guilt which ate at his soul since it was he who had been responsible for the death of his younger brother, Forax the Golden, for the death of his niece, Libia Gentleknee, for the living death of his cousin, Wertigo the Unbalanced, seeking the whereabouts of his lost love, Cyphila the Fair, who had been stolen from him by his arch-enemy, the wizard To'me'ko'op'r, most powerful, most evil, most lustful of all the great sorcerers of this magic-clouded world.

And there were no friends here to give aid to Catharz God-foot. He must go alone, with shuddering terror before him and groaning guilt behind him, and Cwlwwymwn, screaming, vengeful, limping Cwlwwymwn, following always.

And Catharz rode on, rarely stopping, scarcely ever dismounting, anxious to claim his own vengeance on the sorcerer, and the foot of Cwlwwymwn, Last of the Last Ones, was heavy on him, as well it might be for it was at least eighteen inches longer than his left foot and naked, for he had had to abandon his boot when he had found that it did not fit. Now Cwlwwymwn possessed the boot; it was how he had known that Catharz was the mortal who had stolen his green, seventeen-clawed limb, attaching it by fearful sorcery to the flesh of his leg. Catharz' left leg was not of flesh at all, but of lacquered cork, made for him by the People of the World Beneath the Reefs, when he had aided them in their great fight against the Gods of the Lowest Sea.

The sun had stained the sky a livid crimson and had sunk below the horizon before Catharz would allow himself a brief rest and it was just before dark that he came in sight of a small stone cottage, sheltered beneath terraces of glistening limestone, where he hoped he might find food, for he was very hungry.

Knocking upon the door he called out:

'Greetings, I come in friendship, seeking hospitality, for I am called Catharz the Melancholy, who carries the curse of Cwlwwymwn Rootripper upon him, who has many enemies and no friends, who slew his brother, Forax the Golden, and caused the death of Libia Gentleknee, famous for her beauty, and who seeks his lost love Cyphila the Fair, prisoner of the wizard To'me'ko'op'r, and who has a great and terrible doom upon him.'

The door opened and a woman stood there. Her hair was the silver of a spiderweb in the moonlight, her eyes were the deep gold found at the centre of a beehive, her skin had the pale, blushing beauty of the tea-rose. 'Welcome, stranger,' she said. 'Welcome to all that is left of the home of Lanoli, whose father was once the mightiest in these parts.'

And, upon beholding her, Catharz forgot Cyphila the Fair, forgot that he had slain his brother, his niece, and betrayed his cousin, Wertigo the Unbalanced.

'You are very beautiful, Lanoli,' he said.

'Ah,' said she, 'that is what I have learned. But beauty such as mine can only thrive if it is seen and it has been so long since anyone came to these lands.'

'Let me help your beauty thrive,' he said.

Food was forgotten, guilt was forgotten, fear was forgotten as Catharz divested himself of his sword, his spear, his bow and his arrows and walked slowly into the cottage. His gait was a rolling one, for he still bore the burden that was the foot of the Last of the Last Ones, and it took him some time to pull it through the door, but at length he stood inside and had closed the door behind him and had taken her in his arms and had pressed his lips to hers.

'Oh, Catharz,' she breathed. 'Catharz!'

It was not long until they stood naked before one another. Her eyes travelled over his body and it was plain that the eyes of scarlet and crystal were lovely to her, that she admired his silver hand and his nine-fingered hand, that even the great foot of Cwlwwymwn was beautiful in her sight. But then her eyes, shy until now, fell upon that which lay between his legs, and those eyes widened a little, and she blushed. Her lovely lips framed a question, but he moved forward as swiftly as he could and embraced her again.

'How?' she murmured. 'How, Catharz?'

'It is a long tale and a bloody one,' he whispered, 'of rivalry and revenge, but suffice to say that it ended in my father, Xympwell the Cruel, taking a terrible vengeance upon me. I fled from his court into the wastes of Grxiwynn, raving mad, and it was there that the tribesmen of Velox found me and took me to the Wise Man of Oorps in the mountains beyond Katatonia. He nursed me and carved that for me. It took him two years, and all through those two years I remained raving, living off dust and dew and roots, as he lived. The engravings had mystical significance, the runes contain the sum of his great wisdom, the tiny pictures show all that there is to show of physical love. Is it not beautiful? More beautiful than that which it has replaced?'

Her glance was modest; she nodded slowly.

'It is indeed, very beautiful,' she agreed. And then she looked up at him and he saw that tears glistened in her eyes. 'But did it *have* to be made of Sandstone?'

'There is little else,' he explained sadly, 'in the mountains beyond Katatonia.'

(From *The Outcast of Kitzoprenia*
Volume 67 in *The History of the*
Purple Poignard)

The Last Call

Champion! Champion!

In those spaces between waking and sleeping I heard them. Dimly at first. I heard their voices. They were calling. They were distant. Distant and echoing like breakers in a lonely seacave. Somehow I knew they were calling me.

Champion!

I could not bear it.

'No!' I screamed. 'No! I cannot – I will not – I dare not hear you!'

But they were relentless.

Champion!

'Begone!' I cried. 'Begone! I have done too much. There is nothing left of me to serve!'

Champion!

I lay face down. I could not open my eyes. I had the sensation of something wet against my cheek. Had I been weeping? I caught a smell – acrid, bitter and yet also sweet, familiar . . .

. . . your last orders!

'I'll take no further orders. I have fulfilled my destiny. There is nothing left for me . . .'

One more! One more!

'No! I cannot!'

I felt sick. I felt a strange dizziness. My whole body seemed to heave and tremble. And still I could not lift my head. Still I could not speak.

. . . time! Time . . .

'Let me be! Let me lie in space. I have no more to give. And there is nothing more that I can take!'

Champion!

With enormous effort I raised my head, but it was impossible to open my eyes.

Champion!

I could not remember how I had come here. What I had been doing. I could scarcely remember my own name. What was it? I had had so many names, so many faces, so many identities. Why should it be possible for me to know which was which?

We must win. This time we must win. We have the men, we have the experience. All we need is leadership . . .

There is no-one . . .

Only one and he is . . .

There is no way to beat them this year . . .

Only if we can find . . .

Fragments of conversation, of some sort of religious litany. Angry voices. Desperate voices. Defensive voices. Who were they? What did they need? Were they calling me? Or were they calling someone else? Were they calling at all?

Again I raised my head up and tried to open my eyes. For a second I caught a glimpse of a rank of figures, all men, lined before me. They wore strange flat headgear and each one held in his hand a vessel. They were turned, all of them, towards a shining light above their heads. It was bright enough to blind me. It illuminated their faces, but still I could make out no clear features, no details of their garb. I shuddered. There was something about them which filled me not so much with fear as with a disturbing, miserable ennui, a sense that I had come to a place where everyone was dead, where everyone waited, frozen, for something to breathe life into them. Was it me they wanted? Was I to give them life? I could not tell.

I tried to speak. But no words would come.

Champion!

The sickly, bitter-sweet smell increased. I reached out a hand towards the figures.

'Where am I?'

None heard me. Every face was turned to the source of the light. It seemed to me that it changed, that the colours changed, that dim shapes moved in it.

Had they brought me here? Was it all to begin again? The awful struggle? The voices raised in anger? The perpetual fighting? The hideous violence? The savagery? The waves of human flesh pouring over the green earth, turning it to bloody mud? The high screams of the young as their bodies were broken? The tears of the women?

'No! No! I want no more of it. I can stand nothing further. Free me from this. I beg you! Free me! Free me!'

Now at last the heads began to turn. Not many. But still the majority of them were intent on the source of the light, on the vessels they clutched in their fists – vessels full of some reddish, translucent liquid – liquid which foamed. And it was this which gave off the stench which clogged my nostrils and made my stomach heave.

'No!'

Quiet! one brusque voice ordered. But the others continued to observe the flickering light.

Champion!

Magic!

We're bound to win now!

'Please,' I begged. 'Please tell me. Where is this place? I must know. What do you want? What do you want?'

Another head turned. A bloated, half-human face regarded me. I shuddered. Had I fallen amongst the creatures of Chaos once more? Was I forever doomed to find myself in such circumstances? I had thought I was free from my fate at last. But this was worse than anything I had experienced before.

'Please. What do you call this place?'

Why, lad; what canst tha mean?

The voice was rough in timbre but almost kindly. The figure broke away from the rank of its fellows and approached me. It still held the vessel in its right hand. The liquid was almost gone from it, yet still it foamed a little.

'Who are you? And where am I now?'

Ee, lad, tha's had one too many by the look o' yer. You know me. You must know me. Everyone knows Old Enry . . .

'How was I brought here? By what means? What do you call this place?'

By Eck, lad, there's only one way you could 'a come here if tha didn't walk. By the Number Eighty. 'Tis all that passes The Six Jolly Dragoons nowadays, since the privatization.

I tried to ask more of him, but his attention was fading, his head was turned back to the source of the light. He was mesmerized almost as badly as the others. What was this evil which possessed them all?

Come on, lads. Time! Time! Drink up, please.

There came a murmur of protest. Discontented grunts. Then a sudden cheer.

'What is it?' I cried, trying to rise and failing. I fell to my knees. My head was pounding. My mouth felt suddenly dry. My stomach still heaved. 'What is it?'

'Tis two one. Old Enry turned his head. *There's no way they can win now.*

'So you don't need me?'

Why, lad, you're no use to anyone in that state.

'I can go?' An enormous wave of relief came over me. I began to weep. I was free. I was allowed to leave that dreadful place. I was no longer doomed to be part of their struggle.

Old Enry moved towards me. He put a hand under my arm and helped me to my feet. *Come, lad. Where d'you live? I'll get thee 'ome.*

I tried to remember. I recalled a number. A name. I tried to speak. Slowly the two of us moved away from the ranked men. Suddenly the light went out and they turned, staring after us.

It were a great game, that, Enry, said one as he waved farewell.

A huge door swung open and cool air struck my face. I began to feel that I might be able to walk again unaided. I straightened my back.

Aye, said Old Enry, as he signalled goodbye to his compatriots, *it were champion.*

Blackness lay ahead of me. Wet and howling. But anything was preferable to what I had just witnessed. I pulled myself together as best I could and began, with Old Enry at my side, to walk with slow painful steps into the bleak, mysterious dark. Behind me still came the cries of those I had believed summoned me. Then, one by one, the voices died, the lights dimmed and were extinguished.

I gave myself up to the Chaos which heaved within me.

My Life

Apart from a certain warmth (scarcely a *frisson*) felt at the ages of six and seven whilst playing in the company of little girls, the first sexual experience I recall with any great clarity occurred in a remote hill kingdom between the borders of India and Burma when I was eleven. I suppose that white boys must have been something of a rarity, even then, in the seraglios of those corrupt and now largely extinct Rajahs, for I cannot remember meeting another during the time in which I was incarcerated. Captured in the forest (my engineer father and my mother both killed by the same man eating tiger, and wolves my only companions for several months) I was half-wild and had to be chained at wrists, neck and ankles before being led behind the Rajah's huge, jewelled elephants, part of the long triumphal procession, in which the monarch displayed to his subjects the many spoils taken in his recent conquest of a neighbouring state. While I was not regarded as the greatest of his newly acquired treasures, I was given a certain amount of admiration as I staggered, clad only in a thin linen robe, weighted by my gilded chains, through the streets of his capital.

My impressions of the city were primarily restricted to the sparkling white domes and minarets of the palaces and public buildings and I cannot bring to mind much of the poverty which must have existed in the little, white, flat-roofed houses of the common folk. Pale dust rose all around us as we moved to the sound of musical instruments and the cheering of the crowds; there were tall horsemen on white Arab stallions, wearing coats of black and green silk, scarlet turbans, embroidered boots, their wooden stirrups and scabbards decorated with intricate lacquer-work; there were half-naked foot soldiers, in dented, blood-stained brass, their spears or long guns jutting over their shoulders; there were ox-carts, mules and camels, loaded with all manner of boxes carved from the rarest woods, inset with gold, silver and mother-of-pearl, and there were slaves of most ages and both sexes, chained together by means of the collars around their necks, the ends of the chains attached to the traces of the elephants of the Rajah and his generals. I admit to being overwhelmed, as any ignorant peasant, by the sight of this magnificence, and when I was stripped of my robe to be shown to the people in my nakedness I knew a pleasure which was unquestionably sexual. I could not have resisted what next happened to me, even had I possessed any moral preconceptions, for I had no other wish than to enter the service of my captor in any capacity he chose for me.

To a Western reader my fate must seem bizarre, my tale the tale of Innocence Corrupted, but I, of course, did not have (and do not now have) any such feelings. I was taken to the women's quarters and there I was bathed, scented, painted and dressed as a girl. There by means of infrequent but by no means unwelcome beatings I was trained in the manners and customs of a court houri. The Rajah at last sent for me and by the time I had reached his presence and prostrated myself before him I was shaking with the most delicious, weakening emotion. He was not a young man, the Rajah, but he was tall, bearded and elegant. He did not immediately bid me rise, so I remained where I was, my face against the marble mosaic of the floor, while he first discussed some business with his courtiers and then, laughingly, my beauty with one or two of his wives who were waiting on him. At length he dismissed them all and I was alone with my master.

Oddly it was that first emotion, when brought into his presence, that I recall with greatest clarity. Needless to say his interest in me was sexual, but he proved to be gentle and kind and even the beatings I received at his hands were more in the nature of caresses than punishments. I became extremely fond of the old man and, I believe, he of me, for we spent much time together discussing abstract and philosophical matters (he must, I now realize, have taken pleasure in my naïveté) and from him I received my most lasting education.

Towards the end of my stay with the Rajah, I conceived a romantic attachment for a girl of my own age who was not, I think, one of the Rajah's concubines but more likely one of his daughters. The Rajah must have noticed the tenderness of my feelings for the girl and he encouraged them, giving us time together and allowing us to be alone in his beautiful gardens, where all manner of trees and flowers grew upon the lawns, where marble fountains played and where peacocks and birds of paradise moved with their peculiar gait, half stately, half pompous, along tessellated pathways. I remember embracing her as we lay together in the shade of an ancient banyan tree and we made love, after a fashion, with a slow, gentle passion (in my own case imitated from my master), stroking her skin with the lightest possible touch, kissing her perfect little body, from toe to forehead, with the most delicate of kisses. Why we should have decided to leave this paradise I do not know, but one night we took a decorative ceremonial boat from the docks of the Rajah's private Temple and we set off down river.

That night was terrifying as we clung together, listening to the sounds of the jungle, the roaring of the water which bore the boat along at horrendous speed, threatening to capsize it and give us up to the crocodiles and water snakes which, we were sure, greedily waited for us in the black, foam-tipped river.

By morning, however, the river had widened and become quieter. We drifted along hungry, bewildered, regretful, perhaps hoping that the Rajah would send his men to bring us back, but I, at least, was never to see or hear of him again. We had no means of steering the boat and it drifted thus for at least two more days and nights before we were sighted by a small steamer and taken aboard, without any particular gladness, by the Portuguese skipper who delivered us, as soon as he could, to the first British person he came across in a nondescript Europeanized riverside town whose name I no longer remember. From there the girl, I believe, went to a convent orphanage and I was sent on to Calcutta, where my English relatives were traced.

Apart from an almost non-sexual friendship with another little girl on the boat home (she was Danish, I think, with long straight, very fair hair) I was to have no real romance for at least a couple of years. There were one or two panicky, musty moments with the second of several women who looked after me at that time in England. There were giggling revelations of private parts on waste ground or in lavatories and locked bedrooms, but none of this appealed much to me. Without tenderness and romance, I was incapable of intercourse (and have remained so, for the most part, to this day). That cynicism and aggression should replace the qualities I regarded as essential to the enjoyment of love-making always appalled me and as a result I often found myself an outsider at school, though I had many substantial and non-romantic friendships with girls of my own age with whom, it seemed, I had more in common.

My next memorable sexual encounter came when I was fifteen (it was, indeed, upon my fifteenth birthday) after I had left school, but with a schoolfriend who shared with me common tastes in our reading. We had attended a meeting of a literary club and had returned late. It was impossible for him to get home and so it was suggested that he stay at my house for the night. We shared a large double bed and again I felt that companionable, sexually-tinged warmth I had once felt when very young. After a little preliminary talk in which we both hinted how nice it would be if one or the other of us were a girl, we made love. However, his attitude towards sex was slightly shocking to me and plainly his pleasure came from what must have seemed in his terms the perversity of the act, whereas, as always, my feelings were to a large extent romantic. He seemed over-fastidious, too, where certain aspects of love-making were concerned, referring to them as 'dirty'. I soon ended my relationship with him, he later joined the police force and I never saw him again.

A little later I entered London's Bohemian society and began to sleep, little else, with a number of women friends. When mild love-making became full-blooded passion I cannot remember, though I have tried, and my first act of sexual union with a woman could not have occurred until I was sixteen or seventeen. I am sure, however, that I took the same pleasure then as I do now in that first, delicate touch of the penis to the lady's exquisite and beautiful vagina.

(*Extracted from 'My Life', an unfinished memoir*)

The Museum of the Future

Homage to H G Wells and The Time Machine, 1895

The Time Traveller (for so it will be convenient to call him) was explaining a recondite matter to us. It was about what he called 'alternative futures'.

'My own, for instance, where government is able to take better stock of the nation's resources – and then, of course, we have your future. In which, sadly, we are all for the moment marooned.'

He had told us why he'd accepted the temporary post of Curator to the Museum of the Future. Returning to 21st-century Britain for emergency repairs, he made a slightly wrong turn, as it were, in Time and found himself in this slightly different version of the 21st century. 'Which I must admit is a bit of a disappointment.' The repairs to his Time Machine would have taken a couple of weeks in his own 21st century, but here were taking months.

'Only foreign engineering firms have the resources to make the parts. So everything was sent abroad. Like anyone else, I have to live and they said I was ideal to take over from the Curator while he was in Italy getting some decent medical treatment. I thought so, too, before I knew how depressing it would prove.'

He had been here for five months, praying the Czech specialists had correctly refined his quartz components. 'In my own 21st century there were four firms who could have done the job in the Croydon area alone.' A native of Kent, he had returned there only once since his arrival.

'I had expected renewal and optimism, rational farming, ordinary, sane social husbandry, but found instead decay, pessimism, determined ignorance, unadmitted self-disgust – exemplified by that mockery of the Morris dancers on every synthetic village green. They're dancing on the graves of their grandparents' dreams.'

'We were in some ways naïvely optimistic,' he continued. 'Yet we learned our lesson. After 1918 the League of Nations called on the world's best minds to pool their ideas and resources to ensure not only that we never wasted ourselves on wars and pointless national rivalries, but took a *positive* approach to the problems of poverty, famine and so on, by accepting, as most scientists had always done, that the planet was a single system for which every one of us had responsibility.

'Given both the opportunity and the finances previously devoted to military projects, Britain's scientists were fired by a new idealism, a new optimism which, coupled with their traditions and experience, soon earned us the admiration and approval of the world. It is a proud thing to be a Briton in *my* 21st century . . .'

He was escorting us from the gate to the main building.

'At least' – he paused to look up at one of the tall chimneys – 'they found a reasonably dignified function for Battersea Power Station.' He glanced through the glass wall at the Tudor River Fantasia where teams of Russian businessmen dressed in Elizabethan costumes rocked in open boats, feinting with padded lances while, as usual, old Prince Andy was doing his bit for the country's tourist trade as the comic umpire in cap and bells.

From elsewhere came the electronic voices of the Disney marionettes in Dickens world. On some days it was possible to hear the saccharine piping of some extra-wholesome Wendy greeting guests to Kensington Gardens, now renamed Never Never World, while in Royal World a Korean-built Queen Victoria escorted awed visitors on the 'Splendours of Buckingham Palace' Tour.

'Anyway' – he pushed open the great deco doors – 'here we are. Get your tickets at the turnstile, please. And remember, for every pound you pay, a penny goes to buy new boxes for the people of Cardboard City World.'

We were a little surprised by the odour of mould and dust filling a great hall illuminated by shafts of sunlight slanting through gaps in plastic sheets replacing the old glass roof.

'We begin with exhibits from the time of the Museum's founding in the late 20th century. Here are various original British conceptions. For instance, this photocopy thesis of Yusef Ali, the Nobel-winning boy genius of Birmingham, which produced the French "Green" pseudo-crystal which so quickly transformed half the Sahara into grassland and forests.'

'Unfortunately the sample crystal was recently sold to pay for dry-rot treatment. As were the models of Patricia Adamson's "benign virus", which with Swiss backing did so much in the elimination of disease. Oddly enough, both scientists emigrated to Morocco, where they were honoured citizens.'

We passed, dusty cases of papers, figures and drawings, thousands of ideas which were stillborn or adopted by other nations. 'At least,' observed The Time Traveller, 'the objects in the Morlock's museum made a rather livelier display!'

I detected an air of bitter sadness about the place, as if it were haunted by the ghosts of all those thwarted enthusiasts. Beside me a fellow tourist, the Provincial Mayor, whispered that he was ready to leave. It was the most depressing Theme World of the entire tour . . .

The Time Traveller led us past murky display cases full of mouldering green baize and broken plinths. Sometimes we paused, thinking we glimpsed an exhibit, but it always proved to be a dim reflection of our own faces. The Provincial Mayor spoke up irritably at last, asking why 'the damned place is on the itinerary at all?'

The Time Traveller's answer was sympathetic. 'The government ordered it closed "because nobody should be depressed in Merrye Englande" but Lupescu's kept it in their brochure.

'I must admit if it weren't for the confusion I'd have to work at Science World, dressing up as Igor, the mad Professor Frankenstein's genetically unsound servant, exhorting children to shudder at the collection of fantastic gadgets whose noisy quaintness and inefficient idiosyncracy demonstrates the Horrors of Science. You'll see it on Thursday. In 2019 it was the last working factory in England before they turned it, with minimum work, into the present Theme Hall.'

He paused to rub at the dust obscuring a wall plate above an empty space.

'Ah! The British space-plane engine was to have gone there. How *did* this gloomy century come about? After all, the British virtually *invented* the future! When did they lose their way? When did the useful boffin getting us through a scrap become the sinister madman threatening our security with his atomic power stations? What did people blame in scientists which they were too frightened to look for in themselves?'

'In jolly old England we're more interested in the quality of life,' said the Provincial Mayor, 'than in messing about with test tubes and dirty engines and all that pointless theorizing. And as for "controlling nature", it's not exactly Green-thinking, is it? Or even post-modern? Or do I mean post-mode?'

The Time Traveller's attention had shifted back to the river where a red, white and blue plastic replica of Cook's Endeavour ploughed unsteadily up-river towards Empire Park.

'That Chaos and non-linear idiocy was what did it finally,' said the Provincial Mayor, 'and your genetic meddling. But we lost faith long before that, in 1946. You made us *fear* the future!'

'Possibly.' The Time Traveller had learned to hold his tongue when exposed to the type of tribal posturing he often experienced during his visits to the Stone Age. 'You don't feel that a little more scientific education wouldn't have helped perhaps to give scientists improved status, a better self-image, which in turn might have helped them integrate with the community as a whole? Science is only mysterious, after all, to the poorly educated. Wouldn't your citizens feel rather better about themselves if they were still contributing successfully to the world's sum of knowledge and social well-being?'

'We're perfectly happy as we are!' The Provincial Mayor spoke with some heat. 'We're proud of what we've been. We're proud to be Green! My Uncle Denis helped get rid of the last nuclear power station. It's an Edwardian Shopping Mall now.'

The Time Traveller moved away, murmuring about a nation which actually boasted of its scientific illiteracy and whose embracing of the Green movement had more to do with a suspicion of science and technology than any positive will to find positive alternatives to our problems. Discreetly I drew the Provincial Mayor to the window to point out Explorer World and the clattering Golden Hind Roller Coaster Ride.

'We may be poor,' said the Provincial Mayor as a parting thrust, 'but at least we've got our proud past. At least we're not, not,' words failed him for a moment, '*foreign*. You bloody intellectuals were always rocking the boat. We're well rid of you!'

With that he left, saying he would either wait outside or meet us at the House of Commons, where we had tickets for the evening's Democracy in Action game.

'A country valuing neither its artists nor its scientists, and even encouraging a gulf between them, shouldn't have been surprised to discover itself become a country of multinational retail outlets whose chief source of income was tourism,' said The Time Traveller.

'You became obsessed with finding the easiest options and quickest gains. Your past became your only faith, virtually your only morality. To protect it, you turned your backs on the future, on change, on pluralism, on the joys of discovery. You were prepared to spend money on research designed to kill millions, but never willing to spend the same sums on projects designed to save or improve the lives of millions! Is it the inevitable fate of Empire? A decadent society, my dear sir, is a society primarily dedicated to preserving its past, the old *status quo*, at all costs. A country that invests only in its past, soon must have only its past to sell . . .'

He led us to the door. I shook his hand. Sadly, it was too late, I said, to remedy the situation.

He became irritable. 'You people almost instinctively take a positive example and from it derive a negative decision!' he said. 'I'll be very glad to get back to *my* 21st century where optimistically we celebrate our past, present *and* our future!'

We tramped across the courtyard to the waiting 'charabanc', its good old-fashioned petrol engine sending up an eruption of nostalgic smoke. The Provincial Mayor was already in his seat.

As the extraordinary vehicle puffed and wheezed towards Battle World and the Imperial War Experience, I looked back at The Time Traveller, a stocky, determined little figure lifting a rather despairing hand in farewell.

I adjusted my oxygen and prepared to enjoy the trip, while the Provincial Mayor exclaimed how wonderfully preserved the Museum was and how picturesque it looked in the sunset. Then, ignoring the urchins offering to be our 'official guides' to the drug-boutiques and 'craft-markets' of shanty town, he shook his baffled head. 'That chap doesn't know how lucky he is to be living in a country that values her past. In fact, old boy, I'm wondering now if he *was* British at all . . .'

And with that he returned to his information video and his contemplation of a perfectly sterilized past where the Demon of Science was forever banished to that unimportant netherworld, *Abroad*.

And Another Beginning . . .

To Rescue Tanelorn . . .

Beyond the tall and ominous glass-green forest of Troos, well to the North and unheard of in Bakshaan, Elwher or any other city of the Young Kingdoms, on the shifting shores of the Sighing Desert lay Tanelorn, a lonely, long-ago city, loved by those it sheltered.

Tanelorn had a peculiar nature in that it welcomed and held the wanderer. To its peaceful streets and low houses came the gaunt, the savage, the brutalized, the tormented, and in Tanelorn they found rest.

Now, most of these troubled travellers who dwelt in peaceful Tanelorn had thrown off earlier allegiances to the Lords of Chaos who, as gods, took more than a mild interest in the affairs of men. It happened, therefore, that these same Lords grew to resent the unlikely city of Tanelorn and, not for the the first time, decided to act against it.

They instructed one of their number (more they could not, then, send) Lord Narjhan, to journey to Nadsokor, the City of Beggars, which had an old grudge against Tanelorn and raise an army that would attack undefended Tanelorn and destroy it and its inhabitants. So he did this, arming his ragged army and promising them many things.

Then, like a ferocious tide, did the beggar rabble set off to tear down Tanelorn and slay its residents. A great torrent of men and women in rags, on crutches, blind, maimed, but moving steadily, ominously, implacably Northwards towards the Sighing Desert.

In Tanelorn dwelt the Red Archer, Rackhir, from the Eastlands beyond the Sighing Desert, beyond the Weeping Waste. Rackhir had been born a Warrior Priest, a servant of the Lords of Chaos, but had forsaken this life for the quieter pursuits of thievery and learning. A man with harsh features slashed from the bone of his skull, strong, fleshless nose, deep eye-cavities, a thin mouth and a thin beard. He wore a red skull-cap, decorated with a hawk's feather, a red jerkin, tight-fitting and belted at the waist, red breeks, and red boots. It was as if all the blood in him had transferred itself to his gear and left him drained. He was happy, however, in Tanelorn, the city which made all such men happy, and felt he would die there if men died there. He did not know if they did.

One day he saw Brut of Lashmar, a great, blond-headed noble of shamed name, ride wearily, yet urgently, through the low wall-gate of the city of peace. Brut's silver harness and trappings were begrimed, his yellow cloak torn and his broad-brimmed hat battered. A small crowd collected around him as he rode into the city square and halted. Then he gave his news.

'Beggars from Nadsokor, many thousands, move against our Tanelorn,' he said, 'and they are led by Narjhan of Chaos.'

Now, all the men in there were soldiers of some kind, good ones for the most part, and they were confident warriors, but few in number. A horde of beggars, led by such a being as Narjhan, could destroy Tanelorn, they knew.

'Should we, then, leave Tanelorn?' said Uroch of Nieva, a young, wasted man who had been a drunkard.

'We owe this city too much to desert her,' Rackhir said. 'We should defend her – for her sake and ours. There will never be such a city again.'

Brut leaned forward in his saddle and said: 'In principle, Red Archer, I am in agreement with you. But principle is not enough without deeds. How would you suggest we defend this low-walled city against siege and the powers of Chaos?'

'We should need help,' Rackhir replied, 'supernatural help if need be.'

'Would the Grey Lords help us?' Zas the One-handed asked the question. He was an old, torn wanderer who had once gained a throne and lost it again.

'Aye – the Grey Lords!' Several voices chorused this hopefully.

'Who are the Grey Lords?' said Uroch, but no one heard him.

'They are not inclined to aid anyone at all,' Zas the One-handed pointed out, 'but surely Tanelorn, coming as it does under neither the Forces of Law nor the Lords of Chaos, would be worth their while preserving. After all, they have no loyalties either.'

'I'm for seeking the Grey Lords' aid,' Brut nodded. 'What of the rest of us?' There was general agreement, then silence when they realized that they knew of no means of contacting the mysterious and insouciant beings. At last Zas pointed this out.

Rackhir said: 'I know a seer – a hermit who lives in the Sighing Desert. Perhaps he can help?'

'I think that, after all, we should not waste time looking for supernatural assistance against this beggar rabble,' Uroch said. 'Let us prepare, instead, to meet the attack with physical means.'

'You forget,' Brut said wearily, 'that they are led by Narjhan of Chaos. He is not human and has the whole strength of Chaos behind him. We know that the Grey Lords are pledged neither to Law nor to Chaos but will sometimes help either side if the whim takes them. They are our only chance.'

'Why not seek the aid of the Forces of Law, sworn enemies of Chaos and mightier than the Grey Lords?' Uroch said.

'Because Tanelorn is a city owing alliegance to neither side. We are all of us men and women who have broken our pledge to Chaos but have made no new one to Law. The Forces of Law, in matters of this kind, will help only those sworn to them. The Grey Lords only may protect us, if they would.' So said Zas.

'I will go to find my seer,' Rackhir the Red Archer said, 'and if he knows how I may reach the Domain of the Grey Lords, then I'll continue straight on, for there is so little time. If I reach them and solicit their help you will soon know I have done so. If not, you must die in Tanelorn's defence and, if I live, I will join you in that last battle.'

'Very well,' Brut agreed, 'go quickly, Red Archer. Let one of your own arrows be the measure of your speed.'

And taking little with him save his bone bow and quiver of scarlet-fletched arrows, Rackhir set off for the Sighing Desert.

From Nadsokor, South West through the land of Vilmir, even through the squalid country of Org which has in it the dreadful forest of Troos, there was flame and black horror in the wake of the beggar horde, and insolent, disdainful of them though he led them, rode a being completely clad in black armour with a voice that rang hollow in the helm. People fled away at their approach and the land was made barren by their passing. Most knew what had happened, that the beggar citizens of Nadsokor had, contrary to their traditions of centuries, vomited from their city in a wild, menacing horde. Someone had armed them – someone had made them go Northwards and Westwards towards the Sighing Desert. But who was the one who led them? Ordinary folk did not know. And why did they head for the Sighing Desert? There was no city beyond Karlaak, which they had skirted, only the Sighing Desert – and beyond that the edge of the world. Was that their destination? Were they heading, lemming-like, to their destruction? Everyone hoped so, in their hate for the horrible horde.

Rackhir rode through the mournful wind of the Sighing Desert, his face and eyes protected against the particles of sand which flew about. He was thirsty and had been riding a day. Ahead of him at last were the rocks he sought.

He reached the rocks and called above the wind.

'Lamsar!'

The hermit came out in answer to Rackhir's shout. He was dressed in oiled leather to which sand clung. His beard, too, was encrusted with sand and his skin seemed to have taken on the colour and texture of the desert. He recognized Rackhir immediately, by his dress, beckoned him into the cave, and disappeared back inside. Rackhir dismounted and led his horse to the cave entrance and went in.

Lamsar was seated on a smooth rock. 'You are welcome, Red Archer,' he said, 'and I perceive by your manner that you wish information from me and that your mission is urgent.'

'I seek the help of the Grey Lords, Lamsar,' said Rackhir.

The old hermit smiled. It was as if a fissure had suddenly appeared in a rock. 'To risk the journey through the Five Gates, your mission must be important. I will tell you how to reach the Grey Lords, but the road is a difficult one.'

'I'm willing to take it,' Rackhir replied, 'for Tanelorn is threatened and the Grey Lords could help her.'

'Then you must pass through the First Gate, which lies in our own dimension. I will help you find it.'

'And what must I do then?'

'You must pass through all five gates. Each gateway leads to a realm which lies beyond and within our own dimension. In each realm you must speak with the dwellers there. Some are friendly to men, some are not, but all must answer your question; 'Where lies the next Gate?' though some may seek to stop you passing. The last gate leads to the Grey Lords' Domain.'

'And the first gate?'

'That lies anywhere in this realm. I will find it for you now.'

Lamsar composed himself to meditate and Rackhir, who had expected some sort of gaudy miracle-working from the old man, was disappointed.

Several hours went by until Lamsar said: 'The gate is outside. Memorize the following: If X is equal to the spirit of humanity, then the combination of the two must be of double power, therefore the spirit of humanity always contains the power to dominate itself.'

'A strange equation,' said Rackhir.

'Aye – but memorize it, meditate upon it and then we will leave.'

'We – you as well?'

'I think so.'

The hermit was old. Rackhir did not want him on the journey. But then he realized that the hermit's knowledge could be of use to him, so did not object. He thought upon the equation and, as he thought, his mind seemed to glitter and become diffused until he was in a strange trance and all his powers felt greater, both those of mind and body. The hermit got up and Rackhir followed him. They went out of the cave-mouth but, instead of the Sighing Desert, there was a hazy cloud of blue shimmering light ahead and when they had passed through this, in a second, they found themselves in the foothills of a low mountain-range and below them, in a valley, were villages. The villages were strangely laid out, all the houses in a wide circle about a huge amphitheatre containing, at its centre, a circular dais.

'It will be interesting to learn the reason why these villages are so arranged,' Lamsar said, and they began to move down into the valley.

As they reached the bottom and came close to one of the villages, people came gaily out and danced joyfully towards them. They stopped in front of Rackhir and Lamsar and, jumping from foot to foot as he greeted them, the leader spoke.

'You are strangers, we can tell – and you are welcome to all we have, food, accommodation, and entertainment.'

The two men thanked them graciously and accompanied them back to the circular village. The amphitheatre was made of mud and seemed to have been stamped out, hollowed into, the ground encompassed by the houses. The leader of the villagers took them to his house and offered them food.

'You have come to us at a Rest Time,' he said, 'but do not worry, things will soon commence again. My name is Yerleroo.'

'We seek the next Gate,' Lamsar said politely, 'and our mission is urgent. You will forgive us if we do not stay long?'

'Come,' said Yerleroo, 'things are about to commence. You will see us at our best, and must join us.'

All the villagers had assembled in the amphitheatre, surrounding the platform in the centre. Most of them were light-skinned and light-haired, gay and smiling, excited – but a few were evidently of a different race, dark, black-haired, and these were sullen.

Sensing something ominous in what he saw, Rackhir asked the question directly: 'Where is the next Gate?'

Yerleroo hesitated, his mouth worked and then he smiled. 'Where the winds meet,' he said.

Rackhir declared angrily: 'That's no answer.'

'Yes it is,' said Lamsar softly behind him. 'A fair answer.'

'Now we shall dance,' Yerleroo said. 'First you shall watch our dance and then you shall join in.'

'Dance?' said Rackhir, wishing he had brought a sword, or at least a dagger.

'Yes – you will like it. Everyone likes it. You will find it will do you good.'

'What if we do not wish to dance?'

'You must – it is for your own good, be assured.'

'And he –' Rackhir pointed at one of the sullen men. 'Does he enjoy it?'

'It is for his own good.'

Yerleroo clapped his hands and at once the fair-haired people leapt into a frenetic, senseless dance. Some of them sang. The sullen people did not sing. After a little hesitation, they began to prance dully about, their frowning features contrasting with their jerking bodies. Soon the whole village was dancing, whirling, singing a monotonous song.

Yerleroo flashed by, whirling. 'Come, join in now.'

'We had better leave,' Lamsar said with a faint smile. They backed away.

Yerleroo saw them. 'No – you must not leave – you must dance.'

They turned and ran as fast as the old man could go. The dancing villagers changed the direction of their dance and began to whirl menacingly towards them in a horrible semblance of gaiety.

'There's nothing for it,' Lamsar said and stood his ground, observing them through ironic eyes. 'The mountain gods must be invoked. A pity, for sorcery wearies me. Let us hope their magic extends to this plane. *Gordar!*'

Words in an unusually harsh language issued from Lamsar's old mouth. The whirling villagers came on.

Lamsar pointed at them.

The villagers became suddenly petrified and slowly, disturbingly, their bodies caught in a hundred positions, turned to smooth, black basalt.

'It was for their own good,' Lamsar smiled grimly. 'Come, to the place where the winds meet,' and he took Rackhir there quite swiftly.

*

At the place where the winds met they found the second gateway, a column of amber-coloured flame, shot through with streaks of green. They entered it and, instantly, were in a world of dark, seething colour. Above them was a sky of murky red in which other colours shifted, agitated, changing. Ahead of them lay a forest, dark, blue, black, heavy, mottled green, the tops of its trees moving like a wild tide. It was a howling land of unnatural phenomena.

Lamsar pursed his lips. 'On this plane Chaos rules, we must get to the next gate swiftly for obviously the Lords of Chaos will seek to stop us.'

'Is it always like this?' Rackhir gasped.

'It is always boiling midnight – but the rest, it changes with the moods of the Lords. There are no rules at all.'

They pressed on through the bounding, blossoming scenery as it erupted and changed around them. Once they saw a huge winged figure in the sky, smoky yellow, and roughly man-shaped.

'Vezhan,' Lamsar said, 'let's hope he did not see us.'

'Vezhan!' Rackhir whispered the name – for it was to Vezhan that he had once been loyal.

They crept on, uncertain of their direction or even of their speed in that disturbing land.

At length, they came to the shores of a peculiar ocean.

It was a grey, heaving, timeless sea, a mysterious sea which stretched into infinity. There could be no other shores beyond this rolling plain of water. No other lands or rivers or dark, cool woods, no other men or women or ships. It was a sea which led to nowhere. It was complete to itself – a sea.

Over this timeless ocean hovered a brooding ochre sun which cast moody shadows of black and green across the water, giving the whole scene something of the look of being enclosed in a vast cavern, for the sky above was gnarled and black with ancient clouds. And all the while the doom-carried crash of breakers, the lonely, fated monotony of the ever-rearing white-topped waves; the sound which portended neither death nor life nor war nor peace – simply existence and shifting inharmony. They could go no further.

'This has the air of our death about it,' Rackhir said shivering.

The sea roared and tumbled, the sound of it increasing to a fury, daring them to go on towards it, welcoming them with wild temptation – offering them nothing but achievement – the achievement of death.

Lamsar said: 'It is not my fate wholly to perish.' But then they were running back toward the forest, feeling that the strange sea was pouring up the beach towards them. They looked back and saw that it had gone no further, that the breakers were less wild, the sea more calm. Lamsar was a little way behind Rackhir.

The Red Archer gripped his hand and hauled him towards him as if he had rescued the old man from a whirlpool. They remained there, mesmerized, for a long time, while the sea called to them and the wind was a cold caress on their flesh.

In the bleak brightness of the alien shore, under a sun which gave no heat, their bodies shone like stars in the night and they turned towards the forest, quietly.

'Are we trapped, then, in this Realm of Chaos?' Rackhir said at length. 'If we meet someone, they will offer us harm – how can we ask our question?'

Then there emerged from the huge forest a great figure, naked and gnarled like the trunk of a tree, green as lime, but the face was jovial.

'Greetings, unhappy renegades,' it said.

'Where is the next gate?' said Lamsar quickly.

'You almost entered it, but turned away,' laughed the giant. 'That sea does not exist – it is there to stop travellers from passing through the gate.'

'It exists here, in the Realm of Chaos,' Rackhir said thickly.

'You could say so – but what exists in Chaos save the disorders of the minds of gods gone mad?'

Rackhir had strung his bone bow and fitted an arrow to the string, but he did it in the knowledge of his own hopelessness.

'Do not shoot the arrow,' said Lamsar softly. 'Not yet.' And he stared at the arrow and muttered.

The giant advanced carelessly towards them, unhurried.

'It will please me to exact the price of your crimes from you,' it said, 'for I am Hionhurn the Executioner. You will find your death pleasant – but your fate unbearable.' And he came closer, his clawed hands outstretched.

'Shoot!' croaked Lamsar and Rackhir brought the bow-string to his cheek, pulled it back with might and released the arrow at the giant's heart. 'Run!' cried Lamsar, and in spite of their forebodings they ran back down the shore towards the frightful sea. They heard the giant groan behind them as they reached the edge of the sea and, instead of running into water, found themselves in a range of stark mountains.

'No mortal arrow could have delayed him,' Rackhir said. 'How did you stop him?'

'I used an old-charm – the Charm of Justice, which, when applied to any weapon, makes it strike at the unjust.'

'But why did it hurt Hionhurn, an immortal?' Rackhir asked.

'There is no justice in the world of Chaos – something constant and inflexible, whatever its nature, must harm any servant of the Lords of Chaos.'

'We have passed through the third gate,' Rackhir said, unstringing his bow, 'and have the fourth and fifth to find. Two dangers have been avoided – but what new ones will we encounter now?'

'Who knows?' said Lamsar, and they walked on through the rocky mountain pass and entered a forest that was cool, even though the sun had reached its zenith and was glaring down through parts of the thick foliage. There was an air of ancient calm about the place. They heard unfamiliar bird-calls and saw tiny golden birds which were also new to them.

'There is something calm and peaceful about this place – I almost distrust it,' Rackhir said, but Lamsar pointed ahead silently.

Rackhir saw a large domed building, magnificent in marble and blue mosaic. It stood in a clearing of yellow grass and the marble caught the sun, flashing like fire.

They neared the domed construction and saw that it was supported by big marble columns set into a platform of milky jade. In the centre of the platform, a stairway of blue-stone curved upwards and disappeared into a circular aperture. There were wide windows set into the sides of the raised building but they could not see inside. There were no inhabitants visible and it would have seemed strange to the pair if there had been. They crossed the yellow glade and stepped on to the jade platform. It was warm, as if it had been exposed to the sun. They almost slipped on the smooth stone.

They reached the blue steps and mounted them, staring upwards, but they could still see nothing. They did not attempt to ask themselves why they were so assuredly invading the building; it seemed quite natural that they should do what they were doing. There was no alternative. There was an air of familiarity about the place. Rackhir felt it but did not know why. Inside was a cool, shadowy hall, a blend of soft darkness and bright sunlight which entered by the windows. The floor was pearl-pink and the ceiling deep scarlet. The hall reminded Rackhir of a womb.

Partially hidden by deep shadow was a small doorway and beyond it, steps. Rackhir looked questioningly at Lamsar. 'Do we proceed in our exploration?'

'We must – to have our question answered, if possible.'

*

They climbed the steps and found themselves in a smaller hall similar to the one beneath them. This hall, however, was furnished with twelve wide thrones placed in a semicircle in the centre. Against the wall, near the door, were several chairs, upholstered in purple fabric. The thrones were of gold, decorated with fine silver, padded with white cloth.

A door behind the throne opened and a tall, fragile-looking man appeared, followed by others whose faces were almost identical. Only their robes were noticeably different. Their faces were pale, almost white, their noses straight, their lips thin but not cruel. Their eyes were unhuman – green-flecked eyes which stared outwards with sad composure. The leader of the tall men looked at Rackhir and Lamsar. He nodded and waved a pale, long-fingered hand gracefully.

'Welcome,' he said. His voice was high and frail, like a girl's, but beautiful in its modulation. The other eleven men seated themselves in the thrones but the first man, who had spoken, remained standing. 'Sit down, please,' he said.

Rackhir and Lamsar sat down on two of the purple chairs.

'How did you come here?' enquired the man.

'Through the gates from Chaos,' Lamsar replied.

'And were you seeking our realm?'

'No – we travel towards the Domain of the Grey Lords.'

'I thought so, for your people rarely visit us save by accident.'

'Where are we?' asked Rackhir as the man seated himself in the remaining throne.

'In a place beyond time. Once our land was part of the earth you know, but in the dim past it became separated from it. Our bodies, unlike yours, are immortal. We choose this, but we are not bound to our flesh, as you are.'

'I don't understand,' frowned Rackhir. 'What are you saying?'

'I have said what I can in the simplest terms understandable to you. If you do not know what I say then I can explain no further. We are called the Guardians – though we guard nothing. We are warriors, but we fight nothing.'

'What else do you do?' enquired Rackhir.

'We exist. You will want to know where the next gateway lies?'

'Yes.'

'Refresh yourselves here, and then we shall show you the gateway.'

'What is your function?' asked Rackhir.

'To function,' said the man.

'You are unhuman!'

'We are human. *You* spend your lives chasing that which is within you and that which you can find in any other human being – but you will not look for it there – you must follow more glamorous paths – to waste your time in order to discover that you have wasted your time. I am glad that we are no longer like you – but I wish that it were lawful to help you further. This, however, we may not do.'

'Ours is no meaningless quest,' said Lamsar quietly, with respect. 'We go to rescue Tanelorn.'

'Tanelorn?' the man said softly. 'Does Tanelorn still remain?'

'Aye,' said Rackhir, 'and shelters tired men who are grateful for the rest she offers.' Now he realized why the building had been familiar – it had the same quality, but intensified, as Tanelorn.

'Tanelorn was the last of our cities,' said the Guardian. 'Forgive us for judging you – most of the travellers who pass through this plane are searchers, restless, with no real purpose, only excuses, imaginary reasons for journeying on. You must love Tanelorn to brave the dangers of the gateways?'

'We do,' said Rackhir, 'and I am grateful that you built her.'

'We built her for ourselves, but it is good that others have used her well – and she them.'

'Will you help us?' Rackhir said. 'For Tanelorn?'

'We cannot – it is not lawful. Now, refresh yourselves and be welcome.'

The two travellers were given foods, both soft and brittle, sweet and sour, and drink which seemed to enter the pores of their skin as they quaffed it, and then the Guardian said: 'We have caused a road to be made. Follow it and enter the next realm. But we warn you, it is the most dangerous of all.'

And they set off down the road that the Guardians had caused to be made and passed through the fourth gateway into a dreadful realm – the Realm of Law.

Nothing shone in the grey-lit sky, nothing moved, nothing marred the grey.

Nothing interrupted the bleak grey plain stretching on all sides of them, forever. There was no horizon. It was a bright, clean wasteland. But there was a sense about the air, a presence of something past, something which had gone but left a faint aura of its passing.

'What dangers could be here?' said Rackhir shuddering, 'here where there is nothing?'

'The danger of the loneliest madness,' Lamsar replied. Their voices were swallowed in the grey expanse.

'When the Earth was very young,' Lamsar continued, his words trailing away across the wilderness, 'things were like this – but there were seas, there were seas. Here there is nothing.'

'You are wrong,' Rackhir said with a faint smile. 'I have thought – here there is Law.'

'That is true – but what is Law without something to decide between? Here is Law – bereft of justice.'

They walked on, all about them an air of something intangible that had once been tangible. On they walked through this barren world of Absolute Law.

Eventually, Rackhir spied something. Something that flickered, faded, appeared again until, as they neared it, they saw that it was a man. His great head was noble, firm, and his body was massively built, but the face was twisted in a tortured frown and he did not see them as they approached him.

They stopped before him and Lamsar coughed to attract his attention. The man turned that great head and regarded them abstractedly, the frown clearing at length, to be replaced by a calmer, thoughtful expression.

'Who are you?' asked Rackhir.

The man sighed. 'Not yet,' he said, 'not yet, it seems. More phantoms.'

'Are *we* the phantoms?' smiled Rackhir. 'That seems to be more your own nature.' He watched as the man began slowly to fade again, his form less definite, melting. The body seemed to make a great heave, like a salmon attempting to leap a dam, then it was back again in a more solid form.

'I had thought myself rid of all that was superfluous, save my own obstinate shape,' the man said tiredly, 'but here is something, back again. Is my reason failing – is my logic no longer what it was?'

'Do not fear,' said Rackhir, 'we are material beings.'

'That is *what* I feared. For an eternity I have been stripping away the layers of unreality which obscure the truth. I have almost succeeded in the final act, and now you begin to creep back. My mind is not what it was, I think.'

'Perhaps you worry lest we do not exist?' Lamsar said slowly, with a clever smile.

'You know that is not so – you do not exist, just as I do not exist.' The frown returned, the features twisted, the body began, again, to fade, only to resume, once more, its earlier nature. The man sighed.

'Even to reply to you is betraying myself, but I suppose a little relaxation will serve to rest my powers and equip me for the final effort of will which will bring me to the ultimate truth – the truth of non-being.'

'But non-being involves non-thought, non-will, non-action,' Lamsar said. 'Surely you would not submit yourself to such a fate?'

'There is no such thing as self. I am the only reasoning thing in creation – I am almost pure reason. A little more effort and I shall be what I desire to be – the one truth in this non-existent universe. That requires first ridding myself of anything extraneous around me – such as yourselves – and then making the final plunge into the only reality.'

'What is that?'

'The state of absolute nothingness where there is nothing to disturb the order of things because there is no order of things.'

'Scarcely a constructive ambition,' Rackhir said.

'Construction is a meaningless word – like all words, like all so-called existence. Everything means nothing – that is the only truth.'

'But what of this realm? Barren as it is, it still has light and firm rock. You have not succeeded in reasoning that out of existence,' Lamsar said.

'That will cease when I cease,' the man said slowly, 'just as you will cease to be. Then there can be nothing but nothing and Law will reign unchallenged.'

'But Law cannot reign – it will not exist either, according to your logic.'

'You are wrong – nothingness is the Law. Nothingness is the object of Law. Law is the way to its ultimate state, the state of non-being.'

'Well,' said Lamsar musingly, 'then you had better tell us where we may find the next gate.'

'There is no gate.'

'If there were, where would we find it?' Rackhir said.

'If a gate existed, and it does not, it would have been inside the mountain, close to what was once called the Sea of Peace.'

'And where was that?' Rackhir asked, conscious, now of their terrible predicament. There were no landmarks, no sun, no stars – nothing by which they could determine direction.

'Close to the Mountain of Severity.'

'Which way do you go?' Lamsar enquired of the man.

'Out – beyond – to nowhere.'

'And where, if you succeed in your object, will we be consigned?'

'To some other nowhere. I cannot truthfully answer. But since you have never existed in reality, therefore you can go on to no non-reality. Only I am real – and I do not exist.'

'We are getting nowhere,' said Rackhir with a smirk which changed to a frown.

'It is only my mind which holds the non-reality at bay,' the man said, 'and I must concentrate or else it will all come flooding back and I shall have to start from the beginning again. In the beginning, there was everything – Chaos. I *created* nothing.'

With resignation, Rackhir strung his bow, fitted an arrow to the string and aimed at the frowning man.

'You wish for non-being?' he said.

'I have told you so.' Rackhir's arrow pierced his heart, his body faded, became solid and slumped to the grass as mountains, forests, and rivers appeared around them. It was still a peaceful, well-ordered realm and Rackhir and Lamsar, as they strode on in search of the Mountain of Severity, savoured it. There seemed to be no animal life here and they talked, in puzzled terms, about the man they had been forced to kill, until, at length, they reached a great smooth pyramid which seemed, though it was of natural origin, to have been carved into this form. They walked around its base until they discovered an opening.

There could be no doubt that this was the Mountain of Severity, and a calm ocean lay some distance away. They went into the opening and emerged into a delicate landscape. They were now through the last gateway and in the Domain of the Grey Lords.

There were trees like stiffened spider-webs.

Here and there were blue pools, shallow, with shining water and graceful rocks balanced in them and around their shores. Above them and beyond them the light hills swept away towards a pastel yellow horizon which was tinted with red, orange, and blue, deep blue.

They felt overlarge, clumsy, like crude, gross giants treading on the fine, short grass. They felt as if they were destroying the sanctity of the place.

Then they saw a girl come walking towards them.

She stopped as they came closer to her. She was dressed in loose black robes which flowed about her as if in a wind, but there was no wind. Her face was pale and pointed, her black eyes large and enigmatic. At her long throat was a jewel.

'Sorana,' said Rackhir thickly, 'you died.'

'I disappeared,' said she, 'and this is where I came. I was told that you would come to this place and decided that I would meet you.'

'But this is the Domain of the Grey Lords – and you serve Chaos.'
'I do – but many are welcome at the Grey Lords' Court, whether they be of Law, Chaos, or neither. Come, I will escort you there.'
Bewildered, now, Rackhir let her lead the way across the strange terrain and Lamsar followed him.

Sorana and Rackhir had been lovers once, in Yeshpotoom-Kahlai, the Unholy Fortress, where evil blossomed and was beautiful. Sorana, sorceress, adventuress, was without conscience but had had high regard for the Red Archer since he had come to Yeshpotoom-Kahlai one evening, covered in his own blood, survivor of a bizarre battle between the Knights of Tumbru and Loheb Bakra's brigand-engineers. Seven years ago, that had been, and he had heard her scream when the Blue Asassins had crept into the Unholy Fortress, pledged to murder evil-makers. Even then he had been in the process of hurriedly leaving Yeshpotoom-Kahlai and had considered it unwise to investigate what was obviously a death-scream. Now she was here – and if she was here, then it was for a strong reason and for her own convenience. On the other hand, it was in her interests to serve Chaos and he must be suspicious of her.
Ahead of them now they saw many great tents of shimmering grey which, in the light, seemed composed of all colours. People moved slowly among the tents and there was an air of leisure about the place.
'Here,' Sorana said, smiling at him and taking his hand, 'the Grey Lords hold impermanent court. They wander about their land and have few artifacts and only temporary houses which you see. They will make you welcome if you interest them.'
'But will they help us?'
'You must ask them.'
'You are pledged to Eequor of Chaos,' Rackhir observed, 'and must aid her against us, is that not so?'
'Here,' she smiled, 'is a truce. I can only inform Chaos of what I learn of your plans and, if the Grey Lords aid you, must tell them how, if I can find out.'
'You are frank, Sorana.'
'Here there are subtler hypocrisies – and the subtlest lie of all is the full truth,' she said, as they entered the area of tall tents and made their way towards a certain one.

In a diferent realm of the Earth, the huge horde careered across the grasslands of the North, screaming and singing behind the black-armoured horseman, their leader. Nearer and nearer they came to lonely Tanelorn, their motley weapons shining through the evening mists. Like a boiling tidal wave of insensate flesh, the mob drove on, hysterical with the hate for Tanelorn which Narjhan had placed in their thin hearts. Thieves, murderers, jackals, scavengers – a scrawny horde, but huge . . .

And in Tanelorn the warriors were grim-faced as their out-riders and scouts flowed into the city with messages and estimates of the beggar army's strength.

Brut, in the silver armour of his rank, knew that two full days had passed since Rackhir had left for the Sighing Desert. Three more days and the city would be engulfed by Narjhan's mighty rabble – and they knew there was no chance of halting their advance. They might have left Tanelorn to its fate, but they would not. Even weak Uroch would not. For Tanelorn the Mysterious had given them all a secret power which each believed to be his only, a strength which filled them where before they had been hollow men. Selfishly, they stayed – for to leave Tanelorn to her fate would be to become hollow again, and that they all dreaded.

Brut was the leader and he prepared the defence of Tanelorn – a defence which might just have held against the beggar army – but not against it and Chaos. Brut shuddered when he thought that if Chaos had directed its full force against Tanelorn, they would be sobbing in Hell at that moment.

Dust rose high above Tanelorn, sent flying by the hooves of the scouts' and messengers' horses. One came through the gate as Brut watched. He pulled his mount to a stop before the nobleman. He was the messenger from Kaarlak, by the Weeping Waste, one of the nearest major cities to Tanelorn.

The messenger gasped: 'I asked Kaarlak for aid but, as we supposed, they had never heard of Tanelorn and suspected that I was an emissary from the beggar army sent to lead their few forces into a trap. I pleaded with the Senators, but they would do nothing.'

'Was not Elric there – he knows Tanelorn?'

'No, he was not there. There is a rumour which says that he himself fights Chaos now, for the minions of Chaos captured his wife Zarozinia and he rides in pursuit of them. Chaos, it seems, gains strength everywhere in our realm.'

Brut was pale.

'What of Jadmar – will Jadmar send warriors?' The messenger spoke urgently, for many had been sent to the nearer cities to solicit aid.

'I do not know,' replied Brut, 'and it does not matter now – for the beggar army is not three days march from Tanelorn and it would take two weeks for a Jadmarian force to reach us.'

'And Rackhir?'

'I have heard nothing and he has not returned. I have the feeling he will not return. Tanelorn is doomed.'

Rackhir and Lamsar bowed before the three small men who sat in the tent, but one of them said impatiently: 'Do not humble yourselves before us, friends – we who are humbler than any.' So they straightened their backs and waited to be further addressed.

The Grey Lords assumed humility, but this, it seemed, was their greatest ostentation, for it was a pride that they had. Rackhir realized that he would need to use subtle flattery and was not sure that he could, for he was a warrior, not a courtier or a diplomat. Lamsar, too, realized the situation and he said:

'In our pride, Lords, we have come to learn the simpler truths which are only truths – the truths which you can teach us.'

The speaker gave a self-deprecating smile and replied: 'Truth is not for us to define, guest, we can but offer our incomplete thoughts. They might interest you or help you to find your own truths.'

'Indeed, that is so,' Rackhir said, not wholly sure with what he was agreeing, but judging it best to agree. 'And we wondered if you had any suggetions on a matter which concerns us – the protection of our Tanelorn.'

'We would not be so prideful as to interfere with our own comments. We are not mighty intellects,' the speaker replied blandly, 'and we have no confidence in our own decisions, for who knows that they may be wrong and based on wrongly assessed information?'

'Indeed,' said Lamsar, judging that he must flatter them with their own assumed humility, 'and it is lucky for us, Lords, that we do not confuse pride with learning – for it is the quiet man who observes and says little who sees the most. Therefore, though we realize that you are not confident that your suggestions or help would be useful, none the less we, taking example from your own demeanour, humbly ask if you know of any way in which we might rescue Tanelorn?'

Rackhir had hardly been able to follow the complexities of Lamsar's seemingly unsophisticated argument, but he saw that the Grey Lords were pleased. Out of the corner of his eye he observed Sorana. She was smiling to herself and it seemed evident, by the characteristics of that smile, that they had behaved in the right way. Now Sorana was listening intently and Rackhir cursed to himself that the Lords of Chaos would know of everything and might, even if they did gain the Grey Lords' aid, still be able to anticipate and stop any action they took to save Tanelorn.

The speaker conferred in a liquid speech with his fellows and said finally: 'Rarely do we have the privilege to entertain such brave and intelligent men. How may our insignificant minds be put to your advantage?'

Rackhir realized quite suddenly, and almost laughed, that the Grey Lords were not very clever after all. Their flattery had got them the help they required. He said:

'Narjhan of Chaos heads a huge army of human scum – a beggar army – and is sworn to tear down Tanelorn and kill her inhabitants. We need magical aid of some kind to combat one so powerful as Narjhan *and* defeat the beggars.'

'But Tanelorn cannot be destroyed . . .' said a Grey Lord. 'She is Eternal . . .' said another. 'But this manifestation . . .' murmured the third, 'Ah, yes . . .'

'There are beetles in Kaleef,' said a Grey Lord who had not spoken before, 'which emit a peculiar venom.'

'Beetles, Lord?' said Rackhir.

'They are the size of mammoths,' said the third Lord, 'but can change their size – and change the size of their prey if it is too large for their gullets.'

'As for that matter,' the first speaker said, 'there is a chimera which dwells in mountains South of here – it can change its shape and contains hate for Chaos since Chaos bred it and abandoned it with no real shape of its own.'

'Then there are four brothers of Himerscahl who are endowed with sorcerous power,' said the second Lord, but the first interrupted him:

'Their magic is no good outside our own dimension,' he said. 'I had thought, however, of reviving the Blue Wizard.'

'Too dangerous and, anyway, beyond our powers,' said his companion.

They continued to debate for a while, and Rackhir and Lamsar said nothing, but waited.

Eventually the first speaker said:

'The Boatmen of Xerlerenes, we have decided, will probably be best equipped to aid you in defence of Tanelorn. You must go to the mountains of Xerlerenes and find their lake.'

'A lake,' said Lamsar, 'in a range of mountains, I see.'

'No,' the Lord said, 'their lake lies above the mountains. We will find someone to take you there. Perhaps they will aid you.'

'You can guarantee nothing else?'

'Nothing – it is not our business to interfere. It is up to them to decide whether they will aid you or not.'

'I see,' said Rackhir, 'thank you.'

How much time had passed since he had left Tanelorn? How much time before Narjhan's beggar army reached the city? Or had it already done so?

Suddenly he thought of something, looked for Sorana, but she had left the tent.

'Where lies Xerlerenes?' Lamsar was asking.

'Not in our realm,' one of the Grey Lords replied, 'come we will find you a guide.'

Sorana spoke the necessary word which took her immediately into the blue half-world with which she was so familiar. There were no other colours in it, but many, many shades of blue. Here she waited until Eequor noticed her presence. In the timelessness, she could not tell how long she had waited.

The beggar horde came to an undisciplined and slow halt at a sign from its leader. A voice rang hollowly from the helm that was always closed.

'Tomorrow, we march against Tanelorn – the time we have anticipated is almost upon us. Make camp now. Tomorrow shall Tanelorn be punished and the stones of her little houses will be dust on the wind.'

The million beggars cackled their glee and wetted their scrawny lips. Not one of them asked why they had marched so far, and this was because of Narjhan's power.

In Tanelorn, Brut and Zas the One-handed discussed the nature of death in quiet, over-controlled tones. Both were filled with sadness, less for themselves than for Tanelorn, soon to perish. Outside, a pitiful army tried to place a cordon around the town but failed to fill the gaps between men, there were so few of them. Lights in the houses burned as if for the last time, and candles guttered moodily.

Sorana, sweating as she always did after such an episode, returned to the plane occupied by the Grey Lords and discovered that Rackhir, Lamsar, and their guide were preparing to leave. Eequor had told her what to do – it was for her to contact Narjhan. The rest the Lords of Chaos would accomplish. She blew her ex-lover a kiss as he rode from the camp into the night. He grinned at her defiantly, but when his face was turned from her he frowned and they went in silence into the Valley of the Currents where they entered the realm where lay the Mountains of Xerlerenes. Almost as soon as they arrived, danger presented itself.

Their guide, a wanderer called Timeras, pointed into the night sky which was spiked by the outlines of crags.

'This is a world where the air elementals are dominant,' he said. 'Look!'

Flowing downwards in an ominous sweep they saw a flight of owls, great eyes gleaming. Only as they came nearer did the men realize that these owls were huge, almost as large as a man. In the saddle Rackhir strung his bow. Timeras said:

'How could they have learned of our presence so soon?'

'Sorana,' Rackhir said, busy with the bow, 'she must have warned the Lords of Chaos and they have sent these dreadful birds.' As the first one homed in, great claws grasping, great beak gaping, he shot it in its feathery throat and it shrieked and swept upwards. Many arrows fled from his humming bow-string to find a mark while Timeras drew his sword and slashed at them, ducking as they whistled downwards.

Lamsar watched the battle but took no part, seemed thoughtful at a time when action was desired of him.

He mused: 'If the spirits of air are dominant in this realm, then they will resent a stronger force of other elementals,' and he racked his brain to remember a spell.

Rackhir had but two arrows left in his quiver by the time they had driven the owls off. The birds had not been used, evidently, to a prey which fought back and had put up a poor fight considering their superiority.

'We can expect more danger,' said Rackhir somewhat shakily, 'for the Lords of Chaos will use other means to try and stop us. How far to Xerlerenes?'

'Not far,' said Timeras, 'but it's a hard road.'

They rode on, and Lamsar rode behind them, lost in his own thoughts.

Now they urged their horses up a steep mountain path and a chasm lay below them, dropping, dropping, dropping. Rackhir, who had no love for heights, kept as close to the mountainside as was possible. If he had had gods to whom he could pray, he would have prayed for their help then.

The huge fish came flying – or swimming – at them as they rounded a bend. They were semi-luminous, big as sharks but with enlarged fins with which they planed through the air like rays. They were quite evidently fish. Timeras drew his sword, but Rackhir had only two arrows left and it would have been useless against the airfish to have shot them, for there were many of them.

But Lamsar laughed and spoke in a high-pitched, staccato speech. '*Crackhor – pishtasta salaflar!*'

Huge balls of flame materialized against the black sky – flaring balls of multicoloured fire which shaped themselves into strange, warlike forms and streamed towards the unnatural fish.

The flame-shapes seared into the big fish and they shrieked, struck at the fire-balls, burned, and fell flaming down the deep gorge.

'Fire elementals!' Rackhir exclaimed.

'The spirits of the air fear such beings,' Lamsar said calmly.

The flame-beings accompanied them the rest of the way to Xerlerenes and were with them when dawn came, having frightened away many other dangers which the Lords of Chaos had evidently sent against them.

They saw the boats of Xerlerenes in the dawn, at anchor on a calm sky, fluffy clouds playing around their slender keels, their huge sails furled.

'The boatmen live aboard their vessels,' Timeras said, 'for it is only their ships which deny the laws of nature, not they.'

Timeras cupped his hands about his mouth and called through the still mountain air: 'Boatmen of Xerlerenes, freemen of the air, guests come with a request for aid!'

A black and bearded face appeared over the side of one of the red-gold vessels. The man shielded his eyes against the rising sun and stared down at them. Then he disappeared again.

At length a ladder of slim thongs came snaking down to where they sat their horses on the tops of the mountains. Timeras grasped it, tested it and began to climb. Rackhir reached out and steadied the ladder for him. It seemed too thin to support a man but when he had it in his hands he knew that it was the strongest he had ever known.

Lamsar grumbled as Rackhir signalled for him to climb, but he did so and quite nimbly. Rackhir was the last, following his companions, climbing up through the sky high above the crags, towards the ship that sailed on the air.

The fleet comprised some twenty or thirty ships and Rackhir felt that with these to aid him, there was good chance to rescue Tanelorn – if Tanelorn survived. Narjhan would, anyway, be aware of the nature of the aid he sought.

Starved dogs barked the morning in and the beggar horde, waking from where they had sprawled on the ground, saw Narjhan already mounted, but talking to a newcomer, a girl in black robes that moved as if in a wind – but there was no wind. There was a jewel at her long throat.

When he had finished conversing with the newcomer, Narjhan ordered a horse be brought for her and she rode slightly behind him when the beggar army moved on – the last stage of their hateful journey to Tanelorn.

When they saw lovely Tanelorn and how it was so poorly guarded, the beggars laughed, but Narjhan and his new companion looked up into the sky.

'There may be time,' said the hollow voice, and gave the order to attack.

Howling, the beggars broke into a run towards Tanelorn. The attack had started.

Brut rose in his saddle and there were tears flowing down his face and glistening in his beard. His huge war-axe was in one gauntleted hand and the other held a spiked mace across the saddle before him.

Zas the One-handed gripped the long and heavy broadsword with its pommel of a rampant golden lion pointed downwards. This blade had won him a crown in Andlermaigne, but he doubted whether it would successfully defend his peace in Tanelorn. Beside him stood Uroch of Nieva, pale-faced but angry as he watched the ragged horde's implacable approach.

Then, yelling, the beggars met with the warriors of Tanelorn and, although greatly outnumbered, the warriors fought desperately for they were defending more than life or love – they were defending that which had told them of a reason for living.

Narjhan sat his horse aside from the battle, Sorana next to him, for Narjhan could take no active part in the battle, could only watch and, if necessary, use magic to aid his human pawns or defend his person.

The warriors of Tanelorn, incredibly, held back the roaring beggar horde, their weapons drenched with blood, rising and falling in that sea of moving flesh, flashing in the light of the red dawn.

Sweat now mingled with the salt tears in Brut's bristling beard and with agility he leapt clear of his black horse as the screaming beast was cut from under him. The noble war-cry of his forefathers sang on his breath and, although in his shame he had no business to use it, he let it roar from him as he slashed about him with biting war-axe and rending mace. But he fought hopelessly for Rackhir had not come and Tanelorn was soon to die. His one fierce consolation was that he would die with the city, his blood mingling with its ashes.

Zas, also, acquitted himself very well before he died of a smashed skull. His old body twitched as trampling feet stumbled over it as the beggars made for Uroch of Nieva. The gold-pommelled sword was still gripped in his single hand and his soul was fleeing for Limbo as Uroch, too, was slain fighting.

Then the Ships of Xerlerenes suddenly materialized in the sky and Brut, looking upward for an instant, knew that Rackhir had come at last – though it might be too late.

Narjhan, also, saw the Ships and was prepared for them.

They skimmed through the sky, the fire elementals which Lamsar had summoned, flying with them. The spirits of air and flame had been called to rescue weakening Tanelorn . . .

The Boatmen prepared their wagons and made themselves ready for war. Their black faces had a concentrated look and they grinned in their bushy beards. War-harness clothed them and they bristled with weapons – long, barbed tridents, nets of steel mesh, curved swords, long harpoons. Rackhir stood in the prow of the leading ship, his quiver packed with slim arrows loaned him by the Boatmen. Below him he saw Tanelorn and was relieved that the city still stood.

He could see the milling warriors below, but it was hard to tell, from the air, which were friends and which were foes. Lamsar called to the frisking and fire elementals, instructing them. Timeras grinned and held his sword ready as the ships rocked on the wind and dropped lower.

Now Rackhir observed Narjhan with Sorana beside him.

'The bitch has warned him – he is ready for us,' Rackhir said, wetting his lips and drawing an arrow from his quiver.

Down the Ships of Xerlerenes dropped, coursing downwards on the currents of air, their golden sails billowing, the warrior crews straining over the side and keen for battle.

Then Narjhan summoned the *Kyrenee*.

Huge as a storm-cloud, black as its native Hell, the *Kyrenee* grew from the surrounding air and moved its shapeless bulk forward towards the Ships of Xerlerenes, sending out flowing tendrils of poison towards them. Boatmen groaned as the coils curled around their naked bodies and crushed them.

Lamsar called urgently to his fire elementals and they rose again from where they had been devouring beggars, came together in one great blossoming of flame which moved to do battle with the *Kyrenee*.

The two masses met and there was an explosion which blinded the Red Archer with multi-coloured light and sent the Ships rocking and shaking so that several capsized and sent their crews hurtling downwards to death.

Blotches of flame flew everywhere and patches of poison blackness from the body of the *Kyrenee* were flung about, slaying those they touched before disappearing.

There was a terrible stink in the air – a smell of burning, a smell of outraged elements which had never been meant to meet.

The *Kyrenee* died, lashing about a-wailing, while the flame elementals, dying or returning to their own sphere, faded and vanished. The remaining bulk of the great *Kyrenee* billowed slowly down to the earth where it fell upon the scrabbling beggars and killed them, leaving nothing but a wet patch on the ground for yards around, a patch glistening with the bones of beggars.

Now Rackhir cried: 'Quickly – finish the fight before Narjhan summons more horrors!'

And the boats sailed downwards while the Boatmen cast their steel nets, pulling large catches of beggars aboard their Ships and finishing the wriggling starvelings with their tridents or spears.

Rackhir shot arrow after arrow and had the satisfaction of seeing each one take a beggar just where he had aimed it. The remaining warriors of Tanelorn, led by Brut who was covered in sticky blood but grinning in his victory, charged towards the unnerved beggars.

Narjhan stood his ground, while the beggars, fleeing, streamed past him and the girl. Sorana seemed frightened, looked up and her eyes met Rackhir's. The Red Archer aimed an arrow at her, thought better of it and shot instead at Narjhan. The arrow went into the black armour but had no effect upon the Lord of Chaos.

Then the Boatmen of Xerlernes flung down their largest net from the vessel in which Rackhir sailed and they caught Lord Narjhan in its coils and caught Sorana, too.

Shouting their exhilaration, they pulled the struggling bodies aboard and Rackhir ran forward to inspect their catch. Sorana had received a scratch across her face from the net's wire, but the body of Narjhan lay still and dreadful in the mesh.

Rackhir grabbed an axe from a Boatman and knocked back the helm, his foot upon the chest.

'Yield, Narjhan of Chaos!' he cried in mindless merriment. He was near hysterical with victory, for this was the first time a mortal had ever bested a Lord of Chaos.

But the armour was empty, if it had ever been occupied by flesh, and Narjhan was gone.

Calm settled aboard the Ships of Xerlerenes and over the city of Tanelorn. The remnants of the warriors had gathered in the city's square and were cheering their victory.

Friagho, the Captain of Xerlerenes, came up to Rackhir and shrugged. 'We did not get the catch we came for – but these will do. Thanks for the fishing, friend.'

Rackhir smiled and gripped Friagho's black shoulder. 'Thanks for the aid – you have done us all a great service.' Friagho shrugged again and turned back to his nets, his trident poised. Suddenly Rackhir shouted; 'No, Friagho – let that one be. Let me have the contents of that net.'

Sorana, the contents to which he'd referred, looked anxious as if she had rather been transfixed on the prongs of Friagho's trident. Friagho said: 'Very well, Red Archer – there are plenty more people on the land,' pulled at the net to release her.

She stood up shakily, looking at Rackhir apprehensively.

Rackhir smiled quite softly and said: 'Come here, Sorana.' She went to him and stood staring up at his bony hawk's face, her eyes wide. With a laugh he picked her up and flung her over his shoulder.

'Tanelorn is safe!' he shouted. 'You shall learn to love its peace with me!' And he began to clamber down the trailing ladders that the Boatmen had dropped over the side.

Lamsar waited for him below. 'I go now, to my hermitage again.'

'I thank you for your aid,' said Rackhir. 'Without it Tanelorn would no longer exist.'

'Tanelorn will always exist while men exist,' said the hermit. 'It was not a city you defended today. It was an ideal. That is Tanelorn.'

And Lamsar smiled.